BUT ABOVE ALL...
MOUTH THAT C...

That mouth set in... and cruel-looking, ... truded over remarkably ruddy lips which had the effect of highlighting his white skin and giving the impression of extraordinary pallor. The strange thing was, where the teeth protruded over the lips, they seemed peculiarly sharp and white.

The eyes suddenly caught and held mine.

They were large and shone with a curious red malignancy.

'You will come to me,' he said slowly, a smile curving his lips – those, oh, so thin, red lips.

PETER TREMAYNE

Dracula Lives!

DRACULA UNBORN
THE REVENGE OF DRACULA
DRACULA, MY LOVE

A SIGNET BOOK

SIGNET

Published by the Penguin Group
Penguin Books Ltd, 27 Wrights Lane, London w8 5tz, England
Penguin Books USA Inc., 375 Hudson Street, New York, New York 10014, USA
Penguin Books Australia Ltd, Ringwood, Victoria, Australia
Penguin Books Canada Ltd, 10 Alcorn Avenue, Toronto, Ontario, Canada m4v 3b2
Penguin Books (NZ) Ltd, 182–190 Wairau Road, Auckland 10, New Zealand

Penguin Books Ltd, Registered Offices: Harmondsworth, Middlesex, England

Dracula Unborn first published by Bailey Brothers and Swinfen Ltd
and simultaneously by Transworld Publishers Ltd 1977
The Revenge of Dracula first published by Bailey Brothers and Swinfen Ltd 1978
Dracula, My Love first published by Bailey Brothers and Swinfen Ltd 1980
This omnibus edition, under the present title, first published in Signet 1993
1 3 5 7 9 10 8 6 4 2

Signet Film and TV Tie-in Edition first published 1993

Copyright © Peter Tremayne, 1977
All rights reserved

Typeset by Datix International Limited, Bungay, Suffolk
Set in 9½/11½ pt Plantin
Printed in England by Clays Ltd, St Ives plc

Except in the United States of America, this book is sold subject
to the condition that it shall not, by way of trade or otherwise, be lent,
re-sold, hired out, or otherwise circulated without the publisher's
prior consent in any form of binding or cover other than that in
which it is published and without a similar condition including this
condition being imposed on the subsequent purchaser

CONTENTS

DRACULA UNBORN

To Christos Pittas

INTRODUCTION

I am not over fond of visiting street markets. I make this point merely in order to illustrate that it was quite by chance, and not by habit, that I found myself in Islington's Chapel Market, in North London, that hot June afternoon.

I was returning home, having spent a fruitless two hours with my publisher arguing about alterations to various passages he objected to in my latest book, when I decided to stop my car and look around the market. The reason for this step out of character was that the previous evening a friend, a little the worse for the major part of my last bottle of whisky, had collided with an old Victorian lamp bequeathed to me by my aunt. The glass had been smashed and it now occurred to me that perhaps a replacement might be found among the bric-à-brac of Chapel Market.

It was while I was searching among the stalls of the market that a large bundle of old papers caught my eye, buried under a mound of musty Victorian morality books for children. When it comes to old papers, especially manuscripts, I am something of a squirrel, and so I pried the papers loose from the mound. They were tied with what had once been a red ribbon. A crumbling top sheet bore a sentence beautifully executed in copperplate script: *'Papers relating to the estate of the late John Seward, Medicinae Doctor'*. I skimmed briefly through the papers, which consisted of several unimportant letters, some bills and an obscure medical treatise. But it was the main part of the package, consisting of a manuscript dated 1898, that caused my throat to go dry with excitement.

I turned to the old woman in charge of the stall and

asked, in a voice that must have been trembling, how much she wanted for the papers. She looked me up and down through narrowed eyes, cleared her throat, and said, 'One pound, mister.' She then thrust her jaw out aggressively, as if expecting me to challenge her, but I merely pressed two fifty-pence pieces into her hand and made for my car, gratefully clutching my prize.

All thoughts of my Victorian lamp were forgotten.

Once in the sanctuary of my home, I sat down to examine my acquisition. The manuscript was written in a fairly poor English, clearly by someone whose first language, judging by the sentence construction, was more severely Germanic. Indeed, the introductory note, attached to the manuscript, was signed by Professor Abraham Van Helsing of Amsterdam.

I caught my breath. I had always thought that Dr John Seward and his colleague, Van Helsing, had been fictional characters, figments of the imagination of Bram Stoker, author of that classic tale of horror, *Dracula*, which was first published in 1897. In Stoker's book, Seward and Van Helsing were instrumental in tracking down the great vampire, Dracula, and eventually destroying him; now here I was holding a bundle of papers described as coming from the estate of the late John Seward, MD. Not only that, but here was an entire manuscript written by Van Helsing himself. And such a manuscript!

I read the introductory note with growing excitement.

Explanatory note by Abraham Van Helsing M.D., Ph.D.,
D. Litt., of Amsterdam

In the year 1898 I found myself travelling in Russia. I had gone there to listen to a great scientist, Konstantin Tsiolkovski, lecture on a new means of transportation, a method he called rocket reaction propulsion. While there I was privileged to be allowed research facilities in the

4

Kirillov-Belozersky Monastery in northern Russia. It was thus, while looking for a tract by the monk Elfrosin on the infamous Dracula, who ruled Wallachia in the fifteenth century, that I discovered an ancient, crumbling manuscript dated AD 1480.

The manuscript, which was lengthy, was written in the Italian of the age, though the quality differed greatly by its poorness to Dante Alighieri's *La Divina Commedia*, which had its first printing at Foliguo a mere eight years before this date. I checked the catalogues of the Monastery Library but could find no reference to the manuscript. However, the reason why this poor Italian manuscript seized me with an almost unbearable excitement was its fading title:

'A memoir of Mircea, son of Vlad Tepes, Prince of Wallachia, also known as Dracula, who was born on this earth in the year of Christ 1431, who died in 1476 but remained undead. God between us and all evil.'

My hand trembled as I looked at the faded writing. Here was the very beginning, the Genesis if you like, to the undead monster that was to scourge the earth for centuries and whose end I had witnessed that sixth day of November in 1890. That terrifying time when my English friends and I fought the powers of darkness was revealed to the public last year when a Dublin gentleman of Dr Seward's acquaintance persuaded him to authorize that gentleman to edit some extracts from journals and papers relative to the affair. Only last year, 1897, did this volume appear under the title *Dracula*. Most people have dismissed it as a fantasy; others merely as a classic Gothic novel. Yet the English have a saying that truth is stranger than fiction . . .

That is why this manuscript excited me. I spent months, as the guest of the Abbot, painstakingly translating the manuscript, not into my native Dutch, which I warrant would have been easier for me, but into a passable English, the language by which Dracula has now become known to the world.

I am a man of science, of medicine, not of literature,

and therefore I have neither edited nor altered the manuscript by so much as one iota. I have, however, taken liberties by the insertion of some footnotes whereby the reader may appreciate certain references rendered unclear by the passage of time. Thus do I give it to you to read and reflect upon.

I ask none to believe me. I do not wish to prove anything. All I ask you to do is consider the story of Mircea.

As Ambrosius Hüber of Nuremberg commented as early as 1499, it is 'a very cruel, frightening story about a wild, bloodthirsty man, Dracula the Voivode'.

This introductory note alone was enough to determine me to publish the work, leaving Van Helsing's manuscript almost as I found it, seeking only to correct his grammar and spelling, and deleting his more pedantic footnotes. Where I believe they aid the reader's understanding, I have left certain of the footnotes in.

I did make several attempts to verify points of the work, and in this I was helped by the Romanian Ministry of Tourism and the authorities of the USSR. For instance, Konstantin Tsiolkovski did start lecturing in Russia on the principles of rocket reaction propulsion in 1898. However, the library of the Kirillov-Belozersky Monastery no longer exists, though the manuscripts that were contained there when Van Helsing did his research are now housed in the Saltykov-Schredin Public Library in Leningrad under the title of the Kirillov-Belozersky Collection. Again, much as I tried, I could not find the fifteenth-century original manuscript from which Van Helsing made his translation, and was told that a large quantity of the papers went missing at the time of the October Revolution. I did, however, find the manuscript by the monk Elfrosin, referenced as MS. 11/1088, and written in 1488, which contained several tales on the evils of Dracula. And I did trace Ambrosius Hüber's pamphlet entitled *About the wild bloodthirsty berserker, Dracula*

Voevod. Needless to say, the 'Dublin gentleman of Dr Seward's acquaintance' was Bram Stoker, who was born Abraham Stoker in November 1847, at Clontarf, north of Dublin Bay.

Of the authenticity of the story that follows, I cannot make any statement. However, it is true that in 1431 there was born in present day Romania one called Vlad Tepes the Impaler, who was also called Dracula. This same Dracula (the name means 'The Devil' in Romanian) ruled in Wallachia in 1448, again in 1456–62, and briefly in 1476, at which time he died, horribly and as bloodily as he had lived. It is also true that Dracula had three sons – Vlad Tepelus, Mihail the Bad, who ruled Wallachia from 1508–10, and Mircea, of whom nothing is known save that Van Helsing claims he wrote the story which now follows.

Peter Tremayne
London, 1974

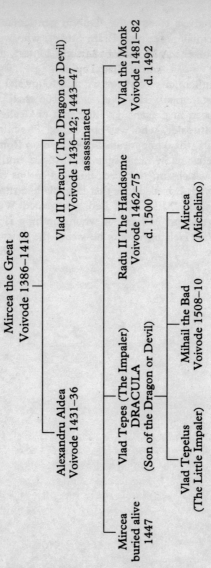

THE HOUSE OF DRACULA

VOIVODES OR PRINCES OF WALLACHIA

Mircea the Great
Voivode 1386–1418

Alexandru Aldea
Voivode 1431–36

Vlad II Dracul (The Dragon or Devil)
Voivode 1436–42; 1443–47
assassinated

Mircea
buried alive
1447

Vlad Tepes (The Impaler)
DRACULA
(Son of the Dragon or Devil)

Radu II The Handsome
Voivode 1462–75
d. 1500

Vlad the Monk
Voivode 1481–82
d. 1492

Vlad Tepelus
(The Little Impaler)

Mihail the Bad
Voivode 1508–10

Mircea
(Michelino)

The male line of Dracula continued as Viovodes of Wallachia from Mihail the Bad to Mihail Radu, also known as Gioan Bey, who was Voivode in 1658–59, was deposed and had to flee to Transylvania where he died in 1660.

A Memoir of Mircea,
son of Vlad Tepes

BOOK ONE
Journey to Wallachia

CHAPTER ONE

Should I be called upon to apportion the blame to any singular incident which became the direct cause of the strange and terrifying adventure that I am about to narrate, I would say it lay directly with the indiscretion I committed with the Principessa Cinzia Lusignolo. Having decided to be scrupulously honest in my narrative, even though it now brings the blush of embarrassment to my cheeks, this fact I admit: it was my seduction of the fair princess and its consequences that drove me from the indolence of my life in Rome to the terrors of the principality of Wallachia and the evils of my ancestral home, Castle Dracula.

What made me embark on the amorous conquest of the princess, I know not; but I must hazard a guess that there were, perhaps, three reasons: boredom, infatuation and revenge – in that order.

My boredom was a prime cause. Indeed, a young man of twenty-two summers can still find himself bored, even in a city such as Rome.

Not long before my nineteenth birthday my mother, her name be blessed, had died and left me with an allowance with which I could indulge in a moderately comfortable way of life – a small palazzo near the Piazza Venezia and enough servants to care for my modest wants. Similarly, I had no need to worry about seeking a means of earning a livelihood, for the allowance, paid to me annually by a trustee, was enough to ensure I did not want for anything that reason dictated. Under such circumstances I became bored, as there seemed little that was not mine for the wanting. The only time I really enjoyed myself was the time spent in study at the University of Rome in the Palazzo della Sapienza, where I studied Latin, Greek, Hebrew and German, and was also tutored in art and mathematics. There, too, I dabbled in the sciences, learning a little of alchemy and natural philosophy.

But of what use was this learning to me? I was no scholar; nor had I any inclination to take to the cloisters where such learning would have stood me in good stead. I had recently decided that the martial arts were worth pursuing and therefore made the decision to travel to the Republic of Venice to join her armies. (Venice had been plunged into bitter warfare with the Turkish unbelievers of the Ottoman Empire since the year 1463 when the Venetians had refused to surrender to the Turks their trading colonies on the Aegean coasts.) Hardly had I made this resolve to become a soldier when I chanced to see the Princess Lusignolo – and all my resolutions crumbled.

I first saw her in the chapel of St Constanza while attending mass, and even before I knew who she was, I was captivated by her beauty.

There, before me in the tiny church, was a figure of such elegance and loveliness that I moved nearer to examine more closely its owner. In spite of a black veil, her long fair hair spilled beneath it almost to her waist. I was transfixed by her beauty; and then her eyes, as she turned away from the altar rail, caught mine. At first I thought they were green, but even as I gazed unashamedly into them, they seemed to flash and change colour while, at the same time, her pale cheeks reddened. She stared fully into my own eyes for a few seconds before she passed out of the church. I watched her trim figure, which would have graced any visualization of Helen of Troy or Aphrodite herself, as she swept through the doors, leaving me trembling with a mixture of desires.

It is not directly part of my narrative to recount how I contrived to regularly attend mass at the chapel of St

Constanza nor how I finally drew into conversation with the princess, all of which took me nearly two weeks. Nor shall I recount how our friendship grew. However, what I must recount is that my amorous intent was strengthened when I learned that she was the wife of the Prince Giuliano Lusignolo, and that this strengthening came through a desire to revenge myself on the man.

I had known Lusignolo during my days at university when he was being tutored in the classics. I had known him and grown to hate him. What better revenge could I have than to show him to the people of Rome as a cuckold?*

Lusignolo was but a year or two older than me, well connected with particular contacts with the great anti-Medici families of the Pazzis and Salviatis who were now in the ascendant and, indeed, whom the Pope, Sixtus IV, favoured. The prince owned a large palazzo near the old Aurelian Wall behind the Piazza Navona and, I have heard it told, his estate was worth 200,000 *scudi*.

Lusignolo would always seek me out to make me the butt of his jokes, and he knew that inevitably my temper would rise to all his discourtesies. When a man loses his temper he always loses his argument, and countless times I was reduced to impotent rage at the cleverness of his tongue and wit. Sometimes he was merely content in calling me a foreigner; other times he called me 'the Slav'; but more often than not he would mockingly call me 'Slavato', playing on the word that means colourless or drab. He would mock at my title of baron, for when my mother brought me to Rome as a child we sought to hide our real identities and somehow Lusignolo had learnt of it.

---

* Here, in Van Helsing's translation, he uses the phrase 'to put the horns on him', obviously translating literally the fifteenth-century Italian *cornuto*.

15

(It was not true that I was a Slav, although I came from the Slavic provinces. In Rome I was styled the Barone Michelino, but my real name was Mircea and my ancestors were rulers of the principality of Wallachia, a small country bordered on its north and east by the great mountains of Transylvania and to the west and south by the river Danube. The country was named from the Volokh or Vlachs who are descendants of the ancient Romans who founded the province of Dacia just to the north of the country many years ago. So in my veins, I warrant, flowed purer Roman blood than in Lusignolo. Indeed, in honour of their ancestors, the Wallachians called themselves Romanians. Now, however, Wallachia had become a vassal state of the Turks, a wasted Ottoman province called Iflak, because of the curse of the house of Dracula which ruled it from the time of my illustrious ancestor Mircea the Great. Therefore, in my veins ran the noble blood of princes, though my mother had taught me never to speak of such things.)

Lusignolo was typical of his breed. A vain man who strutted like a turkey-cock down the *Corso* in his fine clothes, appraising the young ladies as they took the air with their families. I have heard it said that he kept two mistresses. Ah, but he was a fine *Romano di Roma*. He was also a man determined to bribe and befriend his way into high office. It was even rumoured in certain quarters that this was the only reason he had married the Princess Cinzia, for she had been Cinzia della Rovere and related to Francesco della Rovere who now bore the august title of Pope Sixtus IV.

I confess that I know not exactly what her relationship was, for I heard it said that Sixtus was but a Franciscan of humble origin – though the noble bearing of the princess belied any notion that noble blood did not run in her veins. However, as all Rome noted, the Prince and Princess Lusignolo were wont to dine three or four times a year with the Pope.

Whatever the origin of the princess, I was now en-amoured with her, both as an object of my own amorous desires and as a person through whom I might humiliate the hated Lusignolo.

I did not immediately press my amours upon the girl, but instead acted the sympathetic friend with her over her confessed loneliness, enforced while her husband played politics against the Medicis. Indeed, several times she hinted at the unhappiness of her life, and once she even admitted that the prince subscribed to the Italian proverb that a woman is like an egg: the more she is beaten the better she becomes.

Such confessions increased my ardour, not only because they placed emphasis upon the frailty of the princess's relationship with Lusignolo – and thus strengthened my own position – but because they also filled me with genu-ine pity and touched my cold calculations with the warmth of a genuine friendship. Nevertheless, I could not let myself forget the real purpose of my seductions, and thus the need for vengeance, rather than pure love, shadowed my every thought and deed.

While the prince was away, I twice attended dinner parties at the Palazzo Lusignolo. These affairs took place with at least thirty other guests and so I had to bide my time, watching and waiting until the princess would be alone and receptive to my advances. I knew that soon, like the grape, she would be ready to fall into my hands, and I did not want to miss any opportunity. The moment had to come – and come it did when the Palazzo Lusignolo was given over to a great party in honour of the prince's name day.

The Palazzo stands off the Piazza Navona. You make your way there through the squalid narrow streets of the *rioni*, the districts, of the peasants which, thanks to the dictums of Pope Sixtus, are now being pulled down, the streets widened and paved, and new buildings put up to replace the original crumbling structures. The Palazzo itself lies close to the Aurelian Wall on the flat plain in a bend of the Tiber which was the Campus Martius of classical times and where, until some twenty years ago, stood Domitian's great circus. (I tell you this to show you what a fine, great edifice the Prince Lusignolo lived in.) It is surrounded with great gardens, carefully laid out and tended by the best husbandmen that the prince could pay for.

There were some three hundred guests present that night, so it was without difficulty that I avoided being formally introduced to the prince and managed to stay in the background for much of the evening, chatting superficially on this and that to my fellow guests.

All the while I hovered near to the princess and her group, until, having played the dutiful wife, she drifted towards her own circle of friends, leaving the prince to rage against Lorenzo de' Medici and the brigands of Florence. Then, when I saw Lusignolo swallowed up by his faithful admirers, I moved towards the princess and bathed in her radiant smile of welcome.

As the wine flowed and the guests grew more interested in one another, we slipped away into the garden. It was such a night that Rome alone knows, the blue-black sky lit by a multitude of brilliant white pin-points and the great orb of the moon lighting the garden almost as if it were day. The air was warm and the fragrance of rosemary almost overpowering. We walked to the summer-house, entered, and sat for a while looking at the sky without speaking. After a time I felt her hand find mine and grasp it lightly.

'Ah, Michelino, Michelino,' she murmured, her voice like a soft caress.

'You are unhappy, Cinzia?' I asked, bringing a tone of sympathy into my voice, hoping she would not hear the excitement that must surely be edging it.

'It is Giuliano,' she replied, holding my hand tighter, sitting up and letting fire flash in her eyes. 'He is a pig! He angers me more with each passing day.'

'Poor Cinzia,' I said, reaching forward and letting my fingers trace the delicate outline of her cheekbone. 'I wish I could do something. Believe me, I would do anything to make you happy.'

She reached one hand up and held mine and pressed it to her cheek. I felt her warmth at my fingertips.

'I am always happy with you, Michelino,' she whispered.

Indeed it was the time. No man can blame me for taking what was freely offered. And who could deny that as much as I took from her, she, in her turn, took from me?

Ah, but she was beautiful! I had known only two women before Cinzia, but their love-making had consisted of lying back passively, resigned and still, whereas Cinzia was a veritable goddess of the art. I unveiled her pale skin. Her body gleamed in the moonlight. The shadows fell around her face and I saw her moist lips and my need made me blind to all else. The memory is too vivid. My hand trembles as I write. She was lovely and she flowed all around me and our bodies were joined. How much she seemed to know! How much I was to learn! My desire was like a furnace and my lips found her throat and I felt the pain of sorrow and rage, of pure need and vengeance. The experience was confusing. I felt grief and triumph. I felt sorrow and the cold thrill of victory and my nerves were on fire. And yet she was insatiable. She would not let me go. There, in the silence of the moonlit summer-house, we struggled fiercely with one another, mouth to mouth, flesh to flesh, until we had satiated our desire and fell apart, gasping torturedly.

The moonlight fell upon the summer-house. The fragrance of rosemary was overpowering. We were silent and our shame and satisfaction had the stillness of dread. Finally, as if in a dream, she whispered my name.

'Ah, Michelino,' she whispered, 'what do we do this night?'

I had no words to offer in return and my silence condemned our love. Indeed, she, too, must have understood this truth, for she sighed and turned her head to look away.

No more need be recounted of this matter beyond the fact that what had been freely offered had been gladly accepted and both of us now knew what we had wanted: she, escape from the brutalities of her husband; and myself, the cauterizing of old wounds.

Nevertheless, through the chill of this truth, our desire for one another was undiminished. After a while she began to tug me towards her, and I, beyond resistance, reached out for her.

'*Bastardo!*' a voice suddenly hissed.

I turned quickly, but not quickly enough. Prince Lusignolo had already launched himself at me, his two hands outstretched to grasp my throat, spittle forming around his mouth as he screamed abuse at me. The princess shrieked. The prince's body bowled me backwards. We rolled across the floor while the princess sprang back into a corner, her two hands in front of her mouth, her eyes wide with horror. How long the prince and I grappled on the floor I know not. It seemed an eternity, but it could only have occupied the passing of a few seconds. The princess shrieked again.

Voices were now raised in response to the prince's cries of rage. Soon all would be lost. With a sudden surge of strength I pulled Lusignolo's hands apart and threw him back across the floor of the summer house. Then, leaving him no time to recover, I reached down and drew my sword, springing across the floor after him.

'*No!*'

The plaintive wail of the princess stayed my upraised hand. The prince lay before me, breathing heavily, watching the point of my sword with venom in his eyes.

'*Bastardo!*' he hissed again.

I brought down the pommel of the sword, smashing it against the side of Lusignolo's head. He groaned and collapsed unconscious to the floor.

The princess, white-faced, looked silently for a moment at the inert body of her husband; then she raised her wide eyes to mine.

'Mother of God!' she cried, distraught. 'He will kill you for this!'

We both quickly dressed and then I raised her hands to my lips. I kissed her wrists and then I kissed her palms, but before I could offer some reassurance, I heard the guests calling out.

'Lusignolo! Where are you? What is it?'

Cinzia gasped. There was fear in her eyes.'Quick!' she said. 'You must leave here!' She pointed to the garden wall. I saw the moonlight washing over it. 'Over there!' she exclaimed. 'It's the only way! Hurry! *Hurry!*'

I nodded, bent my lips to hers once more, and then very quickly left the summer house. I swung myself at the creepers, was over the wall in a trice, and within moments had put distance between myself and the despised Palazzo Lusignolo.

I walked home that night with a sense of achievement. In one act I had relieved my boredom, satisfied my lust and revenged myself on a worthless poltroon.

Yet little did I know that my trials were just beginning; that my flight from Lusignolo would lead me to an adventure whose dark culmination would haunt me for the rest of my days.

CHAPTER TWO

On my return to my house my *maggiordomo* informed me that some hours before a messenger had delivered a letter for me. I did not send for it until I had bathed and taken a glass of wine, because I presumed that it was merely a package I had been expecting from Naples, a first copy of Masuccio's *Novelino* straight from the new printing press. The buying of the new printed books was becoming a great fad in Rome and I had decided to follow the example of my friends by purchasing the book of Masuccio's whose short stories were being printed in Naples that year.

When my *maggiordomo* brought me the letter, I found it was not the expected book but a thin piece of paper – a paper of rich texture such as only the brothers of holy orders use in their endeavours to record learning for posterity. On it hung a large wax seal with a symbol and motto – a seal that had haunted me from childhood and which had caused both my mother and me much suffering.

I recall that my heart began to quicken and my face flush with a surge of blood as I broke open that dread seal.

The seal was round, the size of a large coin. In the centre was a tree and on one side of the tree was the bust of a king. On the other side of the tree was the bust of a queen. The inscription that encircled it was in an old Slavonic language, the language of my ancestors which my mother had forbidden me to learn.* The letter contained

---

*I have seen this seal in the Monastery Library of St Gall, Switzerland. The inscription is, indeed, in Old Slavonic, though not the language of Wallachia, and reads thus: 'Vlad the warlord, Prince of Wallachia, by God's grace'. Van Helsing.

therein, addressed to me in my real name of Mircea, was written in an exceedingly good Latin hand.

Written at Castle Dracula, Poenari, on the second day of the month of January, in the year 1477.

Brother – it is with much sadness in our hearts that we write this, our first letter to you, bearing the news that our father, Dracula, Prince of Wallachia, is dead. He died as he lived, spilling the blood of the enemies of our house. Brother Mircea, now that this is so and your mother no longer lives, and the quarrel they had lies in the tomb with them, we entreat you to return to Castle Dracula and your home.

For sixteen long years you have been a stranger to your brothers. This castle, its estates and revenues, aye, even the principality of Wallachia itself, are your birthright to share with us. So return to your family and claim that inheritance.

Prosper, brother Mircea, until we meet at Castle Dracula.

Your loving brothers, Vlad and Mihail.

I sat a long time meditating on this letter from the brothers I could scarce remember. What strange thoughts and half-forgotten memories that message from Castle Dracula evoked!

It is now incumbent on me to recount a little of my history and that of my unfortunate country, Wallachia, in order that you may attest to the feelings that this communication aroused in me. Did I not believe in the vagaries of history I would merely record that I am a Dracula and that my father, who but lately ruled Wallachia, was the fifth prince to bear the name of Vlad and is known throughout Europe as Vlad Tepes, the Impaler. But knowing full well the caprices of history, where memories grow dim or events become distorted or confused, I feel I must explain more of the history of the family of Dracula.

The house of Dracula is an ancient one springing, it is said, from the loins of the great Genghis Khan. Their blood had run in the veins of the voivodes, or princes, of Wallachia since the prince Radu Negru crossed the Transylvanian Alps to carve out the principality in 1290.

My father, Dracula, was born in the old German fortified town of Schassburg,* in the country of Transylvania because his father, my grandsire, Vlad II, was in exile there while his half-brother, Alexandru Aldea, ruled Wallachia. It was in that year that Vlad II went to Nuremberg to be invested with the Order of the Dragon by the Holy Roman Emperor Sigismund. (It was this Order of the Dragon from which we now take our family name Dracula, for in the language of Wallachia the name *dracul* means dragon and thus Vlad II adopted as his escutcheon a dragon on a cross.) When he returned to Wallachia as ruler in 1436 he became known as Vlad Dracul – Vlad the Dragon. But the name had another meaning for the people. Dracul can also mean the devil. Therefore my father became known as Vlad Dracula: Vlad, the son of the dragon or the son of the devil. It was the latter meaning that most people adopted.

History, as I have cause to know, can be boring, but I must ask you for patience while I explain the history of my father's life in order that a better understanding of my subsequent narrative can be achieved.

When my grandfather, Vlad Dracula, became ruler of Wallachia he showed great friendship to the Turks who, many years before, had expanded their empire north of the Danube and claimed Wallachia under their suzerainty. In return for tribute, however, the Ottomans allowed Wallachia to retain its own dynasty, territory and religion. And to ensure that Vlad Dracul paid his tribute, the Turks took my father, Vlad Dracula, and his young

*Now Sighisoara. Van Helsing.

brother, Radu, as hostages. Old Vlad Dracul's enforced friendship for the Turks displeased the rulers of the neighbouring states, such as Transylvania and Moldavia, who were fighting to drive the Turks away. Iancu de Hunedoara, the Voivode of Transylvania and Regent of Hungary, who had often been victorious in battle against the Turks, had Vlad Dracul and his eldest son Mircea assassinated and an anti-Turkish ruler, Vladislav, placed upon the Wallachian throne. As a consequence, the Turkish Sultan, Murad II, freed my father, Dracula, and, after defeating Vladislav at the battle of Kossovo Plains in 1448, placed him upon the throne.

Three months of puppet kingship were enough for my father who fled to Moldavia where he became a friend of the prince Stefan cel Mare. In 1451 the new Turkish Sultan, Mohammed II, unleashed the Ottoman hordes on the citadels of Christendom and his victorious armies entered Constantinople, defeating and killing the emperor Constantine XII Dragases. With this act of infamy the great Byzantine Empire fell into a dark age.

My father, Dracula, now swore to drive out the Turkish horde and he went to Transylvania where he threw himself on the mercy of Iancu de Hunedoara and his son Mathias Corvinus, King of Hungary, the assassins of his father and brother.

In the year 1456, supported by a Transylvanian army, Dracula entered Wallachia and defeated the Turkish puppet prince at Tirgsor and seized the throne. To the Wallachians he promised that nobody would be poor, that all would be rich in the country. He was stern, authoritarian and completely merciless to his enemies.

He was particularly merciless with the Saxon merchants who had settled in many parts of the country and who tried to organize an insurrection against him because he had destroyed their trading monopoly. At the same time he had to protect Wallachia from Turkish invasions. In

May of the year 1458 my father, Dracula, defeated an army led by Mohammad Pasha and set free all the slaves taken by the Turks. But in the following year he had to suppress the plottings of the Saxons who tried to overthrow him and placed a puppet ruler called Dan upon the throne. In Christendom Dracula's reputation for his fight against the Turkish unbelievers was known far and wide. Yet another Turkish army, led by Hamza Beg of Nicopolis, was destroyed by him at Tirgo-viste, and Dracula even marched his victorious Wallachians south of the Danube, putting many Turks to the sword.

In April 1462, Sultan Mohammed began a great campaign to reconquer Wallachia. His aim was to replace Dracula with Dracula's younger brother Radu who had grown to manhood in Turkish captivity as a lover of all things Turkish.

At first my father, Dracula, was successful in defeating the vanguard of the great Turkish army which was commanded by the Grand Vizier Mohmud Pasha. Soon, however, he was forced to retreat northwards, and by November he had to cross into Transylvania thinking, once again, to seek aid from the King of Hungary, Mathias Corvinus. But Mathias had been listening to the stories of the Saxon merchants who held great economic power over his empire. On their advice, Mathias seized Dracula at Piatra Craiului and incarcerated him in the great prison of Vishegrad, which stands in the city of Pest, opposite the Hungarian capital of Buda, which cities straddle the Danube. There Dracula was imprisoned for twelve years.

It was early in that year of 1462, a few months before that great Turkish invasion, that my mother took me to Rome. I was then six years of age and would have been celebrating my seventh birthday, on 2 March. My mother was Dracula's second wife. The first wife had borne him two sons, Vlad and Mihail, and had died bearing the second child. In 1454, while Dracula was living in Hungary, he married my mother who was of the Catholic religion. There was some conflict for, of course, Dracula subscribed to the Orthodox faith, but my mother ensured that my devotions were made to Rome.

Since his imprisonment by Mathias Corvinus the evil deeds of Dracula have become the subject for many a chronicler; indeed, they have been more than emphasized. It should now suffice to say that he was a cruel and merciless man and that his cruelty was aimed at my mother on more than one occasion.

Again, not trusting to the vagaries of history, I must record that my father, Dracula, was a most wild, profane and godless man (though in truth, saints have never flourished in these mountain lairs of Wallachia). It was said that in him, particularly, there dwelt a certain wanton and cruel humour which had made his name a by-word in Christendom. He was a man of dark passions. In his godlessness he often persecuted the church, and it is well documented that in Brasov he burnt the church of holy St Bartholomew and stole its vestments and chalices. There are many stories that I have heard and, indeed, which have been recorded, concerning his evil humours.

It was said that once my father met a peasant who was wearing ill-fitting and tattered clothes. Dracula inquired if the man was married. On receiving an affirmative answer, the Voivode told the peasant: 'Your wife is assuredly of the kind who remains idle. How is it possible that she allows her husband to go forth in such rags? She is not worthy to live in my realm. She must perish.' The peasant begged for mercy for his wife. 'My Lord, I am satisfied with her,' said the poor man. 'You will be more satisfied with another since you are a decent and hardworking man,' answered Dracula. The wretched wife was brought before Dracula and executed on a stake and a new wife was given to the peasant.

There was another time when Dracula was witnessing

the execution of his enemies and a certain boyar stood by him. This boyar could not stand the stench of the rotting corpses and politely suggested to Dracula that the royal party move away a little. 'Over there the air is pure,' explained the boyar, 'whereas here it is impure. The bad smell might affect your health.' Dracula asked: 'Does the stench worry you?' The boyar answered that it did and that it would be well to remove to a place which was not so detrimental to the health of the party. Then Dracula ordered his servants to bring a stake three times as long as those his enemies were being impaled upon. 'Make it up for me immediately in order that you impale the boyar so that he may no longer be able to smell the stench from below.'

Ambassadors and papal emissaries to Wallachia never tired of telling of the evils of the prince of that country; of how he would bury a man up to the navel and use him for target practice or how he had gipsies and others boiled alive. But always there were stories of his hideous executions by impaling people on great wooden stakes. Thus did Dracula become known as Vlad the Impaler.

Such was the husband of my mother.

As the years passed my mother grew lonely and desolate at Dracula's court and it was when she was in such an unhappy state of mind that a boyar of Dracula's ruling council of nobles sought her out and proclaimed his friendship and devotion for her. The man was Dracula's *stolnic*, or high steward. My mother and the boyar grew together in friendship and soon the friendship had deepened into something more.

Early in 1462 Dracula discovered the affair and sent for the unsuspecting boyar. He had the unfortunate man impaled on a high wooden stake before the walls of Castle Dracula, but before he could send for my mother, she seized me and fled from the castle.

I dimly recall the flight, days and nights, sometimes on

foot, sometimes on horseback, and sometimes perched precariously in a boat on some river. How long the journey lasted I do not know, but eventually we arrived at the eternal city of Rome where, with the aid of relatives, we received sufficient funds to live in a degree of comfort. My mother changed our names and tried to expunge the very memory of Wallachia and Dracula from her thoughts and mine.

(It was later discovered that a servant woman, who remained loyal to my mother on the night of our flight, tried to prevent Dracula's soldiers from entering my mother's chambers to delay the discovery of our escape. She was promptly thrown to her death from the battlements of the castle* and my mother was officially proclaimed dead throughout Wallachia.)

I have already recounted how I grew to a somewhat indolent manhood while my father was languishing in the dungeons of King Mathias Corvinus of Hungary. How did I discover all this when my mother refused to talk of it to me?

Well, but a few years ago, when I studied at the great university at the Palazzo della Sapienza, I chanced to meet and become friends with an aged scholar named Antonio Bonfini, who was chronicler to King Mathias himself and knew Dracula and, indeed, wrote a history of the unhappy ruler of Wallachia. I did not acquaint the kindly old man of my relationship to the Voivode, but I pressed him eagerly for stories of my father. Thus did I learn what knowledge I have of my true country and family.

Moreover, I learned that about the year 1467 my father's friend, Stefan cel Mare, had become Voivode of

---

*It is historically reported, erroneously it would seem, that Dracula's wife was thrown or leapt to her death from the castle tower. Van Helsing.

29

Moldavia and allied himself with King Mathias. He took it upon himself to plead for my father's release and his pleas were reinforced by the fact that Dracula had secretly married King Mathias's sister, a Catholic, and had given up the Orthodox religion. This marriage greatly displeased Mathias, but forced him to release Dracula in 1475.

No sooner was Dracula released than he joined with Stefan cel Mare and Stefan Bathory of Transylvania to invade Wallachia and throw out the Turkish puppet Basarab cel Batrin, who had succeeded Dracula's brother, Radu the Handsome. In November 1476, Dracula was reinstated as ruler of Wallachia; but in December came the news of his mysterious death and the return of Basarab cel Batrin . . .

Thus is my history concluded, and I assure you that your patience in following this chronicle will be rewarded by a better understanding of subsequent events.

Now, after such a history, I had received a letter from my half-brother, inviting me to return to Wallachia, to Castle Dracula, in order to claim an inheritance.

Inheritance of what? I wondered as I sat sipping wine and musing before the fire. Basarab was ruler now, albeit on behalf of the Sultan Mohammed, and I would hazard that Wallachia was still torn by bloody war and conflict. Yet had I not a few weeks ago thought to join the Venetian army to fight the Ottoman unbelievers? War and conflict would certainly offer me adventure enough. And yet . . . yet there were in my mind grave doubts and misgivings concerning the advisability of an expedition to the lands that the Turks held sway over.

I know not how long I sat there musing before the clatter of a carriage in the courtyard of my palazzo heralded the arrival of the news which would take the decision from my hands.

Ah, how unkind fate can sometimes be, and in what disguises she comes!

CHAPTER THREE

A few seconds passed before my *maggiordomo* ushered the Princess Cinzia Lusignolo into the room and then discreetly withdrew. I rose from my chair as she impulsively moved across the room and grasped both my hands in hers. She stood for a moment, gathering her breath, the candlelight flickering over her face and shadowing her eyes. There was a pink hue to her cheeks and her bosom rose and fell rapidly under the flimsy material of a light satin cloak.

'It's Giuliano,' she breathed at last. 'He's going to kill you.'

'I would not have expected less,' I said.

She shook her fair hair and began to say something, but I interrupted her by calling back my *maggiordomo*. When he arrived, I removed the princess's cloak, handed it to him, and ordered wine to be brought for the both of us.

'You don't understand, Michelino,' Cinzia said as I seated her on a couch before the blazing hearth. 'Giuliano is arranging a duel.'

'I had expected as much,' I said casually, 'but your prince is not renowned for his swordsmanship whereas I have practised the art with many masters. I would have no fear on my account, Cinzia, nor indeed for your prince. I can handle Lusignolo with ease and I will but prick him a few times in the arm to satisfy honour and there will be an end to it.'

'You still do not understand,' Cinzia said, shaking her head almost impatiently. 'Do you really think that Giuliano will risk his position by fighting you himself?'

I was frankly puzzled. 'What then?' I asked as my *maggiordomo* returned with the wine.

She did not immediately reply. The *maggiordomo* poured two glasses of wine, left the bottle on the tray, bowed low and respectfully withdrew. Cinzia waited in silence until the door had closed behind him.

'What then?' I repeated.

She reached forward and placed a hand on mine. The flames from the blazing fire illuminated her face and I felt her beating warmth at my fingertips. The room wrapped us in silence.

'I overheard Giuliano speaking to someone in his room,' she said finally. 'He was asking them to seek you out and challenge you to a duel in such a way that you would be forced to fight. I waited and I heard the man agree. Only then did I recognize the voice . . . It was Francesco Gullo!'

Had the princess said it was the Holy Father himself I could not have been more shocked. Francesco Gullo di Panerea was the most feared *spadaccino* in all Rome. His sword had accounted for the deaths of forty-seven men in duels, and who knows how many others had fallen before him. Yes, I was shocked. Against Francesco Gullo I would be but a babe in swaddling clothes.

'You must leave Rome,' Cinzia said, articulating my very thoughts. 'You must leave Rome before he discovers you.'

I took a long swallow at the rough red wine and nodded slowly.

'You must go somewhere far away from here until the affair . . . is forgotten.'

She blushed and lowered her eyes. Perhaps she was waiting for me to avow eternal memory of her, but more important thoughts tumbled through my mind. Indeed, at that moment I was as far removed from her as the sky is from the earth; I could scarcely recall the exciting lures of her body, the radiance of her smile, the beating of her heart against mine. Rather, as with all young men who have a large love for life, I was thinking only of my immediate survival. It shames me now to record this, but such was the truth, and the truth is itself like the plague. My love was a lie. My passion was selfish. And she, with that fierce light in her eyes, was obviously aware of this.

'Yes,' I said. 'I must leave.'

I called my *maggiordomo* and ordered him to have my best horse saddled and to pack a *bisaccia de sella*, a large saddle bag, with the items I would need for a long journey, as well as a money belt containing all the available money in the palazzo.

'The baron is going to be away long?' the old man inquired.

'That depends,' I said. 'However, in my absence you will see to the running of the palazzo and the well-being of the servants. I shall send you instructions from time to time until I return.'

'Very good, baron,' the old man said imperturbably, as if my hurried departure were in no way an unusual occurrence. He then bowed and left.

I went immediately to my bed chamber where I changed into clothing more suitable for travelling and where I also picked up my sword – a sword I prized highly as it had been the property of a Roman soldier-priest who had carried it on a crusade after it had been blessed by the Pope. In my turmoil I had all but forgotten the princess, and it was not until she had entered my bed chamber that I actually remembered her presence.

She closed the door behind her and leant against it and looked at me with smiling eyes. She was breathing heavily. Her smooth breasts rose and fell. I was aware of her attractions, and of the desire that grew within me, and I realized at that moment that she, too, had won, that in giving herself to me she had humiliated Lusignolo and released herself from her fears. In her eyes there was wickedness.

33

'Sir,' she said mockingly, 'you have surely forgotten your duties as a host.'

I stood uncertainly in the middle of the room, my feet still bare, my shirt open at the front, the belt on my breeches hanging loose.

'Madam,' I said, 'you have me at a disadvantage.'

'Then, sir,' she said, advancing smilingly upon me, 'we must balance up the affair, if you would demean yourself to act as ladies' maid.'

And so for the second time within hours, but this time with more honesty, the princess and I satiated our desires with one another to such a degree that all thoughts of a hasty departure were driven from my mind and I had to sleep to recover from the exhaustion of my endeavours. Indeed, it was some hours later that I left the princess asleep in my bed and the sun, peering over the distant hills, found me outside the walls of the city and urging my horse southward down the ancient Via Praenestina, travelling towards an adventure more hideous than my wildest imaginings.

CHAPTER FOUR

At that time I had no clear idea where I was making for and it was not until noon, when I stopped to eat, that I contemplated my future prospects. It was then that I pulled from my purse the letter from Castle Dracula and it was then that my destination was settled.

The details of my journey are perhaps of little importance. I rode across the mountains to Barletta and there sold my horse and took a ship across the Adriatic to the city state of Dubrovnik.

The city, with its narrow coastal belt, had become an independent republic when the rest of Bosnia fell to the Turks fourteen years ago. I was extremely curious on my arrival in the city, but things were not as strange as I thought they would be, this being due, in part, to the close contacts Dubrovnik has with Italy and the fact that Dubrovnik passed from a Byzantine dependency in 1205 to Venetian suzerainty and then became part of Bosnia in 1358. It is a part-Latin city, but with a strong Slavic background. Its institutions are all autonomous and its merchants own extensive inland areas. The Turks interfere little with them, for they also own a world-wide maritime trade. They are also the principal entrepreneurs in mining, in which mines a great number of Saxons, known locally as *Sasi*, work.

When I left Dubrovnik I noticed almost immediately a drop in temperature. The short cool summer was ending and I was now entering a region where one could look forward to long cold winters with heavy snowfalls which I gather are typical of the area. The countryside through which I rode was greatly wooded; indeed, the whole country seemed covered with forest which was inhabited by a diverse number of animals such as brown bears, wild boar, wolves, foxes, martens, chamois, red deer, roe deer, eagles and falcons. The wild life was rich and abundant and I was amazed at its profusion.

From Dubrovnik I travelled northwards to the cathedral city of Mileseva. From time to time I saw detachments of Turkish soldiers, but they did not stop me or bother me in any way. However, several times I was stopped by large bands of armed Bosnians who still determine to drive the Turks from their country. Hearing my Italian accent, these good people were convinced I was a Venetian and therefore an ally in their battle against the Ottomans. I prayed that no Turk would stop me and reach a similar conclusion.

From Mileseva I went on to Studenica and up to Kalenic; by this way I came to the city of Vidin on the western side of the Danube, on the borders of Wallachia itself.

Vidin is a medium-sized independent city which was once a great trading centre of the Bulgars within sight of the towering Transylvanian Alps to the north and the Balkans in the south. The area has recently become known as the Balkans, as more people adopt Turkish usage; for Balkan is, I believe, the Turkish word for 'mountain chains'. These southern Balkan mountains gleam white in the sun due to the rocky limestone ridges they form, but by the standards of the Italian Alps, they are not really high.

The city of Vidin is dominated by a great Orthodox monastery which has a claim to great piety since three centuries ago Prince Ajtony, whose domains then stretched from the Korcos to the Danube and from Tisza to Transylvania, was baptized a Christian in the city. Soon after, the Byzantine Emperor Basil II captured the city. Vidin was strong, however, and in 1281 it broke away from the empire and constituted a semi-independent principality until 1322 when the Serbs conquered its Bulgar inhabitants.

I found that in spite of the political eclipse of the area and the domination everywhere of the Turks, the native nobility seem to regard themselves as the spiritual heirs to Byzantium. They still maintain an essential identity with what they consider their religious, artistic and cultural centre: Constantinople.

The capture of Constantinople by the Turks in 1453 has indeed changed the face of this country. Byzantium is now no more, and I believe that history will not prove me a liar when I say that there is little hope of it being raised again. Those who supported the Orthodox Church believed that it was not possible for Christians to have a church and not to have an empire, but I believe they will now resolve their differences with the universal church of Rome.

Some years ago the Orthodox Metropolitan of Moscow declared that the fall of Constantinople was God's punishment for the Greek betrayal of the Orthodox Church at the Council of Florence, when a union between the Greek Orthodox and Catholic churches was tentatively agreed upon. That union, which I understand was never popular with the citizens of Byzantium, collapsed with Constantinople and the remnants of the Greek Church reverted to Orthodoxy. Vidin, it would seem, has now become a stronghold of that Orthodoxy.

The inn at Vidin where I stayed was run by a Saxon named Herder and therefore my knowledge of German, albeit a knowledge of the Minnesänger of the court romances and heroic epics, was enough to let me understand and converse in the rolling southern Germanic tongue. The horse I had bought in Dubrovnik was exhausted and before continuing my journey across the Danube into Wallachia I asked Herr Herder whether he could purchase a fresh mount for me. At this he shrugged his broad shoulders.

'It would be useless to even inquire, young *Herr*,' he said. 'Across the river in Wallachia there still rages a war, even though most of the country is desolate and devastated. Three times in the past month, soldiers, either Turks or Christian, have raided Vidin and carried off practically all the horses. And, young *Herr*, that is the least of the things they have taken from us . . .'

His voice trailed off and he was silent awhile. Then, finally, he drew himself up and spat into the fire.

'Ah,' he said despairingly, 'Turk or Christian, both are equally as bad. No, young *Herr*, there are no fresh horses in Vidin.'

There would be nothing for it, I realized, but to delay my journey for several days in order that my mount might recover. This did not please me. At this stage of my journey I detested the idea of delay and the knowledge that I would have to quell the feeling of excitement that was growing in me as I neared the land of my birth.

CHAPTER FIVE

'Excuse me.' A short, plumpish man pushed himself from a chair, in which he had been relishing the inn's fire, and bowed ungracefully in my direction. 'The *Freiherr* will permit? My name is Strasser, Erhard Strasser. I am a merchant on my way to Tirgoviste and I would be delighted for the Freiherr to join me on the journey, if he so wishes.'

Tirgoviste is the capital of Wallachia and was on my route to Castle Dracula at Poenari. The Saxon merchant looked ill-bred and boring, but it would be even more boring to delay my journey for several days.

'I would be delighted to join you, Herr Strasser,' I said.

Herr Strasser nearly glowed with obvious pleasure. (I was to learn later that he had sought my company for two reasons: firstly, he was a snob and to travel with a *Freiherr*, as the Saxon title for baron is, marked him as a man of distinction and influence; secondly, undisciplined hordes of Turks and Christians still roamed Wallachia and a young man was a welcome addition to the cortège of a fat merchant.) Herr Strasser then called for wine and, out of civility, I drank with him.

Early the next morning, having breakfasted very simply with ale and a loaf of Herr Herder's freshly baked bread and some local cheese, Herr Strasser and I set off for the ferry which would take us across the Danube, which the natives called Dunarea.

Herr Strasser's coach was drawn by four sturdy cobs, but in spite of the size and the large numbers of boxes that Herr Strasser was carrying, the Saxon merchant was attended only by one dour-faced Wallachian called Amza whose only language was Wallachian, called the Valakian.

Although, as I was to find later, my faulty German was enough to get me by in most areas of the country, it was a sadness that my mother had steadfastly refused to let me learn the language of my ancestors. From Amza I did, however, learn certain words that caught my attention because of their similarity to the tongue of the Valakian genesis, Latin, and this engaged me for some part of the journey.

The ferry across the Danube from Vidin was merely a large raft upon which only our four horses could go first and then our uncoupled coach. The whole business of our crossing was a lengthy process and took upwards of an hour and a half. The leader of the four swarthy men who piloted the raft from bank to bank asked Herr Strasser for the payment of two *aspi*, which I understood to be a Wallachian coin of silver. There was some argument, for Herr Strasser had none of the local coinage, but he eventually managed to pay them in German *groschen*. I resolved that at the next town I would endeavour to change a few of my gold *ducats* and *perpers* for *aspi*.

Safely on the Wallachian side of the Danube, the raftmen helped Amza to recouple the horses to our coach and we were soon heading at a brisk trot towards the distant mountains.

It was near noon, a bright, hot day with scarce a cloud in the sky. I had cause to praise the new concepts of fashionable clothes that were becoming popular in the Italian city states. Fashion was now abandoning the ostentatious effects of fantasy and abstraction in clothing and moving towards simplicity in everything. My doublet fell to the natural waist, open at the front to show the soft gathers of a low-necked shirt; my sleeves were fastened loosely on the arms, allowing easy movement; while the shirt puffed through the openings. Had I been wearing the old-style pleated Gothic gowns, so much the fashion a mere five years ago, I would have stifled in the heat.

It was while I meditated on such things, bathing in the fierce golden rays of the sun, that a sudden cold shiver shook me. At once the sky began to turn dark.

Amza brought the coach to an abrupt halt, the horses rearing and whinnying in confusion. Herr Strasser cursed and peered out of the door.

'What is it, Amza?' he demanded in German before repeating the question in the man's native tongue.

I was now leaning out of the coach to observe this peculiar phenomenon. Amza pointed a shaking finger at the sky. I peered up. It was very strange indeed. There was still not a cloud to be seen in the sky and yet, slowly, ominously, the sun was being blotted out from our vision as if a black cloud was being drawn across it. Inexorably, bit by bit, the sun was disappearing, shadows swooped across the land, and the countryside was growing cold and dark. I felt myself shiver.

Suddenly, Amza leapt from the coach and fell to his knees, one hand describing the sign of the cross and the other fingering a rosary. All the while he mumbled in his own language, of which I regret I knew not a word. *One* word, however, I heard him repeat several times with vehemence: *varcolac*.

Then, as I looked, I saw a very strange occurrence. The blackness suddenly left the sun and the dark shadows began to grow bright, growing into a large white light that moved gracefully towards the heavens and descended towards the horizon, forming a glowing curve that spread out and disappeared until, within minutes, the day sky was normal once more.

Herr Strasser and I glanced at each other. Amza was still on his knees, staring fearfully at the sky, still fingering his rosary and mumbling. Herr Strasser slowly shook his head.

'There is no cause for alarm, young *Freiherr*,' he said to me. 'This is a natural phenomenon that I have

41

witnessed once before, some years ago. When was it now? Five years ago. It is called a comet, *Freiherr*. The one I saw was in 1472, but more brilliant than this one. It had a vast tail. Do not fear, *Freiherr*, it is only a comet.'

I found myself bristling at the condescension in his voice. I had heard of such things from the learned astrologers of Rome. In fact, I recall being told of a great comet appearing in 1456 which astrologers said would cause a grievous pestilence or some great calamity. It appeared at a time when Christian was fighting Turk and it is said the common saying was 'God save us from the Devil, the Turk and the Comet'. Irreverent men say that Pope Calixtus III even excommunicated it, though when Christian beat Turk it was felt that it had portended good. This was, however, the first time I had seen one, and although I was bristling at Herr Strasser's condescension, I still felt a little uneasy and glanced up at the sky. The comet had gone.

It was Amza who seemed most affected by the partial eclipse made when the comet passed across the face of the sun, so I asked Herr Strasser what the man was mumbling about.

'Ah, young *Freiherr*,' smiled the merchant, 'it is only a local superstition.'

'What does the word *varcolac* mean?' I insisted.

At the very mention of the word, Amza feverishly crossed himself and began jabbering once more at an alarming rate. The merchant merely shrugged cynically.

'These superstitions, *Freiherr*, are as common as berries in a pail. A *varcolac* is a vampire who climbs to the heavens to eat the sun or moon. Amza is merely saying that the sun was being eaten by the *varcolac*. The Wallachians are a very superstitious people, *Freiherr*.'

Amza was now quieter, watching intently as Herr Strasser was speaking, nodding each time the word *varcolac* was uttered.

Suddenly, as I stood looking upwards towards the sun, half expecting some new phenomenon to materialize, Amza screamed.

It was a strange sound from an old man. He had been kneeling before us, his face turned towards us as we conversed, and Herr Strasser and I now stared at him in bewilderment as, trembling, he rose to his feet, his outstretched hand pointing directly at me, his mouth working frantically but in seeming incoherence until, eventually, I caught the word '*Moroii!*' which he repeated several times as in a dream.

Herr Strasser moved forward and spoke sharply to the man, but Amza ignored him and continued to stare wild-eyed at me, all the while repeating the word *moroii* as if it were some magical incantation. Herr Strasser then raised his walking cane and struck the man violently across the shoulders, shouting at him as he did so, but still the man did not flinch. At this point I moved forward and laid a hand on Herr Strasser's arm to prevent him inflicting further injury on the poor man, but as I did so Amza gasped, threw one arm over his eyes, and backed away like one scalded by hot water.

'*Moroii!*' he hissed, and then, quite clearly: '*Moroii! Moroii! Dracula!*'

I froze where I stood. I could not believe what I had heard. I was amazed that the old man had suddenly discovered my identity, and even more amazed by the depth of his fear of me.

'Amza!' I said.

On the instant he turned and, before Herr Strasser or I could recover from our surprise, darted away through the trees and was gone, leaving silence behind him. Herr Strasser finally spoke.

'Well, *Freiherr*,' he said, pulling himself together, 'it is twelve miles to the next village where we may obtain the services of another coachman who, mercifully, may not be as mad as this one. Alas, I have little knowledge of coaches.'

'Do not worry, Herr Strasser,' I replied, trying to act as natural as possible, 'I believe I can drive such a coach as this.'

He seemed relieved and even offered to ride postillion with me. We climbed aboard the coach and set off, moving at a brisk pace, and I soon learnt the knack of controlling the horses. Again the sun was bright and the day very hot as if nothing unusual had happened . . . yet I still felt uneasy.

'It is incredible, *Freiherr*,' Herr Strasser eventually said. 'Amza has been a good servant to me five years now. What could be the cause of his sudden dementia? He has long been a superstitious old fool and often claimed he had the gift of second sight.'

'What was that word he kept repeating?'

'*Moroii* is a word I do not understand, though I do know the other word he spoke – Dracula. However, *why* he spoke it, I know not.'

'Dracula?' I asked innocently.

'Yes, *Freiherr*.' Herr Strasser turned and spat. 'Dracula! God's curse on the name.'

'Why so?'

'Dracula is the name of the voivodes of Wallachia, but when one speaks the name they refer only to Vlad Tepes who was a scourge to all God-fearing men – a *Wütrich*, a blood-thirsty monster. The evil that this Dracula did before his own death, which occurred last December, would cause the strongest stomach to turn.'

'You intrigue me, Herr Strasser,' I said.

'Do I? Well, let me tell you. My home town was called Berkendorf in Wuetzerland. Should you go there you will not find it, though you may find a few houses settled by Wallachian swine called Benesti. But it is not Berkendorf. Vlad Dracula had that town burnt to the ground; the men, women and children that inhabited it he had burnt or impaled. And why? Because they were Saxons.'

'But isn't it the truth,' I said, 'that Dracula was popular with the Wallachians and simply punished the Saxons because they attempted to overthrow him and place Vlad Dan on the throne?'

'The truth?' Herr Strasser said with obvious agitation. 'The truth is that the man was a bloodthirsty tyrant. True we Saxons supported Vladislav Dan in an attempt to overthrow a bloodthirsty maniac. And Dracula tracked him down . . . tracked him down to Fagaras Castle where the Saxons tried to defend him. Alas, Dracula's hordes overwhelmed the Saxons and Dracula ordered Vladislav Dan to dig his own grave and read his own funeral service before he cut off his head. Then began Dracula's persecution of all the Saxons in Wallachia.'

Herr Strasser reached a hand into his pocket and brought forth a collection of printed pamphlets which he waved in my face.

'Do you read German? No? Well, over the years I have collected many pamphlets concerning the evils of this Dracula. It is the intention of us Saxons that Europe will know of his misdeeds. Good Saxon merchants in several cities have paid for the printing of these pamphlets by which Dracula's evil deeds have become known.'

Herr Strasser was obviously very agitated. He put the pamphlets back into his pocket and gazed straight ahead with his eyes narrowed.

'Let me tell you more,' he said. 'Once he killed almost the entire merchant population of Wuetzerland. Then there was the great Wallachian boyar Albu who sided with our plight: Dracula executed him and his entire family. I recall meeting a man from Hermann-stadt, or Sibiu as it is now called, and he said that the dead were impaled on great wooden stakes like a huge forest.

'This Dracula persecuted us because of his blood lust, and rightly was he called Vlad Tepes, the Impaler.

'Once, I recall, the Turkish Sultan sent some ambassadors to speak with Dracula. They entered the castle and, as is the custom of the Turk, paid tribute to him by not removing their fezzes. Dracula asked them why they did not show him respect by removing their hats. They answered that it was the custom of their country to show respect by not removing their fezzes. Dracula said: "I, too, would like to strengthen your customs so that you may adhere to them more rigidly." He then ordered some nails and a hammer to be brought, and he hammered each fez to the head of its owner. He then told them: "Go tell the Sultan that he may be accustomed to suffer such indignity, but I am not so accustomed. Let him not send ambassadors to me exporting his customs." Ach, such a terrible, uncivilized man!'

I believe that Herr Strasser, like most of the Saxon merchants who had lost their property and position during Dracula's rule, was more motivated by personal feelings than by abhorrence at the blood shed by Dracula – for such blood-letting was not so uncommon in those parts – and I should have carried on the discussion, reminding Herr Strasser of the blood thirst of his forefathers, the Teutonic Knights, had not the little merchant suddenly caught his breath.

'*Ach, mein Gott!*' he exclaimed.

He had raised a hand to shade his eyes and now he pointed to a distant mountain slope. Following his pointing finger I saw a band of horsemen galloping towards the roadway to intercept us.

'Bandits?' I asked the white-faced Saxon.

'Worse,' he whispered. 'Turks!'

I looked upon the approaching horsemen with a shiver of apprehension. At last, after the tales of horror that were circulating in the cities of Christendom, I was to come face to face with the hordes of the unbelievers, those who fought the knights of civilization for countless generations. Tales of Turkish murder, atrocity and rape made the alleged evils of the house of Dracula pale into insignificance.

'Will they harm us?' I asked, observing that the horsemen were drawing close and thinking it might be better to attempt to flee.

Herr Strasser shrugged resignedly.

'It depends, *Freiherr*. Firstly, they might think you are a Venetian with whom they are at war. Secondly, these may not be regular troops of the Sultan but *akinois* – irregulars who are little more than bandits, in which case they will murder anyone if they have a mind to do so.' He shuddered. 'I have seen too many victims of the Turks. 'Twould be best if we humoured them.'

The body of horsemen had formed a scythe-like formation, the extreme points of the scythe extending and closing around to encircle us in a well-disciplined manoeuvre.

Herr Strasser nudged me. 'God be praised, *Freiherr*,' he said. 'These are not irregulars, but *sipahis*, the cavalry of *der Grosse Heide*.' I was puzzled by his reference to 'the great pagan', but I learnt later that most of the German speakers were wont to call the Sultan Mohammed by this title.

The leader of the cavalry had brought his men to a halt in a circle around our coach. He was a young man with heavy black moustaches, dressed in a most outlandish and colourful costume with a back and breast armour plate. He wore a conical helmet with a single spike surmounting it and carried loosely across his saddle bow a short, curved sword with a thick blade which was broadest at the point end, the like of which I had not seen before. Apparently, as I was later told, this sword is a favourite weapon of the

47

Turk who took it from the Persians. It is called a scimitar.*

The Turkish officer studied us in silence for a moment, as well as in obvious puzzlement, since it is not often that those of the higher orders are seen driving their own coaches. The officer then addressed us in his own language. We shook our heads and the officer frowned in annoyance before speaking hesitantly in German.

'I am Murad Bey,' he said, 'servant of the great Sultan Mohammed, blessings on his name. What seek you in Iflak?'

I noted immediately that the officer had used the Turkish name for Wallachia. Meanwhile, Herr Strasser bowed awkwardly.

'Great Bey, I am but a humble merchant of Bosnia seeking to trade my wares in Tirgoviste.'

'And you?' The officer eyed me sharply.

'I am Barone Michelino,' I said. 'A citizen of Rome, travelling also to Tirgoviste in the course of my studies.'

'An Italian, eh? A Venetian spy, perhaps?'

'No, great Bey,' I said, adopting the attitude of Herr Strasser. 'I am merely travelling to Tirgoviste to study the local art of wine making, for in Italy I own great vineyards and I would now like to study how the Wallachians prepare their wines. You see, great Bey, I am trying to perfect a blend of wine . . .'

The lies came easily to my tongue, though it is true that I have more than a passing interest in the juices of the grape. The Turk regarded me with an expression of disgust.

'Pah!' he said. 'Merchants! A man such as you should wear a sword for more than ornamentation. You have the heart of a woman.'

I could see that the Turk addressed me thus, with what

* The word used in the original manuscript was the Italian *scimitarra* from which philologists claim the English word derives and that it is but a corruption of the Persian *shamsir*. Van Helsing.

48

for a Moslem is a great insult, in the hope that I would take offence, his reasoning being that if I were a fighting man I could not let such a slight go unanswered. However, instead of rising to his bait, I merely smiled and said:

'Better to live as a coward than to die a brave man.'

The Turk spat in disgust.

'You are typical of the Italians I have fought with,' he said. 'You all like life too much.'

'Why not?' I replied. 'Is death then so enjoyable?'

He opened his mouth to speak, but before he could do so one of his men urged his horse forward, shouting and waving his scimitar towards the distant hills. We all followed his gaze and saw a large force of horsemen galloping towards us. The Turkish officer bit his lip and turned back to us.

'You may thank the Prophet Mohammed for your safety,' he said. 'We must go. Remember, though, you have no Kazikly Bey to protect you now, and, by the beard of the Prophet, we shall return.'

With that he urged his mount forward and sped away up the valley, followed by his men.

'What did he mean by Kazikly Bey?' I inquired of Strasser.

'It means Impaler – the name the Turks gave to Dracula.'

A few moments later we were surrounded by the second group of horsemen. They wore very simple costume. For the most part they were merely mounted peasants with heavy sheepskin coats belted over rough shirts and trousers. Few wore anything on their feet, but most carried a round metal target shield and a long sword. Their leader was better dressed and equipped. He was a good-looking individual with a stern face but smiling eyes. He exchanged a rapid conversation with Herr Strasser in the Wallachian tongue and then he and his men wheeled their mounts in pursuit of the Turks.

'Who were they?' I asked.

'They call themselves soldiers of the new Voivode Basarab cel Tinara, Basarab the Younger, who is now acclaimed ruler of Wallachia. It seems that last week Stefan cel Mare entered Wallachia again with an army to avenge the death of Dracula, who was his friend. Laiota Basarab, the Turkish puppet, and his supporters were driven from Tirgoviste. Stefan then installed Basarab the Younger as the new ruler and the Turks have since been driven south of the Danube.'

'It is good news for the Wallachians.'

Herr Strasser sighed.

'The Wallachians are sheep. Always they are doomed for conquest. One day the Turks, the next the Hungarians. What matters, providing we merchants can continue to buy and sell our goods in peace? One conqueror is as good as another, and one man's money smells just the same as another's.'

He paused and looked up at the sky. I followed his gaze and saw that the darkness was gathering. Black clouds were forming, shadows crept across the land, and the air had turned grey and quite cold. I know not the reason, but this land now seemed strange and somehow threatening. Again I felt uneasy.

'We must hurry, *Freiherr*,' Herr Strasser said. 'It will soon be dark and it is some way to the next village. There are wolves and bears and other scavengers abroad at night who present danger to travellers such as we. Let us push on quickly.'

We whipped the horses forward through the gathering dusk.

CHAPTER SIX

It was evening when we arrived at the next village, though to call it a village was to do it an honour it little deserved. Even though they were shrouded in darkness I could only make out half a dozen rude cottages clustered around a squat building which was a church, one of those ugly edifices erected by the Teutonic Knights crusaders some two centuries ago. To one side of the village lay a sprawling cluster of buildings which Herr Strasser, having passed that way before, informed me was a tolerably good inn.

The first strange thing I noticed was that no light lit our passage into the courtyard, and despite the clatter of our coach as I reined in the horses before the inn doors, no shutter was removed, no door was thrown open in welcome, and no ostler came running out to relieve me of my burden. The inn remained dark, silent and inhospitable.

Herr Strasser gave an impatient sigh and aired his oft stated view that all Wallachians were lazy swine. He dismounted, not without difficulty as his portly frame was much given to being pampered through the perplexities of life by a host of servants. He strode to the inn door and gave three resounding knocks on the heavy timbers with the head of his cane. There was a faint stirring from within, and then silence again. I climbed down from the coach and joined Herr Strasser at the door.

'A strange welcome from an inn,' I observed.

'Ah,' Herr Strasser shrugged, 'you will find, *Freiherr*, that these lazy Wallachian swine are totally inefficient. You have to stir them into activity.'

And suiting the action to the word, he again beat a resounding tattoo upon the door.

A voice called out in Wallachian. It was obviously a query and Herr Strasser replied curtly. There was some mumbling behind the door and I heard the sound of heavy bolts being drawn. Only then did I notice that there were garlands of flowers hanging around the door.

Although I am not a scholar on botanical matters, I observed that the garlands were made up from thistles and garlic. I drew Herr Strasser's attention to the flowers, suggesting they were a strange choice for decoration and wondering what they symbolized, thinking that perhaps it was some religious festival that had taken place that day, for the flowers were fresh. However, Herr Strasser shook his head and mumbled something about the peculiar superstitions of the peasants.

The door finally swung inwards to where a tall, elderly man stood. He wore simple homespun clothes and a soft leather apron, the universal uniform of the innkeeper. His shirt was open and I could not help but observe the delicately wrought metal crucifix that hung on a chain around his neck.

The man scrutinized us for what seemed a longer time than usual, then he bowed, a half bow, deferential but not subservient. He spoke in German, having correctly guessed Herr Strasser to be of that nationality and having observed me to be a foreigner and therefore probably without knowledge of his native tongue. He waved his hand towards the brightly lit room behind him.

'You are welcome, *meine Herren*. You will forgive my delay in opening to welcome you.'

Herr Strasser snorted and strode in, ignoring the man. For my part, I informed him that our coach stood outside and we had no coachman to uncouple it or put the animals in the stables. The innkeeper looked puzzled for a moment and then politely said he would attend to the matter. He bid me enter while he called another man to take charge of the horses.

I now noticed that there were several people in the inn, which was brightly lit. I also noticed that everywhere, but especially around the doors and windows, hung the strange garlands of flowers.

I could only conclude from this that we had interrupted some village festivities which were not normally opened to strangers. Certainly the atmosphere was quiet and strained, and it seemed to me that the dozen or so villagers had removed themselves to the farthest side of the room from us. Only one or two cast glances in our direction, and these from the corners of their eyes.

But there were no complaints about the efficiency with which the innkeeper's wife moved forward with a smile of greeting and helped us off with our travelling cloaks; nor with the prompt insistence of her husband that we have a glass of local mulled wine to warm us. It was exceedingly rich red wine into which he inserted a red hot poker and which tasted pleasantly warm and sweet. In fact, I suggested another glass, but the innkeeper smilingly warned me of its unusual potency, adding that it would be unwise to drink further on an empty stomach. It was advice well taken and much in keeping with Herr Strasser's philosophy.

'We keep but simple fare here, *meine Herren*,' the innkeeper told us, 'but you are welcome to all we have.'

A table was soon cleared for us in a corner of the large room, a little to the side of the large, roaring fire. A pretty, buxom girl called Maria, whom I later learnt was the daughter of the house, laid the platters and pewter mugs before us. I suppose she was the first Wallachian maiden I had encountered, well built with indications that as middle age approached so would stoutness; but now, in maidenhood, her buxomness quickened the blood. Her skin was bronze, a healthy outdoor quality, never seen among the grand ladies of Rome, and her cheeks had natural dashes of red upon them. Her hair was almost the colour of pitch, and her eyes were a bright, penetrating blue. She smiled often as she bustled about the table, showing her ivory-white, perfect teeth.

The food was in fact far from simple, for to start with we had a sort of caviar which, I was told, was made from aubergines, with onions, cloves and garlic, and which was served to us on lettuce leaves. (It appeared to be a speciality of the area.) This was followed by a roast of pork, and to finish came sweet cakes. All of this was washed down with a white wine, for it is in white wine that the Wallachian usually excels.

As we thus enjoyed the 'simple' fare offered by our hosts, a man detached himself from the villagers and joined us at our table. No word was spoken, but our host placed a glass of wine before him and acted with a marked respect. Certainly the man could be differentiated from the rest of the company by the superior quality of his clothes, an authoritative bearing, and a full black patriarchal beard.

As he reached forward to raise his glass, his coat parted and I noticed a crucifix hung around his neck; it was similar in design to that worn by our host, but there the comparison ended. I caught only a fleeting glimpse, but observed the gold encrusted with flashing stones and superb workmanship. Was this man a boyar? It was only when the man smiled and inclined his head that I realized, with a blush, that my curiosity had caused me to stare at him for several moments.

'God be with you, *meine Herren*,' he said in German. 'You have come far?'

Herr Strasser nodded, his jowls not ceasing their rhythmic motion around a large portion of meat.

'I have come from Rome,' I replied. 'And this gentleman has kindly given me the use of his carriage as I could not find a fresh mount in Vidin. There are no horses here that I could purchase?'

The bearded man shook his head.

'The Turks have taken everything,' he said. 'There was little enough before, but now . . .'

He held out his hands, palms upwards, and shrugged.

'Where are you travelling to?'

'I am going to Tirgoviste,' I replied.

'What does a man of Rome seek there?'

'You ask a lot of questions of a stranger,' I said, frowning a little.

'We are a curious people,' he replied with a half smile. 'We peasant folk have questioning natures and strangers are a rarity among us – especially on nights such as this.'

The emphasis did not escape me, though the meaning behind it did, and his smile was as enigmatic as his words.

'You, a *peasant*?' I said in disbelief.

'You know who I am?' he asked.

'No,' I said. 'But not a peasant. Perhaps you are a boyar, as I understand the nobles of this country are called.'

'No, my young *Herr*, not a boyar.'

Suddenly, from somewhere outside the inn, came a distant howl. I have often heard wolves howl among the hills near Frascati, outside Rome, and such a howl was it that I heard now. In all truth it made my blood turn cold.

Immediately I became aware of a change in the people in the room. It was as if they had all been turned to stone, for they now seemed fixed in the one position, with only their eyes, wide open and fearful, darting here and there yet not seeing. Then a coldness descended.

Again came the long, drawn-out howl. Someone gasped. Several people crossed themselves. And the innkeeper, Grigore, hastened to the side of the bearded man.

'It must be time, Father,' he said.

I started. 'Father?' The question sprang involuntarily to my lips.

The bearded man rose and laid a hand on Grigore's shoulder, ignoring me.

'The people are ready?' he asked. 'They know what to do?'

'Yes, Father.'

'Then it is time. Have them light the torches. We will start this end of the village and work our way towards the church.'

Grigore turned and motioned the villagers to follow him. I noticed that each one wore a crucifix of some description outside his shirt. Grigore, standing by the door, handed each man a bundle of twigs and, as each man went out through the door into the night, these were lit to make torches. Grigore himself then did the same.

The bearded man had watched in silence, but now he also strode towards the door. Half-way there he paused, turned back, and looked directly at me.

'Young *Herr*,' he said, 'this can be a strange country to a foreigner. My advice is that you conduct your business in Wallachia as quickly as possible and that you return to your homeland with all speed. As for now, I should go and rest . . . follow the wise example of your companion.'

He smiled and pointed. Herr Strasser had fallen forward into the empty platters of his feast and was snoring the gentle sleep of the replete.

'He has had a good night,' I said.

There was no reply. When I turned back to face the priest, he was gone. The door of the inn was shut . . . and only the blood-chilling howl of the wolf could be heard in the stillness of the night.

I glanced across the room to see Grigore's wife bustling about, clearing away the remnants of the meal. At first she appeared to be quite normal, but then I noticed that she occasionally betrayed her true nervousness by darting wide eyes towards the shuttered windows or the door, festooned in their strange garlands of flowers. I also noticed that the room still seemed cold and, more important, that I myself felt uneasy.

'Where are the men gone?' I asked the woman.

Immediately her nervousness increased.

'Hunting, *mein Herr*,' she whispered.

'Hunting?'

'*Ja, mein Herr*.'

'But what is there to hunt at this hour?'

Her eyes blinked and grew larger. She glanced at me and away from me. Then she turned perceptibly pale and made the sign of the cross.

'Come, my dear *Frau*,' I said. 'You said they had gone hunting. For *what*?'

Her lips opened and closed, and she looked at me desperately, and then, with the greatest reluctance, she hissed a familiar word:

'*Moroii!*'

I started. It was the same word that Amza, the coachman, had coupled with Dracula before rushing away into the trees. My uneasiness increased.

'*Moroii?*' I asked. 'What is *moroii?*'

'No, *mein Herr*, no . . .'

She was now trembling like a leaf in a storm and, dropping a plate in fright, she suddenly turned and rushed from the room.

'Who are *you* to ask what is *moroii?*'

I became aware of a blast of icy air and turned to see Grigore standing in the doorway. His face was troubled and his eyes watched me in suspicion. He shut the door behind him and then walked slowly into the room, stopping before me.

'What do *you* know of *moroii?*' he said.

I confess I was a little perplexed. Grigore seemed the same, and yet different. He was uncommonly aggressive, but behind the aggression lurked a fear that I could not define. My confusion was deepening.

57

'I merely asked your wife what men hunted at this time of night,' I said. 'She answered *moroii* and I wondered what manner of beast was it that kept such strange nocturnal hours.'

At this Grigore sat down heavily on a bench and buried his face in his hands. Anguished sobs racked his body for a minute or two before he managed to regain his senses.

'No beast, *mein Herr*! No beast! Ah, *grosser Gott*, if only it was a mere beast that it could be killed as such. But no! It is a curse, *mein Herr*, an evil, a stealer of souls, a stealer of young children . . . my own daughter, only twelve years old, *mein Herr*, *my own daughter*!'

Suddenly the eerie howl of the wolf pierced the air, and Grigore, his eyes blazing with fury and hate, immediately sprang to his feet.

'There it is!' he exclaimed. 'The *moroii*! Ah, but we shall be more than a match for it this night!'

He started for the door, but I held him back, saying, 'Grigore, do you mean you are wolf hunting? A wolf that has attacked children in the village?'

He laughed almost hysterically.

'No, *mein Herr*. We hunt a beast that dons many disguises . . . a man who has sold his soul to *der Teufel* – the Prince of Evil himself!'

Then before I could properly digest these words, he had turned and rushed out into the night.

For a moment, as the full implication of his words sank into my brain, I was rooted to the spot. I have heard several times of the superstitions that were prevalent among the village communities (and Herr Strasser had not been loath to remind me of them), but this was my first encounter with a superstition that could lead to tragedy. I have heard of some rural communities outside Rome in which old women with deformities of the body are singled out, denounced as practitioners of the black arts, and stoned to death; in some countries they are even burnt. Now, here in this Wallachian village, it would seem that some poor demented man was being singled out for death because of the fear and superstition of the villagers.

If he had, indeed, been responsible for the death of the innkeeper's daughter, then he should be given a hearing. I shook myself angrily. It was my duty as a civilized man to put a stop to such primitive practices. It was my duty to save the poor man who was about to suffer at their hands.

I pulled on my travelling cloak and leaving Herr Strasser snoring by the fire, went out into the damp chill of the night. A ground mist had risen from the warmth of the day and the entire village was shrouded in it. Here and there I caught a glimpse of a burning torch, held aloft by a villager as he hunted the poor unfortunate. From time to time I heard a shouting, but it seemed that the man they called *a moroii* – which I now presumed to mean murderer – had thus far eluded the searchers.

Pulling my cloak tightly around me, I walked towards the squat, square-towered church. On reflection I know not what drew me there, for the line of searching villagers was still composed of mere shadows at the very far end of the village.

The church was surrounded by a small cluster of graves, and this graveyard was separated from the rest of the village by a low stone wall with wrought iron gates. It was untypical of the kind of church that is usually associated with the Orthodox religion and this was due, as I have previously stated, to its builders being crusaders on their way to the wars in the Holy Land.

The mist swirled about me. I heard faint cries in the distance. The gates swung open on their rusty hinges with a protesting squeal as I pushed through them and made my way up the path. As I stumbled on a stone, half blind in the darkness, I cursed myself for not bringing a torch to light my way.

It seems strange to me now that I should have thought that the poor unfortunate would hide out in such a place as that, yet at the time my footsteps were slow and sure, as if some uncanny power was guiding me to where I would find him.

I did not even go into the church itself; instead, my steps swung away alongside the church walls, towards a patch of land where nothing reposed save a large mound of earth. It was very dark here. There was not the slightest sound. I peered intently through the mist and discerned a freshly dug grave. I suddenly felt fearful.

'*Dracula!*'

I started. It was a sigh, a breath, long drawn out. A shiver ran down my spine and my head jerked around. First I saw nothing. Then the darkness seemed to shift. I heard a soft, mocking laugh and I shivered and the night fell about me.

'Who's there?' I demanded.

'*Dracula!*'

'Why do you call me Dracula?'

Again the scornful laugh. It seemed to echo all around me, to fill me and dissolve me, and I found myself shuddering with dread.

'Who is it?' I cried out.

Again I heard the laughter, sneering, macabre, echoing all around me and dissolving me and leaving me helpless. I tried to step backwards. I was unable to move. The mist hung in chill, white tatters about me and the darkness seemed total.

'*Dracula!*'

Suddenly a figure loomed forward. It was tall and dark as the night. I held my breath. It seemed almost to glide towards me. I wanted to reach for my sword, but I couldn't make a move and the fear only heightened my paralysis. I was shivering and sweating. I could feel my heart pounding. The figure moved through the gloom and then stopped a few feet from where I stood. There was the sound of harsh breathing.

Then, through the darkness and the swirling clouds of mist, I saw two piercing eyes, hellish, hypnotic, luring me, blazing like hot coals from the deepest and most scorching fires of Hell.

'*Dracula!*'

I found myself walking forward. I had no will of my own. The hair was matted across the face, obscuring all other features, and the creature's long cloak, which was dark as pitch, hid him effectively from my gaze. I walked forward in terror.

'*Come, Dracula . . .*'

The piercing eyes burned into me, the obscured face moved nearer, and I suddenly felt drowsy, removed from myself, forgot the night and the cold and the fear and seemed to drift into sleep . . .

'Stop!'

The voice hurled me back to reality, and a hand, holding a crucifix, appeared miraculously before my eyes.

I almost fell backwards into the hands of two village men. The graveyard was now athrong with villagers, all holding their blazing torches and surrounding the dark becloaked figure. The man was twisting furiously this way and that, apparently trying to find some opening through the heaving, unrelenting wall of villagers. Everyone was shouting, and I thought I heard the struggling man screaming.

Finally, the villagers managed to pull the man to his feet and I saw him straining for release. I had now recovered my senses enough to wonder why the man, who was certainly very big, could not simply tear himself free and run. Then I saw that the priest (for it was he who had held up the crucifix) was standing in front of the man, his crucifix in one hand, intoning rhythmically in his native tongue. This succeeded in making the man cringe as if terrified. I know not what the priest said, save that he mentioned the names of God and Jesus Christ several times and, each time he did so, the unfortunate man within the circle flinched as if he had been physically struck.

My previous fear was now fled and I felt sorry for the suffering of this unfortunate creature. I went to move forward, but the hands of the villagers who held me served not only to stay me in a moment of faintness, but to restrain me also. Then, as I watched the priest intoning before the cowering man, his face pale and ravaged and demented in the light of torches, I suddenly saw something that made me cry out in horror and beg the priest to desist.

The circle had opened to allow in a burly villager who carried a pitchfork. He immediately raised it, pointing the iron spikes towards the face of the captured man, who then let out such a pitiful howl of terror that it drained the very blood from my heart.

The man looked desperately around him, vainly seeking some escape, and then he raised his eyes to mine. No longer did his eyes burn with malevolent, seductive fury; now they were glazed and despairing and filled with strange grief.

'Help me!' he sobbed. 'Help me! In the name of your great sire, in the name of the blood that flows in your veins, in the name of Dra . . .'

Yet before he could finish what I did not want to hear, the burly villager had stepped forward and, with his entire weight behind him, thrust the iron spikes of the pitchfork straight through his eyes, and the man, thus impaled, fell backwards to the ground, writhing and shrieking horribly, his legs kicking as the villager leaned forward even further, pressing down on the pitchfork, finally impaling the man's head to the ground while, to my horror, the blood that spurted from the sockets shot upwards like a geyser, saturating those who stood nearby. Then, not content with this outrage, a sullen-faced villager moved forward, holding in his hands a heavy wooden mallet and an iron stake, and without further ado, and with the acquiescence of the priest, placed the stake above the heart of the dead body and drove it in with the brutal force of his mallet, until, to my shocked disbelief, the black blood rose like a fountain and, from the lips of what I had already considered a corpse, came a scream such as I had never heard before.

My heart pounded furiously, my head started to spin, and I sank down into merciful blackness.

CHAPTER SEVEN

'*Fühlen Sie sich besser?*'

I opened my eyes and gazed into Grigore's face. I blinked and looked around. I was lying on a bench in the main room of the inn. Grigore and the priest were bending over me while Grigore's wife and daughter stood silently in the background.

'Are you feeling better?' Grigore asked again in his thickly accented German.

I licked my lips and tried to speak, but only a croak would emerge from my dry throat.

Grigore placed a glass into my hands.

'Drink this, *mein Herr*, but slowly,' he said as I raised the glass to my lips. 'It is a spirit we distil here from the residue of the grapes, and it is strong.'

I took a swallow of the water-coloured liquid and felt a fire-like sensation burn its way down my gullet to the pit of my stomach. I coughed and handed the glass back.

'I'm all right now,' I said, struggling to a sitting position.

'The young *Herr* has had a bad experience,' Grigore said.

Suddenly the memory of those moments in the church-yard came flooding back. I shuddered and reached for Grigore's glass.

'A man has been murdered,' I said, looking at the priest.

The priest returned my gaze steadily.

'A beast has been destroyed,' he said softly.

'Beast! Man!' I cried hotly. 'I saw a man done to death in a most vile manner by a pack of superstitious brutes!'

Grigore went white.

'How dare you speak to the Father in that way! Do you not know that you owe him your immortal soul? Had he not arrived in time and shielded you with his crucifix from the *moroii* . . .'

The priest placed a restraining hand on Grigore's arm, and Grigore, white-faced and ghostlike in the flickering candlelight, seemed to float out of my vision. I glanced up at the priest.

'Immortal soul?' I cried. 'And what of the immortal soul of him that lies in the churchyard?'

'He had none, young *Herr*,' the priest said sorrowfully. 'He was a *moroii*.'

'Since coming to this God-forsaken country,' I said, unable to conceal my agitation, 'all I have heard about is *moroii*, beasts without souls. I demand an explanation!'

Grigore's face floated through the ever-shifting shadows, the candlelight illuminating his eyes and revealing his outrage. The priest motioned him away with an imperceptible nod of his head, then he leaned closer to me.

'I told you before, young *Herr*, that this is a strange country of shadows where blood is cheap and flows like water, where the mountains and plains have for centuries been drenched in the blood of many races. Death is no stranger to the men and women of Wallachia. And, in whatever form it comes, we have no fear of it. No, that which we *do* fear is undeath, eternal suffering and torture; and we know and fear those who have succumbed to live as immortals in the cursed guise of the Undead.'

I raised a protesting hand, to question him, to tell him that I knew not what he talked about, but he spoke like one in a dream, seeing images in the blazing fire before us.

'You ask me, young *Herr*, what a *moroii* is,' he continued. 'I shall answer, and I pray to God that you may never have to utilize such knowledge. It is the belief in Wallachia that when a man dies his soul does not pass into Paradise until forty days have gone by. Thus, three years after all burials, we exhume the bodies to make sure that the spirit has ascended and the body become putrified. For unless we are vigilant, the spirit of a dead person can reanimate his corpse to suck at the life of the living.

'When I was a young priest here, there was a young woman who died and was buried. Yet several weeks later there came reports that the same woman had been seen at night playing with children in the village. At that time, living here, was an old man, wise even beyond his years, but whom I, in my youth, called superstitious and ungodly. This old man came to me and told me that the village was in turmoil, that the spirit of the dead woman had not departed and therefore she had become Undead. He asked that the ancient remedy be invoked. Naturally I laughed. I thought I knew better. Then, one day, the old man came to me and said that the villagers had taken matters into their own hands since I would not act for them.

'A young boy who had not yet committed a sexual act was mounted on a jet black stallion which had never mated with a mare. The villagers led the pair across the churchyard until the horse stopped at the grave of the woman who had died and was reported to have been seen. In spite of whippings, the horse stood at the grave and refused to go on. Two men of the village then dug down and eventually exhumed the body. The old man brought me to the graveside and I looked down at the body, eight months buried, and it lay as fleshy and fair as if the girl were but sleeping. The old man then sat down and honed a spade, sharpening its edge, and then, deeming it sufficiently sharp, he stepped forward, raised it high above his head, and brought it down into that fair white neck, severing the head from the body. The blood spurted forth, florid and fresh, so that I would have sworn that he had cut the throat of a woman in full health and vigour. Then the old man turned away, crying . . . for the woman had been his own daughter.

'The body was reburied, face downwards, with a thorn bush on the grave to stop the corpse from rising. And no more was the woman seen and no more were the strange illnesses that had afflicted the children of the village. This, young *Herr*, was my first encounter with a *stigoi* . . .'

The priest was leaning over me. His eyes were bright and intense. There was the movement of people behind him, and the candlelight flickered. I felt suffocated. My heart was still pounding. I offered a brief, nervous smile and felt my reasoning falter.

'Are you asking me to believe that the man killed tonight was a . . . *stigoi*? A corpse?'

'No, young *Herr*. He was a *moroii*, a vampire, but not yet one of the Undead. A *stigoi* is an Undead vampire.'

'Ridiculous!' I snapped, though my uneasiness tormented me. 'I would not have thought that a priest would give credence to such childish, peasant superstitions.'

The priest merely smiled.

'You think that I fall prey to an unreasoning awe or fear of something unknown, something imaginary which creates a fear founded on ignorance? Does it not occur to you, my young *Herr*, that fear can also be founded on knowledge – a fear and respect for the evil that the unknown can do? To each person, the belief of a fellow which is at variance with his own belief is a superstition. I know the *stigoi* and the *moroii* to be a reality, and I warn you, young *Herr*, to be on your guard, especially at this time of the year.'

'What do you mean?' I asked.

'Why, we are in the last days of November. It will soon be the Eve of St Andrew's Day when the evil forces are at their strongest. There are three times in the year when our defences reach an ebb and when the evil forces ride rampant through the world. In the month of April, on the Eve of St George's feastday, and later that month, on the Eve of St Walpurgis' feastday, and on the penultimate day of November, the Eve of the feastday of St Andrew. Beware, young *Herr*, for our superstitions in Wallachia are not taken lightly.'

I did not reply. I felt tired and truly shaken. The priest rose and smiled, and I saw that he, too, was exhausted.

'I see you are tired from the exertions of the day,' he said. 'I will therefore leave you in the hands of Grigore. May you pass the night in peace and safety, and, should you be receptive to advice on the morrow, I would return to your own country.'

I was, thanks to the drink given to me by Grigore, already asleep before he left the inn. It was a strange, troubled sleep in which I saw a great concourse of people rising from their tombs, rising above the mist and the obscene, shifting darkness, clad only in their burial clothes, crying out in one mighty voice: 'Dracula! Dracula! Save us, Master!' Then, once again, I saw the man in the churchyard, black, eyes glistening, wrapped protectively in the cloak, and, in my dream, I suddenly recognized him as my own father, Dracula . . .

I awoke, cold and sweating, and was thankful to see the grim, grey light of dawn seeping in between the cracks in the shutters. I stayed awake, unable to return to sleep, until I heard the noises of people in the kitchen. The smell of freshly baked bread caused me to wash and then rouse Herr Strasser, who still lay oblivious to the hideous events of the previous night.

As we breakfasted, I let Herr Strasser negotiate with Grigore to hire a man from the village to drive our coach to the capital, Tirgoviste. The arrangement was concluded and it was not long before we climbed into the coach.

It was a cold, bright morning. The sun shone, but without any degree of warmth, and a frost still lay thick on the ground. A few groups of silent villagers stood around us, watching our coach suspiciously, but it was inconceivable to me that the event of the previous night could actually have taken place. A man murdered by superstitious villagers, the act condoned by their priest. Indeed, at that moment I felt a rage against them. Had I been in Rome I would have gone to the authorities, but here, in this strange and unfriendly country, who were the authorities? Yes, I raged against them, their ignorance and their stupidity, but even as I did so I was haunted by the memory of the priest's quiet and unwavering conviction . . .

The coach started off through the village, the villagers staring unblinkingly after us, saying nothing, just watching.

'A strange people,' said Herr Strasser, arranging a travelling rug over our legs. 'Eh, *mein Freiherr*?'

My eyes caught sight of the freshly dug grave in the churchyard. It had since been filled in and had a thorn bush planted on top of it. I saw the sun blazing down upon it, and it all seemed quite natural.

'Yes,' I said quietly. 'Strange indeed.'

Then, as we drove out of the cluster of buildings, I looked back along the road to Tirgoviste. By the graveyard wall I caught sight of the bearded priest. As I watched him, the sun suddenly shone on his figure, flashing all around him, illuminating him in the greatest detail. Slowly, he made the sign of the cross and pointed two fingers at me. Then the coach rounded a bend in the road and, first the priest and then the village disappeared from my gaze.

CHAPTER EIGHT

By mid afternoon our coach had rumbled into the narrow streets of the Wallachian capital. We had crossed two great rivers in our journey, the Arges and the Dimbovita, both tributaries to the Danube yet as broad as any river I have seen. The Dimbovita especially was memorable, flowing through a valley of steep mountain walls, with wild gorges and spectacular grottoes.

Although but a village compared with Rome, nevertheless Tirgoviste is a fair-sized city and stands on the banks of another river called the Ialomita. The town is built around the court of the Grand Voivode, now Basarab cel Tinar, that is Basarab the Younger who, but a few short weeks before our arrival, had overthrown Basarab cel Batrin, the man who had defeated Dracula with the aid of the Turks. Early in November the famous Stefan cel Mare of Moldavia had once again defeated the Turks and placed Basarab the Younger on the throne of Wallachia in place of the Turkish puppet. Now Basarab cel Tinar was in the process of rebuilding the despoiled city with its many churches and monuments. Already work had started on the restoration of a sumptuous looking building which I understood was the metropolitan church of Basarab.

Indeed, the city seems a very pious place, and houses not only monasteries within its walls, but outside as well. One of the most beautiful churches I have ever seen is not far from the city, in an area of vineyards up in the hills. I am told that some of the Voivodes of Wallachia are buried here, including my grandfather, Vlad Dracul.*

* It would seem that this church was rebuilt by Dracula's cousin, Radu the Great (1495–1508) as part of the Monastery of St. Nicholas of the Wines, which was known locally as *Monastirea Dealului*, the

The strangeness of the previous night was soon forgotten as I looked eagerly about the city that had once been the capital of Vlad Dracula, my father. Herr Strasser directed our coach to an inn that he praised highly, called Hanul cu Petru, which means Peter's Inn. The inn, like most of the houses that are not churches or palaces, was built mostly of wood – oak, I believe. Hardly had we settled in than I embarked upon a journey through the city, intent upon learning as much as possible during my stay, but no sooner had I stepped forth than it grew dark, and I had to return to the inn.

The next day I was abroad early and found the day passed exceeding quick. Tirgoviste is essentially a city of churches, though much desolated now with the wars that have taken place in recent years. The monasteries, with cloisters, chapels and decorative courtyards, add to the colour of the city and are rewarding to the students of architecture. Apparently, so I have heard, a traveller from Venice thought it 'a vast, gaudy flower house'. But apart from churches and monasteries, I discovered a surprisingly large number of boyars' palaces, each one a small fortress.

I remarked later to Petru, the innkeeper, on this, and he explained that Tirgoviste was a city of anarchy where people did not know from one day to another who would be ruler and who would be victim to political assassination. The lower orders tried to ignore the changes in order that they might survive, but the boyars sought to fortify themselves.

The main churches were of the Orthodox faith, and in the city lay a grand palace of the primate of the church, called the Metropolitan. But there was also a Franciscan monastery. Here I made myself known to the abbot, a

---

Monastery of the Hill. It became one of the most beautiful ecclesiastical structures in Romania. Van Helsing.

Florentine who had come on a mission to Wallachia and stayed in spite of the troubles. He was generous with his wine and bid me stay for the midday meal.

The abbot was a verbose man and soon he had fallen to reminiscences of Dracula's reign, which appears a favourite topic with Wallachians. I leant forward eagerly, for it was my wish to know more of this supposedly gruesome father whose reputation seemed to stink in the nostrils of Christendom.

'What was this Dracula really like?' I asked the abbot. 'We have heard so many tales of his evil acts . . . but surely they are somewhat exaggerated?'

The abbot shook his head.

'Rather, my son,' he said, 'they are understatements, for truly he was an evil man. Why,' the abbot rose and went to a window, 'down there is a narrow street, and half-way along is an old, dirty house where once dwelt one of Dracula's mistresses. Dracula had merely lusted after her body, but she, poor child, loved him. One day he went to visit her when a mood of despair was upon him, and she, wishing to arouse a spark of happiness in him, told him that she was with child by him. The innocent girl thought this news would bring cheer to Dracula. Ah, the poor creature. Dracula took out his sword and cut open her womb, exclaiming that he wanted to see where the fruit of his loins was. There was no child, and he left her there to die in terrible torment. Such was the evil of his mind.'

The abbot paused to replenish his glass.

'He was an austere man whose austerity for others begat such evil,' he continued. 'If a woman consorted with a man who was not her husband, this Dracula had her skinned alive and her skin tied to a pole in the middle of Tirgoviste . . . right in the market place. This same act he performed against widows and young girls who lost their virginity.'

A feeling of nausea arose in me, and I began to wonder whether such tales were really true or whether they were invented against an enemy to discredit him. I had known that Dracula had won the enmity of the Saxon merchants who had done their utmost to spread such stories, and I knew also that he had sometimes displayed intolerance against the Catholic church. But even so, I began to believe that there must exist some truth in such tales of horror.

Later that day, my uneasiness increasing, I bade farewell to the abbot and returned to the inn.

Early that evening, just after the descent of dusk, Petru, the innkeeper, knocked on my door and told me that there was a man waiting for me downstairs.

To describe the man as ugly would be an understatement. His stockiness belied his height, which must have exceeded six foot, and such was his width that he seemed to block out all the light from the room. His head was set well down on his shoulders as if he had no neck; it was a square-shaped head with an exceptionally low forehead, surmounted by a matted mass of dirty hair that must have once been black but was now streaked with grey. Across one cheek a scar traced a livid red line from ear to mouth, drawing the lips up at one end in a permanent sneer. There was a second scar across the eyebrow which caused the right eyelid to appear semi-closed. From this travesty of a face the eyes that stared out were dark and dead; there seemed little hint of life in them as the man watched me descend the stairs into the room. Then, as I reached the foot of the stairs, the man bowed.

'I am Tirgsor,' he said in a thick accent which made me strain to hear the meaning of the German. 'Tirgsor, the *stolnic* of Castle Dracula.'

'You are the steward of Castle Dracula?' I asked, surprised.

For reply he held out a paper. I took it and broke open the familiar seal.

Written at Castle Dracula, Poenari, on the twenty-ninth day of the month of November, in the year 1477.

Brother – Welcome to our home, your home. We are awaiting your arrival with impatience. We pray you have rested well. Tirgsor, our steward, has a carriage which will take you on the last part of your journey to the home of your ancestors. Be well, come safely.

Your loving brothers – Vlad and Mihail

I raised my eyebrows in surprise.

'How did you know I was here?' I demanded of Tirgsor. 'I only arrived last night and have sent no word to Castle Dracula of my coming.'

The big man shrugged.

'I was sent here to escort the young *Herr* to Schloss Dracula,' he replied simply.

'But who told you I was here?'

'I was sent here, *mein Herr.*'

I dismissed the matter for the moment. The solution of this intriguing riddle would have to wait until I saw my brothers and questioned them. And doubtless Tirgsor was possessed of a simple mind.

'Very well, Tirgsor, I will be ready to leave tomorrow morning. You will find yourself quarters for the night.'

The man shuffled his feet.

'I was sent here to escort the young *Herr* to Schloss Dracula,' he repeated stubbornly. 'The carriage is outside.'

'Tirgsor,' I said firmly, 'I have just arrived in this capital of Wallachia and I counted on several days rest here. But in deference to my brothers' invitation, I shall continue my journey tomorrow.'

The huge man frowned and bit his lip.

74

'I was ordered to bring you at once,' he said slowly. 'The carriage is outside.'

So saying, he took a step towards me, almost as if he would seize me and throw me into the carriage whether I wished to go or not. But at that moment there was a footfall on the stair behind me, and I turned to see Petru, the innkeeper, who was watching us both with frightened eyes.

'Forgive me, *mein Herr*,' he said. 'I could not help but overhear you. The young *Herr* does not plan to continue his journey tonight?'

'Why?' I asked.

'Oh, young *Herr*, know you not what day it is? It is the eve of the feast of St Andrew. Please do not travel tonight for there is much danger abroad.' I must have smiled broadly at this, for Petru suddenly grasped my hand and, almost whimpering in fright, said: 'Please, please, young *Herr*! You cannot imagine what can happen on such a day! Should you be travelling at nightfall, then you will become prey to all the vile and evil things that hold sway.'

Now laughing, I disengaged myself from his clutching hands.

'Have no fear, old man,' I said. 'I do not intend continuing my journey until tomorrow, for I wish to rest this night, not travel in some uncomfortable coach.'

An expression of relief crossed old Petru's face.

'God save the young *Herr*,' he said, 'for a long, full and vigorous life.'

He crossed himself and extended two fingers towards me, even as the bearded priest had done. I have since learnt that, among the Wallachians, it is considered to be a charm against evil.

Then a sound, remarkably like a snarl, broke from the lips of Tirgsor. I swung around to face him. His eyes were resting on old Petru and now, for the first time, I saw some animation in them. And what I saw was black hatred.

'Tirgsor!' I spoke sharply. 'You will find quarters and will then meet me outside the inn tomorrow morning, after I have breakfasted. Only then will we continue our journey. Do you understand?'

The steward's eyes, now lustreless again, looked deeply into mine, and I became aware of something strange in their blackness . . . it was almost as if they had no pupils. Then I became aware of a blue flickering in those vitreous depths, blue and black, black and blue, and I watched, fascinated, as the eyes seemed to dissolve, luring me in, my own eyelids growing heavy, a drowsiness descending, wanting to sleep, to close my eyes and drift away, thinking how simple it would be, how much more rewarding, to let Tirgsor drive me immediately to Castle Dracula, where I could sleep, sleep for a long time, sleep in a large bed with snow white linen sheets, sleep, just sleep . . .

Suddenly I jerked awake, almost falling over myself, as if I were being held by some unseen force and now had to jerk myself free.

I blinked and glanced around me. Old Petru was gazing at me in some alarm. Tirgsor was no longer staring at me, but instead was standing quietly with his eyes downcast.

Then I noticed that two others had entered the inn, and I saw from their apparel that they were priests of the Orthodox Church, for they were resplendently dressed and had large gold crucifixes hanging around their necks.

Tirgsor studiously ignored the crucifixes and he seemed almost frightened.

'You have your orders, Tirgsor!' I snapped in a loud and firm tone of voice.

He bit his lips together and refused to meet my gaze; then he shuffled his feet and looked away.

'Very well, *mein Herr*,' he said. 'I shall be here with the coach first thing in the morning.'

With that he turned on his heel and strode out of the inn, while old Petru stepped closer and laid a tentative hand on my arm.

'The young *Herr* is all right?' Petru asked.

'Yes,' I said, 'but a little travel weary. I will go and rest awhile in my room.'

Alone in my room, I know not what made me rummage in my bags and take out the small velvet-covered box that my mother had given me on her death bed. Inside was a short gold chain to which hung a gold crucifix with a figure of Christ executed in loving and intricate workmanship. I took it from its box and hung it around my neck, under my shirt. This done, and feeling strangely happier, I lay down and closed my weary eyes.

I could not sleep. Strangely, after my extraordinary moment of tiredness downstairs, I felt wide awake when in the bed. Indeed, there was no hint of sleepiness in my mind at all and so, after a while, I rose impatiently from my bed and went out.

There were signs of great activity in the streets. Benches and tables laden with food and wine were appearing, while various musicians stood about in groups, playing fascinating airs on their peculiar instruments.

On asking Petru the cause of the festivities, he explained that the people of the city were holding a *hora*. It would appear that this custom arose from the superstition of St Andrew's Eve when, it was felt, great merrymaking and entertainment kept the evil spirits at bay, for, so they reasoned, the evil spirits only prey on the unhappy and fearful.

It was a custom I heartily endorsed and, perhaps to throw off my own inexplicable fears, I threw myself eagerly into the activities. One particular dance I insisted on joining in was called a *perinita*, the literal translation being 'little cushion', and the dance itself being known as the 'kissing dance'. The Wallachian girls took this in great spirit and, in my honour, the dance was performed three times with much gusto and much drinking and laughter.

Later that evening I found myself seated next to an old man whose name, I seem to recall, was Costel. He was a veteran of the army of Iancu de Hunedoara and told me that he had fought at the battle of Belgráde when Iancu defeated the troops of Mohammed II, a month before he took sick and died of the plague. The old man spoke a voluble German, so voluble that I had difficulty in understanding all he had to say. He gestured at the lines of dancing men and women, whirling down the streets in the flickering light of thousands of torches, and then turned to me.

'I knew a *hora* once,' he said, 'here in this city of ours, but one which was not so joyful.'

'When was that, old man?' I asked.

'Dracula's father, the old Vlad Dracul,' he said, 'was assassinated by certain rich and powerful boyars, encouraged by Iancu de Hunedoara, because he had made terms with the Turks. And Dracula's brother, Mircea, whom, God believe me, I knew well and served with in battle, became the Voivode of Wallachia. This Mircea also treated with the Turks, for Wallachia was almost a desert because of their victorious troops, so the great boyars, by guile and cunning, seized Mircea and brought him in chains to Tirgoviste and had him slain.'

The old man sighed and nodded to himself.

'It was in the year 1456 that Dracula returned to Tirgoviste as Voivode,' he continued. 'The first thing he did was order that his brother's coffin be exhumed from the public burying plot of Tirgoviste to be reburied among the voivodes of Wallachia up in the podgorie, the hilly region outside the city. When the coffin was opened, it was found that Mircea's head was twisted and showed that he had been buried alive and died struggling for breath. Dracula ordered him to be reburied with the ceremony befitting a voivode.

'It was not long after this that Dracula formulated his plans to punish the boyars who had slain his father and buried his brother alive.

'In the spring of the same year there was a great feast and dance in Tirgoviste, then as now, and Dracula had all the boyars of the city go to the great hall of the palace – and there was the Metropolitan himself, five bishops and all the abbots of the monasteries. As the feasting went on, Dracula asked them how many reigns they had experienced in their lifetimes. One of them came forward and said: "Since your grandfather, there have been no less than twenty voivodes, and I have survived them all." Even the youngest boyar said he had known seven voivodes. Now Dracula knew that the boyars had scant regard for a voivode and that they believed they would survive him because they were more powerful – but Dracula was cleverer than the boyars.

'His soldiers surrounded the hall and, at an order from Dracula, seized five hundred boyars who had experienced more than seven reigns, for among them, so Dracula reasoned, would be the assassins of his father and brother. These unfortunates he had impaled on wooden stakes in the vicinity of the palace, until the flesh rotted and blackbirds grew fat on their feeding.'

The old man sighed. He scratched at an eyebrow. I glanced down at the floor because I did not dare gaze at his eyes.

'Aye,' he said slowly, 'that was some feast day . . . just over twenty-one years ago. A strange, terrible man was Dracula, but, by my sword, at least he drove the Turks out. Perhaps he was the best of all our voivodes: you have to be harsh and ruthless to rule a country constantly at war.'

I left him to his musings. I will admit that the more I heard of the bloodthirsty acts of my father, Dracula, the more I began to feel that an injustice was being done. Indeed, were not the stories being enlarged out of all proportion to the real events? I well recall, a few years ago, the Papal Nuncio, the Bishop of Erlau, reporting to the Pope that Dracula had personally ordered the killing of 100,000 people – an entire fifth of the population of Wallachia. Yet who accused Dracula of atrocities? Always his enemies.

'Tis true that the man was cruel – the experience of my mother told me that – but was he really the devil incarnate as they made out?

Old Costel had said that to rule a country constantly at war one had to be ruthless. Wallachia was being squeezed by both Turk and Saxon, while there also reigned internal anarchy, intrigues by the boyars or aristocracy, aided by political plots from Hungary. Dracula's virtual destruction of the boyars had given Wallachia an immediate, albeit horrible, lesson: that the voivode's title, and all that it implied, was not to be taken lightly. A nation should unite behind its prince and be obedient to his commands, his resolution and discipline, in order to defeat its constant enemies. In this light, then, Dracula's actions were no more ruthless or tyrannical than those of Louis XI of France, or Sigismondo Malatesta, the Lord of Rimini. Indeed, even so far west as the kingdom of England, it is reported that my lord the Earl of Worcester, during the current civil wars between the houses of Lancaster and York, impales his enemies to such a degree as to make Dracula seem a saint. Given this, why the reputation of Dracula above all the others?

Thus meditating, I turned in early to be refreshed for the journey I would undertake the next day to Castle Dracula.

CHAPTER NINE

We started our journey early in the morning. Tirgsor, as he had promised, presented himself before the inn at first light and I, after a breakfast of good local ale and warm, freshly baked bread, climbed into the coach. It was an open coach, entirely coloured in black, and even drawn by two black horses. The only relief was the escutcheon – a white dragon's head – painted on the coach door. Although the coach was open, there were plenty of furs, the skins of bears which I gathered were numerous in the mountain regions, and these I tucked about me while Petru handed me a large basket of food and drink which his wife had prepared for the journey.

Tirgsor, who had exchanged but two syllables that morning, climbed on to the raised box at the front of the coach, raised his whip and cracked it, and the horses lunged forward, the coach seeming to fly along the road and out of the city.

I caught a last quick glimpse of Petru, crossing himself and holding the inevitable two fingers in my direction. At this I smiled, and hoped that his charm against the evil eye was successful.

The day was pleasant. A clear blue sky, with a bright if warmless sun, followed us for most of the journey. It was a clear autumn day holding the promise of a cold winter to come; however, I was wrapped up warmly and excited by the thought that this was the last lap of my journey.

We swung northwards along the Dimbovita valley, following parallel to the river. From fairly flat land, which I understand is called the Wallachian Plain, small hills soon began to rise and give way to more sharply rising ground. The area here was quite populated, and there were many fortified large houses which are called *cula*. The people of this area are mainly free men or *mosneni*, as they are called. They work small areas of land which belong to them. There are few boyars in the area and few slaves, a sign that feudalism seems to be declining here.

The journey was very pleasant until we reached Catatenidin Vale, a small cluster of houses standing by a river and overshadowed by a grim castle on a mountain. I demanded that Tirgsor stop here while I refreshed myself, otherwise I am sure the surly brute would have continued driving the animals all day until they dropped.

Actually, I had twice asked the sullen steward whether he was ill, for he appeared so pale and weak for a man of his girth, and I noticed that he seemed almost blind in the light. He wore a heavy black cloak which completely encased him, and a hat which he had drawn down so far little of his face could be seen. The previous night he had given the impression of enormous strength (in spite of his pale face and lustreless eyes), but now I perceived that it was almost as much as he could do to control the horses. Nevertheless, he dismissed my solicitous inquiries with a grunt, and so I gave up trying to communicate with him. Instead, I told him to see to the horses' refreshment and then I set off to explore the place a little.

There were few people about, but one man told me that if I climbed the mountain towards the castle I would find a church built inside the rock of the mountain where three monks hold vigil and say mass each day. Time precluded this interlude, but I was led to understand that there is not a mountain gorge, torrent or river in the area that does not evoke some stormy history or deed of war, and, had I the time available, I would have found willing narrators among the peasants.

Tirgsor was impatient and so I climbed into the coach and again we set off at a fast pace, swinging suddenly away from the river Dimbovita and following a smaller tributary which was called the Arges. The steep hills had now given way entirely to precipitous mountains pushing skywards, which seemed to grow higher and higher as we made our way further into the ranges. These were the formidable Transylvanian Alps that separated Wallachia from Transylvania.

I noticed that we were travelling constantly uphill, and several times the horses stumbled. Every time I offered to alight and assist Tirgsor in leading the horses to surer ground, the monosyllabic steward grunted his displeasure and told me to stay in the coach.

Perhaps it was merely caused by the mountains blotting it out, but it seemed that the sun had already set, so cold and dark it now was. Storm clouds were hurrying across the sky, brushing the mountain tops. Unlike the *mosneni* areas we had passed through, this area seemed sparsely populated. The few villages we encountered were smaller and poorer in appearance, and the houses had less decoration. There were one or two people about, and these wore very simple and dirty clothes. I had grown accustomed to seeing villagers with gaily embroidered jackets, but these people wore no such trappings, which is most unusual in mountain districts.

Once or twice Tirgsor had to draw rein because of cattle in our path. At such times I leant out to greet the drover or ask a question, but the only reply I received was a furtive look and the sign of the cross, before the peasant scuttled away like a rabbit. At this, Tirgsor would laugh and crack his whip after the man. I rebuked him more than once, but to no avail.

It may have been my imagination, but with the growing dusk it seemed to me that Tirgsor began to shake aside the vapours he had displayed throughout the day and instead to show a strength I have seldom seen in his handling of the horses.

We now skirted a place called Curtea de Arges, the

citadel of Arges, a group of dwellings and a few large houses surrounding an ancient cathedral. This was once the capital of Wallachia, many generations ago, and in that cathedral many of the line of Dracula were anointed before the assembled boyars. But here we hardly paused, for darkness was descending rapidly.

Tirgsor, all signs of weakness gone, forced the horses on at a pace that made me cry out in alarm, for I felt that he would overturn the coach if he were not more careful.

Suddenly my prophecy almost came true, for both horses reared and whinnied without warning, rearing and straining in opposite directions. The coach slewed around and wound up half in a ditch. I would have been thrown into the roadway had not the plunging of the horses jerked the coach up out of the ditch almost before it had toppled in. Tirgsor, shouting curses, tried to calm the horses, but still they reared and plunged, their terrified whinnies echoing in the silence of the mountains.

The breath had been knocked from me and I lay back, gasping and wondering what was amiss. Then I saw the cause of the incident.

A man in the dress of a priest, his face white, his eyes blazing, stood in front of the horses, his arms held up as if in benediction. It would seem that he must have leapt out into the road, almost under the hooves of the horses, and frightened them. As I watched, I saw this startling figure of a priest, his face distorted with hatred, run towards the carriage. He held some kind of bottle in one hand, and, as I sat there stunned, he ran towards me, uncorked the bottle, and cried out in a loud voice: '*In nomine patris et fili et spiritu sancti!*' Then, without further ado, he flung its contents in my face.

Naturally I recoiled, and saw a triumphant smile on the priest's face – a triumph that swiftly gave way to disbelief, and then puzzlement. I, too, must have shown my own puzzlement as I sat there with water dripping down my face.

What strange manner of man was this, dressed in the guise of a priest, to run out on unsuspecting travellers and throw water in their faces? Was he mad?

As I was thus contemplating, too stunned to do anything else, the man leaned heavily against the side of the carriage, gasping spasmodically, and peered intently into my face.

'You are not he!' he exclaimed.

He turned away a little, shaking his head in perplexity; then he quickly turned back to face me, his eyes blazing angrily.

'What are you doing in that coach?' he demanded. 'Do you not realize to whose house it belongs?'

I started to reply, but Tirgsor, who had now quieted the horses, suddenly turned around and struck out with his whip. The lash caught the priest full in the face, making him cry out with pain before falling down to the roadside.

'Out of the way, Christian pig!' Tirgsor snarled.

The priest raised himself on one elbow, his face once more distorted with hatred, his eyes fierce and staring directly at Tirgsor.

'Spawn of Satan!' he cried out. 'I know you well, Tirgsor! Tirgsor is well known, as is the evil thing he serves, and God will not forget him!'

Tirgsor snarled. It was a sound that chilled my blood. The gloom was descending and the shadows filled my gaze, and then I saw Tirgsor step forward with the whip and bring it down on the priest again.

'Stop it!' I shouted, suddenly regaining my senses. 'The man is a priest, mad or not!'

Tirgsor paused. He glanced at me and at the priest. He snorted and stepped back, and the priest, still on the ground, peered sharply at me.

'Young *Herr*, young *Herr*,' he said, 'you are not one of them. What do you do in that coach? Know you not that it belongs to the house of Dracula? Yes! Evil spawned them, evil nurtures them, and by evil they live in half-death. I beg you, young *Herr*, listen to me! Do not go to Castle Dracula if you value your immortal soul!'

With this the priest started to crawl towards the coach, and again Tirgsor brought his whip down upon him. I heard the priest cry out, and then Tirgsor had urged the horses forward, so sharply that I was thrown back into my seat. By the time I had regained my balance, and had managed to glance back, the priest was but a blur in the gloom. I watched the darkness devour him.

I made up my mind to report the conduct of Tirgsor as soon as we arrived at the castle. I might be a stranger to the customs of this land of Wallachia, which still labours under feudalism, but no man has a right to whip another as one would a dog. I determined that Tirgsor should be punished for his sullen malice.

Night had fallen with incredible swiftness. One moment there had been an eerie twilight, a quickly gathering dusk, and the next there was a blackness in which not even the surrounding woods could be discerned. Tirgsor halted the coach and lit two torches which were hung on either side, but even with this assistance the journey became slower and more difficult, the horses being forced down to a trot. And then, in white brilliance, the moon came racing over the distant peaks, lighting our road almost as if it were day.

We left the wooded area and went across a small plain. The air had become intensely cold and I was glad of the heavy furs which I had heaped about me. Even so, I could not help shivering. As we emerged on to the plain a sudden cold wind began to blow, causing the trees in the area to bend this way and that, whispering and forming strange patterns. I fancied that I saw several dark shapes slinking across the moonlit expanse, and I was just beginning to wonder what they were when I heard the macabre baying of wolves which, I understand, thickly populate the area.

To my surprise, as I looked across the plain, I caught sight of a faint, flickering blue light and then several more beyond it. I blinked and looked again. Across the plain were some half dozen ghostly columns of blue, dancing and flickering in eerie silence.

Even as I saw them, Tirgsor pulled up the horses and leapt from the coach without a word. I saw him make his way towards the flames and bend over one. Then there was a strange optical effect that somewhat startled me, for although he stood between me and the flame, I could still see its faint blue light as though it shone right through him. He went to each blue light and I could see him doing something at each – bending close to the ground as if searching for something – then he returned without a word of explanation and we drove on.

Strange as it seems, I was glad of this sullen brute's return, for I could see the low, long black shapes drawing closer and closer to the coach, while the horses stamped, tossed their black manes, and rolled their eyes in growing nervousness. Indeed, I could not but wonder how Tirgsor had managed to wander so far from the coach and not be attacked by the grim, carnivorous beasts.

As we moved on, I fell to wondering what the blue lights portended, and then, almost in relief, because I was beginning to think that I, too, was falling a victim to the superstitions of the Wallachians, I recalled attending a lecture in the Palazzo della Sapienza given by a learned Florentine alchemist who called such lights *fuoco fatuo*, or will-o'-the-wisp. His theory was that such lights were caused by a marsh gas, formed by decayed vegetation in swampy land during a drying out process. When this vegetation dried out, it formed a material that could be used as a fuel for fire instead of wood. The light was therefore a natural phenomenon and there was nothing magical or supernatural about it.*

We soon left this plain and began to climb rapidly along a narrow track through steep gorges. Then we suddenly encountered a group of miserable dwellings. There was not a soul about, but uncannily, as our coach rounded the bend into what was sadly a village, a church bell began to peal vigorously, to which Tirgsor threw back his head and laughed a horrible choking laugh. He did not pause to find out what the cause of the bells could be, but merely whipped the poor horses to further exertion, so that we passed through the village almost before we realized it. I did see, by the bright light of the moon, that each poor house was shuttered and each door was shut, and at each shuttered window and each closed door I saw garlands of flowers, the thistles and garlic I had witnessed several times on my journey. In addition, each house had a dark cross painted on the door.

One building, which looked like an inn, had a sign above it which read: ΑΡΕΦΩ . The cyrillic letters, I realized, stood for Arefu, which village, I recalled, was the nearest to Castle Dracula.

The coach was now climbing the mountain track at an

* Friend Jonathan Harker, on his journey to Castle Dracula, encountered a similar phenomenon; see his journal entry for 5th May. The old alchemist's explanation for the blue light is substantially correct. To be accurate, the genesis of our fuel coal is well understood today: some millions of years ago the environment on our earth was warm and humid; swamps and bogs proliferated and as vegetation died and decayed it formed vast compost heaps in which oxygen was consumed by putrefactive bacteria. An anaerobic fermentation took place and a marsh gas – methane – was formed while plant debris was converted to humic acid. The process still occurs in swamps and bogs which give off this will-o'-the-wisp light while the residue forms peat which is used in many areas of Europe for fuel. Dracula told Jonathan Harker that the local belief was that gold could be found where the flames shone, but few peasants had the courage to mark the spot. Van Helsing.

alarming angle. On one side of the narrow path lay a sheer drop into the valley, and I shuddered lest we tip over, for all would be dashed to pieces on the rocks that showed so clearly in the moonlight. And even if we were lucky enough to miss the rocks and fall into the silver strip of river, the impact from this height would have meant at least broken necks. I hung on to the side of the coach grimly, while Tirgsor, not even a tremor in his voice, cursed at each of the horses and urged them on to greater speeds. Thus we went on for nearly an hour, and I was beginning to think that the terrible journey would have no end.

Then, all at once, the coach reached a small level patch of ground and we rumbled over a wooden bridge into a stone courtyard. The abrupt entrance into the castle left me speechless, for there had been no indication of an approach. We had simply swung around a sharp bend in the pathway and were now inside a courtyard with grey-black walls towering on all sides of us.

As I sat there trying to adjust my thoughts to my sudden arrival, a tall man, with long black moustaches such as the Wallachian boyars wear, long and almost drooping, emerged from the shadows.

I discerned no hint of welcome on his face. It was a thin, bloodless face; and the eyes, like those of Tirgsor, were large, black and lustreless in the flickering light of the coach's torches. He made no effort to stretch out his hand in greeting, but instead stood a little way off.

'Welcome, brother Mircea,' he said, in a voice that lacked all emotion. 'Welcome to Castle Dracula.'

BOOK TWO
Castle Dracula

CHAPTER TEN

I must confess that as I stared at the pale anaemic face and black lustreless eyes of my brother Vlad, I felt no fraternal feelings such as I had imagined would course through my veins at our first meeting. I experienced only a strange curiosity. In no way did this Vlad Dracula resemble me, though, of course, it must be pointed out that while we shared the same father we did not have the same mother and therein must lie the explanation. Even so, I had assumed that I would feel some brotherly warmth, and in this I was now proven wrong. In many ways – and this is indeed a curiosity – it was as if I were staring into Tirgsor's face all over again, for the pale, dry skin, the cold, corpse-like temperature of the extended hand, and the blackness of the eyes that revealed no emotion all seemed to be more the attributes of Tirgsor than of our common blood.

As I stared at the dead face of my brother Vlad, wondering what manner of greeting to make, a second man appeared at his side to welcome me and to introduce himself as my brother Mihail. So alike were the two that they could almost have been hatched from the same egg, though I knew that there were several years distance between them, and that they were both my elders.

Both were tall, a good head taller than I, and I am not considered to be below the average height. Both wore their hair long, with large black moustaches that threw their pale faces into sharp relief as did the dull black eyes. The clothes they wore were simple: an embroidered shirt, trousers held by a wide leather belt, woollen-lined sleeveless jacket, called locally a *cojoc*, which was also embroidered, and a pair of *opinci*, which are soft pigskin sandals.

This was the typical 'Darcian' costume much worn by the peasants.

'Welcome, brother Mircea,' said Mihail. 'Welcome. Come freely. Go safely. And leave something of the happiness you bring.'

I understood this strange speech was but a typical Wallachian greeting. My two brothers gathered what few belongings I carried and escorted me to the main door into a great hall whose chilly atmosphere made me gasp for breath. I was led up a vast winding staircase to a landing where they threw open two large wooden doors. I felt relieved at the sight of a well-lit room with a great roaring fire crackling in the hearth and a table spread for a meal.

'We have prepared a small supper for you after your most fatiguing journey,' said my brother Vlad, as he closed the doors behind us. I had in fact noticed that they both spoke excellent German, and on querying this I was led to understand that all members of the nobility used the language as their mother tongue, though not the tongue of their mothers. Vlad continued: 'I suggest you sup first and then retire to rest, for you must be very weary. On the morrow we shall talk and seal our friendship as brothers, as we should have done many years ago had it not been for the ill-starred fate of our ancestors.'

I did indeed feel a tremendous weariness and could not find any words to answer him. I merely nodded and allowed Mihail, who is some three years younger than Vlad, to draw me to the table where there was a simple meal of cold meats and bread. I could only pick at the food and take a glass of wine which, with the roaring of the fire and the change from chill to warmth, caused my eyelids to prick and droop until Mihail raised me from the chair, on an arm that gave the lie to his weak appearance by its considerable strength, and conducted me from the room, along a small gallery to a tower.

We ascended a curving stairway and went through a

door which led into a large bed chamber. Again, it was well lit and had a roaring fire which was throwing sparks merrily into the hearth. A large bed had been turned down and a warming-pan inserted between the crisp white sheets. Mihail himself removed the warming-pan and asked me if I needed anything further for my night's repose. I shook my head, noting that my belongings had already been placed in the room, and, with a sense of strangeness, realizing that I had not yet spoken a word to them.

Yawning, I threw off my clothes and fell into the large, warm bed and, before I knew it, I had succumbed to a deep sleep.

Tired as I was, however, the effects of my excitement at meeting my brothers, the arduous journey, and the peculiarities of my brothers' appearance must have influenced the workings of my mind, for I had one of those strange waking dreams.

I came awake in the darkened bed chamber. The spluttering fire had lapsed into a dull glow which threw grotesque shadows over the walls. And, in this strange half-sleep, I thought three people stood at the foot of my bed, my two brothers and a third man, a stranger much darker than the others, a phantom, who seemed to tower above his companions and yet seemed unreal.

'. . . he is no Dracula,' my brother Vlad was whispering.

'I agree,' came the voice of Mihail, edged with a sneer. 'I feel he has no kinship with our house. He is but a stupid Italian lady's man.'

'Nevertheless,' imposed the sonorous tones of the stranger, 'he is a Dracula. In his veins runs a noble blood. His sires were your sires and he has the right to join us in making our house immortal. Let him rest now. His blood is young and will keep awhile.'

Bewildered, fearful, I sank back into the sleep of the exhausted.

★

When I came awake a small shaft of sunlight had entered through a crack in the shutters and was shining on to my face. I felt as if I had been asleep for a long time and, indeed, when I arose from the bed and threw open the shutters, I found the sun already stood at its zenith.

While I appreciated the courtesy of my brothers in letting me sleep late, I was nevertheless somewhat annoyed that I had missed a goodly portion of the day. However, this was but a passing annoyance, so overcome was I by the breathtaking beauty of the scene that unfolded before my window.

Gone were the shadows of the previous night. Castle Dracula stands on top of a mountain and, as I looked down from my window, I saw that this side of the castle stood right on top of a precipice, falling vertically nearly one thousand feet into a valley through which ran the river Arges, beginning its tremulous descent to join the greater river of Dimbovita. The steep gorge was breathtaking. I could see the tiny houses that made up the village, away beneath me like so many tiny dolls' houses. In all directions were mountains covered in woods which seemed to contain every conceivable shade of green, and I could also see a tremendous amount of blossoms. Also, from my window, I could peer southwards and view the hills sinking away to the sun-scorched Wallachian plains. In the other direction were impenetrable mountain ranges, many snow-capped peaks, which separated Wallachia from Transylvania.

I do not know how long I stood there, breathing in the beauties of the scenery. It was not until the sun reminded me of the lateness of the hour that I turned back into my room and found that I had been so engrossed that someone, without my hearing, had already placed a jug of hot water on a stand beside the bed.

I had washed and was about to commence shaving when I observed that there were no mirrors in the room

– an oversight that surprised me as most Wallachians, while they sport large moustaches, clean shave their beards. I had also noticed that this seemed to be the custom with my brothers.

Once dressed in shirt and trousers, I thought I would try to find a servant and ask for a glass. As if in answer to my thoughts, I heard at that moment a noise outside my door, which was confirmed when I heard a woman's laugh. It was deep, almost velvety in its quality.

Immediately I crossed the room, swung open the door, and peered up and down the stairs of the tower. Surprisingly, there was no one there, and I stood still awhile, quite perplexed. Then I heard the sound of rustling skirts from below and I quickly started down the stairs.

The castle seemed shrouded in gloom, there being little or no light penetrating from the glorious day outside, and, as I made my way down the dark stairs, I found myself puzzling over the fact that, in spite of the lateness of the hour, no servant had opened the shutters. This mystery, combined with the rustling of the unseen lady, made me feel even more confused.

Stumbling a little in the gloom, holding on to the cold walls for guidance, I eventually reached the doorway to the gallery which led to the room where I had supped the night before. As I opened the door I glimpsed, at the far end of the gallery, a figure in a white, billowing skirt disappearing into a room beyond.

I called out, but no one answered. Now slightly annoyed, and just a little uneasy, I followed along the gallery and found myself in the supper room. To my surprise, I found a cold breakfast had been laid and a single place set as if in wait for me. Then, from a door beyond, I again heard the throaty laughter of a woman. I strode immediately to the door and threw it open.

There was nobody in the passage . . . but again I heard the rustle of skirts fading down a stairway.

I was now convinced that one of the servants was leading me a merry dance, and I resolved to follow her and seek an explanation for this unwarranted baiting of a guest. I started down the stairway, which was a small, circular way, as if built inside a very small tower. It led deeper and deeper until it grew so dark that I could scarce see. By the dampness of the walls I could ascertain that the stone steps had led me underground, and I was on the point of giving up my quest and climbing back to the warm room I had just quit when the narrow stairs suddenly opened out.

Spread out before me was a large, cellar-like room, lit by some strange phosphorescent light which seemed to glow from the stone walls. By this light I could see the cellar spreading into an infinity of low arches and stone columns, and could also make out the shape of large wine vats. The place was very chilly and damp, and caused me to cough several times as the musty atmosphere seeped into my lungs. It was very quiet. I could hear dripping water. The sound echoed and it made me uneasy and I felt I should call out.

'Is anyone there?' I called.

My words echoed and came back at me, hollow, disembodied, and the shadows of the vaults stained the floor and the silence was vibrant.

Then, again, came the deep-throated laughter, accompanied by the rustling of the skirts.

It came from the far end of the vault.

'Is anyone there?' I called out again, advancing a step or two and staring into the gloom, stricken by a strange, formless fear and not admiring myself for it. 'I know you are there,' I cried. 'Cease this play-acting at once and tell me why you behave thus to a guest.'

The chuckling ceased. The rustling skirts ceased their movement. The silence seemed to be breathing and I heard the dripping water and the gloom swooped around and was stifling. I stepped forward again.

'*Mircea!*' a voice hissed. '*Son of Dracula!*'

I confess, I was startled, but I swung around to face the voice, peering intently through the gloom and seeing nothing . . . nothing but darkness.

'Do not start so,' said the voice, low, voluptuous, almost whispering in my ear and yet unseen. 'I seek only to welcome you home to your rightful place.'

I was bewildered. Whereas before the voice had been to my right, now it seemed to come from my left. I swung around again to confront the ghostly speaker, but once more, amazingly, there was nothing.

Then, again, I heard the low laughter.

'*Mircea! Son of Dracula!*' The voice was obscene, voluptuous. '*Soon you shall know what we know! Soon all will be shown to you! Come, Mircea! Come now . . .*'

The whispering was receding to the dark depths of the cellar, and at that moment, I am certain, I caught a glimpse of the woman in white.

'Who are you?' I cried out, feeling ashamed of my own fears, peering forward into the darkness and instantly noticing that the walls seemed to be losing their phosphorescent quality.

'*Come, Mircea! Come!*'

At that instant a door suddenly crashed open, and there stood the raging Tirgsor, holding aloft a blazing torch. Then, though I cannot swear to it because the sound of the crashing door was echoing and re-echoing around the cellar, I thought I heard from the gloom at the far end of the cellar a woman's most hideous scream of rage. Silence swooped in before I could confirm this.

'What are you doing here in the *pivnit*?'

Tirgsor's voice resounded like thunder.

'Pardon?' I asked, surprised that he should dare to address me in such a tone of voice.

'What are you doing in this cellar?'

Coldly, contemptuously, I told him about the girl, at

which he seemed unusually troubled. When I had completed my tale, he stepped quickly forward, holding the torch above my head and peering intently at me. Then, before I could resist, he reached out and seized my jaw, twisting my head first one way and then the other, staring with blazing eyes at my neck.

'*Che diavolo!*' I exclaimed, forgetting my German. 'What in . . .?'

Tirgsor took no notice of my outburst. Deep in thought, he heaved a sigh and mumbled: '*Der Hals ... der Hals draussen blutet.*'

His German was poor, but to me it sounded like 'The throat without bleeding'. However, before I could ask him what he meant and how he dared treat me in such an impertinent fashion, the sulky brute seized me by the arm and propelled me from the cellar, slamming the door behind us and shooting home two heavy iron bolts.

'What of the woman in there?' I demanded, trying to shake loose from his iron grip.

'Woman?' he said, as if he had not heard the question properly. 'Ah, do not worry, *mein Herr*. It is my daughter. She loves to joke. Sometimes she does not realize her jokes are in poor taste. I will punish her, have no fear, *mein Herr*.'

With that he ushered me up the stairs and into the room where my cold breakfast still awaited me. Pointing at it, he said, unnecessarily, '*Frühstück.*' Then he turned and left without another word.

In spite of the merry dance she had led me, I was horrified that Tirgsor had left the girl locked in the cellar. Then I realized that the door from this room led down the spiral stairway to the cellar, and that this would provide an exit for the girl. I went to the door and tried to open it, but, to my surprise, I found it locked. Somewhat mystified by these events, I sat down to a light breakfast.

★

I was still puzzling over the events of the day when my two brothers entered the room and, after an exchange of meaningless pleasantries, I told them of the morning's adventure. They exchanged a glance which I interpreted as something akin to annoyance.

'Do not worry, brother,' Vlad said. 'Tirgsor's daughter, Malvina, sometimes is taken with devilment and executes all manner of tricks upon us. She is a simple girl. Tirgsor will punish her.'

'He has no need to on my account,' I said. 'On the contrary, to be locked in that dank cellar will be enough punishment for her, so please tell him not to take the matter further.'

Vlad nodded and then dismissed the subject by informing me of the dangers I could encounter in the castle.

'This is an old, old building, brother Mircea, and beneath it are many caverns leading into the hollow of the mountain. Indeed, a man may travel from our cellar right through the mountain into the valley of Arges, beside the river, if he but knows the way; however, the routes are many and the same man may become lost for eternity in the vaults. Therefore, we pray you, do not wander the castle either in the day or at night, especially, for then the greatest dangers are abroad.'

'What dangers?' I asked.

'As a man might travel to the caves in the Arges valley, so it has been known that wild animals, the wolves and bears, seeking a home in the caves, can enter into the vaults at night for warmth. It would be wise to keep to the confines of your room and those rooms we will show you today. All other doors you will find locked, and those you will naturally have no wish to enter.'

I looked at Vlad closely. His tone of voice was strange. I had the feeling that he was hiding something from me, though I could not imagine what. Nevertheless, it seemed a sensible arrangement if, as he had said, wild beasts had been known to enter various parts of the castle.

'Very well,' I said.

Mihail smiled thinly.

'Good,' he said. 'And now we will show you your home . . . our home. And we will talk of the past and of the future.'

Vlad and Mihail led me through another door which led on to a balcony, part of which was still bathed in the rays of the westward journeying sun. Vlad and Mihail preferred to remain in the shadows of the doorway, while I tried to gather warmth from the dying rays.

In daylight I could observe no change in my brothers' complexions, still pale as if the very blood had been drained from their bodies. It struck me as odd, however, how weak and anaemic they seemed in daylight whereas the night before, though pale, they had seemed a trifle more animated. Then, with a start, I recalled Tirgsor, and decided to observe if they, too, gathered strength and vigour with the setting of the sun.

I wondered if they might be suffering from some malady, for I recall a learned doctor lecturing students in Rome on the case of a man who suffered from a morbid acuteness of the senses. This man was tortured by light, by odours, by noises and by textures of certain substances, even clothes. But such a morbid acuteness of sense was a condition of the mind and not the body so how could both my brothers, as well as their steward, share this strange condition?

These thoughts passed through my mind as I observed my brothers. I felt ill at ease with them: they seemed like total strangers instead of the blood of my blood.

My attention was drawn back to the square stone balcony on which I stood. It protruded from what I observed to be the main tower of the castle and which overhung the castle courtyard, which was some thirty feet below.

'Here, brother,' said Vlad, waving a thin hand around the ramparts of the castle. 'Here is the home of your ancestors, where you were born and from where you were cruelly parted from us as a young child. This, dear brother, is Castle Dracula!'

CHAPTER ELEVEN

I have already given an account of the breathtaking scenery that surrounded the castle, and here I feel compelled to give a description of the castle itself. It stands on the very summit of the mountain, on a small plateau. The castle walls closely follow the precipitous sides of the mountain, as if they were part of the mountain walls themselves. The walls of the castle are thus built on the plan of an irregular polygon, the shape of the plateau at its summit. Only on one side of the castle, at its entrance, does the plateau give way to form a dangerously narrow ledge along which the road, or rather a mere track, to Arefu circles down the mountainside.

From east to west, as I discovered, the actual courtyard, which is entirely encircled by the inner walls of the castle and between which the castle chambers are placed, measures a distance of one hundred feet. From north to south this distance is exceeded by twenty feet more. There are five towers at regular intervals around the castle walls; a donjon or strong central tower stands opposite the main entrance and then in each corner of the walls are four more towers, two of which are of classical cylindrical shape, and it is in the south western one of these towers that my bed chamber lies.

The whole castle comprises of the best features of the grim Teutonic fortresses with the intricate and ornate design of Byzantium structures.

Between each of the towers, which are reserved for the reception rooms and living quarters of the household, run the stables, store rooms and quarters for the castle garrison. In the courtyard itself stands an entrance to the castle chapel and vault which stands at basement level.

The castle is entered by one route only, which I failed to observe when I came across it at night. The great double wooden doors lead to a drawbridge which, when lowered, spans a chasm that drops nearly four hundred feet to the rocks below and then tumbles in leaps and bounds still further towards the valley of the Arges. A strange impregnable setting below which, as I was told, the *privnit* or cellar vaults have been tunnelled out of the very heart of the mountain.

I asked Vlad how many people inhabited the castle.

'In our father, Dracula's, time there were two hundred men-at-arms and two hundred more servants; but now we live frugally with Tirgsor as our *stolnic* – Tirgsor and a few other servants.'

I must confess that I had tried hard to recall memories of the first few years of my life at Castle Dracula, but such memories were few. I can recall the tall figure of my father standing before the fire, a sneer on his face, his voice raised in some accusation against my mother. I can recall the night I was awakened, wrapped in a warm blanket, and carried through long, dark corridors to a carriage, which must have been the night of my mother's dramatic flight from the castle. But apart from these, my remembrance of my life before arriving in Rome has all but faded; so my brothers were as total strangers and everything they showed me was new and alien.

Mihail proved the more expansive in conversation and told me that the room in which I slept was the same chamber in which my mother had pushed me into this world, and that it had been my nursery room until the night of our flight. I asked him why he and Vlad had, in their letters to me, given the address of the castle as being at Poenari when in fact Arefu was the nearest village. Mihail led me by the arm to a window that overlooked the Arges valley and pointed to the far side. I saw some ruins, about a mile down the valley.

'That is Poenari,' he said. 'Poenari is well known, known better than Arefu, and thus messengers are more easily able to find their way there. Poenari is the site of the ancient Darcian fortress of Decidara, where the Romans first built their fortress to dominate this province. Upon that fortress a stronger castle was raised to resist the march of the Teutons in the thirteenth century, but it was almost levelled by the Turks and the Tartars.

'Our father, Dracula, maintained a garrison there, but Poenari was finally levelled by the Turks in 1462 when our father was driven into Transylvania.'

He paused and drew me back into the refectory room. A fire had been lit, for it was now early evening and the storm clouds had turned the day dark and chill.

This refectory room, which seemed the main living-room of the castle, was a large one, very lofty with long, narrow windows, shuttered on the outside. In fact, at no time during the day had I observed any servant remove the shutters from any of the castle windows. The ceiling of the room was vaulted with an abundance of black oak beams. At one end was the large carved stone fireplace. A long oak table dominated the centre of the room, while the rest of the furniture consisted of sideboards and chairs and gave a general atmosphere of comfortlessness. Dark tapestries and a few musical instruments, which lay about, failed to lighten the pervading gloom.

My brother Mihail continued in his discourse.

'This fortress of Arges, as we call Castle Dracula, was first built by our ancestor Basarab. It has a greater strategic position in the valley than that of Poenari, but the castle was ruined by the Tartars in the last century. It was our father, Dracula, who had it rebuilt when he became ruler of Wallachia, for he did not trust living in the towns, since the boyars were crafty and self-seeking. Indeed, they had murdered several of our blood. Do you know the story of our uncle Mircea, after whom you were named?'

I admitted such knowledge. We had seated ourselves before the fire and the silent Tirgsor had appeared with mulled wine.

'You know of the punishment our father meted out to the boyars of Tirgoviste,' Mihail continued, 'for the murder of his brother Mircea?'

'I have heard the story told,' I replied.

'Do you then know that after Dracula slew the assassins of Mircea, the five hundred faithless boyars, their wives and children, he rounded up the remainder . . . three hundred boyars with their wives and children. It was Easter and he marched them to this very spot. Across the Arges were the ruins of Poenari, while on this side were the ruins of the fortress of Arges. Dracula told the boyars who had survived the march that he wanted an impregnable fortress raised on the ruins left by the Tartars. And so those faithless boyars, their wives and their children, were set to work like common serfs. They heaved the stone from the ruins of Poenari to the summit of this mountain, heaved the stone day by day, sweating and grunting like the pigs they were until, finally, Castle Dracula rose proud and strong and impregnable. Those boyars worked until the clothes dropped from their backs, and then they worked without clothes. Thus did Dracula build his castle and, with the same stroke, subdue his faithless boyar class and make them submit to unquestioning obedience to the house of Dracula.'

While Mihail recited this horrific tale, I noticed that his eyes had brightened considerably and that he was now leaning forward excitedly in his chair. His pale face was actually animated.

'Didn't the Turks try to destroy the castle when Dracula fled in 1462?' I asked.

'Of course,' Mihail replied, 'but the castle was well built. While our father was in exile, it was held by his governor, Gherghnia, who perished last year in the fight against the Turks.'

'And how did Dracula die?' I asked.

'As you know, our father married the sister of Mathias of Hungary. In so doing, he renounced the Orthodox faith and accepted the Church of Rome which is the faith of the Hungarian princes who are said to have their descent from St Stephen. It was a political decision, for our father sought to return to his own, but the fools of the Orthodox religion made a great outcry, as if religion were important.'

I was surprised at the sneering tone of Mihail's voice; I had thought that my brothers would be strongly for the Orthodox faith.

'In spite of the outcry from the clerics,' Mihail went on, 'our father's third marriage was celebrated at Visegard. Soon after, in 1474, the princes of Hungary, Russia, Moldavia and Poland decided it was time to launch a crusade against the Turkish Sultan, Mohammed. The prince Radu, our father's weak brother who ruled Wallachia, was but a plaything of the Sultan, and so it was agreed to support Dracula in his claim to the throne.

'Radu died, however, and Basarab Laiota became ruler. At this, Dracula decided to invade from Transylvania. On 25 July 1476, he and Prince Stephen Bathory held a council of war in Tirda, and during November Dracula entered Wallachia through the pass of Bran. Soon Tirgoviste fell, then Bucharest. At Curtea de Arges we saw Dracula come into his own again.'

'But how did he die?' I persisted.

Mihail was silent for some time.

'There was a battle near Bucharest,' he said finally. 'There are two tales about it. One, that the Turks were beginning to break and Dracula descended a hill to observe the position when he was mistaken for a Turk and cut down by his own men. Two, that the boyars, who remembered how he forced them to submit to his will, slew him.'

'So there *is* a mystery about the death?'

'There is no mystery,' Vlad interrupted with a certain fervour. 'His body was taken to the monastery of Snagov where it was interred.'

'Snagov?' I asked.

'It is an island in one of the lakes surrounding Bucharest in the heart of the Vlasie forest,' Mihail explained. 'Our grandfather, when he was Voivode, endowed Snagov with more land than any other monastery in the realm.'

'So our father lies at Snagov?' I mused.

'And now our brother Mircea,' Mihail interrupted my thoughts, 'has returned to his proper place.'

'My proper place?' I smiled uneasily. 'I do not know. I was raised in Rome and I fear there is little Wallachian in me. I do not speak the language; nor do I have knowledge of the history and customs of this land. In truth, I am a foreigner.'

'But in your blood runs that of Dracula,' Mihail said. 'An ancient red blood that has been shed many times for the furtherance of our honourable house. Blood cannot be denied.'

'I appreciate your acceptance of me, brothers, as one of the family, and yet I must confess to you that I feel a stranger in this castle.'

Mihail waved a dismissing hand.

'The strangeness will wear away,' he said. 'You are a Dracula and you are among your own people.'

'But being among them, what then?'

Vlad gave a strange, disturbing half laugh.

'We have plans, brother Mircea,' he said in a tone I did not like. 'Plans to restore the house of Dracula to its rightful place.'

'Its rightful place?' I inquired.

Mihail frowned and looked hard at Vlad, who turned away from my curious gaze.

'It is enough talk for one day, brother Mircea,' Mihail

said. 'We will talk more of this tomorrow. But now, let us eat and offer you the hospitality of our wine cellar.'

I would have preferred to continue the conversation, for it seemed to me that my brothers had more in mind for my visit than merely fraternalism.

What plan could they have? I wondered. And where would I, their brother yet a stranger, enter into such a plan?

My uneasiness increased.

Tirgsor was summoned to lay the table and I noticed, with some confusion, that he laid only one place. When I questioned my brothers about this, they explained that they had eaten heartily at midday.

There was one strange thing I noticed about the meal – for I consider myself something of a *buongustaio* or, as the French would say, a *gourmet* – and this was the total absence of spices such as salt and garlic. This absence I could not attribute to the poorness of the larder, so I wondered if Tirgsor, who seemed to do all the jobs in the castle, acted as cook as well. I made a mental note to go for a walk on the morrow to the village to collect some salt and garlic, after which I could explain to the sullen *stolnic* the art of cooking.

After the meal, and tiring of my brothers' endless questions about the world outside Wallachia, I made an excuse to retire to bed early. At this my brothers made no protest, but bid me sleep well and dream well.

Again, as with the night before, a fire had been lit in the hearth of my bed chamber and a warming pan had heated the bed for my repose. Water had been placed for my toilet . . . and it was as I was washing that I heard a familiar noise at my door.

It was the unmistakable rustle of skirts.

Determined not to be made a fool of twice, I crept quietly to the door, gently turned the iron ring handle and threw it open as quickly as possible.

The girl who stood before the door started back, a cry on her lips, one hand raised to cover her mouth. She then froze before me.

As the light from my room fell upon the girl, I found it was my turn to be surprised. Indeed, I swear by the ancient gods of Rome that she was the prettiest thing I had laid eyes on since coming to Wallachia. She could not have been more than eighteen summers, and she had a fresh pale skin with touches of red on her cheeks which were coated so delicately with freckles that one would have sworn that an artist must have painted them there. Her hair was dark, and the blue eyes that stared at me were lovely, but wide with fright.

I immediately smiled in reassurance.

'And who might you be?' I asked, hoping she would understand my German.

'I am . . . Malvina, *mein Herr*.'

'Ah,' I said, 'the daughter of Tirgsor.'

Silently I wondered how such a brute as Tirgsor could have sired such an exquisite creature.

'Tirgsor is my stepfather, *mein Herr*.'

'And have you come to lead me another merry dance?' I said, warming to her blush and her radiant good looks.

'*Mein Herr?*'

A frown creased her well proportioned brow and her voice was clearly puzzled.

'Ah,' said I, 'you wish to forget this morning? Very well, your punishment in the cellar has erased the matter.'

Her lovely face was torn betwixt puzzlement and fright, and I swear that this seemed genuine. Then she suddenly darted a fearful glance at the stairway, raised a finger to her lips, and pushed me back into the room. She then followed me in and closed the door behind her, and stood for a few moments, listening intently, her head to one side.

'*Mein Herr*,' she said finally and with a certain fearful passion, 'you must leave Castle Dracula immediately.'

'Oh,' I said lightly. 'And why, pray?'

'Do not ask, *mein Herr*, just go. Go now! This very hour!'

Naturally I did not believe she was serious. Fearful though she looked I could not forget what had happened this morning and I even thought to compliment her on her acting ability.

'Malvina,' I said, smiling directly at her, 'I enjoy jokes greatly, but I am tired this night, especially after this morning's caprice.'

Again a frown of puzzlement crossed her brow.

'This morning, *mein Herr*? What happened?'

'Come now,' I said, 'admit it. Your father told me it was you.'

The girl shook her head slowly from side to side, blinked her eyes and looked even more bewildered.

'*Mein Herr*, tell me, what happened this morning?'

Overcome once more by an irrational unease, suddenly sensing that the girl was sincere, I explained. And, as I did so, I noticed the blood drain from those delicate features and saw her vainly trying to suppress her own trembling. When I had finished, she grasped me by the hand.

'Oh, *mein Herr*,' she cried, 'as sure as God watches us, believe me, it was not I who led you down to the cellars! Indeed, all this day I have been with my uncle Toma, who keeps the inn at Arefu. I returned but an hour ago, and when I heard you were here I came immediately to warn you.'

'Warn me?' I said, now shaken by her intensity. 'Warn me of what?'

'To warn you to leave and leave now!' She held my hand tighter and her blue eyes were huge and fear-filled. 'Oh, *mein Herr*,' she almost sobbed, 'there is much evil here. Go! Go now, while you may!'

I started to press her further for an explanation, but she suddenly raised her hand and placed it over my mouth. We stood thus like statues for several minutes, she listening, with her head to one side. At last she looked back at me, and there was dread in her blue eyes.

'I must go, *mein Herr*, lest they miss me. Please, *mein Herr*, for the sake of your unborn children . . . *leave the castle tonight*!'

Then she was gone, swiftly and silently, and, shaking slightly, I sat down on the bed to ponder the strangeness of it all.

Either she was a great natural actress or she was totally sincere. If it were the latter, then who was the woman in white? And why had Tirgsor and my brothers lied about Malvina?

There was one way to prove the truth of the matter. On the morrow I intended going to the village of Arefu to gather salt and garlic for my food. On the morrow, then, I would go to Arefu and ask the innkeeper, Toma, if his niece had been with him all day as she claimed. If the answer was positive, I could then demand an explanation from my brothers.

Thus resolved, and feeling none the easier for it, I completed my toilet and retired to bed.

It was dark when I started into wakefulness. I lay there awhile, still groggy from my sleep, trying to register what it was that had awakened me. Then, from my shuttered window, I heard a strange flapping noise. I listened more intently. Twice there was a soft thud, as if something was banging against the shutters. At this, I frowned. Outside the window was a drop of a thousand feet to the valley floor; how, then, could anything be banging at my window? Yet, as I listened, the noise came again, the strange flapping and the thudding, and then silence. I felt fear creeping through me.

Nervously, cautiously, I rose from the bed and walked slowly across the room to the window. First I had to unlatch the thick glass window and then, leaning forward, I opened the shutter.

At first I saw nothing. The night sky was clear and the moon, round and white, shone down cleanly. Emboldened by this, I leant as far out as I could and peered all around me, trying to trace the cause of my disturbed slumber.

Suddenly, with a start, I heard the flapping noise. I glanced up just as something struck me full in the face. I felt tiny pinpricks in my scalp and forehead, and something like a wet, chilly tissue covered my face.

Releasing a cry, I staggered back into the room, my hands flying up to claw at the thing on my face. I was blind. I felt revulsion. My heart pounded and my flesh crawled. It felt small, soft . . . nay, bloated like a bag filled with water, and . . . it had wings. I cried out again. I tore the thing away and feverishly hurled it from me . . . and, in the moonlight, I saw the black shape of a bat.

It lay stunned on the floor where I had thrown it, and I could see that it was a fairly large species. Its flapping wings must have been nearly eighteen inches long, and its body nearly six inches long. It had large ears, broad at the base but narrowing abruptly to sharp, recurved tips. It also had thick woolly fur extending on to its wing membranes, which appeared ash grey in colour.

It lay there for a moment and then, with a loud, high-pitched, penetrating squeak, rose with slow pulsating motions of its wings and commenced to hover at a height of five feet from the floor. At this distance I could observe, with something of a shudder, conspicuously large, white, canine teeth. But, above all, I suddenly became aware of tiny red eyes boring into me . . . red, malignant and hypnotizing.

I shook my head. I tried to recollect my senses. I looked at the bat and saw the moonlight surrounding it and saw the great darkness beyond. The bat made no attempt to fly away. I had been given to understand that this was the habit with such creatures, so I grabbed my walking cane and moved forward, raising it at arm's length. To my surprise, the bat continued hovering, its tiny red eyes glinting in the moonlit room. Then, to my surprise, so much so that I stopped moving, it began to make a curious motion with its wings, swinging from side to side, slowly, rhythmically, as if in some strange, exotic dance. I stood still fascinated, the fear slipping away from me, an enormous drowsiness descending, seeing nothing but the moonlight, the slow sway of the wings, the red eyes, the night, the white teeth . . .

Suddenly, just as I would have fallen into a deep slumber, a high-pitched shriek, like a demented scream of anger, jerked me fully awake. To my horror, I saw an even larger bat fly through the window, its huge black wings slicing through the air, its canine teeth gleaming white against a blood red mouth, before, still shrieking, it fell on the first bat and sank its teeth into its neck.

I felt myself recoil. My revulsion whipped me raw. I heard shrieking, snarling, saw a brief, shocking struggle; then, to my terror, the large bat swooped around the room, carrying the smaller bat in its jaws, and was swiftly gone back through the window, leaving me dazed.

The silence shook me awake. I blinked and saw the full moon. I rushed forward to draw the shutters and looked up in the direction that the large bat had taken. To my amazement, knowing that bats never fly in formation, I saw what must have been the large bat, now flying in the centre of a perfect, diamond-shaped formation of some twenty or so other bats, winging up towards the sky, black against the brightness of the full moon.

Shaken, shivering, I returned to my bedside, poured some water out of the jug, and bathed the tiny claw pricks in my head.

CHAPTER TWELVE

The morning was bright and warm and, feeling no ill effects from my experience of the previous night, I decided to carry out my resolve to take a walk to the village.

I arose quite early, washed, dressed and made my way down into the courtyard. No one was about and I wondered at the lateness of the hours kept by my brothers and their servants. I have always had the disposition of rising early and find myself a little intolerant of others who do not do so. The castle doors were closed, but I found no difficulty in throwing open the bolts and opening the great wooden doors to a sufficient width to allow the passage of my body. Similarly, there was no difficulty to be encountered in working the well-oiled mechanism that lowered the wooden drawbridge over the chasm.

With the sun now beating hotly down, unusually hot for a November day, I made my way down the steep track. I paused frequently to drink in the clean air and the gorgeous fragrance of the surrounding woods, which seemed like nectar after the dank gloom of the castle. As I stood drinking in the air, I could observe the beauty of the landscape.

Dracula had, indeed, chosen well in making his home at this spot. The autumn flowers bloomed in many-hued abundance, and many of the trees were so overgrown that, in spite of the nearness of winter, it might well have been a summer's day.

I reached Arefu after a slow walk of an hour and a half. Here the sun suddenly deserted me, for the shadow of the mountain fell sharply across the houses that comprised the village.

At first glance it seemed that the village was deserted.

Each house was boarded up, the shutters closed and the doors shut. Yet I had the strange feeling that I was being observed as I walked down the street to the building I supposed was the village inn. By the time I reached it, I was almost convinced in my belief that the place was deserted, for I passed the church whose yard was overgrown while the building itself was clearly in decay, its doors hanging open with goats and sheep huddling for warmth inside.

Each house, I noted, had a large black cross marked in some tar-like substance on the door, and at each door and window hung a garland of flowers. Indeed, even on the cow stalls, alongside the road, were hung numerous bunches of wild roses.

I came to the inn door and found it closed fast. The inhospitality annoyed me and I aimed a hearty blow with my fist at its heavy oak, crying to the innkeeper to open up.

A surly voice within urged the Mother of God to keep the inhabitants from harm. I threw back my head and exclaimed that it would take more than God's intercession to prevent harm coming to them if the door was not opened to a weary traveller.

Slowly came movements within. There was the rattle of chains, the creak of hinges, and gradually the door swung open. I strode in, almost pushing aside the portly man who stood holding a small figure of a Madonna in his hand. A woman stood at the foot of the stairs, a Bible in her hands, her face taut and white. I surveyed this pair with some amusement.

'Lord save us,' I said, 'but you are a superstitious people in this country!'

'Amen to the Lord saving us, *mein Herr*,' grunted the man, as he bolted the door after me. 'But it bodes no good to us if we do not have a care in these parts.'

The woman then asked me what I wanted; and her tone, I felt, was much too surly for an innkeeper's wife.

'If this is an inn, what should I want?' I replied, edging my tongue with sarcasm. 'I need to break my fast with a little ale and some bread, cheese and salami.'

Without another word the woman bustled away. The man put down his statue and knelt before the hearth, where it was obvious he had been laying a fire before my knock had disturbed him.

'And where are you from, *mein Herr*?' he said, trying to overcome the unfriendliness of his first welcome.

'From Rome,' I answered.

'What are you doing in this God-forsaken country? There is nothing here, *mein Herr*. Where are you staying?'

The woman had brought me food and I sat down, eagerly biting into the soft warm bread.

'I am staying at the castle,' I said between mouthfuls. 'Castle Dracula.'

There was a crash of broken china. The woman stood before the resultant mess, her hands to her pale cheeks. The innkeeper had half risen and was crossing himself.

'*Mein Herr*,' he said, almost whispering, 'you are the guest who is staying at Castle Dracula?'

'Yes,' I snapped. 'What of it? Is it so strange?'

The man and woman exchanged a glance.

'Strange?' the man said. 'You have been in the castle and *you* ask if it is strange?'

I sighed and took a long pull at my ale. Had it not been for my own increasing uneasiness of late, I would have assumed that all the Wallachians were half-wits.

'The castle is evil, *mein Herr*,' said the woman, whose frame was quite visibly trembling.

'Good God,' I said with as much authority as I could muster, 'does not your own niece, Malvina, work at the castle?'

At this the woman gave a pitiful cry, a cry of the most awesome anguish, and ran from the room.

'Forgive us, *mein Herr*,' said the innkeeper, Toma, now visibly trembling himself, 'but you are in a strange country and we do have strange ways. Indeed, our niece Malvina is forced to work at the castle.' Here he crossed himself and muttered, 'God between her and all evil!' He then paused a second before continuing: 'It is her step-father, Tirgsor, who so ordains it. Many times have we tried to make her leave, but Tirgsor has a strange power over her.'

'And was Malvina at this inn yesterday?'

'Indeed, *mein Herr*. She spent two days with us, but returned to the castle yesterday evening. Why do you ask?'

I shook my head silently. I drank some more ale. Now I knew that Tirgsor and my brothers had lied to me, and I wondered why this could be so. The innkeeper, Toma, was still nervous.

'For the villagers of Arefu,' he said as I ate, 'Castle Dracula stands as a blight. Twenty years ago this was a happy village. Then the Voivode Dracula decided to re-build the old castle and the unhappy boyars were driven here like cattle. Each day we saw them working, each day we saw them dying. Yes, *mein Herr*! Blood built Castle Dracula and blood will cause its downfall. The curse of the Dracula is sealed by blood; the whole mountainside is a citadel of blood. Young *Herr*, I beg you, leave this place.'

'It is not the first time I have been given such a warning. You Wallachians are not very welcoming.'

'*Mein Herr*, we Wallachians were once renowned for our hospitality; but here, at this time, in this place, we fear for strangers even more than we fear for ourselves, for there is a great evil at work here and strangers could spread it to the four corners of the earth. Then, indeed, all would be lost.'

I must confess that I thought the man to be rambling,

but again the strange mysteries I had encountered in my journeys forced me to listen further to him.

'Come, *mein Herr*,' he said. 'Let me show you something, as I see you are yet a sceptic.'

He motioned me to follow him up the stairs to a room whose large door he unlocked with a thick iron key. As he swung open the door, I heard a strange growling sound from within – a sound that was not quite the growl of a dog, nor quite like any sound I had heard before.

'Look inside, *mein Herr*,' Toma said. 'And please be prepared!'

I did as I was bid – and was revolted by what met my gaze.

Squatting on his haunches in a corner of the room was the hideous figure of what had once been a man. His clothes were now in rags and he was surrounded by his own excreta. His hair, streaked black and white, was matted and filthy, totally obscuring his face, except for his eyes which, in their fearful and nightmarish dementia, could well have made the demons of Hell shudder.

This thing was tearing at something in its hands. Stepping closer, a wave of nausea filled my stomach, as I observed that the creature was tearing at a raw piece of flesh, sucking the blood from the red meat with obvious relish.

I stopped my advance, and the creature raised its hideous eyes to mine. It dropped the meat from its mouth. It gazed at me intently. There was blood around its lips and the light in its eyes was a fearsome light. Then, letting out the most hideous shriek, it sprang at me.

I raised my arm to defend myself, but there was no need, for the thing was chained by its ankle to a corner of the room. Pulled back by this chain, it collapsed in the corner and clawed at the floor with its fingers and snarled like a beast. Feeling shocked and weak, I let Toma pull me from the room and relock the door. We then returned downstairs in silence and Toma poured me a glass of spirits which I hastily, and gratefully, drank down. Toma poured me another.

'By the living God, Toma,' I said, gasping and drying my lips, 'what sort of devilment is this?'

'Devilment is right, *mein Herr*,' he replied. 'That beast which was once a man, and a fine man at that, is my wife's young brother, Liviu. He is nineteen years old this Christmastide.'

'How can it be?' I said, for the thing I had seen possessed the appearance of one pitted for centuries against torment.

'Believe it, *mein Herr*,' Toma said. 'In this very room, only last June, we celebrated the wedding of Liviu to Gaia. They were young, handsome and very much in love. Then came word from the castle that Gaia was needed to work there and serve our lord.

'You may know that feudalism still exists in most parts of our unhappy land, but we, in this province, are *mosneni*, freemen who bow to no feudal lord. Dracula, who never observed the laws of man or God, was no longer Voivode; while he was alive he trampled on the rights of the *mosneni*, but he was dead and we had no feudal lord. Thus, Liviu laughed at the demand from the castle.

'Tirgsor, who serves as *stolnic* at the castle, had come to the inn with the demand, and Liviu just laughed at him. Ah, I well remember that day, *mein Herr*. Liviu, young, handsome, with a temper as hot as red iron, laughed at Tirgsor's anger and told him to crawl back to his masters, for Liviu himself had no master.

'Then, one night, we were awakened by an anguished cry. Gaia was gone. Demented with grief, Liviu strapped on a sword and rode up to Castle Dracula. We tried to stop him, *mein Herr*, but he rode away. We all could hear him crying for the blood of the Draculas, and then his voice was lost in the wind.

'When the village had finally gathered in his support, and collected sticks and stones and marched up to the grey walls of the castle, all was quiet. Liviu's horse stood grazing outside, abandoned. We milled around for a while, irresolute, not knowing what to do. Then a scream, such as I never wish to have offend my ears again, broke the silence of the night and sent us scurrying home like frightened rabbits.

'The next morning, when we ventured out, we found Liviu as you have just seen him. His eyes were inflamed, his hair was streaked white, and he snarled and grovelled like an animal. The one word remaining to him was 'blood'. That one word. And all he could digest was raw, freshly killed meat from which he would only suck the blood. All this happened but a few months ago. And, as for his wife, that poor innocent child, Gaia, no one has set eyes on her since.'

We sat for some time in silence. I was shocked, disbelieving, and finally outraged, and I boiled over with contradictory emotions which made my heart pound. Toma's voice seemed to come from far away and I listened in silence.

'That, *mein Herr*, is why Castle Dracula is evil. And that, *mein Herr*, is why you must leave if you fear for your immortal soul. I beg you, *mein Herr*, I beg you . . .'

'And what of Malvina?' I suddenly asked. 'Does she not live safely at the castle?'

Toma frowned.

'Tirgsor is her stepfather,' he answered, as if that explained all. 'He has some strange power over her,' he added. 'And perhaps he protects her.'

At that moment I felt both anger and shame: anger that my brothers should have deceived me in such a manner, and shame in the realization that I myself was a Dracula and in part shared their accursed guilt. Yet my shame went beyond this simple cause. I was ashamed of my own cowardice, of the fears that now pierced me, and I resolved to return to the castle and brave that which frightened me.

'Toma,' I said, laying a hand on his shoulder, 'there is a mystery at the castle and I am much intrigued by mysteries and I intend to clear this one up. Furthermore, if there is danger to Malvina, rest assured I shall return her to your safe keeping.'

So saying, I bought garlic and salt, strode from the inn, and took the path back to the castle.

CHAPTER THIRTEEN

It was well into the afternoon when I reached the castle. Upon entering the donjon tower I was met by my brother Vlad who started to rebuke me in angry fashion for leaving the castle without permission. I replied hotly that I was not his servant, nor a *mosneni* of Arefu, whom he seemed to regard as his serfs. His eyes blazed in anger at this, and I feel blows would have been struck had not Mihail intervened, laying a pacifying hand on my arm and explaining soothingly that his brother and he had been motivated solely by concern for my welfare, since many wild animals prowled the woods, and also bands of *Szgany*, gypsies who would cut one's throat for the clothes on one's back. Somewhat mollified, I accepted Mihail's argument and again found myself in the refectory room, seated before the fire with my two brothers.

'Yesterday,' I said to Mihail, 'you spoke of some purpose that lay behind your invitation to me to come to this castle. Yesterday you said you would speak of such things today.'

Mihail nodded his head.

'First, brother Mircea, you must know what it means to be a Dracula. If you appreciate that, then you will understand our purpose.'

I settled myself before the smouldering logs of the recently lit fire and waited for Mihail to begin.

Mihail walked up and down the room as he spoke, swinging his arms and gesticulating to enforce and emphasize his statements. It was a strange diatribe, full of what I considered vainglorious nonsense, and yet, at the same time, quite thrilling . . . a story that reviewed generations of forgotten history and set the blood tingling in my veins.

'Since the dawn of time,' began Mihail, 'this country of ours has been inhabited, both physically and spiritually, by man. The *munteni*, the mountain people, have lived and worked in these mountains even long before the tribe of Getae settled on the Wallachian plain, long before the Thracians, Scythians and Celts arrived, each group mingling its blood with the whole. The *munteni* have been in these mountains almost as long as the mountains themselves have been here. And always there has been a house of Dracula here.

'It was one of our house, called Burebista, who united the warring tribes into the centralized state of Darcia and made it secure from its enemies. It was a Dracula, Dicomes, who offered aid to Mark Antony at Actium. It was a Dracula, Decebalus, who strove to hold back the Roman conqueror Trajan and then spilt his own blood rather than submit to the eagles of Rome. Then, in 271, when the Roman Emperor Aurelianus ordered his legions to withdraw from Darcia, it was a Dracula who rebuilt the devastated country. It was a Dracula who repelled the Goths and when, in 375, the Huns from the Asiatic steppes came like a devouring fire, it was a Dracula who mingled his blood with Attila, and this seed reinforced our house.

'The Avars, Slavs, Persians came and went like the wind. Charlemagne and his Franks tried to conquer and were blown like chaff from the wheat. The Bulgars of Khan Krum and, likewise, Arpad and the seven tribes of Hungary, aye, the Magyars too, the Vlachs, Vzes, the Kumars, all went down into the melting pot. Only one house and one name survived out of all. It was *our* house and *our* name.

'We gave birth to the Szeklers who devoured the Carpathians and who, in 1213, swept down on the Wallachian plain to regain what was theirs. It was the Szeklers who halted the Magyars from their advance and then, in 1241, it was our house that threw back the great Tartar invasions. Six years later, two of our house, Litovoi and Seneslau, established the right to be grand voivodes of Wallachia. Soon they had thrown off the suzerainty of the Hungarian rulers.

'The pride of our house is the pride of our name. Its glory is our glory, its fate is our fate.

'Out of this mingling of the races of Europe the house of Dracula springs unsullied, owing allegiance only to its heritage and to the ancient gods who made it. For countless generations our house has been the heart and brain of a million struggles, and always, while others went down into the pit, it has kept its noble crest aloft, challenging the infidels' gods to destroy it and knowing that they cannot.

'And you, brother Mircea, you, like us, are sprung from this noble seed. You are called by destiny, Mircea.'

He paused and looked eagerly at me, as if expecting me to spring up in a hymn of praise for my ancestry. Instead, I stretched indolently and looked bemused.

'Destiny?' I asked. 'What can destiny call me to?'

'Why, the house of Dracula must rise again; the fates decree it and it would be blasphemy to deny the course already charted in the heavens. It is our father, Dracula's wish that we three brothers, the seed of his loins, may join and go forward into the world to seize what is rightfully ours. The world will supply the blood while we supply the brains and hearts, just as we have for a thousand generations before us. The world is but a bauble at our feet. We have only to reach out and it is ours.'

I sat back, trying to disguise my surprise. Were my brothers demented? Were they really trying to tell me that they planned to conquer the world? Or was my knowledge of our common language, German, so inadequate that I mistook their meaning?

'Do I understand correctly, Mihail,' I said. 'You talk

of reaching out to grasp the whole world . . . by *conquest?*'

'Conquest?' Mihail said, smiling benignly. 'Yes, but not by military conquest. A conquest far more lasting, more immortal. . .'

He paused here and glanced quickly at Vlad who seemed to be signalling with his eyes, a slight, warning motion. I sat forward and pressed on with my questioning, now determined to clear this matter up.

'How then?' I asked. 'Even the throne of Wallachia has been given by Stefan of Moldavia to a Basarab not of your own house. How can you start a conquest of the world when you have not even a voice in your own country?'

'Pah!' Mihail exclaimed, his eyes flashing. 'Mortal symbols! I talk of something greater. Our father, Dracula, says . . .'

Vlad suddenly laid a hand on Mihail's arm and Mihail fell silent. It was an uneasy silence, and I looked from one to the other.

'Our brother was carried away,' Vlad said. 'Our father, Dracula, spoke long and often to us of establishing a dynasty that will last into eternity; a dynasty to whom the throne of Wallachia would be merely a plaything. We want to establish that dynasty and, as the seed of his loins, it is your right to join with us in that enterprise.'

'Yes,' I said, 'but how? And why? You leave me perplexed, brothers. Are you plotting some *coup d'état* to remove Basarab and put yourselves on the throne of Wallachia?'

'All will be explained shortly, brother Mircea,' said Mihail, 'that I promise. But as to your first steps, you shall know now. The day after tomorrow there arrives at Castle Dracula the Countess Irene Bathory, who is of the house of Prince Stefan Bathory who spilt blood for our house. The Countess is to marry Vlad and cement our two houses together, and thus will Vlad be made acceptable to the boyars when he sets out to claim the throne of Wallachia.'

My mind in turmoil, I took Vlad's limp, cold hand and pretended to congratulate him on the forthcoming nuptials. The idea of a liaison for political ends is not a new one, but nevertheless, when I encounter it, I am somewhat sickened by the idea of it. However, the whole philosophy of my brothers seemed horrific to me, and I was sure that the solitude of Castle Dracula had unhinged their minds.

And yet Wallachia had had a veritable plethora of rulers. Why was it mad for my brothers to stage some coup and continue the tradition laid down by the successive, and bloody, voivodes? No, it was their dream of world conquest that horrified me, for I am sure they were in deadly earnest. The pride and arrogance of their race (which, thank the saints, I had not inherited) made them capable of contemplating such conquest without a qualm. And was this Countess Irene Bathory privy to such mad dreams?

I confess to a slight malady of the head as I meditated on the strangeness of the many experiences I had encountered since I decided to accept my brothers' invitation. Now, I found any pretensions to fraternal feelings waning, if indeed there had been any in the first place. And yet there was some fascination, some morbid curiosity, that prevented me from laughing in their faces and leaving the castle forthwith . . . some fearful fascination, some inexplicable desire, now conscious of a mystery, of a foul, murderous plotting, that I felt it was my duty to seek out and finally resolve.

Would to God that I had obeyed my instincts and fled the castle there and then.

Chapter Fourteen

During my solitary supper that evening I had expected to see Malvina, but as usual it was the sullen Tirgsor who brought the meal and served it.

It was not until I started to eat that I remembered I had purchased some salt and garlic from Toma in Arefu to aid in Tirgsor's unseasoned cooking; but by then it was too late: my mind had been preoccupied with Mihail's monologue and I had forgotten to see Tirgsor about the addition of the salt and garlic to my food. This being so, I decided to leave the salt and garlic in my room until the following day.

Since coming to the mountains the chill had struck my chest several times, and the smell of garlic has a curious easing quality to chest ailments. Therefore it would do me little harm to spend a night inhaling the incense of my garlic, and indeed it would probably do me some good.

Having had an exhausting day, I again made my excuses to my brothers and started along the gallery to my bed chamber. Half-way along, however, I realized I had left my cloak behind and I therefore returned to the refectory door. I was just about to enter when I heard my brothers speaking.

'. . . less and less he behaves as a Dracula,' said Vlad.

'Nevertheless,' Mihail said, 'he will serve his purpose.'

'They are getting thirsty,' Vlad said. 'We cannot hold them off much longer.'

'They belong to me,' came a third voice, its harsh, chilling accent strangely familiar. 'I will make them obey me as I did last night. He will be kept until the nuptials. His presence will ease the mind of the female Bathory . . . then they can feast.'

A shiver ran down my spine. Who were 'they'? And surely it was I that was the subject of conversation. Squaring my shoulders, and trying to look more courageous than I felt, I pushed open the door.

My brothers were alone in the room.

A coldness seized me as I mumbled an excuse, quickly picked up my cloak and almost ran from the room.

The grim truth began to dawn on me that there was indeed something more than mere mystery here; that there was something evil, monstrous in this house of Dracula.

Once in my room, I bolted the door and made sure the shutters were secure. Then I sat before the fire, my head in my hands, and wondered what course I should pursue.

I could, perhaps, effect an escape, for by now I was beginning to suspect that it was only an accident which had let me out of the grim fortress that morning. But something within me rebelled at the idea of sneaking away like a thief in the night. In spite of their eccentricity, Mihail and Vlad were my brothers – and there was also Malvina, alone and unprotected, not to mention the unknown Countess Bathory who was to be duped into a marriage with Vlad. Surely I could not run from all this?

At that moment a gentle knocking on the door sent my fraying nerves jumping.

'Who's there?' I whispered.

'It is I, Malvina, *mein Herr*.'

Relieved, I unbolted the door and stood aside as the girl came into my room. I closed the door quickly behind her.

'Malvina, I was worried about you,' I said.

'Were you?' she said in a girlish way, placing a finger between her red lips and biting at it gently. She then smiled coquettishly at me and walked to the end of the bed, where she sat down with her legs swinging to and fro. 'Why should you be worried about me, *mein Herr*?'

There was something slightly different about her manner, something about the way she carried herself, the way she spoke. At first I could not place just what it was, but then it came to me: I remembered her small, petite figure, her pale face and frightened manner; now she seemed self-assured, voluptuous, even seductive. Her figure was full, her face redder than before; and her lips, which previously had trembled with nervousness, now pouted in a lascivious smile. Indeed it was as if her whole being had changed, with a seductive grossness replacing her former fragility. Looking at her, I felt hot and cold; and then I felt almost desirous.

'And why should you worry, *mein Herr*?' she whispered in a low, sultry voice. 'Am I then that much in your thoughts?'

Her eyes glittered. They were bold and quite wicked. She ran her tongue along the crimson of her lips and her smile was a challenge.

'I saw your uncle Toma today,' I said.

She gave a brief, nasty laugh, throwing back her head, her body arched and her legs swinging freely.

'Him?' she said. 'Pah! He is an old woman. Why should we talk of the likes of him, *mein Herr*? Come here,' she added, now smiling and patting the bed. 'Sit beside me and tell me about yourself. You are the only decent man I have seen for a month. And I have been so lonely and neglected in this place . . .'

Ah, the proud vanity of man! As in a trance, bedazzled by her beauty and lewd, suggestive posing, my emotions stirred to the point where I was oblivious to danger, I crossed to the bed and sat beside the smiling, wanton creature. How long we sat there I do not know, for the room seemed to disappear, to vaporize around us, and I was conscious only of her lips, of the tongue that lightly licked them, of the white of her teeth and the pale beauty of her bosom and the scent of her breath in my face and the play of her fingers. What was said I do not know, but we murmured tender words, then we embraced and fell down on the bed and her warmth flooded through me. I felt her hot breath at my neck, felt her sharp little teeth tentatively explore my shoulder as I, in my turn, removed from reason and shame, began to pull the blouse from her body and smother her with kisses.

Suddenly she was seized by a paroxysm of coughing, and then, with a gasp, she jerked away from me.

'What is it?' I cried.

'There is an overpowering smell in here,' she hissed.

'Nonsense!' I said, my emotions now roused to fever pitch. 'It is the scent of garlic, that is all.'

I pressed her back down on the pillows and once more began to kiss her bared breasts, but even as I did so, a shocking, agonized scream was torn from her lips.

Aghast, I sprang back. She writhed furiously beneath me. Then I noticed that, as I had leant over her, my mother's crucifix, which I wore around my neck, had dropped on to her bosom. The girl was now making a ghastly hissing sound, and the sudden stench of burning flesh filled my nostrils. Then, as I drew back in horror, I saw that the image of the crucifix had burnt itself into Malvina's flesh.

Scarce able to believe this, I yet moved away from the voluptuous creature that now writhed so desperately beneath me. Her face, which before had been beautiful and wanton, was now distorted by pain and wild hatred. Her teeth, which somehow seemed longer than they had been, bit feverishly at her lips until the blood was trickling from them. And her eyes, which had been mischievous and infinitely seductive, were now wild and demented, hypnotized by the mark of the cross that was burnt on her bosom.

'Malvina!' I cried.

Then, with an angry and most peculiar howl, a howl

which reminded me of the cry of a wolf and sent shivers coursing down my spine, she sprang from the bed.

Still howling like one demented, she ran from the room.

In a dream I raised my hand to my crucifix and gently touched its metal, half expecting to find that it was hot. But it was cold, and this made my thoughts spin. Trembling, in great fright, I walked across to the door, and slammed it shut and then bolted it. I then sat before the fire, trying to collect my scattered thoughts, shudder after shudder coursing through my body in uncontrolled spasms, while the black night threw its mantle about me and left me in terror.

CHAPTER FIFTEEN

I sat there until dawn approached. Since I could no longer help Malvina, and since the dogma of my scholarship refused to let my mind believe what my eyes had witnessed, my resolve was to leave the castle immediately and return to the sanity of Italy.

As soon as the grey fingers of dawn crept through the shutters, I stood up, buckled on my sword, and threw my travelling cloak around my shoulders. Scarce daring to breathe, I left the room and managed to reach the castle courtyard without incident. As usual, no one was stirring and all the shutters remained firmly closed. But imagine my horror when I found that on drawing the bolts of the great gates, I still could not open them. Obviously someone had double-locked them.

There was no other way out of the castle except ... except that my brothers, on admonishing me never to enter the castle vaults, had revealed that wild animals were sometimes found in the vaults. And, if wild animals could enter into the castle vaults, surely I could obtain my exit through them.

My mind did not rejoice at this idea, for I would far prefer to have scaled the impregnable mountain sides than venture through the ghostly vaults of Castle Dracula. However, I could not ... so the subterranean horrors would have to be braved.

You may think me a coward for fleeing the castle, but this is not quite so. No, in my mind there had grown a plan more positive than mere flight. Fearful though I was, I had resolved to return to Tirgoviste and seek an audience with Basarab cel Tinar, the Voivode, and reveal what I knew of my brothers' plotting. In this way, perhaps, I could atone for the evil deeds of my family.

In the castle courtyard lay an entrance to a small chapel, which was sunk into the ground so that its main chamber was below the surface and its gloomy interior was lit by means of small ventilations. I had heard my brother Mihail remark that it was from this chapel and its vaults that a stairway led down into the very bowels of the mountain, and this connected with a tunnel in which had been found the animals. He had presumed that this tunnel emerged into a grotto on the banks of the River Arges.*

The iron gate creaked inward as I gently pushed it forward and started down the short flight of stone steps that led me into the chapel. On a narrow ledge to one side I found flint and tinder and several ready made torches. I had little trouble in lighting a torch, and with this I gave my surroundings a cursory examination. It was obvious that the chapel had not been used in many a year, for all the religious ornamentation had been removed and thick dust lay over the floor and discarded stonework. On the far side of the chapel an iron grating separated the chapel from the vault. I moved forward slowly, holding my torch high above my head.

There was the sound of scampering as the light shone through the grating into the vault. I felt the quickening of my heart when I saw several pairs of tiny bright eyes staring unblinkingly at me. I shuddered; but I knew that I must face the perils of the journey; and, indeed, the sooner I had started, the sooner I would finish. Thus convinced, I resolutely drew my sword and pushed open the protesting grating with my foot.

At once the sound of scampering came again to my ears

* In fact that route can still be taken by the enthusiastic explorer even today. Van Helsing.

and some of the tiny bright eyes disappeared. Some of the others remained, cold, unblinking and strangely malignant, sending a shiver down my spine.

I raised my torch and the light fell on a collection of animals, the like of which I had never encountered before. They were creatures a foot or so in length, with heads proportionately small and pointed; the eyes were predominant and the whole was covered in a fur which I could see was a grey-brown, with protruding, flesh-coloured feet. On some of them I could discern white teeth, and for a moment my will quailed; but, as I advanced more boldly than I felt, I took heart at the sight of those evil-looking creatures fleeing before me.*

I paused to observe my surroundings, and to my surprise found the vault as empty as the chapel. I pressed on to the narrow stairway which started to lead downwards to the mountain. It was extremely small and several times I was reduced to a sitting position, edging my way down the stairs on my nether regions, which was both uncomfortable and cold, for the stairway was coated in ancient slime, and more than once I slipped and bruised myself. In fact, so small did my passage-way become at one time that I had resolved to retrace my steps – but then it widened out again and I pressed onwards.

The mountain under the castle was a veritable honeycomb of passage-ways which must have led into other vaults or chambers, for several times, to my right and left, the passages opened up and seemed to invite me to explore their drier and more level ways. However, I knew

*Except that they are usually of a length 8–10½ inches, it is an accurate description of *Ratus norvegicus* of the family *muridae*, or the common rat. They were certainly not known in western Europe until the first part of the eighteenth century, and it is fairly well substantiated that they did not reach Paris until 1753. It is reported, though I cannot vouch for accuracy, that they crossed the Volga in the wake of an earthquake in 1727. Van Helsing.

that I must continue downwards, and so downwards I went.

After what seemed a great age the downward path stopped and I found myself in a wide tunnel which branched off both left and right with no indication of which way I should take. For a moment I nearly despaired, but by the science of logic, always uppermost in my mind, I recalled that the valley of Arges lay on the northern side of the castle and the direction of the stairway I had entered lay to the east. At no point could I recall the stairway changing its direction, and so the route must surely be to my left. I moved forward and found the tunnel sloping downwards.

I had begun to feel more confident in my journey and was trying to summon up a tune to my cold lips when an unearthly cry echoed along the tunnel. It shocked me into rigid stillness. Then it came again, and this time I recognized the howl of a wolf.

My heart began to pump at twice its normal rate. A choking sensation in my throat forced me to open my mouth and gasp for breath. Alone in a dark cave with a vicious wolf! The hand that grasped my sword suddenly seemed weak, and I could not feel the metal hilt in my palm. Indeed, it was as if all bone and muscle had been drained from my body. Then I found myself running blindly.

I ran down the tunnel, feeling an uncontrollable fear arise within me. Indeed, you, dear reader, may have experienced a similar nightmare, whereby you are running forward along some confined passageway and yet you seem to be standing still . . . and all the while you know that there is something, something terrible, something monstrous, just behind you . . . something about to reach out and lay a cold and clammy hand on your shoulder . . . such a nightmare did I experience at that moment.

Then a stone caught the toe of my boot and I sprawled forward, my sword slipping from my hand and ringing on the stone floor of the tunnel, my torch flying from my other hand as I stumbled down on my hands and knees, and then hit the ground.

There was a momentary blackness. I know not how long it lasted, but after a while I sat up, flexed my bruised limbs to ensure I had broken nothing, and once more peered into the dank blackness. I could see nothing. Indeed, I might as well have been blind for all that I could encompass in my vision. Then, still on my hands and knees, I crawled forward in an effort to find the torch. After a while my groping hand encountered my sword, which made me feel a little better; but as to the torch, I had no luck at all, and a fearful panic began to seize me. At this point I realized that I had placed the flint and tinder in my pocket, and soon, with enormous relief, I had lit a piece of matchwood.

As the matchwood flared up, I could not suppress a cry of terror at the hideous sight that confronted me.

A pair of dead eyes were staring into mine.

When I managed to control myself, I saw that I was kneeling before a corpse which lay sprawled across the floor of the tunnel. The clothing had rotted from the body and the flesh was in an advanced state of decomposition. One of the eyes was hanging crazily down a cheek, yet it still contrived to look at me. And in the middle of the chest, a wooden stake had pierced the body to its backbone.

All of this I took in at a single glance, before I rose and fled again down the passage-way.

In the haste of my journey my matchwood extinguished itself, but to my utter joy I found that I was no longer in total darkness. A faint white glow was emerging ahead, and I was certain that I could hear running water.

I hurried on and soon, to my eternal relief, found myself in a large cave which contained a sanded shore and a deep pool of water. On the far side of the cave I could see an opening into a grotto with a large entrance into the bright sunshine of day.

Pausing only to sheath my sword, I plunged headfirst into the water and, after a few strokes, found myself in the swift current of the Arges. I am a fairly strong swimmer, so it was without too much effort that I swam to the river bank and gratefully hauled myself up.

I lay for some time, trying to recover my breath and drink in the bright rays of the sun; then, having dried my clothes to a fair degree of comfort, I began to walk along the river bank.

The tunnel had indeed emerged into the Arges valley, and looking up I could perceive the great granite walls of the mountain and the tiny black shape of Castle Dracula, perched on its top. About a mile along the valley, in the direction I was going, lay the village of Arefu, and I decided that my best course of action was to seek out Toma and see if he could provide me with a horse. By the time I reached the outskirts of the village, my clothes were completely dry, but I mistrusted the chill November air and made up my mind that my first comfort should be a glass of the local brandy.

It was while I was thus musing that I heard the sound of horses from the road which now lay but twenty yards away. Thinking of my safety, I hastened to a clump of bushes and flung myself down just as the black coach of the house of Dracula rounded a curve in the road. It was empty except for the tall figure of Tirgsor, sitting on the coachman's box, lashing at his team of horses and urging them to greater efforts as the whole vehicle, coach and horses, swung on its perilous descent along the mountain track.

I lay awhile after the coach had disappeared and found my conscience attacking me – for I knew that Tirgsor had gone to Citea de Arges where he was to meet the Countess Bathory and bring her back to Castle Dracula. Shame, my conscience said, for deserting this poor woman; though my rational self told me that I was not in fact deserting her, but effecting the best possible rescue by informing the Voivode Basarab of my brothers' evil plottings.

So engrossed in this rationalization was I that I was oblivious to any noise around me. Indeed, it was only when I heard a threatening growl right beside me that I came to my senses and looked up.

There, towering on his hind feet, fore paws waving in the air with claws extended, stood the tallest brown bear I had ever seen. And no dancing bear was this, but a wild and hungry denizen of the forest.

I turned to stone as it clawed at the air and advanced upon me.

CHAPTER SIXTEEN

I had closed my eyes and commended myself to God's keeping when the bear let out a grunt of pain. Opening my eyes I could not suppress an exclamation of astonishment as I beheld an arrow protruding from one of the bear's eyes. The animal was threshing about in its agony, and I quickly rolled away from its blind grasp. I then heard the twang of a bowstring and a second arrow embedded itself in the creature's chest. It crashed down to the ground, its limbs kicked for a moment, and then, eventually, it lay dead.

With a prayer of thanksgiving, I turned and beheld my strange saviour. A short, stocky man in the habit of a Catholic monk was returning a third arrow to his quiver and smiling broadly at me. He then said something in a guttural language that I did not recognize, and I decided to answer him in Latin, this being the language of the universal church, which indeed he understood immediately.

'The bear will be tough eating,' the monk repeated in Latin, 'but it is better than going hungry, and you are welcome at my camp fire.'

He motioned behind him to where a small fire was sparking merrily. He then drew a knife and hacked two generous steaks from the carcass of my late antagonist and, with me following, went and sat down by the fire. He methodically attended to the steaks and, since I had said nothing, looked up at me and grinned quizzically.

'You can understand my poor command of Latin, I trust?' he said.

'Yes,' I said, smiling. 'It is just that I am unused to monks armed with the accoutrements of war, for indeed, sir, I notice that you carry not only a bow and arrows, but a short, strong sword as well.'

The monk laughed. He had wide blue eyes which twinkled in a fleshy and ruddy face which was surmounted by a shock of sandy hair.

'I am a Dominican and thus the matter may be explained,' he said. 'I am but recently returned from a pilgrimage to the Holy Land, and there, and indeed here in this country, a Catholic brother has to be prepared to defend himself, both physically as well as spiritually.' Here he patted his sword and grinned mischievously, adding: 'It serves me better than prayers.'

I was surprised by his frankness and humour, and, I confess, found it refreshing in a religious. I introduced myself as the Baron Michelino of Rome and he in turn told me that he was Brother John of the Dominican Order from Glasney Prior in Cornwall. I asked him where this was, for I confess I had not heard of it, and he told me that if I saw a map of England it would resemble a boot and that I should look into the toe of that boot and there find Cornwall.

'So you are English?' I asked, perplexed.

'No, young friend,' he replied. 'We Cornish are an ancient Celtic people who lived in Britain long before the English came, and we were the disciples of Christ long before the English turned from their worship of Woden and *Thunor*.'

I sat with this strange monk as he roasted the bear steaks over his fire and learnt that he had been away from England for seven years on his pilgrimage. His priory, the Collegiate Church of Glasney, stands near a town called Falmouth, and he informed me that it was the centre of learning and literature in his native land. The language of Cornwall differs vastly from that of England, and although English was much influencing his people since they were conquered some centuries before, the monks of Glasney were given to writing religious plays in the language.

Gradually our talk turned to what I was doing in Wallachia. It is strange that sometimes one can meet a person and within a few minutes feel they have known them all their lives. Such was the feeling I had for the English monk (his Cornish ancestors will forgive me, for I have grown to think of him as such) and therefore it seemed natural to pour out my story, from my birth to my journey to Wallachia and then to the events at Castle Dracula and my subsequent escape. He listened for the most part in silence, save for a question here and there to clarify a point, and only when I had finished did he speak.

'Friend Michelino,' he said quietly, leaning forward with his blue eyes very bright, 'there is a force at work here that is more evil and terrifying than you have ever imagined. I fear, my friend, that unless it is fought and destroyed it will spread itself over the world and obliterate any hope of salvation for humankind.'

I was surprised at the intensity of his reaction and I sat back a little.

'What do you mean?' I asked.

'You are a learned man, my friend,' said Brother John, 'and I fear that in your new knowledge you may reject the old knowledge which is in the lives and experiences of the ancients. I fear that you will ridicule what I have come to suspect about the strange occurrences you witnessed at Castle Dracula.'

'Brother John,' I said, 'I confess I am not a religious man. I accept the teachings of the church, but I care more for my living body than I do for the thought of life after death. However, I believe, as you do, that something strange and evil is being plotted by my two brothers.'

'More than that,' Brother John said. 'Much more than that. And I believe it is imperative, my friend, for the sake of the immortal souls of all humankind, that you return to Castle Dracula with me to fight this evil. Will you do it? I ask you in the name of all that is beloved by you.'

So intense and sincere was he that all my previous fears vanished.

'I will,' I said.

He grasped my hand tightly and we sat for some minutes, not speaking, each meditating on our decision. Then eventually the monk woke me, as if from a dream, by laughing ruefully.

'Our steaks seem all but burnt,' he said. 'Now let us eat. And once fed, we shall go up to the castle.'

'Would it not be better,' I ventured, observing that he had apparently closed the subject in order to give his full attention to the bear steaks, 'if you told me what evil threatens us? You say I might ridicule your idea, but I have seen enough to know there is something inexplicably strange up at the castle.'

He laid a hand on my shoulder and gave a small smile.

'So strange, my friend,' he said, 'that I do not think you would give it credence if I told you. No, rather you must place your trust in me until I observe the situation; and when I have so observed it, and when I have confirmed my suspicions, I shall tell you what the evil is. I pray God that I may be wrong, but I fear it will not be so. Do you trust me enough, my friend, to place yourself in my hands until I can tell you what I suspect?'

I nodded. I felt no qualms in placing my trust in this stocky, humourist monk who could wield a sword as readily as his rosary beads, who had wit as well as knowledge to back his philosophies, and who was a religious but did not fear being a man as well. This confidence he inspired in a simple conversation while cooking meat over a camp fire.

Thus, when we had finished our meal, we journeyed back to the castle.

★

It was just after midday when we reached our destination. I was surprised to see that the drawbridge spanned the chasm and the great gates stood wide open. Evidently Tirgsor had not thought to close them when he set off for Arges. Brother John and I entered with a certain trepidation and I conducted him directly to the donjon tower.

The refectory room lay as it had done on every occasion that I had seen it. The fire was in the hearth, the table laid for a meal – but this time I was more than a little startled to see that the table had been laid for two. Of my brothers there was no sign, but a note was lying on the table. Wonderingly, I picked it up and read it.

Brother – We regret not being able to join you this day, but urgent business dictates our absence. The castle is your home – use it as such. You and your guest are welcome.
Your loving brothers, Vlad and Mihail.

'You and your guest are welcome,' I repeated aloud as Brother John scanned the same note. 'How did they know?'

The monk smiled.

'The road is visible to the castle all the way down to Arefu,' he said. 'It requires little powers of foresight to see two men climbing the road.'

'But where are they gone?' I said. 'I swear Tirgsor was alone in the coach.'

'We will see,' Brother John answered. 'But first let us explore the castle and see whether we can begin to fit the pieces of our mystery together. Come, show me first your room and we will make that our starting point.'

My room was as I had left it hurriedly that morning, and I found it odd that the fire had been allowed to die out and nothing attended to, as if no one had entered the room since I left it. This I found odd because always the room had been cleaned and the fire relit by the unseen hands of a servant. I remarked on this fact to Brother John, who peered closely around the room and then seized upon the garlic and bag of salt which still lay beside my bed.

'This may explain the matter,' he said enigmatically.

'Explain what?' I said, agitated by my ignorance.

'Trust me,' the monk said in answer to my query. 'All will be explained soon. But it is excellent that you have these things here.'

I conducted him back to the refectory room again and tried to open the door to the vaults. As on the previous occasion, the door was locked. Unconcerned, I went to the main door, explaining that there was a second stairway to the cellars, but on trying to open that door I found it also barred.

I began to get a strange feeling of panic, of being trapped, and I rushed to each door and each window in vain . . . even the door by which we had just come from the castle courtyard was barred and locked . . . only the gallery between my bedchamber and the refectory room stood open, and it was only between these rooms that we could traverse. I turned and looked fearfully at Brother John.

'We are prisoners!' I cried. 'All the doors and windows are barred against us. We are incarcerated! What are we to do?'

Brother John bowed his head and crossed himself.

'God between us and all evil!' he whispered fervently.

CHAPTER SEVENTEEN

In the first two days of our confinement we saw no one during the daylight hours, and at dusk Brother John insisted that we retire to my bedchamber. Here, much to my surprise, the monk took the garlic and hung little bunches of it at the door, the window, and above the chimney breast. Around the bed he laid a full circle of salt and then, and only then, did he resign himself to sleep. At no time did he cross this salt circle. When he wished to move out of it, he brushed a little of it aside as if making a door in it.

Nothing untoward occurred during our first night of imprisonment and, indeed, I passed the night in deep, refreshing sleep. The next day food had been placed in the refectory with another note exhorting us to use the castle as our home.

It was late in the afternoon of the second day that I heard the sound of horses clattering into the courtyard, accompanied by the rumbling of a coach.

Both Brother John and I raced to the window of the refectory room and peered down through a gap in the shutters, for the windows were barred and it was impossible to open them. We were in time to see the black coach of the house of Dracula, with Tirgsor driving, come to a halt below.

Tirgsor dismounted and stood respectfully when he opened the carriage door to help out his passenger. A small figure, muffled in a sweeping blue travelling cloak with a hood that shielded most of the face, emerged and paused a moment on the step of the coach so that for a brief second, just before she had alighted, I caught a glimpse of a determined chin and red lips against a lovely fair skin. It was obviously the Countess Irene Bathory.

In agitation I cried aloud and banged on the window, but the girl had already vanished. Only the malign face of Tirgsor glanced up at the shuttered window, and, for the first time, a gloating smile spread across the sullen lips of the steward.

Brother John was as agitated as I was.

'The girl is in deadly danger,' he said. 'We must seek a way of reaching her immediately.'

He turned back to the window and pointed at the red orb of the sun, now hanging low in the mountains.

'Too late! Too late!' he cried. 'She must now pass this night unprotected. But tomorrow, my friend, we must act!'

I asked him to explain, but again he refused, shaking his head and saying that I must have patience.

'My head tells me I am still unsure,' he said, 'though I feel in my heart that I am right. When I know for certain, I will explain all. Please be patient till then.'

That night we retired to my bedchamber again, but this time, try as I might, I found slumber elusive. There was a fierce wind howling around the castle; and somewhere, far away, I heard a door banging to and fro. These sounds, which made the castle seem alive, kept me wide awake, my thoughts in turmoil, remembering my brothers, the mysterious third voice, the metamorphosis of Malvina, the malign face of Tirgsor, the ghostly lady in the cellar, the bats and the howling of the wolves and all the tales of dark horror. I twisted and turned. The wind groaned beyond the room. Then, just as I thought I might sleep, I heard a woman's voice outside the door.

I sprang from the bed, but before I could move further, Brother John had clasped my arm in a vice-like grip.

'*No!*' he hissed. '*Not for your soul!*'

I froze where I stood, but looked quizzically at the monk, who was now lighting a candle and peering around at the garlic and salt.

'What is it?' I asked.

'All will be well,' he said, 'so long as we do not leave the circle of salt.'

'But this is madness!' I exclaimed, my fear mixed with frustration. 'You must explain!'

'Later,' he said.

Just then there was another sound at the door. A woman's voice called out to me, a whisper of a voice, soft, appealing and helpless.

'*Mein Herr, mein Freiherr! Verstehen Sie mich, mein Herr? Würden Sie mir helfen?*'

I cast an anxious look at Brother John who stood in the flickering candlelight, his stocky frame hurling huge shadows on the walls. I heard the wind howling outside.

'It is a girl asking me to help her,' I whispered.

The voice came again, disembodied, almost ethereal, a soft and most seductive sound that yet gave me the shivers.

'*Ich fühle mich nicht wohl. Ich bin verletzt.*'

'Listen, Brother John,' I said, not quite believing my own words. 'She is ill. The poor girl has been injured.'

Brother John took hold of me again and his grip was unyielding. Then he called out in a loud voice to whoever was behind the barred door.

'*Fräulein!*' he called. 'Do you hear me?'

'Oh, Master, I do!' came the purring reply. 'Please hurry, *mein Herr*! I am ill!'

'*Fräulein*, do you acknowledge the Lord Jesus Christ as your Saviour?'

The seconds ticked by. Fingers scratched at the door. The wind howled and shadows leapt on the walls and I felt my heart beating. Then came a most plaintive wail:

'*Mein Herr*, I am ill!'

'*Fräulein!*' Brother John shouted, even louder than before. 'Do you acknowledge the Lord Jesus Christ?'

Again there was silence, but for the howling of the wind and the strange, mice-like scratching at the door.

'*Fundamenta ejus in mortibus sanctis!*' Brother John suddenly cried out in a loud, almost terrifying voice. 'Creature of salt, I adjure thee in the name of the Living God!'

From behind the door came a hideous scream of anger, echoing up and down the halls, blotting out the howling wind, a cry of rage and anguish and hatred that made me turn cold. Then it died away. We stood a long time in silence. The shadows danced on the walls and the wind howled and nothing else moved. Finally, after what seemed an eternity, Brother John spoke.

'We will have to be on our guard, my friend,' he said. 'I fear they realize that we recognize them for what they are. Yes, we are ranged against the forces of evil, my friend, and tomorrow our greatest trial will come. So rest now, Michelino. For the moment, at least, we are safe.'

I lay back on the bed, both fearful and intrigued, too bemused to ask yet again for a full explanation. I now knew he would tell me in his own time.

The sun awoke me. I rolled from the bed to find Brother John had already washed and was fully dressed, and was now looking thoughtfully out of the window. I dressed quickly and joined him.

'We must go climbing today,' he said by way of greeting, pointing to the sheer drop from the window. 'It is our only avenue of escape.'

'That is a thousand feet into the valley,' I said. 'Exactly how are we to accomplish this miracle?'

He took my arm and pointed downwards.

'Twenty feet below is an open window. We will simply tie the bed linen together and then you shall lower me down. I will climb through the window and then retrace my way to the refectory room and unbolt the door, providing our hosts have had the goodness to leave a key in the lock on the other side of the door.'

I peered out of the window. By some oversight, it would seem, a window had indeed been left open below us.

'It has possibilities,' I said, 'but I am lighter than you are, so I am the one who should be lowered.'

We wasted little time in breakfasting, and before long I was climbing through the window, a sheet tied around my waist, attached to strips of sheet that Brother John had tied to the bed frame to prevent my sudden plunge into the gorge. Brother John then paid out his makeshift rope and soon I was descending dizzily into space. There was little hold I could take of the castle wall, and I suffered a thousand cuts and bruises as I swung to and fro, bumping against the hard granite blocks. When I tried to steady myself by placing a foot against the wall, it only caused me to swing out further, and my heart beat faster as I felt the knots of the sheet slipping. It seemed an age before I finally found myself opposite the window and, thanks be to God, saw that the window stood wide open so that all I had to do was carefully swing my way through and prevent myself swinging outwards again while I untied my lifeline.

The room gave an impression of greyness and smelt strangely musty. Yet I saw it was a bedchamber and noticed that the curtains of a large four-poster bed were drawn. The fire had been allowed to go out and there was an air of chill about the room. With a twinge of horror I suddenly realized that it might be the bedchamber of one of my brothers, or even that of Tirgsor, and I slowly unsheathed my sword and crept up to the curtains. Then, gently, and with hardly a sound, I drew back the curtains and let the sun's rays fall upon the still figure that lay on the bed.

My breath caught in my throat.

It was a girl. She was beautiful. There was no doubt that it was she whom I had seen from the window the night before: the Countess Irene Bathory. She lay like some exquisite marble statue, so pale, so still that I thought for a moment she must be dead. Then I saw the gentle rise and fall of her bosom. Her fair, gold-brown hair was coiled around her pale face, and there was a touch of blue on her lips.

I tried to rouse her with a gentle shake, but there was no response. Then, as I gave her shoulder another gentle shake, I noticed that there were tiny drops of blood on the pillow and across the sheet. The girl was evidently seriously ill, so I raced back across the room and cried out through the window to Brother John. His voice had a calming effect on me, and he told me to hurry quickly to release him.

Sword in hand, wary of meeting either my brothers or Tirgsor, I sped from the Countess's bedchamber and along the gallery, which passed underneath the one which led from my own bedchamber to the refectory room. Then I went up the stairs and found myself outside the refectory room door. It was not locked, but merely bolted, and it took merely a second to throw back the bolts and open it. Brother John was waiting impatiently in the room and bade me lead him quickly to the countess's side.

The young girl lay as I had left her, a disturbing, almost death-like pale. The bones of her beautifully shaped head stood out, and seemed to disfigure her lovely face. Yet her breathing was now different, more marked and painful, and I was sure that she was close to Death's door.

Brother John stooped over her, holding a hand to her forehead, and then he placed a finger on her wrists and checked the beat of her pulse. When this was done, he peered at her face again, bending his head close to hers. Then he turned her head to one side and studied her neck.

'*Sancta simplicitas!*' he gasped, crossing himself. 'It is as I thought! It is as I suspected! There is a great evil here, my friend. And this young lady is in very great danger.'

I leaned forward to peer at the thing that had brought forth this ejaculation. Just over the pale blue mark of the jugular vein, which now stood so prominently from the translucent flesh, there were two small punctures, red marks with white around the edges, not pleasant to look at.

'What is it?' I demanded, somewhat mystified. 'It looks like the bite of an animal.'

'Animal indeed!' Brother John exclaimed. 'But quickly, my friend! I will explain afterwards! For now, we have work to do to save her. Go to your room and bring the garlic flowers and my bag.'

Hardly had he given the order than I was flying to our room, the sight of that beautiful face on the bloodstained pillow lending me strength and resolution. Upon returning with the garlic and Brother John's bag, I found that the monk had lit a fire in the room, that his sleeves were rolled up, and that he was busy boiling water in a pot. He took the bag from my hands and smiled anxiously.

'Pray that the spirit of the ancient healers Hippocrates and Theophrastus and Pliny look down upon us.'

He took from his bag some phials and herbs and, being interested in the practice of alchemy and medicine, I inquired what he was doing.

'The young woman suffers from a loss of blood,' he said, 'from anaemia, and we must restore her blood to her and prevent further loss. Here,' he continued, picking up a phial, 'is the herb bloodroot, from which the juice has been extracted, and this red juice will pour down her throat. It will purge uncleanliness from her body and will relax her so that she may sleep naturally. Next we apply an infusion of hyssop, which will cleanse again, calming the nerves and regulating the flow of blood from her poor heart. This is all we can do for the moment, except to ring her bed with these garlic flowers whose aroma will cause her to sleep peacefully and be protected. Should she wake, we will allow her to drink only the juice of the dandelion leaves and lady's mantle in order that her blood might flow naturally again.'*

He paused from his activity and looked at me sharply.

'And now, my friend,' he said, 'we must leave this evil place and take her down to the village where she will be safer.'

I nodded my agreement. Certainly the sooner we left Castle Dracula the happier I would feel.

'I shall look for the best way out,' I said, 'and check if our path is clear.'

The stairway to the bottom of the tower I found barred by a large black wooden door. Curious, I pushed it open . . . and the sight that met my eyes caused a cry to be wrested from my lips and brought Brother John scurrying down the stairs to my rescue.

He, too, froze, open-mouthed.

We stood on the threshold of the room and gazed about us in wonder. Then, breathing deeply, Brother John crossed himself and stepped inside.

'It is incredible,' he said. 'Incredible! For some years I have been gathering information on sorcery and witchcraft for a learned treatise which two brothers of my order hope to publish as a guide to the justiciary of all

---

* These seem to be the same symptoms as were shown by poor Lucy Westerna for which treatment I immediately prescribed a blood transfusion. In Brother John's day such a transfusion was unimaginable. It was not until 1818 that Dr James Blundell of London attempted a transfusion of human blood from which the patient died. The theory had been put forward, however, as early as 1665 when Sir Christopher Wren suggested to the Cornishman Dr Richard Lower that blood might be passed from one animal to another. I can boast that I was one of the pioneers of blood transfusion. Van Helsing.

Catholic countries – but never in my researches have I come across such a place as this.'*

'What is it?' I asked, stepping inside.

'It is the devil's own temple,' Brother John replied.

The room was hung in black drapes and lined with the most curious symbols I have ever seen. At one end stood an altar-like table, also covered in black, while benches, on which were many ancient manuscripts, stood around the room. Above the black altar, on the wall, was hung a wooden board, and letters were burnt into the board as if with an iron poker. I recall the shape of those letters very well, and have reproduced them as I recall them.

Brother John informed me that it was writing in Runic, the language of the ancients, and that translated it stood for Dracula. In the meantime, he hurried to and fro among the ancient books and manuscripts, exclaiming all the while that never in his life had he encountered the like, saving one time when he saw a few such books in a Dominican library, which works had been confiscated from Pietro de Abano, an Italian philosopher who had studied medicine in Paris and then returned to Padua to practise as a physician. He had written some highly respected medical books, but it was believed that he practised witchcraft; and later, when he wrote a work called *Heptarneron*, or *Magical Elements*, he was tried by the Inquisition. Although acquitted, he was rearrested and

---

* This comment is interesting inasmuch that a few years after the events described, Brother John's order, the highly learned Dominicans, published *Malleus Maleficarum*, or *The Hammer of the Witches*. This was in 1486. It became the minatory text of the Inquisition. Van Helsing.

died while awaiting trial. All this did Brother John tell me as he walked from one object to another, all the while talking as if to himself, for I am sure that I understood little of his excited mutterings.

'*Siddhi*,' he suddenly said, peering at an old manuscript which contained such strange letters that they looked more like a child's jottings than a language. He then explained that this was the ancient hieroglyphic language of the Pharaohs of Egypt. 'It is a book that explains the ways of evoking *Siddhi*, the magical power of *Om*, the root of creation.'

'*Siddhi*,' I said, a little impatient. '*Om* . . . I know not these words.'

'They are ancient Sanskrit words,' Brother John said, 'a language that must go back to the dawn of time. They evoke the ancient power. Look, my friend!' He pointed to a manuscript written on rolls of strange paper. 'This is a copy of the Book of the Dead, the religious scrolls of Egypt's Eighteenth dynasty . . . It must be nearly three thousand years old.'

'What does all this mean?' I asked.

Brother John looked into my eyes – a grim glance that bespoke serious resolution.

'My friend,' he said slowly, 'we stand in the house of the Undead!'

'The Undead?'

'Aye, my friend. You were born of this flesh, but it has pleased God to remove you all these years from the source of a vile damnation. So have no thought that this is the house of your family. It is the house of the Undead.'

'You will have to explain further,' I said, feeling ignorant, 'for I cannot understand what you say.'

'Do you know what a vampire is, my friend?'

I looked stupidly at him for a moment. 'Do you mean . . .?' I could not bring myself to finish the question.

'Friend, in every country in the world, from Asia to

Ireland, each culture has its tales of vampires – stories of reanimated corpses which cannot lie still in their graves, but must go out between sunset and sunrise to suck blood from the living, whereby they live in a state of Undead. On the warm blood of the living they maintain their ghastly semblance of life.'

'But this is a superstition of peasants,' I said, not daring to believe he was in earnest.

'No, my friend,' he said, 'it is the truth. In your native Italy there are few tales of the vampire – although your notorious vendetta is based on the belief that murdered people cannot rest in their tombs until the blood of the assassin or his kin is spilt. But elsewhere, the Undead is known and feared – even in my own country. During the last century the stories of the Undead of England were chronicled by the Augustinian Canon William of New-burgh in his *Historia Rerum Anglicarum*; and Walter Map wrote *De Nugis Curialium* to warn us of the Undead and their ways.'

'And you believe in all this?' I asked incredulously.

Brother John paused and shook his head sadly.

'Ah, my young friend,' he said. 'Scholars of today scoff at the mysteries which the ancients knew and understood well. We think our forebears were primitive and supersti-tious, yet all the while they had more knowledge of the natural and of the lost arts than we can conceive. Euripi-des and Aristophanes knew the Undead as *Iamiae*, while the great poet Ovid warned of the *striges*, or *mormos*, that assumed the shape of the great bats which flew at night, sucking the blood of the living. Do we scoff at the knowl-edge of such men? Do we jeer at the very founding fathers of the church? The blessed St Clemens wrote of the Undead, and explained their need to devour the blood of the living.'

I raised my hands to my head and shuddered.

'Can such a thing be true?' I said. 'God, I pray it is

not, and yet, Brother John, you say it is and you are vastly more learned than I. And, too, I have seen with my own eyes such strange manifestations that I have no explanation to credit them . . . Brother John, my logic tells me such things cannot be true, but that same logic cannot explain the things that I have witnessed since I came to this God-forsaken country. I must place my trust in you, good brother. Now tell me: what are we to do?'

'My friend,' he said, taking both my hands in his, 'we have to destroy this evil before it bursts like a plague over the earth.'

'How can this evil spread?' I asked.

'The vampire gains immortality, but immortality carries with it a curse: they cannot die, but must go on forever multiplying their kind, for all that die from their kisses become as they: *Undead!*'

Suddenly my blood ran cold.

'And the countess .. .?' I began.

'No,' he said promptly, 'she can recover. The vampire took but little of her blood.'

The extent of my relief was such that I knew I now believed all that he told me. And, with the acceptance of this belief, came a deep and abiding fear.

'But what can we do against such supernatural powers?' I asked. 'Is there no way we can destroy the vampire?'

'Indeed there is, my friend,' he replied to my surprise, 'but first let me tell you the nature of the Undead. He casts no shadow, casts no reflection in a mirror; he has the strength of many and can transform his shape into a bat or wolf, or can swirl in a mist, or come on moonlit rays as elemental dust. He can see in the dark.

'But though he is not of nature, he has to obey nature's laws. His power ceases at sunrise; and from sunrise to sunset he must return to lay helpless on his native soil – the soil wherein he was buried. Nor can he pass running water, except at the slack and flood of the tide.

'The symbols of good he abominates – such as the crucifix, which protects the living from the Undead. He can be destroyed by the driving of a wooden stake through his heart, or by cutting off his head and stuffing garlic in his mouth.

'Yes, my friend, he can be destroyed – and we have three powerful weapons to fight him with. First, there is iron. Iron from time immemorial has symbolized purity and protection from evil. Even the great philosopher Pliny says, in his *Natural History*, that iron nails above the threshold of a house give protection from devils.

'Then there is salt. Salt, likewise, incorruptible, medicinal and preservative in nature, is symbolic from the land of Persia to the land of the Finns. Did not the ancient Greeks say, "Trespass not against salt and board"?

'The third weapon is garlic, one of the oldest medicinal herbs in the world. The ancients of Babylon used it over four thousand years ago. Aristophanes used it for virility, Dioscordes, the official physician to the Roman army, recommended it for internal disorders, and Galen used it as an antidote to poison. From time immemorial it has been used to keep the devil and witches at bay.

'Thus we are armed, my friend.'

'But, Brother John,' I exclaimed, 'if what you say is true, and I know you say it in all sincerity, there occurs to me a thought which is puzzling. I have seen and talked to my brothers Vlad and Mihail, and also Tirgsor and his daughter Malvina, when the sun has been up and they have come and gone about the castle with ease. How can you then say, as you previously did, that the power of the Undead ceases at sunrise?'

'This is true,' he replied without pause, 'and I well understand your confusion. But regarding those you mention, it simply means that they have not yet joined the ranks of the Undead. Indeed, because of the restrictions placed upon him, it is necessary for the Undead to have slaves or servants that will protect him during the daylight hours. Yet to be such a slave one has to be in a state of semi-Undead.

'Do you recall how you told me that Tirgsor was so insistent upon travelling on St Andrew's Eve, a night when the power of evil is at its height? And the next day, in daylight, you said he was pale and wan, but as night drew on he became stronger and more healthy. You said that you also noticed the same phenomenon with your brothers who were pale and wan in the daylight but grew more animated towards dusk. Is that not so?'

I nodded slowly, feeling dread coil within me, not wanting to face up to what his words were revealing yet enslaved by a horrified curiosity, seduced by my nightmares.

'Yes, that is so,' I said.

'Then we are agreed,' Brother John said, and the words that he uttered scourged my soul. 'While they are not yet Undead, which in this case they are not, they are limited in their powers also. Perhaps, as time progresses, their strength is gradually drawn from them, so that they can move in the daylight less and less. And if such be the case, then they too must finally become Undead.'

'But if they are the slaves of the Undead,' I said, 'who then is this Undead you speak of? Who is their master?'

Brother John leant towards me. I saw the blazing of his eyes. They were fierce and they held a great compassion and a welter of pain.

'Why, my friend,' he said, seizing my arm, 'who else but your own father whom you thought dead? Who else, indeed, but *Dracula*?'

My senses reeled. I fell against him and wept. I let the anguish and the horror flare up and die away, and then, when I recovered, and Brother John had dried my eyes, we returned to attend to the sleeping countess, secure in our mutual faith and trust.

BOOK THREE
The Undead

Chapter Eighteen

It was in the late afternoon that Brother John and I, carrying the unconscious countess between us, made our way down into the village of Arefu and raised the inn-keeper, Toma, from his shuttered inn. We prevailed upon him to give us a room, and I do believe it was only the priestly vocation of Brother John that persuaded him to do that much for us.

Our prime concern was for the health of the countess, and it was agreed that one or both of us should sit with her through the night. Although garlic flowers and crucifixes were hung in abundance in the inn, Brother John insisted on reinforcing these precautions in the bed chamber. We ate a less than hearty supper and retired early, and took up positions in two chairs on either side of the young girl's bed. A blazing fire made the room warm and induced drowsiness, so to keep from sleeping we engaged in a whispered conversation across the sleeping form of the countess.

'When I was born my father was as we are,' I said. 'Of that I am sure from my mother. How then could he now be as you say . . . Undead?'

'There are many ways, my friend,' Brother John replied. 'A suicide may become a vampire, or an unbaptized child, or, indeed, a seventh son* or a man with a caul or membrane covering his head at birth. Also those who

---

* This is an interesting point, for in Romania and surrounding countries a seventh son is a bad omen, perhaps to do with the fact that offerings to the dead have to be seven in number or in multiples of seven. It is only in Ireland, and subsequently in England, that a seventh son is believed to be a symbol of good luck. Van Helsing.

have eaten the flesh of a sheep killed by a wolf, those over whose dead body a cat has passed, those who have been murdered and have remained unavenged, and those who have dabbled in sorcery and led evil lives. Also those who have been kissed by the vampire. Such, my friend, are the ways in which this disease may spread itself.'

'But my father hardly fitted any of these descriptions. True, it is said he lived a life of evil; but others were just as evil and did not become Undead like he.'

Brother John nodded.

'There are three ways that Dracula may have become Undead. First, he may have fallen prey to the disease; he may have been a victim of a vampire – though that is not likely from the manner of his dying in battle and in the strength of character he had. Second, he did change his religion from the Orthodox Church to the Catholic Church, and the peasants hereabouts believe that a person who so changes his religion becomes without a soul, and thus becomes a prey to the vampire. As a priest of Rome I must discount this belief as nonsense. But third, those who dabble in sorcery and conjure the devil, and seek immortality from the dark powers, can achieve such immortality by becoming Undead.

'You saw the great room wherein were all the ancient books of lore on sorcery and symbols of the ancients. I say that Dracula, by means of sorcery, sold his soul for immortality and his reward was to become Undead – for what purpose I know not.'

We fell into silent contemplation, enslaved by our own thoughts. I knew, now, the evil of my own family and was forced to accept this vile truth. Yet I also knew, with a fresh, clear conviction, that in braving the full horror of what had been unveiled I had somehow discovered new strengths in myself. The truth was a nightmare. The nightmare was my inheritance. Yet by facing this dark-ness, and by braving that which I feared, I was strengthening my own childish spirit and emerging to manhood. Yes, I was pitted against my very own flesh and blood, but I knew that good would come from this incestuous war. Of this I was confident.

As midnight approached the countess grew more and more restless in her slumber and, as if in sympathy, the wind began to rise and beat about the inn, howling almost mournfully down the chimneys. The draught sent the sparks flying and the candles flickering, and it put a fierce chill in the air.

Brother John sat with his rosary in his hands, calmly telling his beads, while I kept my gaze upon the small, helpless face of the countess, now beating restlessly from side to side on the pillow. Her breathing was somewhat stertorous and her mouth was wide open, as if to take in bigger mouthfuls of air. I could see her pale gums and the pinkness of her tongue; and although, perhaps, it was a trick of the light, her white teeth seemed unusually sharp and long.

In her sleep she made futile attempts to push away the garlic flowers, and I called Brother John's attention to the fact, wondering whether the fumes were too much for her tortured lungs. However, Brother John forbade me to touch or remove them.

The wind increased in ferocity, and suddenly, as if from the next room, came the long-drawn-out howl of a wolf.

Brother John sprang from his chair.

'What in God's name was that?' he cried.

I was wondering myself until I remembered the poor madman Liviu, chained like an animal in what indeed must have been the next room. I briefly explained this to Brother John, and we listened together and could hear, beneath the breathless fury of the wind, the dragging of a chain on the wooden floor, and a scratching upon the wall, as if a beast of prey were seeking entrance. Another horrific howl came from the next room, and then a ghastly human voice cried out:

'It comes! It comes! Blood is life! Blood is life!'

Just then there was such a violent gust of wind that it roared down the chimney and in one mighty blast turned the wooden logs into an explosion of flying embers and extinguished all the candles in the room.

We stood for a moment, unnerved by the sudden darkness, and a tingle of cold apprehension shivered down my spine when I realized that the wind had now ceased . . . ceased so abruptly that there was not another sound to be heard. Indeed, so quiet was it that I could almost hear the growing of the grass, the decaying of the inn, even feel the rotation of the earth itself.

'Blood is life!' came the scream of the poor lunatic next door.

Then, horrified, we heard the sound of flapping wings, a scrabbling and scratching in the chimney, and before we could move a monstrous bat flew out of the hearth and hovered malignantly before us.

The stench of corruption filled the room.

'Don't look at its eyes!' Brother John cried. 'In the name of God don't look at its eyes!'

But I had already focused on the tiny red eyes that seemed to grow larger and larger. The room was dark, but the bat was even darker, a shadow upon the shadows, swaying sluggishly back and forth, the eyes cold and blood-red and burning out of the blackness like hot coals in the deepest pits of Hell. It was drawing me in. It was bending me to its will. I felt myself succumbing, vaporizing, floating out of myself. Then Brother John stepped forward. This movement jerked me awake. I remembered the bat in Castle Dracula, its power to enslave, and I hastily forced my gaze to the floor and refused to look up.

The flapping wings moved towards me.

Suddenly Brother John ran in front of me and threw

his rosary at the beast. With a screech, as if in rage, the bat flew swiftly sideways and attempted to swoop down upon the countess. Recovering his crucifix, Brother John again ran towards the bat, which, screeching like a soul in the fires of damnation, suddenly flew back up the chimney and disappeared.

Brother John immediately hung the rosary before the chimney piece.

'It will not enter this way again,' he said.

Instantly, once more, the howl of the madman riveted us both to the spot. It was a scream of hatred, of infinite frustration, and it was followed by the sound of plaster being torn from the wall, and then by the smashing of glass.

'By the Gods!' I cried. 'The poor thing that was Liviu has freed itself and leapt through the window!'

As I turned automatically towards the door, Brother John laid a restraining hand on my arm.

'No!' he said. 'We must not leave this room tonight! You have just seen the powers of the Undead!'

Accepting this wisdom, I nodded at Brother John, but made my way to the window and looked out.

The moon was high and the scene was brightly lit, though this light cast shadows which created a plethora of weird figures which appeared to dash this way and that. For a while I had difficulty in focusing my eyes, but eventually I saw the movement of a man . . . No, surely not a human, but a beast, something that seemed to crawl on all its limbs, something wretched, obscene . . . Then it cried out in a voice not quite human: the cry of a soul in hideous torment.

'*Dracula!*'

The thing had crawled from the shadows and raised its pale, ravaged face to the full moon. It was Liviu: the poor, insane beast that a few months ago had been a handsome youth enjoying his wedding night. Now, Liviu was gone. Only that tortured beast remained. And the broken chain dangled from the iron around its neck and I wondered at the strength needed to sever it.

'*Dracula!*' Again the tormented cry broke from his lips. '*Great Voivode, I am here!*'

The cry was in the language of the Wallachians, but by now I had acquired enough of that speech to understand some simple meanings.

'*Dracula! Great Voivode! Give me life, Master! Life is blood! Blood is life!*'

I stared down in pity at this poor unhappy creature which gestured so feebly towards the moon. My soul cried out that his trembling, demented form might have some peace. Then a cold fear shot through me. I found myself looking skywards. There were no stars to accompany the white disc of the moon, but again I heard the flapping noise of wing beats, the wings of many creatures, and the breath caught in my throat when I saw them. I gasped and cried out. I could not believe my eyes. Brother John rushed to my side and he followed my gaze and we both saw a multitude of bats. They were flying in perfect formation. They were led by a monstrous creature. They sped upwards and raced across the face of the moon, then suddenly turned and plummeted earthwards.

I cried out a warning.

Liviu looked up and saw death racing towards him. He saw death and as he looked he suddenly stood tall and strong, and held his arms high and wide, and threw back his head and laughed crazily. Then they were upon him, a black mass all over him, and he struggled and fell down, and was clawing them off, and then exploded into blood and rent flesh, and was suddenly still.

The silence was hideous. It emphasized their thirsty drinking. The black form was crumpled up and the black mass shifted over it and I thought of cats lapping up their milk. I could not suppress a shudder. It passed through me and left me frozen. I wiped sweat from my forehead and looked again, and my blood turned to stone.

The bats were still there. They were a black mass on the body. But behind them stood a tall man, a pale, ghastly spectre, covered from head to foot in a black cloak.

He raised his white face to mine. His eyes were crimson and luminous. There was blood on his chin and his lips were curled back in a mocking smile.

I knew that face. It floated back from my childhood. It was now a hellish face, but its features were unmistakable; and I gazed out of terror and despair at the face of my father.

Indeed, it was Dracula!

Slowly he raised his cloak, like a huge pair of black wings, and then, as if he had never been, he quite simply vanished.

I blinked my eyes. I felt that I was dreaming. I saw a long line of bats, led by a larger bat, flying in perfect formation towards the full moon.

Then I passed out.

CHAPTER NINETEEN

We were woken in the morning to great cries of lamentation from below. For a moment I was startled, suddenly remembering, as I did, the terrifying events of the previous night, and confusing these lamentations with the tormented cries of Liviu, I jerked awake drenched in fear. It was a moment or two before I fully comprehended that I was actually awake, that Liviu was dead, and the lamentations from below were doubtless related to these facts.

I glanced across to the other side of the countess's bed, where Brother John was just wakening, blinking his eyes and looking down at the chair in which he had slept all night. Then my gaze fell on the sleeping figure of the countess.

She lay amidst the garlic flowers and her breathing now seemed more normal, deep and rhythmic, than her tortured gasping of the night-time. Indeed, there was even a touch of colour on her pale cheeks, and I was reminded of the legend of the sleeping princess who would only wake when the right man kissed her.

Again we heard the lamentations rising up from below our room, and Brother John heaved himself from his chair.

'What is it?' he asked.

'I believe they have found Liviu's body,' I said.

He lowered his head and frowned.

'Then let us go down,' he said quietly.

When I hesitated, looking towards the countess, for whom I now felt a more than common regard, he smiled and added:

'Have no fear. She is safe until sunset.'

We went down into the parlour of the inn and found

Toma trying to comfort his wailing wife. Through the window I could see two men of the village bearing away something on a sheet. Toma looked at me through anguished, red-rimmed eyes and then, almost pleadingly, at Brother John.

'We have no priest here,' he said bitterly. 'It is my wife's wish that her brother Liviu be buried as a Christian.'

Brother John nodded and laid a hand on the sobbing woman's shoulder.

'You understand what has to be done first?' he said.

Toma and his wife exchanged a glance, and then the woman nodded, before sinking her head to her breast in a renewed paroxysm of weeping.

'We understand, Father,' Toma said.

'Very well. Where will you bury him?'

'In a corner of our churchyard, Father.'

'Let us go there then. Do you have the necessary things?'

Toma nodded, and Brother John turned to me.

'It is best if you stayed here and took a glass of my medicinal mixture to the countess,' he said. 'It is dandelion and lady's mantle. She must drink it in order that her blood may flow freely and uncontaminated.'

I did as I was bid, and I must confess that I was glad to escape the grim ceremony of burial. Brother John was to tell me afterwards of the task he had to perform in order to give eternal rest to the victim of the Undead, and avoiding this was something I therefore did not regret.

Firstly, he hammered a wooden stake through the heart of what remained of Liviu's body. Then he hammered an iron nail through the head. Then garlic flowers were spread across the body which was laid face downwards in the makeshift wooden box that passes with these simple folk as a coffin. All this was done to the accompaniment of prayers, and I could hear Brother John's sonorous tones coming from the churchyard that lay opposite the inn.

I stood by the window in the countess's bed chamber, the window from which I had seen Liviu die, and found myself taking comfort from the stalwart figure of Brother John as he stood with raised arms over the grave, defying all the dark powers. The ceremony ended with Toma planting a rose bush on the grave, which belief, as I understand it, arises from the idea that if the occupant of a vampire grave tried to rise from it, the thorn bush would prevent the vampire from so doing. Brother John finished by raising his hands above his head and crying out loudly, in a tone so clear and ringing that I could clearly hear it even from the bed chamber:

'*Gott Vater, Du Schöpfer von Himmel und Erde! Beschirm unsern Ring, behüt unsern Herd!*'

'What is it?' said a bewildered and very feminine voice from the bed. 'What is happening?'

I turned to see the countess propped up on one elbow, a perplexed frown on her lovely face, and I took a hesitant step in her direction.

'It is nothing,' I said. 'It is a burial. Do you feel well?'

She looked at me in bewilderment, her hair tumbling around her face, her eyes large and beautiful.

'I . . . I feel weak. I . . . Oh, my Lord!'

A hand went to her mouth and her eyes went even larger as memories of the past days flooded into her tortured mind. I stepped forward immediately and held her hand.

'Have no fear,' I said. 'You are safe now.'

'Horrible!' she exclaimed, clutching at me like a drowning child, her voice rising dangerously near to hysteria. 'Horrible! It was horrible!'

Involuntarily my hand went up to stroke her soft hair, and I found myself pressing her nearer to my breast, not only to comfort her, but because of a growing emotion in myself.

'You are safe now,' I repeated, feeling an onrush of warmth, a pain and an ecstasy combined, a blind, over-powering need. 'Please be calm. It is all right.'

She lay some time against my breast, quiet but quiver-ing, her breath warm and quickened by fear. Then, abruptly, she pulled herself away from my arms with a bright blush tingeing her cheeks.

'Who are you?' she demanded, surprised rather than angry, and perhaps just a little embarrassed. 'Who are you?' she repeated. 'You say I am safe, and yet I recall being in Hell. Was it a dream? No, it could not be so.' She blinked and glanced around her and I noticed that her eyes, now open for the first time, were like pools of amber, bright and intoxicating. 'You say I am safe,' she continued, 'and curiously I believe and trust you. Please, who are you?'

I told her my story as briefly as I could, sparing her the more gruesome details. When I had finished, she turned pale and lay back on her pillows, a little fear and much puzzlement in her lovely eyes.

'You say you are a Dracula,' she said. 'The son of the evil one?'

I nodded, but not with great pleasure.

'Yet you are not as they,' she said. 'I feel safe here, and your eyes tell me I can trust you with my safety. Truly, it is very strange . . .'

'Yet not so strange, my lady!' Brother John cried, enter-ing the room and smiling broadly. He then introduced himself with a stiff, awkward bow and fell to performing his physician's duties. 'Indeed you have been sick, my lady, but you now appear much better. Our medicines did you no harm and so you must continue to take them for your health's sake.' He pressed his herbal concoction into her unprotesting hand. 'Drink this down now, and then let us hear your story, for I believe that friend Michelino has told you ours.'

She drank the mixture and lay back on the pillows. Her sweet face was relaxed, and it seemed that the terrors of the night had fled.

'My story is simple, dear friends . . .'

Dear friends! How ridiculous that my heart leapt at the words and bathed in the radiance of her smile. Indeed, on this instant, I was enslaved by her.

'I am, as you know, the Countess Irene Bathory. The Bathory family is an ancient one, as old as the Carpathian mountains that suckled them and shelters their castles. We have long been of the first noble house of Transylvania. But there is a tragic side to our house, for there are two branches of the Bathory family: one is called the Ecsed branch and the other the Somlyo. I am descended from the Somlyo branch, but the branch of Ecsed is tainted by madness, epilepsy and cruel aberrations in character . . . and yet, yet it is the Ecsed branch that rules our house. Stefan Bathory, a morbid man who is my cousin and would be Voivode of all Transylvania, is the head of the Bathory house. It was he who rode alongside Vlad Dracula last year in a bid to restore him as ruler of Wallachia.

'Alas, I am but nineteen, my parents are dead, and therefore I am ward to Stefan Bathory and have to obey him. Some weeks ago he sent for me and told me I was to marry with Vlad, son of Vlad Dracula. I knew him not, save that I had heard of the stories of the cruelty of the house of Dracula. Yet I came willingly enough to the Citadel of Arges, where I was told a coach of the house of Dracula would wait for me. I reasoned that my own house was cruel enough, so what harm to go to another and perhaps gain my freedom?

'At Arges I waited. My maid Kata became suddenly ill and died on the very day Tirgsor arrived. Therefore it was alone that I went to Castle Dracula, and once inside things became a nightmare . . . an evil dream . . .'

She shuddered and caught her breath.

'Go on!' Brother John whispered.

'I cannot recount the horrors . . . I recall that I awoke in the night . . . a bat . . . the red eyes boring into my own with basilisk horror.'

She raised both her hands to her face and cried out in the dread of her remembrance. I sprang to the bed immediately and rested a protective arm around her shoulders.

'Do not fear, dear countess,' I exclaimed. 'We will do all that is within our power to protect you.'

She raised her large, tear-stained eyes to mine.

'But where am I to go?' she said. 'What am I to do? The Bathorys will only return me to Castle Dracula!'

I shook my head vigorously.

'No,' I said. 'Brother John and I will take you from this God-forsaken country, do not fear. I have a modest income which will suffice to protect you from the evils of life until you decide on your own future.' I paused, embarrassed by the vehemence of my declaration and wondering if I had gone too far in my boldness. 'That is,' I added, 'if you so wish it.'

The countess smiled, bathing me in her radiance, and raised my hand and pressed her lips to it.

'Brave sir,' she said softly, 'I cannot thank you and Brother John here for the services you have rendered me. My thanks would appear an insult to the nobility of your good deeds.'

Brother John cleared his throat.

'Yes, my dear child,' he said, 'but first we have to earn that thanks, for while we have thwarted the will of the Undead for a while, we are far from winning the conflict.'

'What must we do, Brother John?' I cried, determined to do battle with all the furies of Hell itself for another look of gratitude from the fair countess.

'Why, friend Michelino, we must track down the resting place of the great Undead and there end his existence.

We must find Dracula's resting place and drive a stake through his heart.'

I felt the countess shudder against my arm.

'And what of the Lady Irene?' I said. 'We cannot leave her unprotected.'

Brother John turned and took a hand of the countess.

'We must leave her alone one night,' he said kindly. 'Perhaps more. But we will not leave you unprotected, and we will get Toma and his wife to sit with you. We will leave you surrounded by all the protection available to us. Will you be brave and endure it?'

The girl silently bit her lip.

'I shall be afraid,' she finally said. 'But you are the ones who will be going into a great danger, and therefore I will be brave for your sakes.'

Brother John pressed her hand and I felt a surge of pride at her courage – a pride tinged with love, for indeed, at that moment, it was such I felt, and in a manner I had never felt before.

'Where shall we begin our search?' I inquired. 'At the castle?'

Brother John shook his head.

'You must tell me of the spot where Dracula rests, for you recall that a vampire must lay in his own grave from sunrise to sundown. Between those hours he has to lay helpless in his natural earth – in the earth in which he was buried.'

'If that is so,' I said, 'then he would lie where he was buried and many saw him buried.'

'And where was that?'

'The story is that he was killed in a battle outside Bucharest.'

Brother John shook his head.

'It cannot be,' he said, 'for a man killed in honourable battle does not become an Undead such as he.'

'So goes the story, which I only repeat,' I said. 'It may

be false. But of one thing I am sure: his body was taken to the monastery of Snagov, near Bucharest, and there, in the presence of many, he was laid to rest.'

'I know the place,' Brother John said. 'It is an Orthodox monastery that stands on an island in one of the lakes surrounding Bucharest. It is one of the three largest and most important monasteries in all Wallachia.'

'I know it, too,' the countess said, grasping my hand and filling me with warmth. 'It is a fearful place and I fear you going.'

'We must,' I said, absurdly pleased that she should fear for my safety.

'It is a place where the princes and boyars of Wallachia hid in times of peril,' she said. 'It is a grim place which serves as a prison as well as a monastery, for the buildings are heavily fortified and guarded by boyars as well as monks. How can you hope to get in, accomplish your purpose, and escape the wrath of the monks?'

'Nevertheless, my lady,' said Brother John determinedly, 'we must do it, for many may depend on us.'

I nodded my agreement.

'We will be well protected,' I said. 'Never fear.'

'And now,' Brother John said with an air of impatience, 'we have delayed enough. We must get horses from Toma and depart at once. It is fifty miles to Snagov and a hard ride. I will go and make the arrangements.'

I sat in silence for some time, with the countess's hand in mine, too embarrassed by the depth of my desire for her to offer a word. And she, too, obviously aware of my feelings, was quiet and could not look at my eyes, though a blush tinged her cheeks. Finally, after what seemed an eternity, I said that I must go.

'I wish it were not so,' she replied. 'I feel safe with your presence, and I will not feel happy till your return.'

At this lightly veiled confession I felt my heart leap, and I wanted to rush forward and embrace her.

'I am happy it should be so,' I said, smiling yet making no move, 'but we will be safer when our task is complete.'

Impulsively she leant forward and kissed me on the cheek. Her lips were cool and yet they seemed to burn through me.

'Go then,' she said softly. 'God ride with you and protect you and hurry you safely back.'

I kissed her hand and left her. As Brother John and I spurred our horses away from Arefu on our grim mission I saw her slim figure at the window of the inn, waving after us.

CHAPTER TWENTY

Of our ride to Snagov, I can recount but little. I recall that on that long ride we exchanged few words, each being sunk into his own thoughts. Villages, hamlets, forests, streams and rivers went by all unnoticed until, by the late afternoon, we halted our tired horses on the shores of a lake in the heart of the Vlasie Forest, which is near the city of Bucharest.

On an island in the lake, its grey stone walls towering to the sky, stood the great monastery of Snagov ... Snagov, where Dracula lay.

The monastery was a large fortified complex, more secure than most castles. The island was about a mile wide and a mile and a half long, the outer walls of the monastery following closely the shore line. In addition to the various chapels, cloisters and guest houses, there were farm houses and outbuildings by which the monastic population retained a degree of self-sufficiency from the outside world.

I knew little about Snagov except that my grandfather, old Vlad Dracul, had endowed it with more land than any other monastery in his realm so that it was now one of the three largest and most important monastic establishments in Wallachia. Radu cel Frumos, my uncle, also endowed it with land, and I have heard it said that a mistress of my father became a nun here.

The great monastery walls surrounded the island on all sides, coming right down to the water's edge, and a ferry was the only means of entrance or exit.

Brother John and I sat a time contemplating this forbidding building and discussing the best means of ingress. As it was an Orthodox monastery, Brother John felt it would be useless to try to gain an entrance openly and honestly, and certainly futile to try to convince the abbot of the necessity of defacing a tomb and mutilating a corpse . . . and the corpse of a prince to boot. The situation was indeed difficult.

I suggested that perhaps we could gain entrance as ordinary travellers seeking refuge, and then wait an opportunity to enter the tomb of Dracula to destroy him. Brother John wordlessly pointed to the sun now low on the distant hilltops. There would be little time to succeed before Dracula was able to move freely once again. However, when all was said and done, my suggestion seemed the only feasible one.

Brother John removed his habit and ornamentation, for there is sometimes great hostility to Catholic monks from those of the Orthodox persuasion. Securing them in his saddle bag, he then mounted his horse and we rode down to the jetty, where a fat and indolent boatman, grumbling his protestations, rowed us across for a silver *aspi*, which I felt was more than adequate for his services.

A brother greeted us at the great wooden gates of the monastery and demanded to know our business.

'We are travellers in your country,' Brother John replied, 'seeking hospitality for the night.'

'You are foreigners?' the monk inquired, regarding us in suspicion, though there was no strangeness in this since, at this time, Turk and Christian rode across the country bringing bloodshed and disease wherever they spread their sleeping blankets.

'We are,' Brother John replied.

'Enter then,' the monk said. 'Come in peace, go in peace and leave something of the happiness you bring.'

The monk took us to a cell-like room, sparsely furnished, but with two strong wooden cots on which were two blankets. There was also a small table with a bowl and a jug of cold water for a toilet, and a Bible of Byzantine decoration for the salvation of our souls.

'When you have refreshed yourselves,' the monk said, taking his leave of us, 'you will be expected to join the brothers in the refectory.'

'What now?' I asked Brother John when the monk had departed.

'As he says,' Brother John replied. 'There is little we can do until we find out exactly where Dracula rests.'

The immense refectory hall to which we were summoned was filled with many monks attending their one meal of the day. On a long table at the far end of the hall sat several of the hierarchy of the monastery and a monk came forward to conduct us to this table where we were introduced to a tall, grizzle-haired man who was the abbot.

As Brother John had originally stated such, so we pretended to be foreign merchants travelling through the country, and soon we were exchanging gossip on the political events of the world. We congratulated the monks on the defeat of the Turks, and then Brother John managed to pass a comment on the death of Dracula.

'Ah, yes,' smiled the abbot. 'He was once a great defender of this monastery and of Christendom against the Turkish incursions.'

One of the monks leaned forward. He was lean and very pale and there was something strangely familiar about his face. The abbot waved a hand in his direction.

'Our brother Vlad here,' he said, 'is the brother of Dracula.'*

I gave an involuntary start. I had heard of this brother who had, in fact, been the half-brother of my father, the

---

* This must have been Vlad Calugarul, or Vlad the Monk, half-brother of Dracula, who later became abbot of Snagov but was then defrocked. He claimed the throne of Wallachia in 1481 and ruled until 1482, during which time he betrayed the country to the Turks. He died in 1492. Van Helsing.

third and youngest son of the old dragon. He hated and despised my father, but it was a hatred born of envy. I did not like this Vlad's face: it was mean and envious. It seemed strange that he and I were of the same blood, and yet he did not sense any relationship between us. I thanked God that I favoured my mother more than my father.

'The Voivode, my brother,' said Vlad the monk, 'was buried here.'

'Indeed?' said Brother John, and I could not help but marvel at his acting, for it seemed he had never heard of the fact before, so well did he feign his surprise.

'Yes,' Vlad the monk said. 'After the battle of Bucharest, the Voivode's servants brought his body here and it was entombed in our southern chapel.'

Brother John started to talk casually about the Turkish army and their expansion, as if he were not interested in the burial of Dracula, and for some hours we feasted and talked generally with the monks. But later, in the privacy of our cell, Brother John whispered:

'At first light we will go to the southern chapel and destroy him!'

'Why not now?' I asked.

'It is two hours since sunset. He will not be there. We must wait until he returns to rest here at sunrise.'

'What now?' I asked.

'Now?' he said smiling. 'Well, friend Michelino, we must try to get as much rest as we can. I'll wake you before first light.'

With that, we both lay down and slept.

We approached the small chapel as the first rays of the coming dawn began to shine through the slit windows of the great monastery walls.

The chapel stood in a small corner of the monastery's main courtyard, and we crossed to its small but heavy carved oak door without encountering any of the monks, who must now be rising to the hollow tolling of the great bell. We pushed open the door and found ourselves in a small vault-like chapel, scarce twenty feet long and ten feet wide. The stone floor was cold and damp, and there was an altar at one end on which two candles spluttered, giving forth an eerie light.

Before the altar stood a smaller, slightly raised altar piece.

Brother John pointed silently. There was some writing in the old Slavic script which even I could interpret.

DRACULA

Without a further word we bent to our task of removing the weighty stone slab from the top of the altar grave. The sweat glistened on our faces as we pulled and tugged with all our might. Slowly, grating, stone against stone, the slab swung to one side. With our combined strengths we pushed it over and then peered into the silent sarcophagus to confront the great evil which plagued Wallachia.

It was empty.

Brother John and I looked blankly at one another.

'What does it mean?' I whispered. 'I thought you said . . .'

Then, remembering, I indicated the brightening sky, and Brother John nodded grimly.

'He should have returned,' Brother John said. 'Unless . . .'

'Unless what?'

'Unless he has found another resting place.'

We stood irresolute a moment, crushed and confused, and then Brother John shook himself.

'We must find him,' he said. 'Quickly! Let us push back the slab!' He threw his crucifix into the tomb. 'That will ensure he cannot return here.'

Together we exerted all our strength and slowly swung the stone slab back into position.

'What are you doing here?' a sharp voice barked.

Startled, we looked up. The tall figure of the abbot was framed in the door, while behind him I could see the lean, stooped figure of Vlad the Monk.

'Why,' Brother John said, quickly recovering his wits, 'we were so enthralled about your conversation last night concerning the Voivode Dracula that we came to view his tomb.'

'To view?' Vlad the Monk's voice was suspicious.

'I was merely looking closely at the inscription,' Brother John said, 'to ensure that there was no mistake.'

The abbot looked at us closely.

'And?' he said.

'It seems that this is indeed Dracula's tomb,' Brother John said smoothly, 'and we are honoured at being able to see the last resting place of the great Voivode.'

'Not so honoured,' said the abbot, obviously convinced of our sincerity. 'While it is true that the Voivode Dracula was buried here after the battle of Bucharest, a few months ago his sons sought permission of the Metropolitan to have the body exhumed and reburied in the family crypt at Castle Dracula. The tomb you see is thus empty.'

The abbot turned to leave, and I could see Brother John's face turn ashen, signalling that something, I knew not what, was wrong.

'My lord abbot,' Brother John said, visibly trying to control his shaking voice, 'before we leave on our journey, tell me, was Dracula reburied at the castle with great pomp?'

The abbot glanced back questioningly.

'That is a strange question,' he said.

'It is merely, my lord abbot, that most people think the prince is buried here, and I wondered why this is so.'

'There is no mystery,' the abbot explained. 'Dracula's

body was exhumed during the reign of the late lamented Basarab the Old, who was the arch enemy of Dracula. It was therefore not prudent to reveal such things to the general public. But it was the sons of Dracula who also insisted on privacy – pious sons both. Why, they even had some earth and materials taken from our tomb to Castle Dracula in order that their father's sleep might remain undisturbed. A great Christian symbolism. Such piety!'

'Well, we will take our leave, lord abbot,' Brother John said, now trying to disguise his agitation. 'We thank you for your hospitality.'

The abbot nodded absently and was gone. Reluctantly, Vlad the Monk, with suspicion still in his eyes, followed.

'Come!' Brother John cried, when they were out of earshot. 'We must ride like the wind for Castle Dracula!'

'I do not understand,' I said. 'I thought you explained that the Undead must return to their grave between sunrise and sunset, and that an Undead could only lie in the ground wherein he was buried?'

'But did you not hear what the abbot said?' Brother John said, with an uncommon snort of impatience. 'Do you know what it means?'

I shook my head dumbly.

'It means that your brothers, Vlad and Mihail, have removed the body of Dracula to Castle Dracula, bearing with them the earth from Snagov in which he was buried. It means that Dracula lies with impunity at Castle Dracula!'

'Merciful God!' I cried, once more stricken with fear, but this time not for myself. 'What of the Countess Bathory? If he can get past the protection we left her . . .'

I left the sentence unfinished. I could not bear to think of it. I was shaking and my heart started pounding and my thoughts were in turmoil. There was dread all around me.

'Let us ride!' Brother John urged. 'Let us ride for our immortal souls and hers! And may God give us aid!'

*

The journey to Arefu went quickly and fearfully, while our heads spun with mysteries and questions. Indeed, so hastily did we ride that at one point I rode my horse into the ground, after which the poor beast lay there, unable to get up, blood and foam dribbling from its nostrils. There was nothing to do but leave the unfortunate beast and mount double behind Brother John. This I did and we rode off again. Then his horse, too, fell exhausted to the ground, and another night was upon us before we managed to purchase fresh mounts and ride on as if the furies of Hell were pursuing us.

We came to Arefu at dawn, our horses wheezing beneath us, their muzzles flecked with foam and blood to show that we had ridden them too hard.

The inn was as before, silent and shuttered, wreathed in the cold mists of the morn. Hardly bothering to pull rein, I leapt from my mount and hurled myself against the inn door. To my surprise, it swung open and I rushed into the room, glanced wildly around me, and then, thinking only of the countess, my new love, bounded with all haste up the stairs.

The bedroom was empty.

The despair flooded over me. It swept away my senses. I felt anguish and a cold, demented rage that first burned me, then numbed me. A sob escaped my lips. I hammered my fists against the wall. Then, feeling murderous, beyond reason or logic, I suddenly left the room, brushed aside Brother John, and shouted for all my might down the stairs.

'Toma!' I shouted. 'Toma! *Where are you?*'

There was movement below and then I saw the inn-keeper, standing at the bottom of the stairs, his face drawn and haggard.

'What in God's name happened?' I cried. 'Where is the countess?'

'Young *Herr*, young *Herr* . . .' He raised his hands,

palms outward, and shrugged. 'We know not, young *Herr*. Yesterday morning we found her room empty. That is all we know. We fear that . . .'

He raised his shoulders again and then let them fall resignedly. His red-rimmed eyes gazed at mine for a second and then fell away.

Brother John stepped up to me. He held out the gold crucifix. It was the one we had left with the countess.

'Someone has emptied the room of the garlic flowers,' he said. 'I found this lying in the corner.'

A coldness seized me. This ice pierced my heart. I felt I could not breathe and the walls seemed to spin all around me.

'Who removed the flowers?' I cried out to Toma.

'As God is my witness,' he replied, 'I do not know, *mein Herr*.'

Not pausing to think, no longer dwelling on reason, impelled only by my anguish and my love, I rushed down the stairs.

'Where are you going, Michelino?' Brother John called out.

'Where?' I cried without stopping. 'Why, to the castle, of course! We have rescued her once and I shall do so again! Farewell, my old friend!'

'I am with you, Michelino!' the brave monk cried out. 'Pray she is still of the world! Hold! Let me be by your side! Let us go there together!'

And so saying, he bounded down the stairs after me, and together we ventured back to Castle Dracula.

CHAPTER TWENTY-ONE

The castle stood silent and seemingly deserted as we wound our way up the mountain track. Our entrance was gained easily and no one disputed our passage as we wandered from room to room in the grey light, searching vainly for the countess.

'Brother John,' I said, as we encountered empty chamber after empty chamber, 'there is one thing that puzzles me. You say that my brothers Vlad and Mihail, and indeed Tirgsor, are not Undead and this is proved by the fact that they are able to move in daylight?'

Brother John nodded.

'They act as servants to Dracula,' he said. 'The Undead are helpless during the hours of sunrise to sunset, and therefore it is a great aid to have someone who is faithful to them and who can move in daylight to protect them.'

'And yet,' I interposed, 'I initially saw them during the hours of daylight and now we never encounter them at all during these hours. How can this be?'

'Can you cast your mind back to when Tirgsor brought you here? When you saw him on the Eve of the Feast of St Andrew he appeared strong and healthy, but the next day he was weak and sickly until the sun set, and then he became strong once again. You noticed the same phenomenon with your brothers.'

'Yes,' I said. 'That is true.'

'It is my belief, friend Michelino, that the Undead control them. But the Undead can only exercise full power after sunset, so that during the day this strength is diminished. Perhaps the weakness during the daytime gets progressive as the Undead drain more and more of their energies: each night the Undead must prey on them so that, little by little, their life's blood is sapped and they weaken until they, too, become Undead. I believe that your brothers and their servant are finding it increasingly difficult to move about in daylight and that is why we have the freedom of the castle now.'

Horrific though it was, this explanation seemed logical. Certainly there was no sign of my brothers, of Tirgsor or his daughter Malvina, nor was there any sign of my beloved countess. And, at the thought of the countess, I was immediately overcome with a great sense of grief and an anger that fuelled my courage.

We had entered the large refectory room again, and I was about to suggest to Brother John that we start a search of the vaults when something suddenly flashed by my head. Then there was a thud, and a quivering knife embedded itself in the door not a foot from me.

For a brief second I stood looking at it in disbelief.

'*Look out!*' Brother John cried.

The cry stirred me from my stupor and I turned around quickly, sliding my sword from its sheath.

Two men were moving across the room towards us. One was holding a duplicate of the knife now wedged in the door behind me, and the other was brandishing a cudgel. They were evil-looking fellows, dirty and dressed in rags, and their snarling features displayed yellow, decaying teeth.

'*Szgany!*' Brother John hissed, also unsheathing his sword. 'Gypsies!'

The two men approached cautiously. They were crouched low and they were grinning. I flicked my blade towards their faces, but while they maintained a respectful distance, they displayed no fear at all.

'*Mandi maur!*' one cried suddenly and tried to leap under my guard.

He nearly succeeded and might have crippled me with a blow from his cudgel had not Brother John, who displayed remarkable skill as a swordsman, given him a slash across the arm which caused him to cry out in pain and retreat a step or two.

The other man poured forth a volume of sounds which even to an unknowledgeable ear was obviously cursing. I swung towards him, trying to gain an advantage, but the man backed hurriedly away, seized a candelabra and threw it at me. I tried to knock it aside with my sword, but the man followed so closely that he was upon me before I had disengaged from the candelabra and was able to meet his attack. I had only time to grasp the wrist of his descending knife hand, and we fell to the floor in a struggling mass of arms and legs.

There was the sound of someone shouting and instantly I became aware that the man on top of me had ceased his struggle and was now climbing off me. I came to my feet, ready for action, but the sight that met my gaze sent my heart sinking to my boots.

Half a dozen men had crowded into the room, all heavily armed, and all the same breed as our attackers.

I edged nearer Brother John.

A man, short and stocky with a shock of black hair, his skin dark and his eyes humorous, shining alertly from an angular face which had a hooked nose and high cheekbones, stepped forward and shot a number of rapid questions at our two attackers. The two men, offering monosyllabic replies, stood before him like disobedient children. The stocky man then turned to us and smiled. He said something which neither of us understood and to which we both shook our heads. Brother John then spoke to him in German.

'Who are you?' Brother John asked.

'I understand,' the man said, smiling broadly. 'I speak. Me Putzina. Me *Kako*, chief of tribe.' He waved a hand at those behind him. 'Szgany tribe. All Szgany. What you do here? Here is *doosh* place, evil place.'

He suddenly broke into his own gypsy language in which there was much repetition of the word *doosh* (evil) and *Bang* (Devil) and *choovikin*, which was their word for witch.

Brother John explained carefully that he was a priest and I was his friend, and, when the man Putzina repeated this in his own language, a great muttering broke out amongst his men. Our two assailants looked uncomfortable, and one or two of the gypsies near them jostled them in a threatening manner. Putzina then snapped something to his fellows and the two men were seized and marched out.

'Forgive, Father,' he said with a mischievous smile. 'They punished. They be tried by *Kriss*, elder council of tribe. But what you do in evil place?'

Brother John told him we were searching for a young girl who was ill and who had been kidnapped by the wicked owner of the castle. Putzina's angular face was all smiles.

'Look for *rakli*?' he asked. 'Look for girl?'

'Yes,' I said. 'Have you seen her?'

His bright eyes searched my face. A broad smile split his lips. I found myself blushing and then Putzina broke out in a laugh.

'*Kom rakli?*' he said. 'You love girl?'

I nodded, blushing even more furiously, but determined not to deny what my beating heart told me.

'Good!' He laughed again. 'Girl safe at my camp. Found on mountain road by my *meero romni*. You understand? My wife. Girl found. She ill, but Szgany cure.'

I could not express the relief that flooded through me. Indeed, this whole experience was one of contrasting emotions, from anger to fear, from the urge to kill to the need to love, and it seemed to me that whatever the outcome might be, I would never be quite the same afterwards. As for the moment, I felt only relief and joy.

'Your camp,' I said to Putzani. 'Where –?'

'No worry,' he interrupted, holding up one hand, a broad smile lighting up his face. 'Night before last *rakli* found walking towards castle. She walk as if in sleep. Szgany take her to camp. Look after her. Szgany cure.'

He waved us to follow him and we did so, leaving the castle and quickly entering the forest on the mountainside. It was a walk of several minutes before we entered a large clearing where several tents were pitched by a small stream. Two or three donkeys and a horse were tethered nearby to a tree while a lot of men and women sat round a large smoking fire, preparing to eat some delicious smelling concoction which was simmering in a large pot over the burning wood.

'Putzina's people,' said our mischievous-looking guide. 'Putzina *Kako* of tribe.'

I understand that *Kako* meant chief although, literally, it means 'uncle'. In each tribe, it seems, there is one elder who is accepted by general agreement as chief, but it is not a hereditary title, for the wisdom of the gypsies is great. They prefer to elect a man for his wisdom, strength of character and feeling for justice. The *Kako* governs with a council of elders called the *Kriss*, and these elders hold enormous influence over the people. Obedience is not based on fear, however, but on an awareness that within the tribe discipline is the only way for survival.

Putzina pointed to an old woman, whose face seemed obliterated by a mass of snow white hair which hung in profusion almost to her waist.

'*Phui Dai*,' he said. 'Wise woman of the tribe. She cure *rakli*. Your woman get better.'

The old woman smiled at me, brushing some hair from a weather-beaten face in which twinkled a pair of bright blue eyes. She then inclined her head and said: 'Come.'

The woman, Oraga, for such was her name, led us into a tent and there, the saints be blessed, lay my fair countess. She was pale, but alive, her breath coming out in the deep, heavy rhythms of sleep.

'*Rakli* get well if taken away from the evil place,' the old woman said, peering narrowly at Brother John. '*Dadus* know of herbs that heal?'

Brother John nodded.

'*Dadus* listen,' the old woman said. 'Me purify blood of *rakli* with tea of centaury, and mugwort causes her sleep. The devil that drinks of her blood has twice drank so . . .' She paused, turning her gaze on me, her eyes bright and piercing. 'You destroy evil,' she said, 'but first take her to safe place. She get better.'

Words were little enough with which to thank this wise old woman; nevertheless I offered them and Brother John echoed me. The old woman, Oraga, shrugged.

'Luck be with you, boy,' she said. 'And with you, Father.'

Putzina entered and took us both by the arms, smiling broadly.

'No go before guest,' he said, pointing to those seated around the fire. 'Look! *Holomus!* Feast! Drink and eat, yes?'

Protesting, but quietly grateful for the sustenance, we sat down with the Szgany and enjoyed a simple meal. The food consisted of a meat and vegetable soup ladled from a cauldron. This soup was mopped up with bread and washed down with either a beer called *libena* or a wine called *mol*. Both were delicious.

Over the meal we learnt more of their finding of my beloved countess. It seemed that they had been moving across country from Transylvania and had been journeying several days. They did not know this part of the country at all, but had made camp and, seeing the castle, gone to '*mong, loor, nash*', which is a phrase they use, meaning to 'beg, steal or borrow'.

It had been nearly dawn on the previous day when they

had encountered the countess walking towards the castle; there was blood on her clothes, and strangely she was attired for the night. She walked like one in a sleep and they could not rouse her. Instead they brought her to the *Phui Dai* who told them the castle was an evil place.

Putzina had ordered his tribe to shun the place, but this morning they found that two of the tribe had disobeyed orders and gone to the castle. Putzina and his men had followed, and thus it was that they found Brother John and myself being attacked by their miscreant fellows.

Putzina now jabbed a thumb towards the castle towers.

'When wind high, move tent to other side of hedge.'

I understood this to be a Szgany proverb meaning when all is not well it is time to move on. I wanted to do something more to show my gratitude to Oraga, the wise woman, so I left the encampment and started to pick some flowers to give to her. Putzina, however, stopped me from doing this.

'What you do?' he demanded.

'I am thanking Oraga by giving her some flowers,' I said. 'A small token of . . .'

'Flowers picked, symbol of death coming. Flowers should grow like life. Gypsy say picked flowers unlucky.'

His face was so stern that I dropped the flowers immediately.

'Then take this,' I said, tossing him a silver *aspi*.

He raised it to his mouth, bit it, spat on it and then pocketed it, now grinning mischievously.

'Listen, *gorgio*,' he said, using the term by which the Szgany call all foreigners. 'Cloudy morning often change to fine day. Behind bad luck comes good.' He raised his right hand. '*Kooshko-bok!*'

After this we left Putzina's encampment, I carrying the unconscious countess in my arms. Oraga had promised me that the unconscious state would last but a few hours more, after which the countess would awaken naturally. Once out of sight of the camp, Brother John made me lay the countess on the ground while he examined her.

'It is not that I have no trust in the Szgany, but I want to be sure,' he said. 'However, it seems they are right. She is in a deep and natural sleep and that is good. Her blood, though she has lost much, flows well. It is her young heart that comes to her aid in this, and, given care, she will recover ... if she is not exposed to this evil again.'

'What about those?' I said, pointing to the tiny wounds on her neck, which seemed to be more marked than before.

'They will disappear in time,' he said. 'But I think you should return to the inn. Tell Toma he must protect her with his life, and then return to me.'

'What will you do?' I asked, puzzled.

'I shall return to the castle and continue the search to find the Undead and destroy it.'

'Do you think it wise?' I asked, concerned for his safety.

'I have all the protection I need and there is still six hours to sunset. If she awakens, try to find out all you can from her ... it may help us in our fight.'

With a wave of his hand he started up the mountain towards the castle, and I stood looking after him for some moments. In my heart I silently saluted a brave man.

Then, gathering the sleeping countess once more in my arms, I turned and set out for Arefu.

CHAPTER TWENTY-TWO

Toma greeted me as if I were the very prodigal returning home. Indeed, I doubt that the returning prodigal was made more welcome than I. A fire had been lit in the countess's room and I noticed that the garlic flowers had been carefully replaced and some religious icons had been placed around the room. Toma's wife put the countess to bed while I prepared a brew of the juice of hyssop, dandelion leaves and lady's mantle, as Brother John had instructed me.

'The countess must drink a small glass of this every hour,' I told Toma and his wife. 'I shall go up to her room now and stay a short while, but then I must leave for the castle before the sun sets.'

At this Toma seemed much perturbed.

'Must you go, young *Herr*? It is dangerous.'

'Yes,' I said, 'I must go. Brother John needs my help.'

At this Toma hung his head and mumbled a prayer. I pressed his arm and told him to be of good cheer, for we were not yet dead.

'Some things are worse than death,' he whispered.

I smiled and left him and ventured up to the countess's bedchamber. She lay pale and still, but her face was calm and relaxed in slumber. I poured Brother John's mixture between her lips; but even though she swallowed most of it, she slept on. My heart went out to her, for she lay so small and helpless, and all my protective instincts were roused. I watched and waited some time, hoping she would awaken, and just when I was about to give up, my vigil was rewarded.

She stirred and gave a sigh. I saw a redness tinge her cheeks, saw her eyelids flutter open and then go wide. I quickly leaned across and touched her arm.

'Do not fear,' I whispered. 'You are safe again.'

'Michelino!'

It was the first time she had used my name and my heart leapt at the sound of it. Then she raised her head from the pillows and laid it gently against my shoulder.

'Oh, Michelino,' she murmured.

'There,' I said, thanking God for Brother John's herbal knowledge. 'There, all is well now.'

After a moment or two, when she had choked back her tears of relief and taken a drink of the herbal brew, the countess lay back on the pillows, both hands gripping mine.

'Now, poor child,' I said, 'I must know exactly what happened. God knows, I do not wish to cause you more pain by the remembrance of that which can only be hurtful, but Brother John is even now at the castle, the day is drawing to a close, and we must know how you came to be taken to the castle when we left you so well protected.'

The poor girl shivered, but her hand gripped mine firmly, and she offered me a look of resolution. There was a pause while she ordered her confused thoughts, then she began:

'After you left me and night drew on, I found it impossible to sleep. Indeed the many horrible fantasies that crowded my mind – blood and pain and death and living corpses – seemed to preclude all hope of sleep. Then, after a time, I began to doze. It was a fretful, half waking sleep, filled with dreams and recollections, and the aroma of the garlic flowers seemed to oppress me; they gave me a strange choking sensation in my throat and chest, and I felt my lungs would burst. Finally, unable to do anything else, oblivious to the possible danger, I pushed the garlic away from me.

'Later, I became aware of a thin white mist in the room. At first, in my half sleeping state, I thought it was a night mist which had come in through the window. The window! It was then I sprang fully awake – for I noticed that the window was open. Do not press me how it happened. I know not. All I know is that in my struggle to breathe, to escape the oppressive atmosphere of the garlic flowers, I must have risen from the bed, taken the flowers and deposited them out of the window.'

She gave a groan and held a hand to her head.

'How could I have done this after promising you and the good monk that I would not tamper with them?'

'It was not your fault, dearest countess,' I said, squeezing her hand in sympathy. 'The evil we fight has such powers of mesmerism at its command that it was but the thought implanted in your mind that caused you to act so. You did not do this of your own free will.'

She gave a small, brave smile, held my hands more tightly and, gazing downward, shivering slightly in recollection, continued:

'Horrible! Horrible! As I started awake, staring in terror at the open window, I suddenly became aware of a tall, thin figure in a long black cloak. Indeed, he seemed to step from the mist, and my heart lurched in dread. He made no step towards me, but simply stood there, his two hideous red eyes glaring malevolently at me from a waxen face. Oh, Michelino! Michelino! I would have screamed in terror had not his gaze turned me to stone, paralysing me.'

She raised a hand to massage her slim, peach-coloured neck, as if remembering vividly the sensation. Then, when her fingers touched the wounds on her throat, she shuddered violently.

'I was paralysed. I could not make a move. He stood blackly before me and hissed: "Remove those baubles of a debased superstition." Again, the malevolent red eyes bored into mine and, as if I had no control over my own hands, I felt them rise, take off the crucifix and fling it from me. At this he laughed, so sneering and horrible, and then he moved quickly towards me. Oh, my God! My God!'

Sobs shook her frail body and she pressed herself tighter to me.

'What am I to do?' she cried. 'How can I tell you more?'

'You must,' I urged. 'You must tell me all, for all our sakes.'

She withdrew from my embrace and lay back on the pillows, sighing and gazing forlornly above her. Her breathing was heavy. She licked at her lips. She was seized by a spasm of shuddering and then it subsided. Her voice was a whisper.

'His eyes, those malevolent eyes, bored into mine until I began to feel him inside my very mind. Then I began to feel ... excited, to feel I wanted him, the pain and the pleasure, an ecstasy ... I craved it, I needed it, I could scarce control my own breathing, and ... he approached me and I lay back, closing my eyes, helpless, wanting him, burning, as he bent over me ...'

At this point she paused. Her face was inflamed. There was shame and confusion in her eyes and my heart went out to her. She touched the wounds on her neck once again.

'He was breathing all over me ... his breath was warm and reeking ... I felt his lips, moist, heavy, on my ... skin. Then, a sharp bite ... sharp and thin, like a needle, and ... such pain, such ecstasy, such shame and wantonness ... I felt my strength being sapped and I lay back in a half swoon, delirious, ecstatic, beyond shame or caring, as if ... as if he had made love to me.'

Again she burst into sobs, now ashamed and bewildered, and once more cursing the foul house of Dracula, I drew her into my arms and stroked her hair. Eventually she calmed down and continued:

'I know not how long I lay there with him on top of

me, sucking out my very life, but soon he rose, his sneering mouth dripping with my blood. And even ... Oh, God, the shame! The shame! Even as he rose, I cried out that he must not stop, that he must take more from me, that I would die if he did not allow me to achieve the climax of my shameful desires ... He merely smiled at me. It was a smile of pure contempt. He said: "You are now flesh of my flesh, blood of my blood. I will take no more of you for now, for you will be mine as long as I desire and I take from you only as I wish to." I swear, Michelino, that this he said to me, and I, in my debased need, accepted it.'

She paused again, and I saw tears on her cheeks, and the shame and despair in her face now filled me with rage – rage against Dracula and his accursed house. So thinking, I leaned forward and kissed her burning brow, and she suddenly seized me with both hands.

'Oh, Michelino! Michelino!' she cried. 'I fear for your life, for indeed he knows you. That same night he said to me "My son Mircea thought to protect you, fool that he is. My son! He is no son of mine, but the son of his mother, for he would shun me. Yes, he thinks to pit his puny wits against mine, thinks to thwart me, who commanded armies when he was but an ache in my loins! But he shall soon know what it is to cross my path." Then he turned to me and said: "To seal our bond, my beautiful vine, we shall drink from each other and become one." And, so saying, he opened his shirt and, with long sharp nails, opened a vein in his breast. Horrible! Horrible! The blood, so rich, so red, so vile, began to spurt out, pumping in time to his black heart. Then, with one vice-like hand, he seized the hair on my head and dragged my mouth forward that I might suckle like a baby at the wound. And, God forgive me, I did it, I did it willingly, in some strange dream of ecstasy and despair, after which he turned away and vanished, leaving me spent.'

She cried out and fell into my arms and her whole body shuddered. I stroked her hair. I kissed her eyes and her lips. I felt my love and my anger flowing out around us both, and in the violence of these clashing emotions lay my hope of salvation.

'We shall destroy this beast,' I said. 'Have no fear of that, my love. And then we shall cleanse you of this evil.'

She sobbed pitifully.

'Oh, Michelino, would that it were true! But I am tainted, tainted like a leper, and for that there can be no cure. Who will touch me now? Who will take me to them after I have mated with such a fiend? Michelino, my love, my heart breaks from this!'

I raised her tear-stained face to mine.

'My heart is full of love for you,' I declared passionately, 'and I care naught for what has happened to you.'

'Do not pity me, Michelino,' she murmured, her fingers scratching like mice at my spine. 'Please God, do not pity me.'

Pity her I did not, but rather loved her with all my heart, and proved it by smothering her with kisses, first gently, then more fiercely, my lips to her lips, our limbs intertwining, until, our desires overcoming us, we sank back on the bed and became lost in those passions for which adequate words have yet to be created. Ah, but it was wondrous! It left us spent and it exhilarated us. It cleansed us of fear and opened the gates to the future, and it passed without shame or regret, and it filled us with fresh hope.

Only later, when I had recovered from my ardours, did I remember that I had left Brother John alone in the castle. At this I rose from the bed and hastily dressed myself, resolved to venture forth and aid my brave friend.

'You will remain here,' I told my beloved. 'Toma and his wife will spend the night in the room with you, and you must at all times keep the protective objects around you. Fight off all urges to sleep, and should you feel any attempt of outside influences on your mind, you must resist them with all your powers.'

'Very well, my love,' she said, stretching up from the bed and pulling my head down for another fiery kiss that sent my blood coursing.

'Now,' I said, disengaging from her embrace, 'if Brother John or I should not return by sun-up tomorrow, I shall give Toma instructions that you are to be driven into Tirgoviste. I shall leave you enough money to continue your journey to wherever you decide to go. Tonight we must attempt to defeat this evil, but you must assume, if we do not return at daylight, that we have failed, that we have become as they are. Should this be so, and I pray that it will not, you must find someone to convince of the truth of our story, someone who will be able to release us from this curse. God be with you, my love.'

We kissed and parted. On the way out I paused only long enough to explain matters to Toma the innkeeper, and then I rode hard for Castle Dracula. The sky was quickening and storm clouds were gathering, and I knew I would be lucky to reach the castle before nightfall.

CHAPTER TWENTY-THREE

It was nearly dusk when I drew rein before the castle. The storm clouds were now boiling in the sky, low and ominous, and I heard the distant rumble of thunder and then the rain fell.

I threw myself from my mount and raced into the castle. There was no one in sight. All seemed deserted. Shadows fell all around me from the towering grey walls, and beyond them the thunder was now roaring. Several times I called out for Brother John, but received no answer. All was as before, silent, desolate, though fires blazed in the hearths and the crackling and spitting offered proof that life still went on here.

The thunder roared. Lightning flashed across the window. I saw whiteness and shifting black shadow, and my footsteps were echoing.

Again I called out for Brother John, and again I received no reply.

I raced to the refectory room, then along the gallery to my former bed chamber. Both were deserted. Tentatively I tried the door to the vaults. It opened and I started to descend the stairway, treading carefully lest I stumble in the gloom.

A sudden sound made me whirl around. There was no one there, but I could clearly hear the patter of feet in the room I had just left. Immediately I retraced my steps but, to my surprise, I found the room still empty.

Then, having a sudden idea, I made my way to the tower where we had originally found the countess. The room was dank and cold, but again all was as we had left it.

The noise of someone moving came again . . . this time from below . . . from that profane temple of sorcery.

I turned around. The thunder roared and the lightning flashed. The darkness of the room exploded into glaring whiteness and then the darkness swooped in again. I shivered. It was cold. The room was damp and claustrophobic. Then, sword in hand, I started down the stairs.

'Brother John!' I cried out upon reaching the temple door. 'Are you in there?'

There was no reply. I could hear my own heart pounding. From above me came the roar of the thunder. I pushed open the door.

Kneeling on the floor, his back turned towards me, was a bulky figure in a monk's habit.

'Brother John!' I cried out in relief, sheathing my sword and quickly starting forward.

He rose and turned towards me, pushing back the cowl of the habit from his face.

I stepped back and gasped.

It was, indeed, Brother John, but the change in his appearance now froze my blood. His face was a waxy pallor, haggard and deathlike, and his eyes stared at me without emotion. Also, his lips were unnaturally red; they were parted and I could see two rows of white, sharp teeth, very pointed, and with two canines longer than the rest.

'Brother John!' I cried out, horrified, in despair, feeling fear and frustration all at once. 'Oh, God! Not you!'

'Welcome, friend Michelino,' he said, his voice rasping, hollow, and unreal. 'I knew and prayed you would return.'

My hand went to my sword. I started backing towards the door. His cold and lifeless eyes stared into mine, and then he raised both his hands.

'No,' he rasped. 'Do not fear me for the moment. As yet I can still control myself, but . . .' The alien eyes stared up at the darkening skies. '. . . not for long. And, before I succumb, you must set me free.'

I stopped moving backwards and studied him carefully, in anguish for my lost friend, yet wary that he might now be enslaved by the Undead and seducing me for his own accursed ends. He made no move towards me. I sensed a plea behind the cold eyes. I kept my gaze from the hideous mask of his face and, in that moment, bound by love and affection, I knew that my old friend spoke the truth.

'God have mercy, Brother John,' I said softly. 'How did it happen?'

'When you left,' he rasped, his voice hollow, disembodied, 'I foolishly set out to explore the vaults. I believed that the Undead must rest from sunset to sunrise wherever they were. I now know that even in daylight the Undead can move if they be sufficiently deep underground where the atmosphere of day cannot penetrate. Stupidly I went into the vaults and was seized by two of Dracula's handmaidens – she that was called Gaia, the wife of Liviu, and she that was called Malvina. They drank long and deeply from my blood until I, as Brother John, died and took on the semblance of the Undead.'

'But if Brother John is dead, how . . .?'

He raised a hand to silence me.

'I have studied long hours,' he said. 'My mind is now so attuned to occult conflict that I still retain domination until the sun finally sets on another day. How I prayed you would return before that moment . . . that moment which is nearly come.'

He glanced stonily towards the blackening window. The thunder roared and for a brief moment the window was illuminated in white light before turning dark and bleak again.

'We must hurry, my friend,' he said. 'I will tell you what you must do, and you will do it without question or hesitation. And, when you have performed this task for me, you must then perform it on the other Undead so that they, too, may obtain the peace of the grave.'

'No!' I cried out, tears springing to my eyes, an anguish much deeper than death lancing through to my torn heart. 'Is there no way other than death for you?'

'No!' he exclaimed hoarsely.'Quickly now! In that bag you will find some wooden stakes and a hammer. I will lie here and you must drive the stake through my heart.'

'No!' I cried in horror.

'You must! You must! If you value my soul, it is the only way!'

We looked at one another. The thunder roared beyond the walls. I saw the shadows of the walls fall about me and I felt I was dreaming. Nay, it was a nightmare, and it filled my whole being, filled me with a pain and despair such as no one should know. And yet, in that moment, through my dread and helpless fury, I sensed that I was changing, that all innocence had finally fled, and that I stood on the brink of a renewal and was becoming a man. I looked at Brother John. His eyes were alien and cold. I found courage and I took the stake and hammer from the bag, and with tears in my eyes walked towards him.

'Hurry!' he gasped. 'The sky is dark! I can feel my self-control ebbing! There is no time to lose!' He stretched himself out on the table that served as an altar. 'Strike swiftly, my friend,' he said. 'I will watch over you from the next world. *Strike now!*'

As I stared down at the prostrate form of my friend, over whose heart I held the sharp, pointed end of the stake, I suddenly saw the eyes change. A look of hatred came into them and, as the final shadow passed across the window, as the thunder receded and the rain ceased to fall, the look of hatred turned into vindictive triumph. It was then that I understood that the creature beneath my wood stake was no longer my friend, Brother John; rather, it was a nightmare parody of him. Indeed, the pointed teeth were set in a cruel, voluptuous mouth, smiling a vicious smile, and it was clear to me now that Brother John had gone, that this thing, what he would call *nosferatu*, the Undead, had taken his place. All this passed through my mind in a second and strengthened my resolution.

Even as the trembling departed from my hands, the thing started to rise, its hands clawing up towards me, and I brought the hammer down, heavy and true, pounding the stake into its heart. I heard a shriek. It reverberated around the temple. It exploded in my mind and blotted out all thought, but still I did not cease from my travails. Again and again I struck with all my might, instinctively muttering a prayer as I did so. The thing's shrieks were blood-curdling. It writhed beneath the trembling stake. Its sharp white teeth champed until the lips were torn and bloody, and it shrieked and it heaved and the blood splashed upon it, and still I continued to strike. Then the writhing thing was still and I was done.

I leant against a wall, bathed in sweat and wanting to vomit. My breath came in great gulps and gasps, and again I was weeping. Then, as I gazed down, the thing started to change, its foulness seemed to disappear, the malignancy, the brute hatred, and there, in its place, lying serene and undefiled, no longer a slave to the great Undead, lay my friend, Brother John.

I thanked God for His mercy.

And now, with determined resolution, I realized that I must carry out the wishes of Brother John, that it was now up to me to track down the resting place of the Undead and release them from this vile corruption. Night had come. They would be stirring soon, if not already. I picked up the hammer and the bag of wooden stakes and quickly started towards the door. Once there, I glanced back at Brother John.

'Sleep in peace,' I said. 'Sleep in peace, my old friend, for I shall soon avenge your death.'

And so saying, I left him.

★

I went back towards the refectory room. I resolved that I must go down into the vaults and destroy the things that lurked there. It was now night, and I prayed to the spirit of my dead friend to give me the knowledge and protection I needed for my task.

As I came to the door of the refectory room, I caught the sound of furtive movement. I paused before the door and unsheathed my sword, then I gently pushed it open. No one stood before me, so I slowly edged into the room, holding my sword at the ready.

Suddenly a hand seized my sword wrist in a vice-like grip and my brother Vlad sprang from behind the door. I tried to free myself, but Mihail also appeared, and between them they managed to overcome me and bind me to a chair. Their eyes were filled with malevolence.

'Well met again, brother Mircea,' Vlad sneered.

'I am no brother of yours!' I cried hotly, though a fear gripped my heart.

'That has been arranged,' Mihail said in vindictive triumph. 'You have thwarted our designs too long. Now our father awaits you.'

'Brothers!' I cried desperately, hoping to make them see reason, for indeed they were not yet Undead. 'Come back to the true god and be saved! Renounce your false god!'

'False god?' Mihail laughed. 'It is your god who is false. Where is He to save you now?'

'Dare you reject God's truth?' I challenged.

'God's truth?' Mihail sneered. 'Truth in your Christian prattling? Dear brother, Catholic and Orthodox have fought long over our souls, each proclaiming his own truth. I have my truth already, brother, and that truth is immortality on earth.'

'We waste too much time, Mihail,' Vlad interrupted. 'Let us take him to the vaults where he will confront the one truth.' Vlad smiled like the devil and patted my shoulder. 'Fear not, little brother, you will soon come to love and serve the master, and our blood will be reconciled.'

With that Vlad and Mihail released me from the chair and, with my wrists bound before me, led me down the spiral stairway to the great vault and bound me to a pillar by passing a rope several times around my middle. Mihail smiled as they turned to leave.

'Fret not, brother Mircea,' he said. 'You will not have long to wait for some company. The sun is well down and soon they will come, for they are always thirsty . . . *very* thirsty.'

He laughed, a horrible, mocking laugh, then he followed Vlad back up the stairs and left me alone.

The great vault was gloomy. The flickering torches cast queer shadows. There was silence and it seemed to be alive with a voice of its own. I struggled against my bonds. They were tight and I was well held. I glanced about me and the shadows danced and writhed and the silence was chilling. I was sure that my end had come.

At that moment I heard a scraping noise. It seemed like stone being slid against stone. The hairs on the nape of my neck stood up as I realized that I was listening to the stone sepulchres opening.

Then came the chilling tinkle of soft laughter and, in the gloom, I could see something white moving towards me. I held my breath. I tried not to succumb to panic. The creature was moving stealthily and it was dressed all in white and then it suddenly took on a definite shape.

At that moment I recognized the burn mark on her bared shoulder: the burn mark of a crucifix.

'Malvina!' I gasped.

She stopped in her tracks. Bloodshot eyes stared at me. Her features were distorted by evil and her smile was sharptoothed.

'*Mein Herr, mein Herr,*' she whispered voluptuously. 'Dear, beautiful *Herr*. I knew you would come. I knew you would be mine. My lips have longed for the warmth of your flesh, the sweet wine of your young blood. Ah, *mein Herr*, gently. Do not struggle so. Just one kiss and I swear you will cry out for more. Come, my love!'

She raised her arms. She moved closer to me. The white dress fell around her and I saw her bosom heave and I felt her reeking breath in my face. Suddenly I shuddered. I could not control myself. She had opened her mouth and I saw the pointed teeth and my innards were torn by revulsion.

Her fingertips touched me. Her hands travelled up and down me. I felt dread and then I felt languor and a helpless desire. Her crimson eyes were bright. They were wanton and corrupt. They grew larger and they filled my whole being and my body was burning. I tried to close my eyes. Her very presence held them open. Her red lips stretched back across her white pointed teeth, and then I felt her hot breath at my neck and I wanted to swoon.

Her lips were at my skin. I felt the darting of her tongue. She pressed her body against me and she was writhing and groaning, and then, as her mouth sucked at my throat, a harsh voice rang out:

'*He is mine!*'

Malvina snarled with rage. She whirled around with her face distorted. A tall man in a black cloak emerged from the shadows, and one hand shot out to grasp Malvina by the neck and hurl her across the floor of the vault.

'*I say he is mine!*'

My heart pounded furiously. I heard Malvina hiss. I saw the man's ghastly face and his red, piercing eyes, and I knew that at last, and probably too late, I faced the hellish creature that lurked within the body of my father.

I was in the presence of Dracula.

CHAPTER TWENTY-FOUR

He towered before me, encased from neck to ankle in a long, black cloak that made him appear taller than he was. Immediately, childhood memories of my father came flooding back to me, for indeed this ghastly figure was familiar.

The face was strong, acquiline, with a thin, high-bridged nose and arched nostrils below a lofty, domed forehead. The mouth, which could just be seen under a heavy moustache, was thin, fixed and extremely cruel. The chin was broad and heavy, the cheeks firm yet thin. Around the temples the hair was scanty, but it grew thickly towards the back of the head. The eyebrows were massive and almost met across the nose; and the eyes themselves were a piercing crimson void beyond which was nothing but the charnel house.

Protruding over his lower lip were peculiar, unusually long, sharp white teeth.

The extraordinary pallor of his face emphasized the livid aspect of his hideous eyes, and not until the day I die shall I be able to eradicate the memory of his frightful face as it leaned towards me, the mouth curling back from the sharp, demanding teeth, until even the gums showed, in a revolting smirk.

'Well met at last, Mircea, my son,' he said.

I looked on in helpless horror as he drew nearer, the parody of a smile on his evil countenance and his eyes filled with hunger and contempt.

'At last you have come to join me,' he said. 'At last you have come to take your rightful place in the house of Dracula.'

I tried to avert my eyes from his, in a futile attempt to

free myself from the mesmeric spell he was casting over me. He laughed long and loudly, a sound most horrible, until the hairs on the nape of my neck stood out.

'You thought I was a mere earthly tyrant, my son? Hah! I wish to talk to you, to explain the truth to you, before I finally take you as my own. Earthly power, my son, is but the power of a flea compared to that which is now mine. For years I have pursued the path to knowledge, for indeed in knowledge is power. And, just as knowledge is the pursuit of power, so death is the very inspiration of all philosophy – for it is death that prompts us to consider our brief earthly span and, in so doing, makes us dream and hope of conquering death itself.

'In my life I have contemplated philosophy, alchemy, theology and law in my quest to wrest Nature's secrets from her. The ancients in the days of the early Pharaohs knew her secret and thus believed in material existence after death. They believed we had another body, which they called *ka* or *sekhem*, which had all the characteristics of its original being, which was the real body of man, and which, through subordination to the physical body, could separate and move freely from place to place, reuniting itself at will.

'Only in death could *sekhem* really come into its own, and thus were offerings made in the ancient pyramids to sustain *sekhem* in the after life. The ancients of Egypt pursued their knowledge to its rightful conclusion: the method by which *sekhem* could be released to immortality in this world.

'Years ago those ancients succeeded in attaining this immortality, and those who did so were lauded in the land of the Pharaohs. Indeed this movement came to be called the flowering of the Draconian Cult, for its members worshipped Draco, the fire-breathing beast of the Great Deep, and Setek Ab Ra was the chief of priests in the order of the immortality seekers.

'Our family is old, older than the oldest pyramids, and even our name Dracula still links us with our ancient origins by the Nile – for were we not the spawn of Draco himself? Indeed, our history might have been different had it not been for that puny weakling, Amenhotep the Fourth, who tried to destroy the ancient gods and set up a worship to Aton, the sun god. Because of this the Draconians were killed or driven underground; but their ancient lore scrolls were passed on to their descendants of which the Dracula house were foremost.

'While others pursued the new religions, we of the Dracula blood upheld the old. Your friend, the priest, he who was Brother John, said we worshipped the devil. What devil? I know of no such being. I, and my ancestors, from time immemorial, have worshipped the god of the south whose star is Sothis – Set, the Lord of the infernal region of Amenta, epitome of all subconscious atavisms and of the true will and hidden knowledge.'

His demoniac eyes flashed at me and a sneer circled his gross, blood-red lips.

'I have studied long,' he said, 'until, by my own diligence, I have become a Shamblu in the service of Set.'

'God forgive you!' I cried out.

'Forgive?' He laughed harshly. 'Why, your own Christianity applauds my actions and accepts, in the words of the book of Deuteronomy, that blood is life. Yes, even the gospel of St John quotes your Jesus as saying: "Except ye eat the flesh of the son of Man and drink his blood, ye have no life in you. Whoso eateth my flesh and drinketh my blood hath eternal life: and I will raise him up at the Last Day. For my flesh is meat indeed and my blood is drink indeed. He that eateth my flesh and drinketh my blood dwelleth in me." Ah,' Dracula sneered, 'why should I dispute what your own Christ tells his Christians to do?'

He paused. He studied me. His eyes blazed with

chilling mockery. The torches cast writhing shadows and these black shapes fell upon him and emphasized the starkness of his features. I heard his harsh, hungry breathing.

'But then what do you know of Shamblu,' he sneered, 'the Horn of Plenty, the title of Shiva, our Lord Set? You know of nothing outside your Christ! For years I applied myself to gaining the knowledge that would free my earthly body for all time and enable me to walk this earth forever. Doubtless you call it a pact with the devil; perhaps, in your terms, it is. But to me it was the supreme achievement of the thirst for knowledge – the ultimate goal of man – immortality. And in this, of course, as it is with nature, the strong must dominate the weak. I, therefore, the conqueror of life, am supplied with eternal life through the blood of lesser beings, and in turn I can grant them immortality.

'So, my son, Mircea, you are of my blood and that blood will be my sweetest drink. Then, and willingly, you will join your brothers and me in spreading the will of Dracula over the earth.'

Dracula smiled. He held his hands upwards. The black cloak hung from his arms and he looked like some monstrous, rapacious bat. Then, in a voice that almost stopped my heart beating, in a strange and hypnotic Egyptian tongue, he threw his head back and cried out:

'*Shanti! Shakti! Shambhu!*'

Dracula, the lord of evil, was about to drink.

My soul plunged into despair. I tried to tear myself free. The ropes bit into my flesh and my heart was pounding madly and I felt the blood beat at my temples and the room seemed to spin. Then Dracula bent towards me. His eyes blazed into mine. They were a furnace and the fire drew me in and made me surrender. He placed his hands upon my shoulders. My resistance fell away. He was hissing and his eyes were hypnotic and filled me with rapture. I had no shame. I was his to command. Then, just as he lowered his lips to my throat, Malvina rushed under his arms like some wild, vicious beast.

'No!' she hissed. 'He is mine! You shall not cheat me of him!'

Dracula's fiendish eyes left mine, and thus released me from his hypnotic gaze. He glared at Malvina, who ducked aside and lunged at me. She gasped and then her teeth closed on my wrists and I felt the cord loosen as her sharp canines severed some of its strands.

Suddenly, Malvina's head jerked back.

With a terrible scream of rage Dracula had seized her by the hair and he now flung her violently across the vault. Shrieking, teeth gnashing, she leapt to her feet and desperately hurled herself back upon me. I heard myself cry out. I tried to pull the ropes apart. I saw Malvina rushing at me, and then I saw Dracula's back, as he swiftly placed himself between us both, guarding his prize.

'He is mine!' Dracula roared, seizing her by the throat and, with astonishing strength, throwing her back to the floor.

Malvina hissed at him. She was on her hands and knees. Her mouth reddened with blood and she started to crawl towards him, her lips drawn over her gums, her teeth gleaming in the torchlight, sharp and pointed, with two hideous canines. Then she stood up.

Dracula's right hand shot out. His fingers were outspread. His eyes gleamed and stared directly at Malvina and she suddenly froze.

'No!' Dracula said. 'You cannot disobey me! I am your master and lord, and my will is your will.'

Oh, hideous sight to behold! Malvina's eyes widened, her spine arched and her lips opened; and then Dracula embraced her with a harsh and bestial snarl, his cloak billowing like gigantic wings behind him. Then, revoltingly, his mouth fastened on her neck, and the two rapacious creatures, first struggling, now silent, were bound together in their perverted devil's rite. He drank of her blood. She gasped and begged for more. He opened his shirt and opened a vein in his breast, and then he took hold of her head and pressed her lips to the wound and she kissed it and hungrily drank of it. Dracula's eyes gleamed. They gleamed down upon her head. Then he cried out and wrapped his cloak around her in a vile consummation.

I forced my eyes away from this blasphemous sight and then, with a strength born of fear and desperation, pulled my hands apart and snapped my bonds.

Without another glance, I fled up the stairway, knowing not where I was heading, intent only on flight from this nightmare. As I neared the top of the stairway, which led into the refectory room, I heard a terrible shriek from below.

'After him, my children!' Dracula screamed. 'Find him or you shall all be accursed!'

I bolted into the refectory room, slammed the door behind me, and looked desperately around me.

My brother Vlad was standing by the table.

'Fool!' he snarled. 'There is no escape!'

His lips curled in a condescending sneer as he started to move towards me. I began to back away, not knowing what to do, then I saw my sword lying where I had dropped it.

The sword had been blessed by the Pope, and I saw my salvation.

I launched myself across the room and seized the sword. Once in my grip I suddenly became aware that it had more defensive properties than that of a normal weapon. Indeed, at that moment, I could feel the power flow through it, the power of our blessed Lord and creator. I held it up. My spirit seemed to flow through it. I felt strong and my fears fell away and I knew I could face them.

Even as I raised the sword and waved it before me, the unholy ones passed into the room. I say 'passed' for they did not enter through the door, but rather through a crack in the wood. I stared in horrified disbelief as, through an interstice where only a knife blade could go, Dracula and his two disciples emerged. Suddenly, as if from nowhere, they were standing before me with corporeal bodies as real as my own.

They walked slowly towards me and I held up the sword, and, as I did so, felt some Almighty power vibrate along my arm, and then saw a light, from where I know not, flash on the blade of my weapon. At this the hell fiends immediately recoiled, hissing and snarling, their faces distorted with such expressions of hatred and rage that words could not adequately describe them. Then I saw Dracula staring at me. He was trying to mesmerise me. I held the sword before my eyes and a snarl came to his lips; and his teeth, which were dripping with the blood of Malvina, gleamed in a gory, malign smile.

'Vlad!' he said sharply.

My brother sprang to the fireplace where two swords hung below an ornate shield. He took command of one and advanced upon me.

'There is no escape, brother Mircea,' he said. 'Why not simply join us?'

Then he was at me, swinging his blade viciously, leaping forward and moving very fast and displaying great skill. I backed towards the door. I parried his initial strokes expertly. Yet the Undead held sway over him and his strength was therefore tenfold, and I knew that I must end the contest quickly lest my stamina betray me.

He came in swinging his blade again. I then leapt to the offensive. I feinted at his head, but he parried it with ease, darting away and returning on his guard. We moved across the room. Our swords clashed. I saw Dracula and his wide-eyed acolytes, all of whom were just watching. I cut at Vlad's side. Again he blocked the stroke. My eyes fixed on his forehead and I deliberately raised my sword, and, as I expected, he raised his own blade to counter, and I suddenly leapt forward and pierced his heart.

Vlad straightened up and gasped. I withdrew my blade. He glanced down at the blood pumping out of his chest and then he fell forward to the floor.

Immediately Gaia and Malvina, or the creatures in their bodies, leapt upon him, snarling and pushing, struggling like wolves to get at his fresh, flowing blood.

Only Dracula had not moved.

I backed away towards the door. Dracula watched me with a smile. I held the sword before my eyes and the light flashed upon it, and I knew that this was keeping him at bay. Then I reached the door. I heard the females at their gory feast. I heard the door opening and I turned to find myself facing Tirgsor.

He had a sword in his hand.

'Only disarm him, Tirgsor,' Dracula said. 'This one is mine.'

'Very well, great Voivode,' Tirgsor replied.

He moved in and in the opening moments of our engagement I realized that he had great knowledge of the art of swordplay. A few strokes were enough for me to realize that I had met with a master, and had it not been for Dracula's insistence that Tirgsor merely disarm me, I do not doubt that I would have died with Tirgsor's blade in my heart.

For a long while I fought solely to hang on to my sword. The sweat began to pour off me and I knew that I was tiring before Tirgsor's onslaught. Tirgsor knew it, too, for he smiled and redoubled his efforts.

Then the inevitable happened.

A sudden cut from Tirgsor's sword sent my blade flying across the room. Fear of the consequences lent added strength to my failing limbs and I sprang after it as

Dracula turned on me. Even as I did so I knew I could not reach the blade in time; instead I seized a heavy candelabrum and flung it full in the face of the great Undead. Then, without hesitating a moment, I once more grasped the comforting hilt of my sword.

As I turned, I found Tirgsor almost upon me with upraised blade. God had been good to me, but it was nothing short of a miracle that, at the moment Tirgsor poised to make his final strike, the foot of the *stolnic* slid on the blood of Vlad, which lay wet and slippery on the floor. Thus, with a frustrated cry, Tirgsor fell forward and my blade ran into his stomach.

He coughed blood, his eyes rolled back, and then he fell heavily to the floor. I stepped back and glanced quickly around me.

The candelabrum which had halted Dracula had also struck a hanging tapestry and, as if the room were merely dried tinder, a blaze had started and spread rapidly across the wood panelling of the room. The dark smoke was thickening and, peering through it, I could see the Undead creatures backing away before a bright wall of fierce, yellow flame. I promptly made towards the door and, on going through it, turned to glance back into the room.

The creatures were backing towards the cellar door, snarling and shrieking, and I could observe that they were entirely surrounded by blazing beams and falling tapestries, both of which were spreading the flames even further.

However, the malevolent figure of Dracula still towered above the inferno, and even through the billowing smoke, and across the rising flames, I could see his eyes boring into mine.

'You think to escape me?' he called through the smoke and flame. 'You think to thwart me? You who are sprung from the seed of my loins would dare to turn on his own blood? You fool! You puny mortal! You will find that I am not thwarted yet, that I cannot be so easily destroyed! You will learn that my revenge has yet to begin, that I can spread it with impunity across the centuries! Time is my friend as it is your enemy, and soon you will be a Dracula, soon you will be my slave, to do my bidding, to obey without question, to be one with my will. Remember, my son Mircea! One day soon . . .'

The rest of his tirade ceased abruptly as a blazing beam detached itself from the roof and fell with a great shower of sparks and roaring flames, crashing into the floor and sending up clouds of smoke that obliterated them completely from my view.

The crash had the effect of making me realize the perilousness of my situation, and I retreated through the door, down the stairway and out into the courtyard.

The flames spread up the old tower, leaping and crackling, and the woodwork was ablaze within seconds. I barely had time to get to the courtyard door before the fire ate its way across the wooden floor and stairway. As I passed out, coughing and choking, I saw my brother Mihail, his face a deathly white, running straight towards the inferno.

'Dracula!' he cried out. 'Dracula!'

I threw myself into his path. In retrospect I know not what madness it was that seized me and urged me to save him. Had he not been in league with the devil himself? Had he not tried to steal my very soul? Yet try to save him I did, perhaps because he was my brother, no matter how corrupt and beyond redemption. Indeed, I threw myself at him, clutching him by the shoulders, and tried to prevent him from his suicidal flight.

'No!' I cried out. 'It is useless, Mihail! They have all perished!'

He gave a scream, long and drawn out, and his eyes flashed with terror.

'*No!*' he screamed.

He threw off my clutching hands as if he had the strength of ten, and I fell against a stone wall and lay there, winded and dazed. Then I glanced up. I saw Mihail run forward. His hands were before him and he cried out for Dracula and then, as if oblivious, he threw himself into the blazing inferno.

I rose unsteadily to my feet and staggered after him, but the heat of the flames was now so intense that it stayed me at the door. Through the flame and smoke I could see the distorted figure of Mihail, his clothes all aflame, lurching across the hall and up the blazing stairway to the refectory room. I could hear his voice growing fainter and fainter between violent paroxisms of coughing: 'Dracula! I, Mihail, will save you! Dracula! Drac . . . ul . . . la . . .' His voice disappeared and then the intense heat drove me backward into the courtyard. There I stood for a moment, silent and strangely stricken, cowed by the flames which shot up and gave light to the dark sky.

The sound of frightened horses revived me. The flames were now leaping all over the castle, and I turned and raced for the stables. They were filled with smoke, but as yet there was no sign of any flames. I ran quickly through the stables, undoing the stalls and sending the horses galloping down the mountain road. When I came to the last stall, I threw a saddle over the beast within and mounted. I urged it forward out of the stable, across the smoky courtyard, and finally, heaving a huge sigh of relief, headed down the mountain road, into cold, pure night air, away from the funeral pyre of the voivodes of Wallachia.

It seemed but a moment before I was leaping from the beast in front of the inn at Arefu.

'God save you, *mein Herr*!' Toma cried, rushing out of the inn and grasping my hand.

'Is the countess all right, Toma?' I asked immediately.

'A few moments ago, *mein Herr*, she woke as if from a troubled sleep. The colour seemed to flood back into her face as she saw the flames. She is well, *mein Herr*.'

'Thank God,' I said, and dismounted.

Slowly, one by one, the doors of the houses in Arefu were opening. In ones, twos and threes, silent bands of villagers came out into the street and stood looking up the mountainside. They stood silently. They hardly seemed to move. The flaming pyre on top of the mountain cast its red light on their faces, faces graven with lines of suffering and spiritual torment. But wondrously, with each crackle and explosion of falling wood and masonry, the lines started leaving their faces, the light of relief passing across them, and the spark of gratitude seeming to flicker in their dim eyes.

They stood in silence, as I did, looking to the mountain top until the sun's rays bathed them in a golden glow and Castle Dracula was revealed as a heap of grey-black, smouldering ruins. Only then did the villagers return to their homes, and then, for the first time, at least in my experience, they took down the shutters, removed the blinds, and let in the bright light of life.

Toma smiled and laid his rough hand on my shoulder.

'It is over, *mein Herr*,' he said. 'Now we can live again.'

I smiled and went into the inn and went up to the bedchamber. My beloved, more beautiful than I had ever imagined her, rose up from the bed and with arms out-stretched ran into my encircling embrace.

We left Arefu that same day. Arefu: nestling under the shadow of the charred ruins of the citadel of the Voivode Dracula – Dracula, whose dream of revenge, conquest and immortality had led him into a diabolical tryst with Lucifer himself. Yet the shadows had finally been blown away from Arefu, and we therefore left it happy, the peasants dancing and celebrating, for the first time in years, in the clear, sharp air of a brilliant December day.

There is little left for me to recount. In Tirgoviste the Countess Irene Bathory married Barone Michelino of Rome and, by easy stages, we returned to my adopted country, Italy. I closed down my palazzo near Piazza Venezia in Rome and bought an estate in the prolific wine producing country of Apulia in the south where I now raise vines in the wild, rugged countryside where the fierce sun and the heavy, though poor, soil makes the coarse wines that I produce admirably suitable for blending. I swear that I now produce the finest full red wine in Italy.

And so I watch the vines grow, and soon, so I have been told, I shall be watching my children grow strong and healthy. I pray God that they will never know the curse of Dracula.

I have long debated whether I should reveal that Dracula's blood flows in my veins. But what matters now? The curse has passed away for all time, and so, safe in that knowledge, I have set pen to paper in the hope that some day my children and future generations may know of the evil that nearly shattered the world and give thanks that it was not so.

Deus vobiscum, AD 1480

Van Helsing's Final Note

Alas, as Horace wrote, *Nec scire fas est omnia* – it is not permitted to know all things – for Mircea, or Michelino as he preferred to be called, seems to have remained in happy ignorance.

Castle Dracula was not completely destroyed that night, for its edifice still dominates the village of Arefu even to this day, and I have stood in the shadow of its walls. One may even view it in a painting executed by the Swiss Hensie Trenk in 1865, which is a work of excellent quality.

In spite of that last vision of Mihail rushing into the inferno of the castle, by which Michelino thought his brother had perished together with the Undead thing that had been his father, Dracula, Mihail lived on. He managed to save the greater part of the castle from destruction – how, I know not. But this I do know: Mihail lived on to become ruler of Wallachia, known as Mihail cel Rau, or Mihail the Bad. From April 1508 until October 1509 he held Wallachia in thrall, until the people rose to destroy him. Even then he fathered a son called Mircea who gave birth to a line of Wallachian princes, the last of which was one Mihail Radu who was driven out of Wallachia into Transylvania and exile. This Mihail Radu settled in the Borgo Pass in the Carpathians, and it was to this Castle Dracula that friend Jonathan Harker journeyed to see Count Dracula – for above all, Mihail saved his father, Dracula, from the flames of the castle and, as the world knows to its cost, Dracula survived another four hundred years to spread evil and horror across the face of the earth.

THE REVENGE OF DRACULA

For Ron and Hilary Colbert,
who would agree that if the only vampires on this Earth
were like Dracula, then it might be a happier place

'You think to baffle me – you – with your pale faces all in a row, like sheep in a butcher's. You shall be sorry yet, each one of you! You think you have left me without a place to rest; but I have more. My revenge is just begun! I spread it over centuries, and time is on my side.'
Dracula by Bram Stoker, Constable, London, 1897

INTRODUCTION

A writer receives many varied and often strange packages through his postbox. There are sometimes letters of praise for his work, sometimes abusive letters, copies of reviews to flatter his ego or make him rail at the wretches who dare call themselves critics and, less frequent but more welcome, are royalty cheques from beneficent publishers.

For me, the arrival of the morning mail is the high spot of my day and, depending on what is contained in the oddly assorted envelopes and packages that cascade each morning over my front door mat, my mood is established for the rest of the day. It is probably not a very mature reaction, but nothing puts me more in a good work mood for the rest of the day than to receive some exciting titbit in the mail.

Not long after the publication of *Dracula Unborn*, a book in which I edited and introduced Professor Abraham Van Helsing's translation of an amazing fifteenth-century manuscript written by Mircea, the youngest son of the evil Vlad Dracula, I received a rather bulky package which had been addressed to me care of my publishers and passed on by them. The package contained a lengthy manuscript written on ill-assorted sheets of paper, yellowing around the edges. The hand was a neat copperplate, executed in fading brown ink. The whole thing smacked of the Victorian era and a date, *1866*, written at the beginning of the manuscript confirmed this.

Now, as a writer, it has not been an unusual occurrence for me to receive ageing manuscripts, discovered in some family trunk or forgotten drawer, and passed on by some hopeful scion who felt it contained publishable material. Neither is it unusual for the manuscript to turn out to be some illiterate philosophical ramble written by a bored suburban parson with nothing better to do than inflict his views of morality on an equally bored world.

With that vision in mind I was about to toss the manuscript aside when I observed a covering letter. The letter was addressed from a certain mental health clinic near Guildford in Surrey. Furthermore, it was from the psychiatrist in charge of the clinic. It was a rather unflattering letter, somewhat curt in tone:

I am not in the habit of reading the type of lurid tales that writers of your ilk produce. Vampire stories have always seemed to me to be merely crude and sensational efforts to exploit people's genuinely held fears and superstitions. While such stories, unfortunately, enjoy a vogue, they lack the charm and strangeness of genuine folk tradition.

I have read your book Dracula Unborn *merely because some sections of the press have taken the work seriously. The* Bolton Evening News *of February 1, 1978, for example, devoted a lengthy article to the discussion of its historical merits. While I appreciate that it is an accepted literary custom for an author to pretend he has found a genuine manuscript which he is merely editing, I cannot help but say that* Dracula Unborn *was a very irresponsible book to write. Filled, as it is, with genuine historical detail, it gives the impression of a serious historical document which has fooled even some newspapers.*

Do you realize that there is a serious psychiatric condition called lupomania or a 'werewolf complex'; that people of certain neurotic instability genuinely believe that they are victims of vampires and werewolves and, in some horrible cases, may believe they are the vampires themselves and have committed terrible acts in this belief? Your book and others like it, can only feed these fears.

As a psychiatrist, I take the strongest objection to such fiction. It can have an extremely harmful effect. Need I quote the recent bizarre case of the unfortunate man who died in Stoke-on-Trent in 1973? The cause of death was asphyxiation after the man had swallowed garlic which he had placed in his mouth as protection against vampires. I can refer you to a more recent case of a boy in Stafford in 1975 who killed himself because he believed he was changing into a werewolf. And what of the mass hysteria in London during 1969/70 when people began to report visions of vampires in Highgate Cemetery in North London?

I believe that nothing illustrates my contention better than the enclosed manuscript and shows the suffering of the unstable mind when caught up in this vampire mythology. This manuscript was written by an inmate of this clinic when it was, unfortunately, termed a lunatic asylum in the 1860s. In those days an enlightened attitude towards the mentally handicapped had not permeated Western civilization. The poor unfortunate who wrote this could, in all probability, have been easily cured in the light of modern psychiatric knowledge.

The writer of the manuscript, as you will see, suffered from classic symptoms of personality disassociation and delusions, believing that he was being persecuted by a vampire. The story, an imagining from his fear-crazed mind, is certainly the equal to any horror-fiction of today. There are several interesting parallels to your own Dracula Unborn and it seems obvious that the man had access to the same historical sources as yourself.

I hope a reading of the manuscript will serve as a salutary lesson that such tales can have a harmful effect on a person's mental stability.

It took me a while to recover from this rebuke to my literary endeavours but eventually, more out of curiosity than any real desire, I sat down and read the manuscript.

What I read electrified me!

The doctor was surely mistaken when he said that the

story was just the 'imagining of a fear-crazed mind.' So many things fitted in with Mircea's manuscript which the 'lunatic' could have had no access to. I was convinced that the manuscript I now held was not a lunatic's ramblings but another terrifying chapter in the story of the attempts by that horrifying personification of evil – Dracula – to spread his blood lust throughout the world.

I wrote off immediately to the psychiatrist and asked for permission to publish the work. After all, he had sent it to me to read in support of his case so why not present it to the public and let them judge?

At first he was reluctant and objected most strongly on the grounds that I would turn it into a fictional horror tale. Eventually, after some correspondence and a telephone call, he agreed to the publication on condition that I did not alter one word of the manuscript (a condition I was more than willing to meet); secondly, that I made it quite clear that the writer was a man named Upton Welsford who wrote the manuscript while he was in an asylum for the mentally ill, and undergoing treatment for delusions. This I promised to do. Thirdly, in addition to the foregoing conditions, I would allow the psychiatrist to append, as an afterword, a note on the mental condition which he, in the light of modern psychiatric learning, believed Upton Welsford to have suffered from. That, also, I willingly agreed to do.

Having fulfilled these three conditions, I now leave the story for you to read and decide whether indeed it is merely the ramblings of a lunatic or, if not, whether a great wrong was done to Upton Welsford when he returned from Romania in 1862 . . . some thirty-five years before Bram Stoker collected the material to publish his great work *Dracula*.

Peter Tremayne
London, 1978

CHAPTER ONE

They say I am mad.

And at times, mostly at night, as I stand peering through the small iron grille that blocks the window of my room, and staring at the ominous black clouds that scud across the death-white face of the moon, I find myself wishing that it *was* so, wishing that I were indeed mad. For at such times I experience an unearthly, chilling tingle that vibrates against my spine; I find my heart beats twice as fast; I feel the blood bursting hotly into my cheeks, roaring in my ears, and a mist begins to cloud my eyes. And through it all I hear his voice, mocking, sardonic, telling me that the time is coming . . . soon, soon!

Momentarily the swirling mists clear; I catch a glimpse of *him* – a tall, thin man, all in black. I see his face, that waxen face; the high aquiline nose, the parted red lips with the sharp teeth showing ivory-white between them; and the eyes – those black eyes ringed with red fire, flaming as if I were staring at the very sunset.

And the voice:

'Soon . . . *soon!*'

It is almost a caress.

I wish, indeed, I were mad as they say I am. I wish I *had* embarked on the impossible adventures of lunacy and merely encountered the monsters created of man's first morality which have ever vexed him into the spinning of fantasies by which to elude or do battle with them.

But I am sane; yes, I say it is so. I am sane even though I be committed to this brooding asylum filled with the tragic storage crypts of the unthinkable and the unrealizable deliriums of infantile man. I am suffering from no delirium, I am spinning no fantasy, for I have experienced the unthinkable, I have realized the unrealizable, I have suffered the torture of the damned and now know that soon . . . soon such a monstrous evil will burst forth upon the earth that the Horsemen of the Apocalypse will seem like the riding forth of Cherubim and Seraphim by comparison. Yet who can I warn? Who will believe me? Who will take seriously the ramblings of the mentally deranged?

They have, at last, allowed me pen and paper. Smilingly (oh, how I hate their smiles of superior knowledge) they have told me to commit my fantasies and deliriums to paper. They say it will be therapeutic for me. As if there were some medical cure for a branded soul in torment! But, since I have pen and paper, I will write my story . . . my delirium, my fantasy . . . call it what you will. I will commit it to writing.

Alas, I can no longer hope that it will be believed . . . not now. But maybe one day the world will know the terrible truth of what I shall presently recount for I hear, whispering in my ears, that evil, sardonic sneering voice . . . 'Soon . . . *soon!*'

It all began a few weeks before Christmas, in the early December of 1861. In fact it was the very day after my twenty-sixth birthday which I had celebrated with my father, a widower, the Reverend Mortimer Welsford, at Gisleham in Berkshire, in which village and county I had been born and received my rudimentary education before going to Oxford to take my degree. I recall that I had returned to London on the morning following my birthday, a Tuesday, or so I believe, because the next day I was due to attend an important meeting at the Foreign Office.

Straightway I must point out that I, Upton Welsford, served the British Government only in a minor capacity. I was personal secretary to Viscount Molesworth. Lord

Molesworth's connection with the Foreign Office is such that I need not elaborate on this point. Ever since I had come down from Oxford and started a career in the Foreign Office, I had served under the patronage of Lord Molesworth, whose interest in my career and welfare was prompted by the fact that my father had once been chaplain to the Viscount's father. Therefore do not be deluded that I was in any way a person of great weight or importance. If the brutal truth be known, I was nothing more than a lowly clerk. Nevertheless, Lord Molesworth required my presence for that meeting and his summons caused me to hasten from rural Berkshire into the smoke-blackened mists of wintry London.

Having caught the Bristol–London stage before breakfast, I was in Westminster by midday and walked the length of Whitehall to my rooms by Charing Cross. Depositing my bags, I went out to lunch at a nearby tavern and then discovered that I had an entire afternoon to idle through.

My father, who is inclined to over-generosity on birthdays, had given me five guineas to celebrate my twenty-sixth year of life. The coins jangled comfortingly in my pocket as I strolled through the fog-bound streets that grey, comfortless afternoon. As I walked, my feet turned towards Petticoat Lane. I was in no hurry, so I did not summon a coasting hackney-carriage even though it was a fair measure to tread. Now I must confess that my one vice in life is the collection of unusual *objets d'art* and the reason my feet turned in the direction of Petticoat Lane was because of the collection of junk shops that were found in the area. Sometimes, among the piles of coloured bottles, cordage and dusty bric-à-brac, I have uncovered tiny porcelain figurines, statuettes and vases of such unusual quality that I have added them, one by one, into a modest collection that is the envy of my friends. Thus it was, with this idea of seeking yet another treasure to add to my collection, that I walked contentedly through the gloomy afternoon.

Would to God I had been beset by a gang of footpads and thieves; would to God I had been run down by a flying carriage in the foggy twilight of the city streets; would to God I had never reached my destination!

It was late afternoon when I came upon the shop. The sky had already blackened with the early dusk of winter. An old man in a thick, yellow woollen muffler – I recall him well – was shuffling along the street, lighting the gas lamps.

I recall that I had been staring into the grimy window of some shop, scarcely able to see through the twilight and the dirt of the window-pane, when the old man lit the gas-standard which stood opposite, letting a yellow beam of light play on the window. I was about to turn away when this light caught at something in the corner of the window, causing a myriad white pinpricks of light to dance over its surface. I turned and tried to wipe the dirty pane with my sleeve, the better to see the object. It looked like a small statuette of some animal, some unusual animal.

Intrigued, I opened the door of the shop and entered into a musty interior to the accompaniment of a jangling bell.

Almost directly, a large, red-jowled man appeared from behind a curtain at the back of the shop. He bent to a hurricane lamp on a makeshift counter and turned up the wick, causing his dust-laden wares to be more clearly observed.

Two glistening blue eyes stared at me from a weather-beaten face. The man came forward and as he walked his rolling gait betrayed his former occupation: a sailor, without doubt.

'Ar'ernoon, cap'n,' his voice held the cheery accent of a true born Cockney. 'Wot can I do for yer? Sum'ink toikes yer fancy then?'

He gestured about the shop.

I nodded.

'There is a small statuette in your window. It's some kind of animal in black.'

'I knows the one,' replied the man, going to the window and reaching forward into the bric-à-brac. In a trice he had returned with a dusty object in his hand. He looked at it a moment, then pulled a dirty rag from his pocket and proceeded to dust it after a fashion.

''Ere y'are, cap'n,' he said, thrusting it into my hands.

The object was a figure of a dragon, its serpent-like neck arched and its wings spread out behind it. It was of excellent workmanship and carved from some dark green mineral. Its surface was smooth and cold to the touch. Although I was not by any means an expert, I had been collecting *objets d'art* long enough to recognize nephrite jade. It was a superb specimen.

'Where did you obtain this from?' I asked the man casually, trying not to let him see my greedy excitement.

'Howt heast, cap'n,' he said.

'Out east?' I repeated.

'Port o' Kowloon, cap'n. I served fifteen years afore the mast 'fore planting me stumps ashore. Picked this up on one o' me last trips.'

'Chinese, is it?'

I held up the small carving. It was about six inches long and some three inches high. There was no question that it was a fine piece. The carving had been lovingly carried out and the face of the dragon seemed to bear a malevolent smile, menacing yet triumphant. There was no way to indicate the date of its creation. It could have been a few years old . . . or it could have been a few centuries old.

There was no doubting, however, the quality of the nephrite: that much I did know. I also knew that a great many other coloured minerals have been mistaken for jade and I once knew a colleague who paid an enormous sum for a jade vase only to find out that it was made of serpentine. To be on the safe side I walked to the window of the shop and held it up to the rays of the gaslight which seeped in from outside. I did not dare conduct my experiment by the hurricane lamp in case the seaman-cum-shopkeeper guessed at my knowledge. Carefully removing my cravat pin, without being observed, I drew its point along the smooth green-black surface. Had it been serpentine, or, indeed, verdite, which is a deep green micaceous rock, there would have been a scratch on the surface. Both minerals are softer than jade and liable to scratching. Nor could the mineral have been saussurite, another mineral with jade-like qualities, because the colouring of the piece would have been greyish green and not black green. It was nephrite jade right enough and therefore valuable.

The junk dealer stood looking at me expectantly.

'How much do you want for it?' I asked.

He shuffled his feet and gazed into the distance before replying, a sign by which I deduced that he had not been in his present calling for long.

'Why, cap'n, I was 'oping to 'ave two guineas fer it.'

Two guineas!

I felt a momentary surge of triumph for I knew that certain dealers would have demanded no less than ten guineas for such a piece, even if it were only a few years old.

'I'll take it then,' I said without preamble.

'Aye, aye, cap'n!'

The man was as enthusiastic as I was. He ducked behind a small counter and emerged with a piece of yellowing newspaper. Taking the statuette from my hands, he wrapped it carefully and handed it back. Meanwhile, I removed from my pocket two of my father's golden guineas and laid them in his palm.

'Thank'ee, cap'n, thank'ee kindly,' nodded the man, finger to a vanished forelock.

With the jade statuette under my arm, I bade him a good day and left the shop.

Ah, the proud vanity of man. I strutted home like some vain turkey-cock, delighted in my dealings and sparing no thought of remorse for the man I had, through his ignorance, cheated. Cheated? My mind did not even contemplate the concept. That was business. But had I known then what I know now I would have dashed that little carving into the Thames, taken a mallet and splintered it into fragments, or paid ten times two guineas to be rid of the accursed thing.

For that innocuous little statuette, about which I felt so triumphant, was to be the source of the evils into which I was about to be unwillingly drawn.

I was not aware of having a nightmare. All I know is that I started from my sleep with my heart lurching wildly within me. I felt cold and yet, at the same time, my body was wreathed in perspiration as if I were ill with some fever. I lay for a moment feeling my body beyond the control of my mind, my hands and feet trembling with a curious and indescribable sensation. Slowly I drew myself together and sat up, shaking my head to clear it.

A pain, sharp and unexpected, caught at my brows so suddenly that I jerked forward in the bed, head to my knees, and groaned aloud in agony. I placed my hands upon my temples and massaged them fiercely in order to try to dispel the exquisite agony that seared along my throbbing nerves.

Curiously, too, I suddenly became aware of a smell, a fragrance that was both sweet and sickly. It seemed to fill my bedroom so that my lungs heaved against its odour and I coughed several times.

I reached out of my bed for a match and lit the lamp. A

glance at the clock showed it to be nearly two o'clock in the morning.

With strange pains throbbing through my head, I tumbled out of bed and went first to the windows, throwing them open to dispel the sickly sweet smell that pervaded the room. Then I went to the room I used as a sitting-room in order to obtain some powders for my headache.

To my surprise, the smell in my sitting-room was just as strong as it had been in my bedroom. I opened the windows here as well.

I swallowed the headache powders with a glass of water and sat in a chair waiting for them to work. Although a slight breeze was blowing in through the windows, causing the ingress of the cold night air, the smell remained all-powerful.

The thought crossed my mind that Mrs Dobson the landlady, who also cleaned my rooms daily, must have put some strange plant in my rooms which emitted the disagreeable odour. I knew Mrs Dobson was keen on potted plants and seemed to collect them from all corners of the world.

I peered round to find the source of my discomfiture but the only potted plant I could see was a sulky aspidistra which I had reluctantly inherited from the previous tenant and which stood on a china pedestal to one side of the fireplace in my sitting-room.

Puzzled, I made a thorough search of the rooms. I could find no explanation of the smell which, I had reasoned, must have produced the terrible migraine which assailed my temples. Having completed my search, I suddenly realized that both smell and headache had disappeared and was acutely aware of the December chills which were rustling through the curtains at the windows.

I closed the windows and returned to the warmth of my bed, perplexed at the reasons for my troubled night.

CHAPTER TWO

Next morning, having breakfasted, I decided to walk from my rooms along Whitehall to the Foreign Office. Although my headache had gone, I had a strange feeling of exhaustion and a hot irritation seemed to ring my eyes. I felt as if I had been denied sleep for several nights. The brisk walk through the cold morning air had no effect in reviving me.

Viscount Molesworth was already in the office, standing with his back to a newly lit fire, hands clasped behind him. He was a big florid-faced man with sandy hair and watery blue eyes, which twinkled humorously from his fleshy face. His face, however, rarely mirrored his emotions and assumed a permanent expression of melancholy. I believed him to be unfortunate in his physical appearance in that his chin receded under his fleshy cheeks and his top teeth protruded over thin, bloodless lips. He never seemed to care about his appearance and his clothes always looked as if they had been slept in the night before.

It was a stupid man who judged Molesworth by his appearance. His mind was like a rapier in spite of its outward covering. He was an excellent chess player and this probably stood him in good stead in his role at the Foreign Office for he had been responsible for several successful negotiations on behalf of Her Britannic Majesty's Government. Molesworth was a generous friend but an unremitting enemy.

His eyes narrowed as I entered the suite of rooms we used as offices.

'Morning, Welsford,' he said languidly. It was one of his poses to assert a listlessness and boredom when, in reality, his eyes never ceased to observe and interpret. 'You look deuced tired this morning.'

I nodded agreement.

'I've had a bad night, m'lord,' I replied. 'Seemed to have had a migraine.'

He raised his eyebrows as if surprised.

'Better now, I trust?' he asked and then, without waiting for a reply, continued, 'The Foreign Secretary is due here in a moment. He seems to have some sort of job for me.'

That much I had guessed and it would be foolish of me not to admit that I had pondered a long time, during my journey from Gisleham to London, on what sort of commission the Foreign Secretary had in mind for our department. For those of short memory, the year 1861 had been especially busy for the Foreign Office and our missions abroad. A state of civil war had broken out in the United States of America and, while Britain tended to display a bias towards the secessionist states of the South, it was our job to convince the world of our neutrality. We had been forced to send troops to the American continent, however, with France and Spain, in order to exact payment of financial debts from Mexico. In Africa, the ever troublesome Boers – the Dutch settlers – had moved out of the British colonies in the south and formed an independent republic called the Transvaal. The Foreign Office and the Colonial Office were not sure under whose jurisdiction the matter fell. Closer to home, in Europe, the Italian states were causing concern having, with the exception of Rome and Venice, been united as one Kingdom under Victor Emmanuel of Savoy. Britain was inclined to be slightly suspicious of Victor Emmanuel's political aspirations. Prussia needed watching, for a new Kaiser, Wilhelm I, had succeeded to the throne. Finally, Russia had amazed and confounded her critics when Tsar Alexander II abolished serfdom throughout her empire.

What sphere would our assignment fall in?

I was not to be kept in doubt for long. Hardly had I seated myself at my desk and gathered the papers for the meeting when the door was opened and the Foreign Secretary, Lord Clarendon, was announced.

George Frederick William, the fourth Earl of Clarendon, was not an impressive man. Distinguished, yes; but not impressive. He still had the sprightliness of youth in his lean, handsome figure. His curly hair still fell in profusion over a broad, intelligent forehead. But his dimpled chin and wide eyes, set in a well-shaped head, were more in keeping with a ladies' man than a distinguished, sober, Whig politician and one of the Empire's great statesmen.

As he entered the room and shook Molesworth warmly by the hand, I had a definite feeling of 'presence'. The Foreign Secretary cast a quizzical glance in my direction.

Molesworth extended an arm towards me.

'Allow me to present my personal secretary, Mr Upton Welsford.'

'Delighted, Welsford,' there was a distant tone in the Foreign Secretary's voice.

I did not see the look of inquiry which passed between Clarendon and Molesworth but Molesworth, as if in answer to an unspoken question, said: 'Mr Welsford has my complete confidence in all matters pertaining to my office.'

Clarendon seated himself while Molesworth offered him a glass of port. He then waved me to draw up a chair and indicated I should take notes.

'And now, my lord?' prompted Molesworth gently.

Clarendon put down his glass and leant back in his chair.

'Briefly, the Government want you to undertake a mission to Romania.'

'Romania?' echoed Molesworth.

I confess that, though I prided myself on geography, I had never heard of the place.

'Romania is yet to come into existence officially,' explained Clarendon. 'It is the name by which the united principalities of Moldavia and Wallachia are to become known, following their independence from the Turkish Empire.'

He paused and toyed with his glass of port.

'To put you briefly in the picture, I'd best sketch in some history. You may recall that in the summer of 1853 Moldavia and Wallachia were occupied by the Russian armies. England and France formed an alliance with the Turkish Empire, which has ruled those provinces or principalities since the fifteenth century. The following year saw the outbreak of a war between Turkey and her allies, ourselves, and Russia. The theatre of war was in the Crimea. What grew evident in the conflict was that the people of Wallachia and Moldavia – who, by the way, are more Latin than Slavic in origin – wanted neither Russian nor Turkish rule.

'It occurred to Britain that should these provinces be united as an independent state under native rulers, it would have a distinct influence on the balance of power in Europe. We began to investigate possibilities with the local nationalist movement. We realized, although she was our ally, that the Turkish Ottoman Empire was rather unstable. Russia certainly wanted to pick up the strategic parts of the Turkish Empire afforded by Moldavia and Wallachia. So also did the Austrians, who came into the war on Turkey's side. France, as well.'

He paused while Molesworth replenished his empty glass.

'From Moldavia and Wallachia, Russia could secure a good toehold to Europe and dominate vital trading routes to the Middle East.

'However, when the Crimean War ended in 1856, the peace treaty was so designed that it placed Moldavia and Wallachia under the protection of the European Powers.

A Paris Peace Congress was set up to decide what was to be done. The nationalists, led by a man with some outlandish name – Grigore Alexandru Ghica – demanded that the protecting powers recognize the right of these principalities to break away from the Turkish Empire and form one united country called Romania.'

'Why Romania?' asked Molesworth curiously, lighting a cheroot.

Clarendon waved a hand in the air.

'On account of the natives believing they are descendants of the ancient Romans. The Romans did settle the area and called it Dacia or some such name.'

He paused to collect his thoughts.

'Now, the British Government was in agreement with the establishment of an independent Romanian state. As one of its sponsors we would be able to maintain a presence in the area and secure favourable trading links. On the other hand we were supposed to be allies of the Turks. So we pretended to play a middle game while, by agreement, the French put pressure on the Turkish Sultan Abdul Mejid and his Porte – er, parliament, that is – to allow the principalities to hold a referendum on the matter. The result was that both principalities voted for independence and their union into a single state, with an invitation to a foreign prince from one of the ruling families of Europe to become its titular head.

'The idea was endorsed at the Paris Convention. But in 1859 Moldavia's elected assembly decided to depose its ruling prince and elect, unanimously, I may add, a Colonel Alexandru Iona Cuza as ruling prince. Cuza was the leader of the 1818 insurrection against the Turks. Within a few days Wallachia also elected him as their ruling prince. This election of a prince was rather heady stuff but the British Government decided to go along with it and acknowledge Cuza as ruler.

'He seems a pretty impressive fellow – set to work

immediately on organizing common laws and institutions for both principalities. The Romanian language, a rather odd mixture of Latin and Slavic, was proclaimed legal – it had been suppressed by the Turks – and the country seems to be heading for an industrial reorganization. Why, it is even starting to export refined oil for the first time this year.

'Now a few days ago Cuza, who is officially known as Prince Alexandru, issued a proclamation to the effect that the union of Moldavia and Wallachia had been achieved and that Romanian nationality had been established.

'The British Government's attitude is to welcome this new European state and to give it aid and advice – but with caution. I say 'caution' because its political future is far from clear and there are certain dangerous radical elements near the seat of power. The Prime Minister is particularly anxious to establish a full diplomatic mission in Romania but we must obtain some first-hand accounts of the exact situation in the country before we proceed further.

'For example, Austria has become extremely worried by the situation. The Romanian people are not confined to the principalities of Moldavia and Wallachia. They also populate another principality, a rather large one, called Transylvania, which was a province of Hungary.'

'Was?' queried Molesworth. 'I was under the impression that it still is.'

Clarendon waved an expressive hand.

'Last October the Austrian Emperor, Franz Joseph, promulgated a constitutional document . . .'

Molesworth interrupted:

'Yes, I know. It's called the October Diploma which puts an end to the Austro-Hungarian absolutist system and opens up a constitutional rule more in keeping with our style of democracy.'

'Then you should also know, Molesworth, that the

same document allows Transylvania to become an autonomous state within the Habsburg Empire. However, there is a strong liberationalist movement in Transylvania which wants the principality to unify with Moldavia and Wallachia into Romania – a movement called Astra, I believe. It was to take the sting out of this nationalist movement that Franz Joseph issued his decree of autonomous self-government within the empire.'

Clarendon leant back and smiled at Molesworth.

'In brief, Molesworth,' he said, 'the British Government desire that you, together with a small staff, go to Romania in the New Year. You are to reach there by the end of January when Cuza is dissolving the separate assemblies of Moldavia and Wallachia and instituting the first National Assembly of Romania. Naturally, many European states will have representatives attending the ceremonies that will go with the official declaration of the new state. We are sending an official embassy . . .'

'Then what will be my position?' interrupted Molesworth.

'A special embassy,' replied Clarendon. 'You and your staff will concentrate on building up an exact picture of the political situation in the country. Test out the strength of all the parties and political groups. Also, try to find out what the aspirations of Transylvania are . . . whether the people desire union with Romania or not. You will present a detailed report of how you see the developing role of Romania in Europe. Will you accept that mission?'

Molesworth was quiet for a moment, seeming to contemplate the task before him. Then he inclined his head.

'Very well, my lord,' he said, simply.

'Excellent! Excellent!'

Clarendon stood up and stubbed out his cheroot in a glass ashtray. 'I shall report your acceptance to Lord Palmerston at our Cabinet meeting this afternoon. The

247

Prime Minister will be pleased. In the meantime, I advise you to collect as much background information as you can about the country. Interpreters may be necessary, but on no account are the natives of the principality to be taken into your confidence.'

After a limp handshake with Molesworth and a curt nod towards me, the Foreign Secretary bore down upon the door like some battleship under full sail with Molesworth, like a frigate, trailing in his wake.

'We shall have several briefings before you leave,' Clarendon was saying over his shoulder. 'I suggest the first week in January would be an excellent time for your departure. If there is anything you require, let my office know.'

Molesworth paused a moment by the door, looking thoughtfully after the disappearing Earl.

Then, decisively, he shut the door.

'So, Welsford,' he returned to me with a ghost of a smile puckering his lugubrious features, 'we seem to be in for an interesting journey.'

He took out some maps of Europe and spread them across his desk, tracing the countries' boundaries with a forefinger.

'Moldavia . . . Wallachia . . .' he peered curiously at the map, 'and here is Transylvania . . . H'm, come and see, Welsford. There they are, to the north-east of Greece. Well, we'd better see what we can find out about the area. See what you can dig up from the libraries while I'll try to find if there are any natives from the country living in London.'

'Very well, my lord.'

'Compile a dossier giving a sketch of the history, geography, industrial and mineral wealth and recent political developments. But you'd better not be too long about it. We shall want time to digest it and form a plan of campaign this side of Christmas if we are to set out in the New Year.'

A feeling of excitement began to grow in me as I examined the prospects of the journey to a new and strange-sounding country.

CHAPTER THREE

The next few days would make very boring reading if I rendered them into my account. I spent most of my time at Smirke's rather splendid new buildings which now house the British Museum. The museum has an awe-inspiring collection of books through which I browsed, collecting and collating much invaluable data on the principalities which comprised the new state of Romania. There were also several briefing sessions with Lord Clarendon over the next few days in which he advised Lord Molesworth as to what particular information the British Government desired.

The important thing as far as my narrative is concerned was the development of migraine which always seemed to manifest itself at night, causing me to awake with the most excruciating headaches. And then there was that smell, that curious sickly sweet smell that almost caused me to suffocate in the night. I cannot count the times that I staggered from my bed, chest heaving, head burning, to fling open my windows to escape from that terrible, terrifying odour.

For five consecutive days I was haunted by that smell and cursed by those terrible head pains. There came great hollows under my eyes and my friends remarked on the blackish marks that encircled them.

Things became so intolerable that I consulted a doctor who had rooms in Soho. He was a good natured but bumbling sort of man who gave me some strong powders to be taken for the relief of the headaches. Then he gave me a homily on the stupidity of overwork and the need for relaxation, with plenty of fresh air and exercise, before presenting me with a bill for one florin.

I promised to call back if the insomnia continued but I confess that I had little faith in the good doctor's remedies.

And the insomnia did continue.

It was on the fifth day, when I was feeling very depressed and ready to resign from my work, that I bumped into my old university friend, Dennis Yorke. After an unsatisfactory morning at the British Museum studying columns of meaningless figures on Romania's potential trade in imports and exports, I had turned down Holborn into Chancery Lane and made my way to a favourite restaurant of mine. If I was not going to sleep, I was determined that I was not going to starve as well.

And there it was that I bumped into Yorke.

He was several years older than me, the third son of an Earl, although he was not inclined to discuss his family with anyone. We shared the same rooms at Oxford while he was studying philosophy and theology and other esoteric subjects. He was very much involved with occult matters such as the new and growing fad of spiritualism.

Yorke was a tall man, with black curly hair and a long pale face whose sensitive qualities would have won it a place in a Renaissance painting of the disciples of Christ. He usually puffed at a pipe containing some strange eastern weed and he was given to strange practices such as meditation and the exercise of the body, which practices he called Yoga and which, he told me, originated in the east. I seldom saw him these days for he had a private income and devoted himself to his theosophical studies.

Yorke was, in fact, just paying off his hansom cab as I came up.

'By Jove, old fellow,' he cried, clapping me on the back in that expansive way he has, 'you look as if you haven't slept for a century.'

I nodded miserably for, being a trifle vain, I usually took pride in my appearance.

'I'm afraid I haven't been sleeping too well of late, Yorke,' I replied. 'Headaches and all that sort of thing.'

'Well, a good luncheon will set us up, eh? Come and share my table,' he said, propelling me into the restaurant.

It was as we came through the doors that I reeled as if I had been hit.

That smell! That same sickly sweet smell that pervaded my rooms at night; that haunted my sleeping and waking hours! Was I going insane?

I looked wildly around, my nostrils twitching to ensure the evidence of my senses.

'What's up, old fellow?' demanded Yorke. 'You look definitely unwell.'

'Do . . . do you smell anything unusual?' I gasped.

He sniffed suspiciously.

'Not really – oh, you mean that beastly plant smell – some potted plant they have in the foyer, I suppose.'

At least, then, I was not imagining the smell this time.

The manager came up to conduct us to a table.

'That smell,' I demanded of him. 'That smell, what is it?'

The man looked a trifle disconcerted at the wild look that must have flared in my eyes.

'Smell, sir?' He paused and sniffed loudly. 'You mean the flowers, sir?'

'Whatever it is,' I gasped. 'What is it?'

The manager smiled politely.

'A genus of oleaceous shrub, if I may say so, sir. I am something of an amateur horticulturist.'

I looked at him blankly.

'A genus of what?'

'Oleaceous shrub – jasmine, sir. Jasmine flowers. Perhaps a trifle oriental for some tastes, sir. But they are quite decorative . . .'

I interrupted him rudely.

'Give us a table as far away from the damned things as possible. I can't stand the smell.'

The manager pursed his lips in annoyance, and with one arched eyebrow, conveying what he thought of my taste in flowers, he conducted us to a select corner of the restaurant, wished us '*bon appetit*' and clicked his fingers to a hovering waiter to bring us the menus.

Yorke regarded me over the top of the menu with a bemused expression on his face.

'You really do seem pretty grim, old man,' he said gently. 'What's up?'

'Why should anything be up?' I almost snapped.

'You tell me, old fellow?' he replied, not in the least perturbed by my rudeness.

I suddenly realized that I was being rather silly. After all, it was not Yorke's fault that I was suffering from *insomnia*.

I unbent and confided in him the details of my sleepless nights, the terrifying headaches and the strange smell.

'You always smell the same odour each night?' he asked when I had finished my story.

'Always. I did not know what odour it was until the manager told me just now. It is always the scent of jasmine, which is strange because I am sure I have never encountered jasmine flowers before.'

Yorke scratched the side of his long nose.

'Have you seen a doctor?'

'Yes,' I replied, 'but so far it doesn't seem to have done me much good.'

'Well,' said Yorke, 'if you should feel no better and would like me to suggest a means whereby you might be alleviated from the condition, I might be able to help you.'

At the time I thought Yorke meant that he would be able to recommend some of the strange eastern drugs I knew him to be experimenting with. Not being interested in such things and, if the truth be known, being a little afraid of them, I said no more and we fell to attacking our meal.

That night came the first of the strange, terrifying dreams!

CHAPTER FOUR

I was walking through a garden.

The smell, that sickly sweet smell of jasmine, was overpowering. It was oppressive in its intensity and caused my temples to throb against my head like a regular slow beat on a drum. I was aware of a curious black velvet-like shroud that hung across the gardens and yet ... and yet I was fully aware of the tall dark trees and shrubs that hemmed me into a narrow way, a small path, which I traversed.

A part of my mind rebelled against the illusion, indeed, told me it *was* an illusion. I was not walking through some exotic garden; I was home in bed in my rooms in Charing Cross. Yet my senses: sight, sound and smell, rejected this logic.

Abruptly, as if I had stepped through some hidden veil, I came to the entrance of a tall marble structure. Pillars soared to dizzy heights towards the heavens and were lost in the blackness of a night sky. On the steps that led to this edifice there stood a statue on a marble plinth.

The statue was that of the dragon: an exact replica of the one I had bought in the junk shop.

Even now I can see every detail from that vision. Its surface was smooth, green-black, shining now and then as a rebellious moonbeam glanced through the moving black clouds. I can see its hideous face, the eyes wide and staring, a forked tongue protruding grotesquely between evil, canine teeth. The face, which evoked strange terrors, bore a menacing yet triumphant expression.

And while I looked on I became aware of the monotonous beating, the drumming which grew in strength and volume, seeming to join as one with the throbbing in my temples.

I reached a hand to my head and groaned in my anguish.

Then, above the drumming, I distinguished human voices, chanting, chanting to the very beat of the drum, joining and mingling until voices and drum were indistinguishable.

I knew not what they chanted; all I knew was that their voices filled me with such fear that I stood trembling in the shade of the great dragon-beast, unable to move or speak.

Suddenly, as if materialized from elemental dust, I was aware of a figure standing with its back towards me. It was a small, boyish figure, draped from head to feet in a startling white robe, contrasting vividly with the blackness of its surroundings. Two white arms were raised in supplication towards the malignant dragon statue, two pale hands, palm outwards, paid homage to the beast.

Like the tinkling of crystal in a gentle breeze came a voice, unreal, ethereal, speaking in some timeless tongue which I knew was not my native English but which I understood as clearly.

'I come from the Isle of Fire, having filled my body with the blood of Ur-Hekau, Mighty One of the Enchantments. I come before thee, Draco. I worship thee, Draco, Fire-breather from the Great Deep. You are my Lord and I am of thy blood.'

Then the chanting ceased, died with such abruptness that the silence was like some physical blow to my ears.

The tiny figure before me bowed to the image.

'The time is come when the world must be filled with that which it has not known, when you, great Draco, must come into the world and fill it with abundance. Take then this offering which we, the children of thy blood, give you freely – blood of our blood, life of our life!'

I could see, with sudden dread, a silver glitter in the right hand of the figure, the waning rays of the moon glinting on the blade of a knife.

Like a mouse before a cat, I stood still and trembled, with a dawning awareness of the ordeal to come.

The figure turned slowly towards me, arm raised once more towards the sky, wielding the knife that I knew was about to taste my blood.

I raised my eyes to the face of that figure . . .

My breath caught in my throat. Never have I seen such a serenely beautiful countenance. The pale, heart-shaped face, the wide-set, deep green eyes, surmounted by raven black locks which tumbled in profusion from the drapes that covered her figure. The red lips were parted slightly showing perfect white teeth.

The eyes peered into mine and, for a moment, were full of tenderness and sorrow. Tears welled from them and trickled down that perfect skin.

'Prepare . . .' the words were but a whisper scarcely heard. 'Prepare . . . for this is the way of Draco which is thorny and hard and we mere mortals must obey his will even though sorrow be our lot and despair our inheritance.'

The knife was beginning to descend.

I knew that it was all wrong. I tried to tell her. Tried to open my mouth.

I could feel the point of the knife biting into my flesh and I screamed . . .

I thought at first it was the wild beating of the drums. Then I became aware that the noise was a banging on my door.

I lay in my darkened bedroom wrapped in a twisted profusion of bed linen and blankets, sodden with sweat. My mouth was dry and I felt cold and sick.

'Mr Welsford! Mr Welsford! Can you hear me? Are you all right?'

It was the voice of Mrs Dobson, my landlady, accompanied by another resounding tattoo on my door.

There were other voices outside the door, some raised in annoyance.

Crying to them to wait a moment, I struggled from my bed into a dressing gown and went to open the door.

Mrs Dobson and two gentlemen, I believe they shared adjacent apartments to mine, stood outside wrapped in dressing gowns and bearing annoyed expressions on their faces.

'What is it, Mrs Dobson?' I murmured, my tongue rasping dryly in my throat.

Mrs Dobson was a large, raw-boned woman. She stood like a pugilist awaiting the bell, feet slightly apart, hands on hips, jaw stuck out aggressively.

'What is it?' she repeated, as if she had not heard me properly. 'Why, there have been cries and bangs coming from your room these past fifteen minutes. You have woken up two of my gentlemen,' she jerked her thumb at my two agitated neighbours.

'I say, old boy,' the voice was a near whine from a pimple-faced young man who, I believed, worked as a clerk in the City, 'can't a fellow rest and all that?'

'I'm ... I'm sorry,' I mumbled, wanting to return to my bed, 'I had a nightmare, a bad dream ... haven't slept too well lately. Sorry about the noise.'

Mrs Dobson pursed her lips.

'Well, I can't have it, Mr Welsford. This is a respectable house. My gentlemen must have their rest.'

'I'm truly sorry, Mrs Dobson,' was all I could say, repeating the phrase as if it were some magic charm against Mrs Dobson's wrath.

Muttering to themselves, Mrs Dobson's two gentlemen retired to their own rooms and I made to close my door.

'Are you all right?' Mrs Dobson was reluctant to go without a proper inquest into the matter.

'I'll be fine,' I reassured her. 'It was just a bad dream. A bad dream, that's all.'

The bad dream returned, however. It returned the next night and the night after. It was so vivid; each time I dreamed it the scene took on many new details but always, always ended at the same horrific point. That serene, beautiful face, the welling tears, the soft gaze of compassion, the steeling against something which is distasteful but which has to be done, haunted me in my waking hours. The face of that sweet girl grew more vivid and real to me than the face of any girl I had known.

Yet so fearful did I become of those dreams that I became too frightened to go to bed at night, preferring to pace my rooms, to read or write, catching up on my Foreign Office work until exhaustion overtook me and I fell asleep where I sat. Even so, exhaustion did not prevent the grotesque nightmare from returning. I even became afraid to fall asleep during the day lest the vision haunt me still.

My work began to suffer.

Lord Molesworth, thinking I was pressing myself too hard, warned me to ease up and suggested I take a long weekend's holiday. He did so even though he was being pressured by Lord Clarendon to conclude the arrangements for the trip to Romania which was now a mere few weeks away. Naturally, I protested that I would be fine and returned to the doctor I had consulted. Alas, he did little more than prescribe a stronger sleeping draught and headache powders. He even suggested that I dose myself nightly with tincture of opium or laudanum. Against this I protested most strongly and so the doctor dismissed me with a sigh.

In my desperation for sleep I sought out my friend Yorke and reminded him of his offer to help me if the doctor was unable to cure my insomnia.

'What shall I do, Yorke?' I cried in desperation. 'I simply cannot continue in this fashion. I shall kill myself with exhaustion if I do. I shall be in no condition to accompany Molesworth to Romania nor to complete the detailed study I am doing for him. That would mean that my career in the Foreign Office would be ended.'

Yorke sat in his red smoking jacket, puffing some obnoxious weed in his pipe. He stroked his aquiline nose with a lean forefinger, a trick he has when pondering a problem.

'I can suggest something which might be a solution and yet . . . yet I hesitate to do so because you are the son of the Reverend Mortimer Welsford.'

I frowned.

'What has my father to do with this?' I demanded.

'Your father, old chap, is an excellent minister of the Anglican faith and has more than once lectured against dealings in the occult.'

'What do you mean? What are you suggesting?'

'Well, when conventional medicines fail, I have been impressed by those people who are described as psychic-healers.'

I stared at Yorke in amazement. Yorke, as I have already explained, was interested in matters appertaining to the occult. He had even written a monograph on witch-craft which was strongly decried by my father, who had suggested that my friendship with my old university colleague should cease forthwith. But I knew Yorke to be a level-headed fellow and not given to fantasizing. He had a tremendous wealth of knowledge on occult matters and pursued his subject as a science. If he found the matter interesting, then it was his affair. As for myself, I never was greatly interested in religions one way or another.

I gave Yorke a wry smile.

'I confess, old man, I don't think an old lady waving a magic wand around my head will bring back my sleep.'

Yorke pursed his lips in annoyance.

'That isn't exactly what a psychic-healer does. I can tell you that I have seen people cured, yes, actually cured, of many ailments over which doctors have given up in despair. You've tried a doctor, so why not give this a try?'

I was sceptical and yet I was also desperate and in desperation men do many things which are not generally in their nature to do. Yorke pressed his advantage and, in a fit of weakness, I agreed to compromise and accompany him to a meeting which he called a séance. I would go merely in order to see what the business was all about. There would be no attempt at psychic-healing at the meeting but, if I found the meeting agreeable, Yorke would take me to a meeting where I could be healed.

I must confess that after I left Yorke I felt all kinds of a fool and was half inclined to send a message round to his rooms cancelling the arrangements that I had made for that night. But as the day wore on and I began to build up a fear of the coming night, I was seized with a desperate hope that Yorke might be offering me salvation . . . perhaps I could be helped. I wanted so desperately to sleep and yet my fear of the dark shadows of the night caused me to almost torture myself in my efforts to keep awake.

CHAPTER FIVE

The Hansom deposited us outside a terraced artisan's house in a winding street just south of Hampstead Heath. I believe the road was called Fleet Road, although I am not too sure. There was really nothing remarkable about the street or the house and I have only a vague recollection of the name because Yorke told me that the River Fleet, which rises on the Heath, ran through the sewerways under the road on its underground journey through London down to the Thames.

The paint-peeling door was opened to Yorke's imperious knockings by a homely looking woman who was as unremarkable as the house. She welcomed us in the flat accents which I always associate with south-eastern England and said that 'Madam' was in the front-room. She quickly corrected 'front-room' to 'sitting-room' and took our outdoor coats and hats from us, then bade us follow her.

A door leading into a small, overcrowded room was opened. Most of the room appeared to be shrouded in gloom, a lamp spluttered dimly from the centre of a green baize-covered table. In its glow were ringed six expectant faces, while the figure of a large, and very stout, woman stood in the shadows of one corner. The homely woman who had answered the door to us motioned us into vacant chairs.

'Is that the lot, dearie?' came a shrill Cockney voice.

For a moment I could not place it and then realized that it was the stout woman in the shadows who had asked the question.

The homely woman almost curtseyed.

'Yes, mum . . . er, Madam Bing. That's the lot.'

'Roight ow, luv. We can begin.'

I cast a quizzical look at Yorke, but he had lowered his eyes to the green baize table top. A quick look at the circle showed the rest of the participants had done the same. The homely woman had taken a seat by the door; she was seated slightly forward on the chair's edge with arms folded across her bosom. The stout woman, who had not yet stepped forward into the circle of light, shifted her position slightly.

'Now' (it was almost 'naw') 'fer those wot aint bin before, me nyme's Madam Bing. I fink ternoight will be a good 'un if we get sympathetic (this came out as "symper-fetic") vibrations. But don't hexpect miracles, dearies . . . I don't produce hectoplasm or do hany of that stuff.'

She was interrupted by a loud stage whisper from the homely woman.

'Madam means an emanation of bodily appearance.'

It sounded as if she had learnt some lesson by heart.

'Quite so, dearie,' breathed the stout woman heavily. 'Quite so. I don't go in fer hactual physical manifestation . . .' She laboured the words and I could almost see her shoot a look of triumph at the homely woman, 'not hactual physical manifestation,' she savoured the words again, 'but we gets messages from the hother side none the less.'

There was a pause.

Someone coughed.

'Roight. Let's begin.'

'Er . . . what shall we do, madam?'

It was a small, slightly balding man sitting to the left of me who ventured the question.

'Do, dearie?'

Madam Bing's voice was slightly querulous.

'Some mediums request we sing,' explained the balding man apologetically.

'Not in my séances, you don't!' snapped Madam Bing. 'Now!' She clapped her hands loudly so that several at the table jumped. 'Just sit still, think of yer departed loved ones who 'ave crossed hover . . . concentrate . . . concentrate . . .'

She started to walk around the circle at the table, humming softly to herself.

After a while she stopped, opened a book, and began to read from it under her breath. It sounded like a volume of psalms.

'Is there anyone here whose name begins with J?'

The question came abruptly.

There was a brief pause then the balding man nodded eagerly.

'Me. My name begins with J.'

I fancied I heard a sigh of relief.

'J,' continued Madam Bing in strident tones. 'J, is the name John?'

The balding man shook his head.

'It's Jo . . .'

Madam Bing gave a shriek which cut out the last syllable.

'I 'ave it. Joe! Joseph, that's it, ain't it?'

'No, Madam. It's Jodocus.'

'Well, yer family call you Jo, don't they?' demanded her querulous voice.

'I wish they did,' confessed the balding man. 'It's always been Jodocus.'

There came an annoyed exhalation of breath.

'Ah, I'm losing contact . . . losing contact . . . Wait. Is there anyone here whose name begins with the letter A?'

A woman who had just been wiping her nose with a handkerchief on which the name 'Nancy' was prominently emblazoned, nodded slowly.

Madam Bing moved to the side of the table facing the woman, a pale-faced creature of middle age who looked like a nursery governess.

'The letter A that I am getting is fer a first name,' went on Madam Bing.

The pale-faced creature nodded miserably.

I could almost feel Madam Bing smile.

'Yes, yes. A first name . . . your name . . . it is Amalia, no . . . Adela . . . no, no . . . it's coming clearly now . . . Agnes. That's it. Your name is Agnes, isn't it?'

The pale-faced creature grimaced.

'That's it,' she admitted in a whisper.

A tiny gasp of amazement went round the table.

'Yer don't loike ter be called Agnes, do yer, dearie?' demanded Madam Bing. 'There's a spirit 'ere, a spirit hentity wot tells me yer don't loike ter be called Agnes.'

The woman shook her head again.

'Yer prefer ter be called Nancy, don't yer? That's wot this 'ere spirit tells me.'

'Please,' a look of hope came into the woman's eyes. 'Please, is it my mother – she passed over three years ago. Is it her?'

'That's roight, dearie. It's yer mum,' consoled Madam Bing. 'She says she's very 'appy where she is and don't worry. It's a lovely life on the other side and she's far 'appier than when she was in this life, no disrespect intended to yer.'

The pale creature gave a gulp, which was suspiciously like a sob.

'Dear mother,' she whispered. 'Can you ask her . . .'

'Contact is gone,' thundered Madam Bing. 'Alas, our time is short. Now then, now then . . . is there somebody here . . .'

I shook my head incredulously and tried to catch Yorke's eye.

I wondered how far such people could be taken in by such an old charlatan. Nancy is, of course, a diminutive of Ann or Agnes and it was easy to see how Madam Bing worked up to her revelation. I did not know whether to be amused or annoyed by the whole thing. What perturbed me was that Yorke was apparently taken in by a pack of rogues. And these were the very people he suggested might cure my insomnia.

Madam Bing was rambling on.

She had just assured one earnest-looking youth that she had a message for him from his great grandfather who was 'in spirit'; that his great grandfather was happy in the other world, was leading a life full of greater happiness and fulfilment than life in this world and that his offspring must not worry . . . everything would come right and be resolved as it should. Each message seemed to me to be basically the same. The deceased were happier in the other world than they had been in this one and those they had left behind should not worry. I fell to wondering whether the messages had some central design and origin in our collective subconscious to allay man's primordial fear of death.

I was wondering how much longer I would have to put up with this nonsense when Madam Bing suddenly started and gave a little scream.

I do not know whether it was a stage-effect managed by the homely woman who was still sitting on her seat by the door, but suddenly a window blew open and extinguished the flickering lamp. There were several exclamations but the voice of Madam Bing called us to silence from the darkness.

'I . . . I am in contact . . . in contact . . .' her voice was strangely contorted, and I silently congratulated her on her performance.

'There is one among us who is sceptical . . . and yet he is the most vulnerable of us all. He must seek protection of the inner circle or doom will be his lot, evil his inheritance.'

Her voice was rather uncanny in the darkness and seemed to have lost its earthy, Cockney roughness.

'Who is it, Madam?' came the stage whisper of the homely woman.

'*He* knows that I mean *him*. His ancestors were born where the well stands beside the ford of a river.'

A peculiar sensation overcame me. I felt a sudden chill in the room and shuddered violently. I had told no one my name and, although Madam Bing did not mention it as Welsford, yet surely she had given an accurate derivation of that name?

As if in answer to my thoughts, Madam Bing continued with a triumphant ring to her voice.

'Yes . . . you know, do you not? You know that I am talking to you . . . I have a message for you, a message . . . it is difficult . . . there are others . . . other spirits trying to prevent it coming through . . . trying to prevent it . . . no, it is coming now, it is strong.'

I sat rooted.

'You are soon to cross the water . . . do not do so. Beware of the land beyond the forest. Beware of the land of mountains.'

I frowned in bewilderment.

'Beware of *the land beyond the forest!*'

Madame Bing's voice rose to a cry of desperation.

Abruptly there came a thud of something falling. One of the women in the circle screamed.

There was a fumbling and somebody struck a match, I think it was Yorke, and soon the lamp was relit.

Madam Bing lay crumpled in a corner of the room.

The homely woman sprang across the room with a cry of horror.

Yorke was there before her and bent over the prostrate woman, checked her respiration and thumbed back her eyelids.

'I should go and make a cup of tea, madam,' he suggested gently to the homely woman who stood with fluttering hands. 'Madam Bing has merely fainted, that is all.'

'Goodness me, it's never happened before,' mumbled the woman as she disappeared, presumably in the direction of the kitchen.

There was a groan from the inert figure on the floor. Yorke helped the stout woman into a sitting position.

It was the first time I had seen her features in the light of the lamp, which Yorke had turned up. She was a large, moon-faced woman with lustreless eyes and a big, slack mouth.

''Ere,' she demanded petulantly, ''ere wot's going on?'

'You passed out, Madam Bing,' replied Yorke in tones of gentle reassurance.

She stared at him blankly.

'I did?'

'You did,' affirmed Yorke, accompanied by a chorus of agreement from the rest of the circle.

'Strewth!' exclaimed Madam Bing softly, sitting upright and adjusting her hat, which had been knocked askew.

Yorke turned to the rest of the company.

'I suggest we leave Madam Bing to recover . . .'

There was a murmur of general assent and, with the exception of Yorke and me, the rest of the company moved hesitantly towards the door, dropping florins into a cardboard shoebox that stood on a small table near the door. As the last of them left, the homely woman re-entered with a pot of tea on a tray.

'Crikey, luv,' said Madam Bing, 'I don't 'alf need that.'

'Where have the others gone?' asked the homely woman.

'I sent them away,' explained Yorke. 'I thought Madam Bing needed some peace and quiet to recover by.'

'Too true, dearie. Don't I just?'

The moon-faced woman was already tucking into a piece of fruit cake and throwing back her second cup of tea.

The homely woman had immediately gone to the shoe-box and counted the florins, then gave a piercing glance towards Yorke and myself. With a blush of embarrassment, I hastily took out a florin and placed it in her box, which a moment later was added to by Yorke.

At this the homely woman smiled and nodded.

Yorke turned back to Madam Bing.

'Are you all right now?'

It was a superfluous question for the woman was on her third slice of fruit cake.

'Bit exhausted, dearie. Bit exhausted. Never passed out before.'

'Madam Bing, what did you mean by "the land beyond the forest"?' I suddenly blurted out.

The moon-faced woman looked at me vacantly.

'Wot, dearie?'

'You told me to beware of the land beyond the forest. What did you mean?'

The woman shook her head ponderously.

'Not me, dearie, not me. Wot the spirits say I only repeats, don't I? I don't know wot they're on about, do I?'

'Madam is merely a medium, Mr ... er ...?' the homely woman looked curiously at me.

Yorke cleared his throat.

'Well, old chap, we must be going.'

The homely woman shepherded us out into the hallway and gave us our hats and coats.

'Thanks for coming, ever so lovely to see you.'

Her meaningless words followed us down the street.

We walked in silence for a while before I turned to Yorke.

'Well?' I demanded.

He looked at me and raised an eyebrow but said nothing.

'Hang it all, Yorke,' I insisted, 'the woman was off her head . . . a charlatan . . . even I could see how she did it.'

'Could you?' Yorke let a smile pass across his face.

We walked across South End Green to the South Hampstead railway station.

'Even a child could see that,' I said, exasperated by his mysterious attitude.

'And tell me, my child,' he said with a sardonic note in his voice, 'could you see how she contrived to blow out the lamp, know your name and give you a warning not to go abroad, which I know you are planning to do?'

I bit my lip.

'She must have found out from somewhere,' I said lamely. 'You're surely not trying to suggest that she was genuine?'

'Welsford, old man, I've been studying this sort of thing for quite a while. Now it is perfectly true, as you have observed, that the major part of Madam Bing's séance is merely a performance. She does her "messages" as a conscious act and you have seen some of the tricks she uses. But now and again, in spite of herself, something seems to come over her, seems to take control of her and a genuine occult experience occurs. She is definitely what is called psychic but she does not give herself a chance to develop her powers . . . she prefers the easy way.'

I gaped at him in disbelief.

'You're trying to say that the old charlatan has moments of genuine psychic manifestation in spite of herself?'

He nodded.

'That's about the size of it, old fellow. I've been trying to get to all her séances to catch any patterns that may occur. It's for a monograph I'm writing on unwilling or unknowing mediums,' he added.

'Well,' I said hotly, 'if she is an example of your so-called psychic-healers, I am not impressed.'

It was then I realized that I had not once thought about my frightful headaches or terrifying nightmares, the very reason I had been persuaded to go to Madam Bing's performance.

Yorke grinned.

'I didn't mean you to be impressed, old fellow. I just wanted you to see the sort of thing that happens at a séance.'

Just then the train came in and we climbed aboard. It was fairly late in the evening and there were few people on the train as it trundled towards Gospel Oak and swung southwards to Kentish Town.

I had sat in silence for some minutes.

'Well, having seen a séance, and even received a message, do you want to come with me to a more genuine meeting?' asked Yorke.

'Of course not,' I retorted. 'I have never seen so much chicanery in all my life.'

Yorke shook his head sadly.

'You're rather a narrow fellow, I declare,' he said, musingly. 'But never mind. I'll not press you at this moment.'

I retreated into silence.

Somehow I felt affronted that he – a doctor of philosophy from St. John's College, Oxford – should suggest that such a person as Madam Bing, or some confederate of hers, could possibly cure me of insomnia when a fully qualified doctor of medicine had failed. What I had seen was pure skulduggery . . . except, except I puzzled over Madam Bing's revelation. It even crossed my mind that Yorke might have fed her the information, but I dismissed the thought almost at once. Yorke was not that sort of fellow.

When we reached our destination, I bade a rather stiff farewell to Yorke and hailed a hansom.

As I climbed in, slamming the door behind me, Yorke's voice caused me to peer down at him from the window.

He was staring up at me with a look of concern on his face.

'I say, Welsford . . . do not take that warning too lightly, will you? Beware of the land beyond the forest!'

Then he disappeared among the crowds mingling in front of the railway terminus.

Confused, I ordered the cabman to drop me before my rooms at Charing Cross.

CHAPTER SIX

The nightmares continued without respite. They always centred around the jade statuette and, in my spare moments, I sat in my rooms holding the damnable thing in my hands, peering at it curiously this way and that in a futile attempt to fathom the secret of its connection with my dreams. Finally, I resolved to take it to an acquaintance of mine, Professor Masterton, who was an expert in ancient oriental art at the British Museum. Perhaps he would be able to tell me something more about the little dragon which, in my nightmares, I had heard called Draco.

Masterton seemed pleased to see me when I called on him before lunch the next day. I told him the story of my purchase of the statuette from the former sailor who had bought it in Kowloon but I left out all mention of my strange nightmares and its connection with them. I told him that I merely wanted the statuette dated, if that were possible, and would appreciate any other information he could give me of its origins.

Masterton turned the statuette over several times in his big, bony hands and then asked me if I would mind returning after lunch.

When I returned to the museum two hours later I was immediately shown into Masterton's *sanctum sanctorum*. He jumped up as I entered and was clearly excited. Seizing me by the hand, he dragged me to his desk and pointed dramatically at the grinning dragon.

'So you think it is Chinese, eh?'

His voice trembled with excitement.

'Well,' he went on, barely giving me time to give my opinion, 'well let me tell you that you are mistaken . . . totally mistaken.'

I looked at him in puzzlement.

He nodded in violent affirmation of his conclusion.

'I have had two colleagues examine it in order to confirm my observations.'

'What is it then?' I asked.

'My dear boy, my dear boy . . .' the words seemed to fail him. He paused, steadied himself and walked to a cabinet.

'A sherry? A port?' he asked, pouring a rather liberal glass of port for himself and a more modest sherry, on my instructions, for myself.

'You are clearly excited by something, professor,' I said, in order to prompt him.

'Excited? The statuette you have brought me is Egyptian.'

'Egyptian?'

'Indeed, my boy. Egyptian, dating back to the Thirteenth Dynasty.'

I held up my hand in protest.

'Professor, I am not at all conversant with ancient history. Can you tell me what it means – the Thirteenth Dynasty?'

He gestured to me to sit down.

'What you have here, my dear Welsford, is an ancient Egyptian statuette dating back to the reign of Queen Sebek-nefer-Ra of the Thirteenth Egyptian Dynasty which is, roughly, about three thousand years before the birth of Christ.'

I was astounded.

'You mean to tell me that this little piece of jade is nearly five thousand years old?'

'I do,' he said emphatically. 'Furthermore, I can even tell you what the statuette represents – it is a likeness of the Egyptian god Draco – the Fire Snake or dragon.'

I felt the blood turn to ice in my veins.

Draco! I could hear the words of the priestess, for such

she must be, echoing through my troubled sleep. 'I come before thee, Draco. I worship thee, Draco, Fire-breather from the Great Deep. You are my Lord and I am of thy blood.' Yet how could I possibly have known that the statuette was of the god Draco? I had surely never heard the name before, apart from in my dreams; I had believed the jade to be a Chinese carving until Masterton had informed me otherwise. How, then, could my subconscious relate that fact into my troubled sleep?

Professor Masterton leaned forward and peered at me anxiously.

'Are you all right, Welsford? Are you feeling faint?'

I made a negative gesture.

'It . . . it is just a surprise to learn my statuette is so ancient.'

'Indeed, indeed,' Masterton picked up the green-black jade and caressed it lovingly. 'It is of beautiful workmanship. Beautiful.'

'Tell me something about Draco,' I urged him. 'I really know nothing about ancient Egypt.'

I had no need to ask Masterton twice. He reached for a pipe and, having lit it, he sprawled in his leather padded chair, his eyes taking on a faraway expression as he summoned up his store of knowledge.

'Thousands of years before the birth of Christ, a religion – or perhaps we'd best describe it as a primitive science – flowered in ancient Egypt. This religion became known as the Cult of Draco; the cult of the Fire Snake or dragon. The cult was the first systemized form of the primitive mysteries and natural sciences of Africa and the Egyptians elaborated it into a highly specialized system of occultism which spread across the world and flourished in the tantras of India, in Mongolia, in Tibet and in China.

'The cult was evolved from the concentration of knowledge of carefully observed physical phenomena extending over enormous cycles of time. The knowledge gained was based upon intercourse with manifestations of the occult and spirits said to be seen clairvoyantly.

'Life after death was observed as a natural fact; the Draconians believed it was not only possible to free the spirit for the next world but to free the body as well – in other words to make the earthly body immortal. They called such a freed body *ka* or *sekhem*. The body retained all the characteristics of the original mortal being; it was, in fact, the normal earthly body of the man or woman. The Draconians studied ways of releasing the *ka* in this world – of gaining immortality for themselves and there are references to what are claimed to be successful experiments in which the Draconians created living men and women whom they called the Undead.'

I shuddered.

'It sounds horrible.'

The professor, interrupted in his academic discourse, shot me a look of disapproval.

'No more so than other primitive religions,' he observed. 'Man struggles towards knowledge by his fear of ignorance, but sometimes his fear causes him to act as the animal he undoubtedly is.'

Two years previously, in 1859, a scientist named Charles Darwin had published a very contentious book called *The Origin of Species* which claimed that man was, in reality, a species of animal descended from the apes and not created by God at all. The argument still rages furiously and while I keep an open mind on such matters, I knew that Professor Masterton was a keen supporter of the Darwinian theory, as it is now called.

'Where was I? Ah yes, the cult of Draco flourished for many centuries, becoming exceedingly prominent in the Sixth Dynasty. But it was a rather controversial cult which, so I believe, relied on great blood sacrifices. During the Eleventh Dynasty the ordinary people of

Egypt were turning to the worship of more liberal gods, solar worship, which was perhaps more beneficial to them, gods such as Osiris and Ammon. Under the leadership of the priests of the new liberal religion, the people rose up and drove out the followers of Draco.'

He paused and relit his pipe.

'And was that the end of the Draconian cult?'

Masterton shook his head.

'Queen Sebek-nefer-Ra commenced her reign in the Thirteenth Dynasty, nearly three thousand years before the birth of Christ. She suppressed the worship of Osiris and Ammon and made a blood bath of their followers. She brought back Draco as the official state religion. She was an initiate of the inner circle of the most profound mysteries of the cult and was known to her followers as the Great Mother. During her reign the cult obtained its maximum power, spreading through the known world and especially into Asia. It was during her reign that the priests of the Draco cult were accused of creating Undead monsters in their efforts to prolong life.

'From the Seventeenth Dynasty, about 2410 BC, the temporal power of the cult went into a decline and was finally extinguished when the Pharaoh Apophis, the last of the Typhonian rulers of the city of Avaris, was overthrown.

'From that time on the cult was vigorously persecuted and suppressed by the Osirians, who accused its priests of bestial practices, of blasphemies and so forth. All the scientific knowledge gained by the Draconians was lost to mankind, which now returned to the more primitive worship of the sun!'

I frowned.

'You sound as if you are disappointed that the Draconian Cult was overthrown, professor?'

Professor Masterton pursed his lips.

'I am a scientist, my boy. I disapprove of the loss of

any scientific knowledge. Perhaps mankind would have been better off with the wealth of knowledge of natural science gathered by the Draconians, rather than expending its efforts in propitiating primitive fears by doing homage to a ball of gaseous fire in the sky.'

'And are you sure that my statuette dates back to . . .?'

I paused because I had lost my way through the maze of his historical lecture.

'It dates back to the Thirteenth Dynasty; to Queen Sebek-nefer-Ra when the Draconian Cult flourished.'

He took up the statuette from the table with one hand and took a magnifying glass in the other.

'I take it that you have not observed the base of the statuette too closely?'

I confessed that I had not.

'Take a look, then.'

I took the statuette and the magnifying glass from him and peered at the base. There were some mysterious symbols on it from which I could make out no sense at all.

'What does it mean?'

'Hieroglyphics, my dear boy,' murmured the professor. 'Thanks to the works of Thomas Young of England and Champollion of France, we can now translate that ancient Egyptian writing.'

'And?' I asked, not liking mysteries.

'One of the symbols, that within the oval, is the royal seal of Sebek-nefer-Ra; the other is a short inscription which I would translate as "all power is found in Draco".'

Fascinating and perplexing as the professor's explanations were, it did not really solve the problem of my nightmares but merely added mystery to them. The solution to the frightening nightmares and sleeplessness was certainly not to be found in the dry tomes of the British Museum.

I picked up the statuette and placed it into my case

while profusely thanking Professor Masterton for his help.

'Wait!' he cried, 'I have discussed the matter with my colleagues and we are prepared, that is, the Museum is prepared to purchase the statuette from you for the Department of Antiquities – we will meet any reasonable sum you ask for.'

Even the old scholar could not hide the touch of envious greed that flitted in his eyes as they dropped on the case wherein I had placed the carved animal.

I smiled.

'It's not for sale, professor. I did not want to give you that impression.'

His face twitched.

'It is a rare piece . . . we have few monuments that go back to that particular period.'

I shook my head.

'Consider an offer, my boy,' he pressed agitatedly. 'At least consider an offer.'

'Professor, you have been a great help to me and I am most truly grateful. The statuette is not for sale – at least, not at this time. But I will make this assurance – should I ever want to sell it, you shall have first offer.'

I shook the hand of a disappointed and frustrated man and turned out of the museum with his voice still ringing in my ears: '. . . any reasonable sum, mind you. We will meet any reasonable sum.'

I returned to my rooms to ponder on my perplexity.

Would to God I had accepted the professor's offer there and then.

CHAPTER SEVEN

Having spent another exhausting, sleepless night, I arrived in my office about ten o'clock and tried to struggle through a pile of newspaper cuttings on Romanian industrial development as visualized by some French correspondent. I had not been at my task long when Lord Molesworth entered with a rather self-satisfied look on his face. Behind him strode a short, stocky man with distinctly foreign features – high cheekbones, a broad Slavic face and hair the colour of jet.

'This is my personal secretary, Mr Upton Welsford,' he began as I struggled to my feet.

The stocky gentleman bowed stiffly from the waist.

'Welsford, I want you to meet Mr Ion Ghica. We are, indeed, fortunate in finding this gentleman who is spending a few days in our country. Mister Ghica is from Bucharest, in Romania.'

I murmured the customary formula of greeting.

Molesworth waved us all into his suite and ushered us before the fire and, as if by magic, Molesworth's servant appeared with a tray of drinks.

Ion Ghica proved to be a very talkative gentleman, especially where his own country was concerned. He was widely travelled. He had been educated at the Sorbonne and then taken ship to America where he had spent five years and where he had learnt to speak a peculiar form of English. He was more invaluable than a guide book. From him we learned much of the country to which we were to journey in the New Year. It turned out that Ghica was a prospective member of the Romanian National Assembly and sailed under the political colours of a 'progressive'. He had much to say on the need for the Romanian parliament to make its first task the emancipation of the peasants and the granting to them of smallholdings, which they could use upon some payment to the former feudal landowners as compensation. Serfdom was still prevalent in the Romanian principalities, although in some areas there lived groups of peasants who were free and called *mosneni*.

He was a veritable encyclopaedia of information and dispensed it in an entertaining manner. We gathered that Romania was unique, lying in the heartland of Slavonic Europe but totally different from other Slavic countries. The Romans had bequeathed the Latin language to Romania which had been the most remote easterly outpost of the great Roman Empire. The Romans, in so far as one could judge from Ion Ghica, seemed to have bequeathed much more than language to the Romanians. Not only the close Latin similarities of their language and culture could be heard, but the affinity of character, the sparkle and even the physical appearances can be discerned so that there seemed little difference between a Romanian and an Italian from the plains of Lombardy or the Tuscan mountains.

But Ion Ghica also presented a picture of a tragic country.

Throughout the centuries his country had been overrun by the Celts, the Romans, the Goths, Huns, Avars, Slavs and Persians, all of whom had fought across its mountainous countryside. Charlemagne and his Franks had tried to conquer and failed; Khan Krúm and his Bulgars did not succeed either, nor did Arpad and the seven tribes of Hungary. Magyars, Vlachs, Vzes and Kumars also swept in their war bands over the unhappy land.

Ghica seemed rather proud of that bloody history.

And, no sooner had all these nations gone into the melting pot to create the Romanian people, than the Turks were moving in force across the Danube, incorporating Moldavia and Wallachia into their Ottoman Empire while Transylvania fell to the Austrians.

Ghica assured us that now the people of all three principalities wanted to unite into a common Romanian state. They wanted no more Turkish overlordship nor Austrian overlordship.

'And one day, one day soon,' he said in his accented English, 'I tell you, my friends, that it will be so. The people of the land beyond the forest shall unite with us in Moldavia and Wallachia.'

I was so startled that I dropped my sherry glass on the floor.

With a mumbled apology I bent to pick it up, confused thoughts tumbling through my mind.

'What did you mean, Mr Ghica?' I asked after I had deposited the fragments of my glass in a tray. 'What did you mean just now by the phrase – the land beyond the forest?'

He frowned.

'Mean?'

'Yes. What is the land beyond the forest?'

'Oh,' he smiled. 'It is – how do you call it now – a translation of the name Transylvania.'

It was with a feeling of growing unease and apprehension that I bade the stocky Romanian farewell as Lord Molesworth ushered him off to luncheon at his club while I returned to my paperwork. Try as I would, I could not concentrate. My head pounded with voices.

The squeaky tones of Madam Bing:

'Beware, beware of the land beyond the forest!'

The heavily accented tones of Ion Ghica:

'The land beyond the forest is a translation of Transylvania!'

The voices echoed in my brain with an ebb and flow like the sound of waves cascading over the rocky seashore.

At last I threw down my pen in disgust and began to pace my office wondering what it all meant. I rationalized that the whole thing must be some preposterous coincidence.

I realized that I had become so agitated that I had not noticed the passing of time. It was already six o'clock and the winter's night was heavy and black. I drew on my coat and muffler and made my way into the great thoroughfare of Whitehall where I hailed a cab to take me to the tavern in the Strand where I usually took my evening meal.

Sunk in gloomy thoughts, I hunched back in the cab as the driver sent his horses trotting along Whitehall and through the great square which is dedicated to Lord Nelson's famous victory at Cape Trafalgar. We were passing into the Strand when we happened to halt sharply. I was jolted from my reverie and, from my seat, saw that a large hackney carriage had turned in front of us, momentarily blocking the road and we would have plunged into it had it not been for the sharp reaction of my driver. The drivers exchanged courtesies which are impossible to set down in this record.

While the exchange was taking place my eye was caught by the comely figure of a woman walking rapidly along the pavement near the cab. Although she walked rapidly, I detected some nervousness and indecision in her manner. Once she halted and turned, looking back the way she had come, and then hastened on again. My cab had stopped by a lamp which threw a pale yellow light through the evening mist across the pavement.

The woman walked into the circle of light.

My mind registered that she was wearing a blue costume of some light texture and carrying a matching parasol. A large blue hat of a darker hue hid her head entirely. But I saw that her figure was young, graceful, and mentally argued that she could not be more than twenty.

Then, as she stood under the lamp, she suddenly threw back her head and paused, as if to listen.

My heart beat a wild tattoo and leapt to my throat.

I knew her face well. It was the face of the girl in my grim nightmares. The pale-faced girl with the compassionate gaze, the same whose upraised knife plunged into my breast.

Before I could recover my wits the girl had hurried by.

By the time my paralysis had vanished my cab was moving off at a quick trot.

Standing up, so that I nearly toppled out of the cab, I hammered on the communication hatch and cried to the cabby to halt a minute. He had scarcely done so when I leapt from the vehicle and ran back towards the lamp standard under which she had stood. There was no sign of her. I paused and listened. The mist swirled thick, yellow and cold in the night air. No tell-tale footsteps echoed out of the gloom. I hurried forward a few paces but almost at once I realized the hopelessness of spotting the young woman.

Stunned, I retraced my footsteps.

The cabby seemed rather relieved to see me, perhaps believing that I was merely trying to avoid payment.

At the tavern I ate my meal automatically, neither seeing nor tasting the food that I shovelled into my mouth.

My mind was in a complete whirl. Firstly, I had discovered that there was such a place called 'the land beyond the forest' and that I was shortly to go on a journey there when a medium had warned me against going to that place even before I realized its existence. Secondly, I had been told that a creature, Draco, not only had an existence in my nightmares but in ancient history and that I possessed a statuette of that creature. Thirdly, that a girl whom I thought I had dreamt up in some exotic fantasy had an existence in reality.

What madness was this that was seizing my mind?

I awoke from a semi-doze about seven o'clock next morning and, feeling in the worst physical condition that I had ever felt, I plunged my head under the cold water tap in order to shake myself into some sort of semblance of wakefulness. I had come to the end of my tether; there was nothing I could do, no one I could turn to. Night had become a period of terror for me and yet, in daytime as well, my whole being was seized by the most acute anxiety which caused my heart to race erratically and my limbs to take on a life of their own.

In my despair I sat down on my bed and wept. Yes, a grown man ... I wept helplessly, not knowing what next to do.

It still lacked half an hour to eight o'clock when I finally drew myself together, washed for a second time, dressed and went out into the crisp winter morning. I did not know where I was going; I let my feet take me eastwards into the Strand and then north towards Bloomsbury.

Yorke opened the door to my knocking, sleep still causing his eyes to squint in the morning light as he tried to fasten a dressing-gown about his lean frame.

'Good Lord! Welsford! But it's only . . .'

He gave me a searching look and then silently stood aside as I brushed by him into the hallway of his tiny apartment. He closed the door, yawning away his sleep (blessed sleep!) and turned to regard me with a frown.

'You look pretty tuckered out, old boy.'

I slumped into a chair by the smouldering embers of the previous evening's fire.

'I am desperate, Yorke,' I said simply. 'I cannot go on much longer. The dreams ... the nightmares ... they continue. I cannot take it any more.'

Yorke must have detected the hysteria which edged my words.

'Let me put the kettle on for some tea,' he said and stirred up the embers in the hearth to a partial blaze on which he deposited fresh wood. It seemed only a few minutes before a black iron kettle was singing merrily on the hearth and a delicious hot, sweet liquid was scalding my throat.

'What do you want of me, Welsford?' asked Yorke after a while.

'I need help,' I said heavily. 'I'll try anything . . .'

Yorke put up a long forefinger and stroked the side of his nose reflectively.

'So you're prepared to try my suggestion – psychic-healing?'

'Anything !' I said abruptly.

'Even though you don't believe in clairvoyance? In mediums?'

'I'm desperate, Yorke,' I repeated. 'I'll tell you straight that I don't believe in all that mumbo-jumbo but I am prepared to accept that you believe that there are people who might be able to help me. People who can, perhaps, harness natural forces in some way which can be of help to me. I do not believe in miracles . . . but I believe the basis of a miracle lies in natural causes which we have yet to understand; that a person might be cured simply by the strength of his mind believing in the cure.'

Yorke smiled, perhaps a trifle cynically.

'You think you'll believe in a cure?'

'I'll try anything,' I affirmed.

'I can't say I applaud your motive or your views but I appreciate your desperation. I am, as you know, an occult-ist, a scientific observer of natural forces which have become suppressed or distorted as our civilization gets more preten-tiously sophisticated. But I believe there might be a chance you may be helped by the method I have suggested.'

'Then you'll take me to a proper medium?' I asked eagerly.

'Tonight there is a séance in the East End. Professor De Paolo is the medium. Not only is he an excellent fellow as a medium but he is one of the foremost psychic-healers.'

I held out my cup for Yorke to refill it with his delicious brew.

'What time is the séance?' I asked.

'Not until six o'clock.'

I bit my lip.

'Would you mind terribly if I stayed here for the rest of the day?' I asked. 'I associate my rooms so closely with the nightmares that I feel uneasy about going back to them. I am sure to fall asleep and every time I do . . .'

'Of course you can stay here,' Yorke assured me. 'I have some work to do at the British Museum but I shall return about one o'clock for lunch. Treat the place as your home, there are plenty of books to read.' He indicated his well-stocked bookshelves.

Yorke cooked a delicious breakfast of crisp bacon and eggs which reminded me of our carefree days at Oxford when we shared the same rooms and ate many such breakfasts together. After he had gone, I walked about his rooms, my eyelids heavy and drooping, but trying to prevent myself from falling into that dread sleep. I picked a book from the shelf – I can even remember its title and author. It was a new book, a mystery novel by a writer called Wilkie Collins entitled *The Woman in White*. I tried to concentrate on it, sitting in the chair by the roaring, open fire. My eyelids kept drooping, however, and I experienced a kind of resigned despair as I knew I could not force myself to keep awake any longer. The next thing I knew was that someone was shaking me by the shoulder.

I started up.

Yorke was grinning at me.

'It's nearly four-thirty,' he said.

I gaped at him in astonishment and looked at the ornate, wooden cased clock ticking away on the mantelshelf. It confirmed his statement.

I suddenly realized that I had slept and felt refreshed.

'Jove, Yorke!' I cried, springing to my feet. 'I've been asleep . . . asleep and I haven't dreamed.'

Yorke nodded.

'I came in at one o'clock and found you snoring merrily before the fire. You were obviously so peaceful that I decided to leave you to sleep a while longer. How do you feel?'

I paused to consider.

'I've had the best sleep I've ever had. I feel really rested. The dream has gone . . . gone entirely.'

Yorke reflected: 'I must say you look a little better than you did first thing this morning, old chap.'

I felt exuberant.

'I really feel rested,' I said again.

'I've prepared some tea,' said Yorke, indicating a table on which was a magnificent spread of hot buttered scones, some cakes and a pot of tea. 'It's just a snack before we go to the séance, after which we can go out and have dinner.'

I frowned, my natural reticence returning now that my need was no longer desperate.

'Do you think it's necessary now, the séance I mean?' I asked. 'I really feel fine.'

Yorke was seated, drumming his fingers on the table top.

'You've had one sleep, granted. It's interesting, I admit, but it doesn't give us the cause of your nightmares. I think you ought to see De Paolo, now more than before.'

'Very well,' I agreed, more out of deference to the support he had given me than agreement with his views.

While I tucked into the food, feeling relaxed for the first time in days, Yorke merely picked at his, a faraway look in his eyes. Suddenly he banged the table with his fist, making all the crockery jump and rattle.

'I have it!' He banged his fist again. 'You have only suffered these nightmares while you have been sleeping in your own rooms, haven't you?'

I shrugged.

'You mean I have taken some allergy to my rooms at Mrs Dobson's place?'

'No; the nightmares only started the night, the very same night, that you bought the statuette. Isn't that so?'

I nodded agreement.

'And that statuette is a vivid part of your dreams?'

'Yes, but don't forget the girl – the girl I saw in the Strand last night.'

Yorke made a dismissive gesture with his hand.

'Yes, yes. What I am getting at is this. Today you slept well and hearty in these rooms of mine. Before you bought the statuette you used to sleep well in your own rooms, isn't that so? After you bought the statuette . . .'

He clicked his fingers.

Seeing my blank expression he sighed.

'You slept here but the statuette is not here, it is in your rooms. *And so*,' he emphasized, 'you slept well.'

I looked at his triumphant face and frowned.

'Don't you see, man,' he urged. 'The statuette is some sort of medium in itself – the statuette is emanating the nightmares which keep you awake!'

'Oh come now,' I said slowly, 'that's ridiculous. You've been reading those rather sordid stories by that American – what's his name – Poe. Edgar Allen Poe. The statuette is a medium!'

But Yorke's face was serious.

'You know me, Welsford. We've known each other for a long time. You came to me because you knew I was the only person who could help you, that my knowledge would help you where others – with conventional ways had failed. Believe me, the unknown always passes for the marvellous, the impossible, until someone explains and it becomes commonplace. We maintain our ignorance of the unknown, the world beyond our feeble realities, because this condition is the indispensable condition, the *sine qua non*, of our existence. Just as ice cannot know fire except by melting and vanishing, we cannot grasp that which is beyond our mortal boundaries except by the destruction of our mortality. But the reality of the unknown is a reality nevertheless.'

I smiled a little.

'Steady,' I urged. 'Pretty soon you will be quoting Shakespeare: "There are more things in heaven and earth, Horatio, than are dreamt of in your philosophy".'

Yorke took my sneer well.

'Perhaps you would do well to consider that, Welsford,' he said quietly.

We sat in silence for a little while.

'I'm sorry, Yorke, old man,' I said, regretting my cynicism. After all, he was doing his best to help me.

Yorke grimaced.

'I believe it is important that you come tonight – and bring the statuette with you. There is something strange happening to you, old man, and you need all the help you can get. Believe me.'

'All right, Yorke. I trust you. I'll come.'

Yorke smiled and extended his hand.

'I don't think you'll regret it in the long run,' he said.

It was something I shall regret all my life.

CHAPTER EIGHT

Having picked up the dragon statuette from my rooms, we hailed a hansom and Yorke gave an address off the Commercial Road, Whitechapel. The cabby shot us a curious glance, for few gentlemen are seen in that particular area of London. I must confess that I was more than a little excited by the adventure, even to the extent of momentarily forgetting the reason behind it. The East End of London is like venturing into another country which is dirty, squalid and over populated.

Whitechapel lies immediately contiguous to the old City and was once the centre of a thriving weaving industry at the turn of the nineteenth century which attracted many foreign workers to settle there. It is an area of narrow, disreputable lanes, lined on both sides with cheap lodging houses and dirty little shops filled with children by day and with brawling men and women by night.

Commercial Road, lying to the south of Whitechapel High Street, is a wide and well-kept thoroughfare. When the cabby halted at Yorke's instructions, the street was crowded with people. Paying off the cabby, Yorke took me by the arm and led me down a narrow intersecting side street which ran south towards the River Thames and the dock area.

Women and men, half drunk, mauled each other in vile caresses while others argued with such degrading blasphemies that I turned physically sick in my stomach at the sound. All were bold. Many of the women accosted us, pressing against us with thick painted lips, foul-smelling clothes, and stale alcohol perfuming their breath.

Grimly Yorke pressed through them all and I followed in his wake.

Loathsome vapours rose from the sewer-like gutters which spilled over the pavements, under doors, spreading a murky torrent of offal, animal and vegetable, in every state of putrefaction. The alley was undrained and reeked like nothing I had smelt before.

A thought struck me accusingly: England was the very heart of the world, extending her empire to every known corner of the globe, an empire on which the sun would never set – yet here, in the heart of England's very capital, was to be found such squalor, such poverty, such human suffering that I am sure would never be found elsewhere in the world. It seemed strange to me and very wrong.

Yorke paused before a tall tenement house which stood in darkness at the far end of the alley. It stood a little apart from the other houses, fronted by tall iron fencing in which was a gate. A bell chain hung outside, and this Yorke pulled twice. A light glanced from a window from which a blind had been swiftly drawn back. Then darkness again. But a moment later there came the sound of a bolt being withdrawn and an old woman opened the door and then unlocked the iron gate, standing aside to let us enter.

Yorke had obviously been to the place before because, without hesitation, he led the way through a small dingy hallway and up some creaking wooden stairs to a room on the first floor.

The room, which was a large one, was filled with people. During the meeting I actually counted twenty of them. They seemed a cross-section of people, mainly from the tradesmen classes. The room was lit by two lamps, one standing on each side of a slightly raised platform on which had been placed a comfortable chair. A silver-haired man, in a rough homespun suit which immediately labelled him as a countryman, looked round from this platform and then pulled out a large silver watch.

He sighed heavily.

'Right, ladies and gentlemen,' he said with a soft burr to his voice that I associated with people from the West Country. 'Take your seats, please.'

There was a scramble for seats and Yorke and I found ourselves sitting towards the back of the room with a clear view of the platform.

The silver-haired man in homespuns gazed down on us for a moment. I saw that all the faces in the room were upturned expectantly towards his. Most of them, I observed, were women, women worn with household cares, without legions of servants to pander to their needs.

'My friends,' began the man, 'my friends. Welcome. I would like to commence the evening by singing the hymn "O God, our help in ages past".'

There was a weird ring of exultation in the voices which took up the refrain led by the elderly master of ceremonies. I was surprised to see that Yorke, too, joined in with a lusty voice.

'And now, my friends, a short prayer – a short invocation to help us this night.'

I did not know whether to smile at these earnest but deluded people, or to feel a great pity for them. Did they really believe that they were able to communicate with the dead, defying the laws of science and religion?

'And now, my friends, I want to introduce our guest for the evening – a very famous clairvoyant from Italy who is renowned throughout Europe, Professor De Paolo.'

There was a murmur of appreciation as a curtain behind the platform was swept aside and a tall, dark-haired man emerged. He bore a striking resemblance to Benjamin Disraeli, the politician, whom I had encountered several times in my work at the Foreign Office. The nose was large, almost hooked, the hair thick, black and curly, the eyes kindly.

'*Buona sera* . . . good evening, ladies and gentlemen,' he spoke with a pronounced accent.

The gentleman in homespuns shook his hand, then turned back to the audience and held up a hand for silence.

'Professor De Paolo,' he began, pronouncing the name 'dee-pay-oh-lo', but was interrupted by the smiling professor who corrected it to 'di pow-*lo*'.

'Quite so,' said the gentleman hastily. 'The professor is one of our most successful mediums. He works by clairaudient . . . that is . . .'

The professor coughed loudly and pointedly.

'Er, yes. Quite so,' went on the gentleman. 'Quite so. We hope the professor will be able to commune tonight but, as you know, these events depend on laws beyond our control – a sympathetic atmosphere is most essential to good results. And now, the professor.'

The gentleman in homespuns sat down promptly.

The professor smiled down on us.

'Ladies and gentleman . . . you must do your best to get me the good vibrations, is it not so?'

He sounded so like a stage Italian that I almost laughed, for he seemed to put an extra vowel sound on the end of each word.

'Helpful vibrations, no?'

He stood swaying on the platform a moment, his eyes closed.

'It would help, perhaps, if you all sung a verse of a hymn.'

The audience roared forth another chorus of 'O God, our help in ages past . . .' by which time Professor De Paolo had opened his mouth and started a peculiar gabble. I looked at Yorke in amazement, thinking the man was quite mad. Yorke whispered: 'He's seeking vibrations, trying to get on to the spirit plane.'

Suddenly De Paolo straightened himself and looked towards the audience.

'I have a message . . . for you, *signora*.'

He pointed dramatically at a woman in the second row who smothered a little scream.

'A spirit is building up behind your seat . . .'

She half turned.

'Yes, yes . . . it is a man. A man, a short man, short and slightly stocky . . . a black moustache . . . do you recognize him?'

'Oh me gawd!' moaned the woman. 'It's me 'ubby . . . 'E . . . 'e passed over last year.'

'He has a message for you,' went on De Paolo. 'He says . . . says, do not worry. He is all right. He sends his love and blessings.'

'O me gawd!' exclaimed the woman.

Suddenly I felt De Paolo's eyes on me, then he glanced at Yorke.

'There is someone here who wishes to ask me something . . . yes, I feel definite vibrations . . . someone wants to ask me about something which is worrying them, causing them a lack of sleep. It is something about an animal . . . no, no, a statue of an animal.'

I turned to Yorke, my mouth opened in amazement.

Unperturbed, Yorke stood up and took from my hands the bag in which I had brought the statuette of Draco.

'Yes, sir,' he said. 'I would like to ask you about this.'

De Paolo looked at him and then back at me.

'Yet you are not the one who would seek to know the answer; you are not the one who is affected by this statuette?'

Yorke inclined his head.

'Yet I seek the information on behalf of a friend.'

'Very well. Bring it here. Take it from the bag and place it on the table.'

Yorke did as he was told, placing the green-black dragon on the small table on the platform.

'Now return to your seat.'

We watched as De Paolo went and stood before the statuette, gazing down at it as if deep in thought.

Suddenly he shuddered violently.

'*Dio mio! Cattivo* . . . evil . . . *malvagio!*'

He was standing facing us; the table on which the statuette stood was in front of him. He was standing looking at the dragon without touching it. I could see beads of sweat suddenly standing out on his brow and his face became a mass of twitching muscles.

'*Malvagio,*' he whispered again.

The man in homespuns put on a stage whisper: 'Try to keep in English, professor.'

De Paolo did not seem to hear.

'It is old, ancient almost beyond time,' he whispered, his eyes still on the statuette. 'It emanates great evil . . . such evil as I have never known before . . . it burns with evil. Get rid of it, get rid of it if you value your immortal soul . . .'

Suddenly he was looking up and his eyes were boring into mine.

Icy hands caught at my chest as I knew he was speaking directly to me.

'Get rid of it or you will never know peace in this life or that which is beyond. Be rid of it, my friend. Destroy it, throw it away. But be rid of it . . . above all beware of a journey . . . beware of the land beyond the forest. Does it mean anything to you? Beware of the land beyond the forest!'

His voice had the quality of hysteria to it.

The audience looked upon him in surprised satisfaction. Had they come for a show, they were certainly receiving their money's worth.

'What else can you tell us about it, sir?' cried Yorke.

'There is nothing else!' snapped the professor, starting back as if from the statuette.

'We must know,' insisted Yorke.

I reached up and tugged at his sleeve.

'No, Yorke. It is all right. We know enough.'

Yorke, an excited look in his eyes, shook his hand free.

'Professor, there must be something more.'

I looked at the professor and was puzzled by the sight of him pushing backwards with his body and yet, at the same time, reaching his hands, seemingly unwillingly, towards the jade dragon.

'No, no! *Non posso, non posso!*' he cried, yet all the while his hands seemed to be closing towards the object.

It was as if he were engaged in physical combat with some unseen force which was trying to make him pick up the statuette against his will.

Even as we looked his hands closed about the jade creature and he clasped it to his bosom with a sudden scream.

'Are you all right, professor?' asked the man in homespuns.

The professor stood, a tall quivering frame. Eyes closed, face twitching.

'*Bruciatore, bruciatore, bruciatore . . .*'

His voice became a solemn chant.

'What is burning, professor?' demanded Yorke, who knew some Italian.

The professor did not answer.

Abruptly his eyes opened.

I gasped, for they were no longer the kindly twinkling eyes of a few moments ago.

They were large, black and shone with a curious malignancy.

Even his face seemed to change, it seemed to elongate, become more pointed, the cheeks more pale, almost white, the eyebrows drew more closely across the bridge of the nose, the lips became redder and thinner and through their slightly parted smile, the teeth seemed oddly longer than a moment before and shone with a peculiar whiteness.

My heart pounded within me as those awful black orbs searched me out and held my gaze as if in a vice.

297

'You will come to me.' Even the voice was changed. It was harsher and contained a curious accent which was certainly not Italian.

The silver-haired gentleman raised an excited voice.

'A trance manifestation,' he chortled. 'A trance manifestation. I did not know the professor was able to . . .'

Realizing he was ruining the vibrations, he stopped.

I stirred uncomfortably, unable to release my eyes from the black night eyes which gazed into mine.

'You will come to me, do you hear me . . . come across the seas, over the mountains to my home beyond the forests. You will come to me, do you hear me? You will come to me,' the voice had a soft, almost soporific effect, slow, mesmerizing.

'I am the master, the master who will give you eternal life and blessings. You will come to me when I call you. You will come to me and bring the god Draco. You will come to me. Do you hear me? Do you hear now? I am the master . . . across the seas, over the mountains, to the land beyond the forests. I shall be waiting . . . soon . . . soon . . .'

Suddenly there was a great cry of pain, of soul-searing agony.

The professor threw up his arms, the statuette of the dragon was flung across the room and crashed against the wall near me.

The professor himself seemed to be slammed backwards against the platform and crashed to the floor in a mass of splintering woodwork as it disintegrated under the weight of his impact.

Many of the audience had leapt to their feet and a babble of voices rose in surprise and horror.

I sat, staring numbly in front of me.

Yorke hauled me to my feet, giving me a shake to awake my senses, and retrieved the statuette.

'It's not damaged,' he said, replacing it in the bag and

then jostling forward to the group who were standing around the prostrate form of the professor.

'Stand back!'

'Give him air!'

'Has he fainted?'

'Is he all right?'

'*Please*, stand back now.'

I moved forward in a daze, and joined Yorke in trying to peer over the tops of the heads and look down on the prone man.

The homespun man was leaning over him, his face working. He felt for the pulse, then the heart, tried to pour a drink down the man's throat, felt for the heart again and then turned a horrified face towards the surrounding audience. His mouth opened and closed without saying anything. Then he managed to blurt out: 'My God! He's dead! Dead!'

In the screams and babble that followed I was dimly aware that Yorke had gripped me by the sleeve and hauled me from the room, down the stairs and back out along the putrid alleyway, back to the bright lights of the Commercial Road.

'Come on, old man, pull yourself together now,' he whispered, pushing me forward.

'But, Yorke,' I gasped, 'he died . . . that man died . . .! Was, was I to blame?'

Yorke said nothing but turned and spent his best endeavours in trying to hail a cab. Cabs were few and far between along the Commercial Road and it was some minutes before he found one depositing a fare and promptly hired the man to return us to the Strand.

I was speechless with the shock of what I had witnessed.

Yorke hauled me out at a little tavern, the George Inn, I think it was, and propelled me into a quiet booth where he ordered whisky for the both of us.

'Of course we are not to blame for the man's death,' he said, after a while.

'Then why did we run away?' I demanded.

Yorke shrugged his shoulders expressively.

'There will be police, inquiries, you know the sort of thing . . . it won't look good if we are reported to have been in that sort of area. What would Lord Molesworth say, eh? A personal secretary at the Foreign Office mixed up with spiritualists in Whitechapel . . . what would the newspapers say, eh?'

I thought it over.

'I suppose you are right, Yorke,' I said after a pause.

'Of course I am.'

'But Yorke,' I persisted, 'what killed him?'

Yorke pursed his lips.

'Who knows? A heart condition, some other illness . . . who knows?'

'I find it frightening.'

'Well, old boy, I'll tell you one thing – the thing you should take deadly serious about the whole business.'

'What's that?' I asked.

'You must not accompany Lord Molesworth to Romania next month.'

CHAPTER NINE

The nightmare came to me again that night. But this time it was slightly different.

Again I walked through the exotic night garden; again my stomach heaved at the oppressive sickly-sweet smell of jasmine.

The same monotonous chanting began.

All the while my mind was still conscious that this was some illusion; I knew, behind it all, that I was still lying in my bed in my rooms at Charing Cross. Yet the scene was still vivid to my senses.

Through the velvet blackness of that night garden, towards that white-pillared fantasy of a temple and the evil grinning edifice of the dragon god, my unwilling footsteps were led once more.

But instead of the girl waiting for me in the white moonlight there stood a man.

From head to toe he was draped in black. He bore a strange resemblance to the dead medium . . . Professor De Paolo. Yet I knew that it was not the same man.

He was a tall man, elderly it seemed, for a long white moustache drooped over his otherwise clean-shaven face. Even in the uncertain drifting of my dream I could see his face was strong – extremely strong – aquiline with a high-bridged, thin nose and peculiarly arched nostrils. His forehead was loftily domed and the hair grew scantily round the temples but profusely elsewhere. The eyebrows were massive, nearly meeting across the bridge of the nose.

But above all it was the mouth that captured my eyes. That mouth set in that long pale face: fixed and cruel looking, with teeth that protruded over remarkably ruddy lips which had the effect of highlighting his white skin and giving the impression of extraordinary pallor. The strange thing was, where the teeth protruded over the lips, they seemed peculiarly sharp and white.

The eyes suddenly caught and held mine.

They were large and shone with a curious red malignancy.

'You will come to me,' he said slowly, a smile curving his lips – those, oh, so thin, red lips.

The voice was mesmeric, a strange voice, rich in tone and full of alien accents.

'You will come to me, do you hear me . . . come across the seas over the mountains, to my home beyond the forests. You will come to me, do you hear me? You will come to me.'

I was aware that I stood before this dark, forbidding shape like a rabbit before a fox; my eyes wanting to close, to sleep, letting the drone of his voice lull me . . .

'I am the master, the master who will give you eternal life and blessings. You will come to me when I call you. You will come to me and bring the god Draco, you will come to me. Do you hear me? Do you hear now? I am the master . . . across the seas, over the mountains, to the land beyond the forests. I shall be waiting . . . soon . . . soon . . .'

Suddenly the figure was gone, dissolving before my eyes into elemental dust which suddenly shot like a beam of silver along the pale rays of the moon.

My senses reeled.

Then the dream took on its old form. From nowhere the girl appeared with her accursed sacrificial knife – for such I now knew that weapon to be.

Again the ritual; again the incantation.

Again the knife rose . . .

Something sounded in my ears: a bang, a bump, I am not sure. The next thing I knew was that I sat bolt upright in my bed, my eyes and ears straining in the darkness of my room.

Fully awake, I was aware of the rapidity of my own breathing, sounding deafening in the stillness of the night.

A creak from a loose floorboard in my sitting-room caused my heart to beat in a wild tattoo.

There was someone in the next room!

For a moment I let my imagination loose in strange fantasies but then I pulled myself together. I was letting my nightmares and Yorke's strange behaviour colour my fertile imagination. Who could it be but some common thief? And if it was, I was twenty-six years old and strongly muscled, for I believed in keeping healthy and attended regularly at a school of fencing, a sport designed to keep anyone in excellent physical condition. In a position such as mine, which keeps one seated before a desk most of the day, it is so easy to become lazy and slack, to let the body become little more than useless.

Cautiously, I drew back the coverlets and climbed out of bed.

If it was a common burglar, with an envious eye on my collection of *objets d'art*, he would pay dearly for his insolence.

I walked carefully to my bedroom door and slowly, cautiously, turned the handle, prising the door open a few inches.

My sitting-room was in total darkness, the drawn curtains allowing no light from the lamp-lit street. I opened the door a little wider and slipped swiftly into the room.

The paler shades from my bedroom infiltrated the sitting-room so that, after a while, the darkness was not as pitch-black as it had been before. I stood very still, peering forward to examine each corner of the room.

Then in a corner I saw it!

A small dark shadow.

With a bark of triumph I flung myself across the room and snatched at the figure.

It was far smaller than I was, a good head shorter, and seemed light and lithe. But as my hands closed around the small arms they swung up to repel me and such was the incredible strength they seemed to have that I was propelled backwards for several feet and only my colliding with a sideboard stopped this backward propulsion. For a moment I stood leaning against the sideboard, stunned; not stunned by the actual push that I had received, but by the fact that such a small person could be possessed of such strength.

The figure had flown to the door. Recovering myself, I hurled myself after it. The impact of my attack pushed the figure heavily against the door. For a few moments I was able to bring my arms around those of my assailant. Then that incredible strength reasserted itself and I was flung off as if I had been a mere child attacking a fully grown man.

The figure was fumbling with the door handle.

I recovered myself a second time and tackled the legs of the person.

The impact of my third attack sent the figure hurtling backwards, an object which had been held in one hand went flying across the room with a resounding crash. The figure went over, with me on top of it. I struggled to my knees to meet the counter-attack which I assumed would follow, but the figure lay supine on the floor of my room.

Breathless following my exertions, I rose to my feet and looked down. In the darkness I could make out little except that I could hear stertorous breathing and presumed I had knocked out the would-be burglar. I walked to the table, fumbled for matches and lit the lamp.

'Mr Welsford!' There was a sudden thumping at my door. I groaned inwardly as I recognized the imperious tones of Mrs Dobson. Well, at least I had a good enough excuse for disturbing the tenants of her rooming house this time.

'One moment!' I cried and turned, raising high the lamp to observe my thief.

The blood rushed dizzily about my head, singing in my ears, as I peered down aghast at the beautiful girl who lay on the floor. That face, which I had seen so often, now lay in calm repose. Only the mouth, slightly parted, was twisted unnaturally and issued the sound of uncomfortable breathing. It was the same girl from my nightmares, the same girl that I had seen by gaslight in the Strand a few nights before.

'Mr Welsford!'

Mrs Dobson's knocking sounded once more.

I stirred myself with difficulty.

What was I to do? Firstly, I had to get to the bottom of this amazing situation.

'Mr Welsford!'

The voice of the landlady was high and angry.

Reluctantly I went to the door and opened it.

Mrs Dobson stood in her dressing gown. She was red-faced, blotched in anger. She stood with her massive hands placed on her hips.

'Now then, Mr Welsford, I have warned you before about these noises. I told you they must stop. I won't say it again. You are disturbing my tenants. If you can't stop this noise I must ask you to leave. Do you hear me?'

'Yes, Mrs Dobson,' I replied meekly, not wishing to do battle with this reincarnation of Antiope, Queen of the Amazons.

'Well, Mr Welsford?'

She fixed me with her gimlet eyes.

'Mrs Dobson?'

'What's the meaning of this noise?'

My mind raced rapidly.

'Why . . . I stupidly left my window open last night

305

and a cat must have made its way in over the roofs. I just had a devil of a time chasing it out. I'm sorry I disturbed you.'

'A cat?' There was a heavy suspicion in her voice.

'Yes, Mrs Dobson.'

'Well, I shan't warn you again, Mr Welsford. I keep a respectable house here, and I'm the one who has to receive all the complaints. Never heard anything like it, a cat, indeed! Opening windows in December!'

With a scowl and a snort of indignation, Mrs Dobson turned on her slippered heel and disappeared down the stairs.

With a sigh of relief I closed my door and put my lamp back on the table.

The girl was still lying on the floor, her breathing slow and erratic. I bent over her and felt for her pulse. It matched her breathing.

I picked her up in my arms, registering how light she was and frowning in disbelief as I remembered the strength she had displayed a moment or so ago. I took her into my bedroom and laid her carefully on my bed. The fire was still crackling in the hearth and I quickly built it up into a blaze and turned on the gas lamps.

A careful examination of the girl's head, to see how she had rendered herself unconscious, showed no lumps or bruising. Yet she was clearly not in a natural state; it was as if she were in some sort of stupor.

I tried to awaken her from it by chafing her hands and wrists and applying a cold, wet flannel to her forehead.

There was no reaction.

Wondering what to do, I placed a kettle on the hearth, thinking that maybe I could force her to take a hot drink, for it did not enter my church-raised mind to offer alcohol to a lady.

It was then I suddenly recalled that as she fell something had flown from her hands – released by impact –

and thudded across the room. I went into the sitting-room and picked up the lamp to search the floor.

I had no difficulty in finding what it was.

There in the corner, where it had fallen, was the small jade statuette of the god Draco.

In bewilderment I picked it up and replaced it where I usually kept it on my sideboard.

It grinned evilly at my puzzled gaze.

What could it mean? The strangeness of the events was now so confusing, so perplexing, that for the first time in my life I was really apprehensive as to my sanity. I suddenly realized that for all his esoteric ways and his mysticism, perhaps Yorke was truly the only person who could help me solve this mystery – Yorke and, of course, the girl who now lay unconscious on my bed.

I returned to the bedroom.

She lay, pale and beautiful in repose. How can I describe her? She was in her early twenties, perhaps not more than twenty-one or twenty-two. The face was heart-shaped, the eyes were wide-set, the lids lined with curling, graceful lashes. I knew that beneath those lids there lay deep-green eyes that must have been the sort of eyes that Helen used to ensnare Paris of Troy and his brother Deiphobus, and Theseus and Menelaus before them. The pale face, with its delicate rose red lips, was surrounded by a tumble of raven-coloured hair. She had an exotic, remarkably foreign look about her. And her figure, ah, it was injustice to say it was well shaped; it was a figure that Aphrodite might have been jealous of.

It was while I stood thus, breathing in the essence of her beauty that I suddenly became aware of a fact which had not struck me before. The girl was wearing no outer garments, no coat nor hat, but simply wore a tightly buttoned costume with a white blouse pinned high at the throat by a single cameo brooch. Yet the night outside was chilly and cold.

I would not venture far without a heavy overcoat and muffler.

Had she come far?

Another thought struck me, and I leant over her and unloosened some of her garments to make her more comfortable, blushing even while she lay in her unconscious state. But her health was to be put before gentlemanly breeding and I fumbled at the unfamiliar buttons of her costume coat, carefully unfixing the cameo brooch and loosening the top of her blouse and then the tight waistband of her skirt.

Her skin was white and cold to the touch.

I wondered whether I should leave her and go in search of a doctor but I knew not where to find one at this time of night. I glanced at the clock and saw that it was actually morning, nearly six o'clock. I resolved that if I were unable to rouse her by seven o'clock I would set off to Soho to bring the doctor I had consulted there.

I made some tea and tried to administer a few mouthfuls to the girl in an effort to revive her. While she seemed to swallow automatically, it created little change in her condition.

I drank a cup of tea myself and then paced up and down trying to make sense of the events of the past few days, trying to link them together in some sort of pattern. But the task was too much for my racing brain to cope with.

At last, I pulled up the blinds to watch the grey fingers of dawn creeping up the Thames from the direction of St Paul's Cathedral.

The girl's breathing now seemed slightly more regular, more normal, even her pulse more even.

I sat in a chair by the bed, trying to focus on the forthcoming day, but my eyelids grew heavy and, against my will, I fell into a dreamless but uncomfortable sleep.

CHAPTER TEN

A sobbing caused my eyes to start open.

The winter sun was shining full into the room. I blinked and my next reaction was to peer at the clock which now registered nine-thirty. I was about to rise from the chair when another loud sob arrested me and my eyes were drawn to the lithe figure on my bed and the events of the night flooded into my mind with alarming clarity.

The girl was awake, at least her eyes were open, and staring wildly about her.

'Hello,' I smiled, not knowing what else to say.

She stared hard at me and then raised a pale hand to dash away the tears that lay upon her cheeks.

'Wh . . . where am I?' she asked in a tremulous voice.

'You are safe,' I replied, 'don't worry. But . . . are you feeling all right now? You had me worried.'

A frown of puzzlement crossed her face as she stared up at me.

'I . . . I seem to know you and yet, yet . . .'

She bit her lip as if trying to dredge up some long lost memory.

Suddenly it must have occurred to her that she was in a strange man's room, lying on his bed, her clothes in an unloosed fashion.

She gasped and tried to sit up but appeared a little weak from the effort.

'Don't move,' I admonished. 'You are a little weak after your adventure. I'll make some tea. That should make you feel better.'

Her eyes darted about in alarm.

'Where am I?' she demanded.

'You don't remember?' I asked.

'I remember nothing. I went to bed in my room last night as usual. Then . . .' she frowned and passed a hand across her brow. 'I seemed to have a strange dream. I can't recall . . . I've been having so many peculiar dreams of late. I just can't recall . . . But where am I? How did I get here? And who are you? Have we met before?'

I held up my hands to still the questions that came tumbling from her lips.

'One question at a time,' I implored. 'Firstly, my name is Upton Welsford and these are my rooms. We are near Charing Cross. Now who are you?'

I could see my name meant nothing to her.

'I am Clara Clarke. My father is Colonel George St John Clarke of the Egyptian Rifle Brigade,' she added, as if it were some formula which might protect her. 'What am I doing here?'

I poured out a cup of tea and handed it to her. She sipped at it slowly, leaning back against the pillows.

It was all so strange that I scarcely knew how much to tell her.

I decided to be scrupulously honest and her eyes grew wide in disbelief and then horror as I recounted my experiences, describing in detail what had happened the previous night.

'I don't believe it,' she gasped at the end of my account. 'But . . . but it seems to fit in with those awful, ghastly dreams . . .'

She peered hard at me and I turned a trifle pink beneath her scrutiny.

'Who are you?' she asked again. 'And why is it that I seem to know you? I am sure I have seen you before.'

I sighed.

'I do not wish to complicate matters, Miss Clarke,' I said, 'but I, too, seem to have met you before last night.' It was then I told her the exact nature of my dreams. I recounted everything that occurred and as my narrative proceeded, the girl grew pale and once or twice pressed a hand to her cheeks.

'This can't be true ... this can't be happening,' she gasped.

I thought she was about to faint and sprang from my chair in alarm.

'Miss Clarke,' I cried in agitation, 'it is not my wish to distress you further but we have been the objects of such mysterious events that I feel we must be totally honest with each other.'

She nodded slowly.

'Indeed, you are right, Mr Welsford,' she answered gravely, having recovered her composure. 'Although your tale is most horrific and leaves me in apprehensive bewilderment, I must tell you that, in a peculiar way, it gives me comfort, for during the past week I have found myself similarly circumstanced and so terrifying have been my dreams that I thought that I was going insane.'

She paused and shuddered as she seemed to recall unpleasant memories.

'If you would pour me another cup of tea, Mr Welsford,' she gave me a weak but brave smile, 'I shall tell you my story.'

It was a story which was, in every detail, as perplexing and as terrifying as mine.

Her father, as she had mentioned before, was a serving officer in an infantry regiment stationed near Cairo in Egypt. Some twenty-one years previously, which confirmed my estimation of her age, he had met and married her mother, an Egyptian princess, and married her although such a liaison was greeted with disapproval by both the British authorities and by the princess's family. After Clara had been born, Colonel Clarke and his wife had sent her to England for her education. She had lived with a matronly aunt in Sussex, returning to Egypt for holidays with her parents. Three years previously, her mother, Princess Yasmini, had died from some fever and Clara had gone to Egypt to take on the duties of looking after her father's house.

A month ago her father had been ordered south, into the Sudan, to command a punitive expedition against rebellious tribesmen. Clara had returned to England to visit her aunt.

Her boat had docked at Wapping five days ago and it was from that very date that she had started to fall prey to strange nightmares. The nightmares concerned her home in Egypt and were then mixed with weird images of ancient temples, of her own mother in ancient costumes, of blood sacrifices in which she – Clara – seemed about to plunge a knife into a young man who stood helpless before her.

As she told me this, she suddenly started and peered closely at me.

'Why . . . it is you. You are the man in the dream – but that is impossible, surely?'

Her voice had an unmistakable pleading quality to it.

I shrugged my shoulders.

'If I can dream of you, and my dreams began several days before your boat docked – so it would be impossible to claim that I had seen you before and subconsciously imagined you in my dreams – then it is equally possible that you have dreamed of me. I do not understand it; I cannot explain it; but the facts remain.'

She shuddered.

Continuing her narrative, she told me that the dominating feature of her dreams had been a vast image of some wild beast – a serpent-like beast.

'A dragon?' I interposed.

She nodded eagerly.

'A black dragon, that's it. I am always standing before it in my dream. Could it be the same beast that you said appears in your dream?'

I said nothing and she continued that two days previously her dreams altered a little. She began to hear a voice calling to her, telling her to take the dragon and bring it to . . . to somewhere, to someone, but she could not remember who or where. It was terribly confused.

I went into the next room and returned with that accursed statuette.

'Is this the dragon statue in your dreams?' I asked, thrusting the jade forward.

She gave a tiny scream, suppressing it with the back of her hand.

'That's it . . . why, what does it mean?'

'When you came here last night, you were trying to make off with it,' I said, grimly. 'You must have been answering the call of the . . . the someone in your dream.'

She shook her head from side to side helplessly.

'I must be going mad, none of this makes sense to me.'

'Nor me,' I agreed. 'Yet there must be a sense to it somewhere. Somehow there is logic to all this madness. There is a link, that is certain. But what it is, I have absolutely no idea. People do not dream of people they have not met, and yet who exist, without a reason.'

'Perhaps we are insane?' the girl whispered. 'It is too fantastic, too unreal to make sense.'

An idea was already forming in my mind.

I reached forward and, with a sudden boldness, took her hand in mine.

'Miss Clarke,' I said. 'I am determined to get to the bottom of this mystery; and get to the bottom of it I shall before I depart for . . . for abroad.'

She raised her grey-green eyes to mine and nodded.

'What do you plan to do?' she asked.

'I have a friend, Dennis Yorke, who is something of an expert in matters of mysteries and dreams. He already knows that I have been suffering from such maladies but I think it would put a new perspective on matters were he to know that you exist in reality and to hear your own story.'

'I will do anything to get rid of these terrifying nightmares,' she agreed eagerly.

'Very well. If you are well enough, perhaps we can go to his rooms right away. There is no time like the present for dealing with the matter.'

She gave me a wan smile.

'I am feeling better.'

'But wait.' Another thought struck me. 'Is there not someone who will be looking for you?'

She shook her head.

'No. I am staying alone at a small hotel near here and I have not yet let my aunt know that I am coming.'

'Have you no companion, no servant, who accompanied you?' I asked, puzzled.

'No,' she replied. Seeing my look of amazement she laughed. 'Colonial women don't need the pampering afforded by English society. And now . . . if you have somewhere that I could bathe my face . . .?'

Excusing myself for my inconsiderateness, I pointed to a small closet which adjoined my bedroom and while she was at her toilet I dressed and prepared a modest breakfast.

It was nearly twelve noon before I hailed a hackney and gave the driver Yorke's address.

CHAPTER ELEVEN

Yorke raised his grave face and stared solemnly at Miss Clarke and then at me.

Miss Clarke had just finished her narrative, substantially as she had told it to me that morning, and now we waited expectantly for Yorke to make some pronouncement.

He said nothing for a while to alleviate our suspense, but rose to his feet and took down an old briar pipe from his mantelshelf, filled it from an ageing leather pouch and lit it with a taper held in his fire. He drew several breaths of the perfumed smoke and then sighed.

'My friends, we have a profound mystery here. You, Miss Clarke, and you, Welsford, are both the subjects of some force which is trying to communicate with you both, for what purpose I cannot yet say. But,' he raised a warning finger, 'this I know, and I do not wish to sound melodramatic nor frighten you in any way, that force is evil. Of that I am sure.'

I sighed impatiently for I had expected something more from Yorke, some explanation, some rationale.

'Come, Yorke,' I said, 'we need help, not warnings.'

He turned his serious eyes upon me.

'Sometimes a warning is helpful when heeded.'

The girl looked apprehensive.

'Mr Yorke,' she said softly, 'what are you trying to tell us? That we are in some danger from . . . what? Something or someone?'

Yorke nodded over his pipe.

'Just so, Miss Clarke. Let us say it is something.'

'But from *what*?' she appealed.

Yorke frowned.

'I only wish I knew, Miss Clarke. For many years, as Welsford will tell you, I have been a student of the occult. I have dabbled in natural sciences and in spite of the years I have studied, my sum total of knowledge is infinitesimal. But I do know that the occult is not something to be laughed at. There is a real and powerful force at work here.'

'Look, Yorke,' I interposed, 'a week ago I would have laughed at you. This past week I have seen a few things which have raised my curiosity and, quite frankly, have frightened me. I am certainly inclined to be a little more open-minded on the subject of the occult, and I agree that there is a very real and powerful force affecting us. But I want to know more.'

The girl interrupted me.

'Mr Yorke, as you know I have lived many years in Egypt and my mother is of Egyptian blood. I know enough of some of the ancient mysteries that are even today practised among the ordinary folk of that country. That knowledge makes me accept many strange things as natural and I realize that there are many unknown forces still unaccountable to our modern sciences. So my mind is open to your suggestions. But what *are* your suggestions?'

Yorke seated himself before the fire.

'I believe that in some way, Miss Clarke, you and Welsford are mediums – unwilling mediums, perhaps – and that some unknown force, spirit or what you will is trying to communicate either to you or through you. The link seems to be the jade statuette of Draco.'

'Draco?'

The girl's voice was startled.

Yorke nodded.

'I have given some thought to what you have said and my own observations of Welsford have made me come to the conclusion that the force, or whatever you like to name it, uses, or emanates from, the statuette.'

I looked at him in surprise.

'How do you make that out, Yorke?' I demanded.

'Simply this: you say that you started to get your nightmares on the very day you bought the statuette?'

I nodded.

'You could not sleep for days – and every time you dreamt you dreamt in the vicinity of the statuette?'

'That is so.'

'Then you came exhausted to my rooms yesterday and slept peacefully all day, without dreaming, having left the statuette in your rooms.'

'You propounded this theory to me yesterday,' I reminded him.

'I say it again now,' Yorke said emphatically. 'Did you notice how the medium, De Paolo, went into some sort of trance when the statuette was placed before him and how, when he placed his hands upon it, he became another entity entirely? The shock of mediumship killed him.'

'But what of me?' asked the girl. 'I started to dream before I even set eyes on the jade statuette.'

'Indeed,' said Yorke. 'And yet all your dreams were aimed towards the jade; in your dream state you were directed to Welsford's rooms where the statuette was and he caught you in the act of removing it. It was as if you were mesmerized into searching out the statuette.'

She bit her lip thoughtfully.

'So you think the jade is what links Mr Welsford and myself?'

Yorke nodded.

'That is my theory. What the force is, what it seeks, I do not know. There is something malignant, something evil about it, though. And something which links the forbidden cult of ancient Egypt with modern Transylvania.'

'Why Transylvania?' asked the girl, puzzled. 'And where is Transylvania?'

Yorke threw me a look.

'You have not told Miss Clarke?' he accused.

'Not everything, Yorke. I am a government official and my business in Romania is secret.'

'Some secrets are beyond governmental boundaries, Welsford. You can trust Miss Clarke in this matter.'

The girl turned her luminous green eyes upon me and laid a soft hand on my arm.

'Your secret is safe with me, Mr Welsford,' she said imploringly.

I mellowed in her gaze.

'I quite believe it, Miss Clarke. I really do . . .'

'Good,' said Yorke, a little sharply. 'Transylvania is a principality which lies next to Hungary and is currently part of the Austro-Hungarian Empire. It straddles the Carpathian Mountains.'

The girl was puzzled.

'And what has this to do with this . . . this business?'

'Quite a lot, or so I deduce,' went on Yorke.

Without giving away too many details of the Foreign Office connection, he told the girl of my forthcoming visit to the new state of Romania and the possibility of a visit to the neighbouring principality of Transylvania. Then he told her how he had taken me to the two mediums and how both had warned me against going to Transylvania. He described in detail the metamorphosis of De Paolo during the séance.

I echoed the story by adding how I had dreamt of a tall man in black repeating the exact same message De Paolo had given me.

Yorke banged his hand on the rest of his chair in triumphant agitation.

'There, by Jove! That proves it. There is a connection.'

'But what connection could there be between Egypt and Transylvania . . . and with this ancient dragon cult of which you speak, the worship of Draco?' asked the girl.

Yorke shrugged.

'I do not know . . . yet.'

'But how can we find out?' I asked.

Yorke leaned forward, an eager expression on his sensitive face.

'An experiment,' he said. 'An experiment under carefully observed conditions.'

'How do you mean?' asked the girl.

'What I propose may not be pleasant for either of you . . .'

'But what do you propose, Yorke?' I insisted.

He looked from the one to the other of us for a moment.

'I propose that you, Miss Clarke, and you, Welsford, spend the night here – with the statuette. I shall be here also to observe what happens. I have various instruments which will help me study the psychic phenomena and through clinical observation we may be able to ascertain what this force is and what it is seeking.'

He sat back.

'Well, what do you say?'

I looked doubtfully at Miss Clarke.

'If you think that there is a possibility of putting an end to this nightmare then I am quite willing to undertake this experiment.'

Yorke looked at me.

I nodded slowly.

'If Miss Clarke is prepared then so am I.'

Yorke rose and clapped me on the back.

'Excellent, excellent! I am sure we can get to the bottom of this mystery. And now,' he pulled out his silver hunter watch and glanced at it, 'now I want some time to prepare. Perhaps, Welsford, you would care to take Miss Clarke to luncheon, then pick up the statuette and return here – but return before nightfall.'

He laid a heavy emphasis on the last words.

Yorke ushered us out and already I could see that his mind was miles away, locked in his strange world.

I helped Miss Clarke into a carriage and ordered it to Charing Cross. A thought struck me and caused me to bang my hand in agitation.

'Miss Clarke, what a confoundedly selfish ass I am,' I spluttered.

She turned mildly amused eyes on me.

'I should take you to wherever you're staying. I haven't even asked. You will obviously want a change of clothes and . . . and . . .'

She gave a low chuckle.

'Dear me, in the excitement I forgot all about such things. I am staying at the Nelson Hotel, just behind the hospital at Charing Cross. I certainly would like to change my clothes and pick up a few things for tonight.'

I passed the address to the cabman.

'After I came ashore from my ship,' explained the girl, 'I registered at the Nelson expecting to stay only a night or two before taking the train from Charing Cross station down to Sussex where I was going to stay with my aunt. But those dreams have made me so exhausted during the past few days that I haven't been able to face the journey and,' she lowered her voice confidingly, 'one needs stamina to stay with my aunt.'

Her chuckle was musical and caused my pulse to beat more rapidly. I believe it was about that time that I knew that I had fallen in love with this exquisite creature. I do not know what chemistry it is that works to bind men to women in only a moment's acquaintanceship. We are told such things only happen in works of fiction and are scorned by philosophers and men of sobriety. But this I know, the fabled 'love at first sight' is a fact of life, for I was deeply, irrevocably and almost idolatrously in love with Clara Clarke.

'Won't your aunt be worried by your non-arrival?' I asked.

The girl shook her head.

'I told you before that she doesn't even know that I am in England. My departure from Cairo was sudden, on an impulse, and in the rush of leaving I quite forgot to send her a letter. Even if I had, by the time she received it I would already have arrived.'

'In that case,' I ventured, stumbling a little over my words, 'perhaps, after tonight, you could stay a little in London and I could escort you to a theatre or a vaudeville show or . . . or . . . something before you go down to Sussex.'

She smiled gravely.

'I would like that, Mr Welsford. It seems rather ridiculous to spend two nights with a man,' she gave a mischievous grin, 'and then refuse his invitation to the theatre.'

I blushed furiously.

She leant forward and placed her hand on mine.

'I'm sorry,' she said, with more than a hint of amusement in her voice. 'We colony-raised young ladies are quite shameless and ill-mannered.'

I protested hotly that she made the ladies of England as pale as a winter's moonlight.

She laughed at my lyrical protestations, but not mockingly.

Then a serious look caught her eyes.

'When is it that you leave on your mission?'

'The first week in the New Year.'

'And do you realize what day it is tomorrow?'

I shook my head.

'The day before Christmas Eve.'

I gave a low whistle of amazement. The mysteries of the past week or so, together with my researches on Romania, had so ensnared me in a world where time was of no importance, that I had not noticed its passing.

'I can stay only one more day in London,' she said with what I felt was a genuine regret. 'I really must go to my aunt's for the Christmas festivities. However, if I came up to London for a few days afterwards . . . before you leave . . .?'

I could not suppress the joyous grin that spread over my features.

'That would be wonderful indeed,' I said.

The cabman halted his horse before the Nelson Hotel. I dismissed him and accompanied her into the foyer.

An elderly bespectacled man, obviously the hall porter, shuffled forward and handed her a key, giving me a look of deep suspicion.

'Afternoon, miss,' he said. 'We began to wonder where you were . . .'

She merely thanked him for the key.

'Will you wait down here for me. I have to change. I shall not be long.'

I sat fretfully for a good half hour trying to read *The Times*. Then she returned, dressed in a neat cobalt-blue costume and a matching coat and hat.

Together, arm in arm, we walked to my rooms, overcame the glowering resentment of Mrs Dobson, who was overseeing the removal of another unwelcome guest and his luggage, and collected that hideous, green-black statuette.

We had a late luncheon, for it was fully three-thirty when we sat down at the Connaught Rooms and even before the main course arrived we had dropped the 'Mr Welsford' and 'Miss Clarke' and had become plain 'Upton' and 'Clara'.

I have never spent a happier day; yes, in spite of the grim realities that hung like a dark cloud over the two of us, the terrifying, unfathomable mysteries, we rejoiced in each other's company and for that all too brief span of time we were happy together.

Finally, noticing the pressing gloom of the early winter evening, I ushered Clara to a Hansom and together, clutching that infernal object between us, we made our way to Dennis Yorke's rooms in Bloomsbury.

CHAPTER TWELVE

Yorke greeted us with a wan smile.

In his sitting-room he had placed a green baize covered table in a central position. On opposite sides of the
table he had positioned two comfortable armchairs while,
a little behind and to one side, a third chair had been
placed. Beside this chair was a pile of old books and a few
odd looking gadgets.

We divested ourselves of our outdoor clothing and
warmed ourselves before the roaring log fire which Yorke
had built up in his hearth. Yorke had taken the statuette
of the dragon in his hands and had placed it carefully in
the centre of the table. He then took one of his strange
gadgets, which had some sort of meter attached to it, and
ran it over the jade object.

'What are you doing, Yorke?' I queried.

'Testing for any peculiar currents emanating from the
dragon,' he replied without looking up from his task.

Clara frowned.

'How can you do that, Mr Yorke?'

'I admit this is a very crude method,' replied Yorke,
gesturing at his apparatus. 'I am not even certain that this
is a sure method of testing. This is a galvanometer, for
which we have to thank Luigi Galvani of Bologna.'

'I am no nearer understanding,' I said a trifle
impatiently.

'The air about us is filled with unseen electrical currents, even our bodies contain electricity. A few years ago
electricity was thought to be the source of life. Run a
comb through your hair and place it on a piece of tissue
paper and you will find yourself able to pick it up as if
you were holding a magnet and the paper were iron. The

galvanometer measures these electrical currents. And my theory is that this force which communicates itself to you should create a positive electrical disturbance and can therefore be scientifically demonstrated.'

Clara suppressed a shiver of apprehension.

'Is there any electrical disturbance now?' she asked.

Yorke shook his head.

'Nothing. But I shall attach the galvanometer to the statuette by these wires and bring them across to where I shall be sitting; away from the table and able to observe you both.'

He busied himself for some time fixing up his apparatus.

'Right,' he said finally, 'that's it.'

I pointed to the pile of books.

'Have you been able to find out any connection between ancient Egypt and Transylvania?'

He shook his head regretfully.

'No, I have been able to find several references to the cult of Draco, though. But there is nothing to connect it with Transylvania. Certainly dragon worship was not known there, although dragons, or *balaur* as some Romanians call them, have long been connected with witches and evil events. Strangely enough there was one Romanian prince who lived in the fifteenth century who was called "the Son of the Dragon" or Dracula. But he ruled in Wallachia and not in Transylvania. Although he seems to have gathered an evil reputation among the Saxons and Turks, because of his habit of impaling them on wooden stakes, among Romanians he seems to be regarded as something of a national hero because he drove the Turks out of Wallachia. The Saxons reckoned he was so blood-thirsty that they openly called him a vampire. But there seems no connection between Dracula and Draco.'

'There's a similarity of name,' I pointed out. 'Are there descendants of Dracula living today?'

'Linguistic similarities are often misleading,' Yorke admonished. 'From the Egyptian *draco*, the Greek *drakon*, the Latin *draco* and so forth, we all seem to have similar words for the dragon. No, my friends, I can see no easy connection. We still have to solve the mystery.'

He looked at his watch.

'And now, my friends, I think we should begin.'

Clara cast a worried glance at me.

'Begin?'

Yorke gave one of his reassuring smiles.

'You and Welsford will have to make yourselves comfortable in the chairs before the table. We will stand Draco in the middle. You will merely compose yourselves as if for an ordinary night's sleep. I will stand by to measure any electrical currents in the room so that we can observe whether this force may be gauged. I will also be able to witness anything else that transpires. First we must see what the nature of this beast is.'

Under his gentle reassurances we seated ourselves in the comfortable armchairs. For some hours – certainly, the last time I looked at the clock, it was striking midnight – we could not sleep but sat tensely in our chairs, our eyes on that hideous green-black monster between us.

Even now I cannot recall exactly how I fell asleep.

All I know was that there came to my nostrils that tremendously sickening sweet smell of jasmine, choking and burning at my throat so that I started to cough. I raised my head to warn Clara and Yorke that something was happening.

But when I looked up I was not in Yorke's room at all!

I tried to raise myself from the chair but found some invisible bonds kept me fast.

The dragon, the green baize covered table, Clara, Yorke, the room, had all vanished.

I tried to call out but found such a constriction in my

throat due to the sickly odours that the feat was impossible.

I calmed myself, my brain reasoning that I was still in Yorke's room and that this was a mere hallucination. I must observe clinically, as Yorke would do. I must take in every detail so that I could report fully to Yorke what I had seen.

I was in a high-roofed room, so high that the roof above me vanished in the gloom. Firebrand torches rested in metal fastenings along the walls, illuminating strange murals in blue, red and ochre. They seemed familiar to me and I realized, with quickening apprehension, that I had seen such murals in the Egyptian Rooms of the British Museum. There were a few benches around the walls and I sat on such a bench in one corner. The bonds that held me were shackles of metal.

As if appearing from a swirling mist, Clara stood before me clad in white robes, a tiny golden circlet on her head and a silver chain around her neck from which hung the image of a dragon. She looked down at me and there was sorrow in her eyes.

'So, Ki, Kherheb of the false god Ammon, are you prepared to renounce?'

She spoke in some weird tongue, an ancient tongue, and yet I seemed to understand it perfectly.

'Never, Sebek-nefer-Ra!' I heard myself reply, a harshness in my voice.

Her eyes grew rounder and sadder.

'Will not even your love for me force you to reject Ammon?'

Her voice was tremulous.

'No, I cannot be false to the god of peace and plenty even for love of you, Sebek-nefer-Ra ... great though that love may be; timeless though that love must be. I shall not desert my god to follow yours.'

The girl before me stifled a sob.

'Then there is nothing I can do to save you, Ki. Already the people are gathered for the sacrifice. They call for the blood of all followers of the false god Ammon, especially for the blood of his priests. You are Kherheb of the Ammon, High Priest of the two kingdoms of Egypt. Yet if you renounce and follow the true god Draco, I can still spare you, and you will be allowed to live as a great example to the people.'

'O princess and new-made queen of the two king-doms,' I heard myself say, 'turn aside from this heretical folly. Do not resurrect a god of hate and evil. We who have loved each other know well that this will plunge the kingdoms down into the abyss of ignorance from which there is no return.'

'I have sworn an oath to Draco,' cried the girl, drawing herself up. 'Immortality must be mine! I will not grow old and wither as others have . . . I am Sebek-nefer-Ra, Queen of Egypt, and I shall live for ever!'

She stamped her foot.

'I shall sweep away the old gods, the gods who promise nothing in this life. My god promises everything in this life and that it will last forever. Now, Ki the Kherheb, do you recant your god, will you join me – sit at my side – as the convert priest of Draco?'

'Never!'

'Then so be it.'

She turned and was gone from the room.

My mind raced, the reasoning part, saying that this could not be happening and yet, at the same time, it was all so familiar as if I had lived the experience before.

Then came the part of the dream I knew so well.

I was walking through the garden, through the smell of jasmine. This time I knew that there were two strangely clad soldiers at my side and that my hands were bound.

There was the tall marble edifice, its pillars disappear-ing into the heavens. There was that accursed statue,

328

grinning evilly down on me, the eyes wide and staring, the mouth twisted, showing its evil canine teeth and its obscenely protruding forked tongue.

In the background came the monotonous chanting of unseen people, filling me with fear and foreboding.

Before me, back turned towards me, stood Clara's boyish figure. Two arms were raised in supplication towards the brooding statue of the dragon, two pale white hands, palm outwards, paying homage to the beast.

Her voice, as in my previous dreams, came like the tinkling of crystal, unreal, ethereal.

'I come from the Isle of Fire, having filled my body with the blood of Ur-Hekau, Mighty One of the Enchantments. I come before thee, Draco, I worship thee, Draco, Fire-breather from the Great Deep. You are my lord and I am of thy blood!'

The chanting died away.

Her voice continued:

'The time is come when the world must be filled with that which it has not yet known. The time is come when you must take your rightful place in the world and fill it with your abundance. Take then this offering which we, the followers of our lord Draco, give you freely . . . the blood of an unbeliever, the blood of a priest of the accursed false god Ammon. For blood is life and here is blood of our blood, life of our life!'

And now she turned, slowly turned towards me, arm raised once more aloft with the knife flashing in the flickering torches.

Then, as it started to descend, the girl vanished.

Before me, seemingly surrounded in a mist which billowed and swirled around him, stood a man clad all in black. The same pale-faced man with the drooping, long white moustache, the cruel red mouth and the eyes – those malevolent eyes – glaring balefully down on me.

'You will come to me, do you hear me . . . come across

the seas over the mountains, to my home beyond the forests. You will come to me, do you hear me? You will come to me.'

It was the same, slow mesmeric incantation as before.

'I am the master, the master who will give you eternal life and blessings. You will come to me when I call you. You will come to me and bring the god, Draco, you will come to me. Do you hear me? Do you hear now? I am the master ... across the seas, over the mountains, to the land beyond the forest. I shall be waiting ... soon ... soon.'

I raised a hand, or tried to do so, tried to call out, to demand, to reason, to implore ... then a sudden giddy sickness seized me. I felt myself pitching forward, forward, forward and down, down, down into a blackness to which there seemed no end.

I was aware of something cold and wet on my face.

I pushed up my hands and struggled.

'Steady, steady, old fellow.'

The concerned face of Yorke came into focus, peering down at me, while over his shoulder another face hovered – pale and out of focus. I blinked my eyes and stared hard. Clara, a frightened expression on her features, was peering over Yorke's shoulder.

I lay on the floor of Yorke's sitting room.

I struggled up into a sitting position, my head feeling that it was exploding into a thousand pieces.

I groaned.

A glass of brandy was thrust into my hands by Yorke and gradually I was helped back into my chair.

The first thing I registered was that it was nearly three o'clock in the morning. The room was the same. There was the table and the green jade statuette upon it.

'What ... what happened?' I mumbled. Then, as a thought struck me, 'Are you all right, Clara?'

The girl smiled and reached out her hand to grip mine.

'I'm fine, really I am.'

Yorke nodded.

'You are the one who has given us cause for concern,' he said gravely. 'For the past fifteen minutes you have been shouting and rolling over the floor.'

'Did nothing else happen?' I asked.

I could not conceal the disappointment in my voice, for I had expected Yorke to recount some terrible manifestation.

Yorke shrugged.

'Nothing spectacular happened but I presume we shall know more after we have compared notes of our individual experiences and sought a common denominator.'

He rebuilt the fire and prepared a hot drink for us all while we digested inwardly our thoughts and feelings.

'Let me begin,' he said, as we sat before the fire, sipping the strong hot coffee. 'Just after midnight it seemed as if a gust of cold air blew into the room. I looked up, fully expecting to see a window had blown open. But they were all closed and the curtains were still in place. Then I looked at my galvanometer and the needle was dancing wildly about. All of a sudden, the apparatus burst . . .'

He showed us the meter: the needle was indeed bent and the glass splintered into fragments.

Yorke continued:

'I felt a momentary excitement. I think I even called to you to tell you what had happened. Then I noticed that you were both asleep – but your breathing was stertorous, laboured as if you were unconscious rather than in a natural sleep. I tried to get up from my chair but suddenly felt very tired. So tired that I too fell asleep. I awoke from a doze to find you, Welsford, crashing to the floor, screaming. Miss Clarke was already out of her chair . . .'

He paused and cast a searching look at Clara.

'I've just remembered. You seemed about to pick up the statuette.'

There was a note of accusation in his voice.

Clara nodded unhappily.

'I don't know when I fell asleep but I do recall dreaming . . . I seemed to be in some black room, a cold, dank-smelling place . . . almost a crypt. At one end of the room there stood a very tall man. There was not much light in the place but he seemed elderly in spite of his tallness, with a pale face and long white moustache . . .'

I started.

'Did he have blood red lips, thin and cruel, and protruding teeth?' I demanded.

She turned to me in amazement.

'That would be how I would describe him,' she agreed.

'What happened then?' intervened Yorke.

'He told me to come to him; to take the statuette and come to him . . . "over the seas, beyond the mountains, to the land beyond the forest" . . . those were his words.'

Yorke and I exchanged glances.

'Incredible,' breathed Yorke. 'Then what, Miss Clarke?'

The girl shrugged.

'I do not know. I know that I wanted to obey him. The impulse to obey was stronger than anything I have ever felt before, even though it was against all my rational and moral instincts.'

'And?'

'I suppose I was trying to obey him when you woke up; you saw me reaching for the dragon . . .?'

Yorke made an affirmative gesture.

'And Welsford's cries probably brought you to your senses.'

The girl leaned forward and laid her hand on my arm.

'It seems, Upton,' she said quietly, 'you have suffered more distress than any of us.'

It was then that I recounted my vivid dreams and told them the parts which I had dreamt before. They sat listening to me with incredulous expressions on their faces.

As I finished Yorke stood up and paced the room. His eyes held that faraway expression which characterized the man when his mind was wrestling with a weighty matter.

We watched him in grave silence.

After a while he turned and looked thoughtfully at me.

'I think I begin to see . . . Welsford, Miss Clarke – I implore you to beware; it is as I suspected, you two are mediums, receiving thoughts and orders that are being transmitted by some unknown force which requires this object, this statuette, for some important purpose.'

I looked at him incredulously.

'But what force? For what purpose?' demanded Clara.

'As yet, I do not know for what purpose,' replied Yorke solemnly. 'Nor do I yet know the precise nature of the force . . . a person with immense powers of telepathy, perhaps? But this I am sure of, that force, whatever or whoever it is, represents evil and that evil lies somewhere in Transylvania.'

CHAPTER THIRTEEN

'What shall we do?'

It was Clara who agitatedly voiced my thoughts.

Yorke considered.

'I believe that while you are the receivers of this tele-pathic communication, the actual means of contact is this infernal idol. I propose that I be allowed to keep the statuette for a while to see whether you are troubled further.'

I agreed at once.

'Something has to be done,' I said. 'Your suggestion seems all right to me.'

'But there are several mysteries which remain to be cleared up,' declared Clara. 'If, as you say, Mr Yorke, some unknown force or person is seeking telepathic com-munication with us – and I will admit my ignorance on this subject – the purpose seems to be to entice one of us to take this statuette to this country called Transylvania, which I have never heard of before. But why does Mr Welsford dream so vividly of ancient Egypt as I have done on occasion?'

As Yorke opened his mouth she stayed him with a motion.

'Oh, I know that the statuette originated from there and it features in these dreams. But why does Mr Wels-ford dream of me as Sebek-nefer-Ra and himself as . . .'

'Ki, a priest of Ammon,' I supplied as she hesitated.

She nodded and turned back to Yorke.

'Why do we dream these things?'

Yorke reflectively stroked the side of his nose.

'Do you believe in reincarnation?' he asked abruptly.

'I have lived in Egypt,' said Clara simply. 'Reincarnation is an accepted fact of life. Although it seems opposed to western orthodox Christianity, I am inclined to believe in it.'

I looked at her in surprise. My Anglican Church background rejected the idea.

'And you, Welsford?' asked Yorke.

'What *would* the son of an Anglican minister be likely to believe in?' I asked. 'However, had I not experienced the events of the past few days I would have said we are all mad anyway. So what is your theory?'

Yorke gave me an almost paternal smile.

'You may be surprised to know that reincarnation was once part of early Christian doctrine.'

I sighed.

'Nothing will surprise me, Yorke. But say on, why do you think reincarnation has anything to do with our dreams?'

'This,' Yorke jabbed his forefinger at me, 'I believe you and Miss Clarke are reincarnations of two Egyptians involved with the flowering of the Draconian cult. That Miss Clarke was once Sebek-nefer-Ra and you, Welsford, were once Ki, Kherheb of Ammon. In your dreams, triggered by the vibrations of the statuette which played an important part in your former life, you have relived a dramatic part of that life. The force which is seeking contact with you picked up the vibrations that emanated when you first made contact with the statuette and is now using the power of those vibrations to call you to it.'

'You mean,' Clara was gasping, 'that I was really Sebek-nefer-Ra and that, thousands of years ago I killed Upton?'

'Five thousand years ago, to be precise, Miss Clarke,' agreed Yorke. 'Yes, five thousand years ago Sebek-nefer-Ra became queen of Egypt. She led the overthrow of the more liberal gods, including Ammon, who had replaced the older cult of Draco. Draco was then re-established not only in Egypt but throughout the known world.'

'And what of Ki?' I asked.

'Obviously Ki was the High Priest or Kherheb of Ammon. From your dream it seemed he loved Sebek-nefer-Ra when she was a young princess but when she came to power and led the overthrow of Ammon he refused to desert his god. The people demanded sacrifice. She tried to save Ki by asking him to recant and when he refused she was forced to perform the sacrificial ceremony herself.'

'How awful!' shuddered Clara. 'Poor soul.'

Yorke nodded thoughtfully.

'A poor soul, indeed, Miss Clarke. And it seems that finally, after all these years, the soul of Sebek was reborn in you and the soul of Ki was reborn in Welsford ... strange indeed.'

'But why the mystery concerning Transylvania?' I cried, feeling the frustration well up within me.

Yorke shrugged.

'I have told you: as yet I do not know. But we will learn in time.'

'And in the meantime?' I demanded.

'I am sure that the statuette is the key and while it is safe with me, safe under lock and key, and with you both out of its vicinity between the hours of sundown and sunrise, at which times this telepathic link seems to have its strongest effect, then I think you will have no more nightmares. In the meantime I will do my best to wrest its mystery from it.'

Clara was clearly worried.

'Is there no danger to yourself?'

'I think not,' returned Yorke. 'I have dabbled in this sort of thing long enough to know how to take elementary precautions.'

A thought occurred to me.

'And what of my trip to Romania? Do I refuse to go?'

Yorke massaged his temples with the tips of his lean fingers.

'I think I can answer that nearer to the time you are due to leave. By then I should have reached some conclusion in my researches. I would say, initially, that so long as the statuette remains in London this force has no way of contacting you.'

Clara shuddered and I automatically drew an arm around her shoulders. She made no objection to my boldness.

'Is there any other way we should protect ourselves?' she asked.

'Any symbol of goodness as opposed to evil will more often than not provide the right – how shall I describe it – vibrations to combat the evil. For example,' he rose and went to a drawer in his desk and drew out a small box, 'these things will afford you a degree of protection and I will give you them to wear as an added precaution over the next few days.'

He drew out two tiny silver-white crucifixes of delicate workmanship hanging from thread-fine silver chains. As *objets d'art* they really were exquisite pieces of craftsmanship.

'How beautiful!' ejaculated Clara.

'Take them and wear them at all times,' admonished Yorke, handing one to each of us.

'They are beautiful pieces,' breathed Clara again, fastening hers around her shapely neck.

'They have been blessed by the Pope and thereby have been doubly sanctified,' explained Yorke. 'Do not let that prejudice your Anglican mind,' he added as I looked dubiously at the ornament.

Clara smiled.

'But what use is Christian symbolism in combating an ancient Egyptian evil?' she suddenly asked. 'Christianity was not born until three thousand years after this cult of Draco died out, so how can one combat the other?'

'It is the symbolism that matters, Miss Clarke,' declared Yorke, earnestly. 'Symbols of good against symbols of evil. Today, in our western society, it is the crucifix that symbolizes goodness, peace and all that is worthy in our moral life. Yet two thousand years ago that very crucifix symbolized an ignoble death, degradation, the symbol of the Roman master race throughout its empire. Equally you could wear any other symbol of religion which preached goodness and light . . . yes, Welsford,' he gave a half-scornful glance towards me, 'in spite of your nineteenth-century Anglican morality, there are other religions, even non-Christian ones, which have the same moral code as your own.'

I shrugged. I had long passed the stage of argument. But sometimes I think Yorke despised my unquestioning Anglican faith instilled in me by my father, a most god-fearing man.

Yorke was continuing his illustration.

'You could wear a sprig of mistletoe, symbolic of the ancient Druidic religion of the Celts. That was the first European religion to teach the immortality of the soul. A religion of goodness and light. The ancient Greeks, such as Aristotle, claimed to have picked up much of their own philosophy on immortality from the Celtic peoples . . . the ancestors of the now despised Irish, Welsh and Scots.'

He paused as he warmed to his subject.

'You could,' he told Clara, 'equally wear a swastika . . .'*

'A what?'

Yorke reached into his drawer and came out with

---

* Those who have early Macmillan editions of the works of Rudyard Kipling will see that emblem carried on these books. Similarly, with 1920s George Newnes paperbacks, the emblem was also used as decoration. The symbol was unfortunately adopted by the German Nazi Party and, through it, became debased into an anti-Semitic racist symbol.

Tremayne.

another tiny gold charm hanging on a fine chain. The little object was a cross but with arms bent at right angles running clockwise.

'It's lovely,' said Clara, 'but what is it?'

'This,' said Yorke, holding it up, 'is one of the most ancient and worldwide symbols of goodness. It is emblematic of the sun. It is called a swastika from the ancient Sanskrit word svastika – *sú*, meaning well, and *asti*, being. In fact, I tend to wear it when I need such symbolism for it is far older and thereby more powerful a symbol of good than the cross.'

He grinned at me.

'You had better not repeat my heresy to your father.'

'So any symbol of good, not necessarily Christian, can combat evil?' I asked, ignoring his jibe.

'Yes; even the looped cross of ancient Egypt or any other such symbols from religions where light overpowers darkness.'

'And you think it is all right for us to continue our lives as before?' I pressed. 'From now on these terrible dreams will end?'

Yorke nodded.

'Although I am not absolutely certain, I would say that all the probabilities are in your favour.'

'And how will you be able to find out more of the statuette?'

'Leave that part to me. What I suggest is that you both go and enjoy your Christmas holidays and when you return to London next week, contact me. Hopefully I will have a report to make. If you feel any ill effects cable me directly. Above all, wear those crucifixes and never leave them off for one moment. I do not think anything will happen to you, but one must guard against all contingencies.'

'Look!' ejaculated Clara. 'Why, it doesn't seem possible . . . look!'

She pointed to the curtains where a beam of grey light was filtering in.

The clock chimed the hour of eight.

'Another day,' observed Yorke. 'We'd best all have breakfast and then you had better go and get some rest.'

'Tomorrow is Christmas Eve,' I reflected. 'I have quite a bit of work to catch up on at my office.'

'I shall travel down to my aunt's home later today,' said Clara. 'I'll come back to London next Friday,' she added, catching my anxious gaze. 'You can escort me to a theatre or two before you depart on your mysterious journey.'

I sighed.

'I wish I didn't have to go but . . .'

'But you have your career to think of, Upton,' she replied.

It was true; I knew it. Even now I was worried at what Lord Molesworth was going to say about my protracted absences from the office and my lack of results concerning my work.

We breakfasted together, Yorke, Clara and I, and the mood was light and bantering. I suppose we were filled with a great relief by Yorke's explanation, although I was haunted by nagging doubts, being unable to accept such theories as reincarnation, mediumship, and evil forces without some degree of self-questioning.

After breakfast I took Clara to her hotel and waited while she packed a suitcase and reserved her room for the following weekend, and then I accompanied her to the railway terminus at Charing Cross. I saw her seated on the train to Horsham, a little town in West Sussex, and made sure she was well provided with magazines and chocolates for the journey. Then I waited until the train began to pull out of the station. As it did so she suddenly leant forward from the carriage window and planted a soft kiss on my cheek. 'I am *so* glad I've met you, Upton,'

I heard her whisper before the hiss and whistle of the steam engine drowned any further conversation. She waved until the creaking line of carriages was hauled out of sight round a bend in the track.

I was soon in my office in Whitehall, bending my head to my tabulations of papers on Romania.

It was just before midday when the doors opened and my chief entered. My apprehension died away as he turned a smiling face to mine.

'Good show, Welsford. I need you today. I'm meeting with the PM at one o'clock.'

'With Lord Palmerston, sir?' I asked.

'Indeed, m'boy. Indeed.'

He glanced at the papers on my desk.

'Nearing completion with the background information, are we?'

I put on an air of confidence and nodded.

'Good, good. Will you have them ready first thing after Christmas?'

I swallowed.

'I'll do my best, sir.'

He pulled out some papers and put them on my desk.

'Fine. We shall be a party of ten going to Romania. That's not including all the official representatives from the royal family and others who will represent Queen Victoria at the celebrations for this Prince Cuza chappie.'

I ventured to correct him.

'Prince Alexandru, sir.'

'What?' he snapped.

'Cuza is his surname, sir,' I explained. 'His title will be Prince Alexandru.'

Molesworth guffawed.

'So 'tis, so 'tis. 'S what comes of making an ordinary fellah into a Prince. Nevertheless, glad you're with me to remind me of protocol and all that rubbish, eh?'

I examined the list of ten names that comprised our

Foreign Office delegation. Viscount Molesworth headed the list and my name followed immediately as official delegation secretary. A further party, comprising members of the royal family and military and naval observers, was to travel separately to take part in the ceremonials and the state opening of the Romanian parliament.

'When are we to go, my lord?' I asked Molesworth.

'When? Dear me,' he fumbled with his diary for a moment. 'Ah yes, just over a week, young feller. Gives you time to have a decent Christmas and then 2 January . . . that's when we'll set off for this Romania place eh?'

CHAPTER FOURTEEN

I shall not recount the boredom of that Christmas. I sent a cable to my father at Gisleham, doubtless upsetting him, and informing him that I could not join him for the festive season as work at the Foreign Office had to be my primary consideration. I then locked myself in my room – venturing out only to partake of a second-rate Christmas dinner in a nearby hostelry. All through Christmas I bent my head over the papers which I had neglected and by the following Thursday I, at last, had everything in order for my superior to check before we embarked.

One thing needs to be said: Yorke was totally correct in his prognosis. No dreams came to me, no fantastic nightmares, no summonses from across the water, no ceremonial sacrifices in ancient Egypt – just deep, dreamless, refreshing sleep. I slept the sleep of the just, never waking from the time I placed my head on my pillow until the time I stirred with the morning sunlight on my face. Yet, just in case, I always made sure that I wore Yorke's little silver crucifix.

The journey to Romania was going to take several weeks and would depend on the winds and the tides. At the most, the journey could last four weeks, and, at the least, it could be as little as two weeks. The idea was to embark on the *Agrinion* out of Tilbury and bound for Gibraltar. There, as a British diplomatic mission, we would change ships for a fast naval frigate which would take us through the Mediterranean, the Aegean, entering the Sea of Marmara, protected by the fact that Britain was still legally an ally of Turkey, and then turn into the Black Sea for disembarkation at the port of Constanta, which was the largest seaport possessed by the new

Romanian state. From Constanta we would journey by coach or train to the capital at Bucharest.

It was quite an exciting prospect, this journey to a strange new country, for a young man embarking on his career. But the prospect paled as I thought of Clara and I grew panic-stricken as I thought of being absent from England for one long, long year.

I could scarcely conceal my impatience that Friday morning as Lord Molesworth's voice droned on and on explaining the arrangements for our journey. But suddenly the clock was striking one and Molesworth, remembering he had a luncheon engagement with Lord Clarendon, left in a flurry of hurried instructions. No sooner was he gone through the door than I, too, departed and managed to arrive at Charing Cross just as the one-thirty train from Horsham was approaching the platform. My heart was bumping wildly within me as I stood watching its slow approach.

Many people spilled along the platform but I had eyes for only one – the girl with the pale heart-shaped face and the tumble of raven black hair.

Her face, anxious, saw me and the anxiety was driven away by her smile like snow before the sun. She waved and called to me, and I laughed at the startled disapproval of her fellow passengers edging their way towards the ticket barrier.

'Upton! I'm so pleased you are here.'

We stood awkwardly for a moment, looking at each other and smiling, saying nothing, expressing everything; then a porter snorted in my ear and muttered about people who have nothing to do but block platforms. Red-faced, I seized her baggage and ushered her to a cab.

'The Nelson?' I asked.

'Please, Upton,' she replied. 'I want to dump my baggage and then you can take me to luncheon. I am really starving . . . you haven't eaten, have you?' she asked anxiously.

'No,' I assured her. 'I thought I would wait for you. How was your Christmas?'

'Terribly boring,'she confessed, 'but I suppose that is just as well. No dreams, no visions, just good peaceful sleep. And you?'

'The same.'

'After I had been in Horsham a day I almost began to regret not having a dream,' she went on. 'My aunt, who is elderly and matronly, has not altered with the years. She still disapproves of me and everything about me. I nearly came back to London immediately.'

'I wish you had,' I said fervently.

She laughed delightedly.

'How scandalous it would have been. London society would have crumbled and the Empire too, no doubt. Your father would have had the hounds out to hunt you down.'

I grinned.

'But are you sure you had no dreams?' Her face suddenly grew serious.

'No,' I replied. 'I never slept better in my life. Mind you, I wore Yorke's crucifix constantly.'

'And I,' she confessed. 'It seems rather ridiculous now.'

She paused, a hand coming up to absently finger the little cross at her throat.

'Have you seen your friend, Mr Yorke, recently?' she asked.

'Not since before Christmas.'

The cab pulled up outside the hotel.

'Maybe we had better call to see him after luncheon,' she said, alighting.

I waited while she registered and had her luggage taken upstairs to her room and then we went to the Strand and had a magnificent luncheon.

It was a gorgeous day for late December. After

luncheon we even walked by the river; yes, even the muddy, brown-coloured Thames could not daunt the happiness of spirit which possessed us that afternoon.

We talked of many things, things I cannot even recall now – of our childhood, our prejudices, things we enjoyed and things we disliked. It was not until six o'clock that we guiltily recalled our resolve to visit Yorke and see how he was progressing in his investigations. We strolled arm in arm across the city to Bloomsbury and were soon knocking on Yorke's door.

He opened it and stood for a moment staring at us in some surprise. He was puffing his usual foul-smelling briar and wore a red smoking jacket that I recalled from our Oxford days.

We accepted sherry and told him how things went with us.

'Me?' he responded to our queries. 'Yes, I have been working hard. But I feel unable to make any pronouncement as yet. The fact that you have suffered no further unpleasant experiences makes me sure that we have this force, whatever it is, under control now. I suggest that you both carry on as you have been doing. Now, let me see . . . Welsford, you leave on the second of the month, don't you?'

I nodded, a melancholy feeling catching at my breast.

I saw Clara bite her lip.

'Well,' continued Yorke, obliviously, 'the day before you sail I want you and Clara to join me for dinner. I shall have some news by then . . . and I think I can assure you that it will be interesting. Very interesting.'

Then before we knew it, Yorke had dismissed us and we were standing outside his rooms.

As if by some unspoken agreement we turned and walked down to the Strand.

I must confess that my thoughts were not on Yorke, nor on the terrible experiences to which he was engaged in seeking a meaning. My thoughts were of my departure, of my losing Clara when I had only just found her.

Her hand found mine and squeezed it. It was as if she knew and understood my thoughts.

'Will you be away long?'

'Probably the best part of a year,' I replied morosely.

I heard her slow intake of breath.

'It is too long,' she said simply.

'I know,' I replied, almost harsh in my fervour.

'Perhaps, after you have gone out there and discovered what it is like, and if you think the country is suitable, perhaps . . .'

'Yes?' I encouraged eagerly.

She gave a little laugh of embarrassment.

'It's just that I am used to travelling.'

I stopped and pulled her close to me.

'Upton!' she rebuked. 'We are in a public street. Everyone will see!'

'Let them!' I said savagely, lowering my lips to hers. With a sigh her arms came up to encircle my neck and she responded with a soft lingering kiss. I felt myself go weak at the sensation of those two soft lips on mine and that curious, gentle, darting tongue. Then I felt her pulling away, casting a nervous glance around and straightening her hat.

'Goodness me, Upton,' she rebuked. 'I swear you'll have to make an honest woman of me now.'

I laughed joyously.

'Anything you want, my dear.'

She gazed at me coquettishly.

'Anything?'

'Anything at all,' I affirmed.

'Then I want . . . the best meal in London followed by a vaudeville or music hall!'

Laughing gaily, much to the horror of the passers-by, we linked arms and set out to find a cab.

The evening passed in a dream, a wonderful never-ending dream. If you were to ask me what I ate or, indeed, what music hall we went to see, I could not tell you. The time passed in a wonderful carousel of sounds, tastes and laughter.

When we came out of the theatre I hailed a cab and helped Clara into it. 'The Nelson Hotel,' I ordered but, to my amazement, Clara, though blushing furiously, told the driver to go to my address.

'You see, my love,' she whispered as she nestled close to me in the leather upholstery of the Hansom, 'you are going soon and who knows how long it will be before I see you again. I . . . I want to remain with you as long as I can. Is that so wicked?'

I kissed her gently on the forehead.

'I love you, Clara,' I declared.

She sighed and closed her eyes.

It was late when the Hansom deposited us before Mrs Dobson's rooming house. I paid off the cab and we entered stealthily and did not dare to draw breath until we were in the privacy of my own rooms. It took a while to raise a blaze in the hearth of my bedroom and Clara asked if she could freshen her face. While she was at her toilet I went into my sitting-room and selected a bottle of malt whisky from my cabinet, placed it on a tray and, polishing two glasses, set the tray ready. I mused that if my father could see me he would have taken his horse-whip as an aid to teaching me morals.

I suddenly realized that Clara had been a long time.

'Clara?' I called softly through the door of the bedroom, 'Are you all right?

There was no reply; but I heard a gentle rustling sound like the movement of starched cloth.

'Clara?'

A little alarmed, I pushed into the bedroom.

The first thing that caught my eye was Clara's coat and

hat strewn across a chair. The second thing was the dress which she had been wearing and which now lay in a pile on the floor alongside some garments which, frankly, I could not describe.

I must have stood looking at them in perplexity for some moments for there suddenly came a low rich chuckle from the bed.

There, between my sheets, with only her head showing and her black hair tumbling across the whiteness of my pillows, was Clara.

My throat went dry and the blood sang in my ears.

She gazed at me with a smile of amusement on her face.

'It's cold, Upton,' she whispered, but there was an edge to her voice, a tone which I could not place. 'It's cold. Come to bed.'

Like one in a dream, I turned down the lamp so that the room was lit only by the flickering fire from the hearth. My hands trembled, not from fear but from a strange desire which had seized my whole body, as I carefully unbuttoned my clothes and, finally, naked as I was born, climbed in beside her.

For a second she drew away, but only for a second, before she nestled close to me.

I leant on one arm looking down at her exquisite face which gazed up, childlike and trusting, wanton and yet innocent.

'Be gentle with me, Upton,' she whispered, 'it is . . . I have not . . it is my first time.'

Could I tell her that I, too, had yet to know the opposite sex?

I bent down and kissed her softly on the mouth. Our lips parted and it was as if a charge of electricity passed between us. Suddenly we were gasping, snatching, hungry and demanding, feeding from each other. When we paused for breath I let my hand stroke the soft coldness of her well-rounded shoulder, then slip down to her firm breasts whose nipples were raised hard with desire. Then my hand went further, across the cold flatness of her stomach, feeling the tautness of anticipation in the hardening muscles as my hand slid further to that mysterious cavern between her thighs.

She groaned, a sound hard and unreal.

Then she suddenly pulled me to her.

Never in all my experience was there such enjoyment, such pleasure, such feelings of love which through that act linked two people. This, surely, was the pinnacle of all human experience.

After it was over, we lay against each other, our bodies still fiercely intertwined, and fell into a gentle sleep.

All the feelings of guilt associated with such an act which had been impregnated on my young mind, with the morals and religious teaching of my youth, fell away; I realized how evil were the people who would try to make us feel ashamed at such a thing. This was natural, this was Nature herself, and they were debasing Nature, debasing mankind's creativity, by their narrow prudery. They were debasing God Himself.

I lay back feeling, for the first time in my life, complete.

The next day passed in a dream; what we did I have little remembrance of except that we made love, went for a meal, returned and made love again with the passion and enthusiasm of thirsty wayfarers in a desert who, coming upon an oasis, drink from the well as if it were the first and the last water that they would ever taste in their lives.

On Sunday evening Clara had to return to her hotel. Our plan, concocted in our starry bliss, was that Clara should accompany me to Romania as my wife. My sailing date was Tuesday and I reasoned that I could obtain a special licence and be married on the Monday. If that plan failed, I determined that Clara would accompany me anyway and we would get the captain of the ship to marry us once it was standing out to sea.

We moved in a delirium of happiness.

Having made our plans that Sunday evening, Clara said she would return to the Hotel Nelson, pack her luggage and return to my rooms in preparation. She laughed outright at my suggestion that it would create a scandal if Mrs Dobson saw her return with luggage. 'How so,' she demanded, 'when we shall be man and wife tomorrow?' I realized that there were some aspects of my narrow moral upbringing which would take some time to replace.

I started to get ready to accompany Clara, but she said that she would collect her bags by herself. After all, the hotel was not far away and she had only two cases with her. I could utilize the time by getting started on my neglected packing.

We kissed fondly and she left to accomplish her task.

In a rapturous dream I mooned about my rooms, trying to concentrate on filling my suitcases with the items I would need for my journey. It was done with much contemplation, sighing and dreaming, for I am of a romantic turn of mind.

It was while I was searching the bedroom for a lost cravat that my eye was attracted to a tiny flash of silver from the bedsheets. I bent down and discovered, with a degree of surprise, one of Yorke's tiny crucifixes. My hand went automatically to my throat and felt my own little cross still in its place. It must have been Clara's, I realized, and – ridiculously – I kissed the blessed thing for her sake. With an inward blush I realized that the cross must have come loose in the excesses of our lovemaking. Well, there was no need for charms now. The nightmares had long stopped. I scooped up the silver object and placed it in my pocket.

An hour later I began to expect the return of Clara.

Two hours saw me pacing the room in nervousness, eyes upon the clock to assure myself of the passing of time.

When three hours had passed I was sick with anxiety and my hands fluttered with agitation, for I could not keep them still.

On the striking of that third hour I grabbed my hat and coat and went down the stairs to the street. It was about nine o'clock in the evening and the streets were fairly deserted. I set off at a brisk pace towards the Nelson Hotel and was soon standing in its dimly lit foyer, agitatedly ringing the bell on the reception desk.

A prim-faced woman of fifty came through a curtained doorway and stood regarding me with hostile eyes glinting from behind rimless spectacles.

'I wish to see Miss Clarke,' I said

I could scarcely keep the impatience from my voice and the woman looked at me with deep suspicion.

'Miss Clarke?' There was a nasal drawl to her voice.

'Yes, yes. Miss Clara Clarke. Which room?'

The woman shook her head.

'I am afraid Miss Clarke left this hotel two hours ago.'

I staggered back as if I had been hit. Two hours! Plenty of time to return to my rooms. There must be some mistake.

'She . . . she's gone?' I asked incredulously.

'That is what I said, sir,' said the woman, stonily.

'When will she be back?' I pressed, not understanding.

'Miss Clarke vacated her room in this hotel,' said the woman heavily, as if talking to a child.

'Well, where has she gone?' I almost shouted.

'The lady would not be likely to confide in the staff of this hotel as to her movements,' was the unhelpful reply.

I backed out into the street in a daze. My world was suddenly shattered.

How could she have left without saying a word to me?

And where would she have gone to? I suppose, ridiculous as it was, my first thoughts were to the effect that I was an injured lover – deserted by my love, that Clara must have been using me to some purpose. No sooner had the angry thought flashed into my burning head than I rebuked myself strongly for giving even momentary credence to such an uncharitable thought. I stood on the pavement, outside the hotel, trying to decide where she had gone.

A cab came idling by. I hailed it and directed it back to my rooms. Asking the man to wait, I raced up the stairs to my apartment, but they were still desolate. I scribbled a hasty note to Clara, lest she should return from some perfectly innocent mission in my absence, and pinned it to the door. Then I hastened back down the stairs to the waiting cabman and gave him Yorke's address.

I do not know what moved the feeling within me but, as we trotted through Bloomsbury Square and turned up the small thoroughfare in which Yorke had his rooms, I had a strong feeling of disquiet. On reflection I think it was sparked off when my hand strayed to my pocket and started to nervously finger an object there. It was some moments before I realized what it was – Clara's silver crucifix.

Then, as I alighted and told the cabby to wait once again, I heard a terrified feminine scream from the house in which Yorke's rooms were situated. I wheeled abruptly towards the door, and finding it open, I pushed my way into the building. I took several stairs at a time and reached Yorke's landing in a moment.

Outside his door was a dowdy little woman whom I recognized as the housekeeper.

'Oh sir, oh sir,' she sobbed as she caught sight of me.

'What is it?' I snapped.

'It's Mr Yorke, sir,' and she began to sob in a frightful manner.

'What's wrong?' I almost shouted.

'He's groaning in there something awful, sir. I heard it not long after the young lady left . . .'

'Young lady?' I cried, seizing her by the shoulders. 'What young lady?'

She backed away from me looking frightened.

'I don't know, sir. I came up here but the door was locked and I went away again. That was an hour ago. But a short while since I heard a banging on my ceiling, my rooms being immediately under Mister Yorke's, and I came up here to find out what the matter was. A few minutes ago he gave such a terrible groan . . . oh sir, something is awfully wrong.'

My blood running cold, I tried the door. It was locked.

'Do you have a master key?' I asked.

She shook her head.

'Mr Yorke is very particular about who has his keys, sir.'

'Then there is only one thing for it,' I told her. 'I must break down the door.'

Without waiting to hear her protests, illogical protests in view of the situation, I put my shoulder to the door. It was heavy and would not budge. The noise, by now, had attracted a police constable who, ascertaining the position, and finding it to be somewhat dire, leant back and used his heavy boot against the door. Three kicks had the lock snapping and the door swinging open.

'Seeing you're a friend, sir, you'd best go in first,' advised the constable.

I entered and stood appalled.

To say that the room was in disarray would be an understatement.

It looked as if a whirlwind had struck it. China and ornaments lay in smashed profusion; furniture was broken and splintered wood was littered everywhere.

A heart-rending groan brought me to the figure of a man lying face-down on the littered floor.

My first reaction was one of relief.

It could not be Yorke because the figure had a mane of white hair.

I bent over the man and slowly turned him on his back. It was then that my world started to spin rapidly. Behind me the housekeeper let out a squawk of horror and fainted dead away for I heard her body slump heavily to the floor.

I reached out a hand to grasp a support.

The face of the man before me was old . . . lines cracked across a bloodless, white parchment skin. The mouth was twisted back as if in terror, the eyes were wide and staring, the shock of white hair was like snow . . . but it was the face of my friend Yorke.

CHAPTER FIFTEEN

'My God!' I exclaimed aghast.

The policeman looked from the prostrate housekeeper to my ashen face in bewilderment.

'Your friend, sir?' he asked quietly.

I nodded, unable to speak. I breathed deeply several times to recover control of my senses and then advised the constable: 'You had best call a doctor . . . oh, and take the lady downstairs.'

'Right, sir.'

The constable lifted the unconscious woman from the floor and went out.

I bent and felt for Yorke's heart and, incredibly, I felt a faint flutter.

'Yorke, old fellow. It's me, Welsford. Can you hear me?'

The terrified eyes tried to focus.

That ghastly twisted mouth moved. I heard a faint breath and bent my ear to his lips.

'Welsford . . .'

It seemed a great effort for him to speak.

'Yes, old friend. It's me,' I replied encouragingly.

'Failed, Welsford . . . underestimated the power . . .'

He paused gasping for breath.

'Don't worry, old man. A doctor will be along shortly.'

He moaned and shook his head.

'No . . . no good. Too late.'

'Can you tell me what happened?' I urged as gently as I could.

'Power made contact . . . she . . . she came . . . unprotected . . . power made contact . . .'

My heart lurched.

'She? Clara?' I fought hard to keep the agitation out of my voice.

'Yes . . . unprotected . . . power, underestimated power. She obeyed . . . statuette . . . taking it to . . . land beyond the forest . . . controlled by power . . .'

He was racked by a rasping cough.

'Tried to stop it . . . power rebounded on me . . . power through Draco . . . through statuette . . .'

I felt myself growing cold with horror.

'Clara came here?' I pressed him. 'Clara came here and the power which you say emanates from the statuette took control of her mind? She is taking it to Transylvania?'

He nodded weakly.

'Yes, yes . . . tried to stop her . . . power rebounded on me. Done for.'

Suddenly he grasped my wrist in an almost superhuman grip.

'You must stop her, Welsford. The statuette is the key . . . destroy it. If you fail . . . evil will spread into the world like waters bursting through a dam . . .' His voice was strong now and a fierce light burned in his eyes. 'Welsford, do not underestimate the power as I did . . . remember to protect yourself with the symbols of goodness and light.'

'Yes, I understand, Yorke,' I gulped. 'Try not to talk anymore. The doctor . . .'

He gave an abrupt rasping cough and fell back.

I did not need to be told from his glazed, staring eyes that Yorke was dead.

A moment later the constable re-entered.

'A doctor is on his way, sir,' he said.

'Too late,' I sighed, getting up from the floor. 'He's dead.'

The constable let out a long, low whistle.

He looked around the room with a professional eye.

'Looks like a burglary, sir. Was he attacked or was it his heart, sir?'

I hesitated.

'I don't know,' I said heavily. 'He didn't say anything.'

The constable regarded me thoughtfully for a moment.

'Thought I heard you talking to him a moment ago, sir?'

I shook my head.

'I tried to rouse him but he didn't respond,' I lied, realizing that if I told the truth he would think me as insane as I nearly believed myself to be.

'Look here, sir,' the constable had found a new interest, 'this tin box . . . do you know what he kept in it?'

It was the box in which I had seen Yorke place the jade dragon.

'Some valuables, I believe,' I hedged.

The policeman gave a snort of triumph.

'Nothing in it now.' He held it towards me. 'Look at the way it is dented and look at the black burn marks on it . . . it's as if someone used some explosive to open it, or as if it was struck by a bolt of lightning. Curious, eh?'

He placed the box aside and took out a notebook.

'Now, sir, I'd better get some details before my sergeant arrives.'

It was nearly two hours later before I returned to my rooms. My heart was cold within me and I was gripped by a terrifying apprehension.

The police had regarded the matter as one of simple burglary with Yorke suffering from some form of heart attack at the shock of it. I did not amplify on his ghastly change in physical appearance and I understood the house-keeper was in a state of shock and would not be able to be questioned for several days . . . by which time, I reasoned, I would be on the high seas and therefore unable to answer the obvious questions which would arise.

I must have sat through the night locked deep in

thought, for it seemed but a few moments before the sun was sending brilliant cascades of light through my window.

I stirred myself and tried to finalize my thoughts.

Firstly, I had to find out if Clara was still in London. Yorke had said that she was under control of the strange power emanating from the jade dragon and that she was taking it to Transylvania – 'the land beyond the forest'. I had no reason now to disagree with Yorke's explanation that some mysterious force was calling her, controlling her and forcing her to take the ancient statuette of the dragon god.

No one could surely scoff at the idea after witnessing the scenes that I had seen.

There was no doubt in my mind that I, Upton Welsford, was Clara's only salvation in this weird nightmare. I must track her down and destroy the dragon god before it destroyed her. It was as simple as that.

Having made that resolve, I felt better and the adrenalin began to flow once more in my veins.

I ate a meagre breakfast and went immediately to Lloyd's Register of Shipping to make inquiries about vessels sailing directly for the Black Sea ports. The clerk looked through his ledgers.

'There is one vessel, sir. In fact it is the only vessel that will make the direct voyage for a fortnight. But,' he gazed at the clock, 'I don't think you will make it, for it is due to sail on the morning tide from Tower Wharf.'

A surge of excitement went through me.

'The name of the ship?' I demanded.

'The *Psyche* out of Liverpool, sir.'

I had no complaints about the way the cabby thrashed his horses through the narrow streets towards London Bridge and then along the north bank through Billingsgate Fish Market to the Tower of London. He did not draw rein until we had raced through the dockyard and on to the Tower Wharf itself.

My heart sank within me.

The wharf was deserted.

An old man in a sailor's grubby jersey and cap sat on a bollard whittling at a piece of stick with an old clasp knife.

'Has the *Psyche* sailed already?' I demanded.

The old man gave a toothless grin.

'Reckon so, mister,' he said and jabbed his stick towards the empty wharf.

'Has she just gone?'

'Nope,' he said, intent on his whittling again.

'Here,' I said, pressing a shilling into his hand. 'Tell me, what time did she sail?'

He pocketed the coin and gazed at me reflectively.

'Happen about midnight. 'Gainst regulations, too, but her captain is a greedy man, so he just slipped her cables on the night tide.'

I frowned.

'What do you mean by that?'

'Happen like this: I'm in the Black Anchor over there, see? I'm having a drink with a friend o' mine, Chalky White, when old Ben comes across and says the *Psyche* has upped and slipped her cables. Old Ben works on these docks, you see. He says about an hour towards midnight a cab drives up with a woman – a pretty young woman at that, says Ben – she's all alone with only a couple of pieces of baggage with her. Old Ben hears her book a passage on the *Psyche* then she tells the captain that there is a nice bonus in it for him if he slips his cables there and then.'

'Where did she book to?'

'You interested in the *Psyche* or in the girl, mister?' asked the old sailor, a flicker of amusement in his eyes. 'If 'tis the girl then I can't help you. Old Ben didn't hear. If 'tis the *Psyche* then she's bound for the port o' Varna carrying a cargo of corn seed.'

'Varna?' I gasped. 'That's near Constanta on the Black Sea.'

'Aye, that it be. I sailed into Varna and Constanta many a time in my day. Turkish ports they be, though not in Turkey-land proper.'

'How long do you estimate it will take for the *Psyche* to get to Varna?' I asked.

'Oh, two weeks mayhap. More likely three weeks because she's a slow enough vessel even in calm seas. She carries too much weight on her beams.'

My mind raced. There was still time then. If, as scheduled, we – Lord Molesworth and the Foreign Office party – sailed tomorrow and made the transfer to the British naval frigate quickly at Gibraltar, then the frigate might have us at the Black Sea ports before the *Psyche*.

I thanked the old sailor with another shilling, climbed into the cab and returned home.

It was a chance, but it was my only chance.

CHAPTER SIXTEEN

The *Agrinion* sailed from Tilbury on the morning tide the day after my futile attempt to follow Clara aboard the *Psyche*. On board were Lord Molesworth, myself, and the entire British Foreign Office delegation to Romania. Of the journey to Gibraltar there is little to recount except that during our stormy crossing of the Bay of Biscay Lord Molesworth took me aside in his stateroom and, without preamble, demanded:

'What the devil is the matter with you, Welsford?'

'Matter, sir?' I feinted.

'Matter,' he echoed. 'You have worked for me for some years now and I have never seen you in this state before. You are nervous, even fretful . . . if you continue this way, Welsford, you will be worse than useless to me when we reach Bucharest.'

How could I tell him what my situation was?

It was while I fumbled for my response that I decided to tell him a half-truth.

'Well, sir,' I began, my mind rapidly forming my story, 'I became engaged to be married at the weekend.'

Molesworth looked startled.

'The deuce, you say!' he exclaimed.

'I do say, sir.'

'And who is the . . . the young lady in question?'

'Miss Clara Clarke, sir, the daughter of Colonel George Clarke.'

One of Molesworth's gifts was an incredibly retentive memory for certain types of information such as people in the British service, serving abroad.

'Clarke, eh? On the Egyptian staff? Good man. Congratulations, Welsford. But how does that fact explain your attitude?'

'I discovered that Miss Clarke, my fiancée, thinking no doubt to surprise me, sailed for Varna on a ship called the *Psyche* yesterday. I am naturally fearful for her safety.'

Molesworth chuckled.

'Damn me, she sounds a spirited girl, Welsford. Headstrong family, the Clarkes, you know. Must take after her father. Held back a whole tribe of Afridis single-handed during the war in . . . well, never mind. Any girl who will do that for a man is not to be treated lightly.'

He clasped my shoulder.

'Don't worry, Welsford. She'll be all right. We'll soon find her, don't worry. Get it out of your mind. Now, how about a little snorter to celebrate the betrothal, eh?'

I felt pleased because, when we reached Constanta, I would at least have an excuse to leave the delegation to go in search of Clara at Varna.

The rest of our passage to Gibraltar passed uneventfully enough, apart from the continuing high winds and seas which seem to be a feature of the coast of Biscay. It was calm enough when we reached Gibraltar but we did not go ashore, for which – in my fretful state – I was thankful. Instead we transferred to a naval ship, which turned out to be a sloop not a frigate, although I am not sure what the difference is exactly. It was a sleek black and white coloured vessel named *Centurion*.

The captain was a ruddy-faced, youthful lieutenant-commander who had spent most of his life sailing in the waters of the Near East and had many a tale to tell about slave trafficking between Africa and Arabia. In other circumstances I would have been a fascinated audience. But I had no cause to complain about delay, for the *Centurion* was a fast enough craft which, with the trade winds behind her, cut through the water like a knife. The navy had orders to put the delegation ashore in Romania in time for the state ceremonials at the end of the month and the captain was determined to carry out the orders to the letter. The first officer, an even younger looking man than his captain, a Lieutenant Brown, took a pride in praising sail over the 'new-fangled steam', as he called it.

'Mark me, Mr Welsford,' he would say, thumping his hand on the taffrail, where we were standing, 'steam will never replace a good set of sail in the Royal Navy. A good set of sail handled by experts will run rings round steam and ironclads any day.'

It was common talk that new steam ships were being built on the Mersey for the young Confederate States of America and designed for use in their war of secession against the Union. These ships were equipped with heavy iron armour plating. The navies of the world were witnessing a revolution on the sea. In fact, it is worth noting that, within a few months of our conversation, on 8 March 1862, the first great naval engagement between ironclads was fought between the American Confederate ship *Merrimac* and the Union American ship *Monitor* which was to mark the greatest change in sea fighting since a cannon fired by gunpowder was mounted on ships four hundred years ago.

Such conversations helped to pass the hours as the *Centurion* sped through the calm blue waters of the Mediterranean.

We made fast time from Gibraltar and passed the Balearic Isles to the north, passed the southern coast of the island of Sicily and were bearing south of the Ionian Sea when there was a yell from the lookout at the foremast top.

'Sail ho! Bearing off the larboard bow!'

I was on the quarterdeck at the time, trying to find shelter from the hot rays of the sun and unable to bear the stuffy close-quarters of my cabin. The cluster of officers raised their glasses towards the black pinprick which was some miles in front of us.

'Lugger, sir,' sang out one man. 'She's weathering all her canvas. Must be in a devil of a hurry.'

The captain nodded curtly.

In the monotonous life at sea, a passing ship was at least something to look at and converse about and Lord Molesworth joined me at the taffrail watching the black speck grow larger and slowly take on the aspect of a low-bowed ship under full sail.

During the late afternoon the first officer made another examination of the ship, which we were fast overhauling. His remark set my pulses throbbing.

'I recognize her, captain. It's the old *Psyche* out of Liverpool. She often trades in these waters.'

'The *Psyche*?' I gasped. 'May I borrow your glass?'

With amused surprise at my eagerness, the lieutenant handed me his telescope.

The *Psyche* must have been two miles away, still bearing in front of us under full sail. I could make out only her silhouette and see some tiny black figures moving on her decks.

'We're overhauling her sure enough,' said the lieutenant over my shoulder. 'Another two hours should see us abeam of her.'

I swallowed hard. An idea flashed into my mind.

'Do you think it possible to lay alongside her?' I asked.

'Alongside?' There was amazement in the first officer's voice.

'Do you think it possible that you could put me aboard her?' I persisted.

'Good Lord! Put you aboard the *Psyche*, Mr Welsford?'

The captain, overhearing my remarks, joined in the conversation.

'It is imperative I go aboard her,' I said somewhat lamely.

It was Molesworth who drew the naval officers aside and told them, I suppose, the story that I had told him. They turned back with sympathetic grins.

'Tell you what, Mr Welsford,' said the captain with a smile, 'if the weather holds, I can put a skiff across . . . maybe you would like to bring your fiancée back aboard and continue the voyage with us?'

I grasped his hand and blurted out my thanks.

'Think nothing of it, Mr Welsford,' said the naval officer with a ghost of a wink. '*Cherchez la femme* and all that, eh?'

In agony I stood by the rail watching the *Psyche* looming closer and larger, trying to hide my impatience at the slowness of the process.

Abruptly, the blue-blackness of the velvet Mediterranean night started to sweep across the horizon, like the sudden rolling down of a blind.

'Break out the skiff,' called the captain who turned to me and added, 'We have time to put a boat across before it becomes too dark to see.'

I echoed my gratitude once again.

The skiff was lowered into the water and four burly seamen and the first officer clambered down into it. I was given a hand down and sat in the stern of the little craft, next to the first officer, as it started to gather speed over the still black waters, propelled by the firm strokes of the sailors at their oars.

The *Psyche* seemed to be standing almost motionless a hundred yards or so to our larboard side. The wind had died down and although she still had on every stitch of canvas there was not a sufficient breeze to fill them.

As we started away from the side of the naval sloop, the captain leaned across the rail with a megaphone in his hand and hailed the *Psyche*.

'*Psyche* ahoy! This is Her Majesty's Sloop o' War *Centurion*. We are sending a boarding party across.'

There was no reply from the now dimly-seen shape of the lugger, standing hove-to in the twilight.

I cannot quite recall what happened next.

One minute we were rowing swiftly across the calm sea, through the twilight but still with an excellent degree of visibility of both our own ship and the *Psyche*, then the next minute we were surrounded by a mist, almost a fog of some obnoxious green-brown substance. I swear it had some sickly sweet smell to it, which for the moment, I could not place.

'Avast pulling!' snapped the lieutenant.

The sailors rested on their oars and looked round in bewilderment.

'Where did this stuff come from, sir?' asked one.

'Jesus, it don't 'alf smell putrid,' commented another.

'Silence!' ordered the first officer.

The silence surrounded us as completely as the mist or fog. There was no sound except for the gentle slapping of the sea along the bottom of the boat.

'Is it usual to encounter such mists in the Mediterranean?' I whispered.

The first lieutenant shook his head.

'It doesn't seem to be passing, whatever it is,' he said.

He sat back in his seat and cupped his hands to his mouth.

'Ahoy! Ahoy there!'

We listened.

The voice seemed to be lost in the thickness of the mist.

'*Psyche* ahoy!'

There was no answer.

The lieutenant turned in the direction we had come from.

'*Centurion* ahoy!'

There was no sound but the slap, slap, slap of the waves on our keel.

'Blamed me if I sees anything like it,' swore the sailor.

'Shall us row back, sir?' inquired another.

The lieutenant plucked at his lower lip.

'No, we might have swung right round in the fog and then where would we be?'

I could see the logic of this.

'What shall we do if it doesn't clear,' I asked

'Of course it has to clear,' retorted the officer but I could see worry etching his face.

We sat for a while in complete silence: it was so uncanny, that silence, the slapping of the water and no other sound except the occasional cough as the putrid green-black mist swirled into our lungs.

The faces of the sailors gradually formed expressions of annoyance and then apprehension.

'Rooney,' the lieutenant finally said, 'you'll find a storm lantern in the bow locker behind you. Better light it, it might be seen by the *Centurion*.'

The seaman nodded and executed the order.

The storm lantern was a futile gesture; even from our position in the stern we could barely make out its flame in the bow which was only twelve feet away.

The first officer was perplexed.

A chilling feeling began to grow within me. I could hear Yorke's agonized voice: 'I underestimated the power!' Could the power, whatever it was, of the force that held Clara an unwilling servant be so strong as to be able to create such conditions? A shudder of horror ran through my frame.

Lieutenant Brown, observing my shudder, attributed it to the wrong cause and clapped my shoulder reassuringly.

'Don't worry, Mr Welsford. We'll soon be out of this mess.'

His bonhomie sounded strangely false.

'Hold hard, sir!' snapped a sailor. 'I think we are nearing a ship . . . listen there!'

We all strained our ears.

There was a slight difference in the sounds of the sea. I was too much a landlubber to pick them out but I understand that a trained ear can make out the hollow smack of the waves against a big ship's hull, the running water from the cable lines and other queerly distinctive sounds that can only be associated with a larger vessel.

For a moment there seemed a break in the mist and the lieutenant gave a cry of exultation.

'Over there!' he pointed. 'Pull, you swabs. It must be the *Psyche* for she's a large vessel squarely rigged fore and aft.' He raised his cupped hands again. 'Ahoy! *Psyche* ahoy!'

The silence was still unbroken by a reply.

'Curse them all for deaf idiots,' swore the lieutenant.

The sailors strained fiercely at their oars and brought our skiff nearer to the great silent vessel.

My apprehension of a moment before returned like a deep gnawing pain in my stomach.

'Do you smell anything, lieutenant?' I whispered anxiously.

He sniffed cautiously.

'Great guns! It smells like dead fish and decaying seaweed. Ugh! What can they have aboard?'

Abruptly, without warning, our skiff bumped into the solid black side of the ship.

One of the sailors put out a hand to steady the skiff and drew it back uttering a cry of disgust.

'Slime, sir,' he said, holding out his hand in the light of the storm lantern. 'Bloody slime! The sides of the ship can't have been swabbed down for ages.'

'Ahoy!' The lieutenant raised his voice once again, standing up in our small craft and peering towards the deck.

There was no answer.

'I don't like the look of it,' muttered one of the seamen.

The lieutenant sat down in the stern again, a worried expression on his face.

'I can't make this out, Mr Welsford. The ship seems deserted.'

The four seamen started to mutter among themselves.

'Avast!' snapped the lieutenant.'Quit your blubbering and take the oars.'

'What are you going to do?' I queried.

'We shall row round the vessel and see if we can raise anyone; if not, I propose to board her. We can then wait until the mists clear, make contact with the *Centurion* and claim prize money . . . remember that, you fellows,' he admonished the seamen.

Bemused I asked: 'What prize money?'

The lieutenant jerked a thumb towards the black hulk towering up beside us.

'If she's deserted then we are entitled to salvage.'

Under his guidance, the skiff was rowed alongside the vessel, which stank in a terrible fashion. There was no light on the ship at all and it soon became obvious that the ship must be a derelict. We passed round her stern but could see no name plate at all. One thing was certain, this was not the *Psyche* which we had been rowing for. But where had this strange vessel appeared from? There had been no sight of it before we set out for the *Psyche*.

As we rowed up the other side of the vessel we came to a rope ladder hanging from an open gangway.

'Make fast,' ordered the first officer.

The skiff secured alongside, the lieutenant grasped the rope ladder and started to draw himself up.

'Careful as you come,' he called over his shoulder, 'the ladder is wet and rotten.'

A sailor, who I noticed had stuck a belaying pin into his waistband, followed the officer up to the deck. I was next. The deck was shrouded in gloom and even when the sailor, Rooney, followed us with the storm lantern, it cast little light on the ship. The deck was wet and slippery beneath our feet and the whole superstructure seemed to be covered with a slime such as usually appends itself to breakwaters and suchlike which are almost permanently under water.

'Well, one thing is certain,' said the lieutenant, 'this is a derelict and by the look of her condition she must have been drifting for years.'

'But what's become of the *Psyche*?' I demanded. 'There was certainly no other vessel near us when we left for her.'

The officer shrugged.

'Devil I know, Mr Welsford. But there's not much we can do for the time being, we'll just have to wait until the mist clears or the sun comes up.'

'Guess we'll have to spend a hungry night, sir,' observed a broad-faced, well-muscled seaman – the one who had been wise enough to arm himself with the belaying pin.

'Right enough, Hampden,' replied the lieutenant. 'Still, now we are here, we might as well explore the vessel. We can at least find out who she is and what happened to her.'

There was a murmur of reluctant assent.

'Hampden, you take two men and search for'ard. I'll take Rooney and Mr Welsford and search the stern.'

Hampden knuckled his forehead.

'What about the lantern, sir.'

The officer swore.

'As you were. We'd best see if we can find any other means of lighting.'

In a body we moved towards the stern and entered what must have been the chart room and captain's day cabin. It was fairly dry inside and there were several storm lanterns on a shelf. Hampden seized a couple and checked them for fuel. He made a taper out of a piece of crumbling chart and lit them.

'We'll go for'ard and check things out, sir.'

The lieutenant, the seaman Rooney and myself were left to explore the papers in the cabin.

'Well, I'll be . . .' the lieutenant suddenly gave a whistle. 'This is the old *Ceres*, a Russian ship out of Varna. She's been missing for five years or more. The crew were saved, abandoned her during a storm off Crete . . . they were a bit mad, complained of peculiar happenings on board, you know what foreign sailors are like.'

His voice was tinged with all the superiority that a British Royal Navy Officer has towards a foreign seaman.

'Well, well. I'll bet we're in for a tidy penny in salvage. The crew thought the *Ceres* had foundered off Kásos. I wonder if her manifest is still . . .'

Just then a terrified scream echoed from the forward part of the ship.

CHAPTER SEVENTEEN

We turned with startled glances.

The lieutenant was the first to recover his composure and grabbed at a rusty sword which hung in a rack in the cabin. Then, followed by Rooney and myself, he pushed his way out on to the slippery deck.

The three seamen, led by Hampden, were slipping and falling along the deck towards us.

'Jehosephat!' swore the lieutenant. 'What on earth is going on?'

Hampden collided heavily with the officer, unable to stop himself on the slippery planking. The lieutenant grasped at the rail and managed to retain his balance, thus preventing them both from falling.

'There's something back there, sir. Hoskins saw it.'

The seaman named Hoskins turned a white fear-ridden face towards us.

'Saw it? I'll say I did. The eyes, sir, oh my Gawd, those eyes . . . red, 'orrible, they was!'

The lieutenant snorted.

'For heaven's sake control yourself, man! Eyes indeed! What eyes? Whose eyes?'

'The very devil himself, sir!' swore the seaman with some vehemence. 'Tiny red eyes, sir, red and small, staring unwinkingly at me sir.'

The lieutenant, much to our surprise, suddenly threw back his head and bellowed with laughter.

'Hoskins, Hoskins,' he laughed helplessly. 'Have you never seen ship's rats before this? Tiny red eyes, indeed! This ship has been adrift for five years, it's the old *Ceres*, and it must be acrawl with rats.'

Hampden turned on Hoskins with anger replacing a momentary look of sheepishness.

'You blamed fool, Hoskins!' he snarled.

'Enough of that, Hampden,' admonished the lieutenant. 'Rats can be dangerous too, especially on a derelict. They might have been without food for a long time, so don't dismiss them too lightly.'

Hampden lapsed into silence.

'You'd better continue to search for'ard but keep a careful watch.'

The sailors returned to the forward part of the vessel while the lieutenant, Rooney and myself went back to the chart room.

I watched while the officer sorted through a pile of papers which had been scattered about: they were wet and soggy and had been partly eaten, obviously by rats in search of food.

'Nothing here of interest,' he pronounced after a while.

For my part, I was still pondering on the mystery of the fog and the *Psyche*.

'It seems strange,' I said once again, 'that we did not see this vessel before the fog closed down on us.'

Lieutenant Brown nodded.

'Strange things do happen at sea, Mr Welsford,' he said, a trifle too glibly. His smile indicated that he was probably thinking of the salvage money which would be due to him come the morning when the *Centurion* could take us in tow.

'Isn't this ship too rotten to salvage?' I wondered.

'Probably it is too rotten to refit, but salvage is salvage,' replied the officer.

We walked out on to the deck and stood peering around in the mist-shrouded gloom.

'The smell is really vile,' commented Lieutenant Brown.

'Ay,' mumbled the usually silent Rooney. 'It's as if the

ship has been dragged up from the bottom of the ocean after lying there for who knows how long.'

I agreed with Rooney's description.

Hampden and the others rejoined us and admitted to seeing nothing of interest apart from the odd glimpse of baleful red eyes staring at them in the darkness.

'Must be thousands of the bloody little creatures below decks, sir,' observed Hoskins with a shudder.

'So long as they stay there,' replied the lieutenant lightly.

It was then that the gloomy silence around us was split with a long mournful howl. It froze us like stone statues, so unexpected was the sound. It was the mournful howl of a hound hunting its quarry.

But here? Here on an old derelict, five years adrift in the ocean?

'Christ! Look, sir. Look there!'

Hoskin's finger was raised and trembling towards the quarter-deck.

Standing on the raised deck, seeming to tower high above us, stood the grotesque black shape of a dog. But it was a dog so large that it dwarfed even an Irish wolf-hound, the biggest of the species. It was gazing at us with large luminous eyes. It was something I had never seen before and a sight that I never want to see again. Even as we watched it, it threw back its muzzle and howled again . . . long, drawn-out . . . echoing like a thousand banshees in the gloomy mist.

It was the lieutenant who was the first to recover his power of movement.

He brandished the rusty sword in front of him.

'Careful, men,' he whispered softly, 'draw back for'ard, a step at a time now and slowly does it. Don't frighten the beast now.'

'Frighten it? Me frighten it?' croaked Hoskins. 'Lawd! What d'you think it's doing to me?'

'Shut up and move back there!'

We started to edge back along the deck. Our three lamps were held high. We had not gone back many paces when the huge brute suddenly leapt from the quarter deck and landed on the main deck not ten yards from our group. I registered unconscious surprise at the agility of the great beast which must have sprung a distance of twenty feet, landing in the thick slimy wetness of the deck without one slip or falter in its step.

With the lanterns held high, the light from them spilled across the ghastly vision as it glared malevolently at us from those vicious red eyes. It was a hound. No! It was more a grotesque parody of such an animal, large as a lion and as black as jet. Its eyes gleamed with an unholy aura like glowing red coals. Its great white fangs were bared and its muzzle and dewlap were dripping with saliva and tinged with blood.

We had barely gone back a dozen more paces when the creature began to gather up his hind legs beneath the sleek black body and I knew that the beast was about to spring.

In desperation my hands clenched in my pockets.

My hand closed on the tiny silver crucifix which had reposed in my coat pocket since that frightful evening when I found it after Clara had left me. Dimly I seemed to hear Yorke's rasping breath: '. . . remember to protect yourself with the symbols of goodness and light.'

With a terrifying howl, the great beast sprang forward.

Two things happened. Rooney suddenly hurled his lantern full at the creature at precisely the same moment as I flung the tiny crucifix into its gigantic maw.

I know not which was the cause of what followed, nor do I precisely know exactly what happened.

There was a terrific flash of blinding light and even as I averted my eyes the great beast seemed to dissolve into thin air. Yes, one moment it was there and the next it had vanished. And a strange thing seemed to happen – even now I am not sure whether it was a strange trick of the gloomy light – the great black shadow of the hound seemed to dissolve in flames, dissolve and then twist itself into a tiny winged creature – the shape of a small black bat – and flit upwards into the blackness, uttering strange human-like cries, as if of rage.

At that instant the derelict gave a lurch and a strange creaking seemed to echo from all sides.

The lieutenant gave a warning cry.

'My God! She's breaking up! Back to the skiff!'

The sailors needed no second urging for, above the creaking of the spars and deck planking, and the strange lurching of the doomed vessel, we could hear the high-pitched and terrified squeals of hundreds of thousands of rats. And even as I hesitated in following the seamen towards the gangway, below which the skiff was fastened, the rats started to erupt on to the slime-covered deck. I paused appalled by the sight of the countless black creatures with their red darting eyes, spilling through doors, portholes, hold covers, even through gaps in the planking itself.

'For God's sake, Mr Welsford,' screamed a seaman.

But I stood rooted in horror.

Someone – I think it was Hampden – grabbed me by the collar and bodily heaved me over the side into the skiff. Rooney was already untying it and, as soon as Hampden flung himself aboard, the rest of the men were working the oars and sending the craft shooting away from the doomed derelict; away from the frightful noise of the squealing of the drowning rats which rang in our ears so loudly that I thought my very brain was on fire.

Even so, so desperate were some of those terrible creatures that many of them leapt from the deck and several even fell into the skiff.

Disgust governing all reason, the lieutenant and I seized

belaying pins and laid about us with a will, smashing viciously at the animals before they could recover from the impact of landing.

It seemed that the entire ocean heaved and boiled around us as countless rats leapt into the water and swam for their lives, seizing upon any floatable objects they could find, fighting each other for the possession of the smallest oar or plank of wood.

There was a great gurgling sound and the sea seemed to open up and swallow the dark shape that had once been the *Ceres*.

We rowed into quieter water and, examining the waters around us and observing no wreckage nor any sign of the rats, the sailors rested on their oars while the lieutenant and I bowed our heads in a silent prayer of thankfulness.

'Look, sir!'

It was Hoskins.

We looked up.

As if by some miracle the green mist had completely evaporated. The white moon shone with a pale brilliance down out of a rich blue Mediterranean night sky which was littered with a myriad of white pin pricks where stars shone. The sea was perfectly calm and clear and a mile away we could make out the lights of a ship and even its dark silhouette against the lighter blue-black of the night.

Of the wreck of the *Ceres* there was no sign at all.

The lieutenant wiped his mouth with the back of his hand. I could see a faint tremble in it and saw the sweat standing out on his brow.

We had all been through a lot that night.

'Stand out for that ship,' ordered the lieutenant. 'Put your backs into it now.'

The sea was peaceful and the skiff made rapid progress across the intervening distance.

As we approached, Hampden swore.

'Bless me, sir, ain't that the old *Centurion*?'

Hardly had he spoken when a voice hailed us.

'Skiff ahoy!'

We could make out some of the crew hanging over the rails. It was the *Centurion* right enough. Willing hands pulled us aboard. The lieutenant made his report but his precise naval manner conveyed none of the terrors of that strange ship.

We were soon taken below for a hot toddy.

Molesworth was there, clapping me on the back and smiling.

'Thought we'd lost you, dear fellow,' he murmured.

The captain looked thoughtful: 'Damned strange thing,' he remarked. 'There was the Psyche and ourselves in sight when that beastly mist came down. Then, when it lifted, there was no sign of anything. Thought you'd vanished or at least made it aboard the *Psyche*. Then you suddenly appear out of the night, so to speak. Damned strange.'

There seemed no answer.

'Well, we'd best get under way . . .' the captain turned reluctantly out of the cabin. 'Don't forget to write a report for the log entry, mister,' he told the lieutenant who, like me, was tucking into a hot stew in some effort, I should imagine, to re-identify with reality.

The captain paused at the cabin door and looked back at us with a worried expression.

'Damned strange,' was his parting remark.

CHAPTER EIGHTEEN

The rest of the passage passed uneventfully. I had a lot of time in which to examine the strange affair from the very beginning. I had now come to terms with what I was doing. I was facing some terrifying occult power which was so colossal that it could control mists and mirages. I was now firmly convinced that it was the throwing of Clara's crucifix into the maw of the hell-hound which had destroyed it. Rooney swore that the lantern he had thrown had smashed against the beast, soaking it in petrol and incinerating it. And the lieutenant had rationalized that the hound was nothing more than a ship's dog, left behind when the crew of the *Ceres* abandoned ship. The beast had then grown wild and primitive in its instincts during the five years of drifting, probably prolonging its existence by eating the rats that populated the ship.

It seemed that only I had seen the swiftly flitting shape of the bat spring from the flames and flap its way into the gloom of the night.

I shuddered. If I had rationalized this way a few weeks ago I would have had myself committed to some asylum. I fingered the remaining silver crucifix which never left my throat and pondered a long time on what Yorke had told me. The evil power which had ensnared my beloved Clara had to be tracked down and destroyed. But how? And was I strong enough to accomplish the task?

The captain, ironically enough, apologized to me for missing the *Psyche* in the mist. He seemed a trifle puzzled as to how he had come to miss the ship and I did not venture any explanations.

It was his guess that the *Psyche* was now way behind us and that it would be ruinous to the success of the British delegation's mission should we attempt to circle back to try to sight her. I was inclined to agree. If the *Psyche* was, indeed, a slow ship, then the sooner we made for Constanta the sooner I could arrange to have the ship met at Varna. In this the captain was quite helpful and – after the proposition had been placed before Molesworth and met with his approval – it was suggested that I should be put ashore at Varna which is, in fact, a little south of Constanta and therefore would be passed by the *Centurion* on its way to the Romanian port. Molesworth agreed, stressing that I must press on from Varna as soon as the *Psyche* docked and join the delegation in Bucharest at the earliest opportunity.

The journey was now given up to relaxing and trying to revitalize my anxiety-torn mind and body. From Cape Matapan, the most southerly point of the Morea Peninsula in Greece, the voyage was somewhat idyllic and I began to relax a little. I found time to speculate that I could appreciate how Odysseus must have felt on his return to Ithaca after his voyages in the balmy Aegean seas. No wonder he stayed away so long in such waters, dreamy, blue and restful. I had always suspected that Penelope must have been a rather boring person; any woman who waits twenty years in chastity for a man who might never return, all the while sewing some ridiculous tapestry to keep prospective lovers at bay, must have little love of life. Perhaps Odysseus was in no hurry to return?

Through the Aegean, which the sailors called the Archipelago, we crossed into a small channel named the Dardanelles which cuts through the Turkish territory into the Sea of Marmara. Some Turkish naval craft stopped and boarded us in spite of the Union flag at the jackstaff and the ensigns of the Royal Navy fluttering from our mastheads. We were not held up long and soon entered the hot Marmaric Sea. Here we were somewhat slowed by lack of wind and twice the captain, in order to make time, had the ship's boats hoisted out and the sloop towed for a few miles before the wind came up again.

At the eastern end of the Marmaric Sea we could see the great city which the Turks now call Istanbul. It had once been Constantinopolis, capital of the Byzantine Empire and chief city of the Greco–Roman world. In other circumstances I would have given anything to have been allowed to wander ashore, to walk through its fascinating streets, see its fantastic mosques, its colourful Orthodox churches and its other historical monuments.

Soon we found ourselves once more in a tempestuous sea – the great Black Sea across which so many of our brave lads recently travelled to their deaths in the Crimean Peninsula. Once into its choppy waters we turned northwards across this huge inland sea and stood out for Varna. Two weeks and five days after leaving Tilbury in London, I stood by the rail of the *Centurion* looking on the exotic eastern seaport.

I was rowed ashore at Varna and stood at the quayside of this strangely Mediterranean-looking seaport, watching the skiff speed back to the *Centurion* which was already hoisting its sail for Constanta. My arrival did not seem to excite much curiosity, for the port was apparently a busy one. Standing off its harbour waters I could make out a menacing squadron of Russian warships, sleek and deadly, for these ships of Tsar Alexander dominated all the Black Sea trading routes. There were merchantmen of all types in the port, loading and unloading. Large, cumbersome vessels from the Ukrainian seaport of Odessa, trading cargoes of iron ore from Krivoi Rog; there were sleek and exotic-looking vessels from Georgia, weather-beaten ships from the Crimea, oddly alien-looking vessels from the north Turkish coast and many others. The quayside was filled with all manner of men in many varied costumes and the variety of languages would have done justice to a visualization of the Tower of Babel.

I became aware of a small, sallow-skinned man with a long drooping black moustache. He stood before me waving some sort of a ledger and speaking with a raised voice. He was flamboyantly dressed, wore a fez, a red brimless conical cap of wool from which a black tassel leapt in time to the jerking of his head. Over a white shirt hung an embroidered waistcoat and once-white pantaloons were tucked into black shiny boots. A long, curved sword hung at his waist. Incongruously, he wore a small pair of rimless spectacles perched on the end of a large, bulbous nose. The whole effect was comical but I am glad that I had the sense not to laugh.

Behind him stood two bored-looking men in a sombre type of uniform which pronounced them to be soldiers of some description.

The man, or so I presumed, was some official . . . perhaps the customs officer of the port. I asked him if he spoke any English at which, to my amazement, he spat on the ground and set off in a tirade of what I judged to be Turkish. I then addressed him in French and, when this failed, I spoke in German. By this time he had gone red in the face and the two soldiers were grinning at his anger.

I was wondering whether I was going to be hauled off to some police station when a ship's officer came across and addressed me in German.

'You are English?'

I admitted that I was.

'Permit me, Graf Von Hubeck, *Kapitän-Leutnant* of the *Otto Klaus* of Bremen,' he waved his hand towards one of the vessels in the harbour. 'I understand you have trouble in interpretation, is it not so? I will interpret.'

He was a clean-shaven, red-faced man of thirty-five, or so I guessed, meticulously dressed and obviously used to giving orders.

He snapped a series of sharp questions at the Turkish

official who seemed to deflate before him. The Turk's replies were offered in an apologetic manner.

'This man,' said Von Hubeck, nodding towards the Turk, 'is the customs officer of the port. All foreign travellers entering here must show their passports.'

I smiled.

'Ah, I guessed as much but could not seem to find a common language as a means of communication.'

'*Ach*,' grunted Von Hubeck, 'usually in these parts you can get by with German. From ancient times Saxon merchants and traders have travelled and settled extensively in the area. You won't have much trouble once you travel among the ordinary people, the Bulgars or the Wallachians, or go north into Transylvania. The Turks are the exceptions – they never seem to learn any language but their own. Your German is excellent,' he added as an afterthought.

I bowed.

I suddenly noticed the Turkish official waiting somewhat impatiently and I drew out my passport.

'Will you tell him that I am travelling on a British diplomatic passport . . . that I am one of an official British delegation *en route* for Bucharest? I am in Varna for only a few days, waiting to meet someone from a British ship, the *Psyche* out of Liverpool, which should be calling in here shortly.'

The German Count, for such is the meaning of the title Graf, repeated this in his excellent Turkish.

The Turkish official grunted, examined my passport, drew some sort of rubber stamping device from his pocket, spat on it, and pressed it firmly on the visa section. He handed it back to me and said something in Turkish.

'He says,' interpreted the German, 'that the Government of the Emir Abdul Mejid welcomes the representative of the British Government to Varna and trusts your stay will be fruitful.'

I bowed towards the Turk, who elaborately returned it.

'He also says that if you require any assistance, he will be honoured to receive you at the harbour entrance where his office is situated.'

The Turk and his bodyguard hurried away and I was left to thank the German for his aid. He saluted and extended an invitation for me to take wine aboard his ship at any time I felt like paying him a visit.

Taking my single bag, which I had brought ashore with me, I made my way through the busy harbour environs into the town, up the sunbaked streets in search of a hotel. I decided that I had two priorities; firstly, to find myself a room and secondly, to find myself somebody who would act in the function of guide, interpreter and servant.

The problem of a hotel was almost immediately solved. Walking up a wide thoroughfare, I came across a building on which large lettering proclaimed it to be a hotel. Attached to this sign was an intriguing postscript: 'Inglez speaken' which I interpreted as being 'English spoken'. Indeed, as I found out on entering and making my wants known, 'Inglez' was certainly 'speaken'.

A fat little man, bald but with a full black beard and a permanent smile distorting his formidable features, bustled about me.

'Inglez? I spoke fine no? You a Jollee Jik?'

I frowned and then enlightenment dawned.

'Oh, you mean a Jolly Jack Tar – a sailor? No, I'm merely a traveller.'

He led me to a plain room which had a commanding view of the harbour.

'You stay in Varna . . . wait for ship?'

His pronunciation was actually '*Yo wet fi sheep?*' but, after a while, I grew accustomed to the meaning of his strange diction.

'I wait to meet someone from a ship,' I replied. 'Then I go on to Bucharest.'

'Bucharesti, no?' he nodded enthusiastically. 'Is good. New capital. Brother lives there.'

I finally escaped a long lecture on his brother's noble character and the fact that his brother owned a grand café in Bucharest. My problem now was to find an interpreter and then wait patiently for the arrival of the *Psyche*. I was in Varna for two days without discovering a suitable person.

After a light luncheon on the second day I decided to explore a part of the town I had never been to before: a dingy little district which fronted on to the wharves and was clearly the slum area. I had traversed several streets when I realized I had made a mistake: it was not the sort of area for a well-dressed foreigner. I started to walk quickly along a side street, hoping to break out into a main thoroughfare when I found my way blocked by three vicious-looking brutes, one of whom held a cudgel in front of him and muttered in a menacing way.

I turned rapidly back the way I had come but another man appeared at the other end of the street and started to walk slowly towards me.

I halted and decided to try to bluff it out. I ordered them to desist in every language I knew, none of which was Turkish or Bulgar, the local languages. Suddenly I heard a street door open and, idiotically, I cried aloud for help in English.

A young man of perhaps twenty-two years was coming out of a house further up the street. He paused and turned at my voice and then, seeing what my situation was, his hand suddenly slipped into the pocket of the coat he was wearing and came up with a small pistol. He walked swiftly along the street, levelling it at my would-be assail-ants and called to them in a loud, commanding voice.

All four paused, open-mouthed, and then turned tail and ran off.

I mopped my brow and, feeling a little weak about the knees, turned to thank my rescuer.

He was a pleasant-faced man, with the high Slavic cheekbones, twinkling greeny-blue eyes and a mop of tousled black hair.

'That's okay, sir,' he silenced my stumbling thanks with a soft Transatlantic drawl. 'You should never be out in these parts without a pistol handy, though.'

He thrust his weapon back into his coat pocket.

'I guess you could do with a shot of liquor.'

He pointed back down the street.

'I have a room there and, if the animals haven't raided it already, I guess I still have the best part of a quart of malt liquor there.'

I followed him into a decidedly derelict-looking building.

'You're an American?' I asked.

To my surprise he shook his head violently.

'No sir, don't let my English fool you none. I'm a Romanian from Buzau.'

He pushed open a rotting wooden door and led the way up a rickety stairway to a room that was appalling in its dankness and squalor.

He ushered me in and then dropped to his knees by the bed. After a moment's frantic search he finally pulled out a bottle of amber-coloured liquid and gave a sigh of satisfaction. He poured two generous glasses and handed me one.

'Scotch!' I exclaimed, tasting it.

'No sir!' he ejaculated. 'That there is pure American.'

'Whisky, anyway,' I smiled.

'Mebbe, mebbe. But there are whiskies and whiskies.'

'How does it happen that you are a Romanian from Buzau and yet speak like an American?' I asked.

'Both my parents were killed in the insurrection in 1848. My uncle decided to go to the States and take me with him. I was nine years old at the time and so I've gotten most of my education in Richmond, Virginia. Two years back, when there was this talk about finally setting up a Romanian state, I decided to come back to my homeland. I still consider myself to be a Romanian, still talk the language as well as a smattering of Turkish, Bulgar and German. Another shot?'

Without waiting for an answer he refilled my glass.

'So I came back. My uncle, he stayed on. Said at least he had peace and security in America. Then he goes and gets himself killed last July fighting under Colonel Pergam at Rich Mountain down in West Virginia, trying to defend his new homeland. Ironic, ain't it?'

He sighed.

I was looking round his squalid room and he noticed my gaze.

'Yeah, you might say I've fallen on hard times,' he said as I flushed with embarrassment. 'Fact is, I *have* fallen on hard times. I've been working up at Bucharest as an interpreter and odd-job man for the past two years. Then I undertook to take a party from Bucharest down here and see them safely on a ship. So here I am. Been here ever since, trying to pick up something.'

It was too good an opportunity to miss, even though I acted on the spur of the moment.

'You've worked as an interpreter?'

He nodded.

'You know the country between here and Bucharest?'

'Sure I do. Why?'

'How would you like to work for me? I need an interpreter, a sort of guide, translator and odd-job man. How about it?'

He grinned.

'Now that depends on what you're paying.'

'Can you afford to be that fussy?' I asked, unused to financial frankness.

'I can always afford to be *that* fussy,' he smiled.

It demonstrated something of his character and I took a sudden liking to the man. Soon a bargain was agreed and I learnt that his name was Avram Murgu. I told him a sketchy version of my story, confining myself, more or less, to what I had told Lord Molesworth – that I had to meet my fiancée off the *Psyche*. We agreed that he should come and take a room, at my expense, in the hotel where I was staying and, the following day, start to earn his keep by making inquiries for a coach and horses to transport us northward to Bucharest.

It was the morning of the third day after our meeting when my general factotum, for I know not how else to call him, shook me awake.

'Up you get, Upton,' there was no distinction of man and master, or creed, class or nationality in Avram's up-bringing. 'Up you get. It's the *Psyche*. She put into harbour during the night.'

That brought me leaping from my bed and hastily throwing on my clothes. I did not even pause to breakfast but rushed down to the harbour with Avram trailing in my wake.

The *Psyche* was easy to find, tied up alongside the quay.

I went up the gangplank and was met by a surly-faced man at the rail.

'I wish to see Miss Clara Clarke,' I announced.

To my surprise, the man almost winced.

'That 'un! Bad cess to 'er!'

I felt the hot blood course through my cheeks as he turned and spat over the side of the ship.

'Mind your manners, fellow,' I admonished.

The man glowered at me.

'I 'appen ter be the master o' this 'ere ship, matey. Captain Raikes. An' I tell ye, bad cess to that woman, if woman she be. Two men dead, the rest o' the crew a

389

feared o' their own shadders. Two spars lost. Stranded in a weird fog. Me cargo 'alf eaten by rats. Never 'ad a worse trip and why? Never take a lone female on board ship . . . it ain't natural. We've 'ad the luck o' the very devil. All hell's to pay on this trip.'

My fears were mounting at his recital.

'Where is Miss Clarke?' I demanded, a catch in my throat. 'Is she safe?'

The man laughed, a snarl of a laugh.

'Safe? I guess she is. Thanks to my stupidity. I should 'ave throwed her overboard in Biscay. 'Stead of that I stand to lose me boat.'

'Where is she then?' I persisted.

'Gone.'

He drew out a plug of vile-looking tobacco and bit off a chew.

'Gone?' I repeated stupidly as if not understanding.

'Ay, can't 'ee talk plain English, mister? Gone, I say, and curse her too.'

I fought to control my rising temper.

'Gone where?'

'Who cares?' snarled the surly master.

I reached forward and grabbed him by the collar.

He gave a yelp which ended in a fit of coughing as he swallowed his chewing tobacco.

'If you value your life,' I hissed at him, 'as well as you value your ship, you'll tell me where she's gone.'

'I don't know, mister, and that's God's truth. 'Swelp me! We docked afore midnight and not long after a carriage arrives on the quayside. Next thing I know she – Miss Clarke – is climbing into it with never a please nor thank you, captain, for the voyage. Lucky she paid her passage money in advance, though small good that will do me.'

I let him wriggle free from my nerveless hands.

'Gone,' I whispered incredulously.

Avram, who had been watching my exchange with bewilderment, caught me by the arm.

'Perhaps we can find out where she went from the harbour master?' he suggested.

In a daze, I followed Avram to a building where the same Turkish official, who had greeted me on my arrival, stood – the epitome of politeness itself.

No, he replied to Avram's question, he had not been on duty the previous night. A Bulgar had been in charge and, by coincidence, the man arrived at that precise moment. He was a stocky, pleasant-faced man. I was surprised to see that his face paled at Avram's questions. Yes, he had seen a coach. It was about one o'clock, or near enough. A black coach and four had entered the harbour and gone straight across the quayside where the *Psyche* from England had just tied up. Intrigued by the late arrival, he had watched and seen a young lady come from the ship and climb aboard. Yes, she did carry some luggage. The coach then left and, against all regulations, had refused to stop to let the lady's passport be checked and registered. He had written his report in his record book. What direction had the coach taken? Why, it had turned along the road which led to the main Bucharest highway. Could the English gentleman hazard any guess as to why the young lady had refused to stop in compliance with passport regulations?

Avram said something which appeased the officials, I am not sure what, and led me white and trembling back to the hotel where he forced me to eat a hot breakfast.

'Seems as if you have a mystery on your hands, Upton,' he drawled. 'Guess the lady thinks she is meeting you in Bucharest. What do you say?'

I tried to pull myself together.

For a moment I wondered whether I should confide the whole of my story to him but then I realized how ridiculous such a tale would seem, told in the pure light of day to someone as earthy and stolid as Avram. Even as I thought about it Clara's beautiful face flitted before my eyes and I could hear Yorke's dying breath as he urged me to rescue her and destroy the dragon god.

I forced myself to smile.

'That must be it, Avram,' I said. 'She has gone to Bucharest, thinking to meet me there. Perhaps, if we set off immediately, we could overtake her? Can you cancel the arrangements for a coach and get two good horses here within the half hour?'

I pretended not to see the look of deep suspicion which Avram gave me as he left the room to attend to our needs.

CHAPTER NINETEEN

By midday Avram and I were cantering our horses at an easy pace along the highway which led to Bucharest. The day was fine and the way fairly easy, the road for the first leg of the journey followed the course of a large river from Varna. Several times along the route Avram stopped and made inquiries concerning the passage of the black coach. More often than not his inquiries were met with sullen looks and the shaking of heads. One old woman gave a cry and made the sign of the cross before slamming her door in our faces. But several times we encountered peasants who were courteous and helpful, assuring us that a black coach and four had passed on the road not more than twelve hours before.

We spent the first night in a sleepy hamlet called Sumla and the next morning turned north for Bucharest. We were annoyed to learn that the coach had halted at a village called Isiklar for the day. Instead of stopping the night at Sumla, had we ridden for another six hours we would have overtaken the coach because it did not set out from Isiklar until midnight.

'It seems odd,' commented Avram suddenly, 'that this coachman prefers to travel by night and rest by day.'

I nodded without speaking. It was some moments before the fact suddenly struck me with some significance. Was there a limitation to this strange power which, Yorke said, was based in Transylvania? Could it be that the power, whatever it was, was weakened by day and could only exercise its strength at night? Surely a telepathic power as incredible and as strong as I had witnessed it to be, would not suffer such limitations. But the coach was laying up by day and travelling at night. And, thinking more closely on the subject, all the manifestations which I had witnessed had occurred *after* sunset.

'Tonight, Avram,' I announced, 'we'll continue to ride until we overtake the coach.'

Avram gave me a puzzled stare.

'You seem certain that what the coachman did last night he will do again tonight?'

There was a question in his statement.

'I think he will,' I replied, refusing to say more in spite of the penetrating look the American-Romanian gave me.

Along the route, through the town of Ruscuk which we reached during the late afternoon, we continued to ask about the coach. From this point onwards the peasants did not seem as forthcoming as before. Many doors were slammed to our inquiries and many men and women crossed themselves, some holding out two fingers towards us which Avram afterwards told me was a sign of protection against the evil eye.

Avram grew more unhappy and paled by these reactions and finally he pulled his horse up and looked me firmly in the eye.

'Upton, you must tell me, who is it or *what* is it we are following?'

'Don't be ridiculous, Avram,' I snapped. 'I have told you – we are following my fiancée, Miss Clarke.'

For the rest of the day we rode in silence and when evening came, sending its chill black fingers entwining around the landscape, we stopped for a meal at a small wayside inn. Then, by mutual consent, we rode onward. All through that silent, freezing night we rode, through the long dark hours until the early hours of the morning. Our horses were blowing and clearly reaching the end of their endurance.

Avram cast a worried look at me.

'We cannot continue far in this manner, Upton,' he chided gently.

I admit I was uncaring for the needs of the poor beasts. My one thought was for Clara. In this manner we might overtake her and destroy whatever it was that held her ensnared in its power.

'We must push on,' I said stubbornly, 'at dawn the coach is bound to halt and we will be able to overtake them.'

'But the horses . . .' insisted Avram. 'It is no use killing the animals under us!'

I was about to damn the horses when we came to a rise. The road suddenly plunged downhill into a valley, twisting and turning around the contours of the hill. It was as we breasted this rise that the full moon shot out from behind a cloud bank and the valley glinted white in its rays. It was almost as clear as a dull, cloudy day.

Involuntarily, a cry was wrested from my lips.

In the distance I could see a black coach drawn by four black horses thundering along the road ahead. The tall figure of the coachman could be clearly discerned, a black cloak billowing around him, flapping like great wings. In one hand he held a whip and I could hear its crack, crack, crack in the night air as he flayed his beasts unmercifully.

'It is them!' I cried to Avram and, without waiting for a reply, I kicked my horse forward down the hill.

Then it was that I made a mistake.

In my triumphant jubilation I gave vent to the childish cry of the hunter who sights the poor fox.

For an instant I saw the coachman turn his head, caught a glimpse of a deathly pale face turned to mine, and then heard the renewed cracking of the whip. For a while we rode grimly on, although I could feel the beast beneath me growing weaker and weaker. I knew that if I did not stop soon the heart of that stout animal would surely burst . . . but Clara was only a few hundred yards away and surely one can sympathize with my desperate efforts to reach her?

We were passing through a small copse which straddled the roadway. I was aware of a large river to my left, the Arges as I subsequently learnt. The moon had passed back behind the low-hanging, black storm clouds. A rather fierce drizzle started to patter down which I could hear even above the thunder of hooves and the gasping of my horse.

Then, causing all the other sounds to die away, came the long drawn out howl of a dog – hound or wolf, I know not.

My horse suddenly shied, whinnied and reared, pawing frantically at the air. I lost my grip and slid backwards from the saddle. The impact of my hitting the ground stunned me but did not hurt me. Avram had ridden up and dismounted, trying to quieten the horses, both of which were shying and pulling away. He managed to get them fastened to the branch of a tree, to which he tied them in such a fashion that they could not rear, but they continued to buck and kick out with their hind legs in a clear state of terror.

'Are you all right, Upton?' he asked as I struggled to my feet swearing, more at the shock than at the injury.

'Confound that dog!' I snarled. 'Just when we were so near . . .'

The coach had already disappeared.

Avram said nothing but stood peering about him.

'The horses are too exhausted to continue,' he pointed out. 'You'll kill them if you go on.'

Reluctantly, I nodded.

We stood under the shelter of a large tree, away from the rain.

Avram had bent down and scooped up a handful of some peculiar white flowers which I had not seen before. I wondered what he was doing and was perturbed to see his face was pinched with anxiety.

'Wolfbane,' he whispered.

'What's that?' I asked. 'I have not heard of it.'

'Even he who is pure of heart
And says his prayers at night
May become a wolf when the Wolfbane blooms
And the moon is full and bright.'

The ancient rhyme, which Avram recited in a hollow voice, sent a chill through my body.

'Nonsense, Avram,' I scoffed, purely to keep up my own courage, for I could believe anything now. 'You don't believe in that sort of thing, do you?'

'Upton,' he said slowly, 'this land is very ancient, here all the beliefs and instincts of primeval man still survive . . .'

'Well, I am a modern nineteenth-century sophisticated man, so the writ of primeval man does not run with me,' I said, turning towards the horses.

Another long, low howl riveted me to the spot.

A flash of lightning coincided with the ending of the howl and there, standing glowering in the rain on the far side of the clearing, stood the same massive brute that I had seen aboard the ill-fated *Ceres*.

I heard two shots in quick succession. Avram had drawn his revolver and fired at the beast.

The animal did not even flinch. I could see its ghastly luminous eyes fixed upon me.

It moved forward slowly.

Avram fired again. He might just as well have thrown flowers at the beast for all the good it did. The bullets seemed to pass right through the creature.

I knew that I was lost. Like Yorke, I had underestimated the strength of the power that I was contesting. Like a fool, I did not even know what that power was.

The eyes of the creature caught and held mine. They seemed almost human, assuming a glare of malevolent satisfaction, of triumph. I could hear the rasping of its fetid breath, see the bloody saliva dripping from its dewlap, see its hackles rise, see its yellowing teeth, sharply pointed, see the ears flatten on its skull and the muscles ripple in its back as it gathered itself for the leap.

I was lost. I had no will of my own. I was a sacrifice. There was nothing to struggle for.

I was aware of Avram yelling something.

Then the beast sprang. Automatically my hands went up in a futile gesture of defence, my eyes closed and I tensed my body for the impact of those tearing jaws.

It never came.

Avram stood before me, in one hand a large crucifix of the Orthodox persuasion and in the other hand an empty phial.

Of the beast there was no sign.

'What . . . what happened?' I gasped, collapsing against a tree.

'What happened, my friend?' said Avram in a voice which was curiously calm. 'What happened is that you are lucky to have met me and employed me for your guide.'

I looked at him to gauge the deeper meaning behind his words.

'What do you mean?'

'I think we had best begin by getting out of these woods and finding a dry place. Then you had better tell me the real reason why you are in this country and whose carriage we follow.'

I followed him meekly to the horses.

'Tell me one thing, Avram,' I said. 'What was in that phial you flung at that beast?'

'Garlic salt, that is all,' he returned curtly.

The horses were quiet now, standing trembling and blowing, with steam rising from their glossy coats.

'We will have to walk them awhile,' said Avram. 'It will not be far . . . there is a little inn not far away. I know this part of the road. Bucharest is within an easy ride if we can get fresh horses.'

We walked along the road without speaking. It was three miles before we came to the tiny inn and knocked resolutely at its door.

I could not help but notice that affixed to the inn door was a large iron crucifix and I wondered why a mass of some strange flowers, whose perfume reeked of garlic, were placed in profusion around the windows. Avram confirmed later that these were, in fact, garlic flowers.

A window above us was opened and a harsh voice echoed down to us. Avram answered in the same language. He later told me that the voice had demanded to know who we were and what we wanted. On Avram's reply, the voice then demanded if we acknowledged Jesus Christ as Lord and Saviour. Only on Avram's assurance that we were Christians was the window shut and, after a few moments, a frightened and elderly innkeeper ushered us inside his warm parlour. Soon a fire was roaring in the hearth and a meal and wine were brought to refresh our needs. The man then went to bed down our horses for the night, regretting that he was unable to supply us with new mounts. We would have to wait until morning before we could continue our journey.

It was while the innkeeper was thus engaged that Avram looked at me and said, simply: 'Well, Upton?'

Suddenly I felt the urge to tell him the whole story, to unburden this ghastly nightmare which seemed to have begun oh, so long ago, long ago in that junk shop in London.

Avram sat and listened to me gravely, throughout the whole of my narrative which I recounted up to the time I had fallen in with him in Varna.

Having finished I sat back and eyed him apprehensively.

'Go on,' I prompted, as he sat silently. 'Go on, tell me that I am a madman and should seek the advice of a doctor.'

He smiled gently and shook his head.

'No, my friend. That is not my intention. I believe you.'

I looked at him in surprise.

'You do? And you a hard-headed American?'

He snorted with mock indignation.

'Haven't I told you that I am Romanian?' Then, without waiting for further comment, his face and voice grew serious. 'It is the Romanian who now talks to you, friend Upton, and more than a mere Romanian. When I was sixteen I went to New York where the Romanian emigrant priests and monks have a seminary which teaches the Orthodox religion of this country to the emigrant community. I studied for the priesthood there. Does that surprise you? Oh, I admit that the priesthood was not for me. I left without taking my final vows. But the seminary gave me an education and taught me to believe many things that are unbelievable to the finite mind . . .'

He paused, as if trying to find simple words to explain a complex concept.

'As a Romanian I tell you that this is a country of shadows, where blood is cheap and flows like water and where the mountains and the valleys and the great plains have been drenched in the blood of many nations and many cultures. This, my friend, is the crossroads of the world. Through the Carpathians came many conquering peoples . . . Celts, Huns, Goths, Mongols, Vandals . . . every nation that ever rose in Europe came out of these mountains of ours. They came from many quarters of the world to this crossroads of civilization.

'They came, intermixed their blood and learning with the blood of those they found here, and then pressed on to their destiny . . . the Celtic tribes who were destined to spread Christian civilization across Europe when civilization was dying under the yoke of the Germanic conquerors, the Angles, Saxons, Vikings and others who rose to create new empires. If you like, the genesis of Europe was in the Carpathians.

'And although they passed on, always passed on, it is here that were left behind the beliefs and the superstitions of mankind's pre-history. Here you will find beliefs in religions that were centuries dead before Christ, before Buddha found enlightenment and before Mohammed came into the world as the Prophet of Allah. And who knows how powerful are those creeds of primitive man . . . and who are we to call them primitive?

'What we know is that there are some beliefs which are morally right and some beliefs which are morally wrong. There is always the struggle of good over evil. The Roman creed of Mithras, god of lightness banishing darkness and evil, was a righteous creed compared with the sacrificial beliefs of Jupiter. Whatever the belief, if it is morally good and beneficial to man and to human progress, then it represents the force of light as opposed to those creeds which keep mankind in subservient ignorance and fear. No one religion has a monopoly of good.'

'But what of this power which has ensnared Clara?' I demanded, interrupting his philosophizing.

Avram shook his head.

'I don't know the cause of it, my friend, but I share with you the belief that it is evil and deadly and must therefore be destroyed. We, you and I together, will join forces and I will supplement your strength of purpose with the knowledge I gained as a postulant in the priesthood.'

He reached his hand across the table and gripped mine in a firm, warm grasp.

We called for another bottle of wine and silently toasted our venture . . . the rescue of Clara and the destruction of the evil power which had her in its thrall.

We had, however, made a bad start to the new venture by losing the coach.

Our exhausted horses enforced our delay at the inn until late the following morning. But I was sure, and Avram grudgingly agreed with me, that the coach seemed to travel only by night. Therefore it was fairly certain that it had not gone far between the time we saw it on the moonlit road and the approach of dawn. Avram seemed certain that the coachman would have been able to make for the shelter of Bucharest itself and, as the new Romanian capital lay so short a distance away, we decided to ride there by lunch time that morning.

We trotted our mounts carefully on the journey for, although they had had several hours rest, the beasts were still fairly weary. But the journey to Bucharest did not take us long and we soon passed over the River Danube, a great river which the natives call Dunarea, and it was not long after that when we found ourselves in the city.

It was a strangely built city to my English eyes; from its architecture one could almost identify the different conquering nations which had passed through its blood-splattered thoroughfares. Here was a mosque, with sullen-faced Turks grouped at its door. Once conquerors, now they were merely immigrants in the new land. There was a simple Catholic church while a street away was a magnificent gold-roofed edifice whose flamboyant columns declared it to be of the Orthodox persuasion. Civil buildings, hotels, fountains, markets, all seemed to be as if Rome itself had suddenly been given rebirth in the middle of Istanbul or Damascus.

The city was athrong with soldiers, all armed and imposing as they paraded through the streets and squares. The streets were consistently crowded by carriages and men and women on horseback. Everywhere I saw signs of foreigners – Prussian officers, Turks, Frenchmen, Italians, Russians all attending the birth of the new European nation. At any other time the air of excitement would have seized my imagination, for this was history in the making.

The people, for the most part, were good natured and cheerful. Here and there small huddles of them were to be found around the latest news bulletins or proclamations.

The Hotel Concordia was by far the largest edifice in the central part of the city and this was where most of the foreign delegations were staying, including our British delegation. Avram and I made our way there through the excited throng and left our horses at the hotel's stables.

'I'll register at the hotel, Avram,' I said, 'while you start making inquiries to see if the coach has arrived in Bucharest.'

'Hopefully the task won't be difficult,' he said. 'I'll be as quick as I can.'

I watched him hurry away into the crowds and then turned into the magnificent marble portals of the hotel.

CHAPTER TWENTY

As I was being conducted to my room in the hotel the first person I encountered, and whom I had no wish to meet at that time, was Viscount Molesworth. He welcomed me with a hearty bonhomie.

'Welsford! Thought you'd disappeared off the face of the earth. You've missed several important ceremonies, you know. Can't be helped . . . but where is the lady in question, you young dog? Hiding her somewhere, eh?'

I wondered how I should react to this and, in my embarrassment, I asked Molesworth to join me in my room for a drink. There, in order to stop his persistent questions, I told him that somehow I had missed Clara at Varna and learnt that she had come on to Bucharest.

Molesworth snorted.

'Good God! Odd behaviour . . . what? She hasn't arrived at the Concordia and everybody who is anybody comes here . . . all the overseas visitors. Even the top men of the Romanian Government are staying here, Welsford. Are you sure she has come to Bucharest?'

I nodded and told him that Avram, who I explained I had hired as a guide and interpreter, was making a search of the town at that moment.

'Well, then, Welsford, you've nothing to worry about. She'll be with you before long, eh?'

I kept my uncertainty to myself.

Oblivious to my anxiety, Molesworth rambled on about the state opening of the new parliament which had taken place on 22 January. He told me he had encountered Ion Ghica, the Romanian we had seen in London, who was now a prominent 'progressive' member of the National Assembly.

'Can't say I like the way things are developing,' muttered Molesworth. 'Been talking the matter over with the French Consul, chap named Béclard, who agrees with my concern. Lot of radicalism here, you know, the spectre of this new-fangled communism has got quite a hold.'

I could see that he wanted to talk about the matter and forced myself to concentrate on what he was saying. After all, it was my job which had financed my journey here and, if I did not fulfil my obligations, Molesworth could easily force me back to London on the next ship and God knows what would happen to Clara then.

As if divining my thoughts Molesworth gave me a sympathetic look.

'See here, Welsford,' he said, 'I realize how anxious you are about Miss . . . er, whatsis. Tell you what, I'll let you have the next couple of days to yourself to get yourselves settled down, but in three days' time we have an important meeting with the new prime minister of this country, Babu Catargiu, a rather prickly nationalist type. I'll need you for that.'

Molesworth wasn't a bad sort and he had to hold up his hand to stem my gratitude.

'In the meantime,' he continued, 'you'd best know how the situation is shaping up.'

He went on to 'put me in the picture' as he expressed it. The British delegation had arrived in Bucharest to hear Prince Alexandru open the National Assembly, consisting of members of the former assemblies of Wallachia and Moldavia meeting as a single chamber. Prince Alexandru has told the people that the union of the principalities would be 'such as Romania wishes it, such as she feels it should be'. A new age was opening up for the country and 'progressive development of all institutions' was promised.

The majority political group was the National Party, a group of conservatives led by Catargiu who had, on that basis been designated the prime minister of the new state. Catargiu was all in favour of the social *status quo*, of keeping the majority of Romanian peasants in serfdom and of allowing the boyars, or great landowners, who had survived four hundred years of Turkish occupation through wealth and influence, to continue their powerful hold on the country. But there was a strong party of moderate conservatives and liberals in the parliament, led by N. Cretilescu, which favoured moderate reforms to lead the country into a more democratic Western democracy. There were more radical liberals who wished for the emancipation of the peasants and the confiscation of the large estates owned by the Church. Our friend Ion Ghica was among those advocates.

'The most worrying factor,' explained Molesworth, 'is a man called Mircea Malaieru. He is the leader of a peasant movement aimed at radical revolution. Peasants under his command have been put down once after an attempt to overthrow Prince Alexandru and establish some sort of republic . . . in fact, so far as I understand, the Bucharest regiments put them down with rather an unnecessary amount of bloodshed. The local police chief, a rather nasty piece of work named Bibescu, has simply created martyrs for their cause.

'Unless the situation is handled rather carefully, this country could be split into a rather bloody civil war between peasants and landowners. If so, the Porte and the Turkish Army will simply rush troops into the country on the pretext of keeping the peace and point out that the Romanians aren't ready to govern themselves. After all,' he gave a cynical grin, 'Her Majesty's Government have used that ploy before now. But what will happen to our buffer state in eastern Europe?'

I promised to turn my mind to such matters as soon as I could.

He stood up shaking his head sadly.

'You know, Welsford, it was bad strategy to mix affairs of politics and women at this time. Women and politics simply do not mix.'

'Isn't that a conservative attitude, my lord?' I was stung into replying. Having taken my degree in history I knew that European history was full of instances where women made better politicians than men.

'Nonsense, Welsford,' laughed Molesworth in answer to my rebuke. He poked a playful finger at me. 'At this moment you are prejudiced. But women have no head for politics. That is why they don't have the vote. Indeed, they never will have the vote.'

I decided to say nothing to encourage Molesworth to climb on his favourite hobby horse. But I recalled reading a weighty treatise, published by some Irishman named Thomson in 1825, a contemporary, I believe, of the advocate of the cooperative movement, Robert Owen. As I recall, the book was entitled *An appeal of one half of the human-race, women, against the pretensions of the other half, men, to retain them in political and thence in civil and domestic slavery*. 'Shall man be free and woman a slave . . . never say I!' cried Thomson, advocating female emancipation. I wondered what Thomson would have made of Lord Molesworth and decided to renew the debate at some future date.

'Take my word for it, Welsford,' said Molesworth, pausing at the door, 'women and politics do not mix. But we cannot cry over spilt milk. I hope you are able to get your affairs sorted out quickly because the delegation is in need of your services.'

He took his departure and I groaned a prayer of gratitude. There were more important things to think of than even the political affairs of the new state or the emancipation of women.

I waited at the hotel until late afternoon, fretful and impatient. I could not sleep or rest. I was just beginning to think about going out to join the search myself when Avram knocked at the door. He carried a small black bag such as doctors are wont to use.

I searched his face intently for signs of news as he came in and poured himself a drink.

'Well?' I finally demanded.

He threw back his head and drained a tumbler of whisky in one gigantic swallow.

'Well indeed, Upton,' he returned. 'I have traced the coach.'

I was halfway to the door.

'Not so fast!' admonished Avram. 'Remember the saying about fools rushing in?'

'But we must rescue her at once!' I cried.

'Wait, man!' snapped the American-Romanian. 'First we must review the situation. We must consider exactly what we are up against.'

He poured a second drink and sipped at it gently.

'I questioned some peasants who, just before dawn, saw a black coach and four enter the city. I managed to follow its path, by questioning people who were abroad early this morning, to a small suburb where there are several grand town houses that belong to rich boyars, or nobles. Men of wealth and power who usually made their way by collaborating with the Turks. Men,' here to my surprise he made a motion of spitting, 'men who are still in power in this land as the so-called native government.'

There was a bitterness in his voice.

'Continue,' I pressed him. 'What of Clara?'

'I'll come to that. The coach was seen entering the grounds of a house belonging to a boyar family whose main estates lie in Transylvania.'

My heart quickened.

'A peasant boy,' continued Avram, 'recalled seeing a pale-faced lady, with black hair, in the coach as it drove into the grounds just about dawn this morning. The boy works as a stable lad in a house opposite and he swears that the coach has not left since sun up.'

'Then we must go there at once . . . it will be dark soon.'

'Don't worry, my friend,' Avram returned. 'I don't think the power we seek gathers full strength until sometime after sundown.'

There was a tone in his voice that made me look closely at him.

'You sound as if you now know what that power is, Avram? What else have you learnt?'

'I don't know for certain . . . but I think I know.'

Avram's face was serious.

'Then tell me!' I cried, exasperated.

'The house to which the coach was driven has an emblem on its iron gates. I examined the outside of the house very carefully. The emblem was in wrought iron . . . it was a small grinning dragon.'

I felt suddenly weak and slumped into a chair.

'Draco,' I breathed.

Avram nodded.

'The stable boy who saw the coach enter also told me that the coach carried the same emblem on its doors . . . a white dragon which was the only relief to that black vehicle.'

He reached forward, opened his bag and drew forth a sheet of paper. It was a page torn from a book . . . a book of heraldry.

'I removed this from the local library,' he explained.

My eyes were on the leering head of the white dragon, rampant against a black background.

I gasped. It was the head of my statuette, the head of Draco, the dragon god of ancient Egypt.

Gathering my scattered thoughts, I peered down at the piece of paper.

'It does not say to whom the emblem belongs,' I commented.

'It doesn't need to,' said Avram softly.

'How so?'

'It belongs to a family as old as this land itself, whom everyone in this part of the world has known and feared for centuries. If folk tales and legends are one per cent true, then the family represented by the dragon symbol is the source of the evil power which we must fight.'

His voice, tinged with horror, set my flesh acrawl.

'Who is this family?'

'A family that once were princes of this country . . . and one particular prince who was possessed of an extraordinary power, a man – if you can call him that – whom legend has it has lived more than ten times his normal span of years.'

I suppressed a shiver.

'Nonsense,' I rebuked without conviction in my voice.

'Maybe. Remember I said that it's what legend records,' returned Avram calmly. 'Yet here, among the black shadows of the Carpathians, legend and truth are so intermingled that you can't tell which is which.'

I rose to my feet impatiently.

'You said you knew who this family is?' I said, pointing to the escutcheon.

'I do.'

'Then tell me.'

'The dragon crest is the symbol of the House of Dracula.'

CHAPTER TWENTY-ONE

'The House of Dracula?' I echoed. 'I seem to have heard that name before.'

Even as I spoke I recalled that Yorke had once mentioned the name.

'The Draculas are one of the oldest families in the land, perhaps as old as the Carpathians themselves.' Avram's voice had a strange intensity to it. 'They were the voivodes or ruling princes of Wallachia. The dynasty was actually founded by Mircea the Great who died in 1418 but the family took their name from Vlad III, who was called Vlad the Impaler. He also became known as Vlad Dracula, the son of the Dragon or the Devil. He was known as the Impaler for, although he drove the Turks out of the country, his very name stank in the nostrils of Christendom because of the unholy and inhuman practices he had of impaling the bodies of his enemies and even his friends on sharp wooden stakes.

'He was vile and bloodthirsty but he was also cunning and brave. He had a mighty brain and iron resolution which went with him to his grave. He died, no one knows how, at the very height of his power in 1476. It was said of him that he had a learning beyond compare, he knew no fear and no remorse and even attended the Scholomance . . .'

'What is that?' I interrupted.

Even Avram, whom I suspected was something of an atheist, raised a hand and crossed himself.

'The Scholomance, my friend, is a school which exists in the heart of the Carpathians where the secrets of nature, the language of animals, and all the knowledge of science is taught by the Devil in person. Only ten scholars are admitted at a time and when the course of learning is ended, nine of the scholars are sent to their homes but the tenth is kept by the Devil as his aide and rides about the mountains mounted on a dragon!'

'The dragon again,' I observed.

'Even so. Dracula was as feared as he was hated throughout the country.'

'And there are Draculas even to this day?' I asked.

'Dracula had a son, Mihail the Bad, who was Voivode or Prince of Wallachia until 1510. Then his sons Alexandru II and Peter the Lame succeeded him. There was a line of direct male heirs to Dracula until the time an Alexandru, who died in 1632, became Prince of both Wallachia and of Moldavia.'

'You know your history well,' I observed.

Avram smiled gently.

'When your country is conquered and your history becomes a forbidden thing, a thing to be belittled and sneered at, then you tend to cherish it all the more. In America I've met countless Irish whose knowledge of their history would put a scholar to shame. It isn't a quality unique to the people of Romania.'

He sighed and then continued: 'The Draculas were never good rulers. The last of them was Mihail Radu. He took the throne of Wallachia on 5 March 1658, and started his reign of terror by murdering thirty of his boyars because of his jealousy of them. In November, or thereabouts, in 1659, there was a great battle at Fratesi and the people overthrew this Dracula and forced him to flee from Wallachia. Mihail was the last Dracula to rule.'

'What happened to him?'

'He fled to Transylvania and settled in some great estate among the Carpathians, somewhere near the Borgo Pass. The descendants of the Dracula family have continued to live there in isolation, shunning the world, since those days. They call themselves "counts" these days, no longer "princes". And I'm told that a Count Dracula still rules these Transylvanian estates. Strange stories have been told about him . . . stories which even go so far as to say that Dracula himself, the same evil Prince of Wallachia, still lives and rules his family . . . but that is only a peasant legend.'

'But what could this House of Dracula want with a statuette of an Egyptian god and with Clara?' I demanded. 'And from what source comes this evil power they seem to exercise?'

Avram's face was grave.

'If the evil power we seek comes from the House of Dracula and is what I now suspect it is, then, my friend, we're battling against the curse of the ages . . . vampirism!'

'Vampirism?' I cried aghast. 'You mean dead men who leave their graves to prey upon the living?'

I looked upon Avram's face to see if this were some ghastly jest, but the deep-etched lines of his face told me he was deadly serious. A few weeks ago I would have laughed outright if a man had told me that he believed in such things but now, now after all that I had witnessed, I merely suppressed a shudder.

'What you say, friend Upton, is a simplified idea of what vampirism is. Going back to ancient Egypt, each nation has its tales of vampires . . . of corpses that become reanimated by blood from the living, of corpses that cannot lie still in their graves but flit about the world from sunset to sunrise sucking the blood from the living. They live in a state of Undeath.

'I have told you that this was the crossroads of the world where blood is a cheap commodity and flows like water from the mountain streams. The fields have been fertilized by the blood of many peoples. Death is no stranger to the people here and, in whatever form it comes, they do not fear it. Look how they fought continually and at great sacrifice against the Turks, shedding rivers of their blood to be free of the curse of foreign domination. But what they do fear is the terrible Undeath, eternal suffering and torture.

'From time immemorial we Romanians have known of those creatures of the night, those who have succumbed to live as immortals in the cursed guise of the Undead.'

'Is it possible that such things exist?' I whispered.

'It is possible and they do. You, yourself, have witnessed many manifestations of their powers. And I believe that the legends about the Dracula family are true ... perhaps Prince Dracula did attend the Scholomance and attain such powers as the peasants claim.'

'But,' I cried, 'what has this to do with the statuette? What had the ancient Egyptian god Draco to do with vampires?'

'I've given some thought to the matter,' replied Avram. 'I don't know for certain but I can guess at the answer. Perhaps this cult of vampirism started in those far-off days among the ancient Pharaohs of Egypt. You told me that your friend Yorke said that the followers of the god Draco believed that life after death was a natural fact, that it was possible not only to free the spirit from death but to free the body as well ... in other words the ancient Egyptians thought they could make the body immortal.

'The vampire, too, has a mortal body. Didn't your friend say that all those thousands of years ago in Egypt, the Draconians studied ways of releasing themselves from their mortal span? That they experimented with ways of obtaining immortality? Did he, your friend, not say that it was written that the Draconians claimed to be successful in their experiments by which they created what was called – even by the ancients – Undead?'

I nodded slowly, recalling that conversation.

'Then, perhaps,' continued Avram, 'the answer lies in the fact that these followers of Draco created a race of

Undead men who needed living blood to prolong their immortality . . . that five thousand years ago, or more, in ancient Egypt the first vampire was created?'

He paused.

'That could be why they were driven underground by the enlightened religions. And perhaps, seeking refuge, they trudged to the Carpathians, like many before them and many who have followed them. They came here, to the crossroads of the world, and their achievements were spread across the face of the earth like some noxious plague as nations came and went among the mountain passes. That is why every country in the world, from Asia to Ireland, has its tales of the Undead, the vampires. That is why Euripides, Aristophanes and Ovid all knew and wrote of the Undead and why St Clemens warned the early Christians to beware of them.

'Yes,' he concluded, emphatically, 'the more I think of it, the more I'm convinced that this is the way it happened.'

'And Clara is in the hands of such evil?'

I was sick with apprehension.

Avram laid a hand on my arm.

'Friend Upton, I'd prepare myself for the worst. Maybe we are too late to save her.'

'Too late?' I looked at him in bewilderment. 'But you said that the young boy saw her alive this morning.'

'He saw her, yes.' Avram reached out both hands and held me by the shoulders, looking me squarely in the eyes. 'The Draconians sought immortality for their followers. They created the Undead, the vampires. The vampire is immortal but immortality carries with it a curse: they cannot die but must go on forever multiplying their kind, for all that die from their kisses become as they are – Undead!'

A red fire began to whirl around my brain.

'And Clara . . . is she in the power of the Undead . . . will she . . .?'

Avram nodded solemnly.

The chair seemed to slide away from under me. I seemed to swim down, down, down into a black whirlpool of screaming voices.

I was lying on my back when I opened my eyes. Avram was standing over me with a wet towel which he was applying to my temples.

I tried to start up but he held me down.

'Careful, Upton,' he said gently but firmly. 'You'd best gather your strength for you'll need it.'

'My God,' I cried in anguish. 'Clara . . . is there no hope?'

'It's possible that the worst hasn't come yet,' said Avram, cautiously.

'Explain yourself,' I demanded.

'The Undead are constrained by bonds of nature. Their power ceases at sunrise; from sunrise to sunset they must return to lie helpless on their native soil, the soil where they were buried. They can't pass over running water except at the slack and flood of the tide. They also hate all symbols of goodness and light, such as the crucifix I see around your neck. They can be easily destroyed by a man of courage, with a steady hand and firm eye and a belief in right over evil. They can be destroyed by driving a stake of wood through their hearts, or cutting off their heads and stuffing the mouths with garlic . . . for garlic is one of the oldest medicinal herbs in the world, used throughout the ages to keep the devil at bay.'

'And why would this make you think that Clara has not become . . . become . . .'

'They may need her to do their bidding, to protect them during the hours that they're weakest.'

'But she wouldn't . . .' I began to protest.

'Not willingly, of course. But she is under their control.'

'Then we must destroy them,' I cried, sitting up.

'But we mustn't rush into the affair without knowing our adversary's power. You've heard his weakness. Now hear his strength. The Undead have the strength of many, can transform their shapes into those of bats, wolves, or can swirl in a mist or come on moonlight rays as elemental dust. They can see in the dark. They cast no shadow nor a reflection in a mirror. They have powers of mesmerization . . .'

'And they can control Clara . . . even sending telepathic commands across thousands of miles from here to London,' I added.

'It's possible,' agreed Avram. 'But they must have some powerful leader to do such things, a leader of astonishing qualities.'

'All the dreams I had, that Clara also had . . . these emanated from the hypnotic power of these creatures.'

'I'd say that psychic vibrations from the jade statuette also played an important part,' pointed out Avram.

'Then what must we do?' I cried, a surge of anger bursting through my veins. Deep down I knew that my anger was born of the great chill fear that was gripping at my throat. But I kept seeing an image of Clara before my eyes, reinforcing my resolve.

'It's a terrible task, my friend,' said Avram. 'Death isn't the worst thing that can overtake us. And if the curse of the Undead overtakes either one of us, we must resolve to save the soul of the other by driving a stake through his heart. Agreed?'

Silently we shook hands upon that terrible proposal.

Avram picked up his black bag.

'I've purchased a few things that'll arm us against these creatures.'

He drew forth two fairly large crucifixes of the Orthodox Church style and handed me one.

'Keep it in your pocket for protection always.

He then showed me that in the bag was an abundance

of garlic flowers and also a wooden mallet and several heavy wooden tent pegs which, he explained, would serve us as wooden stakes.

'Well now, Upton, my friend, now's the time. Evening is wearing on and we must put our faith in the powers of goodness and light. We must go out to contend with this evil cancer.'

I braced my shoulders.

Without another word we passed out into the darkening evening.

CHAPTER TWENTY-TWO

The house was in an isolated part of the city.

Avram had hired a carriage, which bore a marked resemblance to our own English hansom cabs, and he directed the driver to a wide, tree-lined avenue along which high walls ran. Behind these high walls I could just make out the tall edifices of gaunt, forbidding buildings which, so Avram informed me, were the town houses of the boyars of the country. Apart from the grim architecture, the prospect was not altogether unlike some avenue in Hampstead.

Evening had descended with its wintery blackness by the time the driver dropped us at the end of the avenue. Avram thought it best not to journey further by the carriage lest our coming rouse suspicion within the household. Instead we walked the last three hundred yards and halted before the great iron gates.

I, too, then saw what Avram had seen. The dragon emblem on those forbidding portals. There was no doubt about it, the image was exactly the same as the jade statuette – the same as Draco, the dragon god.

The house itself stood only twenty yards from the gate and rose perhaps three storeys, which was a remarkable height compared with most of the houses in the outlying areas of Bucharest. There seemed to be no movement within the house. It was dark and, in fact, the overall impression was one of centuries-old decay. All the windows were shuttered but here and there a shutter had rotted away from its hinges and hung flapping gently like some broken bird's wing in the faint evening breeze.

I will not hide the fact that it took courage to follow Avram through the squeaking iron gates. Avram bent his head to mine and whispered: 'You'd best stay here and watch the front of the house. I'll go round to the stables and see if the coach is there.'

I silently envied Avram's courage as he disappeared towards the back of that deserted building. My heart seemed to pound uncomfortably loudly in my ears. The evening air was cold and I gently stamped at the ground, hoping to attract the pumping blood to my feet. There was no moon and everything was shrouded in black gloom, even my breath in the coldness seemed like puffs of dark grey smoke.

An owl hooted on a nearby tree causing me to jump.

It was then I noticed that the door of the house was half open and in the gap stood a small feminine figure.

'Clara?' I gasped, cursing the fact that I had no lantern.

The figure stirred and I fancied I heard a soft laugh.

'Who . . . who's there?' I demanded, a trifle brusquely in my nervousness.

A sweetly feminine voice answered in what, I presumed, was the local language.

'I do not understand,' I replied.

'Do you speak this language, *mein Herr*?' asked that soft, caressing voice in German.

'I do. Who are you?' I demanded again, resorting to my schoolboy German.

'Do not be alarmed, *mein Herr*. Come in where it is warm.'

The figure opened the door a little further and behind it I could see the hallway was lit by a lantern which silhouetted the figure of the woman, no, no more than a girl whose shape, aye even in silhouette, caused me to catch my breath in admiration. Never have I seen a figure come so close to perfection before. Then I thought of Clara and felt a pin-prick of guilt.

'Come in where it is warm, *mein Herr*,' she repeated softly. 'It is cold in the night air.'

I took a hesitant step forward and then my mind remembered our mission to that house and immediately registered alarm.

'Who are you?'

'My name is Malvina, *mein Herr*. I am the *Hausmädchen* to the Count and look after the property in his absence.'

My suspicions eased somewhat. At least I did not have to fear this innocent-sounding girl. She could only have been eighteen at the most.

'Is the Count at home?' I queried.

'Why no, *mein Herr*,' replied the girl. 'He seldom comes here . . . but he may be found at his estates at Borgo.'

She shivered suddenly.

'But please come in, *mein Herr*. I am sure you are cold standing there.'

I hesitated still.

'I am with a friend . . .' I began.

'Ah yes, *mein Herr*. Do not worry. He has entered the house at the rear and is upstairs . . . going over some papers in the Count's rooms . . . he sent me to fetch you.'

'Ah!' I cried. 'Why didn't you tell me this before? I thought . . . ah well, never mind. Lead me to him, *Fräulein*.'

She stepped back and I entered the great hall. Apart from the lamp burning on a side table, the hall was dark and cold. I turned to the girl to ask why, as *Hausmädchen*, or housemaid as we would say, she did not keep a fire burning by which to receive guests. But the question was not framed. My mouth hung open as I gazed upon the beautiful young creature before me. My estimation of her age as eighteen years seemed to be an accurate one. She had a fresh pale skin with touches of red on her cheeks which were speckled with tiny freckles so delicate that an artist might have spent hours placing each freckle to its greatest effect. Her hair was dark and her eyes blue and wide. She stood there smiling almost coquettishly at me.

'That is better, *mein Herr*, is it not? It is so cold out there ... so,' she paused to find the right word, 'so inhospitable.'

I did not point out that the house inside seemed just as freezing as the night air outside.

'Where is my friend, *Fräulein*?' I asked.

'Do not be alarmed, *mein Herr*. I shall take you to him.'

She smiled a smile of such sweetness and innocence that I was amazed a girl like her could be employed in the services of the family which Avram had so vividly described to me.

Her face was that of a young innocent, without blemish, without corruption. Even her coquettishness was without studied affect.

For one wild moment I felt an insane surge of desire which thrust from me all thoughts of Clara. For a second I fought to control my wild emotions, closing my eyes and leaning heavily against the wall. When I opened them I saw her still smiling at me, red lips parted a trifle, showing beautiful milk white teeth over which she momentarily ran the tip of a pink tongue.

'Where is my friend?' I demanded, a harshness in my tone to dispel the wicked desires within me.

'If you will pick up the lantern and follow me, *mein Herr* ...?'

She turned and walked swiftly into the gloom of the hall. I hastily took up the lantern and hurried after her, thinking that she must have the eyes of a cat to walk into that darkness with such assuredness. She led the way up a winding flight of stairs and then from the first floor up another stairway. She paused before a door, threw it open and entered.

The room was empty, without fires in the hearth nor light except the rays of the lantern I carried.

I looked around in puzzlement.

'He is not here,' I said, stating the obvious.

The girl, Malvina, smilingly shook her head.

'He will join us, never fear.'

I set down my lantern and peered about. The room lay under a thick covering of dust. Bed, chairs, dressing-table were covered in dirt and, to my horror, several items of furniture were rotting away.

'How long have you been *Hausmädchen* here, Malvina?' I asked, amazed that anyone could allow such advanced decay to go unchecked.

'Oh, a long, long time, *mein Herr*.'

'But not long enough to clean the place, eh?' my natural fastidiousness formed the rebuke in my voice.

She pouted, oh so prettily.

'Pah, what is a little dirt? The Count never comes here.'

'You are a poor housemaid, Malvina.'

She gave a low, gurgling laugh.

'Yet I am much better *in other things* . . .'

The emphasis in her voice left no doubt as to her meaning and it startled me that I should hear this from a child of her innocent mien.

In my embarrassment I turned to the mirror and started to wipe away the dust from its surface, pretending to be interested in its ancient workmanship.

I know the room was dark and the rays from the lantern threw many strange shadows across the room but, as I bent towards the mirror, with Malvina standing smilingly behind me, a cold terror gripped my throat.

I could not see the reflection of Malvina in the mirror!

In growing fear I rubbed harder at its surface, sending cascades of dust this way and that, and when I had cleared a sufficient portion of the surface, I pressed close.

Great gods! I cannot record that terrible feeling as I saw that I stood alone in that room.

I whirled round and saw Malvina standing there, laughing silently as if at some great joke.

Dimly I recalled the words of Avram: 'They cast no shadow nor reflection in a mirror.'

The gentle, innocent face of the girl looked at me in sudden concern.

'Why do you start so, *mein Herr*? Why do you look at me so? I am but a poor girl. Yet why do your eyes stand out in fear? You need have no fear of me.'

Yet, as I stared, her innocence seemed to vanish. Now she seemed so self-assured, so voluptuous. The desire I had but a moment ago vanished in the chill fingers of fear which gripped my heart.

'Who are you?' I breathed.

'I am Malvina, as I have told you. Have no fear of me . . . rather let your desires suppress your fear.'

She made an obscene, seductive gesture with her body.

'Come, young *Herr*, young, vital *Herr* . . . come to me. Let me love you for I worship the warmth of your body, the warmth of your blood, rich young blood . . . for blood is life . . . and life is all . . . come young *Herr* . . .'

The voice that I had thought so innocent was edged with a grossness, the smile, so beguiling, was now merely lascivious.

Her voice droned on, gently, coaxing, coaxing . . . I knew I was being mesmerized. I jerked up my head and bit my tongue to let the pain add sharpness to my wits.

'No . . . in the name of God!'

My hand struggled down to my coat pocket to grab for Avram's crucifix which nestled there.

It froze halfway.

A strange transformation seemed to come over that once lovely creature . . . aye, lovely – yet spawn of the devil!

Into those softly dreaming blue eyes there sprang the red fires of hell . . . the eyes seemed to become glowing red coals, blinding me as I stood frozen in time. The lips, now blood-red, obscene things, pulled back from those white, oh so white, teeth. And the teeth themselves seemed to grow longer, sharper, the incisors like flashing knives, and a ghastly red tongue lashed hungrily over them.

A snarl erupted from that once beautiful throat, a snarl that reminded me of the cry of a hunting dog about to spring on its prey.

Hands forward, like grasping claws, the girl moved slowly towards me.

Even as those hands grasped my coat, my fear . . . pumping adrenalin through my limbs, galvanized me into action. One hand shot out to grasp the soft white throat of the girl, another fumbled in my pocket. But I had not counted on the strength of the creature; she seemed to be possessed of the strength of ten full-grown men.

I crashed backwards against the mirror under the force of her attack.

All the while those eyes – livid hungry coals – burned into my very soul.

I found myself sobbing with fear as I felt her mouth, with those dreadful grinding, snapping teeth, closing towards my neck, felt the awful odour of her fetid breath, whose warmth seemed to burn my skin. Closer, still yet closer, came that obscenely gnashing mouth, that licking tongue, against my neck.

Somehow, just as her lips touched my skin, I managed to swing my left arm around so that, as those terrible teeth closed on my arm, I could feel them, needle sharp, piercing through my skin.

I gave a terrible cry of anguish.

Suddenly the creature pulled back from my body, mouth working, eyes wide in terror.

Avram stood on the threshold of the room, one hand clutching at a crucifix that seemed to mesmerize and terrify the creature.

'Upton . . . are you all right?' came his anxious voice.

'I think so,' I replied hesitantly.

'Then hold up your crucifix and keep this devil's spawn at bay for a moment.'

I did as I was told.

The creature's terrified eyes turned to the symbol I drew forth and held up. Under Avram's guidance I moved forward until the thing was imprisoned in a corner of the room.

It was like keeping some hissing, snarling beast at bay.

What happened next was my fault. For an instant I turned my gaze to see what Avram was doing and the she-devil was at me, my arm went back and my crucifix, knocked from my hand by the impact, went flying across the room. Then the creature had knocked me to the floor and, in terror, I threw up my hands to protect myself.

Abruptly the creature stiffened and gave a long scream, a howl like the night cry of a wolf.

Her body fell away from mine.

I shall never forget that ghastly scene, lit by the rays of the solitary lantern in that dusty old room.

From the heart of the creature there protruded a wooden tent peg and from it blood pulsated like a terrible geyser. The creature was gnashing its mouth, tearing at its lips until they were red and bloody. It had fallen back on the floor. Avram leant over it and gave the wooden peg a resounding blow with a wooden mallet.

The scream was awful to my ears yet, in fascinated horror, I had to watch.

Avram was mumbling something, which I afterwards understood to be some prayer. Before my horrified gaze the girl . . . that girl of eighteen years . . . started to grow old. Yes; incredible as it sounds, her struggles ceased. For a second she seemed young and innocent. Then her skin was wrinkling, aging, the hair growing grey, white and then – horrors – falling from her shrinking skull in great tufts. Then the skin itself became dried and cracked, and withered to dust before my eyes. Even the bones turned brittle and before long there was nothing but a pile of dust upon the floor, indistinguishable from the other dust.

I bent over and vomited.

CHAPTER TWENTY-THREE

The next thing I knew was that Avram was helping me away from that accursed place and soon I was in my hotel room with the American-Romanian bending over me and bandaging my arm.

'Are you feeling better?' he asked anxiously as my swimming eyes finally focused on his anxious gaze.

'I feel terrible,' I confessed, as, groaning, I forced myself into a sitting position.

He handed me a glass of brandy.

'Is it poisonous?' I asked, looking at my bandaged arm.

'I don't think so,' replied Avram. 'I've cleaned it as best I could. The teeth tore the flesh open but didn't strike a vein or artery. In any case, a vampire must drink long and deeply before it has an ill effect.'

I shuddered at the memory.

Then:

'My God! What of Clara!'

She had been the whole purpose of our visit to that monstrous place and I, in my distraction, had forgotten.

'We were too late,' Avram said softly. 'No, no,' he added quickly in answer to my hoarse cry of despair. 'We may still be able to save her. The coach must have left a moment before we arrived. In the stables I found signs of it having been there during the day. But when we arrived it was gone.'

'Gone?' I whispered fearfully. 'Gone where?'

'I'd say that it has left Bucharest, taking Miss Clara with it, and is now heading for the Dracula estate in Transylvania.'

'Then we must follow!' I cried, leaping from my bed.

Avram agreed.

'I've already given the hotel clerk the order to hire us a carriage for it's too far to ride comfortably on horseback. If one of us takes turns to drive, then the other can sleep in the carriage and, that way, we might overtake the coach fairly soon. There are enough post-houses between here and the Transylvanian border to supply us with fresh horses when they're needed.'

As he spoke I flung my belongings into my bag and was soon following Avram to the front of the hotel where the clerk had already obtained a landau drawn by two well-muscled horses.

I did not even spare a thought for Viscount Molesworth or the British delegation, even though it was goodbye to my career with the Foreign Office. Clara, and the fighting of this evil were of greater importance than the machinations of nations playing puny games with each other. But I will say this in passing; later, at the inquiry, Lord Molesworth did speak up on my behalf and tried to get me reinstated in the services of the government, albeit unsuccessfully.

I should also add that Molesworth's political foresight proved correct as regards the new Romanian state. A few months later the conservative prime minister of the new state, Cartargiu, was assassinated outside the Metropolitan Church in Bucharest, soon after leaving the National Assembly. Mircea Malaievu, the head of the radical peasant movement, was blamed. In the turmoil that followed, the Romanian parliament voted by sixty-two votes to thirty-five to grant freedom to all the peasants in the country and free them from the feudal obligations of the landowners. But Prince Alexandru, true to his principles, refused to endorse the law. The birth pangs of the Romanian nation became violent. Alexandru was forced to abdicate and a new 'moderate government' was formed. Unfortunately for the British interests, represented by Molesworth, the throne of Romania was offered in 1886 to

Carol of Hohenzollern-Sigmaringen, a relative of the King of Prussia. Our support of the unpopular Alexandru lost us our hold on the country.

By dawn the following day, Avram – taking first shift as coachman – brought our landau and two restless mares to the town of Ploesti within sight of the brooding white peaks of the Carpathian mountains. This particular range, so Avram told me, was the Transylvanian Alps which separated Wallachia from Transylvania. At Ploesti we found a peasant who had been early in the fields and had seen the black coach rumble through the town in the direction of Kronstadt, a town which lay over the Alps, beyond the border. Avram further learned from the man that the Austrians had closed the frontier between Transylvania and Wallachia an hour earlier due to the agitation by some Transylvanians to be allowed to secede from the Austro-Hungarian Empire and join the Romanian union. Even now groups of guerrillas fighting for this end were at large in the mountains.

'It'll be difficult to get through to Kronstadt,' said Avram worriedly. 'Still, I think it proves that the coach is heading for the Dracula estates near the Borgo Pass. My guess is that from Kronstadt they will head for Bistritz and then into the Borgo Pass.'

'What shall we do?' I asked. 'How can we follow?'

'To avoid trouble at the frontier, I think our best plan is to keep to this side of the Alps; a few miles east of here the mountains swing northwards. We can follow the eastern spurs of the mountains as far as the town of Piatra on the River Bistrita. There we can cross the border, swing around through the mountains and enter the Borgo Pass from the north-east ... in the opposite direction. If we make good time, we can arrive before the coach reaches there and ambush it.'

I looked at him in amazement.

'Ambush it?' I repeated stupidly.

'Exactly, my friend,' he smiled. 'We can abduct Clara from the coach and take her to a place of safety before we're suspected. They'll be thinking that we're following the coach, not sweeping round into a semicircle to intercept it.'

I realized the strategy of the idea and caught something of Avram's enthusiasm.

Now I took my turn at the reins while Avram dozed in the open carriage. I sent the landau hurtling forward under its new team of horses towards the Piatra road.

Three days of travel, stopping only to change horses and obtain food, saw our landau to the north-east of the Borgo Pass, a flat, desolate expanse which ran through a mountainous crag- and torrent-filled terrain leading down at its south-western extremity to the town of Bistritz. Bistritz was an ancient town, so Avram told me, of some twelve thousand souls. It was surrounded by the ruins of old bastions and towers which, for the most part, had been badly burnt down about five years before. Near the southern entrance of the Pass itself stood a ruined castle which once dominated the entrance and surrounding countryside. According to Avram, only the great Dracula estate still stood to dominate the passage through the Carpathians which led from the main reaches of Transylvania proper up to the small territory of Bukovina where the actual Castle Dracula was situated.

It was the dark side of twilight when we entered the Pass and Avram pointed out a gloom-enshrouded tract of land to the west which disappeared into a valley of its own. That, he told me, was where the Dracula lands lay. It certainly looked a gloomy and forbidding area but we did not halt here. Avram drove on a few miles and, where the road from Bistritz narrowed and rounded a bend with rock walls on either side, we drew up and made preparations for our ambush.

In spite of the length of our journey, I felt strangely refreshed. Perhaps it was the anticipation of the forthcoming encounter. We had carefully worked out the passage of the coach and knew it must arrive sometime during that evening, even allowing for unforeseen delays.

Our plan was a simple one. As soon as I, posted on a protuberance of rock, heard the approach of the coach I was to signal Avram who would then drive our landau across the narrow roadway. Having halted the coach we would overpower the driver and then flee in the direction of Bistritz with Clara.

It seemed so simple.

It was ten o'clock when I heard the first rumble of the carriage wheels along the rocky roadway. Then, through the shrouding gloom I could make out a dark shape. There was no mistaking the black coach, for its image had been burnt into my mind ever since our first encounter before Bucharest.

'Now!' I cried, the excitement cracking my voice.

Avram promptly leapt upon the landau's driving seat and guided the horses across the roadway. Then he leapt down and, to my surprise, I saw him grasp his small derringer revolver.

'Just in case,' he whispered.

The black coach was suddenly upon us, thundering at full speed around the narrow bend. At the last minute the black-clad coachman saw our barrier and heaved back on the reins of his four black beasts. From his mouth came a stream of profanities, or so I guessed his invective to be.

The coach wheels locked as he slewed the vehicle round, the brake hard on. The coach itself spun into the rocky walls, snapping the shafts. The horses reared and whinnied and pawed out in a dozen different directions. Then, suddenly, they broke free of their traces and flew off down the road northwards taking, to my horror, our own beasts – trailing our landau – with them.

But there was no time to lament our loss.

The coachman had leapt from his box with a snarl of rage and launched himself at Avram who had no time to use his revolver. The man knocked him back on the ground and I saw the derringer fly off into the night and fall among the rocks. Avram seized the two hairy hands which were gripping his neck and began to prise them apart. Spurred into activity, I rushed up behind the man and kicked him in the lower spine. With a cry of agony he turned from Avram and made a lunge towards me. But Avram, quickly recovering, seized the man from behind.

'Quick, Upton,' he cried. 'Take care of Miss Clara!'

I ran to the splintered carriage and peered inside.

Dear God! Clara was there, just sitting, a faraway look in her eyes and holding that accursed dragon statuette before her.

'Clara, my dear,' I cried, clasping her to me. She was like a marble statue in my arms, cold and immovable.

'Clara, are you all right?' I cried.

But she stared right through me.

I waved my hand before her eyes. There was no reaction. She seemed to be in some strange hypnotic trance. I tore the statuette from her grasp and sent it crashing to the roadway, but with no effect. She sat there, unseeing, unhearing.

'Upton!'

A cry of dismay caused me to look back at Avram. The coachman had seized Avram once more by the throat and was pushing him back against a rock. His hands clawed desperately at his assailant.

Seizing my crucifix, I raced to the man and pushed it into his face, thinking he might be some creature of the night, a pawn of his evil master, as Malvina had been.

To my horror the man leered up at me and then, with one gigantic paw, sent the crucifix hurtling into the night.

The man was human . . . or enough so as not to be afraid of such symbols.

With one blow of his hand he sent me crashing to the ground and turned back to finish Avram.

'Find my gun, Upton,' cried Avram in despair. 'My gun . . .'

Panic-stricken, I scrambled over the rocks. It was more by good luck than judgement that I found the cold metal and, clasping it in my hand, I pulled myself up.

How can I forget that sight?

As I pulled myself up and levelled the pistol, the tall coachman had heaved Avram above his head, as if he had been but a child, and then threw him bodily at a sharp, rocky crag. Avram's scream was cut short by the sickening thud of the impact and I saw his inert body slither to the ground. Even in that gloom I could see his head was oddly twisted and the eyes were wide and staring.

A red rage filled me.

I turned to the coachman. He was grinning oddly at me, walking slowly towards me, his arms hanging loosely by his side.

I pulled back the safety catch and fired the gun. The bullet hit him in the chest. He halted in surprise and looked down at the trickle of blood that was spreading over his shirt. A coldness gripped me as he started forward again. With clenched teeth I fired all the remaining chambers of the gun in quick succession. He stood still, and for a horrified moment I thought he was going to come on again, but slowly, ever so slowly, he sank down to the ground and lay there without a sound.

A cold sweat upon my brow, I stood trying to fight the weakness in my legs.

My eyes moved from the still-smoking gun to the bloody corpse before me and then travelled to the poor twisted body of my friend Avram.

'Upton . . .?' Clara's hesitant voice broke the stillness.

I glanced up, startled.

Clara had descended from the coach, her eyes were wide with fear and her clenched fist was stifling the scream in her mouth.

'What has happened? My God, Upton, what has happened?'

Her voice was on the verge of hysteria.

'Clara?' I cried, wild with relief, 'Clara? Are you all right?'

She collapsed, sobbing helplessly as I clasped her to my breast.

'A nightmare . . . since I left you, Upton . . . I have been in some terrifying nightmare . . . oh my God! Is it true? Is it true? Am I . . . am I one of . . . of them?'

'No, Clara, no!'

I tried to comfort her sobbing body.

'You're safe now, everything will be fine. Just fine.'

But fear gnawed my mind.

'We must leave here immediately, Clara. It's a long way to walk but we must try to get to Bistritz.'

'Anything, anything,' she gulped, 'so long as you are with me now.'

I made a hurried search of the wrecked coach but could find no provisions nor anything else to protect us from the perils of the night. There was only Clara's long travelling cloak and this I placed around her trembling shoulders.

I gave her a rather wan smile.

'Come on, dearest, we'll have to step it out . . . it's a long walk . . .'

I became aware that her eyes were not focused on mine and were staring wide with fear on something behind my shoulder. I swung round in a defensive attitude and pushed her behind me.

On a little rise, a few yards away, stood an elegant calèche, illuminated by two side lanterns which threw out

435

an eerie red glare. The calèche was black and blended with four great coal-black horses which stood patiently in their traces. But before the little coach stood a man. He stood looking down on us, giving an absurd impression of a great height. He was clad from head to toe in a long black travelling cloak which disguised all his features in black shadows. Only his eyes shone out like two pinpricks of red light, the reflection, I reasoned, of the glare of the calèche's side lights.

'You have had an accident, my friends?'

To my surprise he spoke English, an English strangely accented, his voice deep, almost sonorous.

'You would appear to be in some distress,' he said, when I did not reply. 'My calèche is at your service and my house lies not too far from here. This is a bad place to be during the hours of darkness. Perhaps the lady and yourself will accompany me so that I may bring you some relief from your plight?'

I recovered my manners and gave a bow.

The man's offer was better than walking to Bistritz through that inhospitable countryside. I stammered out my thanks to the stranger, wondering how I could account to the authorities for this affair, for there was bound to be some inquiry about the shooting of the coachman and the death of poor Avram.

Courteously, the tall man handed Clara up into the calèche and, as I climbed up after her, I heard a sharp intake of breath.

The stranger had bent down and picked up the jade dragon and was holding it up in the light of the calèche's lamps.

'Why, this is a superb piece of workmanship, is it not so? It would be a shame to leave it on the roadway for any scavenger to take.'

Carelessly, he tossed it up on the driver's seat and swung himself after it.

'How far is it to your house, sir?' I called anxiously.

'Not far, my friend, not far,' was the reply.

I heard the crack of the whip and the horses jerked forward.

It was then, just as we were leaving the scene of that terrible encounter, that I heard a terrible howling of wolves seeking their prey. The moon suddenly, for the first time that night, slipped from a cloud and laid a pale white light over the ground. Low black shadows were slinking towards the bodies of the coachman and poor Avram, and I cried out to the tall stranger to stop.

He halted a moment and asked what the matter was.

Leaning out of the coach, I pointed to the snarling creatures who were already beginning to fight over the remains of the coachman.

'We should protect their bodies from those vile beasts, sir,' I began.

To my amazement the man threw back his head and laughed.

'Vile creatures, you say? Poor creatures of the night . . . and you would deny them their sustenance? They, like man, must live and must kill to live. They have earned their right to feast this night.'

He suddenly cracked his whip and I was thrown back into the calèche as the horses sprang forward and the coach flew into the night.

'Upton!' Clara uttered a shrill cry of horror and I followed her pointing finger towards the upholstery of the carriage.

Embroidered on the black satin cushions was the image of a white dragon. Underneath it was one word . . . *Dracula!*

CHAPTER TWENTY-FOUR

The speed with which the calèche travelled made any thoughts of escape nonsensical and it did not seem long before the grim coachman drew up in some dimly lit courtyard. We were ushered through a large door, along several stone passage-ways into a surprisingly bright room. A roaring fire crackled in a great hearth at one end of the room, before which a large table was spread, as if for the evening meal. Only two places were laid and the tall coachman ushered us to them, bade us be seated and poured out some drinks.

'I have been expecting you both,' he said softly. 'You must be tired after the distress of your journey, so eat and refresh yourselves.' I looked at him in puzzlement.

'*You* have been expecting us?' I queried. 'Then you are . . .?'

'I am Dracula,' the man acknowledged with a bow.

It was then that recognition flooded my brain.

The dreams, if such they were, that I had experienced in London, flooded back into my memory. Here stood the same man; the man who had whispered to me in my dreams. Yes, from head to toe he was draped in black; the very same man.

He was tall, elderly it seemed, although his pale face held no ageing of the skin, only the long white moustache which drooped over his otherwise clean-shaven face gave the impression of age. His face was strong – extremely strong, aquiline with a high-bridged thin nose and peculiarly arched nostrils. His forehead was loftily domed and the hair grew scantily round the temples but profusely elsewhere. The eyebrows were massive and nearly met across the bridge of his nose.

As in my vision, it was the mouth which captured my eyes. That mouth set in the long, pale face; fixed and cruel looking, with teeth that protruded over the remarkably ruddy lips whose redness had the effect of highlighting his white skin and giving the impression of an extraordinary pallor. And where the teeth protruded over the lips, they were sharp and white.

Even in this brightly lit room I could not discern the natural colour of his eyes. They still seemed red in the glow of the flickering fire.

'And so . . .' he smiled softly. 'So you have both come to me.'

Clara shuddered.

I forced myself to meet his smile.

'And now you owe us explanations, Count Dracula.'

He chuckled without mirth.

'I do?' he bantered.

He pointed to the table: 'Eat, and while you eat, my friends, I shall talk. You have many, many questions which you want to ask of me. I feel it. But you shall eat and I shall talk.'

I looked across at Clara and tried to smile.

'We had better do as he suggests. It is no good starving ourselves in the midst of plenty . . . and we may need our strength.'

I added this last sentence *sotto voce*, implying a deeper meaning.

The count did not appear to have heard and was standing with his back to the fire.

Clara was unable to do anything but pick at her food and I must confess I felt no better an appetite.

While the count seemed to be lost in thought I suddenly dared venture a question.

'What is your connection with Draco? Why do you seek the statuette?'

He looked sharply at me and then smiled.

'You ask me why I seek the image of Draco, the fire breather from the great deep, the giver of immortality?'

He paused as if contemplating how best he should answer.

'Countless years ago, there arose in ancient Egypt a set of earnest inquirers of the sciences, observers, if you will, of all natural phenomena. They followed the cult of the life-giving force of Draco – The dragon god, Draco, the personification of the elemental life force. As they studied and experimented, those ancients found that not only the spirit could achieve immortality but, if a man had courage and possessed the correct rituals and knowledge, a man's body, too, could obtain perpetual life. The ancients found the forbidden secrets of life, discovered ways to release what they called *Ka*, the spiritual body of man. They pursued their science to its rightful conclusion and they prospered. There came the years of the great flowering of knowledge, the days when the Draconian Cult was followed from the shores of the Atlantic Ocean to the shores of the Pacific Ocean.

'But others,' his eyes flashed in vicious hatred, 'puny mortals full of petty prejudice and pretentious morality, others came and condemned without understanding the great achievements of Draconian science. They said it blasphemed against the true gods, against Nature herself and against man. Thus a great persecution of the priests of Draco commenced in the ancient land of Egypt and by the force of that bloody persecution new, weaker gods like Ammon and Ra and Hathor were raised in place of the one true creator of life. In their hundreds, the priests of Draco, keepers of the great secrets of Nature, fled from the land of Egypt. They fled east and west, north and south . . . to Asia and Persia, to the bowels of Africa, and to the cold north wastes and beyond.

'And some of them took their learning and, in the dark forests or windswept plains, they raised up the image of the dragon god again and once more began their search for the secret of life.'

We sat listening to his amazing narrative, mesmerized by the intensity of his voice, seeing the images which he sketched as vividly as if we were witnessing them at first hand.

Clara reached out a hand to mine for comfort.

'I am a Dracula,' he said, raising himself to his full height. 'Our family is ancient, more ancient than you can ever guess, for we are the very spawn of Draco and our name links us with him. We are descended from the loins of Setek-Ab-Ra who was his greatest priest and philosopher. The children of Setek-Ab-Ra fled Egypt with others of the cult and made their way to the fortress of the Carpathian peaks, bastions against the blood-thirst of Amenhotep the Fourth who tried to destroy Draco and set up a worship to Aton, the sun god. And here, my friends, among the defences of the Carpathians, the seed of Draco prospered.'

He struck himself on the chest with a clenched fist.

'And I, I am proof that his seed still lives!'

A fierce fire blazed from his eyes.

'We Draculas settled this country when the people wore animal skins and hunted with implements of stone. We watched and saw the land become the crossroads of civilization; we saw the Getae come and settle on the Wallachian plain, saw the coming of the Thracians, Scythians and Celts ... each nation mingling its blood with the whole to sire a new race of people.

'And when there *was* a people to command, a Dracula it was who commanded them. It was a Dracula who offered aid to Mark Antony at Actium. It was a Dracula who held back the Roman conquest, who repelled the Goths and the Huns from the Asiatic steppes when they came like a devouring fire to eat up Europe. Attila himself bowed his knee before Dracula.

441

'The Draculas are a proud house bearing a proud name. Out of the mingling of the nations of Europe, the house of Dracula springs unsullied, owing allegiance to none save Draco who spawned them.'

He suddenly snarled.

'But what does this new Europe know about such things? What do you – foreigners from some accursed north land – know or care?'

'You have told us that you claim to be a descendant of priests of Draco from ancient Egypt,' I ventured. 'But you have said nothing of . . .'

I fell silent as his baleful eyes bore into mine.

'Claim?' he spat the word. 'Claim? I *am* descended from Draco. When I was a young man, a prince of Wallachia, I pursued the Draconian path of knowledge, for in knowledge there is power. I contemplated on philosophy, on alchemy and theology and law. With the aid of Draco I wrested Nature's secrets from her. Aye, one by one I looked into the secrets of Nature and they opened to me like flowers before the sun. And the time came when I could dare to challenge the gods themselves and gain immortality as they . . .

'I took myself off into the mountain peaks and performed the ritual . . . step by step, line by line, but something went wrong, wrong!'

He smashed his fist into the palm of his hand.

His eyes glared round wildly as if seeking someone to accuse for the error.

'I achieved immortality, true, but not the complete immortality that I sought. I found myself but a mockery of an immortal, an Undead creature with great constrictions upon me. I could only move by night, and each day I had to return to a cursed sleeping-death, hidden from any who knew the secret of my destruction. And each night I was forced to find warm, living blood to drink, to sustain my existence, for in that blood was the essence of life for which I hungered. Without it I would eventually fade into the elemental dust of my creation. And, cursed be my fate, each person that I drank from became as I . . . and we were called vampires!

'Vampires!' he screeched the word. 'A Dracula, a follower of the true life force, made into a mere creature of the night, little better than a wolf or bat, a prey to those who could stalk me in the sunlight!

'The ritual for immortality was wrong, I knew it. I have been cursed as you see me now for a span of four long centuries . . .'

'What?' I cried aghast.

Clara gave a cry and sank into merciful unconsciousness.

My eyes did not leave this strange, terrifying being who claimed he had walked the earth for four centuries. God! Could it be true?

'Impossible!' I cried.

The count threw back his head and bared his teeth in a parody of a laugh.

'The only impossible things are those which have not yet been mastered! You cannot conceive of immortality? But I tell you that I am Vlad Dracula whom the men of my time once called Vlad Tepes, the Impaler, who ruled Wallachia for many a year and made it great. Did I not drive out the Turk and the Saxon who came to dominate the Carpathians?'

I felt my body turn to a trembling jelly.

'The seed of my loins ruled Wallachia for near two centuries after – shall I call it my death? Yet the ungrateful Wallachians rose up and drove out Mihail Radu, drove him out of Wallachia and out of Castle Dracula at Arefu. Mihail, as all other Draculas, knew my secret and took me with him, carrying the earth of my burial ground in large boxes so that I could rest at my ease during the accursed daylight hours. We fled from Arefu across the

Carpathians to this castle where, for the past two hundred years, I have rested.

'Long have I fretted in my confinement, long have I pondered on my mistake in that ritual. And, at last, I discovered my mistake . . . a discovery born of four hundred years of contemplation. Now I know the remedy, the ritual which will set me free of this . . . this constriction! Soon I shall no longer be restricted by the rising or the setting of the sun. Soon I shall walk the earth freely. True immortality shall be mine!'

I shuddered at the prospect.

'Then the house of Dracula shall rise again!' he was staring into the fire, his voice full of vehemence. 'The fates have decreed it and it would be blasphemy to deny the course already charted in the heavens. I shall go forth into the world and seize what is rightfully mine. The world will be but a bauble at my feet. I have but to bend down . . .'

It was like listening to the ravings of some megalomaniac . . . the old desire of world conquest! Yet what chilled me with a sense of dread and awe was that I knew him to be no maniac bent on fanciful dreams. He had a power so terrible, so ghastly, that I knew my poor friends Yorke and Avram had been right. That evil power must be destroyed at any cost! But how?

'Where do we, Miss Clarke and I, fit into your plans?' I ventured to ask. 'And what of the dragon statuette?'

He smiled like some benign schoolmaster to a backward child.

'You will know all about reincarnation, so I will not bother to explain. Let me merely state that your spirit once walked the earth as a priest of Ammon. Many centuries ago you were Ki, Kherheb of Ammon, and you were eventually executed as a foul traitor and blasphemer against the true god, Draco. Miss Clarke,' he smiled thinly at Clara's still insensible form, 'was once Sebek-nefer-Ra, a magnificent queen of Egypt who placed Draco above all else, aye, even though she loved Ki the Kherheb, she sacrificed the false priest with her own hand because he refused to turn away from his heresy.'

I felt another spasm of shudders run through me as I recalled my early nightmares.

'If you refuse to admit belief in reincarnation, then consider the matter thus: in you there are the same components, the same electrical forces, the same life spark, that dwelt in Ki the Kherheb and in Sebek-nefer-Ra. Then, by accident, there came into your hands the very statuette of Draco that was made by the first worshipper perhaps some six thousand earthly years ago. The very statuette that was placed in the sanctum of the great temple at Thebes.

'Let me explain it this way . . . the statuette possessed a power, an essence. You were the negative element and she,' he motioned to Clara, 'was the positive element. Between you, you comprised both parts of a conductor of the force. When you met, with the statuette as transmitter, the circuit was complete. The force was all-powerful and through it I was able to extend my thoughts across the continent to guide your steps hither.

'And why do I need the statuette? As the statuette acted to complete the circuit with you and the girl, so will it complete my circuit . . . it will allow me to complete the ancient ritual which will allow me to strike off these fetters I have worn for four hundred years. I can strike them off and walk the earth in the sun once more and be, at last, omnipotent in the eyes of puny man. The world shall be mine at last!'

'But what of the girl and me?' I pressed.

'The girl I need for the ritual. As I have said, she is the positive element. You, I do not need now that the girl has brought me the statuette. That was why I tried to prevent you from following her, in case you succeeded in stopping her. That was why I tried to stop you on the ship, on the road and in Bucharest.'

'But you sought me out at first,' I said, not understanding. 'Through the dreams and through the mediums you enticed me to come to you and bring the statuette.'

'That was before I found her,' he said, nodding to Clara once more. 'You were a difficult subject, but she was easier to control and came without trouble. I needed you no longer.'

I suddenly became aware of another presence in the room.

I turned, startled, to a corner of the room where it seemed as if three people had suddenly materialized out of nowhere. I could have sworn that they had not entered by the door, for I had been sitting facing it. A tall, youngish-looking man, bearing a striking resemblance to the count himself, stepped forward and examined me with burning eyes set in his pale face. With him were two voluptuous young women, so remarkably like Malvina that for a moment I thought my eyes were deceiving me. They smiled, nay – leered, at me like hungry cats waiting for their meal.

The young man turned to the count. He was dressed in a grey cloak that enveloped him from feet to neck, leaving as a relief only the pale white of his face and the blackness of his hair.

'It is nearly sun-up, lord,' he said.

An anxious frown gathered on the dark brows of the count. He glanced towards the window.

'You are right, Mihail. We must show our guests where they must rest until . . . until the ceremony.'

One of the women, the smaller of the two, whose rich red lips seemed obscene against the white of her skin, crept closer to me.

'But why, lord,' she breathed in a purring tone, 'why not let us enjoy them . . . they are so young, so rich in blood . . .'

I pulled back as she came nearer me. I could feel her dank, putrid breath hot on my cheek.

In two strides the count had crossed the room, seized the creature by her white, gross neck and – with a strength that appalled me – lifted her bodily and sent her crashing across the room.

'These people are mine,' he snarled. 'Mine! No harm shall come to them until after the ceremony! Do you hear?'

'We hear, lord,' the young man answered for the trio.

'Very well. You understand the importance of the ceremony . . . they must not be touched.'

The two female creatures, hissing terrifyingly in their disappointment, crouched back as the count towered over them.

'Begone, you sluts! Begone, you vile creatures, back to your lairs. The sun comes!'

He raised a forefinger at the window and, sure enough, I could see the pale cast of dawn against the black sky.

No greater horror was mine when the two creatures vanished as if in a wisp of smoke . . . dissolving into some vapour-like substance which sped in a tiny stream through a crack in the door.

The count turned and swept up the still mercifully unconscious Clara in his arms.

'Follow me,' he said curtly, and led the way from the room.

I looked back to where the young man, Mihail, had been standing but he, too, had vanished.

The count led the way to a small bedchamber and laid Clara on the bed. Then he ushered me, protesting, from the room and locked the door. An iron grip on my shoulder, he ushered me to another door, opened it and pushed me, none too gently, into a second bedchamber.

'Tonight!' he said, smiling through thin lips.

Then, with an anxious glance at the light now streaming

through the window, he slammed the door shut. I heard the key turn and his ringing footsteps echoing down the passage.

CHAPTER TWENTY-FIVE

No sooner had the count gone than I was at the door twisting the handle this way and that. But it was to no avail. I do not know how many centuries that castle had withstood the storms of war, but the mighty portals were secured with great oak doors many inches thick and intricately fastened with iron hinges and locks. Even as I struggled I knew my task was futile.

My brain now burned with the thought of one endeavour. I must rescue Clara and seek a way out of this vile prison and, before nightfall, must put as much distance as I could between ourselves and Castle Dracula.

My attention focused on the window and, to my excitement, I found that the iron lattice work opened to my touch. I peered out and my excitement gave way to a groan of anguish. It must have been all of fifty feet down to the tiny cobbled courtyard below. Again, excitement stifled my anguish as I caught sight of a ledge, not more than six inches wide but a ledge nevertheless, which ran six feet below my window.

I leaned out of the window and cupped my hands to my mouth.

The sun, now standing well above the eastern horizon, beat hotly down on me as if mocking my endeavours.

'Clara!' I yelled. 'Clara, can you hear me? Come to the window!'

I paused.

Suddenly the next window to mine was pushed open.

A trembling voice cried: 'Upton, is that you? Where are you?'

'At the next window.'

Her face peered out.

'Upton, what are we to do? What has happened?'

'Don't worry,' I cried, full of false courage. 'I have a plan. Look, I shall try to come along to you.'

'But how . . .?'

'The ledge below. I shall drop down to it. I think it is wide enough to take me. Then I shall come along towards you, but you will have to find some means of giving me a hand up to your window.'

She nodded.

'A bedsheet rope.'

'Clever girl,' I cried.

She disappeared and shortly was heaving a torn sheet out of the window.

I applauded her endeavours.

'Now for the difficult part.'

Taking my courage in my hands, I climbed out of the window and slowly let my body down towards the ledge. For a moment I thought I was slipping and my body hung swaying in the air with only my fingers gripping the window ledge.

Hanging at the full reach of my arms, my fumbling feet found the ledge and I stood unsteadily upon it. I paused for several moments to recover my confidence and then began to edge my way along the ledge towards her window. It seemed an eternity before I was grasping the torn bedsheet and hauling myself up into her prison. I lay a while gasping on the floor while she bent anxiously over me.

'We must escape,' I said, recovering and stating the obvious.

'Yes, but how?' she wailed with despair in her voice. 'Even if we can make it down to the courtyard, the castle gates are probably locked. And, look, you can see the great iron bolts shot home from here.'

What she said was true enough.

'Nevertheless,' I insisted, 'we must try.'

But her mind was thinking more clearly than mine. My thoughts were only of physical flight, of placing geographical distance between us and the grim fortress of this evil monster. She, however, was more logical.

'Escape to what, Upton?' she pointed out. 'Did this Dracula not call us here to Bukovina all the way from London in England? If we escape, surely he will merely call us back to him again. We will never be free of him until we have destroyed him.'

She was right. I agreed and, at her insisting, I recounted the terrible story the count had told me while she lay in her swoon. 'He was only able to call us, to control our minds, while the accursed statuette was near at hand.'

'Nevertheless, Upton,' she said firmly, 'he must be destroyed. If he succeeds in his evil plan then no one in the whole world will be safe.'

How my heart went out to her for her fortitude and courage, a greater courage than any I had witnessed. I seized her hands and kissed them.

'We must find his lair and destroy him and his kind,' she said. 'He has already confessed that he is vulnerable during the day. Let us put the day to good use.'

'Yes,' I replied, recalling my conversation with Avram. 'I have the knowledge of how his kind may be destroyed thanks to my poor friend who was slain by the coachman.'

'Then let us commence this grim task, Upton.'

I tried the door but with as little success as my own.

'The only way out is down to the courtyard,' I told her.

In silence we sat knotting the sheets into a rope which reached into that cobbled courtyard.

The descent was easier than I had imagined. The stones of the castle walls under her window were large and roughly cut and the mortar had by process of time been washed away between them. Thus a secure foothold could be easily attained by an enterprising climber. It was not long before we both stood safe and secure on the ground.

It was true, as Clara had predicted, that the great doors of the castle were closed, bolted and locked by heavy padlocks which might have been centuries old.

Clara squeezed my hand in encouragement.

'We must find his lair,' she whispered.

Squaring my shoulders I pushed at a side door, which opened into one wing of the castle containing bedchambers. But such chambers . . . most of them were entirely empty, others were barely furnished and all seemed never to have been used in ages, for everything was covered in a profusion of dust and grime.

One room caused Clara and me to gasp aloud for, although empty, there lay in one corner a pile of gold of all kinds – gold coins, from every part of the earth and covered with a thick film of dust as though it had lain long in the ground. None of it was less than three hundred years old. And next to this amazing treasure trove were chains, ornaments, some jewelled, but all of them of incredible age.

I do not know what drew me, but there was a door in a corner of that particular chamber. It was a heavy door, of the same dark oak and iron fittings that were found throughout the castle. With Clara at my side I tried its rusty, screeching handle and, to our surprise, it swung gently open. It led through a stone passage-way to a circular stairway which went steeply down as if driving towards the very bowels of the earth.

I called to Clara to keep behind me and mind her step, for the stairs were dark, although a faint gloomy light spread through a series of loopholes which pierced the heavy masonry to the world outside. Slowly, carefully, we went downwards and came to a dark, tunnel-like corridor.

'Upton, what is that dreadful odour?' gasped Clara, coughing as she breathed in some obnoxious fumes.

The air smelled of a sickly perfume, the odour of musty old earth newly dug. It was quite oppressive and grew in its intensity as we pushed our way down that passage. At the end of the corridor was another heavy door. Surprisingly, the handle seemed well oiled and it swung open quite easily before us.

We found ourselves in a chapel-like vault. Everywhere were fragments of old coffins and piles of dust. We could clearly see them in the dim light which seemed to filter in through cracks in the roof.

And everywhere were piles of earth.

'Upton!' cried Clara in horror. 'Look!'

With a quivering finger she pointed to a darkened end of the chapel vault.

There were several coffins resting on trestles in the gloom, but without lids covering their contents.

'It . . . it looks like people newly interred,' I said, aghast, as I perceived each coffin contained a body, but a body not yet in the process of decay.

Then I drew nearer and recognized one of the figures that lay stretched on a pile of that putrified earth.

I stifled a cry of terror.

There lay the count in some catatonic trance, or so I judged it to be. His eyes were fully open and stony, but lacking the glaze of death, and his cheeks were not the colour of parchment as in death. The lips were as red as ever but there was no other sign of life.

'This is what they meant, Clara,' I whispered. 'This is what they meant – Avram and the count. He lies confined in this box from sun-up to sunset.'

Clara's face was drained of blood and I could see she was fighting hard to control her twitching nerves.

'They must be destroyed,' she choked the words out.

I searched that terrible vault for some weapons and

chanced upon a spade, a wooden shaft with iron blade, and with this I turned back to those gruesome creatures. Firstly, I bent over the count. There seemed a mocking smile upon his pale face, the thin red lips were drawn back, showing those terrible sharp teeth. I felt a revulsion so great that I wondered for a moment whether I should fall insensible. But sanity gripped me from the abyss.

In the other coffins were the two female creatures and the grey-clad being called Mihail.

The sooner I commenced my work then the sooner it would be ended.

The blade of the spade was sharp enough.

I raised it over my head and struck downward. With one blow it split through the white fleshy neck of Mihail.

I was unprepared for what happened.

A great scream of anguish came from that monstrous body, echoing and re-echoing through the close confines of the dank vault. And, horror upon horrors, a fountain of black blood sprayed from that corpse, splashing on my sleeve as I stumbled to escape from its ghastly deluge.

I fell back, near swooning.

Then, as I looked on in naked terror, the body of Mihail, as Malvina's body had done before it, crumbled slowly away into dust.

A strange itching in my skull caused me to turn back to the count's coffin.

Great God! The count's head was turned towards me and the eyes . . . the eyes were boring into mine in a blaze of basilisk fury.

I dropped the spade from my nerveless hands and stood paralysed in terror.

Clara's iron composure suddenly crumbled at the terrible sight. Hands to her cheeks, she emitted scream after scream and suddenly went stumbling back towards the door, along the passage-way, away from this fiendish nightmare.

Anxious for her safety, I sped after her and finally caught her in the great dining room where we had eaten the night before.

She collapsed senseless in my arms for a moment and, on recovering, gave vent to the most heartrending fit of sobbing that I ever want to hear from a human being again.

I do not know how long she lay sobbing in my arms, and all the while with me trying to offer her reassurance and comfort. I do not know how long it was nor do I remember when the sobbing faded and, not having slept the previous night, we sank into a sleep of sheer exhaustion, comforted by the nearness of each other.

I recall springing awake abruptly, my heart pounding in sudden dread.

'My God, Clara!' my voice rose to a hysterical note as I saw the dark shadows at the window. 'Clara, the sun . . . I must finish the job before it is too late!'

Wide-eyed in terror she, too, peered at the evening shadows creeping round the window.

'Quick, Upton!' she cried, 'we must . . .'

There was a sudden passage of cold wind into the room.

In terror we glanced up.

There, standing before the door, his dark cloak flapping behind him like some gigantic bat's wings, stood the count.

'You are already too late,' his thin red lips curled in a sneer. 'You are already too late. The sun has set.'

CHAPTER TWENTY-SIX

I know not what passed that night in reality nor what passed in my fevered fantasy. I see images of the count, who spoke no word of my destruction of Mihail, and those images will haunt me until the day I die. I recall his tall figure conducting us into a vault, furnished in strange exotic trappings. This time the putrid smell of mouldering earth did not pervade the air but rather that terrifying sickly sweet smell of jasmine, the smell which had haunted my nightmares, hung in the atmosphere. Whether Clara and I went willingly with the count or whether we were propelled by his powerful will and ability of mesmerization, I cannot be sure.

I do recall that Clara and I, though not physically bound, were held in some kind of bondage.

The vault was like some grim replica of my nightmares. At the end of the room stood a large figure of the accursed Draco, whose dragon features I knew so well. Flickering torches lit the scene. Before the statue stood a black-draped altar on which sat the jade dragon which had been the cause of our ghastly adventures. It seemed to be dwarfed by the bigger replica behind it. Also on the altar, I recall that there were chalices filled with certain flowers and herbs. There was an ancient manuscript, like some papyrus I had seen in the British Museum, as well as other paraphernalia whose function I could not guess at.

The count stood before the altar, hands upraised in supplication, mumbling in a strange tongue.

At his side stood the two voluptuous devil-women who seemed to act as his servers in a terrifying parody of some ancient mass.

The deep sonorous voice of the count began to intone:

'I come from the Isle of Fire having filled my body with the blood of Ur-Hekau, Mighty One of the Enchantments. I come before thee, Draco. I worship thee, Draco, Fire-breather of the Great Deep. You are my lord and I am of thy blood.'

I strained my head to look at Clara who was standing opposite me, on the other side of this terrible temple.

Her face was flushed and her eyes were glazed as if she were in a trance.

The count turned and followed my gaze, a smile sneering across his thin lips.

'Sebek-nefer-Ra! Do you hear me?'

To my horror, Clara's eyes were forced towards the count's stare. Her lips opened.

'I hear, lord.'

'Then the time is come when the world must be filled with the *Ka* of Draco. When the spirit of Draco must enter the world through my body and fill it with abundance.'

'It is the will of Draco,' intoned Clara's voice.

I struggled feebly with my invisible bonds.

A strange green fire seemed to be playing over that accursed jade statuette.

A voice was beating in my head, telling me to do something, to stop this evil bursting forth into the world.

And yet what could I do? I was held in the thrall of a force so powerful, so evil . . .

'I come before thee, Draco,' came the count's voice again. 'I who have been faithful to thy service over the centuries . . . I come before thee to demand my reward.'

The strange green fire was almost obliterating the statuette.

All about me was a strange drumming sound and I could distinguish in this percussion human voices chanting, chanting to the very beat of the drum, joining and mingling until voice and drum were indistinguishable from each other.

It was like my nightmares.

But I was no longer asleep.

'I call upon Sebek-nefer-Ra to exhort thee, Draco, to bestow on me the reward of thy office.'

The count flung up his arms towards the image behind the altar.

With numbed emotions, I saw Clara walk towards the altar. She walked slowly, like one in a dream; walked forward and genuflected towards the statuette. Then she climbed upon the altar and lay full length upon her back, hands across her breast as if in repose, her eyes closed.

'I am thy servant, Draco. I, Sebek-nefer-Ra, willingly do offer myself to thee, creator of life, so that in my blood judgement may be made on this, thy servant Dracula.'

The women harpies, teeth churning at their fleshy lips until the blood trickled down their chins, gave frightful chuckles of delight and drew near the girl's still figure.

The count waved them back.

'To thee, Draco, I take this drink of life . . .'

I saw his mouth open, the elongated teeth bared, saw him bend slowly forward.

Clara gave a languorous sigh and arched her neck to met the sharp prick of those teeth!

I tried hard to cry out but no sounds would come.

It was then I felt a curious burning sensation at my throat. I felt my hand fused with some strange power, felt it recover its power of movement and felt it come up to my neck to feel the object at my throat.

It was the small silver crucifix that Dennis Yorke had given me for protection. I had worn it every day since that time and forgotten about it completely. It had been Clara's crucifix which I had thrown at that ghastly wolf-beast on the decks of the derelict *Ceres* but I had continued to retain my cross about my throat, under my shirt.

Not knowing exactly what I did, I reached up and snatched it from my neck. Then, mustering all the force I could, I flung it straight into the grinning green-black face of the dragon.

It was as if I had thrown a stick of dynamite at the beast. There was a terrific roar as if from an explosion. The statuette seemed to shatter into a million tiny splinters of green crystal. The blast flung Clara from the altar table.

The count gave a scream of fury and tried to run towards the smashed altar but now great sheets of flame were bursting over it, consuming the splinters of the statuette as if they were merely dried wood, wrapping the accoutrements and ancient papyrus in sheets of hungry flame. Eager tongues licked at the large dragon replica until it, too, cracked and splintered into fragments.

'The formula! The formula! The statuette!' Dracula was screaming. 'I cannot succeed without them.'

He tried to enter the consuming fire but the flames caught at his great black flapping cloak until he was forced to desist.

Fear sped adrenalin through my frame.

Clara lay at my feet moaning as she seemed to rouse herself from her hypnotic trance. I bent down and seized her in my arms and ran towards the stairs.

I heard a vicious snarl behind me.

'So you think you have thwarted me . . . thwarted the work of four centuries by a moment's caprice? You will know my revenge now, I shall not spare you!'

The count, his face working in obscene hatred, rushed towards the steps calling to his two screaming harpies.

'Come sisters! Do not let them escape! You have wanted to drink from their young blood . . . drink then! They are yours! Drink your fill, my sisters, let vengeance be ours!'

They gave cries like wolves on the scent of their prey.

I do not know what lent me strength but, with Clara semi-swooning in my arms, I hurried through the corridors of the castle with those unholy demons of the night shrieking after me.

How I managed to keep ahead of them, whose strength and guidance gave me support, I will leave it to the readers to make their own observations. Somehow I reached the door leading into the courtyard. A joyous exultation filled me as I saw that the ceremonies which the count had performed had lasted through the night. Day was already breaking, the courtyard was filled with grey light and over the eastern walls of the castle, the sun's rays were starting to stream.

With Clara still in my arms I ran out into that light.

One of the female fiends was at the door before her sister and the count and, to my consternation, rushed straight into the courtyard after me.

For a long horrified moment, as she bore down on me, I thought that Avram's knowledge of these phantoms had been wrong. Perhaps they could move in daylight?

The creature, that vile creature of the grave, neared me, a blaze of unholy triumph in her red, burning eyes.

Then I heard the screams of warning from the count and his companion.

A black shadow passed across her contorted, hate-ridden face. She glanced up and appeared to see the light of dawn for the first time. Her mouth twisted in terror. She made to turn back.

Abruptly, as if her legs had lost their power, she collapsed on the ground. Her black hair suddenly streaked with grey and, even as I watched, turned white. The skin crinkled, became dry and cracked as the rays of the rising sun swept across her body.

'Help me . . . help me . . .!'

It was the last plaintive shriek I heard from her decomposing body.

Then, as the rising sun blazed down in its morning strength, that terrible body collapsed into the dust from whence it came and was blown hither and thither in the gentle morning breeze.

I looked towards the doorway where the tall, black figure of the count hovered in the protection of the shadows.

'Puny humans!' he screamed in rage. 'You with your pale, stupid faces. I shall make you sorry yet . . . you have destroyed the dragon god . . . you have destroyed the ages-old formula by which I could have attained true immortality . . . you think that you have thwarted me? You have not yet destroyed me and while I exist I shall find a way to make you pay. You shall yet be sorry. My revenge will be sweet and time is on my side. Though you go to the ends of the earth . . . though you go to the ends of time . . . time is my friend and the centuries are mine to control. I shall be revenged!'

With another wild scream of anger the great castle door slammed shut and I could hear the bolts thrown.

I stood for a while unmoving, how long I did so I cannot recall. An insane terror rooted me to the spot and I stood in that courtyard in the golden warmth of the morning sun, babbling and trembling in my fright.

It must have been Clara who, recovering from her swoon, gathered new strength and guided me from that accursed place. I cannot even recall how we managed to open the great outer gates of that grim castle, nor, indeed, whether the outer gates were barred as they had been the previous day.

I know little of what followed. I dimly recall a long walk through some green valley, lit in the bright sunlight, of meeting with a band of strangely clad people – gypsies, perhaps – who gave us food, shelter and warm clothing and on whose strange wagons we eventually came to Bistritz. Clara afterwards told me that my hair had become streaked with white. I kept babbling, I know, as the enormity of the horror of what I had witnessed burst like a flood over my sensibilities. God knows how Clara managed to keep herself sane, perhaps it was my greater need that made her control her shattered feelings, for she nursed me day and night in my deliriums. By easy stages we went from Bistritz to Klausenburg and from thence to Budapest and on to Munich. From there the railway brought us to Calais and thence to Dover. All the while it seemed as if I continued to exist in some dark nether world, only half-realizing what was going on about me.

At times I would rave and rant and cry on people to help me destroy the evil before it was too late.

And they would sorrowfully shake their heads and cluck sympathetically as if I were some lunatic.

Some times the terrors seized me with such force that not even Clara could control me.

And now . . .

How long I have been here I cannot recall exactly. I do not resent Clara allowing them to take me to this place for, though they do not believe me, the doctors have, at least, been able to calm my fears, sedate my terrors so that I am now able to control them and face the future with a more positive frame of mind. No longer do I shriek uncontrollably as the sun sinks below the western hills, nor do I start at the sight and sound of bats, dogs and rats.

Yet they say I am mad.

And at times, mostly at night, as I stand peering through the small iron grille that blocks the window of my room, staring at the ominous black clouds that scud across the death-white face of the moon, I find myself wishing that it *was* so, wishing that I were indeed mad. For at such times, I experience an unearthly chilling tingle that vibrates against my spine; I find my heart beats twice as fast; I feel the blood bursting hotly into my cheeks, roaring in my ears, and a mist begins to cloud my eyes. And through it all I hear *his* voice, mocking, sardonic, telling me that the time is coming . . . his will shall triumph, his revenge can extend to the tranquil shores of England . . . soon, soon . . .

God! What will happen to us if he finds a way to escape from the confines of his castle in the Borgo Pass . . . if he finds a way to come to England! The thought is too horrible.

Even as I look on, in my vision the swirling mists clear momentarily and I catch a glimpse of him – a tall, thin man, all in black. I see his face, that waxen face; the high aquiline nose, the parted red lips, with the sharp teeth showing between them; and the eyes – those red basilisk orbs, burning as if I were staring at the very sunset.

And the voice.

'Soon . . . soon . . .'

Oh Clara! How shall we protect ourselves if *he* finds a way to come to England?

CHAPTER TWENTY-SEVEN

At the end of Upton Welsford's manuscript were pasted three yellowing newspaper cuttings. The first read:

> *The Westminster Gazette, 10 June 1862*
>
> We regret to report that Mr Upton Welsford, a former senior official at the Foreign Office, has been committed to the Netley Heath Sanatorium for the Insane. Mr Welsford was committed on his recent return from Romania where he had, apparently, suffered a mental breakdown.
>
> Mr Welsford was one of the British delegation to go to Romania early this year to witness the formation of the new Romanian state. Colleagues said that overwork was probably a contributing factor to his illness. A spokesman for the Foreign Office told our reporter that they have accepted Mr Welsford's resignation from office.

Following this cutting there appeared a note, written in a precise copperplate, which read: 'Welsford was released in September, 1868. His delusions apparently no longer exist or trouble him. He left this manuscript behind. It is a remarkable example of the imagination of a brainsick individual which students of such disorders will do well to read.'

The other two newspaper cuttings then followed.

> *The Westminster Gazette, 10 March 1869*
>
> The marriage of Mr Upton Welsford and Miss Clara Clarke took place on Monday last at St James's Church, Westminster.
>
> Mr Welsford was formerly personal secretary to Lord Molesworth at the Foreign Office. He resigned due to ill-

health which he has suffered in recent years. Miss Clarke is the daughter of . . .

At this point the rest of the cutting had been torn away.

The Westminster Gazette, 27 September 1890.

ANOTHER HAMPSTEAD MYSTERY*

We regret to announce the deaths of Mr and Mrs Upton Welsford of Devonshire Road, Hampstead Heath. The unfortunate couple were found dead in their home yesterday by a domestic servant. A doctor was called and pronounced life extinct, the cause of death being put down to exposure due to progressive anaemia, a lack of haemoglobin or red blood corpuscles. The servant afterwards recalled that this condition had been prevalent for some days, the couple showing a peculiar spiritlessness and languor. The servant expressed regret and remorse that she had not been able to attribute these symptoms to serious illness.

Our correspondent learns, from a reliable source, that the throats of the unfortunate couple showed tiny wounds of the kind which have been associated with the recent cases of injured children who have been found in a distressed condition on the nearby Heath after disappearing in mysterious circumstances for often as much as twenty-four hours. The facts in these mysterious cases have been reported in the columns of this journal.

The attending doctor has disclaimed any significance or connection between the couple and the children, although a police spokesman suggests that the same animal, thought to be a rat or a small dog, which attacked the children on the Heath, also attacked the couple who lived close by the Heath. The police spokesman told our correspondent that

---

* Articles from *The Westminster Gazette* of 25 September 1890, giving an account of 'A Hampstead Mystery' and 'The Hampstead Horror' were quoted by Bram Stoker in his *Dracula* (1897) in Chapter XIII. Tremayne.

a group of rat catchers will shortly be investigating the vicinity for the animals.

Mr and Mrs Welsford were well known for their charitable work in local circles, especially in their efforts to raise finances for medical research among the insane as well as supporting work for the upkeep of hospitals for the mentally ill.

Mr Welsford was fifty-five years old at the time of his death. The son of the late Reverend Mortimer Welsford of Gisleham, Buckinghamshire, he graduated from Oxford University and became personal secretary to Viscount Molesworth whose work at the Foreign Office is well known. Mr Welsford accompanied Lord Molesworth to Romania at the time of the establishment of the Romanian State. On his return, an illness forced his resignation from public office.

Mrs Welsford was formerly Miss Clara Clarke, daughter of the late Colonel George St John Clarke of the Egyptian Brigade of Rifles.

Psychiatrist's Afterword by Hugh Strickland, MD, FACP, FAPA

In allowing Mr Peter Tremayne to publish the foregoing manuscript – which was written by Mr Upton Welsford when an inmate of the Netley Heath Sanatorium for the Insane sometime between 1862 and 1868 – I have stipulated that I, as present director of the sanatorium, be allowed to contribute a few observations to this case.

Mr Welsford's story is horrific; but it is by no means unusual for someone to suffer delusions of being persecuted by vampires and werewolves or, indeed, even believe that they are changing into such mythological creatures themselves. If Mr Welsford were alive in this day and age we would have been able to cure his psychiatric disorder without too much trouble. 'Lupomania', the werewolf or vampire complex, is still known today. In my initial letter to Mr Tremayne, quoted in his introduction, I have listed some modern occurrences.

In this post-Freud period the sexual basis of vampirism and lycanthropy has been recognized by psychiatrists. The Jungian psychologist, Robert Eisler, in his excellent study *Man into Wolf* (1949) also advances a creditable hypothesis.

Man was once a peaceful herbivorous ape, living on roots and berries. But as an imitative creature, in his battle for survival against wild animals, he acquired the ferocity and bloodlust of a wild animal. So intense was this experience that man sees the mark of masculinity, a form of behaviour to impress women, as being violence. The great men of history are not usually peacemakers but those who are warriors, conquerors, full of this terrible primitive bloodlust. Soldiers are made heroes by an adoring society because they represent mankind's collective bloodlust. And when man feels frustrated, that frustration usually manifests itself in aggressive behaviour.

Bloodlust in man is often combined with an animal identification hence the phrase 'as strong as a lion' etc., for it is the hunter-animals, the killers, who are most respected by man.

Respect for the hunter-animals has led man into animal worship. There still exists, in Africa, a leopard cult because the leopard is one of the most bloodthirsty beasts of prey. But the leopard's equivalent in Europe is the wolf. In mediaeval Europe, it was the wolf which was the commonest and most dangerous hunter.

Therefore numerous sexually repressed men identified with the wolf as the hunter and believed themselves to be werewolves as their justification to attack young girls in order to fulfil these repressed lusts. There are many historical cases which one is able to cite. Perhaps the most famous was that of Gilles Garnier who was executed as a werewolf in 1574 at Dole in France. In recent times, in New York as late as 1928, Albert Fish, and in Wisconsin about the same time, Ed Gein, attacked young girls, sucked their blood and ate their flesh because they believed themselves to be werewolves or vampires.

These attacks arose out of a suppressed sexual desire but, unable to come to terms with it, the perpetrators of the deeds seemed to convince themselves that they were victims of a terrible destiny – that what they did was out of their control and attributed to some strange mystic disease called vampirism. And the same basic sexual drive lies behind both vampirism and werewolfism.

It is my belief that Upton Welsford, who admits in his manuscript to a rather narrow Anglican upbringing during the worst excesses of the Victorian Age, had an inverted sexual frustration. The sexual drive is obvious in his descriptions of his love-making to Clara and of his near seduction by the vampire Malvina. These were not so much incidents that happened but incidents that he wished would happen. His whole fear of being attacked by vampires was expressive of a desire to be seduced by women, yet, at the same time, a fear of what that seduction might bring. Victorian society had taught him that sex was something sinful, that it must be repressed. This conflict with his sexual frustrations grew more acute and, with increasing overwork, he suffered a serious mental collapse in which his mind created a fascinating fantasy whose symbolism is now obvious. I find it significant that, having married Clara Clarke, and thus enjoying a normal sex-life, Upton Welsford seems to have undergone a complete cure.

DRACULA, MY LOVE

For Elizabeth who gave me the title
and for Dorothea who gave me her advice

'And you . . . are now to me, flesh of my flesh; blood of my blood; kin of my kin; my bountiful wine press for a while; and shall be later on my companion and my helper. You shall be avenged in turn; for not one of them but shall minister to your needs.'
Dracula by Bram Stoker, Constable, London, 1897

INTRODUCTION

Perhaps it was some premonition, or perhaps it was the icy cold of that wild winter evening stirring images in my mind that brought the lines of Byron's poem *The Giaour* unbidden to my lips.

> Thy corpse shall from its tomb be rent;
> Then ghastly haunt thy native place,
> And suck the blood of all thy race;
> There from thy daughter, sister, wife,
> At midnight drain the stream of life;
> Yet loathe the banquet, which perforce
> Must feed thy livid living corpse.

It was London's coldest night for sixteen years. As I walked home across Hampstead Heath snow flurries were blowing across the bleak landscape and driving as particles of ice against my face. I drew my scarf across my mouth and bent into the sharp fingers of the wind. By the time I reached home I was as chilled as a corpse.

Later that evening, with some semblance of life restored, I was roused away from the fire by an insistent buzzing on the door-bell. A short figure in black, looking like a benevolent Rasputin, stood upon my doorstep.

'Mr Tremayne? My name is Mitikelu, Serban Mitikelu. I would be grateful for a few moments of your time to hear a tale that I am confident will be of interest to you.'

For a moment I hesitated. His accent was a mixture of middle-European and American. He wore a long black coat, ankle length, trimmed with astrakhan, and his head was guarded by a black fur Russian-style hat. He was an elderly man, his hair very thin and silver-grey. His beard was full and wiry and fell as a grey cascade to his chest. He had black piercing eyes, deep-set in a white face that had only a slight tinge of red about the cheeks. The face itself was angular, almost bony. His figure was slight. In his right hand he carried a bulky briefcase. His tone of voice, however, was courteous and his manner undangerous, and so I invited him in, divested him of his coat, and led him to the fire. Devoid of his big coat he looked pitifully thin.

Made comfortable in one of my armchairs and given a cup of coffee, he said: 'You are Peter Tremayne who has written the Dracula books?' and when I nodded he went on: 'Good. I was given your address by your American publisher.'

I said nothing, wondering what was coming. Publishers do not usually make free with authors' addresses.

'My name,' he said, 'is Serban Mitikelu. I am a Romanian by birth and upbringing although since 1948 I have lived in America. I am a priest of the Romanian Orthodox Church, ministering to a small flock of émigrés in New York. As I am on a visit to the Orthodox community in London I have taken the opportunity to call on you.'

'I am flattered,' I said, 'but may I ask why?'

'Because of your books. But let me tell you my story and then you will appreciate the reason for my visit. When I was a young man I was a monk in the great monastery of Snagov.'

'Snagov?' My head jerked in surprise. 'Where . . .?'

'Exactly,' said the old man, 'where Dracula was buried in 1476. I was a postulant there in the 1930s, took my vows and was ordained in 1940.' He sighed heavily. 'They were terrible years, the war years. Romania was governed by Fascists, the Iron Guardist movement being led by General Ion Antonescu who established himself as a military dictator, leaving the poor weak-minded King Mihail I as merely a figurehead. Antonescu inevitably brought

Romania into the war on the side of Nazi Germany, and anyone in Romania who opposed Antonescu's Fascists was sent to concentration camps. Murder was the order of the day. It was a terrible period in our history – terrible.'

He paused to sip his coffee. 'I am ashamed to confess that during that time the Church either stood passively by or openly supported Antonescu, with many priests inciting the people against the Jews, the gypsies, the Communists, and any others who were not wholeheartedly Fascist. Great evil was done in my country in the name of the Church.

'Antonescu fell in the summer of 1944 and two more generals came and went before the Fascists were finally toppled. King Mihail was forced to abdicate, and in the last month of 1947 the People's Republic of Romania was proclaimed under the leadership of Dr Petru Groza. Feelings were running high against the Church, with the Communists blaming us for what the hierarchy had done. Monasteries were closed in Wallachia and Moldavia and there were wild tales of trials, imprisonments, and executions. One night I awoke to find our monastery in an uproar. It was said that the partisans were on their way to arrest the brethren and loot our treasures. We were urged by the Abbot, all of us, to seize what we could, particularly our ancient, priceless manuscripts and flee with them to our missions abroad. I and others hastened to the library and gathered what we could and escaped only a few minutes ahead of the partisans.'

Again he sipped his coffee. 'I will not bother with too many of the subsequent details of our flight. Suffice to say that after six months of hardship I eventually arrived in New York and have remained there ever since. It was only after arriving in New York that I was able to examine in detail the manuscripts that I had been able to rescue. All save one were ancient and of great value to our faith, and these I handed over to our Metropolitan, or bishop you would call him. One, however, I kept. It was not ancient, nor was it Romanian. It was a late nineteenth-century handwritten manuscript in English, a language that I could barely understand at the time, and so I kept it until I could learn enough of that tongue to read it properly.'

I poured him some more coffee. 'What was the manuscript about?'

'It was a story about Dracula,' he said, watching my reaction.

My eyes widened. 'In English – written in the nineteenth century?'

'Precisely. Written by a woman and purporting to be her memoirs. When I was able to read and fully under-stand it I considered it a lurid and even blasphemous piece of fiction. I put it away and did not bother with it again – that is until I read some of your books. The details were so similar, so horribly similar.'

He suddenly bent to his briefcase, snapped it open, and brought out a large bulky envelope. 'I have brought that manuscript for you to read,' he said simply. 'I would like you to read it and see whether it should be published in an effort to come to a closer understanding of the horrific legends that surround the name of Dracula.'

Serban Mitikelu stood up. 'I have to go now,' he said abruptly. 'I shall be in touch with you in a week's time, which is when I return to New York. You can give me your opinion then.'

When he had gone I carefully placed the manuscript in a drawer of my desk, fully intending to read it at the first opportunity. But the next few days were extremely busy to such an extent that I had almost forgotten it. My memory, however, was shocked into life by an article in the local newspaper. The body of an elderly man, that had apparently been discovered in Highgate Cemetery, had been positively identified as Serban Mitikelu of New York, a priest of the Romanian Orthodox Church. A medical report confirmed that the man had died of a severe heart attack. The article went on to say that a spokesman for the Coroner's Office had issued a sharp denial that the expression on the dead man's face had indicated that he had died from terror.

I put the newspaper down and rushed to my desk and drew out the manuscript that the old man had left with me. There was no title or date, except that on the first page, ringed in the top right-hand corner, were the words 'Morag MacLeod: Her Memoir.'

I began to read, and I did not stop reading until I had finished it. No wonder Serban Mitikelu had thought it lurid and blasphemous, but the references in it fitted so remarkably with those in the other Dracula manuscripts that have come into my possession, and which I have edited and published, that I am convinced that it is yet another authentic chapter in the bloody and ruthless history of that Undead fiend, Count Dracula. Or was he such a fiend after all?

Peter Tremayne
London, 1980

CHAPTER ONE

The fall of a leaf in autumn is a whispered warning to the living. All things must pass, must pass and be no more. Yet I have lived; have suffered; have cried; have fought; have loved and, oh, I have had so much ambition burning within me. Must it all pass into forgetfulness, into oblivion, as if I had never existed? How I would love to believe that it were not so. And, in spite of the logic of intellect, perhaps in the innermost recesses of my mind I have a yearning, a hope, that I shall not die; for it is surely *other* people who die and as I am not another, I shall not die.

The fall of a leaf in autumn is a whispered warning to the living. And the leaves fall by my window, rustling and whispering in the gentle breeze, whispering a knell, *my* knell.

What answer should I give? An acceptance of my mortality or to pursue man's age-old hope for immortality? Mortality and morality or immortality and immorality. Perhaps there is no difference?

He has allowed me time to consider; to reflect. To think on what he has proposed. No harm nor danger shall come to me during my hours of reflection. It is his promise and he is one whose word can always be trusted.

The decision is mine; mine alone.

I went to see him a while ago, to sit by his side as he lay pale and peaceful in repose. How strong, how handsome he looked as he lay there resting. It is indeed strange to think that he does not lie in a natural sleep. But, then, what is natural; what is normal? It was comforting to sit by his side awhile gazing on his face and drawing from it some of that colossal strength of purpose which has served him so well in his struggle for existence. I am sure he knew that I was there, for his pale face seemed relaxed and tranquil.

But a decision is wanting.

Now I have returned to my room, taken pen and paper, and resolved to set down a brief memoir of my life. By so doing I hope, I pray, that my chaotic thoughts may become ordered; that I may see the logic and reason of my purpose, *his* purpose; that I may clarify my fears and ambitions; that I may clearly hear what the falling leaves of autumn whisper to my heart.

Where shall I begin? On the day which is sketched in vivid colours on my heart? Each hour, each minute of that day, I can recall as if it were only a moment ago. I felt that my life had begun on that chill autumn day.

We strolled hand in hand, Ernst and I; hand in hand through the brown-red autumn woods of Weissenfels. We made plans as we strolled under the falling leaves; gay, carefree plans for the future. We had to part that day, so Ernst told me, but it would only be for two months, perhaps three months at the most, for by then the stupid war would be over and Ernst would return from the army and we would be married. Yes, married, in spite of the punctilious snobbery of Ernst's parents. We strolled through the woods. Then he held me close awhile, kissed me on the lips, leapt to his horse and was gone.

I never saw him again. Yet now it does not seem to matter. Ernst no longer matters, though the day is still burnt on my memory. Perhaps Ernst's death marked my rebirth?

Yet, I suppose, a memoir should begin at the beginning even though it is now hard for me to see back beyond that day at Weissenfels.

I was born in the city of Edinburgh, the capital of Scotland, in the year 1843. My father, a MacLeod of

Loch Moy, wanted a son who would achieve some distinction in the world. But he had to reconcile himself to the birth of a daughter and, as a compromise to his ambition, named me Morag which means 'great' in the old Gaelic tongue of my country. Our family life together was a short one. My father was an officer in the 43rd Highland Regiment and was killed during the disturbances of 1848 when Scottish Radicals attempted to raise an insurrection. It must be told now that my father was a spendthrift who squandered his income as fast as he earned it. At the time of his death he had mortgaged his army pay for five years plus the residue of a small private income from his father's estates.

My mother and I were left destitute and were it not for relatives of my mother, the family of Cluny of Invermallie, we would surely have starved. My mother, a proud woman who was greatly shamed by her enforced poverty, did not long survive my father and I was left an orphan to be raised by the whims of my relatives. Yet, with all due fairness to them, I admit they gave me a sound education and I attended lessons given by the governess who instructed their own children. But my life was not a happy one. My cousins resented me and made fun of my poverty-stricken disposition and my uncle and his wife would often lecture me on the need for displays of gratitude for their charity.

At the age of sixteen I was informed, without prior warning, that the time had come for me to repay my relatives for their generosity in raising me. I was despatched to the city of Perth to an 'Academy for the Ladies of Gentlefolk' which was conducted by a Dr and Mrs Smout. I was to be trained as an assistant teacher at the grand sum of one shilling and sixpence per month. I shall not recount the misery of my life at Dr Smout's academy. I will quickly pass over the four years of torment that I suffered at that establishment and mention only that I initially survived the doctor's rapacious liaisons because his lusts were adequately catered for by three other girls who were employed as assistant teachers. These girls, their shame be it, took a wicked delight in this obscene man's attentions. Finally, late one night, the doctor dared push his way into my attic bedroom and force his attentions on me.

The next morning, in my shame and anger, I packed my few belongings and fled from that evil place. I had just turned twenty and was so marked by the violation of my person that I vowed never to befriend a man again for I deemed all men as lecherous and licentious as Dr Smout.

With scarcely more than the few pence I had managed to save, for most of my wages had been deducted by Dr Smout and sent directly to my uncle and aunt, in repayment for their fosterage of me, I decided to journey south to England. Chance saw me arrive in the city of York and, as luck would have it, I immediately obtained a position with the family of a blunt-mannered colliery owner and his kindly wife. They had four children and were seeking a governess. I was with the family for three years and my duties were such that they left me plenty of time to employ to my profit, striving to perfect my French and German and my general knowledge.

Soon after my twenty-third birthday, my employer called me into his study and asked me whether I wanted to change my situation. A friend of his, the Earl of Fylingdale, was looking for a governess for his five daughters. The new situation would mean an increased remuneration and an opportunity to travel because, so it seemed, Lord Fylingdale often wintered abroad in Switzerland and the south of France. I seized the opportunity with delight, for here was the very chance to improve my fluency and command of French and German. I was soon on my way to Lord Fylingdale's estates just outside Scarborough.

Three idyllic years were spent with Lord Fylingdale's family, each year we spent long periods in St Moritz and in Altdorf. It was in Altdorf, in Switzerland, that we met a family of Prussian aristocrats, the Graf von Stoffel and his *Gräfin*, or countess. They were both red-faced, stiff-necked and distant to the point of unfriendliness but they had two delightful daughters, both under the age of ten years.

Much to my surprise I learnt that the old Graf had asked Lord Fylingdale whether he would be willing to part with my services because he wanted his daughters to have an English governess – the poor Graf never learned the difference between the Scots and English. I must confess that it took me a little time to consider the prospect but my ambition overcame my natural reluctance to move into an unknown and foreign land. But, I reasoned, with a few years' experience as a governess abroad to a titled family and a fluency in German resulting from that experience, there was no telling what situation I could obtain on my return to my homeland.

Thus it was that I, Morag MacLeod, found myself as governess to the house of the Graf von Stoffel at his vast estates at Weissenfels, in Germany, in the early spring of the year 1870.

Since my unhappy experience with Dr Smout I had avoided all friendship with men and, indeed, shunned any familiarity like a plague. Do not think that this was because of a lack of opportunity on my part. Several would-be beaux had tried to seek me out but I rejected all advances. I must, at once, state that I am not a plain creature. I am possessed of a shock of blonde hair which, I confess, I rather detest, a pale skin and eyes that are a deep blue, some would even say they are of a shade of violet. My features are not irregular but are well appointed and my figure pleasantly proportioned. I took a pride in my appearance but rejected the fashionable stupidities to which other females submitted themselves in order to attract the attentions of men.

It was then that I met Ernst von Stoffel.

He was the eldest son of the old Graf and Gräfin, a shy young man of twenty-three who was an *Ordonnanz-Offizier*, an assistant adjutant of a cavalry regiment which was permanently stationed in Weissenfels and so he lived at Schloss Wohlhabend, the von Stoffel castle. He was tall with thick, curly black hair, piercing dark eyes and a face which always seemed moulded in a smile. Physically he was the total opposite of me and I believe, even now, that this was the foundation for my initial attraction to him. Of course, he was also the first man to treat me as an equal, with kindliness and courtesy, and not as a species of some lower order or an object for physical gratification.

How it began, I cannot now remember. I only know that by the time the budding blossoms of spring gave way to the radiance of summer, I was deeply in love with him and the intensity of my emotions was heightened by the fact that I made him the object of the natural feelings I had had to stifle during the loneliness of my childhood and early years. But this I only judged in retrospect. In justification, I must say that I did not precipitate myself blindly into the affair. I tried to tell myself that the relationship should not be. After all, he was a Prussian noble and I was merely a governess. But my heart said that our different stations had nothing to do with the matter. After all, I was a daughter of a MacLeod of Loch Moy and only my impoverished situation had forced me to work for my livelihood. Anyway, was there not an old Gaelic proverb which states: 'We are all Kings' sons!'? I tried to tell myself that I was nearly twenty-seven and Ernst was only twenty-three, but what does a difference of years matter when the minds and hearts are one? I also tried to tell myself that Ernst was but a man and were not all men to be scorned for foul licentious creatures? Yet little by little Ernst overcame my doubts and fears and soon I knew I was deeply and rapturously in love with him.

Throughout the summer he courted and wooed me with a courteous passion and all my self-inflicted prejudices crumbled. Finally we were making passionate love in the summer woods, in my room, or anywhere away from the prying gaze of the Graf and Gräfin. Our relationship grew in secret for I did not doubt what the old Graf and his countess would do if they discovered the liaison between Ernst and myself. The von Stoffels were social snobs of the worst order, disdainful and superior to all except those whom they considered their equal in rank. In my position as governess I was treated as only one grade above a domestic servant. Had we been discovered I would have been summarily dismissed and sent in disgrace to Britain. But that thought, which passed briefly through my mind, did not really concern me much during the balmy weeks of that short, oh so incredibly short, summer.

I did not know it then but the inevitable storm clouds were gathering on the horizon. A war between France and Prussia had broken out on 15 July. I forget now what the cause was. I think there was some dispute about who should succeed to the throne of Spain and both sides were willing to back their opinions by force. Napoleon III of France declared war on Wilhelm I of Prussia. It was one of those silly squabbles between two power-crazed men in which the ordinary people had no interest but, inevitably, it was the ordinary people who had to lay down their lives in settlement of the disagreement.

Towards the end of July I recall that Ernst became excited because General Helmuth von Moltke, the Prussian commander-in-chief, had launched three German armies across the frontier into France. Then there followed daily news of French defeat after French defeat, much to the delight of the von Stoffels who were patriotic supporters of von Bismarck, the Prussian chancellor. By 14 August the French had suffered defeat in four disastrous battles and a few days later we learnt that two more battles had been fought which might have stopped the rapid advance of the Prussian armies but, because of the incompetence of the French general, Marshal Achille Bazaine, the French forces were now besieged in Metz and Sedan. Everyone thought the war was over.

Towards the end of September Ernst received orders to join his regiment. A final offensive was being launched to crush the French opposition.

The news came as a great shock to me for I had news of my own.

There, walking through the autumn woods with Ernst, just before he left to join his regiment, I had to confess that I was to bear his child. Ernst saw my white, trembling face, and smilingly chided me for the fears which showed plainly in my eyes.

'Come, Morag,' he said gently, his arm around my waist. 'Why do you confess it as if it were some guilty secret? It is great news. Joyous news! This war is almost over and I shall be back within a month or two, certainly before Christmas. Then we shall tell my parents and I shall tell them I love you, that I shall marry you – yes, marry you in spite of their prejudices. We shall go away from Weissenfels, perhaps to Switzerland. That is a good place to raise our son, eh?'

I looked up into his smiling face and all my fears vanished, and I nodded, dumbly happy.

'Come, *liebling*, do not worry any more. I shall soon return.'

Then he was gone; gone forever.

I had four letters from him, all reassurances and protestations of his love. He also told me how his regiment had joined von der Tann's army and how that army had managed to win a further victory over the French by capturing the town of Orléans on 11 October. The last letter was written on 20 October and Ernst's boyish enthusiasm came through its every line. He said he was expecting leave any day because, so tremendous had been the impact of the German victory over the French, they were expecting an armistice or surrender to be signed daily.

Then I heard no more until 12 November.

I was in the schoolroom of the castle that morning teaching geography to little Hilde and Anna when the sound of a horse's hooves galloping into the stone-flagged courtyard made me peer out of the window. It was a young hussar officer whose face was set into a serious mask and who clutched a white envelope in his gloved hand. He disappeared from my view and, within seconds, there came an imperious knocking on the doors of the castle.

Curious, I left the children to their books and went out on to the landing which overlooked the main hall where the old butler was opening the door.

'News of utmost urgency for the Graf von Stoffel!' snapped the young hussar officer, brushing aside the old servant and striding into the hall.

The Graf came out from the library.

The young officer removed his hat, clicked his heels and bowed. 'Leutnant von Harben, mein Graf,' he announced. He paused to clear his throat. 'Sir, it is my unfortunate duty to bring you news of your son, the Freiherr Ernst von Stoffel.'

Cold hands began to clutch at my heart.

'Well?' the old count stood cold and impassive.

'Sir,' began the young officer punctiliously. 'I have to report that on 9 November a French army commanded by General Louis d'Aurelle de Paladins launched a fierce attack on the army of General von der Tann at Coulmiers. The army was decimated. The Freiherr von Stoffel was among the casualties. He died bravely and with honour.'

Suddenly I heard a scream from what seemed a long way away. Somewhere, in some recess of my mind, I registered surprise because the scream came from my own mouth and, abruptly, my world collapsed into a kaleidoscope of vivid, flashing colours and then darkness. Complete. Utter.

CHAPTER TWO

I recovered from my swoon to find Frau Schmidt, the housekeeper, bending over me in concern. I was so numb with grief that I could not speak. A great pulsing black depression seemed to hem me in. I was led stumbling to my room. The only thought that registered in my mind was that Ernst was dead! Ernst was *dead!*

I can recall little of the next few hours but I was told afterwards that I had given way to a sobbing fit of hysteria, crying over and over again for Ernst.

I dimly recall a man making me swallow a glass of some bitter concoction. Afterwards I learnt that Frau Schmidt had summoned a doctor who dosed me with laudanum, and that I had remained in a drugged state for forty-eight hours.

I think I must have screamed a lot in my hysteria, and mumbled a lot about Ernst and me. Not long after I had awoken the Gräfin von Stoffel herself came to see me. She was a tall woman, erect of carriage, cold and imperious. She came to my bedside and looked down at me disdainfully with chill grey eyes. 'You are better, Fräulein MacLeod?' she asked in a voice that held neither warmth nor concern.

I edged myself to a half-sitting position in the bed. Countess von Stoffel's eyes were red rimmed but, apart from that, there was no mark on her cold features to show that her only son had just been killed. I shuddered slightly at her lack of feeling.

'Yes, much better now, Countess,' I replied. Better! My whole life had disintegrated into a million fragments and yet I had to speak of feeling better! The whole world was one vast black abyss.

'Well, *Fräulein*,' said the old Countess in her slightly querulous voice. 'I have an unpleasant task. I must ask you some questions about my son, the Herr Freiherr von Stoffel. In your delirium you said some pernicious and scandalous things. You spoke of – of love,' she said it as if it were a dirty word. 'You spoke of the Herr Freiherr and yourself as lovers.' She sniffed and narrowed her eyes. 'What makes matters worse, so that it becomes a slight against the house of von Stoffel, is that these things were alleged in front of the servants. The very fact that you could make such allegations, even in a delirium, indicates that you are not a fit person to continue as governess in this household.'

I stared open-mouthed at the Countess and the hypocrisy of the thing hit me with a sudden fury. In retrospect, her attitude acted as the best therapy for me in my morose condition. 'Madam,' I said, with slow deliberation, 'I have little recollection of what I said in my delirium, but let me tell you this – I loved your son, Ernst, and, what is more to the point, he loved me.'

The old Countess winced and stepped backwards.

'Yes, madam,' I continued brutally, 'I am prostrate with grief at the news of Ernst's death. I grieve for him because I loved him. We were going to marry when he returned from the war.'

The old woman suddenly barked with laughter as if she found this amusing. 'Marriage? You? Why, you are nothing more than a servant!'

A fury spread through me and I wanted to hurt the old woman as much as I could. 'Perhaps, madam,' I replied, 'you will not laugh so heartily when I present you with the proof of Ernst's affections, when I bear his child.'

If she could have turned a shade more pale, the old Countess would have done so. She moved to a chair and suddenly collapsed in it, gazing at me with baleful eyes. 'You lie!' she whispered viciously.

I shook my head and smiled, assured of my triumph.
'It is no lie, I assure you.'

'Ernst could not love you. He was a von Stoffel and
knew his place in the world,' the old woman said slowly.

I confess, I laughed in her face.

The Gräfin tried to reform her features into her usual
mask of cold expressionless composure but she remained
a shocked and hurt old woman.

'Ernst may have had an affair with you,' she said angrily,
'that I am prepared to accept. He was a growing boy and not
above temptation. But to suggest he could love a servant . . .'

At this I scrambled out of bed, weak from the laudanum, and withdrew the bundle of Ernst's letters from my
writing box and flung them at her.

With a growing smile of satisfaction I watched her
reading them.

The emptiness and pain of Ernst's death had curiously
subsided. The ambition to hurt these arrogant and self-
righteous people, with their ridiculous prejudices and
haughty disdain for others, drove all else from my mind.

After a long pause the Countess peered up at me with
tired eyes bleared by a suspicion of tears. 'But he was
only a young boy,' she whispered defensively.

'He was twenty-three. A grown man. Old enough to
die for his country.'

'I must speak to the Graf,' she said helplessly, attempting to rise.

'I will keep these letters, Countess,' I said, taking them
from her hand.

She looked at me as if she no longer saw me. 'The Graf
will know what to do,' she whispered.

After she had gone I collapsed on my bed in nervous
exhaustion. Frau Schmidt came in and presented me with
a bowl of hot gruel.

'Poor dear,' she murmured. 'You have made yourself
some powerful enemies in the Graf and Gräfin.'

'I do not want enemies, Frau Schmidt,' I sighed. 'I just wanted Ernst and peace to live my life as I see fit.'

The housekeeper stroked my hair soothingly. 'Remember that soon you will have a little one to take care of, and you will need all the friends you can find. Do not trust the Graf, he can be an evil and cruel man.'

The next morning the doctor came again and, although he said nothing to me, I knew from his careful examination that he was testing to confirm whether I was pregnant. The following day, having recovered my equilibrium, I was allowed up and, in the afternoon, Graf von Stoffel sent for me.

He sat in his study, white haired and looking almost like a masculine replica of his wife. He did not stand as I entered but merely waved me to come forward to his desk. He watched me from under hooded eyelids, his hands lay palm downward on the desk before him. On the desk I noticed several papers, including a red leather-bound volume which I recognized as Ernst's diary. It must have been part of the effects returned from Ernst's regiment.

The Graf's face was expressionless as I walked to the desk. He did not invite me to be seated but sat looking me up and down. 'Well, *Fräulein*,' he said after a long silence. 'It appears that this house has nursed a viper in its bosom.'

The blood sprang immediately to my cheeks. 'I am not your slave that you can speak to me like that. If you cannot raise yourself above such childish abuse, there is no point in continuing this conversation.' His eyes flew open and his jaw dropped in amazement. 'I presume, Graf von Stoffel, you wish to speak to me about the fact that I carry your grandchild?'

He opened and closed his mouth several times. 'My wife and I are both exceedingly shocked by your immoral behaviour,' he began.

'By *my* immoral behaviour?' I arched an eyebrow at him. 'And, I presume, similarly shocked by Ernst's immoral behaviour? You disapprove of two people falling in love, Graf? Or is it that you disapprove of Ernst daring to fall in love with me – a mere servant, as your wife expressed it?'

The Graf clasped his hands together. 'My son is dead, *Fräulein*, and beyond my condemnation. Were it not for the intercession of my wife, I would have had you thrown out of this house and horsewhipped for your impudence. You have betrayed the trust of your employers. Naturally, I cannot allow someone like you to continue in any position in this household let alone a position of trust as governess where you might contaminate the minds of my children. But my wife has interceded on your behalf . . .'

I sneered openly at his hypocrisy. 'Interceded? You mean she has told you that I have letters proving how Ernst felt about me? Proof that Ernst accepted the child as his and was going to marry me on his return from the war? Perhaps,' I nodded towards the diary, 'you have also found proof in Ernst's own words.'

The Graf bit his lip and stared at me but I remained oblivious to the dislike in his eyes. 'What do you mean to do, *Fräulein*?' he asked coldly. 'Are you hellbent on a scandal?'

In that moment I saw that he was frightened of me; that he was scared that I would use Ernst's letters to create some scandal or even blackmail him. Suddenly I felt exhausted by the whole affair. 'Whether you believe me or not, Graf, I loved Ernst. All I want now is to have his child quietly and then be able to earn enough to bring it up and give it a good chance in life.'

The Graf drummed his fingers on his desk top. 'Very well, *Fräulein*,' he said eventually, as if making a weighty decision. 'I will not go into the moral questions nor into the hurt and disgust that my wife and I feel. I accept that my son was led astray in a moment of weakness which has, unfortunately, resulted in your carrying his child.

'Let me make this very clear to you, however – there is no way in which the House of von Stoffel will recognize your child as a member of this family – or you, *Fräulein*. There never could have been any marriage if my son had survived the war. It would not have been allowed. Neither will you be allowed to besmirch our family name. Should you ever intimate outside this house that Ernst von Stoffel is the father of your child, the family will fiercely dispute your claim. Is this clear?'

I did not reply but waited for him to continue as I knew he would.

'Nevertheless, I have read my son's diary, and my wife has told me of your letters. It appears my son admitted some affection for you and a responsibility for the child. That being so, I am duty bound to accept a moral responsibility. Therefore, I have a proposal.'

Again he paused and again I waited for him to continue.

'I have a brother, the Herr Baron Heinrich von Stoffel, who has an estate in Siebenbürgen which is a province of the Austro-Hungarian empire in the Balkans. I propose that you go there and stay on his estate while you undergo your confinement. After the child is born, we can come to some arrangement with regard to a small allowance which will ensure the child has a start in life. This much I owe to Ernst.'

My mind whirled. If I had my way I would not have accepted one *pfennig* from the von Stoffels. But I was alone in the world. Moreover, I was pregnant and it would be impossible to secure another position now. What other choice had I but to accept Graf von Stoffel's offer.

'Very well – as you wish.'

'Good,' he said, with evident satisfaction. 'You will leave in the diligence for Siebenbürgen the day after tomorrow.'

How I was to bitterly regret not paying closer attention to old Frau Schmidt when she warned me to beware of Graf von Stoffel. His cruelty knew no bounds. But that fact I was not to discover until later.

CHAPTER THREE

Two days later I bade farewell to my lovely Weissenfels where Ernst and I had been so happy during that long summer of 1870. Now the thin ice-cold fingers of a winter's wind unkindly ruffled the bleak landscape. Ernst was dead and the sky was grey and sombre as if in mourning and snow storms threatened along the distant horizon. Only kindly Frau Schmidt wished me a friendly 'God's speed!' as I climbed aboard the diligence which was to take me to Munich. I hardly had time to wave my farewell to the old housekeeper before the great swaying coach, which seemed to have no springs at all, was bumping and bounding away from Weissenfels along the southern road.

It would be tedious for me to recount my journey to Munich, a truly beautiful twelfth-century city which abounded in graceful squares, handsome buildings, and spacious gardens. In other times and circumstances I would have insisted on staying at least a week to explore the city. But I was more concerned with reaching my destination and placing as much distance between Weissenfels and myself as possible.

I took a train at Munich and was subjected to a long and tiring journey for, while the scenery was wild and exciting, my mind was preoccupied with thoughts of my future. After all, I was going to stay with Graf von Stoffel's brother. What if he were as arrogant and unfriendly as the Graf? I tried hard not to form any opinions or even think about it, but time and again depressing thoughts kept springing into my mind. Thus it was that I hardly noticed when we crossed the Austro-Hungarian frontier at Salzburg and pressed on to Graz. At Graz I took a train to Budapest, and then another from Budapest to Klausenburg, which is the provincial capital of Siebenbürgen.

Imagine my surprise when I alighted at Klausenburg and, on making enquiries for a good hotel, was directed to one imposingly called the 'Queen of England' or, rather *Königin von England*. I passed a pleasant night there and the next morning asked at the reception desk how best I might make my way to Schloss Stoffel at Schassburg, which I understood lay some miles to the south of Klausenburg.

Before the receptionist could instruct me, a somewhat hollow voice spoke from behind me. 'Are you the *Fräulein* from Weissenfels?'

I turned in surprise to see an old man dressed in faded livery regarding me with bright, twinkling blue eyes. His face was a leathery brown and he had an open and ready smile.

'I am,' I assented. 'Who are you?'

'Bucar, *Fräulein*. The Herr Baron von Stoffel has sent me to collect you and bring you safely to the Schloss.'

'Why, that is excellent,' I said. 'But how did the Baron know when I would be arriving?'

The old man shrugged. 'There is only one train from Graz during the week. The Herr Baron was told to expect you this week.'

'Very well. I'll arrange to get my baggage and we will leave within the hour.'

'As the *Fräulein* wills.'

Now I noticed that although our conversation had been carried on in German, the language was not Bucar's native tongue any more than it was mine. Later, when he had recovered from his surprise at my insistence on sitting beside him on the driving seat of the monogrammed coach and four, I asked him if he was a Hungarian. Knowing little of the history of this area, I seemed to recall that

Hungary had once been a subject territory of Austria and that it was only recently that it had become a state equal with Austria under the same monarchy.

The old man shook his head fiercely and spat. 'Neither Austrian nor Hungarian, *Fräulein*,' he said in a scornful voice.

'Oh,' I said, interested. 'Where do you come from, then?'

He waved his whip to the surrounding countryside. 'Here.'

I was puzzled. 'But isn't this a province of the Austro-Hungarian state?'

'By right of conquest only. This land, which the German speakers call Siebenbürgen, is called "the land beyond the forest" – Transylvania. To the people it is Transylvania still.'

'Then what language is spoken here?'

'Romanian.'

I was about to pursue my questions when he abruptly stopped the coach and turned an earnest face to mine.

'Fräulein, I intend no discourtesy to you but I have a feeling for people. You are a kind person, a nice person. When I picked you up from Klausenburg I thought you were either a creature of von Stoffel's or some new servant. But you are a nice young lady. Why do you go to Schloss Stoffel?'

I frowned.

'I may be flattered at your compliments, Bucar, but I cannot see that it is any of your business.'

'Believe me, I mean no discourtesy. I do not think you realize what sort of place you go to! The Baron is an evil man – the castle is no suitable place for one such as yourself.'

I laughed nervously. 'Come now, Bucar, I know and have worked for the Graf von Stoffel and, if his brother, the Baron, is like him, I know what to expect. They are arrogant and stupid people but I think you exaggerate their qualities.'

'Let me drive you back to Klausenburg, *Fräulein*. Please do not go on.'

'And what am I to do when I return to Klausenburg? I am many miles from my own country and have little money. And – as I am sure you can observe for yourself – I am carrying a child.'

The coachman shook his head obstinately. 'For the sake of the unborn child you should return to Klausenburg.'

'It is precisely for the sake of my unborn child that I must go on. The child's father was a von Stoffel.'

Bucar drew back with an incredulous look on his features. 'A von Stoffel?' he almost whispered.

'I was to marry Ernst von Stoffel,' I said, wondering why I was confiding in this coachman. 'He was killed in a war and now I only have his child.'

Bucar bit his lip. 'God look down upon you, *Fräulein*. But I beg you not to go on.

'Nonsense!' I said, drawing myself up and wearying of the argument. 'There is nothing else I can do. Drive on.'

The old man flicked the reins and the coach rumbled forward.

For some time I was silent, filled with some strange sense of foreboding at Bucar's strange behaviour.

After some hours of travelling we came within sight of a large town, built around a hill on which some fortifications stood dominating the landscape.

'We are not far from the Herr Baron's Schloss,' Bucar informed me with a wry expression.

'Is this Schassburg?' I asked wonderingly, for I had expected a small hamlet and not this busy-looking township.

Bucar spat disgustedly. 'That's what the German speakers call it.'

'What is its proper name?' I asked, deciding to humour him, for it would do well to have a friend in this strange land.

'It is called Sighisoara, *Fräulein*.'

I confess the German name sounded easier on my ears.

Bucar drove the carriage into the township and a cry arose in my throat at the beauty of the place. It was surely one of the most perfectly preserved medieval towns that I have seen. It was surrounded by thick stone walls, towers, bastions, churches, cobbled streets and exquisitely painted houses. In the centre of the town, a hill stretched up to a church which had a fortress-like appearance and, on closer inspection, seemed to form part of a citadel.

I asked Bucar to halt and let me inspect the place, giving a cry of delight at espying a clock tower. I asked the old coachman if he knew something of its history.

'A Saxon invention,' he observed sourly. 'This is a Saxon town now. The Saxons came here in the twelfth century, *Fräulein*, and have made the town their own. A local Saxon craftsman named Kirschel erected that clock tower about 1648. At midnight, a figure, maybe three feet tall, emerges to represent the day of the week by a sign.'

'What sort of sign?' I asked, intrigued.

'The moon for Monday; Mars for Tuesday, and so on. But that is no longer the original clock for many fires have devastated the citadel and a new clock had to be installed by someone called Devai in 1812.'

'You know a lot of the local history, Bucar!' I observed.

'Subject people have an affection for their history,' he returned.

The township was crowded and I would see many gypsies selling copper pots and kettles. They were colourful people but very shy and when I was drawn to inspect their wares both men and women covered their faces. I afterwards learnt from Bucar that they did this from fear of being laid under a charm by the non-gypsies.* Bucar spoke sourly of gypsies and for all his lamentation of the plight of his own people it soon became apparent that most Transylvanians think little of oppressing the large gypsy population of the country. I learnt that until recent times the gypsies were regarded as slaves, beasts of burden, and bought and sold like any other marketable animal. If a man killed a gypsy, he was not punished by law unless the gypsy happened to belong to another man. Then the crime was not 'murder' but merely injury to another man's property.

The carriage took us swiftly out of the town and, as we left the outskirts we passed by a strange solitary tower which was perched on the overhanging cliff of the river that ran by the town.

'What is that?' I asked Bucar.

'Catherine's Tower,' he answered. 'They say that it is where a Turkish pasha, riding a white elephant, was buried many years ago. They say that if you climb to the top of the tower and look down a small hole in the roof, you may still see the pasha on his elephant.'

A few miles later we entered a great wood of spruce and fir trees which was so thick that the day seemed to turn into night. It took us half an hour to traverse this wood and then we entered a bright, sunlit plain of cultivated fields and areas where flocks of sheep grazed. In the distance stood a tall grey building which promptly reminded me of many of our own Scottish castles. It was a building with towered minarets, pointed roofs and battlements – like some story-book castle.

'That is the Schloss von Stoffel,' said Bucar pointing with his whip.

* The fear still exists today and when members of the British Dracula Society visited Sighisoara and tried to take photographs of gypsies they were bombarded with clods and other missiles. Tremayne.

We drove up at a rapid pace and I suddenly became aware of a number of people by the roadside and in the fields, obviously field workers on the Baron's estate, doffing their caps and bowing low as the carriage clattered by. It was either a sign of deep respect and courtly manners or something else – perhaps fear.

Bucar guided the carriage through the open gateway of the castle and into a small courtyard, which was filled with fifty or more people who did not even look up as the carriage clattered in and halted. Their silent eyes were on another sight.

Before them, face against the stone wall of the castle, and hanging his full length by his wrists from an iron ring six feet from the ground was a man stripped to the waist, his bare back criss-crossed with ugly red welts and wounds.

I raised my hand to my mouth in horror and even as I did so a short, stocky man brought his whip down on the shoulders of the hanging wretch with such violence that a scream of anguish echoed around the courtyard, and the tormentor laughed in obvious enjoyment of his task.

Bucar caught me by the arm. 'Come inside, *Fräulein*. This is not a sight for a young lady.'

Feeling sick, I allowed the coachman to lead me into the castle.

CHAPTER FOUR

A sour-faced woman, who answered all my questions in grunts and monosyllables, led me to a shabby room. Looking at it in dismay I doubted whether a servant at Weissenfels would even stay in it. There was a peculiar coldness in the castle and yet, as far as I recall, there was absolutely no reason why the chill should strike me. Fires burned in every room and the place was clearly lived in. And yet there was a coldness, a feeling of neglect.

I bathed in tepid water, brought to my room after much insistence on my part, changed my clothes and ate of the sparing meal that was brought to me. I was wondering what my next priority should be when the sour-faced woman returned. She was thin lipped and her colourless hair was screwed back in a bun. She wore a long dress and a belt on which a large bunch of keys jangled as she walked. I conjured up a picture of a jailer but in fact she was the housekeeper. I forget her name; perhaps I never heard it for the von Stoffels never addressed their servants by name.

'The Baroness would like to see you in her drawing room immediately,' the housekeeper said curtly to me.

'Very well,' I tried to smile and make the best of the shroud of unfriendliness which cloaked the castle and its occupants.

I followed the housekeeper down a flight of stairs and along several corridors before she stood aside to usher me into a large room. I stood on the threshold, staring at the luxurious tapestries which bedecked the walls with vivid colours.

'Well, girl?' snapped a brittle voice. 'Don't just stand there. Come here!'

Baroness von Stoffel, or so I judged the woman to be, was a plump rather grotesque creature. Her hair was mousey and set ill against her pale eyes buried deep in her broad fleshy face. Ugly was but a poor description for her. She stood, hands on hips, at my approach as if I were some wilful child found guilty of a misdemeanour.

'So? You are the English girl, MacLeod?'

'Scottish,' I corrected automatically.

'What?'

'I am Scottish not English,' I repeated with some spirit, determined not to let this overbearing fat woman browbeat me.

The Baroness frowned. 'No matter. You have been sent here by my brother-in-law, the Graf von Stoffel?'

'Graf von Stoffel suggested I should come here during my confinement,' I corrected. It was only then that the thought struck me – how could they have been expecting me? There had been no time to send a letter announcing my coming before I left Weissenfels.

The Baroness appeared to read my thoughts and pouted in a smile of superiority. 'The Graf and the Baron communicate with each other every week by means of carrier pigeon. We knew of your coming even before you left Weissenfels.' She drew herself up. 'And now, my girl, in this house you will learn to be respectful and address me correctly. As a servant your manners leave much to be desired. You will soon learn where your proper place is with us.'

I stared hard at her, not believing my ears. 'I am no servant of yours,' I bridled immediately. 'I regret that you should have been informed otherwise. I thought that suitable arrangements had been made for my confinement here. I see otherwise and shall leave immediately.'

The Baroness flushed scarlet, opened her mouth but remained in speechless outrage as I swung on my heel and walked away from her. In retrospect I did not know where I was going for I had little money on me and where could I have gone in that strange country? I thought of Bucar's warnings. He had been right; I should not have come to this chill place.

'Come back!' the Baroness screamed. 'Come back here, at once!'

I ignored her but before I reached the door it was flung open and a short, stocky man entered. I recognized him immediately as the evil-faced creature who had been wielding the whip so unmercifully on the back of the poor wretch in the courtyard. It was obvious now from the slight resemblance to the Graf that this was the Baron von Stoffel.

He was thick-boned in spite of his shortness and, on closer inspection, what I thought was stockiness was, in fact, mere fat. He had a heavy red face and tiny black eyes. His thick lips hung permanently open showing yellowing teeth. His black hair was greying and thin. And though he was dressed in clothes that were obviously expensive, they looked tasteless and ill-fitting on his figure. It was his hands that made me shudder; stubby hands, with long, dirty finger nails.

'What is this?' he said, in a voice which held a particular whining quality. I could smell the stale tobacco and wine on his breath even from a distance of some feet.

I took a hesitant step backwards before him.

'She insulted me!' shrilled the Baroness. 'This slut insulted me!'

I faced the Baron hotly. 'The only insults uttered have come from your wife,' I said determinedly. 'I am Morag MacLeod from Weissenfels. The Baroness appears to have mistaken me for some servant whom she is evidently expecting.'

The Baron raised an eyebrow, grinned, and to my horror began to nibble absently at his dirty finger nails. 'Mistaken?' he said with a supercilious smile on his face. 'Surely not?'

A chill feeling began to grow in my heart. 'I was governess to Graf von Stoffel's children,' I pressed on desperately. 'Ernst von Stoffel and I were going to be married when the war with France ended. Surely the Graf told you this? When Ernst was killed I was bearing his child. Graf von Stoffel suggested that I came here for the remainder of my confinement. He said that you, his brother, would see to my comfort during this period and until the child was strong and then the Graf was to furnish me with money to go to London.'

The Baroness let out a shrill peal of laughter. 'A pretty tale, a pretty tale, is that not so, Heinrich?'

The Baron nodded with a sneer. 'Now listen, my girl,' he said. 'As far as we are concerned you were a servant at my brother's castle in Weissenfels. Like many a slut of a servant you allowed someone to have his way with you, doubtless you led them on, and now you bear the consequences of your wickedness.'

My face drained of blood. A wild desire to scream grew within me. I could not believe what I was hearing.

'My brother, out of the goodness of his heart, instead of throwing you into the street, as you richly deserve, has sent you to me. You will work in my kitchens as a scullery maid until the time comes when you bear your bastard. Then we will allow some of the peasants on our estate to nurse it until such time as it can work for a living. As for you, if you serve us well, you can remain as a kitchen servant.'

I looked at him in speechless horror. My mouth opened and closed but no words would come forth to express the emotions that beat within my heart. If I had only listened to Bucar's warning. But surely, surely the Graf would not go so far?

'This is ridiculous!' I stammered. 'I have never been spoken to so rudely in my life! I shall leave here at once.'

The Baron laughed. 'Oh, no. Here you are and here you stay.'

The sour-faced housekeeper appeared at the door. 'Take her to the kitchens and show her what duties she must perform,' snapped the Baroness. 'And while you do that make sure she is given clothing more suitable for her station.'

The housekeeper went to take me by the arm but a blind rage seized me. I tore myself away. 'This is criminal!' I cried. 'Monstrous! You're insane! You have no right to hold me a prisoner. I shall not work for you nor be your servant. I am a citizen of Britain. I demand that you let me leave here immediately or I shall inform the police.'

The Baron giggled. 'My dear girl,' he sneered, 'you are not in Britain now. You are in Transylvania. My word is law for fifty miles in either direction. Now, go with the housekeeper.'

I turned, my mind still whirling at the sudden nightmare world into which I had been precipitated. I suddenly started to run, to run towards where I considered the main doors to be but it was a vain, futile effort. The Baron snapped a command and, as if by magic, two sturdy peasants, their moustachioed faces leering evilly, appeared and pinioned my arms to my sides. One of them grunted a question to the Baron in a language I knew not and the Baron replied in the same tongue.

Without more ado they hauled me down a corridor, forced me up several flights of stairs and flung me into a barely furnished, cell-like room. All the while I screamed and raved at them in my impotent fury. I tried to kick and bite at my captors until, alone at last, I finally gave way to hysteria and did not know how long I passed in that condition.

Perhaps it was the next morning that there came a grating of bolts and the door was thrown open to display the sour countenance of the housekeeper. She held a dress in one hand; a coarse thing which was made from sacking.

She threw this at me and then pointed to my own dress. 'You will change and be ready to come to work in ten minutes.'

'Never!' I cried at the closing door.

What madness was this? I still could not believe that the von Stoffels could imagine themselves to be above the law, to be able to act with impunity. I cursed them. I cursed all men for my plight. Such a rage burned within me that I felt I had the strength to tear down that castle stone by stone. I beat and cried against the stout wooden door until I fell back exhausted.

After a while, the door swung open again and the housekeeper looked in on me. 'You have not changed,' she said slowly.

A renewed wave of fury swept through me. Stupidly, I threw the sackcloth dress at the woman and then launched myself to the attack, hands clawing.

She stepped back quickly and banged the door shut in my face leaving me to fall to my knees sobbing in anger and frustration.

It was not long before I heard another step in the corridor outside and, with a grating of bolts, the door opened again. I moved backward as the figure of the Baron entered and thrust the door shut behind him. In his hand he carried a short riding crop and his face glistened with his vile sweat. I tried to pull myself together; to show him that he did not intimidate me. 'I warn you, Baron von Stoffel,' I cried hotly, 'I shall inform the authorities, including the British ambassador. You shall not keep me here against my will.'

He leant back against the door and I could feel his piggy eyes examining me. 'You seem to have become confused, my dear,' he said slowly. 'I am the only authority here and as for a British ambassador – well, there is one in Vienna, there may even be one in Budapest, but that is far away. And what could he do? Here I am lord. Here my word is law.'

'You have no right,' I began lamely.

The Baron chuckled. 'Come, come. You are only making things worse for yourself. Why not gratefully accept the charity we offer you and your bastard? You are young, pretty too. Things need not be so bad as you fear. I could quite like you, if you made yourself attractive to me.'

For a moment I did not understand the drift of his remark. Then the horror, disgust and anger must have showed themselves in my face. He moved forward and gripped the riding crop. 'Listen, slut!' he snarled. 'You will obey me, *you will*!' He raised the crop and brought it down against the upper part of my arm. It stung terribly and I screamed. The scream seemed to please him for he smiled. A sickness spread through me as I realized that I was facing a sadist.

'By the time I have finished with you,' he drawled, 'you will be begging me for the charity of a room in my stables, let alone my kitchen.'

His crop fell again and, although I tried to prevent myself from adding to his pleasure, I screamed once more. I crouched on the floor before him while he aimed blow after blow on my unprotected back. Oh God, how I prayed for the torment to stop; how I wished I could conjure up Ernst, someone, anyone, to save me from this awful nightmare.

Then I felt a violent pain; a pain from the pit of my womb. It was needle hot and numbing. I screamed, screamed more loudly than ever as it darted through my entire body. I clutched at my stomach and rolled about screaming, screaming until I was sick.

The baby, oh God, the baby!

A wave of blackness swept me into a merciful unconsciousness.

CHAPTER FIVE

My baby! My baby!

The next week passed in a hell of torment and anguish. My labour, induced prematurely by the sadistic assault of the Baron, was painful beyond my wildest fantasies. And my poor baby, Ernst's baby, came into this evil world and died without a sound, without even drawing one breath.

I was confined to my bed for a fortnight and nursed (if such a word could be used) by the sour-faced housekeeper until I recovered from the pain and delirium of that agonizing stillbirth. I was given enough food to exist, warm watery soups, stale bread, mouldering cheese and weak ale. On such a diet, I survived. And there, locked in my cell-like room, I nurtured my hatred for the male species which had caused me to fall to such an extremity in life.

At the end of three weeks I was well enough in body to get up and pace my room. They had taken my clothes and my portmanteau and left me with only a sackcloth dress. Then, one morning, the housekeeper announced that I was to start work in the kitchens that day and commence to earn my keep for, she added, I had been a burden on the Baron's charity for long enough. At once my eyes flashed in anger and I refused. The woman twisted her thin lips into a smile and said that she would go and fetch the Baron to persuade me. Knowing full well what she meant, for I could still feel the sting of his riding crop on my back, I hesitated. No, I decided, I would have to be more cunning. I would have to await my opportunity to escape. In the meantime I would sullenly acquiesce.

Weeks passed as I laboured in the kitchens of the

Schloss Stoffel. The other poor wretches who laboured there were natives of the area and I could not communicate with them. There was little or no time to learn their language even if they had the desire or ability to teach me. They were too wrapped up in their own misery to have sympathy with mine. The housekeeper, who spoke some German, would sometimes come and supervise the work but would not exchange any conversation with me. My loneliness was complete. It was as I had often imagined a prison to be.

One day I suddenly saw Bucar come into the kitchen on some errand and he looked with sorrow on my emaciated form.

'Did I not try to warn you?' he whispered as he passed by me. 'Did I not tell you that the Baron was evil? God's peace upon your dead one.'

I caught him by the arm. 'I must escape,' I cried.

He threw an apprehensive glance about him.

'There is no escape from Schassburg. The Baron is the feudal lord in these parts. It would have been better had you never come.' Then he threw off my restraining hand and was gone leaving me to my despair.

Words cannot convey the utter despair and loneliness that I felt. I even contemplated secreting a kitchen knife to my room and ending this foul experience which was my life. But my ego, my sense of survival, was too developed for such a vain gesture.

There had to be some other way; another way by which I might escape from the castle and live to revenge myself upon the family. For many weeks I brooded on the subject.

My working day started at four-thirty each morning when I, with a raw-boned peasant woman, had to scrub the vast floors of the kitchens. This took an hour. Then we had to wash the kitchen utensils ready for the breakfast. After which there were a hundred-and-one other chores. After breakfast was served to the von Stoffel family and any guests who were staying, the scraps were given to the servants to eat. Then came the cleaning again, then luncheon, cleaning and dinner, until the day ended about ten o'clock when we went exhausted to bed.

Day passed into day, and at weekends and even on the sabbath there was no respite from the endless routine. The weeks passed into months until the faint gold of early autumn swept across the countryside. But the weather in that land was fairly changeable and irregular and on several days during early September great carpets of snow lay across the land as if it were mid-winter.

There was no time, nor opportunity, to explore the castle or its grounds to seek a way of escape. One night however, during the first week of September, an event happened which made me realize that I could not endure another moment in the castle.

I had gone to my room exhausted as usual about ten-thirty and had fallen into a deep sleep. The next thing I knew was that someone was fumbling at my door. I came awake swiftly and sat up in bed in time to see the door swing open and then, framed in the faint light, the bulky figure of the Baron.

'What do you want?' I cried.

He moved into the room, closing and locking the door behind him. My blood ran cold. From the manner he swayed towards the bed I knew that he had been drinking. He gave a deep, throaty chuckle. 'And what would I be wanting, my pretty?'

The stale perfume of alcohol made me retch. 'Leave me alone or I shall scream,' I cried desperately.

'Scream? And who would hear you?'

Suddenly he lunged towards the bed. I struggled furiously but the more I did so the more that monstrous man seemed to enjoy the contest. In my ill condition, weak after my ordeal, there was nothing I could do to avert the inevitable. After he had gone, I felt like some leper, unclean and disgusting. I think it was then that I came very near to attempting my own life. By morning I had reasoned that I must make a bid to escape. The Baron would not have his way with me again.

That day I smuggled a large meat-knife from the kitchens. It was used to carve sides of beef and therefore was sharp as any razor. I hid the knife in my skirts and took it to the safety of my room where I laid it beneath my pillow. It gave me a comforting feeling of protection.

A few days later I made a heartening discovery.

It was during the dinner period and the servants were engaged in a tremendous amount of work because the Baron had several guests that night. There had been some stag hunts during the course of the day and many of the local gentry had converged on the castle to enjoy the Baron's hospitality. With all the cleaning involved it was discovered that we had run out of fresh linen towels and the housekeeper ordered me to go to the kitchen linen cupboard and get some fresh ones.

I knew this cupboard. It had the proportions of a good-sized room and lay at the end of a short corridor where various pantries were situated. I took the key sullenly enough and went off on my errand. I found the cupboard but just as I was entering I saw a door on the opposite side of the corridor standing ajar.

Perhaps it was simple curiosity or perhaps it was an underlying desperation to see whether this was a new opening that could lead to my freedom, I cannot remember now, but some instinct compelled me to push open that door. As a means of escape it was a disappointment. It was merely a junk room of sorts. Large numbers of boxes and parcels were stacked about the place gathering dust.

What caused me to catch my breath was the sight of my own portmanteau in one corner. It was a familiar and comforting sight in the nightmare world into which I had descended. I went eagerly to it and opened it. Yes, there were all my possessions as I had left them. My clothes and other items.

No plan of escape then entered my head but some instinct made me remove the portmanteau from that room and place it in the linen cupboard. I knew that the room from where I had removed the bag was usually locked but the key to the linen cupboard was always kept among other domestic keys hanging on a board in the kitchen. I hid the bag in one corner under a pile of linen and hurriedly grabbed the towels and returned to the kitchen.

Slowly, during the course of the evening, I formed a plan. I would rouse myself just after midnight, go to the linen cupboard and change into my own clothes. Then, taking my portmanteau, I would make my exit from the castle through the scullery door. It would be bolted but I could stand on a stool to withdraw them. For the first time in months, perhaps for the first time since I had learnt of the death of Ernst, a strange lightness gripped my heart and I looked forward eagerly to the coming of midnight.

It was a long time coming but at last I heard a distant clock chime the hour. I waited a further half an hour to make sure that no one was stirring and then, taking the kitchen knife with me as a protection, I made my way quietly down the corridors to the kitchen. From the board on the wall I selected the linen cupboard key, entered and recovered my portmanteau from its hiding place. With a smile of joy I threw off my sackcloth dress and hurriedly pulled on my own clothing. I was nearly dressed when I heard a low chuckle.

The Baron stood in the doorway smiling, his face glistening with sweat. 'Very pretty, my dear,' he said in his curious whine of a voice. 'Very pretty indeed.'

I shrunk back like some trapped animal.

He entered the big cupboard and heeled shut the door. 'And where were we going, my pretty?' he said wheezily.

I felt as if I were frozen to the spot.

'You do not say? Well, no matter. Your trip has just been cancelled.'

He raised a hand to touch my body.

I bent down to the shelf where I had laid the kitchen knife and held it before me. He drew back startled.

'You shall not touch me again!' I hissed.

He recovered his composure and came towards me again, his hand reaching out to seize the knife. A fury lent me more strength than I dreamed I could possess. In rage, in despair, I thrust the blade forward. It sank into his chest, just below the rib cage. A dazed expression crossed his face, he clutched at the knife and fell whimpering at my feet as the blood ran from the wound.

Then there was a silence.

For some moments I stood like a statue, unsure whether he was dead or not. Then, seeing that he was, I dropped the knife, turned away and was violently sick.

I did not feel remorse at the death of the Baron, only a horror that I had been the instrument of that death. Had anyone else slain the monster, I would not have cared one jot.

Had he not murdered my child? Had he not defiled me? Would he not have used me again? No, there was no remorse for him. I would have danced joyously on his grave.

Controlling my shaking limbs, I finished dressing, trying hard not to look down at the bloody body. Then I took my portmanteau and was halfway to the door when a sudden thought stayed me. The instinct for self preservation is very strong in the human mind and it was this that sent me back to the side of that awful corpse and made me rummage through its pockets. I came across a number of gold and silver coins and thrust them in my bag. It would help pay my passage away from this place. Do not think I felt guilt – what that man owed me by way of compensation was immeasurable.

I walked swiftly to the door and looked up and down the empty corridor. All was silent.

Once in the kitchen I lost no time in seizing a footstool and throwing open the bolts of the door which led onto a moonlit yard. I closed the door behind me and waited a moment while my eyes attuned themselves to the darkness and then I hurried forward, through an arch and across a minor maze of courtyards until I came to the main entrance of the castle. The great gates were not closed and there was no one about. It was so easy. I hurried through the open portal and walked rapidly down the road, along the route which Bucar had driven so long ago.

Although it was early September, as I have mentioned before, it was as cold and bleak as a midwinter night and the snow lay as a white carpet across the countryside.

The night air became increasingly cold and in spite of trying to maintain a rapid march I began to suffer from the chill. The snow began to fall so thick and whirled around me in such rapid eddies that I could scarcely keep my eyes open to focus on the road ahead. At one point the wind gusted so strongly at my back that I was forced to run awhile before it.

And then to my terror and discomfiture the heavens were torn asunder by vivid flashes of lightning and the crack of thunder was so loud that it hurt my ears. In one flash of lightning I saw a glimpse ahead of a mass of trees heavily coated in snow. I resolved to rest in their shelter a moment for the icy air was taking the breath from my body.

I reached the trees, great yews, spruce and cypresses, and soon found an area which was dry and devoid of snow, so thick did they spread their canopy. I sat down on a fallen tree, my back against a spruce, and closed my eyes, gasping in the slightly warmer air around me.

Then I started up.

Far in the distance I heard a strange sound, a long low howl which rose slowly until it reached some crescendo and ceased abruptly. A moment later the sound started again. At first I thought it was a dog and then I realized with a shudder that it must be the baying of a wolf. A strange tingling feeling crept down my back and I decided to forsake the shelter of the wood and get back to the roadway and continue my journey, cold or no cold.

I moved a few paces but found to my growing apprehension that my feet seemed racked with pain and that I could barely move them. It was as if I were rooted to the spot. Around me I became aware of a vast stillness. The storm seemed to have died away and there was not even a hint of the wind whispering among the trees.

Then I heard a warm rasping, the low panting of some animal close by. With an effort of will I turned and my mouth opened. I struggled to raise a hand to my mouth. But no cry came.

There, a few yards from me, stood a gigantic wolf. Its eyes – two great flaming eyes – fixed me to the spot. Its sharp white teeth glistened in a gaping red mouth and I could almost feel its hot breath fierce and acrid upon me. How long that beast and I stood gazing upon one another I do not know.

Suddenly it moved, moved cautiously and trotted in a full circle around me. Then it gave a strange yelp, a sound that seemed to hold no threat in it but even a note of friendship, if such a word could be used to describe a wolf's cry. Then it turned and vanished through the forest as abruptly as it appeared.

At the same time I found that I was able to move my limbs again. I expect that it was my fear and anxiety which had frozen them to the spot.

Again I was aware of the storm breaking and the fierce whispering of the wind. But I could delay no longer. If I was lucky the Baron's body would not be found until the castle started to stir at four-thirty, hopefully the find might even be delayed until later for there might be no call for anyone to go to the linen cupboard until the day had grown late. But I dared not count upon that. I had to reach Schassburg and seek some form of conveyance out of the region as swiftly as I could before a hue and cry was set up against me.

Grasping my portmanteau, I made my way back to the road and hurried on as fast as I could through the drifting banks of snow. After a while my mind seemed to grow numb, its one thought was how to place one foot in front of another and, by so concentrating my mind to performing this function, the long hours of night passed until the cold grey fingers of dawn appeared in the eastern sky. Soon, I saw the snow-capped roof-tops of Schassburg.

Dawn spread with sudden swiftness as I entered the picturesque township but there was no time for me to appreciate its medieval beauty.

I made my way swiftly through the deserted streets to where a sign bore the legend '*Bahnhof*' and an arrow pointed the way to the tiny railway station.

To my great joy, there was a light in the station office, which stood beside a single trackway that ran to the outskirts of the town. There were three or four people about, obviously country-folk, who greeted me with a nod and a look of suspicion. I found the station-master in his office, roasting himself before an iron stove into which he was feeding small logs of wood.

'Good morning, *Fräulein*,' he said, straightening himself and staring openly at my bedraggled appearance. 'A cold morning to be up so early.'

'Does a train go from here to Klausenburg?' I asked, ignoring his opening pleasantry.

He nodded. 'A train arrives in twenty minutes, *Fräulein*, and then goes on to Klausenburg immediately. But it is not a passenger train. A few people travel in one of the wagons for a reduced fare but it is not a comfortable ride. It is a goods train, *Fräulein*. The passenger train leaves at midday.'

'I would like to take the first train. How much is it?'

He examined me carefully, somewhat suspiciously, I thought. But he nodded. 'That will be a *krone*, I'm afraid, *Fräulein*. Are you sure you wish to travel on it?'

I took out von Stoffel's purse and selected a coin. The station-master took it and then handed me a printed form on which he scribbled an initial, my destination and date. 'You'd best wait in here until the train comes, *Fräulein*,' he said. 'It will be little enough comfort that you'll get in the wagon.'

He was right. When the train arrived, half-a-dozen peasants and their women crowded into a box wagon, seating themselves on the straw-covered boards. There were large gaps in the wooden sides of the wagon through which the wind blew unmercifully. One of the peasant women, shyly smiling, offered me the protection of a large rug which I shared with her. None of these warm country folk had more than a few words of German but they were friendly enough. One of them offered me a drink of some warming local spirit. All in all, I did not mind the discomfitures of the journey one bit. At least I was free. I was escaping. That was all that mattered.

And little by little we came to Klausenburg.

CHAPTER SIX

I alighted at Klausenburg station as one in a dream. No; not a dream, a nightmare. I felt sick and weak, weak not only from my dreadful experiences but from ill-nourishment. My mind still whirled with a thousand panic-stricken thoughts, which were not eased when I learned from the station-master who struck me as oddly surly and unfriendly, that it would be three days before there was a train for Budapest. Clutching my portmanteau, I wandered through the station and into the main square. Food became a pressing necessity and I espied a small café, entered and sat down.

I ordered coffee and rolls from a waiter who was as surly as the station-master. His aloof hostility made me wonder until it suddenly crossed my mind that the attitude of these city-types, unlike the natural friendliness of the country people, might derive from the fact they thought me to be an Austrian or Saxon against whom they appeared to nurse a bitter resentment.

I sat sipping the hot, strong coffee and contemplating my situation. It was obvious that I had to leave Klausenburg. When the baron's body was discovered, it would not take long before the authorities traced me to the railway station at Schassburg and from there to Klausenburg. But where was I to go?

I had carefully counted the money I had with me and, while it would pay for a ticket to Budapest, it would certainly not keep me for three days and then get me to Britain. My best plan was to place as much distance as possible between Klausenburg and myself and, having done so, obtain some temporary position in order to raise the rest of the fare to London.

Sitting, contemplating the situation over my coffee, I let my eyes wander over the tiny café as if seeking some inspiration among its chequered tablecloths, its hanging salamis and cheeses and stacks of wine bottles.

Apart from myself there was only one other occupant in the café. It was a man also engrossed in his breakfast. It was his face that made me give him a second, closer, scrutiny. He had what is called a striking appearance. One could not say it was a handsome face. It was craggy with a prominent nose, slightly hooked in the Roman manner. The jaw was firm and aggressively positioned. The brows were bushy and beneath them I could discern a pair of piercing blue eyes. His hair was a sandy-yellow. It was obvious that he was not a native of the place, though, I suppose, he could have been Austrian or Saxon, or even British.

I suddenly realized that he was smiling at me and had inclined his head slightly as he caught my examination of him. I felt my cheeks grow hot at thus being discovered and turned my head immediately. Men are so apt at receiving the wrong impression.

At that moment the door of the café jangled noisily open and a large, broad-built man entered. He was prosperously clad and carried a silver-topped walking cane. A monocle was screwed into his right eye and he glowered at his surroundings before banging on a table with his cane and crying, in a raucous voice: 'Kellner, Schnaps bitte!' Then he flung himself into a chair and proceeded to open a newspaper.

There was no sound from the waiter and the man looked up, annoyed at being ignored. Again, the jangling door caused me to look up. Two young men stood hesitantly on the threshold. They were dressed in the clothes usually worn by peasants but there seemed something odd about them. Perhaps it was their well-groomed features.

There was a sudden movement behind the small bar at the back of the café. The waiter entered, stared at the prosperous-looking man and then the two youths and dived behind the bar for shelter.

When I turned back to the youths they were holding pistols in their hands and even as I turned there was a succession of three or four explosions, sounding for all the world like thunder in the narrow confines of the café.

There was the crash of an overturning table. The prosperous-looking man struggled to his feet, his eyes staring, his mouth open and working. Across his broad chest several stains of deep crimson were spreading.

'*Mörder!*' he gasped. '*Meuchelmörder! Hilfe! Hilfe!*'

His voice was interrupted by another explosion and, in horror, I saw the man's face disintegrate into a mask of red pulp as he fell among the débris of broken tables and chairs.

The two youths turned and fled and I could hear their footsteps running down the street. Then, somewhere near at hand, came a hoarse cry, the sound of a whistle being blown and a pistol shot.

A hand grasped my arm, making me jump and give out a startled cry.

It was the craggy-faced man with the blue eyes.

'What do you want?' I gasped, tugging to release my arm from his grip.

'To save you a great deal of trouble, *Fräulein*,' he replied grimly. 'Come, this is no place to be seen now.'

He grabbed my portmanteau and propelled me across the café, through the narrow passageway behind the bar where the waiter was still cowering.

'There is a back entrance?' demanded my guide.

The waiter nodded dumbly and pointed.

'Good. Remember, when the police come, you did not see us. There were no other customers in your café.'

The man merely stared and my guide pushed me

through a small kitchen, past a scullery and into a small back yard which led into a narrow street. The man walked at such a pace that I almost had to run to keep up with him. It was as if he appeared to know every alleyway in Klausenburg for he turned rapidly down one side street after another until we finally emerged into a quiet square.

Only then did he pause and smile down at me.

'I am a doctor, *Fräulein*,' he said, inconsequentially. 'What I would prescribe is a good glass of Schnaps.'

Weakly, I let myself be guided to a café where this doctor ordered not only a bottle of Schnaps but fresh coffee and hot rolls. 'It does not pay to interrupt breakfast,' he observed with satisfaction as he began to butter the rolls.

I sat there dumbly. What land had I come to? What sort of country was this where cruelty, death and evil were so commonplace? I was beyond further shock. I was drained of emotion.

'Who are you? What happened?'

The craggy-faced man gave a smile. I admit, it was a rather attractive smile. Boyish and innocent. It reminded me a little of Ernst's smile.

'Ah, forgive me, *Fräulein*. My name is Van Helsing. Abraham Van Helsing of Amsterdam.'

'You are Dutch?' I said, trying to concentrate on one fact at a time.

'Just so, *Fräulein*. But presently I am working in Klausenburg at the hospital pursuing a study of herbal medicines which are used widely in these parts.'

'What happened?' I said, still trying to concentrate. 'What was all that about – that horrible murder. Why did you take me out of the café?'

The man, Van Helsing, poured out a glass of Schnaps and handed it to me. 'Drink,' he ordered. I did so because my mind refused to function on its own. 'Now,' he gave me a friendly look, 'why did I take you out of the café?

Because, *Fräulein*, I observed that you, like me, were a foreigner. Is that not so?'

'I am Scottish,' I replied.

'Ah, a Scot. I have met many of your countrymen in Europe. The Scots seems to be natural emigrants – doctors, engineers, soldiers – all serving other countries. Is their own country so bad?'

'You have not explained, Doctor Van Helsing, why you took me out of the café. Were you involved in that murder?'

The thought had suddenly occurred to me. After all, why had he fled so quickly from the scene before the police arrived, and why had he exhorted the waiter to remain silent about his presence?

'My God!' he cried, in mock horror. 'You think me an assassin? Listen, my Scots *Fräulein*, what you saw was a political assassination. There have been many in Klausenburg of late. Had we not fled from that scene, we would have been arrested by the Austro-Hungarian police, who are getting disagreeably hysterical about such events.'

'But we, or *I* at least, had nothing to do with it,' I asserted vehemently.

'That is true, but the Klausenburg police have taken to arresting anybody and, indeed, everybody, at the scene. They stand little chance of finding the real assassins so they make arrests indiscriminately. At best, we would have spent several days in their disagreeable police cells answering a lot of nonsensical questions. The easiest solution to our predicament was to remove ourselves as quickly as possible.'

I suddenly realized that he had, unwittingly, done me a bigger favour than he realized. I certainly had no wish to encounter the Klausenburg police and, had I been arrested on suspicion of complicity in the café murder, I would have been detained long enough for the police authorities at Schassburg to catch up with me.

Grudgingly, I thanked the Dutchman.

'Ah,' he smiled in that boyish way of his, 'it is not every day that one has the honour of serving such a pretty *Fräulein*.'

I returned this compliment with a scowl. Men are all the same. Why is it that they always think they flatter a woman by making veiled sexual advances?

'You said that this was a political assassination,' I said, ignoring his flattery.

'Indeed, it is,' said Van Helsing. 'Ah, poor Transylvania or, as the Germans call it – Siebenbürgen. It is a very unhappy country. Very unhappy.'

'Why?' I demanded.

Van Helsing stirred his coffee. 'It was once a proud, independent state ruled by its own voivodes or princes. Then came conquest and exploitation. The Turks invaded and for many years Transylvania lay under the yoke of the Ottoman Empire. The natives tried to wrest back their freedom from the Turks many times. Each time they were unsuccessful. Finally their leaders accepted the "protection" of the Austrian Empire. Austria fought a war with Turkey and took Transylvania from her in 1686. Since then Transylvania has languished under the tutelage of the Habsburgs. The Austrians proved no better than the Turks, the Habsburgs were just as rapacious, greedy and dominating as the Ottomans.'

'And the Transylvanians,' I said, remembering Bucar, 'are a different nationality to the Austrians and Hungarians.'

'Very distinctly so, *Fräulein*. They speak a mixture of a Latin and Slavonic language which is called Romanian. The same language is spoken to the south in Moldavia and Wallachia, two principalities which joined together ten years ago, freed from Turkish rule, and formed the kingdom of Romania.'

'Then the Transylvanians are the same nationality as the Romanians?' The Dutchman nodded.

'And I suppose the Transylvanians want to break away from the Austro-Hungarian Empire and join Romania?'

Van Helsing smiled. 'You have an exact grasp of the political situation, *Fräulein*. You are as intelligent as you are pretty.'

'And that is the basis of the murder?' I pressed, ignoring his male stupidity.

'At one time, my dear *Fräulein*,' said Van Helsing, 'Hungary was also a subject nation of Austria. Then, after numerous rebellions, Austria gave Hungary self-government, recognized her language and took her into the Austrian Empire as a co-equal partner.'

He sighed. 'It is strange, you know, how often an oppressed people, fighting off oppression and winning freedom then oppress someone else in turn. It seems the lessons of their own struggle are never learned. No sooner were the Hungarians given self-government than they promptly set about oppressing other nations which they had been given jurisdiction over – the Slovaks to the north and here, in Transylvania. They have ruthlessly tried to stamp out these peoples' languages and cultures and all national aspirations. Transylvania was forced to become an integral part of Hungary in 1848. Of course, this "union" was not made without some opposition – a long and bloody opposition. But, of course, the new Hungarian army, reinforced from Austria, eventually destroyed all opposition. It was in December, 1849, that Transylvania became a mere province of Hungary ruled by a governor from his residence in Sibiu.

'But, as you rightly said, dear *Fräulein*, the Transylvanians do not wish to be Hungarians nor Austrians. There are two national movements. There is a moderate group led by the Metropolitan Andrei Saguna, a bishop of the Orthodox Church, whose party wants to establish a home-rule government. A domestically independent Transylvania within the Austro-Hungarian Empire. But the other party is more extreme. They are led by George Baritiu and Ioan Ratiu, both of whom have been elected to the Hungarian parliament for Transylvanian constituencies, but both have refused to take their seats. They are organizing their movement for the total overthrow of the Austro-Hungarian Empire in Transylvania. They plan to unite the province with Romania to the south.

'I think you will find that those youths were members of the latter group. The man they shot was a local *Ratsmitglied* – a town councillor who was a staunch unionist. Actually, he was no great loss to society. I believe he was a cousin of the Baron von Stoffel, who is quite a power in these parts and an evil man.'

Van Helsing broke off alarmed by the agitation on my face. 'Do you know von Stoffel, *Fräulein*?' he asked, curiously.

'No, no,' I returned vehemently. 'It is just that the thought of that murder or assassination is still upsetting to me.'

'I would sit here awhile,' he said solicitously. He drew from his waistcoat a gold watch on a chain and looked at it clucking his tongue. 'Alas, I have to return to the hospital. The time has passed swiftly. It is the first time I have talked politics for so long with such a charming and intelligent young lady. But I would try to forget what you saw; try to avoid local politics altogether. There is a war going on in this country, guerrilla groups are gathering, assassination is rife. They even say that to the north-east, in Bukovina, the guerrillas have fielded an army and the regular troops are hard pressed to contain them. Of course, no one really knows. There is too much censorship.'

The Dutchman stood up and handed me a small white card. 'Here is where I may be reached. If, during your stay in Klausenburg, I can be of any assistance to you, please do not hesitate to call upon me. It will be my pleasure.' He bowed low over my hand, his lips just brushing it. 'Until we meet again, *Fräulein*,' he said and then was gone.

I stared after his retreating figure as it swung jauntily down the street and vanished around a corner. It was odd what an acute feeling of loneliness came over me after he departed.

CHAPTER SEVEN

For a moment I wondered whether to race after the friendly Dutch doctor and explain my predicament. But how can you confess to a stranger, however sympathetic and friendly, that you have just killed a German nobleman? No, I reflected; I had only my own resources to rely on. Once again, one thing was abundantly clear to me. I had to get some sort of post to raise my fare to London. But what? And where?

Beside me on the seat was a discarded newspaper. Absently, I picked it up and started to turn its pages. It was a local paper, the *Gazeta Transilvanei*, and it was that which nearly made me set it down again for it was mostly in the Romanian language with one or two articles in German. Yet something made me turn to the columns of advertisements and the following was the one that sprang immediately to my eye.

> Governess of gentle breeding required: To teach and foster the education of nobleman's children. The successful applicant should be versed in arithmetic, geography, some history and a knowledge of languages, in particular, a knowledge of English is essential. Applications should be made to Castle Dracula, care of the Post Office at Bistritz.

The blood coursed through me in wild excitement. It was almost as if the advertisement had been meant for me alone. At the time I did not question why such an advertisement should appear in German in an obviously Romanian nationalist newspaper or why I had been prompted to pick it up. I have been described as impulsive and headstrong; had I not been impulsive I doubt whether

I would have escaped the confines of Dr Smout's academy and would probably have wound up teaching in some poor village school, or even worse. Besides, my impulsiveness was given an impetus by my situation. I determined, therefore, to travel to Bistritz and present myself at Castle Dracula before the unnamed nobleman could receive any other applicants.

Without any more ado, clutching the newspaper and my portmanteau, I left the café and made my way back to the station. My heart skipped a beat when I saw the main square and station patrolled by policemen. It soon became apparent that they were looking for the Transylvanian patriots (for the local people regarded them as such) who had assassinated the town councillor. I was given no more than a passing scrutiny as I made my way to the ticket office.

I saw hostility clouding the eyes of the man behind the desk as I asked for a map of the area. I decided to pre-empt any wrong conclusions the man might draw from my accent.

'I am a Scottish visitor to your country,' I explained, 'and want to get to Bistritz but am unsure of the way.'

The man paused, puzzled 'Ah. The *Fräulein* is not Saxon nor Austrian?' he pressed.

'Scots,' I confirmed, and then seeing he did not understand added 'from Britain.'

His eyes lightened. 'Ah . . . Britain. Inglezi.'

I refrained from trying to explain the difference.

From then on he was all politeness and took out a well-thumbed map which he spread before me. 'Here is Klausenburg, *Fräulein*. Bistritz is here to the east and slightly north – a distance of about ninety kilometres. It is a pleasant enough city but, alas, for the tourist there is little to see there. A great part of the old city was burnt down some ten years ago.'

'How would I get there?' I asked.

'You are in luck,' he smiled. 'There is a train from here in two hours. You would be in Bistritz by about six o'clock this evening.'

Without giving the matter any further thought, I bought a ticket and then took myself to the *Königin von England* hotel, recklessly spending some of my few precious coins on an adequate luncheon.

Two hours later, feeling increasingly nervous lest the murder of Baron von Stoffel now be public knowledge and the hue and cry already up for me, I returned to the station. The ticket collector now greeted me with a marked degree of friendliness and conducted me on to the station platform where a two-carriage train was drawn up behind a rather ancient-looking engine. He led me to a compartment and wished me a pleasant trip.

I had hardly settled back in my seat than the whistle screamed and, with a shuddering jerk, the train began to push forward. For a while I watched the countryside flying by the windows and with each passing mile I began to sense a feeling of growing relief, of well-being that I was finally leaving Klausenburg behind me. Then it occurred to me, idiot that I was! The police authorities from Schassburg would have no difficulty in tracing me to Klausenburg and once there I had left them a further open trail to Bistritz. I should have been more circumspect. The ticket collector at Klausenburg would undoubtedly remember the 'Inglezi' woman and her destination.

But soon the rattle and sway of the train began to have its effect and so I closed my eyes and began to doze. Before I realized it, I had fallen into a deep sleep.

In retrospect it was merely a dream. At the time it was strangely real even to the appalling musty smell of decay and corruption that permeated it. I can remember the dream even now in vivid detail.

It seemed, after a short while, I awoke alone in the

train compartment and found myself gagged. I tried to free myself but my arms were pinioned to my sides.* Then, there appeared before me a vision – an image of a man. He seemed to be standing in the shadows of the compartment. I had an impression of a tall man whose eyes seemed to gleam with a strange brightness. The image lasted but a few moments and then vanished to be replaced with strange whisperings in my ears – no, not just in my ears but in my head itself, in my very brain. I tried to speak but the gag prevented me. The voices seemed to be asking questions of me, questions about me.

There came to me an image, long forgotten, of my father taking me upon his knee in the little apartment we once had in Edinburgh. Then it was gone and the self-satisfied faces of my cousins milled around me and opened a path for me to where a coffin lay open. Inside lay the frail, pitiful body of my mother. Then that too was gone and in its place came the sweating red lecherous face of Dr Smout, his heavy, vile body pinning me to the bed.

Each image came and went in swift succession and was gone before I realized it. It was as if the images were being dragged unwillingly from my subconscious, dragged up against my will by some outside agent.

Ernst's boyish face came before me and vanished; the pain and screams as my body contorted over my dead baby echoed in my mind. The malignant ugly face of the Baron von Stoffel appeared followed by the surprise in his eyes as he staggered away from me with death touching his evil soul.

Then, once again, came the vision of the tall man, still

* It is interesting to note that, according to *The Interpretation of Dreams* by Zolar, to dream one is bound is a forewarning of obstacles to be overcome and for a girl to dream she is gagged is an indication of a meeting with a man with whom a deep and close relationship will be established. Tremayne.

shrouded in gloom; the eyes only were alive, bright and piercing. The shadow-draped head nodded, as if in approval, and then a thick swirling grey mist clouded my vision.

I began to doze dreamlessly once more.

'Bistritz! Bistritz! Come, *Fräulein*, this is Bistritz!'

The shouting of the guard through the carriage window caused me to jerk fully awake and scramble from the carriage compartment.

The platform was athrong with soldiers. They all seemed young, with coarse red faces. They shouted loudly to each other and some of them leered at me as I stood uncertainly in their midst. Some said things, laughing lewdly with their companions. Oh, how vain and ridiculous is the male animal. If only they realized how stupid their sexual bravado makes them seem. Ah, but I was coming to dislike men to an extent that bordered on hate. God, had Ernst behaved in this lewd fashion when he was in France?

An officer sprang forward, saluting me and clearing a way towards the station office where a ticket collector stood looking sourly at the soldiers. 'Hungarian soldiers,' he said, taking my ticket. 'Going up to Bukovina. They say there is a full scale uprising going on up there.' His eyes caught mine and he frowned. 'Austrian?'

'No. I'm a visitor – from Britain.'

'Ah,' his face lightened. 'Well, have a care, *Fräulein*. With this rabble on the streets of Bistritz no one is safe.'

'Is there an hotel here?' I asked, thinking that it would be fruitless to try to find Castle Dracula that night.

'There is the municipal hotel, the *Stadt Wirtshaus*,*

---

* Bistritz was predominantly a Saxon town. The *Stadt Wirtshaus* belonged to the municipality. The traveller, George Boner (Transylvania, 1865) stayed there and said it was one of the worst inns he had visited. 'The business is, in fact, not conducted at all; everything goes on in a

across the square as you come out of the station, *Fräulein*. You cannot miss it.'

I thanked him and came out of the station and stood looking across the main square of the old town.

Dusk had descended, laying a carpet of grey across the vista of the old black towers which stood like minarets against the night sky. I could see hundreds of lights about the place and from these I judged the town to be of a fair size. I wondered whether the Post Office would be closed at this time and decided to leave my inquiries about Castle Dracula until the morning. With my few remaining coins I was, at least, assured of one night's stay at the hotel.

Suddenly I became aware that a man was watching me from a few yards away. He was tall with a long brown beard and a great black hat which effectively hid his face. I could only see the gleam of a pair of eyes that seemed to glow red in the lamplight.

'Is the *Fräulein* bound for Castle Dracula?' he asked in a German which was at once both cultured and yet had a strangely foreign intonation to it.

A slight shudder of surprise ran down my back. 'I . . . I am,' I stuttered. 'But how did you know?'

I could almost see a thin-lipped smile spread over his features. 'My master has sent me to meet the train from Klausenburg and transport the young *Fräulein* who would arrive to the castle.'

'Oh,' I smiled. 'Then this is a coincidence.'

'Coincidence, *Fräulein*?'

'Yes. Although I am going to Castle Dracula, my coming is not known. I am going to answer an advertisement in the newspaper. Your master must have sent you to meet someone else, not me.'

---

happy go lucky style, no one in the house caring anything about it.' The Golden Krone, in which Jonathan Harker stayed (*Dracula*, 1897) does not appear to have been built until later. Tremayne.

'Nevertheless, the *Fräulein* has come from Klausenburg and is bound for Castle Dracula.' He made a pantomime of looking up and down the square before the station. 'And there is no one else.'

'Wait,' I replied, and hurried back into the station building to where the ticket collector was stoking his iron stove.

'Excuse me,' I said, breathlessly.

'You have forgotten something, *Fräulein*?' he asked.

'No. But can you tell me whether there was any other lady on the train from Klausenburg?'

The ticket collector smiled and shook his head. 'No. You were the only one.'

'There was not another young lady who wanted to go to Castle Dracula?' I pressed.

The ticket collector stepped backward and I swear he turned pale. Suddenly he did an extraordinary thing. He crossed himself and held two fingers towards me, exclaiming, 'God between us and all evil! There was no one else on the train.'

Frowning, I thanked him, puzzled by the fear which had suddenly grown in his eyes.

Outside the station the tall man still stood as if he had not moved from the spot. 'There was no one else,' I said weakly.

He nodded gravely. 'I have a coach and horses waiting,' he said, 'and the journey is quite long. The castle lies in the Borgo Pass towards Bukovina. We have to be there before sunrise.'

Puzzled but uncaring, I followed this tall coachman across the square to where a splendid black calèche was drawn up. In the harness, snorting with impatience, were four coal-black horses. I noticed as the coachman went to the door of the calèche to open it for me, that on the black varnish was painted a crest. It looked like a dragon in white relief and underneath the name 'Dracula' was inscribed.

The coachman handed me up into the calèche and I had a passing awareness of the tremendous strength of his hands.

'You will find rugs and furs inside for the journey,' he said, as he shut the door behind me. 'Also there is a small hamper with food and a bottle of *slivovitz* to keep out the cold, a plum brandy, *Fräulein*, a national drink in these parts.'

He turned and mounted the driving box. 'Come, my beauties, home now,' I heard him whisper softly to the neighing beasts. And then the calèche seemed to fly into motion, clattering across the cobbled streets of the town and out into the dark countryside with incredible speed.

CHAPTER EIGHT

The calèche sped with amazing lightness along the dark road and away from the comforting lights of Bistritz; it was as if the carriage had suddenly sprouted wings and scarce touched the road, so smooth was its journey. I lay back among the warmth of the furs and for a while watched the jagged black shadows of the mountainous horizon standing out in relief by just a shade from the night sky. Then a drowsiness overcame me but this time the sleep into which I fell was dreamless and refreshing.

When I awoke the moon was high in the sky, sparkling over the snow-carpeted countryside in a strange, eerie, silver glow. I yawned and stretched and looked about me. It seemed that we were passing through a narrow valley of tall, precipitous mountains and from the angle of the carriage and its slightly slower pace, I deduced that we were journeying upward.

I leant forward and reached into my portmanteau for my small travelling clock. The moonlight was bright; bright enough to see the face of the clock. I was quite surprised when I saw the time. It was seven full hours since we had left Bistritz. Seven full hours! How had I managed to sleep that length of time in a fast-moving carriage without waking?

I began to feel tiny pangs of hunger and remembered the picnic hamper which the coachman had indicated.

Strange, but it seemed as if the driver read my very thoughts for the coach abruptly swung off the road on to a small area of land which must have been especially constructed as a resting place for carriages ascending the narrow mountain roadway. The tall figure of the coachman swung down from the driving box and looked up at me. 'The *Fräulein* may eat and drink here. A half-hour, no more. We have three more hours upon our journey and must reach the castle before sunrise.'

It was the second time he had alluded to the sunrise but I was more startled to learn that we still had a long way to go. 'Three hours?' I asked. 'But that would mean we will have journeyed some ten hours from Bistritz. I thought the castle was near the town?'

'Distances do not mean much in this country, *Fräulein*,' was the coachman's response. Again, the only impression I had of the man was of the reddy glow of his eyes. All other features seemed to be shaded by his black, large-brimmed hat and cloak. 'Bistritz *is* the nearest town to the castle.'

He turned to the horses and began to inspect them, caressing them and talking to them soothingly while they stood quiet and docile under his touch.

I was eating ravenously of the cold meats and cheeses within the picnic hamper when I suddenly realized the man was not eating. 'Will you eat also?' I called.

The coachman looked back at me inquisitively and then shook his head. 'I ate while I was driving – while the *Fräulein* was still asleep.' He paused and then stared at me a moment. 'Is it the custom in your country that a lady offers to share her food with her coachman – that mistress and servant eat together?'

There seemed a mocking quality to his voice. 'No,' I replied. 'But on a long journey why should the lady eat and the coachman go hungry just for the sake of affected etiquette?'

The coachman gave a sardonic snort of laughter. 'The *Fräulein* has a quality of humanity in her that is not to be found in the boyars of these parts.'

'Boyars?' The word was new to me.

'The nobles – like my master, Count Dracula.'

I sipped at the *slivovitz*, the plum brandy, which I

found warm and comforting. 'What place is this?' I inquired, pointing to the valley.

'We are entering the Borgo Pass, *Fräulein*,' replied the coachman. 'Those peaks to the south are the eastern Carpathians. Those to the north, the tall black peaks, are the mountains of Birgau.'

I looked at the forbidding peaks and shuddered. 'How bleak they look.'

'Bleak? Yes, to the stranger who does not know them. But those of us who know their passes, their caves and shelters, are not dismayed by their bleakness. They are both home and fortress to us. The snow that lies on them from autumn through to mid-May gives us protection from the ravening hordes of invaders while in summer the rocks and precipices are like the unscaleable walls of a castle.'

He spoke with a strange passion, like a general assessing his defences against an enemy who were even then attacking.

An eerie scream suddenly broke the silence of the night, rising, rising until it ended in a shrill crescendo. The sound – so strange, so unexpected – made me shudder in fear. Then the single scream was joined by others until an awful cacophony of noise echoed and re-echoed through the deep, dark valleys, among the mountains. It took me some moments before I identified it as the baying of wolves.

I was aware of the coachman smiling at me. True I did not see his parted lips but, I suppose, I felt the smile rather than saw it.

'Ah,' he said softly, almost benignly. 'Isn't it beautiful music they make? They are the children of the night, *Fräulein*. The night is theirs. We intrude in it. Come, we have delayed long enough. Let us leave them to their own.'

I shuddered and agreed.

We sped on through the snow-carpeted landscape, climbing here, descending there, always keeping close to the floor of the valley. In all the time we journeyed, I only once saw the black outline of a few scattered houses forming a village. The whole area struck me as the loneliest spot on this earth; an empty dramatic landscape inhabited only by wild animals. I once saw a great bear rearing up at the side of the roadway as we sped by. Now and then groups of wild boar would run snorting from our path. Once, in the distance, lit by the silver light of the great moon, I saw the stately figure of a Carpathian stag, surely one of the most beautiful creatures on this earth. Not even in the highland country of my native Scotland had I seen anything so remote, so terrifyingly beautiful.

If anything, the night grew more chilly as we drove on. I was forced to snuggle down into the furs but I could still see well by the incredibly bright moonlight. We now entered an area which hemmed us in with tall spruces and pine trees which grew so close together that the roadway seemed to enter a long tunnel. A wind, which had risen, whispered and keened its way through the serried ranks of the trees and now and again the branches crashed against each other with an angry, frightening clatter.

The baying of wolves continued sporadically, sometimes close and sometimes far away. Sometimes it even seemed that we were surrounded by them. But the coachman never faltered nor spared his horses as we sped onward.

As I was wondering whether the journey would ever end, we crossed a white plain of snow, turned the shoulder of a mountain and entered a small valley.

It was not long before we were clattering through great stone portals and into a cobbled courtyard where tall black stone walls rose on every side. The courtyard was dimly lit by a storm-lantern which hung over a tall wooden door.

The coachman dismounted and opened the door of the calèche, handing me out of the carriage. Again, I was aware of the strength of his grip. I was unsteady for a moment, having been confined for so long in the coach. Indeed, we must have journeyed for all of ten hours since leaving Bistritz for already I could see a faint hint of dawn in the eastern sky. The same thought must have struck the coachman, who had been so keen to arrive at the castle before sun-up. He glanced quickly up at the sky and muttered something under his breath which sounded like a curse. He swung my portmanteau down from the calèche and placed it on the doorstep before the wooden door.

'Wait here, *Fräulein*. They will open directly,' he said and, without another word, climbed back on to the driving seat of the carriage and sent it clattering into the innermost reaches of the castle's maze of passageways and courtyards.

I stood on the stone flagged steps before the great wooden door, shivering slightly in the early morning air. I could see, now, in the gloomy light of the storm lantern, that each section of the iron-studded wooden door held the figure of a dragon; the same design as in the crest on the calèche. It was obvious that this was the family crest of the mysterious 'Count Dracula' to whom the coachman had referred as his master.

The thought now flashed through my mind that the remoteness of Castle Dracula was greatly to my advantage, should I be successful in obtaining the post of governess here. Should the Schassburg police track me to Klausenburg and then from Klausenburg to Bistritz, the trail would surely end there? Castle Dracula seemed to me to be an ideal hide-away until I had saved enough money to allow me to travel to London in comfort.

There was a rasp of bolts being withdrawn and the click of a lock being turned. Slowly the great wooden door swung inwards.

A tall man stood on the threshold, holding a flickering candelabra in one hand. For a moment I thought it was the coachman, so closely did this figure resemble his.

Then the figure spoke.

'I am Dracula.'

CHAPTER NINE

He stood, a tall shadowy figure, holding aloft in one hand a great silver candelabra of some antique design whose candles spluttered and flickered but shed little light in the gloom. He made no motion to step forward to greet me but stood well within the threshold of the door.

'Welcome to Castle Dracula, *Fräulein*,' he said in a curiously accented voice. 'Enter freely and of your own will.'

Clutching my portmanteau, I obeyed this strange invitation, and entered across the stone flagged threshold while the Count closed the heavy wooden door behind me.

I turned and examined my prospective host carefully and immediately felt that there was something unusual about the man who now confronted me. It is hard to describe the impression, a feeling that he was no simple person, for he emanated a powerful aura, a charisma that made me feel almost child-like in his presence. Perhaps subsequent events have coloured my first impression of the man but I certainly recall that my first encounter left me breathless.

At first I thought he was old, for he had white hair and a long white moustache; yet his face, though pale, was etched in sharp features and had no marks of ageing at all. What immediately impressed me was the strength of his face. His nose was thin and had a high bridge and strangely arched nostrils. The eyes – well, I had an impression of wide-open green eyes but these so often appeared to reflect the light, especially from the candles and fires, that they often appeared to glow with some red aura. The effect was made more threatening by the bushy eyebrows that met over the nose. His forehead was high domed and the only unpleasing aspect was his mouth. Under his moustache it showed rather fixed and rather cruel, as if nature had twisted it into a permanent sneer at the misfortunes of lesser men. Also, the lips were very red and I had a wild passing thought that the count might use lip rouge.*

I suddenly realized that the Count was regarding me with a somewhat sardonic smile, aware of my close scrutiny.

'Welcome to my house, *Fräulein*,' he said, giving a half-bow which exuded some measure of old world courtesy. 'Welcome. Come freely. Go safely; and leave something of the happiness you bring.'

There seemed a strength of sincerity in his voice and I at once decided to correct his obvious misapprehension.

'You are most courteous, Count Dracula,' I began. 'However, there has been some mistake.'

'Mistake?' he arched one eyebrow.

'Yes. There was a mistake at the station in Bistritz. It was not your coachman's fault,' I added hastily. 'But I am not the person that you were expecting. You see I was in Klausenburg when I saw your advertisement in the newspaper and I came to Bistritz to apply for the position on an impulse. Your coachman was at the station and said he had been sent there to meet a young woman from Klausenburg – there was no one else who fitted that description on the train – but, you see . . .'

The Count stood in an attitude of deferential attention until I trailed off lamely.

'Do not trouble yourself, *Fräulein*. My exact order to my coachman was to pick up *any* young lady alighting at

---

* Morag MacLeod's description of Dracula makes an interesting comparison to the detailed description of Dracula by the Papal Legate Nicolas Modrussa who met the Wallachian ruler during his captivity in Hungary 1462-1474. Tremayne.

Bistritz and asking for Castle Dracula. Because of the advertisement, I suspected that someone might arrive on the train from Klausenburg in reply to it.'

'You sent your coachman all that way to Bistritz just in case?' I asked astounded.

The Count shrugged. 'There was some other business to be conducted in the town and since he was there . . .' The Count dismissed the subject and reached for my portmanteau. The explanation seemed plausible but I could not help feeling suspicious. I had an uncomfortable feeling, a ridiculous feeling, that the coachman and the Count had known that I was coming, but I dismissed the matter, silently rebuking myself for being childish.

The Count turned towards the stairway in the great hall. 'My servants are still abed,' he said, as if in explanation for his action. He suddenly paused on the bottom steps and cast a look through one of the tall windows of the hall through which there was a hint of grey light.

'Ah, the sun rises soon. How annoying that life is governed by its rise and set.' He began to mount the stairs. 'A room has been prepared for you,' he said as we ascended.

'For me? But . . .'

The Count read my thoughts. 'For anyone who came in answer to my advertisement,' he smiled.

'Then should we not discuss my application?' I asked.

The Count waved his hand, as if dismissing the idea. 'That can be done later, after you have rested. It has been a long, long journey and you must be in need of rest. Here, in the Carpathians, time is of little consequence.'

We reached the landing to the upper chambers of the castle and passed down several corridors which were hung with remarkable tapestries, mostly depicting scenes of violent destructions and bloodshed.

The Count seemed to observe my examination of them. 'They are old tapestries which reflect the history of my so-unhappy land, *Fräulein*. It is, unfortunately, a land in which much blood has been spilled, wasted like a surplus of water gushing from a pump. One day that pump may run dry.' He paused before a door and pushed it open with one massive hand. 'Here is your room, *Fräulein*. It has been made ready for your ease. You will find all that you need to refresh yourself and for making your toilet after so long a journey. There is a light breakfast laid. Then I suggest you sleep and, afterwards, we may talk about those things which have led to your coming to my house.'

I was far too tired to analyse the Count's words but I had a passing feeling that they conveyed some hidden knowledge.

He placed the portmanteau within the room and gave another bow.

'A few hours sleep will see me refreshed,' I said, not wishing to disturb the routine of his house.

'Do not worry, *Fräulein*. We are late risers in this household. I, myself, have yet to sleep and will not arise until late afternoon. So take your ease as long as you desire.' He turned towards the door. 'Ah,' he turned, as if struck by a further thought, 'to ensure that you are not disturbed until you wish it, I would advise that you lock your door.' With a thin-lipped smile he turned and left.

I stood for a moment and surveyed my room. It was an old oak-panelled bedroom in which a huge fire crackled merrily in a great stone hearth. In front of this fire stood a small table on which stood a great silver tray containing a meal. But such a meal! For months now I had become accustomed to the terrible slops and leftovers at von Stoffel's castle. This meal was a feast. There was fresh bread, butter, and a dish of preserves. To my delight I found that the remaining silver dishes contained hot bacon, eggs and sausages, the like of which I had not seen since leaving Britain. On the hearth there was also a hot pot of coffee.

In spite of the picnic on the road, I realized that I was very hungry, and I fell to with a will.

And while I ate I examined my surroundings.

The bedroom itself, as I have said, was panelled in dark oak. There were several tapestries depicting the same central theme as those I had seen in the corridors – bloodshed, war and murder. They probably meant something specific to those acquainted with the history of the country. The bed was an old four-poster covered with exquisitely embroidered quilts and fresh white pillows and sheets. The furnishings were generally old but each item was obviously of great value. Count Dracula was evidently a nobleman of great substance if he could furnish a governess's room in such fashion.

I began to consider the strength and warmth of the welcome with which the Count had received me, contrasting it to the terrors of Schloss Stoffel. And, although I felt an odd pricking feeling of disquiet, I also had an overall sense of contentment and relaxation.

It must have been some slight noise that made me glance up. There, a few feet away from me, stood a small boy. I had a passing wonder that I had not heard him enter the room. He was certainly a most odd looking child, dressed in a black suit, with only a snow white ruffle at his throat to offset the sombreness of his appearance. The boy regarded me with deep-set eyes, eyes that seemed black but filled with a myriad other lights. The face was broad, almost Slavic, and the skin was stretched and taut over high cheekbones. The hair was the colour of pitch and swept straight back from the forehead where it centred in a very pronounced widow's peak. The eyebrows, like the Count's, were bushy and met across the bridge of the nose. The lips were thin and red, with peculiar-looking sharp white teeth protruding over the bottom lip.

I smiled at the boy and said 'Hello' in English.

The child stood regarding me in silence for a moment, his eyes seeming to bore into my mind. It was an oddly uncomfortable feeling. Then he spoke in a language I did not know, presumably in Romanian. 'I'm sorry,' I replied in German. 'I do not understand. Do you speak this tongue?'

The child nodded. 'Who are you? Are you my new governess?'

'I hope so,' I said. 'But that is up to the Count to decide.'

The child examined me solemnly. 'You are very pretty, aren't you? Perhaps a little thin, though. You have not been eating well lately.'

The remark astonished me for the little boy could hardly have been eight years of age.

'Yes,' continued the child without waiting for my comment, 'you are pretty. That is good. But you must eat well. Are you married?'

I laughed gently at his directness. There is a quality in the simplicity of a child's directness which makes a mockery of our adult pretences. 'No, I am not married,' I replied in a solemn tone.

'And your name, *Fräulein*?' pressed the child.

'My name is Morag, Morag MacLeod.'

The child frowned 'What sort of name is that?' he inquired.

'It is a Scottish name,' I replied. 'I come from Scotland, a country which lies in the northern part of the island of Britain. And what is your name?'

'My name is Radu.'

'And is that a Transylvanian name?'

The little boy drew himself up with grave dignity.

'My ancestors, who bore my name before me, were once princes of this country.'

'And Count Dracula is your uncle?' I asked, hazarding a guess.

'He is . . .' The child paused and bit his lower lip. 'He is Dracula.'

He moved close to me and peered into my face. 'You are indeed pretty, *fräulein*,' he said softly.

It may have been the two days and nights that I had passed without proper sleep, or the change in temperatures from the cold of the carriage to the warmth of the bedroom, or the heaviness of the breakfast I had just eaten, for as I looked down at the boy, those large black eyes of his seemed to dissolve into pools of swirling mists through which strange coloured lights seemed to flicker. I began to feel terribly sleepy.

'May I kiss you, pretty *Fräulein*?' I heard the boy saying, his voice seeming to come from many miles away.

I felt him reaching upwards, his hot breath against my neck. 'Radu!' A harsh voice cracked across the soporific quiet of the room.

It seemed that an icy cold wind blew through the room jerking me from my drowsiness. Count Dracula stood framed in the doorway, his eyes flashing with a peculiar red fire. His face was contorted by anger.

To my amazement the young boy spun around, snarling like some animal. 'She is mine!' he yelled, defiance in his voice.

'Yours?' sneered the count. He came forward and seized the child by the scruff of the neck and flung him bodily across the room. A finger pointed to the growing intensity of light at the windows. 'Do you not realize the time? Back to your resting place and let us have no more talk of "mine" and "thine" in this house. It is I who rule here.'

I watched this drama in petrified amazement as the boy picked himself from the floor whence he had been hurled and spat angrily at the Count. Then his features formed into a sulky grimace and he left the room. The Count turned to me and the anger of his features suddenly dissolved into a mask of grave courtesy. 'Your pardon,

Fräulein,' he said, giving a half bow, 'but did I not tell you to lock the door and thus prevent yourself being disturbed?'

Then, to my surprise, the Count bent forward and took my chin in his hand and turned it first one way and then the other, apparently examining my neck. There was nothing familiar in this action. It was done with the same detachment as one might use in inspecting a coat for dirt.

'What is it?' I asked.

'It is well,' he sighed.

I frowned and tried to collect my thoughts. 'There was no need to act so cruelly to the boy on my account,' I said, remembering the way the Count had flung the child across the room and feeling no little indignation. 'After all, it is in a child's nature to feel curious at the arrival of a stranger.'

The Count's lips twisted in a smile. 'Radu was told not to enter this room. He disobeyed, *Fräulein*. Therefore he must be punished.'

'There is no need to punish him on my account.'

'That is not my intention, *Fräulein*. He is to be punished on his own account. He must learn to obey. One has to learn to obey before one can command.'

'But he is so little,' I protested. 'And . . .' I halted as I noticed that the Count was glancing frequently towards the windows where the first rays of dawn were creeping in.

He held up his hand. '*Fräulein*, I promise I shall discuss this with you at a later time. But now you must rest, as I must also rest. Be sure to lock the door behind me. Rest well and may your awakening be a pleasant one,' and he turned abruptly and left the room.

I crossed the floor and turned the key in the lock behind him.

For a moment I paused – I thought I heard a whimper, the whimper of a child, somewhere in the dim recesses of the old castle. But then there was silence. I turned back into my room and made a hurried toilet before falling into my bed and succumbing to a deep, dreamless sleep.

CHAPTER TEN

I awoke feeling marvellously refreshed. Oh, how I must have needed that sleep. I lay in the warm, comfortable bed and gradually allowed my senses to slowly awaken and my eyes to open, smiling with an inner contentment.

Then I started upright for I could not believe my eyes.

The room was shrouded in dusk. Outside, the black skies of night were gathering. Surely I could not have slept so long?

I scrambled from the bed and reached into my portmanteau for my travelling clock. In the glow of the firelight I examined its hands and was assured that I had slept well into the early evening. I felt a surge of guilt and went to the door and listened. I could hear no sounds from the rest of the castle. It was then my eye caught sight of a small door on the far side of my bedroom which stood ajar. It had escaped my notice that morning but now I saw it led into another room from whence came the glow of a lamp. Pushing it open I discovered a small dressing room filled with toilet requisites and, more importantly, there stood a steaming bath of water. I frowned for I was sure I had locked my bedroom door and there was no other means of ingress into this tiny chamber.

However, the panic of creating a bad impression with the Count drove all other thoughts from my mind and I had a hurried bath, my first real bath in months, for the cold pump at Schloss von Stoffel could hardly be called a bath. I dried myself and dressed quickly and arranged myself in such a manner as to present a pleasing prospect to the Count.

I had hardly finished making myself ready when I heard a soft knocking on the door. 'Who is it?' I called.

'The Count has sent me to bring you safely to him,' answered a strange male voice.

I opened the door and found a short, squat-looking man with a broad Slavic face, pale with lustreless eyes. He bowed low. 'I am Tirgsor, the major-domo of the castle. The Count awaits you in his library.'

My head full of apologies for the lateness of my rising, I followed the stocky figure of Tirgsor along the corridors and down the wide stairway into the main hall. Here he paused before two great oak panelled doors, knocked and then threw them open, calling something in Romanian. There, standing before a blazing fire, stood the tall, dark figure of the Count.

Some weird optical illusion made me pause and blink my eyes because, for the briefest moment, I thought I could see the roaring fire clearly through the body of the Count. I blinked and when I opened them again the Count had moved forward to greet me. 'Come in, *Fräulein*. You have rested well?'

I blushed a little in my shame. 'I fear that I have rested so well that I have over-slept. I must apologize for my discourtesy in not joining your family during the day.'

He laughed. 'It is of no consequence. We are late risers in this household. The dark mists of the approaching winter offer little encouragement to those who love the sunshine. But we prefer the evening gloom, the night's blackness to shroud our winter melancholy.'

He closed the library doors behind me after dismissing Tirgsor with a nod and a word and led me to a great wooden table which had been laid out with yet another sumptuous feast. 'Please be seated and eat. I and my family have already dined.'

I began to apologize again but he cut me short. 'Nonsense. Your journey yesterday was arduous. No blame can attach itself to you for obeying the law of Nature. All creatures need to rest when Nature tells them to. Nature is the supreme arbiter of our fate.'

He stood apart while I set to and tackled the dishes of cold meats, exotic cheeses and dishes of varying salads which were washed down with a delicious dry white wine. The Count noticed me savouring this wine and inclined his head towards the decanter.

'I compliment you on an excellent taste in wine, *Fräulein*. That is the best our little country has to offer. We have a long history of wine-making in Transylvania; our vines have been here since time immemorial and our soil conditions and climate create the best white wines anywhere in Europe. Yes, in white wines we excel, though our red wines tend to be soft and rather dull on the palate. They suffer from an over-sweetness. That wine you are now drinking is from the central plains of Transylvania, from the beautiful area of Tirbava where the vineyards slope down to the rivers from which they take their nourishment. Beautiful . . .' He sighed and closed his eyes.

'You are a connoisseur, Count?'

He smiled wistfully. 'When I was younger. The wine of the grape, alas, no longer agrees with my constitution. But come, if you are finished, draw up to the fire and we will talk. But first . . .'

He reached out and pulled a bellrope near the fireplace. Somewhere, a long, long way away, a bell jangled. After a moment or two, Tirgsor entered with a silver tray on which was a decanter and a large goblet.

'Allow me, *Fräulein*,' said the Count as Tirgsor withdrew, having placed the tray on a small table near the fire. The Count poured out a small measure and handed it to me. 'A Cognac, *Fräulein*; a brandy wine straight from the wood and about forty years old. Alas, I no longer have a taste for it and so it is reserved for the pleasure of my guests.'

It was sweet and relaxing, but I was not a guest in his house. I was merely an applicant for the position of governess. 'You have been very kind, Count,' I mumbled awkwardly. 'I am grateful for your kindness and hospitality.'

'The unfortunate need people who will be kind to them; the prosperous and strong need people to be kind to. You, I feel, have been unfortunate in life, *Fräulein*.'

I stared open-mouthed for I was a little taken aback by this directness.

The Count shrugged at the implied question in my face. 'I have lived a long time, *Fräulein*. In that while I have learnt to read people's faces and expressions as others might read a book.'

'You are right,' I said. 'My circumstances have indeed been unfortunate.'

'Then why not tell me your story? From the beginning.'

There seemed a warmth of encouragement in his voice. Perhaps it was that. Perhaps it was the relaxing spell of the meal and the wine. Perhaps it was his gentle questioning and sympathetic encouragement. But soon I found myself, almost as if I had no will in the matter, confessing all the intimate secrets of my unhappy childhood, my terrible experience at Doctor Smout's academy, my career as a governess, my *affaire de coeur* with Ernst von Stoffel and then, as if unable to help myself, I told him of the baby, my journey to Transylvania and my reception at the Schloss Stoffel. But even more – while part of my mind registered caution, to my astonishment I found myself confessing everything! Everything! Even to the death of Baron von Stoffel.

The Count sat back, his eyes half closed, his hands held before him, the fingertips pressed together with his chin almost resting upon them. 'Another glass of brandy wine, *Fräulein*,' he said. I was amazed that I had confessed so much to this stranger. What on earth had possessed me to make such an honest confession? What strange magnetism did this man possess that he could bring a confession of murder so easily to my lips? 'What now?' I whispered. 'Will you contact the authorities?'

The Count laughed, so that his sharp white teeth flashed in the fireglow. 'Authorities? Foreigners, you mean, who misrule this ancient country. No, no, *Fräulein*. I knew of this Heinrich von Stoffel. He was a jackal. He had not even the courage of a wolf but merely followed in the wake of the wolves to scavenge what they did not want. He was a foul leech fastened on the neck of my beautiful Transylvania, a leech who exploited my land and people and crushed them under foot without mercy. He was an evil man. I knew as much without your tragic tale to give me evidence. Mere death was too good a fate for such as he.' He paused and looked long into the fire. 'No, *Fräulein*, rest easy on this matter. Let me give you the sanctuary of my house for a while. Here, within the walls of my castle, no one dare touch you lest they be answerable to me.'

I leant forward eagerly in my chair. 'I accept your offer willingly, but do I not endanger you? After all, the authorities will be searching for me.'

'They can search but they will not find you here. Here you have asylum.'

'Then I may remain awhile as governess to your children?'

'My children?' For a moment he seemed surprised and then he smilingly shook his head. 'Ah, I had children once. They died, all of them. Mircea who betrayed me; Vlad and Mihail who were devoted – all dead.* No; these children are the children of my, er, cousin. You will meet them shortly.' There was a passing sadness across his broad countenance. 'Yes,' he continued, 'if you will teach

* See *Dracula Unborn*, Peter Tremayne.

these children the rudiments of an education, it would suit my purpose well.'

'Should I not tell you of my qualifications for the post?'

'You have already told me enough of your history. Qualifications are not as essential as personality. You will make an ideal governess. This, I feel. And as it is my wish that the children be given some tuition in the English tongue, no one is better qualified.'

'But,' I said, 'perhaps we should speak of routine?'

'Routine?'

'At what hours should I teach?'

'Ah,' the Count nodded. 'This is a most important point and in this matter you will have to adapt yourself to the eccentricities of the household. We have, over the years, grown used to some particular ways. We rise late, all of us, so that most of the day – especially during the hours of daylight – the time will be your own. At dusk we have our meal and knowing this will probably not suit you, I suggest that you dine as and when you like. After the evening meal, I suggest that you take the children for instruction. There are three children – the boy Radu, whom you have met; Vlad his brother; and their sister Tinka.'

Concealing my surprise I asked how old the children were. He frowned as if I had asked some absurd question and seemed at a momentary loss as to how to answer, which I attributed to an incomplete command of the German language.

'The boys are eight years of age and Tinka is ten.'

'It is merely to know what level of instruction they are at,' I explained.

'Oh, you will find them excellent pupils and perhaps more intelligent than most. Anyway, the routine will never vary. Two hours of instruction each evening after the evening meal. Apart from that you will have little contact with them.'

I decided it was time to make my point. 'You forewarned me that your routine is eccentric, Count, but surely this regime would be harmful to the children? Would it not be better to send them to bed early and get them up first thing in the morning so that their minds will be fresh and alert?'

For a moment an angry fire smouldered in the Count's eyes. '*Fräulein*,' he said coldly. 'We must understand each other better. The regime of my household is rigid and unalterable. Do not question it. Your routine will be as I have stated.'

I flushed and opened my mouth to retort but the Count, seeing the indignation forming in my face, suddenly smiled, disarming me. 'Forgive me, *Fräulein*. As absolute master in my home, I have grown used to issuing orders without them being questioned. You have a right to an explanation. Very well. The children have been ill – a sickness which, if it is to be contained and remedied, needs this routine to be carried out to the letter.'

I was puzzled. 'A sickness?'

'Have no fear. It is not serious if the precautions are observed. Daylight tires them and the cool air of the evening is more conducive to keeping the virus dormant.'

I confess that I had never heard of such a sickness but there was concern and sorrow in the Count's face and so I bowed my head in acquiescence. After all, I was grateful to obtain this position so who was I to question the eccentricities of the Count's household especially if they had been created by sickness?

'One other duty that I would ascribe to you, *Fräulein*,' observed the Count. 'I would like to perfect my knowledge of the English language, for it is my wish to go there some day when conditions permit it. So, each evening, perhaps you will have the courtesy to talk with me a while.'

It was a duty that I did not find disagreeable.

'So now, I shall introduce you to my household.'

I rose and, as if on cue, there came a movement outside the door. I looked up to see an elderly woman enter. She was dressed in a long white robe which was almost funereal in its design. She had a pale face, piercing black eyes and long snow white hair. She was almost as tall as the Count and carried herself with chin tilted in haughty disdain.

'I want to present Fräulein Morag MacLeod who is to be our new governess,' announced the Count.

As the old woman inclined her head a fraction in my direction, Count Dracula announced: 'This is the Countess Bathory, a distant relation of mine.'

'I am pleased to meet you, madam,' I said.

The old Countess peered at me coldly. 'She is not one of us,' she spoke to the Count. It sounded like an accusation.

'What matters?' snapped the Count. He suddenly resorted to a short speech in Romanian at the end of which the old woman nodded slowly.

There was a giggling and two young women, more like girls, entered. They seemed, to my eyes at least, strangely voluptuous and smiled constantly with sharp white teeth, leering like hungry cats. The image stayed with me a long time. They hurried towards me, arms outstretched. 'Welcome, welcome sister,' cried one of them and made as if to embrace me.

The Count's dark form came before me and the young women fell back. 'This is my guest!' the Count thundered in a strange tone.

I smiled towards the women but they now backed away sullenly.

'These are my cousins,' announced the Count, jerking a hand towards them. Then he turned to them. 'Where are the children?'

One of the women shrugged. 'I am not their keeper.'

'Get them!' snapped the Count.

I was a little surprised at the shortness of temper and positive rudeness which the Count displayed towards his relatives, but before I had time to reflect further one of the women did something which caused my eyes to widen. She had not left the room but merely raised her face upwards, closed her eyes and frowned in concentration. A moment passed before her face relaxed in a smile and she opened her eyes. 'The children come, lord.'

I think I shivered for the Count turned to me. 'We are a close family, *Fräulein*. Between us there has grown a close telepathy, our minds can sometimes unite. You have doubtless heard of this phenomenon.'

I nodded. 'They say it is a common occurrence among the Highland people of my country,' I said, 'but I have never encountered anyone who could perfect it to the extent of . . .'

Three children entered the room and stood gazing solemnly at me. One of them I recognized as Radu. The other was assuredly his twin brother, but not identical for while Radu was dark haired, Vlad was fair. The third child was older, and one of the prettiest young girls I had ever seen. This, of course, must be Tinka.

The Count came and stood by me. 'I have gathered you here to present Morag MacLeod who will be governess to the children. She will not only be governess but will be my guest. Her safety is therefore precious to me. No harm must befall her. No harm at all. Should aught happen to her, should she be missed, nothing is to be spared to find her and ensure her safety.' He turned to the elderly woman, his eyes holding hers for a lengthy period. 'Is this understood?' he asked.

The old Countess inclined her head.

'And you, and you?' He turned to the sullen women. 'Is this clear to you?'

'Yes, lord,' they said as one.

'And you, children?'

The little girl, Tinka, came forward and smiled up at me. It was a sweet, friendly smile and I found my heart captivated by her. 'Are we not to kiss her at all?' she asked in a plaintive tone.

I was just about to say that although I was governess I also wanted to be a friend to the children and, of course, they could kiss me, when the Count almost snarled the word: 'No!' I looked at him in surprise. 'I shall explain in full later, *Fräulein*,' he said to me. 'But, as I told you, the children have recently been ill with a virus, a virus which is highly contagious, particularly if a sufferer kisses someone not immune. I would not wish you to succumb to such an illness.'

He turned back to the children. 'Each one of you will swear that they will treat the *Fräulein* with honour, will obey my wishes and respect the *Fräulein*'s wishes in the matter of tuition.'

The three children repeated 'I swear' one after the other and looked so dejected that I felt sorrow for them. I was surprised by the Count's dramatic oath-taking but I made no observation on this rather eccentric behaviour. The Count was undoubtedly a kindly man, but in the matter of raising children he seemed sadly deficient. What he understood to be discipline bordered on tyranny and cruelty where a child was concerned.

'Remember,' insisted Count Dracula, as he dismissed his family, 'remember that her safety is precious to me. Woe betide any who transgresses my commands.'

As I returned to bed in the early hours, I decided that I must make every allowance for the odd behaviour of the Dracula family. I determined to do my utmost to fit into the family environment until I had earned sufficient to take me to London. My willingness to overlook each oddity of behaviour was largely due to the warmth and gratitude I felt for the Count's courtesy and sympathy towards my plight and his offer of the sanctuary of his castle.

CHAPTER ELEVEN

Though I tried to wake early the next day it was well past midday when I stirred and found the soft pale glow of the winter sun bathing my bedroom, creating an impression of warmth where it struck against the dark oak panelling. But the warmth was illusory and, as I found the fire dying in the hearth, I lost no time in jumping out of the bed, hauling on a dressing gown and setting to rebuild the fire. Within moments it was roaring heartily again.

I reached forward and tugged on the bell rope to announce that I was astir. I wandered into the tiny dressing room but there was no sign of the arrival of my bathwater. I waited some time fully expecting a servant to appear, even the dour-faced Tirgsor, but no one appeared. I listened and could not hear any sounds in the old castle. I strode back to the bell rope and sent forth several peals but none of them provoked the slightest response.

It was then I noticed, on a small sidetable near the door, a great silver tray laid, as on the previous day, with some breakfast dishes but, unlike the previous day, these were cold. On the tray was a note from the Count. 'Breakfast well. We do not stir until late in this household and thus we do not eat hot foods until the evening meal. Make free with the rooms of the house that you find open to you. Dracula.' I frowned; presumably this eccentricity of late rising also applied to the servants.

I grumbled silently as I splashed my face and arms in ice cold water and then completed my toilet and dressed. I sat down to my breakfast and found dishes of cold ham, with fresh bread followed by preserves and fruit. A jug of coffee was quickly heated on the hearth, and this did much to mollify my bad humour. I had fared far worse at Schloss Stoffel.

After breakfast I was at a loss to know what to do. If my duties did not start until the evening then I had several hours of leisure at my disposal. I went to the windows of my bedroom to see what I could of the surrounding landscape but, to my regret, this side of the castle merely opened on to the main courtyard and stood almost directly before a low arched wall in which the main gateway was situated. There was little to see except a cobbled courtyard.

I left the room and made my way along gloomy corridors, retracing my pathway to the head of the great stairway in the main hall. As I moved down the corridor, with no set purpose in mind other than to explore my surroundings, I tried the doors to my left and right but found them all locked and so presumed that they belonged to the other inhabitants of the castle and were their bedrooms.

In the main hallway of the castle I paused. An antiquarian would have been moved to joy in such a place for the hall was a veritable museum. There stood suits of armour and weaponry from every age. On either side of the door stood two iron cannons, culverins I think they are called, while along the walls hung shields and swords, javelins and ancient muskets. Everywhere was evidence of the Count's own family crest – the coat-of-arms showing the white dragon's head on a black background.

I spent a while in the hall wandering around these artefacts but, of course, they held but passing interest for me being weapons of war, of death and destruction. There were several oak panelled doors which faced into the hall but most of them were locked. Even the tall, iron-studded, wooden door into the courtyard was barred. The library in which I had eaten the previous night was open and a fire was still smouldering. I stirred it into life and replenished it with logs.

I then examined the library more thoroughly than I had been able to on the previous night. It was furnished with a superb collection of books from all parts of the world and in many languages. The Count would be possessed of a remarkable mind if he were able to digest all these works in their original tongues. There were volumes in ancient Greek, in Latin, Hebrew or Arabic; there were volumes in French, German, Spanish, Italian and even some in English; there were volumes in many other languages at whose origin I could not even begin to guess.

I came across a section of volumes that were entirely devoted to occult subjects, to astrology, to witchcraft, necromancy and alchemy. I found myself smiling at this strange taste in literature for I was sure, by the well-thumbed appearance of these volumes, that this was a special interest of the Count's.

One book in particular caught my eye for it was lying on a small sidetable, a piece of paper marking the spot on which there were some notations made. The book was a volume of poetry in German and I saw that it was a work of Goethe, a poet who it has been said founded German literature.

Peering closer I saw that the Count was trying to render the poem into his own language, for the notations, as far as I could tell, were in Romanian. One particular verse of the German text had been underlined several times and this was the verse that he was clearly trying to render. In German the verse read:

> From my grave to wander I am forced,
> Still to seek God's long severed link,
> Still to love the bride I have lost
> And the lifeblood of her heart to drink.

I shivered slightly as I read and wondered why the Count had picked so morbid a subject.

After some time wandering through the library I decided to explore further and returned to the main hall, pausing to listen whether any sounds denoted the household stirring yet. The silence was complete, heavy and omnipresent. Through the tall windows of the hall the sun was lowering itself behind the outer walls of the castle, casting shadows through the interior.

I tried the doors once more with the same lack of success but, in a corner, I came upon one smaller than the rest which opened to my inquisitive hand. Beyond the door was a small flight of circular stone steps leading upwards. I decided that this must be a way up to one of the castle towers from where I might view the surrounding countryside. So, without more ado, I started upwards.

I had not risen far when the steps ceased at another small door which gave access on to a very low corridor. At one end was a dust-begrimed window while at the farthest end was another flight of steps which spiralled downwards.

I paused at the top wondering what to do. Outside the castle I could discern, through the grimy window, that the sun had disappeared and, while it was not totally dark, the gloom was dense and great black shadows shrouded the castle. I looked around for some candle or other means of light but there were none. I turned and was about to retrace my steps back to the main hall when, from the black interior of the stair well, I swear I heard a soft laugh.

I paused and listened, and there came to my ears a soft whispering. At first I thought it was the wind but then I became positive that it was the whispering of some women. Perhaps the stairway led to a living room?

I began to move softly down those stairs, moving carefully for one false step would have precipitated me to the bottom. Carefully, slowly, I felt my way down until I could go no further and stood trying to accustom my eyes to the darkness. It seemed that some long corridor stretched before me into the blackness. But what made me catch my breath was the awful stench, a musty smell of new-turned earth, the smell of corruption, of putrefaction. I coughed as my lungs tried to adjust to those awful fumes. I would have turned back even then but, along the corridor, came a soft laugh – a laugh and then sibilant whispering.

Hands touching the wall on either side to guide me, I moved forward down the corridor. Gradually the blackness was dispelled by a faint light until I could see that the corridor opened into a great vaulted chamber which reminded me of a chapel. I paused wondering which way to go. Here the stench was really overpowering and I began to regret my reckless adventuring.

Suddenly, from the far side of the chamber, there came a peal of laughter; there was no mistaking it this time. It was soft yet vibrant and it echoed hollowly in that crypt.

'Who's there?' I asked. There was no answer but I could hear the soft swish of silk, as if someone moved. 'Who is it?' I called anxiously. Then the laughter came again and I swore I saw across the far side of the chamber, the movement of some figure in white. I moved forward hesitantly.

A soft, sibilant voice whispered: 'That's right. That's right, little sister. This way – this way.'

'Who is it?' I asked curiously. 'What game are you playing with me?'

With a scream of rusting metal and a crash like thunder, a tall door at the far end of the vaulted chamber was flung open and framed in its portal, holding aloft a lantern, stood the dark figure of the Count. I thought I heard a low cry of anger and the rustling of silken material as if someone had fled the place. The Count's face was turned upon me. 'What are you doing in this place, *Fräulein*?' His voice was sharp and demanding.

I replied with a nervous laugh. 'I seem to have lost my way.'

He stood back against the door and motioned me forward with one hand. 'Come.'

By the light of the lamp I moved across the vaulted room and out into a corridor. The Count pushed the door shut behind us.

When he turned to me his face showed anxiety mingled with anger. 'It is obvious that the *Fräulein* likes to explore,' he said heavily.

'I apologize if I have been where I should not have been.'

The Count pouted his thin lips. '*Fräulein*, you may go anywhere you wish in the castle except where the doors are locked, where of course you will not wish to go. There is a reason that all things are as they are, and did you see with my eyes and know with my knowledge, you would perhaps better understand. Remember, *Fräulein*, Transylvania is not your so beautiful country of Scotland. Our ways are not your ways and there are many things that will be strange to you.'

I replied that I understood this and would do my best not to trespass against the rules of his household again.

He stared at me for a moment and then nodded. 'Come then; your meal is ready . . .' He turned and started to lead the way along a corridor.

'Shall I commence the children's lessons tonight?' I asked, hurrying to keep up with his long paces.

'Tomorrow is time enough. Here time becomes almost meaningless and we do not hurry as they do in the world outside. Tonight I would talk with you. I would appreciate some instruction in English and to hear about your country, its history, topography and customs. I am a curious man, *Fräulein*. I thirst for knowledge, for knowledge is the very bread and wine of life to me. Sometimes I grow bored within the confines of this castle.'

'Perhaps travel is the answer?' I suggested.

He shook his head. 'Alas, travel also presents me with difficulties that one day I hope to surmount but, until then . . .' He fell silent and explained no more.

He led the way into the library where, as on the previous night, a meal was laid for me. This time I did not ask why he, or any of his family, did not join me. The Count removed himself to one corner of the library, apologizing that he had some papers to see to. The meal, as before, was an excellent one to which I did full justice.

When I had eaten my fill, the Count put aside his papers and joined me before the fire, pouring brandy and, again, excusing himself on the pretext that beverages before sleep seldom agreed with him.

As I sat there I found myself thinking that the Count was, in all respects, a highly attractive man. The nobility with whom I have been employed, both English and German, have had greatly overrated opinions of their own importance, and no concern for those of lesser station. But the Count was in every sense a gentleman, a man such as I had begun to believe did not exist. For, in spite of the obvious eccentricities of the man, he seemed deeply concerned with people; concerned and caring and I had every reason to thank my good fortune for bringing me to Castle Dracula. His old-world courtesy and charm made me feel like some princess in a fairy tale. In truth, I found stirring within me some affection for the Count. I appreciated him for his gentleness and concern, for his knowledge yet modest use of it, for his strength of command yet lack of an overbearing quality and for his quiet handsomeness. I bit my lip at the forwardness of my thoughts and caught myself from my reverie as I became aware of the Count speaking to me.

'I beg your pardon?' I said with some embarrassment. 'My mind seemed to wander for the moment.'

The Count laughed, 'It is a habit that I am well

acquainted with. I was only asking whether I may henceforth address you as Fräulein Morag? Mere *Fräulein* sounds too sharp and Fräulein MacLeod is too distant.' I gave my permission and the Count bowed gravely. 'I was wondering if you had been able to see much of our country?'

I shook my head. 'Schassburg and Klausenburg I saw briefly but that is all. My stay at Schloss Stoffel did not permit . . .'

The Count waved a dismissing hand. 'It would be wise to forget those unfortunate incidents at von Stoffel's castle. For your own sake it would not do to dwell on the unhappy side of life. A young lady as pretty as you should not dwell on such remembrances but look forward to the future, is it not so?'

'But I did take a life, albeit in self defence.'

'Have no regrets, and do not place yourself in the same role as you would in your own country. Here you are in a country that is under the heel of a foreign tyrant. It is his laws and his rules that you break and those rules and laws are enforced against the will of the people. Von Stoffel was one of a band of foreign tyrants, invaders who settled on confiscated land, confiscated from the Transylvanians that he murdered. Is it not a saying that those who live by the sword shall die by the sword? So, also, shall the murderer meet his end by murder. Is that not just?

'Should you, in remorse, surrender yourself to the authorities, you would have no sympathetic ear to listen to your plea. You would be tried by the kin of von Stoffel – the jackals and despoilers. And their day will come. Egypt, Persia, ancient Greece and Rome, the empire of Charlemagne, that of Sweden and that of Spain – they have all passed away. And soon, one day soon, the empire that is Austro-Hungarian must wither and decay. That is Nature's law. No empire lasts, no one nation can rule another for eternity.'

He paused and smiled, 'Forget your experiences, Fräulein Morag. Here you will be safe. You have my word on it.'

I began to thank the Count once more for all his kindness but he would have none of it and helped me to another glass of brandy.

'I am pleased, however, you were able to see a little of Schassburg – it is one of the gems of our country. In that town I first opened my eyes upon the world.'

'You were born there? Then you have not always lived in Castle Dracula?'

'Ah no. I have lived in many places though none so beautiful as Sighisoara.' He sighed. 'You must find this a strange country, Fräulein Morag? Perhaps full of strange people, eccentric people?' His white teeth flashed a sudden smile that was almost boyish and showed that he could, at times, make fun of his own eccentricities. 'Well, you are right. This is a strange country, especially here in the citadel of the Carpathians. We have a strange history and there is none more conscious of it than we boyars, the nobles of this land.'

'Is your family very old?' I asked.

'Sometimes I believe that we are as old as time itself,' replied the Count, but there was no false modesty nor pride in his voice. 'The legends of my house are innumerable. It is said that we Draculas settled this country when the inhabitants wore animal skins to cover their nakedness and hunted with crude implements of stone. It is said that the Draculas were prominent here long before these great mountain passes became the crossroads of civilization. From here we saw the Getae settle on the Wallachian plain, saw the coming of the Thracians, Scythians and Celts, saw the conquest of the Romans, of the Goths, the Huns and, from the Asiatic steppes, saw Attila come like a devouring fire to eat up Europe. We saw nation after nation pour through the Carpathians in unending streams and mingle their blood in the whirlpool that was to become Europe. We Draculas are a proud house owing allegiance to no one save ourselves.'

There was a quiet dignity in the manner he spoke, a dignity which impressed me far more than the boast of his lineage. While I sat there fascinated the Count warmed to his subject and as he spoke of the travails and turmoils that had beset his country, of the battles, of leaders and rulers and peoples, he spoke as if he had been present at each historical epoch, so vibrant was his voice, so clear his description. I sat enthralled as he spoke of the various invasions that his country had endured and of the long fight to gain freedom from the thralldom of the Turkish empire and from the yoke of the Habsburgs.

'Bah!' snorted the Count, thumping his fist into the palm of his hand. 'Today the warlike defence of my land is over. Blood is accounted too precious a thing in these days of dishonourable peace; and the glories that once were Transylvania are now tales that are told by old men beside some tavern's hearth.' He paused and again smiled his boyish smile. 'Forgive me, Fräulein Morag. You will think me too warlike and uncaring of spilling the blood of my people. On the contrary, blood is life. Blood is sacred to me. But man is a strange creature. Sometimes he must spill blood to remain free. It makes me suffer to see my people beneath the boot of a vile tyrant whose vaunted empire is run by so many clerks entering figures in financial ledgers far away in Vienna or Budapest. Empire is the spawn of finance. Transylvania must fight.'

I recalled what I had witnessed of the country, and what the Dutch doctor and old Bucar had told me of the politics of this corner of the world. I pointed out that I thought the Transylvanians were fighting in the only way they could and that there appeared to be many in the country who wanted Transylvania to join with Wallachia and Moldavia in the new Romanian state.

The Count complimented me on my knowledge, which I think impressed him a little. 'But my people chase illusions. True, I rejoice to see a Romanian state. True, I would like to see the old principalities united into one historic Romania, fulfilling its rightful role in the European community of nations. But what angers me is that the Romanians do not seek to implement the will of the people. A small band of clerks and businessmen invite a German princeling to become a monarch – a member of the household of their hereditary enemies! What stupidity could instigate such a thing?'

He laughed harshly. 'How the seeds of Attila and Arpad must be laughing. How the tribe of the Huns that swept into Europe from the Russian steppes must be sacrificing in joy to Thor and Woden! For what they failed to gain by their blood-thirsty conquest, their descendants have gained by other means.'

I failed to understand him.

'Reflect; reflect, dearest *Fräulein*,' he chuckled. 'Look at the great royal houses of Europe. Is there one that is not a German house? Are they not all the children of Attila and Arpad? Even the queen that sits on the throne of your beloved country, even the British queen herself – is she not German? Are the British monarchs not seeds of the house of Hanover and, in future generations, will they not be fortified by the seeds of the house of Saxe-Coburg? And when Greece became independent scarce forty years ago did not the same clerks and businessmen invite a Saxe-Coburg to sit on its throne? And did the Belgians not invite the Saxe-Coburg house to become monarchs of their country? Examine the monarchs of Europe and you will find they are but one big family sprung from the loins of Attila.

'And boyar though I be, noble that I am, I would rather that each country declared for a republic than let them rejoice in the worship of these children of the hordes that tried to destroy them.'

'Do you dislike the Germans so much?' I asked.

The Count had arisen and had been agitatedly pacing the rooms. He paused and shrugged. 'Forgive me; I do not hate the Germans. But I hate the German monarchy which has conquered Europe. But, I lecture. I have been alone too long to know the proper way to entertain ladies.' With this he took my hand and bowed low over it, his cold lips gently brushing it.

I replied that, on the contrary, I found his conversation most stimulating.

'One great lesson can be learnt from history, Fräulein Morag,' the Count said, 'and that is that people never learn from history. History becomes one great spiral, often repeating itself. People are all too often content to react for the moment, not to analyse, not to judge, not to see the way things are formed, the various processes by which a situation is arrived at. No; they are content to react, and action and reaction continue, and thus history repeats itself.'

The Count bowed again. He glanced towards the curtains where, following his suddenly anxious gaze, I saw a faint shaft of light hinting at the coming of the dawn. 'Forgive me,' he said penitently. 'Here is the morning once again. How remiss I am to let you stay up for so long. You must make your presence less appealing to my vanity, for I become so wrapped in my own ego that I do not notice how the time flies by.'

He lent me his arm and escorted me to the landing, at the entrance of the corridor which led to my room. Here he gave me a courtly bow and left.

It was with strange emotions that I went to bed in the early dawn light. I found that I experienced a feeling of regret when our conversation came to an end. I felt that I could sit and listen to the Count discourse for hours without any conscious feeling of time passing; listening to the Count speaking and watching the animated expressions chase themselves across that broad, handsome face of his. Yet, in spite of this, there were also contradictory feelings. Whenever he was near I found that I had begun to experience vague feelings of unease – perhaps it was unease at myself, at my own feelings? Why should this strange, rather eccentric nobleman have such an effect on me? I, who had come to regard all men as tyrants? Was it merely an over-reaction, after my terrifying experiences at Schloss Stoffel? Surely not? There must be something else.

CHAPTER TWELVE

It was difficult to adjust to the strange time-table kept in the castle, especially in teaching the children for two hours each night after the evening meal which I inevitably ate alone. This was actually a puzzling ritual because, in my attempts to fit in with the family, I staggered the times of my evening meals in order to join them at their own. But on no occasion did I do so. Each time I entered the library, the lethargic-looking major-domo, Tirgsor, would inform me that I must eat alone as the Count and his family had just eaten. I never saw the dining table laid other than for me and it crossed my mind with some amusement that perhaps the family never ate at all! Certainly I had no objections to the fare provided by the Count's kitchens; it was of the best and there was always wine and brandy to follow. I began to feel like a spoilt child.

Each evening, after the meal, I would go straight to the schoolroom. The previous governess must have had some strange notions. There were no brightly covered walls, no illustrations from childhood myth or fairy tales, no touch of colour nor gaiety anywhere. As a schoolroom it was a most sombre place indeed. The walls were furnished with pictures that dealt mostly with strange beasts, pictures of creatures that seemed half-man and half-wolf, of symbols that appeared to be some necromancer's nightmare.

I resolved to confront the Count on this matter, for surely no child should have his mind turned by such ominous surroundings. The Count smiled at my request to have more brightly coloured walls and for the removal of the more morbid objects and their replacement by fairy tale scenes. But he shook his head and was firm. 'I regret, Fräulein Morag, my intellect cannot allow such things as you propose. To educate children one must adopt an attitude of honesty with them.'

'But is it healthy that the children should be concerned with death?' I pressed. 'Surely, with the illustrations in the schoolroom, they need some lightness?'

'The illustrations are the children's own choice,' replied the Count. 'If you speak to them on this subject, *Fräulein*, you will see that they are merely passing through a phase where death intrigues them. I believe that they should come to know death and understand that it is natural to die as it is to be born. Unfortunately most people fear death, would prefer not to think of it merely because they are frightened. When you live as long as I have, *Fräulein*, you will find death a friend.'

I confess I smiled broadly as I looked into his face.

He seemed puzzled. 'You laugh?'

'I laugh,' I hastened to explain, 'because you sound as if you have lived a great age. Yet in spite of your white hairs I am sure that you cannot be much more than forty years of age.'

He pursed his lips and for a moment his eyes glazed. 'I was forty-five years in coming to this physical state,' he murmured. He then shook himself and gently dismissed me.

I must be completely honest and state that the children were highly intelligent and easy to teach. They had the sort of minds that, when they grew into adulthood, would soon overtake their humble teacher. They had a clear grasp of language and I need only explain a problem once and they understood it completely.

But intelligence apart, they were not as other children, although it is difficult for me to touch on the cause of that difference. Perhaps it was that their minds seemed too old compared with others of that age whom I have taught. Perhaps it was their lack of jollity, the skittish humours of children of that age. They all seemed so sombre and never once did I hear their voices raised in laughter.

Each time I presented myself in the schoolroom they would already be there, seated at their desks, hands folded patiently before them, their dark eyes staring solemnly from their pale faces.

Tinka, the eldest, was not given to playing with dolls, which I found a delightful change from the traditional female role. It is too often the case that the sexes are forced into their roles by parents' encouragement – dolls for girls and toy soldiers for boys. Fantasy should always play a large part in the development of a child. We learn morality and codes of behaviour by means of mythology, and this fantasy I found lacking in my charges. They never played games together, so far as I could see, nor ever created a play world which is natural to children.

One night, after the regular lessons, I asked Tinka: 'Don't you ever play?'

She regarded me gravely. 'Play?'

I smiled down at her frowning face. 'Don't you ever have games, play things like hide-and-go-seek?'

It was Vlad who answered. 'Why should we?'

I was somewhat shocked. 'But how do you enjoy yourselves?' I pressed.

'Enjoy?' repeated Vlad slowly. 'You mean, what do we do to extract pleasure from our existence?'

'I suppose I do,' I said, wondering how any eight year old could form such a philosophical expression.

'Our pleasure is in our existence,' said Tinka.

'I do not understand,' I said, perplexed.

'We exist, we gain nourishment to exist, we exist further. That is our pleasure,' replied Vlad.

'But surely something else gives you pleasure, enjoyment . . .' I began lamely.

'The other day, *Fräulein*,' said Vlad suddenly, 'you were speaking of a great poet of your country – Robert Burns.'

'That's right,' I said, pleased, in spite of myself, that he had remembered my passing remarks about the poet.

'I found a volume of his poems in the library,' went on the child, 'and I read them. In one of the poems he wrote:

> Pleasures are like poppies spread:
> You seize the flower, its bloom is shed.'

'I understand what he means. All pleasure is balanced by an equal degree of pain or languor. Is that not so, *Fräulein*?'

I marvelled and was at a loss for words to answer this phenomenal child.

It was Radu who interrupted my thoughts. 'But there is a game we like to play, *Fräulein*,' he said, a tone of excitement edging his voice.

I seized at the straw offered. 'Ah, and what is that?'

'Why not come and play with us now, now that the lessons are over?' went on Radu.

Now here was something that I understood. If I could get on a playing relationship with the children, it would also help me in my understanding of their minds and therefore how I would instruct them through their lessons in the future. 'I would love to come and play with you all.'

Tinka, however, shook her head. 'I don't think we should. *He* said we shouldn't.'

Radu said something harshly in Romanian and then turned back to me. 'Will you come and play with us?'

'Of course,' I smiled.

Radu and Vlad arose and each took me by the hands, their own hands were marble cold to the touch and I shivered involuntarily. They led me from the schoolroom with Tinka sullenly bringing up the rear. In solemn procession they led me down several long corridors and down a long flight of dusty steps.

'Where are we going?' I ventured to ask, noticing that thick dust and cobwebs hung in profusion around the place.

'Down to our special room, the room in which we play,' replied Radu.

Every child that I have known has a special playspot. Mine used to be a cave, more a hole really, set in a hillside in which I escaped from my cruel uncle and made into my fantasy home. For an adult to be willingly accepted into a child's special playspot shows how much the child trusts the adult in question. I was extremely pleased by this development. But I wondered at the gloom of their surroundings as they led me further down the stone stairway into what must surely be the vaults of the castle. It became cold and damp and the dust and cobwebs were so thick that, stirred by our progress, they hung heavy on the air irritating the throat and lungs.

'Do you really play down here?' I asked amazed.

'Of course,' replied Radu as he and Vlad conducted me through an iron door into a large chamber. It was pitch black and, at my insistence, the children stopped awhile for me to strike a match. 'There is a candle behind you,' observed Radu.

I laughed. 'You must have eyes like a lynx to see in this gloom,' I told him as I found the candle and lit it.

The spluttering candle cast little light in this dusty vault. Across to one side of the vast room I saw a small glimmering of light and made my way across to where a narrow slit opened through the wall. It was one of those slits used by archers in ancient times when they were defending the castle, a slit in the shape of a cross set in the wall. I peered through and to my surprise, found that we were not below the main castle but still some distance from the ground level for I was peering out on snow-covered fields which glowed with faint silvery luminosity in the light from the bright moon.

I turned back into the chamber and found that there were several more cross-shaped slits along the walls and, now my eyes adjusted to the light, I found that these cast a soft moonlight through the room.

'This was the armoury in olden days,' announced Tinka. 'The archers used to shoot from those positions by the slit windows.'

'And this is your special room, where you play?' Radu nodded. 'And what sort of games do you play?'

The boy looked at me and his mouth moved in a soft smile. 'We play kissing games, *Fräulein*,' he said softly.

I confess I was shocked. I thought maybe I had not heard the boy correctly. 'You play – what?'

'Dearest *Fräulein*,' the boy said sweetly, his eyes suddenly seeming to glow like coals in the reflected light of the candle, 'dearest *Fräulein*, we play kissing games.'

I bit my lip, unsure how to deal with this situation. Sexuality in children sometimes develops at a remarkable early age but surely . . .

'Do not be alarmed,' came the soft, purring voice of Tinka. 'We shall not hurt you. But you did so want to play with us.'

The softness of her voice held some other, indescribable, quality which caused me to shudder violently.

'Come, won't you let me kiss you?' said Radu softly. 'I would so love a kiss from your warm lips, *Fräulein*.'

The boy's eyes seemed to have grown enormous, they burnt with such intensity that I stared at them almost mesmerized by the dancing red light that shone directly into my own eyes. 'No!' I heard my unwilling voice. 'The Count . . . he told you . . . the virus . . . said you must not kiss . . .'

'Sweet *Fräulein*, dearest *Fräulein*, do not be alarmed. The virus is quite gone now. Now I want a kiss. Come, please; come to me . . .'

Part of my mind was clear and rational. I tried to

express my indignation but to my horror I found myself moving forward towards him, towards the glowing coals of his eyes. I saw his small red tongue darting over his lips, those rich ruby red lips. It seemed as if his teeth were longer, whiter, sharper. My conscious mind kept crying for me to stop this nonsense, yet I seemed compelled by some strange force to move forward towards the young child as he continued to whisper terms of endearment to me.

God knows how it would have ended, that awful childish game, but an extraordinary thing happened. It seemed so strange; so weird; I can only recount it as it appeared to me, yet there must surely be some logical explanation to it.

I mentioned before that the moon was full and bright and shone with a powerful silver light. As I was about three or four feet away from Radu, the moon – which must have been sheltered behind a cloud – suddenly broke through and its beam shone straight through the cross-shaped slit, projecting an image of a great silvery-white crucifix on to the chest of Radu.

The reaction to this was incredible. Even now I am not sure what happened exactly.

Radu glanced down at the shape of the cross against his chest and let out a piercing shriek of terror. Then, although I must have still been in a somnambulant state, it seemed to me that where the moonlight struck the boy, smoke was curling upward as if the light was causing the child's clothing to burn.

At that moment the door opened with a crash and there stood the Count. Even in my state I had the impression of his face working in great rage and his eyes blazing in anger. 'You have dared disobey me!' he thundered at the children. 'If she is harmed you will pay, you will pay dearly.'

Then he saw Radu and jerked a hand before his eyes as

if to screen out the sight. With one hand held before his eyes, he strode to my side and with his other arm scooped me from the floor. He turned and then lifted me into his powerful arms and strode out of the room without a backward glance at Radu.

In my hazy, half-wakening curiosity, I peered over the Count's shoulder. It must have been a trick of the light; some fantastic illusion. It seemed as if Radu had collapsed and miraculously disappeared for all I could see was a small bundle of clothes on the dust-laden floor, still lit by the moonlight cross. But there was no sign of Radu. Just the clothes. And the dust.

CHAPTER THIRTEEN

The Count strode up the cobweb-strewn staircase to the upper living rooms of the castle as I lay, still somewhat dazed, in his powerful arms. He set me down in a chair and poured a small glass of brandy from the decanter. 'Are you all right, Fräulein Morag?' he asked anxiously.

I nodded. 'I seem to have come over faint for some reason. What happened?'

'Did the children touch you?'

I shook my head.

The Count sighed with audible relief. 'I warned you, *Fräulein*, that the children have suffered from a virus which is contagious.'

He now turned to the door and I saw that Tinka and Vlad had followed us into the room and now stood in apprehension before the Count. 'I warned you!' he snapped at them. 'Did I not warn you?'

I recovered sufficiently to reach forward to lay a hand on his arm, for I read the fear in their faces as they looked at him. 'Yet no harm has been done. I am sure they will not disobey again. But what has happened to Radu? Was he taken ill?'

The Count gave a characteristic shrug. 'Yes, but do not worry, Fräulein Morag, I will go to see to his welfare. Remember what I say, and avoid close contact with these children. The virus can be fatal if contracted by a kiss but other than that the virus is not contagious. So have a care, *Fräulein*. Your welfare is precious to me.'

Before I could reply he had swept from the room, ushering the children before him. I frowned as I tried to recall what had happened in the old armoury room. Why had I been overtaken by a strange dizziness during that ridiculous children's game? What had happened to Radu?

A sudden swish of silks made me glance up. The old Countess Bathory stood in the shadow of the doorway. She gave me a long, hard look. 'Let me offer you some advice, *Fräulein*,' she whispered harshly. 'Leave Castle Dracula! Leave now before you regret it. There is nothing here for you except endless pain, suffering and eternal loneliness.' Then she turned on her heel and was gone leaving me greatly perplexed.

What strange household had I come to? Well, I had been in strange households before and, in spite of the eccentricities, Castle Dracula contained none of the nightmarish qualities of the Schloss Stoffel. Perhaps it was in the light of that experience that I was looking for drama where it did not exist. Yes, that was it. I fell then to reflecting about the Count for I had experienced a wanton thrill when he had told me 'Your welfare is precious to me'. The sensation bewildered me, I thought I detested men, I who had suffered so cruelly at the hands of male arrogance. Yet, in spite of this, in spite of my inner protestations, I felt a delight in the Count's attentions. I looked forward eagerly to our nocturnal conversations. Why? What was it that attracted me to this man of brooding loneliness and melancholy?

The Count did not return, and that night we did not have our usual conversation. I stayed in the library a while reading a rather fascinating work in English entitled *Transylvania: Its Products and Its People* by a Mr Charles Boner. The book explained much of the topography and also the strange folkloric beliefs of the country, some of which I found quite gruesome. When the Count had not returned by the early hours of the morning, I went to my room, somewhat disappointed, and retired to bed.

The next evening Radu did not turn up for his lessons with the others and I asked them whether the child was ill. Vlad said nothing and was quite sulky while Tinka merely said he had 'gone'. After the lesson I sought out the Count in his study and asked whether anything was wrong with the boy.

'It is the virus, *Fräulein*,' replied the Count gravely. 'His condition has worsened and he will be unable to attend lessons for a while.'

'Is there anything I can do?'

The Count shook his head. 'There is no need to concern yourself with his nursing, *Fräulein*. He is being well looked after.'

'May I visit him then?'

'No!' The Count's voice was harsh and I took an involuntary step backwards for it resounded in my ears like some physical blow. He saw my reaction and forced a smile of apology. 'I say it for your own sake, *Fräulein*. In his current condition the virus could spread.'

I tried to press the Count as to the nature of this strange virus. 'I know a little of medicine and may know something of its treatment,' I said.

His white teeth flashed briefly but he shook his head. 'I think not, *Fräulein*. But I thank you for your concern. It demonstrates that I am wrong to think the world is still only motivated by self-interest and greed. Your concern for the welfare of my family touches me deeply.'

'But the virus?' I pressed again.

'A rare blood disease, *Fräulein*, which is only manifest in these granite barriers of ours – the Carpathians – and therefore would be unknown to the outside world. Do not trouble yourself further on the matter.'

The next night and the next there was no sign of Radu and, each time I questioned Vlad and Tinka, they would shake their heads and say they knew nothing of their brother. On the fourth night, at the end of a long and most interesting discourse with the Count during which he had displayed an amazing knowledge of Byzantine art in its late period, I questioned him about Radu once again.

'Alas, *Fräulein*, you will not see Radu for a long while now. He has been despatched to some relatives who live further up in the mountains where the air is purer than the thick brooding mists which surround this castle.'

It came out so glibly that I had a passing feeling that the Count was lying for some reason but, unable to think of a justification for such a thought, I dismissed it from my mind. Our conversation almost immediately turned back to art.

The next day I rose at twelve noon, which was early for me. Ever since my arrival at the castle, due to my work and the long fascinating talks with the Count, often lasting until sun-up, it seemed that I never went to bed much before dawn. Then, in a state of exhaustion, I usually slept all day until dusk. I tried to point out to the Count the unhealthiness of this regime but he insisted that it was essential to the children's wellbeing due to the strange virus.

Why I woke at midday on this morning, I do not know. I lay in my bed blinking in the bright rays of sunlight which flooded into my room and realized that I had not seen the sun for several days. It stirred the blood within me and lightened my heart. I rose and went to the window, opened it and looked out. It was then I caught the sound of a wailing, a sobbing lamentation, whose tones of utter despair caused my blood to run cold. Peering down into the cobbled courtyard I tried to place the direction of the sound. 'Who's there?' I cried, English coming readily to my tongue.

The cries of lamentation suddenly ceased. There came a scuffling sound and the figure of a middle-aged peasant woman came into view around a corner. She was colourfully dressed, as all Transylvanian peasants seem to be. But her hair was wild and unkempt and her face red and tear-stained. In one hand she held out the most beautiful carved crucifix that I had ever seen.

On seeing me at the window, she gave a scream, fell to her knees on the cobbles, crossed herself and raised the crucifix towards me. Then she broke into a weird wailing, a dreadful crying sound that horrified me. 'What on earth is the matter, woman?' I cried.

A torrent of strange words rushed from her mouth. I picked up some of them but they made no sense to me. Some of them she repeated clearly over and over again. *Strigoi* ... *pricolici* ... and *halak* were among them. 'Wait!' I cried in German. 'Do you understand this language? What is it you want? What is the matter?' I wondered that her lamentations had not aroused the whole castle by now.

The woman paused in her tirade and looked at me, obviously trying to find words. 'Monster!' she suddenly screamed in German. 'Witch! Return my child! My child! What have you done with my child!'

She suddenly went off again into a screeching tirade of her own tongue, shaking her fist towards me, and it took no linguist to understand that she was condemning me with every curse her tongue could utter.

'I know nothing of your child, good woman,' I tried to pierce through her wailing. 'Is your child lost?'

'Lost?' she repeated the word and then paused a moment before shaking her fist at me. 'Aye, lost! Fiend, monster, witch! You have caused it to lose its immortal soul. My child! Return my child!'

I supposed the woman to be demented for she continued to kneel on the ground, sobbing and wailing, cursing and shaking her fist and giving way to all the violences of extravagant emotion.

Then came a sound which caused my blood to run cold. It was a pitiless howl of a hound taking the scent. I cried a warning to the woman but so intent was she on her curses that she did not hear. The next moment I saw a pack of hounds, hounds as large as any wolf, pouring into the cobbled yard, their huge jaws agape. The woman now heard them, too. She turned and uttered one shrill shriek before going down beneath their tearing jaws.

I screamed also. I turned and ran from my room, raising my voice to rouse the household. But only silence met my cries; a strange, eerie silence as if the castle were empty of all humankind.

In despair, I seized a great javelin from the wall, where it hung above some shield, and raced into the main hall, sobbing in my exertions to throw back the bolts. I had no thought of myself but of that poor, wretched woman, being savaged to death by those terrible beasts. Even as I swung open the doors I could hear their savage, triumphant snarling.

But when I recklessly ran forward into the courtyard, javelin held to defend myself, there was no sign of the woman nor of the pack of hounds. I halted, bewildered. All was utterly still as if I had imagined the entire affair. I walked forward cautiously to the spot on which I had seen the woman kneeling but a moment before. The only sound I could hear was the faint breeze blowing through the trees of a nearby forest. Could it be that I had witnessed some amazing hallucination? Perplexed beyond reason, I turned back to the castle and as I did so my eye caught sight of something on the ground, something that caused the bile to swim into my throat and me to retch there and then.

It was a severed human hand surrounded by a little pool of blood.

I spent an anxious moment looking to see if there were any more remains of the wretched woman but there were none and neither was there any sign of the hounds. Sick and faint, though in control of myself, I returned to the castle and pushed shut the great door behind me.

What amazed me in all this savage turmoil was that no one was apparently stirring within the castle. Of the servants, of Tirgsor, of the Count and his relations, there was no sign or movement. I cried aloud once, twice, thrice, but no one answered my calls. A curiosity overcame me and I started to wander along the corridors examining each room I found open. Most of the rooms I entered were not only empty but incredibly laden with dust as if they had stood thus for centuries. Many were entirely empty, save for rotting floorboards and crumbling draperies at the windows, whereas others contained furniture of sorts but in various stages of decay. The library, the schoolroom and my own bedchamber were the only rooms that I could discover that were properly furnished and clean. I tried to explore further but the other doors were barred against me.

I returned to my room with my mind in a whirl and helped myself to a large glass of plum brandy, hoping it would aid my reason in finding some logical explanation to my situation. Where was the Count? Where was Tirgsor, the taciturn major-domo of the castle? Where was the old Countess or the young females I had encountered on my first night? And where were the children? A thousand questions milled in the whirlpool of my mind until I threw my hands to my temples in despair.

I could not believe that a woman had been torn to pieces while I had been hurrying to her aid. Nor could I accept that the castle was deserted and that most of the rooms had not seen a living soul in centuries! What strange mystery was there here? What should I do? Where should I turn?

CHAPTER FOURTEEN

I must have fallen asleep exhausted by the mystery because a knocking on my door awoke me. My room was shrouded in darkness. 'Who is it?' I cried, struggling up and lighting the lamp by my bedside.

The door opened and Tirgsor surveyed me with a bland expression on his Slavic features. 'My master requests your presence, *Fräulein*,' he said in his heavily accented German.

'I'll come now,' I said, determined to get to the bottom of the terrifying events of the day. I bent to the mirror on my dressing table and straightened my hair. I had just finished this operation when I caught sight of the open door behind me. Tirgsor had vanished. I frowned because it was unlike the dour major-domo not to wait and accompany me to the Count's library. I spent a moment or two more at the mirror and then turned. The gasp escaped me before I could control it. Tirgsor was standing waiting in the doorway. He eyed me impassively. 'Is there something wrong, *Fräulein*?' he asked.

I paused a moment to allow my heart to slow to a regular beat. 'You startled me, Tirgsor,' I confessed. 'I thought you had gone on.'

The major-domo looked at me disdainfully and said nothing.

I cursed myself for a fool. It is ridiculous what imagination will do. Having had this terrifying experience that day I was beginning to let my mind run amok with all sorts of fanciful notions.

I swear that Tirgsor had not been reflected in the mirror, but presumably he had merely moved out of the range for a moment. What a child I was becoming.

Nevertheless, it was curiosity which made me ask Tirgsor whether he had been disturbed that afternoon.

'*Fräulein?*' he inquired politely.

'What I mean is, did you get woken by any disturbance outside the castle?'

The major-domo shook his head. '*Fräulein,*' he said gravely, and I swear I saw the hint of a smile play at his mouth for the first time, 'when I rest the lamentations of the dead would not raise me.'

He paused before the library door and held it open for me. The Count rose from his high-backed chair as I entered. 'Ah, Fräulein Morag,' he came forward and bowed over my hand. 'I trust this evening finds you well?' He gave me a searching look and I swear he knew that something was amiss already.

I allowed him to conduct me to a chair. 'Were you disturbed at all while you slept today?' I asked pointedly.

He waved a hand in the air, a vague gesture. 'To be truthful, my sleep was somewhat fretful. I thought I heard sounds of some disturbance but it is very hard to awaken me. I trust you were not disturbed?'

With a sudden rush of words, I told the Count all that I had witnessed from my bedchamber window, of the horrible manner in which that wretched woman had met her death. The Count seemed struck by concern mingled with anger. 'Alas,' he cried, 'my pack of hunting hounds must have got loose from their kennels. Thanks be that you were not harmed by them.'

'But the peasant woman . . .' I began.

'Ah, her,' nodded the Count. 'Peasants – they should have more sense than to wander the countryside unprotected.'

I stared at his callousness.

'Forgive me, *Fräulein,*' he was at once contrite at my expression. 'You have a soft heart, a gentle heart. Here in the Carpathians we live in a cruel world. We become –

how do you say – brutalized by continuing human disaster. Death is no stranger to us, nor the violence of death.'

'But shouldn't someone be notified – the police or the authorities, so that the woman's family can be informed?' I cried aghast.

'Ah, the police,' echoed the Count, a suspicion of a twinkle in his eyes. 'We are not respectful of the police in this land as you know to your advantage.'

I felt my cheeks crimson for I knew what he meant. 'But . . .'

He held up a hand. 'Nevertheless, the unfortunate's relatives shall be notified.'

He tugged the bell rope and remained silent until Tirgsor entered. 'There has been a disaster,' the Count announced. 'A peasant woman was wandering in the castle grounds and has been killed by our pack of hounds. They must have broken out of the kennels. Unfortunately, the *Fräulein* was a witness to the distressing incident. See to it that the hounds are rounded up and safely returned to the kennels. Then try to retrieve the unfortunate woman's remains. Lastly, the *Fräulein* is anxious that the woman's family be notified. See to it that the local captain of police is acquainted with the facts and efforts made to inform the relatives of the sad occurrence. Also, as the hounds were mine, see to it that adequate compensation is offered.'

Tirgsor's face did not change expression. 'It shall be done even as you instruct,' he murmured and left the room.

The Count turned back to me with a smile. 'Was that satisfactory, *Fräulein*?'

I nodded, feeling a little foolish. 'But,' I insisted, 'what could have made the woman so demented? Why should she accuse me of taking her child?'

'Fräulein Morag,' interrupted the Count. 'You ask the impossible. Who knows what was in the mind of the poor

593

unfortunate? Why did she venture from her home and come to this inhospitable countryside? What turned her mind? It is surely a fruitless exercise to seek reason from unreason. I suggest that you try to forget this sad and terrible occurrence. We have done all we can to alleviate the distress this has caused and that must surely end the affair.'

But I refused to be swayed from my purpose. 'There is another thing,' I said, stubbornly. 'The noise of the woman's lamentation aroused no one in the castle save myself. And when the hounds attacked the woman I cried aloud for help and no one came.' The Count made to speak but I continued. 'Afterwards – after it was all over – I returned to the castle and tried to discover why no one answered my calls for help. I searched the castle . . .'

The Count's head jerked up and he glared fiercely at me, anger suddenly flashing in his eyes. 'You searched?' There was a threatening note in his voice.

'Many of the doors were locked but others I opened and discovered rooms in all manner of decay. Only the rooms which I use, this room and the schoolroom, showed any signs of occupancy. I thought at first I might be alone in the castle. I searched the rooms because I wanted help for that poor woman.'

The baleful look in the Count's eye was fading. 'You think you have discovered some great mystery, is it not so, Fräulein Morag?' he smiled. 'The answer is more mundane than your imagination tells you. The answer also accounts for the fact that no one else was disturbed during the unfortunate incident. Castle Dracula, *Fräulein*, is a very ancient castle, a big, rambling edifice, in which a person could become lost unless they knew the way through its rambling corridors.' He waved his hand to encompass his surroundings. 'These rooms are situated in one wing of the castle which we have made especially hospitable for you and for the teaching of the children.

There are so many rooms in the castle, and we are such a small household, that it is impossible to maintain them all. You will appreciate the logic of this?'

I did, though unwillingly. 'Yes, I can see that it would be impossible to maintain every room in a building of this size with such a small staff. But why couldn't you hear my calls or the disturbance outside?'

'The rooms which we, my family, occupy, are in the furthermost recesses of the castle, *Fräulein*. Through these thick stone walls we can hear little of the outside world. So your mystery is no mystery at all. But I deeply regret that you should have been so alarmed. I should, perhaps, have informed you of the arrangements from the beginning and also warned you about the possible consequences of wandering through the castle on your own?'

'Consequences?' I queried apprehensively.

'In future it will be best if all the rooms, saving those now known to you, are locked for your own safety. Keep to the rooms that are open and let me offer you a word of warning. Should you by chance find yourself in another part of the castle, have a care that you return to these rooms before the twilight hour, and before you are overcome by sleep. No, no,' he went on, seeing my expression. 'I do not mean to be dramatic. But, in seriousness, this is an old castle, a castle which has witnessed much bloodshed and terror. There are many ancient memories which linger in its cobwebbed corners, many bad dreams for those who sleep unwisely and who are sensitive to atmosphere. Keep to these chambers for here you have my word that you will be safe.'

'I will certainly do as you advise, Count Dracula,' I replied, not understanding why he was so serious. 'I certainly have no wish to trespass into the private chambers of your castle.'

He smiled. 'Then we are in agreement. But come, you have not dined yet. We will pardon the children from the rigours of their lessons this evening. You will dine and tell me more of your intriguing country. It borders on to England, is that not correct? I knew an Englishman once, Welsford was his name. We parted bad friends, he and I. Yet it is my hope to meet him again one day for we have a debt to be balanced.'*

The Count ushered me to the dining table and rang for Tirgsor to bring in the meal. I looked expectantly at the Count but he shook his head. 'You will excuse me,' he said. 'I have dined early. But feel at your ease. I will sit here and entertain you with some reminiscences about my poor country.'

I confess I was in little mood to eat in view of the day's events but I forced myself to pick at the food which Tirgsor brought. While I ate the Count talked, and I noticed that this evening he talked with rapidity as if nervous, using his hands to emphasize the various points.

He began to talk first of his love for the countryside, of his pride in being a boyar, the pride in his family's history which, he claimed, was older than any European monarchy. He mentioned, to my surprise, that his family had once been the ruling princes of Wallachia, the principality which lay south of Transylvania and is now part of the Romanian state. Soon I had forgotten the events of the day and became mesmerized by his anecdotes and tales of his family and their history.

He made so many references to the ancient origins of his family that, at one point when he seemed to pause for breath, I asked: 'What are the origins of your family? What does Dracula mean?'

'Some say it means the Devil's spawn,' he replied with a smile. 'Some say it means "son of the Devil". Others, more correctly, say it means "son of the Dragon". There is a legend in my family that we originated in the Egypt

* See *The Revenge of Dracula* by Peter Tremayne.

of the Pharaohs. Many thousands of years ago, long before the advent of the Christian God, the people of ancient Egypt worshipped the god Draco, the fire-breathing dragon of the great deep, the creator of all life. There came a time when this god fell out of favour and was persecuted, as all gods are eventually. Those of his followers who remained faithful fled before the four winds.

'It is said that the family of the hereditary high priests of Draco settled within the protection of the Carpathian mountains and survived, taking the name Draco as their family name in honour of the god whom they did not forsake. The name has remained as Dracula.'

There was a curious light in his eyes and, I confess, I was held spellbound as he continued, making two thousand years of history seem like only yesterday.

'Fräulein Morag,' the Count suddenly leant forward and took my hand, 'ever since my first talk with you I have judged you sympathetic. I have known many women but in you I see a friend and equal. Perhaps the first and only one who may come close to understanding the great purpose of my existence.'

I sat dumbstruck by this sudden familiarity.

'Dear *Fräulein*,' he continued unperturbed at my expression, 'allow me to show you something which few people have been allowed to see. Even those of my household are forbidden to behold it.'

I confess to a nervousness as he drew me from my seat and, taking a candelabra in one hand, preceded me from the room. I followed his tall, black-suited figure bewildered by his sudden intimacy. We passed along a corridor until he came to a small door which he unlocked and ushered me through. This led into other corridors like a maze, and then down a small stairway to a small iron door.

Here he paused and smiled at me softly. 'It is ten years or more since I last came here. There is hardly anyone to whom I have shown this room; to no one outside my kin and even few of those. You, I believe, will appreciate that which I am about to reveal. You will understand.'

He took a great iron key and turned it, protesting, in the rusty lock. With a rasp of metal on metal, he drew back the door and stepped inside, motioning me to follow.

I looked around the room, now lit by the flickering light from the candelabra which he held aloft. I could not suppress a gasp of startled wonder. It was the most amazing, most puzzling room that I have ever beheld.

CHAPTER FIFTEEN

The room had been furnished to resemble a temple of ancient times. Like other chambers I had seen, it was vaulted with many arches and gave the impression of the crypt of some church. But black drapes hung from walls that were decorated with the most curious symbols that I have ever seen. At the far end of the room there stood an altar-like table, also covered in black on which stood a carving of a large dragon which grinned in a most hideous fashion. It was the very same symbol which I had seen adorning the coach of the Count and which appeared to be his family's crest. Also along the walls were benches on which reposed piles of ancient manuscripts and books in a variety of languages which I did not know but which, from their appearance, I guessed to be quite ancient.

'What is this place?' I asked in wonder.

The Count stood to one side, watching my reactions with a slight smile. 'This, Fräulein Morag, is a whim on my part, my pleasure, my what shall I call it? – my indulgence.'

'I don't understand.'

'As I told you, my family claims descent from the high priests of the temples of ancient Egypt – from the temples of the god Draco, symbol of the all-powerful Nature and creator of all life forms. From Draco we took our name. This room has been made sacred to him.'

I stared amazed. 'You hold a room sacred to a *pagan* cult?' I said, a little awed, for the 'fire and brimstone' of the Kirk of Scotland had conditioned me to view such matters askance.

'Cult?' The Count moved forward and set his candelabra on the altar. 'Perhaps, but it was a cult of true science, one which sought to find answers to the mysteries of Nature and one which spread across the world – to India, Mongolia, Tibet, China as well as south through Africa.

'The ancient priests of Draco knew far more than the so-called scientists and holy men of this day and age. The cult of Draco evolved from a great concentration of knowledge, a knowledge of carefully observed physical phenomena extending over enormous cycles of time. By such observation the high priests of the religion knew that life after death was a natural fact long before the Druids of northern Europe influenced Pythagoras the Greek to evolve his doctrine of immortality. The followers of Draco came to the conclusion that it was not only possible to free the spirit of man for the next world but to free both spirit and physical body in this one, to make the earthly body immortal.'

As the Count spoke I wandered around the room examining the artefacts gathered there, strange carvings, each repeating the dragon motif, ancient statues, manuscripts by the score. It was obvious that the study of this ancient cult and the connection of his family with it was a subject dear to the Count's heart.

'You have kept this room as a sort of museum to your ancestors?'

'Not just to them,' nodded the Count, 'but to a scientific cult that I respect. Remember, the cult of Draco was not a religion, it was a science. It was not a mere primitive recognition of a higher and unseen controlling power, not a blind worship of a god nor the obedience of a specific code of morality enforced by the priesthood. It was a realization that, if man willed, he could control the powerful forces of Nature which were symbolized by a fire-breathing beast from the great depths. Did we not all have our genesis in fire and will we not be destroyed by fire?'

'When did this cult flourish?' I asked, intrigued by the Count's intensity.

'Three thousand years ago before the birth of the Christian god.'

'And you keep this room as a reminder of the belief of your ancestors, of the continuity of their thought and endeavour?'

'Yes, Fräulein Morag,' he paused, 'but also because I too believe in the science of Draco.'

'*You believe?*' I was surprised.

He regarded me thoughtfully a moment. 'Do you ever meditate on immortality, *Fräulein?*' he suddenly asked.

I reflected. 'I suppose all human beings do. Yes, I probably share what is common to everyone – fear of old age and death; a regret that our span of life is so short.'

'Ah, you do not share the Christian belief of life after death, the belief in a beautiful heaven – crystal-clear streams, green meadowland, golden-haired, white-robed angels with their harps? These images, which doubtless arise from Nordic conceit, have no appeal to you? No Elysian Fields, no Valhalla, no Tir na nòg?'

I laughed. 'I suppose I would like to believe. But I do not, in spite of a church upbringing. I suppose I reject the church of my childhood along with the cruel uncle and his family, along with all the other influences of my unhappy childhood.' I was surprised that I could talk so freely about my past. 'Yes,' I continued, 'I believe that when we have achieved our mortal span there is an end to it; an end to our intellect, our hopes, dreams and fears. No, I do not believe in the life after death, only in the sense that we are all part of Nature and that Nature is immortal, we come from Nature and we return to Nature.'

The Count nodded slowly and seated himself on a bench. 'Your thoughts are quite profound, *Fräulein.*'

I smiled at his compliment. 'In truth, I have not thought greatly on the subject. All I know is what I observe with my own eyes. I know that the Christian doctrine has little appeal for me. Perhaps I am really a follower of Nature? It is only fear that makes men invent religions to explain away what they do not understand. Yes, if I must follow a godhead, I would follow Nature. Nature is all-powerful and often mysterious. Over the years we have wrested many of her secrets from her grasp in our search to answer the mysteries which surround us. Many things we have attributed to the will of the gods have proved to be the will of Nature.'

I warmed to my subject. I had never been able to speak of these things before because of the prejudice of those in my environment. But the Count was different. He could understand.

'I believe it is because of man's fears that he started to invent his gods in bygone ages. Because he could not understand Nature, he had to invent Supernature, attributing the inexplicable to the will and force of mystic beings and gods. And man's fear of accepting how unimportant his species really was in this great universe has made him devise all kinds of philosophies, especially the philosophy of immortality. Man cannot, in any time or culture, accept that he will die and that is an end to him. So he must believe, he *does* believe, that he will live forever. But I also believe that the borders of our minds are ever shifting and extending and widening. Perhaps one day a great deal which we, at present, fear because we do not understand it, will be revealed to us. We are still like children grasping in a darkened room for means to light it.'

My speech, which even surprised myself, had a profound effect on the Count who leant forward and took my hand in both of his and raised it to his lips. '*Fräulein*, I have been too long closeted in this vile castle. I did not know that there existed a mind outside these portals whose broadness could encompass such philosophical conceptions.'

I blushed at the admiration in his voice. 'There must be many who feel as I do,' I admonished.

He shook his head vigorously. 'There used to be in the days when mankind recognized Nature as a great force. But religion has stunted their growth and their intellect. The will to shake off the petty restrictions of fearful moralizers and seek out science, to grasp the truth of Nature once more, has been sapped over the centuries. To even state the thought is considered a great blasphemy.'

He sat back and looked reflectively around the temple room. 'Let me ask you this, Fräulein Morag – do you really feel that man, unrestricted by the confines of his fear, which he has consolidated into religious taboos, can reach out his hands and grasp the secrets of Nature without fear and guilt?'

I pouted. 'In theory he can. But all men and women are restricted by religious morality, and moral philosophy differs from religion to religion. What is right for one may be wrong for another. Though, of course, there is a central code of morality which seems to spring out of the core of man's genius, a code of reason and understanding. But the world and its societies have bathed in religious fears for thousands of years, years of fear of punishment by some omnipotent godhead. That is why I say "in theory" for what man or woman can stand up today and say he is entirely free from his environmental development, free from the culture in which he was raised?'

The Count sighed. 'A reasoned answer. But let us allow there was such a person – free of all religious and cultural restrictions – do you believe that there might be no limits to the secrets that Nature would offer him if he had the mind to grasp them?'

'I don't understand.'

The Count seemed to be suppressing a growing excitement. 'Nature contains many things that are wonderful and miraculous, is it not so? Already man has started to make attempts to journey under the sea . . .'

'*Under* the sea?' I was astonished.

'Yes, yes,' the Count said hurriedly. 'As long ago as 1614 a ship called a submarine was constructed and sailed in the Thames river in England. But, don't you see, soon man will learn the secret of bird flight, grasp things considered impossible, supernatural even. That being so, do you not think that Nature can offer man the secret of immortality as well?'

I smiled. 'I agree that science is making rapid strides but immortality? No, I do not think so. I think our preoccupation with immortality is merely our fear of accepting the law of Nature, that death is as inevitable as birth. We fear the "nothingness" of death. We fear returning to the blackness from which we have sprung. We fear the forgetfulness of our life and its experiences, its loves, its hopes. We cannot, with our finite minds, encompass the infinite. So we hope, we cling to the belief that when we die we continue to exist, somewhere, in some form. Even as I say it now, I hope – in my heart of hearts – that I am wrong and that I will live forever after death.'

Count Dracula shook his head vigorously. 'No, Fräulein Morag. I speak not of hopes nor of vague yearnings created by man's fears. What I say is this – do you think it possible that a man, a man skilled in the sciences and relentless in pursuit of the secrets of Nature, could find the secret of life from Nature and, by using it against the moral condemnation of his fellows, seize it, use it and perpetuate his own earthly existence?'

I began to see his point. I nodded my head towards the carved figure of the dragon god, Draco. 'You mean in the way the ancient Egyptians believed? Immortality as a *natural* fact of existence, once Nature's secret was discovered?'

'Precisely so.'

'Put that way, it is scientifically possible. We have already conquered many of Nature's secrets. Yes, it is possible but not probable.'

'But you would not fear such a discovery?' pressed the Count.

'Fear? No, I don't think so. Such a discovery would be a great milestone on man's road to a real understanding of himself and his universe.'

'But it would not make you fear to meet someone who has lived for hundreds of years?'

I laughed. 'It is hardly likely that I would. And by the time man could make such an achievement the fears and prejudices of society will have altered so that the question of that particular emotion will not arise.'

The Count looked pleased. 'Fräulein Morag, in you I have found someone with whom I can speak, with whom I can unburden the secrets of my thoughts. I, who have been twice married and twice widowed, have never thought to find a woman in whom beauty and intellect walk hand in hand. Perhaps it is male prejudice. But you honour my house with your presence.'

I blushed at this speech and felt ridiculously pleased by the Count's declaration. Again the question flashed in my mind as to why I should feel such a wanton attraction to this strange brooding man.

'Fräulein Morag,' he continued, 'I have studied science, alchemy, the laws of nature and theosophy for many years. What would you say if I declared that the secret of immortality has already been found and proven?'

For a moment I did not realize what he meant. I stared hard at him. 'Why . . .' I found my voice after a short while, 'I would be surprised, very surprised indeed.'

The Count laughed uproariously. It was the first time that I had heard a genuine pleasure in his voice. 'You are possessed of a sense of humour, Fräulein Morag. In truth, also, you say that you would not fear the revelation of the secret, you would not be revolted by it nor raise your hands in horror and denounce it as a creation of the Devil?'

My mind raced. 'Nothing that is natural can be considered a creation of the Devil,' I replied, hesitantly, wondering what game he was playing with me. 'But surely you are not suggesting that you believe that someone has really achieved . . .'

'Not only do I believe it,' interrupted the Count, 'but . . .'

'My lord!' the voice of Tirgsor was raised in alarm. He was standing at the entrance of the temple room.

The Count turned with a snarl disfiguring his lips. His change of temper was so sudden that I started. 'Do you not know that this place is forbidden to you?'

Tirgsor blinked but did not retreat before the Count's apparent fury. 'My lord,' there was a slight tinge of terror to his voice. 'Do you not know the time? The sun is already on the rim of the eastern mountains.'

To my surprise the Count sprang up with a startled exclamation. 'Get you gone then!' he snapped to Tirgsor. He turned and bowed over my hand. 'Forgive me, Fräulein Morag. Please forgive me. Time is sometimes an enemy, especially when one has such enjoyable company. Today the sun governs my actions. I have to leave you immediately. I will not return to the castle before sunset. Perhaps then we may continue our discussion.' Then he whirled around, eyes staring in dismay at the soft grey morning light that was filtering through the castle into the very vault. He had turned and fled before my gaze.

I sat bemused for a while, pondering on the strange room, before returning to my own bedchamber. My mind was in a turmoil of conflicting thoughts as I prepared for bed. What I found strange was that in spite of my experiences with men, in spite of my unhappy life, I found it easy to open my heart to the Count. Yes, in spite of myself, I found the Count growing in my affections. His mind puzzled me and attracted me; his wide range of knowledge, his reasoning, his intellect, his courtly and manly attitude towards me. Yet, at the same time I also felt that there was something awesome about him, something that made me uneasy, something mysterious which, in a less rational person than myself, could be found frightening. Something was not quite natural in the eccentric habits of the inhabitants of Castle Dracula.

CHAPTER SIXTEEN

I awoke with the firm resolve that I would pass no more late nights in conversation with the Count. While I enjoyed the conversations immensely I realized that I should be more concerned with my duties as governess. The eccentric lifestyle of the household was not one that I, in charge of the teaching of the children, could really adhere to. The family never seemed to stir between sunrise and sunset. What sort of troglodyte existence was this? I had already observed how strangely pale the children were, indeed how strangely pale the Count and his cousins were. It was surely a result of being subjected to this existence and I determined that I would speak to the Count strongly on the subject next time we conversed together.

The sun was high in the sky and I observed that a cold breakfast had already been laid in my room and that a kettle of water had been simmering on the hearth for my morning wash. I breakfasted hurriedly for, I reasoned, it was high time that I went for a walk around the castle grounds and enjoyed what sun I could.

It was already late in the day and the sun was one of those pale gold, almost white wintry suns that shone with little warmth but with a fierce intensity of light. I wrapped up warmly in a heavy coat and scarf and set out from the castle gates. Castle Dracula lies in a horseshoe valley, away from the main valley called the Borgo Pass which cuts through the towering snow-peaked Carpathian mountains. The valley is quite wide, rising to a little knoll on which the gaunt grey towers of the castle push skywards, each tower being topped by a cone-shaped black roof. The castle itself is very large. I do not doubt that three hundred men could hide themselves in the vast building and remain undiscovered. The Count's household was certainly a small one and I realized fully how a disturbance at one side of the building could fail to raise a response from anyone elsewhere in the castle. Thankfully the Count's hound pack had been returned to their kennels and were now secure, otherwise I would not have ventured out.

Alongside the castle there runs a fairly broad river which, to the north of the castle, meanders along the walls and makes an effective moat. It was probably from this river that the castle drew its water supply although I am not sure. I could observe, having learnt of such matters from poor Ernst, that the castle must have originally been built as a guard post on the Borgo Pass. The garrison, in olden times, could sally out, down the valley and into the Pass, cutting off any invading force entering from either direction.

From the castle gateway I made my way over a broad, wooden beamed bridge which spanned the river. The temperatures both during the night and day must have been considerably below freezing for the river, broad as it was, was frozen over and the ice looked thick enough to skate on.

I continued on my way across the crunching snow and entered a great wood of spruce which stood like a regiment of great snow-capped giants. I smiled with delight and decided to explore. It was with a light heart that I crunched along enjoying the winter beauty of that marvellous forest, without thinking of the passage of time nor of the distance I travelled. After a while I was aware that I must have walked a considerable way into the woods and I sat down on a nearby log to rest a moment before retracing my footsteps back to the castle. It was then I became aware of a sighing all around me, of the wind whispering urgently through the tall trees.

Looking up through a gap in the great canopy of the forest I could see great thick clouds, edged with black, drifting rapidly across the sky at a great height. The brightness of the day was going and I began to realize that it must be near the onset of twilight. I had been out longer than I had anticipated.

The snow began to fall softly at first and then with more urgency, flurrying its way even through the protecting branches of the trees. I rose and began to trudge rapidly backwards on my path, my eyes following my footprints. But, after a short while, the prints disappeared under the fresh fall of snow and, I confess I grew a little panic-stricken. But I realized that sooner or later I must reach the forest's edge and would then be able to get my bearings for my return to the castle.

In the distance there broke upon my ears a strange eerie wailing. I halted, perplexed. The wailing rose to a shrill climax and then died away on the wind. It took me several moments before I realized that I was listening to the distant howling of a wolf. What a stupid fool I was not to remember that in this desolate country there still roamed great wolf packs, and here was I gaily marching out from the protection of the castle alone and unarmed. And now, with dusk falling, I was lost in the forest.

I cursed myself for being all kinds of simpleton and recalled the Count's condemnation of the peasant woman who had walked abroad without protection. Overcome with fright, I started to run, stumbling into clawing bushes, through thorns, pushing against the whipping branches of trees, stumbling, falling, rising and running onward. This panic lasted only for a few moments until I halted for want of breath and stood gasping heavily in the thin cold air.

I became aware that I was in a small clearing, a clearing which still had a heavy canopy of branches sheltering it so that the snow had barely carpeted the ground. My ears became aware of an eerie stillness and in that deep silence – a silence in which it seemed Nature herself had ceased to breathe – I felt awed.

I examined the clearing carefully and saw what seemed to be a small building on the further side of the clearing. The earth had been raised up into an embankment into which had been set an ornately carved stone portal. I walked towards it and saw that the pillars were of marble, intricately worked into figurines that at first glance seemed to be cherubims and seraphims. However, when I peered closer it seemed as if the stonemason had executed some weird and tasteless joke for these cherubs had grotesque faces, leering with twisted lips and oddly long teeth.

Set squarely in the centre of this structure was a thick wooden door, studded with iron. The door had a small grille and an ornate iron handle, and across the top was set a metal plaque. Intrigued, in spite of my nervousness at the place and its surroundings, I raised my hand to brush away the dirt so that I could read the words more clearly. The language was German and I could see that it was some ancient form or, perhaps, the rolling south Saxon of those who had settled the area centuries ago.

Here Rests He That Was
Mihail Radu
of
The House of Dracula
sought but not found dead

At the time I thought it was a strangely archaic way of expressing the belief in life after death.

So this was the crypt of the Dracula family?

I do not know what it was, some ghoulish instinct perhaps, but I found myself testing the iron handle of the door. Finding that it swung open easily to my touch, I moved forward and peered into the gloomy interior of that strange sepulchre.

In my handbag I had a box of matches and I took these out and struck one, holding it before my face. I cannot explain the odd compelling instinct that made me actually enter the tomb, yet I moved a pace or two into it as if my will were not my own. In the small interior stood a central bier. The lid had been taken off and cast to one side and, scrawled on one side of the plinth, were some words in illiterate German.

My match went out with a splutter and I bent down to light another. It took me some moments to decipher the sense of the scrawl. 'Drive him quickly to his grave – for the dead travel fast!'

I paused in surprise. What sort of person would come and desecrate a grave in this fashion? I rose up, striking a third match and found my eyes forced by some unseen and unheard command towards the open coffin. My breath caught in my throat as I looked at the skeleton that lay there.

A huge wooden stake was embedded through the jumble of smashed ribs into the base of the coffin. Out of the grinning mouth of the skeleton hung a small rusty crucifix while the skull lay unnaturally, the vertebra smashed around the neck as if the head had been struck from the body.

The compulsion moved me still. It seemed as if a voice was whispering deep within my brain, urging me, cajoling me, imploring me. The voice seemed to want me to reach forward and remove the crucifix and drop it to the ground. I did so, finding myself unable to disobey. Now the voice urged me to take the wooden stake and remove it. I leant forward, both hands unwillingly clasping the stake and started to move it.

Perhaps it was a trick of the light, it must have been, but the skeleton began to take on what I can only describe as an *animated* aspect.

At that moment a sudden gust of wind blew shut the door of the sepulchre, shutting me in a complete darkness. I gave an involuntary scream, its sound breaking the strange mesmeristic spell. I let go of the stake, stepped back and felt a panic surge within me. I fled from that place, out into the clearing and then away, stumbling once more through the thick snow that carpeted the floor of the forest.

After a while, I paused to recover my breath. I shook my head feeling a little ashamed of my behaviour. What was there to be afraid of in the place of the dead? The dead were dead and the living were the only ones to fear. Yet what on earth had possessed the person who had desecrated that tomb to perform such an act of blasphemy? They must have driven a wooden stake through the heart of the corpse, cut off the head and placed a crucifix in its mouth. It was horrible! Perhaps it was some strange peasant form of witchcraft. I wondered whether I should mention the matter to the Count. As Mihail Radu was probably one of his ancestors he might be sensitive on the subject.

Anyway, there had certainly been no need for me to fly in panic like some silly schoolgirl.

In spite of the years of our Christian veneer we, as a people – the Irish, Scots, Manx, the Welsh, Bretons and Cornish – have never wholly lost our psychic sensitivity; we have never wholly rejected the cosmic terrors of the Old Religion which are depicted so clearly in our mythology, our fairy tales and folklore.

Twilight hung like a shroud over the forest now. I became aware of the wolves howling again; there seemed several of them, their voices raised in unholy chorus. I looked skywards and realized that dusk was lowering fast and, the supernatural apart, I had cause for concern as to my physical welfare. I began to walk rapidly through the forest, trying hard to ignore the incessant howling that seemed to grow nearer and nearer. At one point I stopped and picked up a length of a branch which I thought might make a suitable weapon. It was, at least, better than nothing at all.

My heart beat faster as I came abruptly to the edge of the woods and found myself, thankfully, not more than a mile away from the tall black shadows of Castle Dracula. I could just discern its tall snow-covered spires in the gloom.

I was about three quarters of a mile towards it when a chorus of yelping and snarling made me halt and look backwards. Emerging from the wood, close to my trail, was a host of long grey shapes which slunk through the snow towards me. They espied me and suddenly began to give voice; a sound that almost froze me where I stood. But I turned and hurried forward, running as swiftly as I dared.

I was almost in tears and gasping wildly for breath as I neared the frozen river. The huge snow banks seemed to have slowed down the speed of the pursuing beasts, but even so I knew that I would not have enough time to run the hundred yards along the river bank and across the bridge. There was only one thing to do. I must chance the thickness of the ice and cross the river itself.

But even as I resolved this, I knew my time had run out for the wolves were at my very heels. With a cry of despair I raced forward but my foot caught in a shrub and I sprawled on my face upon the river bank just as the leader of the wolf pack reached me.

I lay petrified as I watched his foam-flecked hackles, the sharp yellowing teeth and tiny bloodshot eyes set in his great grey head, loom close. The beast stood over me, saliva dripping from his panting red tongue. Then the others came bounding up and formed a semi-circle behind him. The beast astride me raised his head towards the blackening sky and a low rumble came from deep within his throat, growing louder and louder until that awful plaintive cry stirred the evening air with terror.

Then, suddenly, a sharp cry of command cut through the evening air. The great beast looked up with his tiny bloodshot eyes and stared in the direction of the river. I turned my head and saw, on the far side of the frozen river, a tall figure in black, a long black cloak flapping around it like the wings of some monstrous creature.

The harsh voice came again, and to my utter amazement the wolf leader dropped its great grey head and let out a whimper. It backed away from me and suddenly sat on its haunches. The other wolves followed the example of their leader and all sat like obedient dogs looking towards the tall black figure on the far side of the river.

I raised myself slowly on one elbow. 'Fräulein Morag, are you all right? Have you been hurt?' The voice was clearly that of Count Dracula. In a dream I nodded. 'Then raise yourself slowly, *Fräulein*, and come towards me.'

I looked curiously at the wolf pack, wondering with what strange powers of command the Count could control such beasts as if they were pet dogs. I climbed slowly to my feet, half expecting the savage beasts to spring at my throat. But again the harsh cry came from the Count and, whimpering like curs, the entire pack abruptly rose and loped off towards the forest.

Believing that they would return any moment I started hurriedly forward across the ice crust of the river.

'No, Fräulein Morag! Go by the bridge!' There was an urgency in the Count's voice. 'The ice is too thin. The beasts will not attack you now. They are my creatures.'

However, my fears of the wolves blinded me to all else and I ignored his plea and hurried forward. By the bank the ice was thick but as I ventured near the centre of the river I realized the extent of my foolhardiness as the ice rapidly thinned. I paused and was about to turn back when there came a sudden cracking like a volley of pistol shots. Great cracks appeared in all directions and I was precipitated into the cold waters. I gave a wild cry for help and scrabbled for a hold, trying to resist the dragging current of the black waters which threatened to draw me under the ice to inevitable death.

The black-cloaked figure of the Count stood on the river bank and even from that distance I could see the horror register on his pale face. He made to cross the ice towards me but, even as his foot touched the ice near the bank, he yanked it back as if it had touched red hot fire. He stood wringing his hands and moving up and down in agitation. Suddenly he stretched up his clenched fists to the sky, threw back his head and cried in a loud and angry voice: 'A curse! A curse on the fate that so confines my earthly movements!'

As I felt my strength giving out and my hands slipping from their freezing hold, I saw him run to a tall tree, a young sapling that grew close by the river bank. Never had I seen a man possessed by such demonic strength, for the Count grasped the sapling in his mighty hands and, with a great cry of exertion, he pushed it down, tearing it from the ground, roots and all. Then he dragged it to the bank and pushed it out across the ice until it was within grasp of my hands.

'Can you reach it, Fräulein Morag?' he called anxiously. 'Can you pull yourself upwards?'

I reached out and grabbed at the branches. Slowly, hand over hand, I dragged my frozen body upwards, out of the black swirling water, and along the trunk towards the bank.

After what seemed an age, I reached the bank, shivering and sick, and as I felt Count Dracula's strong hands pull me to the safety of the river bank, I swooned.

CHAPTER SEVENTEEN

I suppose it was only a few moments before I recovered my senses and found the Count carrying me – as if I were a baby – towards the castle. For a moment I lay passively in his arms watching his strong, aquiline and handsome face from lowered lids. The face was etched with concern and, lying there against his broad chest, I felt a curious feeling of comfort, of security, which – in my fatherless life – I had never experienced before; not even with Ernst.

I stirred at last and opened my eyes.

The Count looked down and smiled. 'How do you feel?'

I shuddered, aware of the intense chill of the river. 'I am cold,' I said feebly.

He strode swiftly through the corridors of the castle, brushing aside the sullen-faced Tirgsor. 'Fetch hot water to the *Fräulein*'s room,' he snapped.

Tirgsor looked blankly for a moment at the Count and then at me. 'Very well, lord,' he growled as he departed on his errand.

At the door leading to my room the gaunt figure of the old Countess barred our progress. When she saw me in the Count's arms, a strange smile cracked across her pale parchment skin. 'The girl?' the old woman's voice almost chortled in delight. 'Have you . . .? Is she . . .?'

The Count waved her from his path with an angry jerk of his head. 'No!' his voice cut like a whiplash. 'She fell into the river.'

The Countess' face dropped, as if this news somehow disappointed her. But I had no time to dwell on it for the Count swept me into my room and laid me gently on the bed.

'I regret,' he bowed uncomfortably, 'that there are no maid servants at present in the castle to attend you. Tirgsor will fetch water for your bath which I suggest you take immediately to offset the chill of the river. I will have food brought directly to you.' There was a deferential knock and Tirgsor entered with a tray on which was a bottle and a single glass. 'Ah, excellent!' exclaimed the Count. 'A glass of *slivovitz* will help mend matters.'

'I have prepared the water for the *Fräulein*'s bath,' announced Tirgsor.

'See to it then,' snapped the Count. He poured a drink and handed it to me. I raised myself and sipped gently at the warming liquid while Tirgsor made several trips to my dressing room with scalding buckets of hot water.

'How do you feel now?' inquired the Count.

'Much better,' I sighed. Then, reflecting on matters, 'You saved my life. How can I thank you?'

The Count shrugged in embarrassment. 'I did what I could, Morag . . . er Fräulein Morag,' he said.

Some impulse made me reach forward and clasp his hand. It was ice cold, like mine. 'I would be happy if you would call me Morag, although it is a difficult name to pronounce.'

The Count shook his head.

'I do not find it so,' he insisted. 'And if I could presume upon your friendship, my name is Vlad. It is so long, so very long since anyone called me by that name. Yet I would be happy if you would do so.'

There was something almost pathetic about the way he made his request, something boyish and shy. I think it was then that I realized that I was falling in love with this grim, sometimes awesome Transylvanian nobleman. I could not tell you exactly why. Perhaps he represented strength, firm resolve, security, comfort, a courtesy which I had never really enjoyed from the men in my unhappy life. Perhaps it was these factors; perhaps, in some strange way, he represented the father that I had never had.

I felt a surge of tenderness towards the man and, without thinking, I took his strong, firm hand in both of mine and squeezed it tightly. 'I would be honoured to call you Vlad and be counted among your friends.'

He looked down at me, a smile quivering on his lips, and then he gave a sigh and patted my hands. 'Ah, Morag, Morag,' he said. 'You are my only friend; how delightful it is to have someone with whom I can talk as an equal, someone whose intellect I respect; someone who does not want to feed on me nor I on them. You do not know how lonely I have been throughout the years.' He paused. 'One day I hope to confide in you all of my unhappy existence.'

'Unhappy?' I asked, surprised. 'But you are your own master. If you are unhappy here, why not go away?'

'Away? Perhaps. I do not know. Maybe one day I shall find the means to leave this spot. But I am not yet fully my own master for men can still dictate to me. There are always limitations and boundaries.'

I had a sensation of intense melancholy and I suppose it was that which caused me to shiver. But the Count looked down at me and became profuse in his apologies. 'How unthoughtful of me, how discourteous. You are still in your wet clothes. Forgive me. I will retire. Have your hot bath and eat well. I will come and see you by and by. Perhaps, if you are not too distressed by your experiences, we will talk further.'

He withdrew leaving me with a multitude of new and curious emotions. Yet, on the whole, my emotions were happy ones and it was with a light heart that I stripped off my sopping wet clothes and went into the dressing room where the hot tub of water was waiting me.

I spent half-an-hour at my toilet and with the aid of the warming water, the blood was soon surging through my limbs again. It had a soporific effect and I was yawning when I made my way back into my bedroom. My wet clothes had been removed in my absence and a small table had been laid before the roaring fire with a repast fit for a queen. In spite of my tiredness, I ate heartily and just managed to make my way to my bed before my eyes closed and I fell into a long, deep sleep.

Afterwards I realized it was a dream. It must have been. I awoke, or seemed to awake, hearing the crackle of the blazing fire in the hearth of my bedroom. The flickering flames were the only form of light in the now darkened room. I lay warm and comfortable in my bed knowing that something had prompted me into wakefulness and yet not knowing exactly what.

Then came the sound of laughter, a throaty, voluptuous feminine laugh. I tried to move my head and found, to my puzzlement, that I could not. My whole body felt warm, comfortable, but sluggish and not responding to my commands. I lay in a stupor, my senses aware of my surroundings through some hazy mist, yet remaining incapable of movement or speech.

Then I had an awareness that I was not alone in my bedchamber. At the bottom of the bed, lit by the bright white rays of the moon which shone in through my uncurtained window, stood two young women – the young women I saw when I first arrived at the castle. They stood looking at me and smiling. My brain commanded my body to rise but it would not. I had only seen them once, once on my first day in the castle, when the Count had introduced me to his family. I could see now how like the Count they were, more like sisters than cousins. They were dark, with high aquiline noses like the Count, and great piercing dark eyes that seemed to glow unnaturally red in the fireglow. As they smiled down at me I saw their brilliant white teeth set against the redness of the voluptuous lips.

There was something about them that conjured up the fear in my heart and yet at the same time I felt a wicked burning desire, an unnatural desire, that they would come and kiss me, caress my throat, with those red lips of theirs.

One of them pushed back her head and laughed, the deep, throaty laugh of the wanton. 'She is young and strong. We may feast a little.'

The other looked at me with an odd yearning in her face. 'But *he* has forbidden it.'

'He forbids everything that would give us pleasure,' returned the first, scornfully. 'What is he that we must obey him?'

'He is our lord,' responded the second girl.

'Our lord?' sneered the first. 'He created us, that is true, but that does not make him our lord. Since he created us in his own image, we owe him nothing. He owes us existence and pleasure. He must provide it. What is there left for him to do to us? Nothing. Why fear him?'

The second girl shuddered.

'But I do fear him. Aye, and rightly so.'

The first laughed mockingly. 'Then fear him if you must, but I do not. Tonight I will have my meat and my drink!'

She advanced slowly along the side of the bed until I could feel the gentle warmth of her breath upon my cheek. Then I felt that intolerable pain of desire again. I swear the skin of my neck tingled for the touch of those soft red lips, the darting tongue, the bitter-sweet caress of her mouth.

'Why should he have her all to himself? Why must he feast of the best and leave us nothing but the blood of peasant's offspring?' the first girl was demanding without taking her dark glowing eyes from me. She bent towards me, arching her neck, her mouth opening and a sharp red tongue lapping at those brilliant white teeth of hers, licking her lips like some animal before its meal. I closed my eyes in a languorous ecstasy and lay back waiting, waiting for that bitter-sweet caress, feeling her hot breath on my neck, and the gentle touch of those soft cold lips. The desire grew within me making my heart beat wildly. Now! Now! I almost wept for the desire that surged through my body.

A harsh voice cracked me into reality. 'Dare you touch her? Dare you touch her when you know I have forbidden her to you?'

The first girl sprang back like an animal at bay; sprang back from the bed to turn in a crouching position towards the speaker. The second girl let out a whimper and started back towards the window. The first girl now let out a deep-throated snarl. For a moment I thought I was hearing the snarl of the wolf-pack on my heels once again. 'What right have you to tell us what we cannot do?'

A figure strode into the glow of the firelight. It was the Count. Never could I imagine that handsome, saturnine faced man in such a light as I then saw him. His eyes glowed like the fires of hell, the mouth was twisted in passion. 'Right? You speak to me of right?'

'You created us,' cried the girl, defiantly. 'Your duty is to provide for us. What right have you to keep her from us?'

'She is mine. Hear me? I have forbidden you to harm her. Defy me and you shall feel the weight of my punishment.'

'But three days have gone by since last we feasted,' cried the second girl by the window in a plaintive wail.

'You shall feast again,' cried the Count. 'I have brought you sustenance. Go to the vaults below and there you may feast.'

Then, in this strange dream of mine, the girl by the window seemed to dissolve into a shimmering haze which faded into the moonlight and disappeared completely.

The first girl, still crouching defensively, was defiant. 'Why should she not join us? Why do you wish to protect her?'

The tall figure of the Count threw out an arm in an impatient gesture. 'You question me, *me*? Begone, vile slut!'

'You call me a vile slut!' shrieked the girl suddenly. 'Once I was young. Once I was beautiful. I strode in the gentle sunshine, was adored by young men, loved art, beauty, music and food. Yet look what you have reduced me to?'

'Have I not given you the world?' replied the Count.

'Aye, that you have. You have given me a world of eternal night; a world of shadows, a world that exists forever and forever. Do you expect gratitude?'

'No. I expect obedience.' Then the Count strode across the room and in one great powerful hand he seized the defiant girl by her long, slender neck and hurled her with savage violence to the floor. 'Begone, slut! Begone, I say!'

The girl thudded to the floor with a cry of pain and rage. Then she was up, hands claw-like, reaching for the Count, her eyes glowing an unholy red, her teeth gnashing horribly until the blood ran down her chin. The Count turned upon her and grabbed her hair, forcing back her head until the neck was exposed. Then, dear God, the terror of that nightmare! I saw his thin-lipped red mouth open, saw the flash of bright white teeth, and the Count suddenly bit deeply into her white neck, as a wolf might take its prey. For a while the two struggled before my horrified gaze; struggled this way and that like animals locked in ferocious combat. Then the girl fell away and lay motionless on the floor.

The Count stood looking down at her. There was no pity, no emotion at all, in that broad, handsome face of his.

Finally, the girl sighed and stirred. 'Go now!' snapped the Count. 'Go to your feast before your sister denies you your share.'

The girl rose, rubbing gently at her neck with one

hand. There was a languorous smile upon her lips as she looked at the Count.

'Yes, lord,' she said softly. 'Yet if only you could love. But you have never loved.'

'Go!' cried the Count. Then, like her sister, the girl seemed to dissolve into some silver sparkle which hung, mist-like in the room for a while before vanishing in the light of a moonbeam. For some moments the Count stood looking at the spot and then he shook his head. 'Never loved? Ah yes, I have loved. It was a surfeit of love that brought me to such misery.' He turned and came to my bedside. 'I still love, although I thought the centuries had destroyed such feelings forever.'

He gazed down upon me with his face now composed to its former handsome self, the savage beast gone and in its place the pathetic, helpless look of a little boy lost. Even in that moment my heart went out to him. Yet in this weird dream I still could not move.

He bent forward and I felt his gentle hand under my chin, moving my head this way and that, examining my neck. 'No harm is done,' he said as if to himself. 'They would rue the day if any harm came to you.' Then he lowered his face to my forehead and I felt his cold lips brush my brow.

'Sleep on. Sleep on now. Soon you will return to a natural sleep, a deep, deep refreshing sleep. And when you wake, my love, you will remember nothing of this save as some elusive, half-forgotten nightmare. Rest well, my love. Sleep well.'

CHAPTER EIGHTEEN

The next morning found me tired and melancholy. I could recall parts of the strange dream of the night before but it seemed so fragmentary as to be illogical and I tried to force it out of my head. But the fragments, the incidents, kept returning to my mind, and in a depression, I spent the whole day dozing fretfully until the evening when I bathed and dressed and went to the library where, as usual, my solitary meal was laid.

Without doubt I now felt that there was something strange, something sinister, about Castle Dracula. Eccentric habits were one thing but I experienced an odd feeling, almost of dread, as I reflected on the events which had occurred since my arrival. Yet that sinister oppression vanished when I thought of Vlad Dracula. Even his name caused my blood to quicken and bring a gentle hue to my cheeks.

The door opened, and the Count stood on the threshold. 'Did you sleep well?' he asked, as he strode into the room and stood smiling at my side.

I shook my head. 'I had such strange dreams ... Vlad.' I said his name a trifle breathlessly after a short pause.

'Ah, my poor Morag, I fear you have suffered the consequence of your adventure. You must swear to me that you will never journey far from this castle again, not at a time when sunset is approaching. Within the castle, under my protection, you will remain safe.'

'You need have no fear that I will venture far again,' I averred. 'I will never forget those fearful wolves.' I suppressed a shudder.

'Well,' he said, his voice adopting a boyish tone, 'enough of such melancholy. Rather let us speak of that which is within our hearts.'

And, indeed, we did. I told him more of my life, my experiences, my hopes and ambitions. He clicked his tongue in sympathy and here and there offered comments and analysed events and characters in my story to such an extent that I began to see people in a new light, yes – even my own father and mother. With them I could now sympathize and mourn as I had never done before. Vlad Dracula's gentle probing and comments caused me to increase my admiration of his perception and intellect and made me even more a willing victim to his charismatic charm.

I asked him about his own life.

'I will confess I have known many women,' he said, causing me to blush at his directness. 'In truth, though, Morag, not one of them did I respect as I now respect you.'

'But you mentioned that you were once married?' I said, trying to lighten the import of his words.

'I have been married twice, but both of them are dead. The first wife died of a wasting sickness, the second ran away with her lover. She went to Italy where she, too, died eventually.'

'Were there children?'

He nodded. 'Two fine sons by my first wife – Vlad and Mihail. They gave their lives in my defence. In the Carpathians one finds many enemies and once, when my enemies converged to bring about my destruction, Vlad and Mihail sacrificed their lives for me.'

'But you mentioned another son, a son who betrayed you.'

'The son of my second wife, a young man raised in Rome as an Italian fop and popinjay; he betrayed me. Not understanding, and being fearful, he tried to deliver me into the hands of my enemies. But it was such a long, long time ago.'*

'But you are not old!' I asserted. 'It cannot have been so long ago.'

There was a long silence and then he sighed. 'One day, Morag, when you have achieved a full understanding of my life I will tell you more. I thought, during the long years of my loneliness here, that all feeling in me had died. But that is not so, Morag. From the day you came to Castle Dracula, there has stirred within me feelings of attraction and then, later, affection. Would it be an insult to you if I were to admit a feeling deeper than friendship . . . of love?'

My heart beat wildly and I leant forward. 'Vlad, your words echo my very own thoughts.'

He stared at me in surprise. 'Can it be true?' he asked.

I felt like a wanton; all my upbringing and my prejudices were abandoned. I only knew that I had to be honest with this man – and with myself – and bare my very soul to him and freely admit of the fierce emotion that stirred within me.

He reached forward and thoughtfully tugged at his lower lip. 'There is much you must know. For a long while I have composed myself to think that I had no feelings. Now such feelings awake within me and stir more fiercely than I have ever known. Yet what would I have to offer to you – a young, normal woman of sunlight? Can these feelings be possible?'

He stared long and hard at me. His eyes were deep pools possessed of a probing quality that pierced beyond my eyes, probing deeply, until it seemed they pierced my very soul. It was as if I stood naked before him. His gaze came back from its wanderings and he gave a smile, small and sad.

'Ah, it is so. I can feel it. Yet what must I do?'

I frowned. 'Should there be anything to do?' I wondered.

* See *Dracula Unborn* by Peter Tremayne.

'One day you will understand, Morag. One day. But I cannot explain it yet. Beware of me, my innocent Morag. I seek myself through what I desire.'

'I do not understand.'

'It is my nature, Morag. I have to impose my will on others. I freely confess my faults. I am an egotist; I am avaricious; I am desirous of power and possessed of pride. Beware of me, Morag,' he insisted. 'My gifts are two-edged: I can raise you from a path of self-destruction and guide you to a positive and creative existence. Yet I am also a seducer who takes the vital but uncommitted and unrealized energies of your being to use for my own goal no matter what the cost to you. I can either be the healer or the being which drains your life-essence. Beware, Morag, and do not allow yourself to take the chance of eternal destruction.'

I only saw what my life had been like before I had met Vlad Dracula and then the *new* path he had opened to me. I knew, even then, that chance did not enter the matter. 'It is not chance,' I said, smiling at him reassuringly, 'but my own free choice.'

Vlad saw my smile and sighed again. 'I was born under the sign of Scorpio which has been called the accursed sign, the harbinger of death and destruction. Thousands of years ago the great Roman poet, Marcus Manilius, wrote:

Bright Scorpio, armed with poisonous tail, prepares
Men's martial minds for violence and for wars.
His venom heats and boils their blood to rage,
And rapine spreads o'er the unlucky age.

'Have a care, Morag, have a care of my poisonous tail.'

For a long while he sat in silence, brooding at the flickering flames of the fire. And I, I in my new-found ecstasy, was content to sit there at his side in silent companionship, neither demanding nor taking from him; only sustaining comfort from his silent image.

At last he stirred. 'Alas, I have to go now,' he said, rising to his feet. 'But tomorrow I swear that all things shall be answered to you. Then I will tell you what lies between you and me. Sleep well.' He departed with such a look of anguish on his face that he left me bewildered.

In retrospect I began to see the unhappiness that brooded within the Count. Yet why? What was the secret of that unhappy man? What strange mystery dwelt within the walls of this castle, within the tormented face of Vlad Dracula? If only I could reach out and help him. What was the secret that seemed so awful to him? He had warned me of his character, of strange dangers to myself if we pursued our emotions to their logical conclusion. Yet he was no demon. The true demon is one who is aware of his evil and joyfully practises it. Yet Vlad Dracula was not taking joy in what he saw as the evils of his character.

The desire to help him was uppermost in my mind as I made my way back to my room. We had talked away another night and I had not gone to the schoolroom to teach the children. No one had come to fetch me to my duties nor had Vlad rebuked me for not remembering them. It was odd. I undressed for bed dazed by the complexity of my thoughts, by a thousand unanswered questions. I lay awake for a long time before I sank into a fretful slumber.

CHAPTER NINETEEN

A roll of thunder, distant and menacing, brought me to my senses. I suppose I had been awake for a little while, lying with my eyes closed. The thunder rolled again, this time nearer and more angrily. I opened my eyes and, to my disgust, I saw that once more I had slept the entire day away. The sky outside was black, covered in dark storm clouds which were racing before the wind. Without warning a sudden streak of lightning shot across the heavens and, for a brief moment, illuminated my room.

I sat up repressing a cry of alarm for a tall figure in white stood at the foot of my bed. 'Who is it?' I cried, reaching out to light my bedside lamp.

'It is I, Elizabeth Bathory,' replied the old Countess's hollow voice.

Shivering in the chill evening air, I struck a match and lit the ancient lamp by the side of my bed. 'What is it?' I asked. I had never felt at ease with this strange, gaunt woman. In fact, I had hardly seen her more than two or three times since I had been at the castle.

The Countess's thin lips parted slightly and twitched into a smile that held no warmth in it. 'Child,' she replied, 'I have been watching you these past nights. I have seen you growing fond of my cousin Dracula.'

I started from my bed and threw on a dressing gown. 'Fond?' I said, making it seem a question yet knowing full well what she meant.

The old woman did not move but her deep eyes, glowing oddly in the lamp light, gazed into mine. 'My cousin, Vlad Dracula, has had the company of many women, but he has always been alone. He has a great intellect, a sensitive mind, but he has never shared his dreams, his hopes nor his fears with anyone. His will is his self, and in that self there is no room for anyone else.'

I frowned. 'What are you trying to say, Countess?'

'I am saying, my child, that any feelings that you think you have for Dracula cannot be. Must not be. There is much you do not understand and that is why I come to you. You have spent many an hour talking with Vlad Dracula and, it seems, that he has delighted in your company. That is strange. It is a thing he has not done for many a long year. He usually scorns the company of women except for what they can provide him with.'

A colour rose to my cheeks for I thought she meant that Vlad used women merely for his physical gratification.

'I have never known him to treat a woman, nor even a man, as an equal in intellect.'

'Then I am flattered, indeed, Countess,' I interrupted. 'I am flattered that the Count finds our conversations worthwhile.'

The old woman bit her lip. 'You are young, my child. You are in love with Dracula, of course? Ah, yes. Of course. I can see that.'

There seemed nothing I could reply.

'Yes, you are like all the rest, captured by his magnetism; ah, that accursed magnetism against which nothing is sacred; against which nothing can stand.'

'What do you mean?' Was the old woman demented?

'I warned you to leave this castle days ago. You did not obey me. I told you that there was nothing for you here but an eternal loneliness and pain. Now you must see for yourself why your love for Dracula cannot be fulfilled. Come, child, put on your clothes and follow me.'

The imperious tones seemed to warn that no argument would be tolerated and, I must confess, I felt uncomfortably disturbed by the Countess's words. What could she show me that would alter my feelings for Vlad?

It took me a few moments to dress myself, but at last I was ready and the old woman turned to the door. I followed her down the interminable corridors, up steps, and into a grim, musty-smelling part of the castle which I had not seen before. We went through a low wooden doorway and emerged into a courtyard so large that within its boundaries grew a cluster of cypress trees and one large spruce. It seemed a desolate spot, and the leaves blew hither and thither in the wind of the storm that now raged about the castle. Several times, as we passed through that musty courtyard, the sky was lit by brilliant flashes of lightning.

My curiosity growing, I followed the old Countess as she walked across the yard to a large wooden door. She paused, produced a large rusty key, and turned it in the lock. Then she swung the door back and motioned me to enter.

Inside was a strange room, almost like a child's nursery. It was already lit by a dimly flickering oil lamp. I walked forward hesitantly. The Countess followed me in and closed the door. 'What is it you wish to show me?' I asked inquisitively.

The Countess gave me her thin-lipped smile. 'It is here in this room.'

I peered around and could see nothing. 'What is it?'

'In good time, child. In good time.' The Countess's face was wrinkled as if laughing at some hidden joke. 'You must forgive me if I savour this moment. It is so long, so very, very long since I enjoyed myself.'

I stared at her shaking shoulders in amazement. Was the old woman mad? Was she playing a joke on me? 'Why is it you say that the feelings I have for the Count cannot be fulfilled?' I demanded, trying to get her back to the purpose of our coming to this gloomy place.

'Oh *that*!' The old woman smiled as if she had forgotten. 'Do not think my cousin, Dracula, acts from pure altruism. He always has a purpose behind his words and actions.'

'I remember,' her eyes seemed to glaze a little in reflection, 'I remember how people used to sneer at my knowledge. But I could read people as I could read books, and what was more I knew the real secret of life – I knew the source. Finally, the ignorant peasants led by Count Thurzo came and arrested me for witchcraft and walled me up in my own castle to die. And it was Dracula, my cousin, who came to release me from that bondage and guided me to the true path, to that which I had been seeking all along.'*

I gazed at the old Countess horrified. 'People walled you up in your own castle because they thought you were a witch?' I cried aghast. 'But such things have not happened since the Middle Ages!'

The Countess laughed. 'Aye. But Dracula rescued me.' She frowned. 'But his motives were not of altruism. He needed me, he needed people who *knew* – who knew the secret of life.'

'What do you mean?'

'Listen, child, Dracula has had you to himself long enough. Why he continues to play a game with you I do not know. But there are others in this household whose need is just as great as Dracula's. We must all survive.'

I sighed in my exasperation; I could humour the old woman no more. 'Listen, Countess,' I said, 'with respect, I have no time or inclination to play games with you.' I turned and started towards the door.

'Games?' The old woman threw back her head and gave a loud peal of laughter. Yet there was no humour in

---

* Could this be the Countess Elizabeth Bathory? The facts seem to fit. Countess Bathory was tried in 1611 at Bitcse where she was accused of slaughtering between 300 and 600 women in her castle of Csejthe. All her servants were beheaded and King Matthias II had her walled up inside her castle. Tremayne.

the laugh. 'It is a long time since I played games, not since they walled me up to die.' I decided to ignore her. 'Stop!' she suddenly cried. 'Do you not want to see what I have to show you?'

I hesitated and turned. 'What is it?' I demanded.

'Why, I have to show you the secret of life, the secret of eternal youth, of immortality!' I almost screamed from frustration. 'Blood is the secret,' she went on. 'Yes, child, blood! Blood is the drink and food of life!'

I turned away in disgust. This tall, aristocratic Countess, was reduced to a slobbering old woman raving about blood and eternal youth. I had nearly reached the door when she suddenly screamed at me: 'Stop! Do you think you can treat me with such discourtesy! I am the Countess Bathory, you peasant child! Be grateful that I have chosen you to propagate my existence!'

There was a sudden metallic clinking. I spun round and peered about me. Something was moving in the shadows in one corner of the room, and as I looked the shape of a young girl emerged from the shadows and with curiously jerking movements moved forward into the light. I stood rooted to the spot unable to believe my eyes. As the dim light of the lamp fell on the figure, I beheld a life-sized doll. The face was waxen, and its head was covered by red hair which was undoubtedly a wig. It was dressed in a dainty blue frock, which gave it an air of innocence. Its arms, once painted a flesh colour, were of some metal substance and they were held out stiffly before it. Each finger was hinged and the whole hand was thus able to clasp and unclasp in a menacing fashion. It moved on jerky metal legs but I know not how.

But this was the horror of it:

From the breasts of this metal creature there protruded two long sharp metal spikes, perhaps two feet in length, that jerked out in a stabbing motion and disappeared each time the monster took a step forward. The jaws were also hinged, and the large mouth kept opening and shutting, displaying two rows of large, bloodied sharp teeth that snapped up and down with fierce regularity each time the figure moved.*

I raised my hand to my mouth to stifle a scream. Then I turned and tried to open the door but the old woman had locked it behind her. With a chill of fear and anger sweeping through me, I turned like an animal at bay. The old Countess was laughing hysterically. 'Stop it!' I cried. 'For God's sake, stop it!'

I had to dodge away as the monster's arms swept close to me. This only caused the old woman to cackle even more and I could see, with disgust, that she chewed her lips in excitement so that the blood gathered on them. Her tongue darted in and out to lick the blood as it trickled down her chin. I swerved aside from the metal creature's arms and ran to the far side of the room seeking a means of escape. God alone knows how that creature was contrived to work but it turned slowly after me, its jaws snapping, its metal hand clenching and unclenching, the spikes on its breasts moving in and out. I dodged the monster once more, screaming at the old woman to make it stop. Then I slipped. I tried to regain my balance but fell into the path of that terrifying metal creature.

* On the manuscript Serban Mitikelu had scribbled a note: 'This must be pure fantasy for the very idea of robots in 1870 is beyond belief.' On the contrary, Countess Elizabeth Bathory did possess such a creature in 1610! It was made for her by a German clocksmith and was designed to clutch anyone who came near it in a tight embrace, transfix them with its spikes and teeth so that the blood would run down special channels in the spikes. This was then collected and used for the Countess's bath. Bathory's psychotic mania was a belief that the blood of virgins would act as an excellent skin conditioner and she literally bathed in their blood gathered by means of this gruesome robot. This was revealed at her trial. The first published account of the trial was written by Laszlo Turoczi in a work entitled *Erzebet Bathory* published in Budapest in 1744. Tremayne.

Abruptly I was aware of a tall figure in a black cloak, of a mighty hand that reached out and hauled me from the path of the monster while, at the same time, a second hand caught an arm of the creature, lifted it high and sent it smashing into a thousand pieces on the far side of the room.

I was looking up into the face of Count Dracula. It was a wild, angry face. The eyes were bloodshot beyond belief and blazed in fierce hatred at the old woman. The mouth was a reddened, twisted shape of fury. With scarce a glance at me, he set me aside and advanced a pace on the old woman, who stared wide-eyed in fear at him. 'Did I not warn you that no harm was to come to her?' whispered the Count ominously.

The old woman drew herself up. 'Why should you keep her for yourself? Why should I be denied?'

The Count's brows gathered in anger. 'Did you not swear that no harm would come to her?' he went on remorselessly.

It was as if the Countess suddenly read something in the Count's features. She started back. Her eyes widened and there was no mistaking the terror that now shadowed her face. 'No! No!' she let out a wild shriek. 'I was justified! You wanted her for yourself. My need was just as great!'

Without waiting for a reply, she turned and ran towards the wooden door which I had tried a moment ago.

To my utter disbelief she appeared to slip between the door and the jamb as if she possessed a body composed of nothing but air.

With a snarl of rage the Count darted after her. One massive hand jerked at the door handle, and with a gigantic heave that splintered the wood around the lock he wrenched the door open and ran into the courtyard beyond.

Weak with shock, yet compelled beyond either fear or

caution, I followed the flapping black cloak of the Count to the threshold and peered out.

The white figure of the Countess was moving swiftly across the piles of decaying leaves, seeming to glide like some spectre. The effect was heightened by the storm which still resounded unabated about the grey stone walls of the castle.

What happened next I shall never forget. As the Countess reached the clump of cypresses and the tall spruce there was a terrifying crack of thunder and a great white streak of lightning burned down into the courtyard and struck the bole of the spruce tree. The great tree creaked, toppled and fell. I had a glimpse of the Countess's pale face, wild with fear, turned up towards the falling tree, heard her scream, and then all was drowned in a mass of falling, splintering wood and a noise like hell let loose upon the world.

For a moment there was total silence. The Count raced before me across the courtyard and tore away the great branches with those strong hands of his until he reached the side of the Countess. I stood behind him and looked down in horror on the pale figure of the old woman. The sight made me sway and nearly swoon in sickness. A great branch had splintered off into a sharp stake which, in its fall, had transfixed the Countess through the breast. Blood spurted like a geyser across her white dress.

The sight was bad enough. God knows what could be worse? But worse came!

Slowly, as I gazed upon that fearful sight, the Countess's body seemed to bloat, decay and then crumble until there was nothing left but a pale white bloodstained dress and a small pile of white-grey substance that dispersed swiftly in the blowing of the storm wind.

I staggered back a step or two, trying hard to control my pounding heart, the welling red mist before my eyes, and the irresistible impulse to scream.

CHAPTER TWENTY

Later, how much later I do not know, I sat in the warmth and comfort of my bedchamber with the Count sitting anxiously before me. 'Gently, Morag, gently,' he was saying in that soft, comforting voice of his.

I reached out and grasped his strong hand. 'Am I going mad, or did it really happen?' I asked.

'Be at peace, Morag. Be at peace. Nothing is going to harm you; no one shall ever harm you. Do you believe me?'

I looked into his strong, handsome face and nodded. There was no mistaking the sincerity of his expression. 'But you must tell me, Vlad, the truth now. Since I came here there have been many strange happenings and each one I have either ignored or found reasons for because of what I feel for you.' An expression of joy mingled with pain crossed his face as I said this. 'Vlad, you know that I am not a child to be frightened. We have talked enough for you to realize that I do not believe in supernature. I believe that all things are natural and can be explained scientifically. This much we have discussed. Now I must know the truth of the mysteries of Castle Dracula – of you.'

He nodded. 'Yes, the time has come for the truth. I have given you my heart, the heart I thought I no longer possessed. Ah, Morag, since you came here the burden and woe of my heart has been lightened. I love you, Morag; I love with what power of emotion is still left to me. Yet it cannot be.'

I frowned. Deep within me there dwelt the growing realization of what was meant by the mysteries of Castle Dracula yet I needed to know from his own lips. 'The truth, Vlad.'

He sighed. 'The truth you shall have, Morag; the truth

as I have told no other person. But before I tell you, believe this if nothing else. I love you and swear while you are under my protection no power shall ever do you harm. Do you believe that?'

'I have believed it from the first,' I nodded.

He stood up and paced before the fire. 'Then let me tell you a story; a story which will make all things clear. Many years ago, many centuries ago, there was a young boy who had been born to rule his country. The boy was introspective and therefore studious. He thought deeply on matters appertaining to philosophy and metaphysics and grew to manhood with a knowledge and intellect superior to his fellows. Now the country in which he was born was an unhappy one. It was torn by continual invasions and bloodshed for it stood at the crossroads of three great empires, each hungry to tear the throat of the other. The boy's own father, a ruler as wise as most, fell to the petty greed of his neighbours and then brother warred against brother for the right to rule the kingdom which had become a bloodstained province of the Turkish empire.'

Vlad paused a while and then continued his tale. 'The young boy, younger than his brothers, swore that one day he would become ruler and free his country from the invaders, throw out his despotic brothers, and teach all a lesson which would not be forgotten. The boy grew to be a handsome youth. The youth became ruler in time but his country was still in turmoil and he was deposed. He fought back, and later, as a young man, he was restored to the throne of his country. This time he secured his position, ousted his rivals, destroyed the intriguers who plotted against him and began to drive out the invaders until his very name was feared the length and breadth of Turkey. Fat Saxon merchants, who grew rich upon the blood-stained soil of the country, and cruel Turks whispered his name in fear.

'The country prospered and his name resounded

throughout Europe as the saviour of his people. But, after many years, he was deposed through the treachery of a brother raised in the Sultan of Turkey's court. He fled to Hungary where an avaricious king imprisoned him because that king, too, coveted his kingdom.

'In prison, at the age of thirty-one years, he had time to ponder and reflect. He was allowed servants and access to those family possessions that were his. Twelve years were spent in that prison in the ancient city of Buda overlooking the Danube. For twelve years he had nothing to do but study those books and manuscripts that were brought to him and reflect.

'It was during this time that he discovered that his family was an ancient one with its origin in the Egypt of the pharaohs. They had been high priests of the god Draco and, when Draco had been overthrown, they had fled to the Carpathians bringing forth manuscripts containing forbidden knowledge, knowledge that only the high priests knew. He studied the manuscripts eagerly, mastering their secrets, mastering the mysteries of nature, striving towards the moment when he could finally reach out his hand to grasp the forbidden rituals of the ancients – the secret of life itself.'

Vlad paused and laughed, a short gruff laugh. 'Then, after twelve years of incarceration, the Hungarian king gave him his freedom once more. It was simple petty intriguing again for the Tartar Khan of the Crimea had become a vassal of the Turks and had begun to fight the Hungarians in Bosnia. The Hungarian king freed him and gave him a military command. He took it, but not to protect the Hungarian king. He took it and with his army invaded his own country, driving the Turks before him like the chaff from the wheat. As the Turks fled in bewilderment and he was proclaimed ruler once again, he retired to his family's great castle by the Arges in Wallachia which lies to the south of Transylvania.

'He had come home to rule and now he was determined to rule in justice and peace forever. During the years of his confinement he had experimented in alchemy and studied the ancient texts so that, one by one, like flowers before the sun, the secrets of Nature opened to him.

'I have already told you, Morag, how the followers of Draco in ancient Egypt believed it possible to make the earthly body immortal; that the body could retain all the characteristics of the original mortal being after its so-called death. For thousands of years the followers of Draco devoted themselves to the study of releasing the immortal body – the *ka* as it was called in ancient times. It was during the reign of the great queen Sebek-nefer-Ra, in the Thirteenth Dynasty – three thousand years before the birth of the Christian god – that the high priests of Draco succeeded and created the first immortals, the Undead, as they were known.'

I stared hard at Vlad in amazement. His face was grim. 'Oh yes, Morag, I said they succeeded. I almost told you this the other night when we spoke of it. But then, in the Seventeenth Dynasty, the temporal power of the cult of Draco went into a decline, for the Pharaoh Apophis, the last of the Typhonian rulers of the city of Avaris, was overthrown by superstitious sun-worshippers and the cult was persecuted until its high priests fled the country and dispersed to all the corners of the earth.

'Among those who fled were the children of Setek-Ab-Ra, the greatest of the Draconian priests and philosophers, a scientist far in advance of his time. He and his family fled from the blood lust of the Pharaoh Amenhotep IV, who had become a convert to the worship of Aton, the sun-god. They fled to the bastion of the Carpathians where their seed prospered and, in remembrance of their origins, they took the name of their god Draco as their own. Dracula – the sons of the dragon.'

I cannot confess to be truly shocked by his revelations.

I was curious, intrigued, and the mysteries were beginning to fit into a pattern, however incredible.

'The ruler, at his castle by the Arges, was a descendant of the children of Setek-Ab-Ra. From his ancestors he had learnt that if a man was possessed of courage, and not frightened by the prejudice and superstition of his time, he could obtain perpetual life from the performance of the correct scientific rituals; he could release his *ka* and walk abroad on the face of the earth forever.'

Vlad paused and looked closely at me. 'Morag, you must know, must suspect, that *I* was that ambitious ruler, the boy grown to manhood, the ruler who dared challenge the gods themselves.'

There was no surprise in me, just a numb acceptance. There was no horror nor even a questioning of the truth. Too many things had happened to substantiate what Vlad was calmly telling me. 'When did this happen?' I asked quietly.

'I performed the ritual in the month of December, 1476.'

I felt a cold shiver thrill through me. Suddenly it all became clear to me; the talk of immortality; the cult of Draco; the science of Nature. Then he, Vlad, was . . .

'I performed the ritual, Morag, but something went wrong.' Suddenly his eyes flashed and he smashed his fist into the palm of his hand. 'I achieved immortality, Morag. I became immortal, but it was not the complete immortality that I had sought. I found myself but a mockery of an immortal. I became merely an Undead creature. There were great constrictions upon me. I could only move by night, and each day I had to return to a cursed sleeping death, hidden from any who knew the secret of my destruction. And each night I was forced to find sustenance for my existence.'

I listened numbly, realizing that I believed him without question. Nor was I really afraid of what I heard. Not even shocked.

'Poor Morag,' he whispered. 'I must tell you now that part of my story which will distress you. But I tell you now for in being cruel with the honesty of my confession I will spare you further pain later. The principle of the Draconian ritual is that blood is life. Blood is the source of all mysteries of life in animals. But because I failed in my ritual, I – Undead as I am – am forced each night to find warm, living blood to drink in order to sustain my existence. In blood is the essence of the life-force for which I hunger. Without blood I would eventually fade into the elemental dust. And though my body would fade to dust my mind would linger on, my thoughts would remain in an agony of purgatory knowing neither rest nor peace until this great universe finally gives up its very existence. Cursed be my fate, my quest for immortality made me into a vampire and each person that I drink from becomes as I.'

I could not control the shuddering gasp that came from my throat.

'Alas, Morag. I, a Dracula, a follower of the true life force of the universe, made a mistake and am now a mere creature of the night, little better than a wolf or bat, over which creatures I have been given dominion. I am a prey to those who can stalk me in the sunlight.'

'And the others?' I asked. 'The Countess? And Radu, what happened to him? And Tinka and little Vlad? Tirgsor and the others – are they . . . all as you are?'

He nodded solemnly. 'We are all Undead, beings of the night who exist for all eternity unless some mishap destroys us. The Countess is no more for the wooden stake that pierced her heart let loose the blood which sustained her. And little Radu is no more for we are prey to the symbols of those religions which condemn us. The symbol of the Christian cross destroyed him.'

I shook my head. 'Vlad,' I whispered, 'my emotions tell me to believe you but my intellect rebels. How can I believe it fully?'

'Watch, Morag,' he said softly. 'Watch and do not be afraid for no harm shall come to you.'

He rose, his tall figure shrouded in blackness, until he seemed to tower above me. Then it was as if his figure suddenly shattered, dissolving into a million shimmering specks of silver which raced into a column towards a shaft of moonlight, gleaming in through the open window of my room. The shimmering light sped, turned and twisted, and then returned.

Suddenly, to my horror, a great monstrous black bat hung before the door of my room. Its large flapping wings must surely have measured some eighteen inches across and I could see every detail of its powerful, smooth black body. It had large ears, broad at the base but narrowing abruptly to sharp recurved tips. It also had thick woolly fur extending on to its wing membranes which appeared ash grey in colour. It hung there with slow pulsating motions of its great wings, showing conspicuously large white teeth. Its tiny red eyes seemed malignant and bore deeply into mine.

Then it was gone; gone in a shimmering silver glow and I caught my breath again as in its place stood a great wolf. It was a beast so large that it would have dwarfed even the great Irish wolfhounds, the biggest of the dog species. It gazed with large luminous eyes, gleaming like red coals. Its great yellowing fangs were bared and its muzzle and dewlap were dripping with saliva and tinged with blood.

I fought to retain my sanity at such horror and I closed my eyes to shut out the sight. As I opened them the form of Vlad shimmered into being before me.

'It is part of the curse of the Undead, that we may change our shape and guise. One more thing will convince you – go to the mirror and gaze into it.' I did so, seeing my pale face in the flickering light of the room, strained, white and staring. 'Do you see yourself?' asked Vlad's voice.

'I do,' I replied quietly.

'Very well. I shall now come and stand behind you.'

I felt him move behind me but I could see nothing reflected there. I turned. Vlad stood behind me smiling. Startled, I turned back to the mirror. He cast no reflection. My mind raced back to the similar occurrence with Tirgsor.

'You see,' said Vlad gently, 'that I have spoken the truth?'

'How is it possible?' I whispered.

'It is the nature of my existence, Morag,' he said. 'I cast neither shadow nor a reflection in a mirror; while I have the strength of many, I can also transform my shape into a bat or a wolf, or swirl in a mist or come on moonlit rays as elemental dust. I can see in the dark, being a creature of the night. But I am powerless between sunrise and sunset. At that time I have to return to lie helpless on my native soil, the soil wherein I was buried. Nor can I pass running water except at the slack and the flood of tide.'

In all this horror a light of understanding dawned in my memory. 'When I fell into the river, you could not cross to rescue me, and that was why you cursed your bondage?' He lowered his head, and with that another realization dawned; one that I had really known all along. 'Then it *is* true – your love for me? I have felt it all along.'

'But it cannot be,' he sighed. 'It cannot be for I am a creature alien to you.'

I reached forward and grasped his hand. 'Surely you, above all others, are not accustomed to restrictions?'

'The Undead should not be prey to the emotions of a human mortal. Yet I cannot deny the feelings I harbour in this shell that was once a man.'

'And *still* is,' I cried, realizing that I was tossing aside all reason, all the morality and beliefs of my upbringing.

'You have shown me that with courage and lack of prejudice and fear, man may strive towards great scientific advances. Your intellect could rule the world.'

He smiled softly. 'I thought so once, but my enemies are powerful and many. My limitations are too severe. In daylight I can be hunted out and destroyed with a wooden stake through my heart, or my head cut off and placed about with wild garlic to prevent my rising. My enemies can confine my movements with the symbolism of their religions which I abhor. Yet they have tried and failed to destroy me. I have triumphed and exist still!' He nodded as if in agreement to his thoughts. Then he turned and looked at me as if seeking some answer. 'These revelations do not make you fearful?'

'No,' I replied. 'I feel no horror or fear because when a mystery is explained it is no longer something to be feared.'

'I rejoice in your wisdom, Morag,' sighed Vlad. 'I truly love you as I have never loved another.

'I do not mean, as others often mean, that I want to possess you, to imprison and control you. I mean that I care for you, care for your future even if that future should be without me. We cannot be as other lovers, you and I. So should you wish to leave you may do so, with my sorrow but my blessing and love.'

'Vlad,' I cried, 'I am more selfish. I want to be with you, know you, care for you. I do not care why you exist but that existence is in itself enough for me.'

He smiled softly. 'If we make a mistake, we have all eternity to regret it and unlike other human mortals we cannot rectify that mistake once made.'

'I don't understand, Vlad.'

'Admitting that we love each other truly, then what? I will continue to exist in my present form until someone stumbles on the secret of my destruction and . . .'

'I shall grow old, wither and die,' I cried in despair. 'But I want to share your existence!'

'Unless . . .'

He spoke the word softly. I looked up. I knew, a deep burning feeling within me, that I wanted more than anything to share his existence for eternity. 'Unless?' I prompted.

'I can prevent your mortal decay, can give you existence for all time.'

'How? How can it be done?' I asked slowly, suspecting full well the answer.

'The choice must be yours and yours alone,' he replied. 'But I can claim you as mine with a kiss, a gentle sighing kiss which could perpetuate your earthly existence as surely as mine. For everyone I kiss must become as I – Undead – and with that goes all the restrictions that confine my world. But I will not kiss you nor drink of your blood without your full knowledge and consent. Rather, because of my love, I say to you shun these haunted solitudes, return to your own world of sun and blue sky and light.'

'No, Vlad!' My heart beat wildly but my intellect was calm and reasoned.

He reached out and took my hand, holding it tightly for a moment. 'The choice I give you cannot be decided by emotion alone. It must be decided with the intellect as well.' He looked towards the window and frowned. 'The sun will be rising soon, setting the boundaries to my existence once again. I must leave you. But during the hours of daylight yet to come, consider and make your choice. When the sun sets, if you are in your room and willing to join me, I shall come to claim you with my kisses. But if you rebel at the great weight of your choice, if you have any reservations about the enormity of your commitment, you are free to leave the castle with my blessing and love.'

'I could not part from you now, Vlad,' I cried.

He held up his hand and smiled. 'The emotion still

speaks, Morag. Let it be still awhile. The intellect will come to you when I am gone. And to help it, I wish you to come with me now and see the place where I and the others of my kin must rest!'

I stood up willingly. 'Nothing you can say nor show me can make me falter in my choice, Vlad. I am determined that I shall be by your side.'

He stood looking down at me, then he shook his head and placed a fingertip to his smiling lips. He turned and beckoned me to follow. 'Come; come and see in what place you would have to dwell.'

CHAPTER TWENTY-ONE

There was no fear in my heart as I followed Vlad Dracula along the musty corridors of the old castle, through countless chambers, many of which were entirely new to me. Some of them, like others I had seen, were entirely empty but for dust and cobwebs while others were still furnished but whose furniture was covered in a profusion of dust and grime. In one room through which he led me I had to pause and gasp aloud in astonishment for, although empty of furniture, there lay in one corner a pile of gold coins of all kinds, from every part of the earth. They were covered in a thick film of dust as though they had lain there a long time. Close by them was yet another surprising treasure trove, chains, ornaments, some jewelled, all made of gold or silver and all of them an incredible age.

Vlad paused and watched me examine them with an indulgent smile. 'Baubles, my dear,' he said. 'They mean little in my existence.'

He beckoned me onward, glancing anxiously towards the brightening windows. He led me through a heavy panelled doorway. Its lock was rusty and the handle screeched in protest as he swung it open. It led through a stone-paved passageway, damp with mildew, to a circular stairway which spiralled down deeply as if driving into the very bowels of the earth.

He preceded me slowly, a step at a time, for the stairs were in total darkness, until we came upon a black tunnel-like corridor. 'Keep close to me now,' Vlad called in a low voice. A dreadful odour assailed my nose. It was of sickly perfume, the musty smell of old earth newly turned, the stink of corruption and decay. It grew oppressive and intense as I followed Vlad's dark form down the corridor.

He paused before a door which ended the corridor. 'Courage is needed, Morag,' he said softly, 'for you are about to see what none may see and survive in the sunlight of the old world. But I have given you my word that none may harm you, none of my kin that populates the nether world with me. You are about to see that place wherein I must rest during the hours of sunrise until sunset.'

He threw open the door and entered. I found myself in a chapel-like vault. Everywhere were fragments of old coffins, boxes, piles of earth and dust. Grey rays of light were filtering downwards, lighting the gloom through cracks in the ancient roof.

'This is my resting place,' whispered Vlad, and there seemed a sadness in his voice. I stepped forward uncertainly. In the gloom I could make out the dark, long shape of several coffins resting on trestles but without lids covering their contents. I raised a hand to choke back a cry. Each coffin contained a body, but a body not yet in the process of decay. 'Yes,' sighed Vlad, as if answering my thoughts, 'they are all here – the others.'

I drew nearer the coffins, curiosity forcing my gaze on the figures that lay stretched on the piles of earth. Yes, there lay the two voluptuous girls; there lay the sullen-faced Tirgsor; and there lay the two children Vlad and Tinka. Beyond them lay a large empty coffin and, near by, an empty child's coffin. Were these the beds of the old Countess and young Radu? I shivered. Nearer still I drew to them like one in a dream.

'Vlad!' I started back with a scream as I realized that the eyes of all those living corpses were opening, blood-shot, red and staring at me with fury.

'Fear not,' he whispered. 'They will not harm you. They cannot. It is already dawn's light that drifts into this chamber and there they must lie until the set of the sun. I still have yet a moment longer for I am stronger than they.'

At that the two young women began to writhe in their coffins as if they would get up. Bloodstained lips chewed and threshed against their sharp white teeth. 'Help us, lord!' implored one. 'It is not fitting that she should look upon us and remain without our world so that she may do us harm while we rest.'

'Quick, lord! The sun is coming and you will soon be as us – helpless. Kiss her and make her of our blood and flesh!'

A coldness went through me and I found myself grow tense but Vlad's voice was reassuring. 'Silence, you wantons! I have sworn no harm shall come to her from me and mine. She will make her choice when the time is meet; hers will be the choice, not mine or yours. On this I have sworn.'

'Why hers?' came a plaintive wail from one. 'We had no choice!'

I stood aghast at their threshing. 'Is this how it must be for eternity?' I whispered. Then I frowned as a thought struck me, something Vlad had said. 'But you said you had to lie in your native soil – the soil wherein you were buried?'

'This is so,' replied Vlad.

'But you ruled Wallachia and it was there that you became Undead.'

He smiled. 'That is true. I remained in my castle near the Arges, guarded by the successive generations of my family – the house of Dracula – who ruled Wallachia after me. Then, in 1659, my descendant Mihail Radu was driven from the throne and had to escape here to Transylvania. He took me and mine in great boxes filled with the earth of my native soil. And here we have dwelt ever since.'

Mihail Radu! I had seen his crypt. I turned back to the creatures in the coffins. 'And this is how it will be – for eternity? Must I rest here, as they, only to emerge in the hours of sunset to sunrise? Must I live in darkness for ever?'

The tall black figure bowed his head. 'It must be so, Morag, if you would join me. Alas, it must be so. Yet in my existence I entertain the hope that I shall discover where I went wrong in the ritual and that one day soon I may complete my experiment and become a true immortal; that I shall stride the earth in sunlight once again. That day must come soon; I know it. Then we shall all return to the surface of the earth and woe betide them that would destroy us.'

'You have sworn the choice shall be mine?'

'If I remain true to anything, Morag,' averred Vlad, 'it will be to that oath.'

I smiled. 'I believe it.'

He nodded. 'But remember, Morag, and be warned. I am the tempter and buyer of souls. I offer the promise of power and lust fulfilled. I am the catalyst who gives the searching soul a way towards growth. Man often finds it difficult to merge with the forces of light for this means that he has to labour hard and long and sacrifice his seeming pleasures in order to obtain goals which are often unreal and impractical. Easier, therefore, is it to merge with the Darkness for there he can keep all his possessions and desires. Was it not Milton who wrote "Better to reign in hell, than serve in heaven"?'

Suddenly he doubled forward and gasped.

'Vlad! What is it?' I cried in alarm.

'The sun ... the sun comes ... I must get to my refuge.'

He staggered forward, like a man drunk, grasping the wooden coffin and heaving himself into it with obvious physical pain. As he lay there his face became relaxed.

'The sun sets boundaries to my existence,' he spoke the word with great difficulty. 'Yes, Morag, the choice is yours. Leave while you can, during daylight, but if you would join me I shall come to your room at sunset and find you there and claim you with a kiss. The choice is yours!'

His body seemed to stiffen slightly. His eyes still stood fully open and turned towards me but they became stony, lacking the glass of death but not being fully conscious. The redness did not leave his lips and his skin maintained its parchment colour.

So this was how they slept! I turned and looked from coffin to coffin. All of them seemed in that strange catatonic state, neither dead nor living, all staring upward with those solemn stone eyes.

I moved back to Vlad's coffin. The face before me was still as strong and handsome as before and with the intellect of four hundred years behind it. Should I cringe in fear? A week ago I might well have done. A week ago I did not know Vlad Dracula. It is hard for anyone to understand my reasoning, my thoughts, my lack of fear. I saw nothing supernatural in the existence of these Undead creatures; they were as much part of nature as I was.

There was now but a simple choice to make, to join that being whom I loved, or to flee from that spot and join my own world again. My world? What had that world ever offered me but unhappiness, cruelty, lies and hypocrisy? I turned and looked down at Vlad's face and drew from it some of that colossal strength of purpose which had served him so well in his struggle for existence.

Yet it was not possible to throw off the prejudices of a lifetime. As Vlad had said, without his intellectual presence to reinforce my emotional courage, my intellect had taken over creating nagging doubts. When all was said and done, were not the Undead vampires, alien creatures – creatures of the nether world – who preyed upon the living to perpetuate their existence, draining the blood of the living to create a legion of Undead? Should I not champion the side of light, the side of humankind, against

653

these creatures? Should I not destroy these aliens before they destroyed the world? A wooden stake, Vlad had said, piercing the heart of these creatures would destroy them. Should I not perform that deed for the sake of the survival of my own kind?

A low soft moan escaped from Vlad's lips as if his great mind had read my thoughts and, even in his confines, he sought to dissuade me.

'The choice is mine,' I repeated in a low voice which, nevertheless, seemed to echo through that chamber.

Aye, and was my own kind worth saving? Who was I to say that the existence of the Undead was evil because it differed so much from the existence of my own species? Who was I to say that Vlad's philosophy was wrong because it differed from the philosophy of human kind?

The choice was mine. 'I think I shall go for a walk,' I said slowly, peering down at Vlad's face. 'I shall keep near the castle but I must have one last walk in the sun, a walk to clear my head and come to my decision.'

I turned and left that chamber, making my way slowly back through the dust-laden rooms and corridors to the great hallway of the castle. I returned to my room to throw a shawl about my shoulders and then went down and unlocked the great doors, moving out into the soft warmth of the autumn sunlight.

It did not enter my head to recall the dangers that lurked outside the castle walls, the wild animals and wolves. My mind was too keenly honed to the problem I had to face before the day was over. I did not even consciously guide my feet, nor did my mind take in the surroundings as I walked. Instead my mind sought to wrestle with the problem of my choice.

My emotions assured me of my love for Vlad Dracula. That emotion was so strong I wondered whether I really did have a choice. But what of that nagging feeling that I was betraying my kind? No, I argued, let superstitious fools rant and fear; Vlad was no alien in mind and soul. He was a great scientist who had embarked on an experiment to grasp what was the greatest of all Nature's secrets. True, he had only partially succeeded and by that partial success he had suffered disabilities.

I walked, head forward, down the valley road, not knowing where I went as the questions churned within my mind.

An abrupt movement halted me. Out of a nearby clump of bushes a heavy black shape stepped out into my pathway, so suddenly that a startled scream escaped my lips and I threw up my hands in self-protection.

CHAPTER TWENTY-TWO

'Why, if it isn't the pretty young Scottish *Fräulein*!'

I stared at the man who had materialized before me. Where had I seen this craggy face before with its prominent nose, firm and aggressive jaw and sandy-yellow hair? The twinkling blue eyes looked at me in friendly fashion. Of course! The doctor from Klausenburg. 'Doctor von . . . van . . .?'

'Van Helsing, *Fräulein*,' he supplied, bowing low. He looked at me inquisitively. 'If I may venture a question, *Fräulein* – what are you doing in this Godforsaken spot?'

I suddenly felt the weight of great exhaustion upon me. Van Helsing appeared so normal, so mundane. 'Is there anywhere we could go, for I am badly in need of something to refresh myself?' I asked.

He nodded thoughtfully. 'I have tethered my horse further down the valley. In my saddle bags I have a good bottle of Schnaps and some food for my luncheon.'

He turned and wearily I followed him to where a bay horse stood tethered to some trees. We sat on a grassy knoll, behind the shelter of some grey granite rocks, and Van Helsing unpacked the contents of his saddle bags. I swallowed a mouthful of the fiery liquid and felt its warmth coursing through me.

'I am here collecting species of wild garlic that grow in abundance in this region,' confided Van Helsing. 'The locals here seem to use it both as a herb and in some kind of symbolic folkloric way but for what purpose I have yet to find out.'

He turned and smiled. 'But what brings you to this wilderness, *Fräulein*? Are you staying in this area?'

I nodded. 'I am a governess at the castle at the end of this valley,' I said. 'I was out walking.'

The Dutchman shook his head. 'Surely, *Fräulein*,' he said, 'you do not expect me to believe that you go for walks in this fierce cold with nothing more than a shawl about your shoulders?'

From the turmoil of my mind there arose within me a wild desire to confess my story to him, perhaps it was not just to him, but anyone of my kind who would listen to me. 'You are right, doctor,' I said. 'Something weighs heavily on my mind which made me come out in this condition and I must tell you or burst with my desire to tell someone. Do you know what the Undead are?'

The effect on Van Helsing was electric. He crossed himself and peered long and earnestly at me, as if, perhaps, to see whether I was playing some joke with him. 'What do you know of such evil things?' he said grimly.

'I know a great deal now, doctor,' I replied. 'And I must tell you so that my thoughts may become ordered in my mind.'

He bowed his head. 'Speak then if you must.'

Leaving aside my sordid experiences at Schloss Stoffel, the nightmare of which had now paled into insignificance, I told the Dutchman of my coming to Castle Dracula, though I made no mention of its name nor referred to the name of 'Dracula' at all. I merely spoke of the nobleman and his quest for immortality and the pursuit of the natural sciences which had made him the thing he was, an Undead being, a vampire.

'My God!' whispered the Dutchman after I had finished my tale. Then he did a curious thing. He suddenly reached over and held my chin, twisting my head this way and that so that he could observe my neck.

I smiled. 'No, doctor, you will not find the mark of the Undead upon me.'

Van Helsing muttered to himself. Then he reached

into his pocket and suddenly tossed something towards me. Automatically, I caught it as it fell into my lap and examined it. It was a tiny silver crucifix.

Van Helsing peered closely at my hands. 'No, no,' he whispered, 'it is as you have said. You are unsullied and not of their kind as yet. Thanks be to God. Keep the crucifix, *Fräulein*. It will be of protection to you.' Shaking his head he took the bottle of Schnaps and swallowed hard. 'Thank God that I came across you in time before this so-called nobleman renders you great harm.'

Smilingly, I shook my head. 'Oh no,' said I quickly, 'on that account I am not worried. That is not his way. He has promised me that no harm shall come to me.'

Van Helsing stared at me aghast. 'But, *Fräulein*, he is a creature of evil, something that should have departed this earth long, long ago. I know of the Undead, believe me, *Fräulein*.'

'But you do not know him,' I protested.

'I know *them*,' returned Van Helsing earnestly. 'I have studied them, believe me. Did not the Lord say to Job –

Who is this that darkeneth counsel
By words without knowledge?

'I say to you, *Fräulein*, that you do not know them for they are as a pestilence that must be extinguished from the world forever.'

'But they are living beings,' I cried.

Van Helsing sprang to his feet in agitation. 'Great God, has the creature mesmerized you? I tell you that they are wicked, evil. These vile lepers of our kind must be destroyed, and there is an end to it!'

My soul cried out in protest. Is everything so black and white? Are there no shades of grey? Is there *just* good and evil? Who decides what is right or wrong, good or bad?

Van Helsing was pacing up and down in an agitated

manner. Suddenly he stopped and stared down at me. 'This castle, it is the one at the end of the valley? Can you gain ready access to it?' I nodded. 'Of course, but why?'

'I will have to ride back to the inn at the foot of the valley where I am lodging and collect some equipment. I am sure of one thing, *Fräulein*, that I must enter that castle and destroy this evil blot on our humankind.'

I sat in silence for a while. The prejudices of my upbringing told me that I should convince myself that Van Helsing was right. How could I change my life for an alien existence? How could I contemplate the future Dracula offered me? To reject the light, to reject the sun and live in darkness forever? Would it not be better to live with one's own kind, even if they were often cruel, vicious and brutish?

I looked at the Dutchman, waiting expectantly, and nodded. He smiled. 'Praise God! Abandon your fears of the Undead and help me destroy them.'

'Yet I do not fear him,' I protested.

Van Helsing looked at me pityingly. 'Take the crucifix I have given you and wear it for your protection. Meet me by the castle gates. I shall come within the hour. That will give us two hours of daylight to complete the work of God.'

I stood and watched him mount his horse and spur away like some excited schoolboy after a new adventure. As I turned and walked slowly back to the castle I had a strange feeling that I was betraying Dracula, even though I had given him no promise. He had, by sheer power of will, overcome the mortal confines of human life. Did that not make him better than mankind? According to Van Helsing it made him sub-human, an evil canker to be rooted out and destroyed.

To survive he had to drink human blood. Well, to survive the great majority of mankind lived on the flesh and blood of other animals. I noticed Van Helsing enjoying his blood sausage with a degree of relish while, at the same time, throwing up his hands in horror at the idea of living off human blood. Were humans and the Undead so very different? Suddenly I felt angry at men like Van Helsing with their moral posturings. Good and evil are not immutable. The difference between them is often a matter of human expedience. Van Helsing can wrinkle his face in disgust at the vampire's need for life-giving blood; but would no doubt smack his lips at the succulent bloody softness of a rare steak, or the savoury tang of a thinly cut slice of beef. With such thoughts running through my mind, I retraced my footsteps up the valley towards the rising towers of Castle Dracula.

What was it that Vlad Dracula offered me? That which everyone secretly or overtly desires – immortality! The opportunity to live forever; never to face that dismal day when everything must cease. Man refuses to come to terms with death and so in all his religions he has made himself immortal in the next world. But what if there is no next world and the only place to gain immortality is in this one, an immortality offered by Nature herself?

Suddenly I saw a world opening before me; through Vlad I could attain the only immortality that is open to man. Was it so abhorrent to become Undead? The confines of that existence were nothing compared to the confines that society had placed upon me.

What did I want to achieve in my brief span of life? To struggle for existence? To spend the years of my life grubbing for pennies to simply exist? Or did I want to live to enjoy the quality of what the world has to offer, to appreciate the arts, philosophy, music and literature, and all those things that are denied to the great majority of us because we are concerned with securing enough bread to exist another day and have no leisure for anything else?

I walked to the gates of the castle, paused and looked up at the sun. The final answer for me lay in the love that

Vlad and I shared. I walked into the castle, pushed the gates shut behind me and secured them. I stepped lightly through the gloomy rooms of the castle with a strange singing happiness bursting within me.

An hour or so later I heard someone calling outside the walls of the castle. I peered down from my window. It was the Dutch doctor Van Helsing. He stood peering up and calling my name, wailing it like some tormented soul. His eyes caught sight of me and he started waving his arms. I could hear his voice quite clearly. 'For God's sake, *Fräulein*, open the gates! Quickly! There is little time to lose before the sun sets. The evil monster must be destroyed. Let me in, *Fräulein*!'

I became suddenly aware of Van Helsing's tiny silver crucifix at my neck. I reached up and undid it. Then I threw it out of the window. I saw it flashing downwards, sparkling in the late afternoon sunshine, until it landed at the feet of the agitated Dutchman. He stood staring down at it a moment, his body tensed in a grotesque mime of horror. His white face peered back to mine. 'My God, *Fräulein*! Have you lost your senses? For the sake of your immortal soul, open this gate.'

'No, doctor,' I called down to him. 'No, I have not lost my senses and it is for the sake of that immortal part of me that I will not let you in.' I turned and closed the window on his frantic crying and walked to my bed.

Soon the sun will sink below the mountains.

Soon it will be night.

Soon Vlad will come.

The fall of a leaf in autumn is a whispered warning to the living. All things must pass, must pass and be no more. Yet I have lived; have suffered; have cried; have fought; have loved and, oh, I have had so much ambition burning within me. Must it all pass into forgetfulness, into oblivion, as if I had never existed? How I would love to believe that it were not so. And, in spite of all logic, perhaps in the innermost recesses of my mind I have a yearning, a hope, that I shall not die; for it is surely *other* people who die and as I am not another, I shall not die.

The fall of a leaf in autumn is a whispered warning to the living. And the leaves fall by my window, rustling and whispering in the gentle breeze, whispering a knell, *my* knell.

Mortality or immortality? Well, now I have made my choice. Morality or immorality? – there is no difference except in our prejudices and fears.

He has allowed me time to consider, to reflect, to think on what he has proposed. Now I have decided. The decision is mine.

I went to see him a while ago, to sit by his side as he lay pale and peaceful in repose. How strong, how handsome he looked as he lay there resting. It is strange to think that he does not lie in a natural sleep. But then what is natural? What is normal? It was comforting to sit by his side awhile gazing on his face and drawing from it some of that strength of purpose which has served him so well in his struggle for existence. I am sure he knew that I was there for his pale face seemed relaxed and tranquil in his repose.

Ah, now the sun is setting.

The autumn leaves have ceased to fall.

Soon *he* will come.

THE END

SIGNET

Published or forthcoming

Ira Levin
author of *Rosemary's Baby*

Thirteen hundred Madison Avenue, an elegant 'sliver' building, soars high and narrow over Manhattan's smart Upper East Side. Kay Norris, a successful single woman, moves on to the twentieth floor of the building, high on hopes of a fresh start and the glorious Indian summer outside. But she doesn't know that someone is listening to her. Someone is *watching* her.

'Levin really knows how to touch the nerve ends' – *Evening Standard*

'*Sliver* is the ultimate *fin de siècle* horror novel, a fiendish goodbye-wave to trendy urban living … Ira Levin has created the apartment dweller's worst nightmare' – Stephen King

SIGNET

Published or forthcoming

BASIC INSTINCT

Richard Osborne

A brutal murder.

A brilliant killer.

A cop who can't resist the danger.

When San Francisco detective Nick Curran begins investigating the mysterious and vicious murder of a rock star, he finds himself in a shadowy world where deceit and seduction often go hand in hand. Nick can't stay away from his number one suspect – stunning and uninhibited Catherine Tramell – a novelist whose shocking fiction mirrors the murder down to the smallest, bloodiest detail.

Entangled in love and murder, Nick is headed for trouble, with only his basic instinct for survival to keep him from making a fatal mistake...

SIGNET

Published or forthcoming

THE RATING GAME

Dave Cash

Behind the glass-fronted walls of CRFM's 24-hours-a-day nerve centre in the heart of London, three people fight for control of their lives as the tycoon powerbrokers of international finance move in for the kill...

Monica Hammond, the radio station's beautiful and ruthless Managing Director – nothing was allowed to stand in her way ... until one man discovered her fatal weakness.

Nigel Beresford-Clarke – CRFM's greatest asset – hopelessly betrayed by his love for a schoolgirl...

And **Maggie Lomax**, uncompromising and tough as nails – then her outspoken broadcasts pushed the wrong people too far ...

They're ready to play ... *The Rating Game*

SIGNET

Published or forthcoming

THE GLITTERING STRAND

Judith Lennox

The Levant trade of the 1590's offers wealth and danger in equal measure. And, always, dreams ...

A dream for Serafina Guardi, captured by corsairs and sold into slavery *en route* to her profitable betrothal, struggling with the intrigues of the Italian cloth trade to reclaim her heritage – and revenge herself. And for Thomas Marlowe, the English pilot wrecked on the Barbary Coast, dreams of a ship such as the Mediterranean has never seen and wider seas to sail her in.

Chance and treachery conspire against their hopes while irretrievably entangling their fates. There will be long, hard years before either Serafina or Thomas comes near to their dream – only to find the dream is no longer the same...